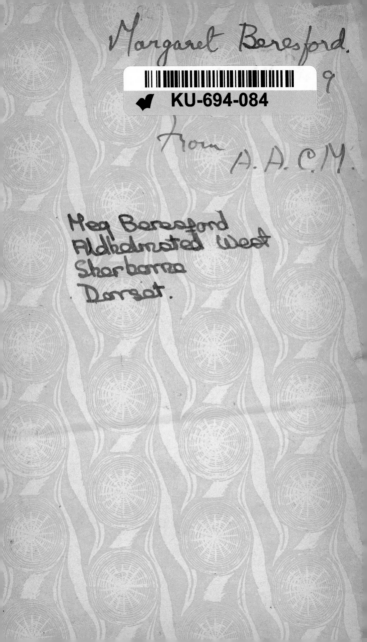

Everyman, I will go with thee, and be thy guide,
In thy most need to go by thy side.

EVERYMAN'S LIBRARY

Founded 1906 by J. M. Dent (d. 1926)
Edited by Ernest Rhys (d. 1946)

FICTION

THE COUNT
OF MONTE CRISTO
BY ALEXANDRE DUMAS
IN 2 VOLS.   VOL. 1

ALEXANDRE DUMAS, known as 'the elder,' born at Villers-Cotterets on 24th July 1802. Early life spent in poverty, but playwriting obtained for him the position of librarian of the Palais Royal. Left Paris in 1832, travelled abroad; returned to journalism and to write historical novels. Assisted Garibaldi at Naples in 1860. Returned to Paris in 1864 and died at Puys on 5th December 1870.

THE COUNT
OF MONTE CRISTO
VOLUME ONE

ALEXANDRE DUMAS

LONDON: J. M. DENT & SONS LTD.
NEW YORK: E. P. DUTTON & CO. INC.

INTRODUCTION

DUMAS was in the very midsummer of his invention when he wrote the following romance, which appeared in the year 1844, the year also of his *Three Musketeers*. He took the title of *Monte Cristo* from the small island of the name which he had espied on a trip to Elba and Corsica with the young Prince Napoleon in 1842. In the late Mr. Harry Spurr's excellent *Life of Dumas*, he tells the first outline of the story, viz., that a rich count living in Rome should do a great service to a young French traveller, and beg him to repay the kindness when his new acquaintance should visit Paris in turn. When Monte Cristo reached that city, he was to find enemies waiting there, who had condemned him in his youth to ten years of captivity. The young Frenchman's fortune was to furnish the count with the means of revenge.

But now, having got so far, Dumas acquainted Maquet, his collaborator, with the story, who pointed out that he was missing the best part of the story, the prologue, in which should be told not only how those enemies betrayed the count in his youth, but also the story of his years in prison. From that moment the story developed: Dumas seized the idea, took for his text three cities—Marseilles, Rome, Paris—and the romance was made.

Monte Cristo owed part of its enormous success to its verisimilitude. The details were most convincing, and had, indeed, been studied on the spot.

" There is one thing I cannot do," Dumas tells us, in his preface to the *Compagnons de Jéhu*, " I cannot write a book or a drama about localities I have never seen. To write *Christine* I went to Fontainebleau; to write *Henri III.* I went to Blois; to write *Les Trois Mousquetaires* I went to Bethune and Boulogne; to write *Monte Cristo* I returned to the

Catalans and the Château d'If. This gives such a character of truth to what I write that the personages I plant in certain places seem to grow there, and some people have been led to think they have actually existed; in fact, there are persons who say they have known them."

Once the material, the plot, and the local colour were made secure, the romance fairly flew from the pen.

" I believe," said Charles Reade, " they still show at Trouville in a fisherman's cottage the chamber and table where the pair (*i.e.*, Dumas and Maquet) wrote the first four volumes of *Monte Cristo* in sixteen days."

This almost rivals Sir Walter Scott's writing of *Guy Mannering*.

Alexandre Dumas Davy de la Pailleterie, grandson of a French marquis and a negro woman, Louise-Cessette, was born on July 24, 1802, and died on December 5, 1870.

1909.

The following is the list of his published works:—

POETRY AND PLAYS.—Elégie sur la Mort du Général Foy, 1825; La Chasse et l'Amour (in collaboration), 1825; Canaris (Dithyramb), 1826; La Noce et l'Enterrement (in collaboration), 1826; Christine (or Stockholm, Fontainebleau et Rome), 1828; Henri III. et sa Cour, 1829; Antony, 1831; Napoléon Bonaparte, ou Trente Ans de l'Histoire de France, 1831; Charles VII. chez ses grands vassaux, 1831; Richard Darlington, 1831; Térésa, 1832; Le Mari de la Veuve (in collaboration), 1832; La Tour de Nesle, 1832; Angèle (in collaboration), 1833; Catherine Howard, 1834; Don Juan de Marana, ou la Chute d'un Ange, 1836; Kean, 1836; Piquillo, comic opera (in collaboration), 1837; Caligula, 1837; Paul Jones, 1838; Mademoiselle de Belle-Isle, 1839; l'Alchimiste, 1839; Bathilde (in collaboration), 1839; Un Mariage sous Louis XV. (in collaboration), 1841; Lorenzino (in collaboration), 1842; Halifax, 1842; Les Demoiselles de Saint-Cyr (in collaboration), 1843; Louise Bernard (in collaboration), 1843; Le Laird de Dumbicky (in collaboration), 1843; Le Garde Forestier (in collaboration), 1845; L'Oreste, 1856; Le Verrou de la Reine, 1856; Le Meneur des Loups, 1857; Collective Eds., *Théâtre*, 1834-36, 6 vols., 1863-74, 15 vols. Dumas also dramatised many of his novels.

TALES AND NOVELS, TRAVELS.—Nouvelles Contemporaines, 1826; Impressions de Voyage, 1833; Souvenirs d'Antony (tales), 1835; La Salle d'Armes (tales), 1838; Le Capitaine Paul, 1838; Acté, Monseigneur Gaston de Phébus, 1839; Quinze Jours au Sinaï, 1839; Aventures de John Davy, 1840; Le Capitaine Pamphile, 1840; Maître Adam le Calabrais, 1840; Othon l'Archer, 1840; Une Année à Florence, 1840; Praxide; Don Martin de Freytas; Pierre le Cruel, 1841; Excursions sur les bords du Rhin, 1841; Nouvelles Impressions de Voyage, 1841; Le Speronare (travels), 1842; Aventures de Lyderic, 1842; Georges; Ascanio; Le Chevalier d'Harmental, 1843; Le Corricolo; La Villa Palmieri, 1843; Gabriel Lambert; Château d'Eppstein; Cécile; Sylvandire; Les Trois Mousquetaires; Amaury; Fernande, 1844; Le Comte de Monte-Cristo,

1844-5; Vingt Ans après, 1845; Les Frères Corses; Une Fille du Régent;
La Reine Margot, 1845; La Guerre des Femmes, 1845-6; Le Chevalier de
Maison-Rouge, 1846; La Dame de Monsoreau, 1846; Le Bâtard de
Mauléon, 1846; Mémoires d'un Médecin, 1846-8; Les Quarante-cinq,
1848; Dix Ans plus tard, ou le Vicomte de Bragelonne, 1848-50; De
Paris à Cadix, 1848; Tanger, Alger, et Tunis, 1848; Les Milles et un
Fantômes, 184c; La Tulipe Noire, 1850; La Femme au Collier de Velours,
1851; Olympe de Clèves, 1852; Un Gil Blas en Californie, 1852; Isaac
Taquedem, 1852; La Comtesse de Charny, 1853-5; Ange Pitou, le Pasteur
d'Ashbourn; El Satéador; Conscience l'Innocent, 1853; Catherine Blum;
Ingénue, 1854; Les Mohicans de Paris, 1854-8; Salvator, 1855-9 (the two
last with Paul Bocage); L'Arabie Heureuse, 1855; Les Compagnons de
Jéhu, 1857; Les Louvres de Machecoul, 1859; Le Caucase, 1859; De
Paris à Astrakan, 1860.

OTHER WORKS.—Souvenirs de 1830-42, 1854; Mémoires, 1852-4;
Causeries, 1860; Bric-à-brac, 1861; Histoire de mes Bêtes, 1868; Memoirs
of Garibaldi, Reminiscences of various writers, historical compilations,
etc.; Children's Tales; Histoire d'un Casse-Noisette. La Bouillie de la
Comtesse Berthe, Le Père Gigogne.

PUBLISHERS' NOTE

MONTE CRISTO—the most celebrated work of its celebrated author, not even excepting the D'Artagnan romances—has hitherto been known to the English-speaking world only through the medium of a very imperfect translation, which from time to time has been republished without any material improvement. The great story is worthy to be presented in a better form. If readers have found it admirable in a crude presentation they will find new excellences in it as they follow, in an improved translation, the inimitable style of its author,—observing his peculiar success in the employment of words fitted to his thought; his light humour, often so delicately conveyed that a careless rendering must lose it altogether; and, regarding the work as a whole, his artistic skill in proportion and perspective, which may easily be made of no effect by omissions in translating.

In the present edition omissions have been supplied; expansions have been rigorously reduced to the author's own crisp form of statement; erroneous and misleading renderings of words and phrases have been corrected; and where, as in many instances, the translator had usurped the functions of the author, he has been remanded to his proper subordination.

"The style is the man;" and no small part of one's pleasure in reading comes through the sense of a personal intercourse with the man who thus pervades the book. It is therefore with a peculiar satisfaction that in publishing this work we create an opportunity to make, or renew, acquaintance with ALEXANDER DUMAS, through a translation which follows him instead of running away from him, and reproduces his forms of thought with as much precision as the differences between English and French idioms will allow.

PUBLISHERS' NOTE

Monte Cristo—the most celebrated work of its celebrated author, not even excepting the "D'Artagnan romances," has hitherto been known to the English-reading world only through the medium of a very imperfect translation, which from time to time has been republished without any material improvement. The great story is worthy to be presented in a better form. If readers have found it admirable in a crude pre-eminent they will find new excellences in it as they follow, in an improved translation, the inimitable style of its author—observing his neater niceties in the employment of words studied to his thought; the, with humour, often so delicately conveyed that a careless rendering must lose it altogether, and rounding the work as a whole, his stately skill in proportion and perspective, which may be fully made of no effect by omissions in translation.

In the present edition mistakes have been supplied, errors have been corrected and misleading renderings of words and phrases have been corrected; and where, as in many instances, the translator mistaken the intentions of the author, he has been remanded to the proper subordination.

The style is the man, and no small part of one's pleasure in reading comes through the sense of a personal acquaintance with the man who thus pervades the book. It is therefore with a peculiar satisfaction that in publishing this work we secure an opportunity to make, of renew, acquaintance with ALEXANDRE DUMAS through a translation which follows him instead of running away from him, and reproduces his forms of thought with as much precision as the difference between English and French idioms will allow.

CONTENTS

LIST OF CHARACTERS

Period, 1815-1838.

EDMOND DANTÈS, a Marseilles sailor, mate of the *Pharaon*, afterwards Count of Monte Cristo, assuming the names of Lord Wilmore, Abbé Busoni, and Sinbad the Sailor.

LOUIS DANTÈS, his father.

MERCÉDÈS, a catalan, betrothed to Edmond Dantès.

FERNAND MONDEGO, her cousin, afterwards Comte de Morcerf.

VICOMTE ALBERT DE MORCERF, his son.

DANGLARS, supercargo of the *Pharaon*, afterwards Baron Danglars, a Paris banker.

BARONNE DANGLARS, his wife.

MADEMOISELLE EUGÉNIE DANGLARS, their daughter.

LOUISE D'ARMILLY, her music-teacher and friend.

M. MORREL, owner of the *Pharaon*.

MADAME MORREL.

MAXIMILIAN MORREL, }
JULIE MORREL, } their children.

EMMANUEL HERBAUT, } clerks in the house of Morrel and Son, Marseilles
COCLÈS, }

GASPARD CADEROUSSE, a Marseilles tailor, afterwards landlord of the Pont du Gard Inn.

MADELEINE, his wife, otherwise known as La Carconte.

THE EMPEROR NAPOLEON.

LOUIS XVIII.

BARON DANDRÉ, Minister of Police, } Royalists.
DUC DE BLACAS, }

M. NOIRTIER DE VILLEFORT, an adherent of Napoleon.

M. GÉRARD DE VILLEFORT, his son, *procureur du roi*.

MARQUIS DE SAINT-MÉRAN.

MARQUISE DE SAINT-MÉRAN.

MADEMOISELLE RENÉE DE SAINT-MÉRAN, their daughter, betrothed to M. Gérard de Villefort.

COMTE DE SALVIEUX, friend of M. de Saint-Méran.

GENERAL FLAVIEN DE QUESNEL.

BARON FRANZ D'ÉPINAY, his son.

LIEUTENANT-COLONEL LOUIS JACQUES BEAUREPAIRE,
} members of the
BRIGADIER-GENERAL ÉTIENNE DUCHAMPY,
} Bonapartist Club in
CLAUDE LECHARPAL, keeper of streams and forests,
} the Rue St. Jacques.

MARÉCHEL BERTRAND.

M. DE BOVILLE, inspector of prisons.

THE GOVERNOR OF THE CHÂTEAU D'IF.

ABBÉ FARIA, a prisoner in the Château d'If.

A JAILOR, at the Château d'If.

THE MAYOR OF MARSEILLES.

CAPTAIN BALDI, of *La Jeune Amélie*, a Genoese smuggler.

JACOPO, one of his crew.

MAÎTRE PASTRINI, proprietor of the Hôtel de Londres, Rome.

GAETANO, a Roman sailor.

CUCUMETTO, a brigand chief.

CARLINI,
DIAVOLACCIO, } of Cucumetto's troop.

RITA, betrothed to Carlini.

LUIGI VAMPA, a shepherd boy, afterwards a Captain of Roman brigands.

TERESA, his betrothed.

PEPPINO, a shepherd.

ANDREA RONDOLA, a condemned murderer.

COMTE DE SAN FELICE,
DUC DE BRACCIANO, } Roman noblemen.

CARMELA, Comte de San Felice's daughter.

COMTESSE GUICCIOLI.

MAJOR BARTOLOMEO CAVALCANTI, an adventurer.

BENEDETTO, passing under the name of Andrea de Cavalcanti.

M. LUCIEN DEBRAY, private secretary
  to the Minister of the Interior,
M. BEAUCHAMP, an editor,
COMTE DE CHATEAU-RENAUD, } friends of Albert de Morcerf.

HÉLOÏSE, Villefort's second wife.

EDOUARD, her son.

MADEMOISELLE VALENTINE, Villefort's daughter by his first wife, in love with Maximilian Morrel.

DOCTOR D'AVRIGNY, Villefort's physician.

M. DESCHAMPS, a notary.

ALI TEBELIN, Pacha of Janina.

VASILIKI, his wife.

HAYDÉE, daughter of Ali Pacha and Vasiliki.

SELIM, favourite of Ali Pacha.

BERTUCCIO, steward to the Count of Monte Cristo.

ASSUNTA, Bertuccio's sister-in-law.

BAPTISTIN, Monte Cristo's valet.

ALI, a Nubian mute, slave to Monte Cristo.

ABBÉ ADELMONTE, a Sicilian.

GERMAIN, Albert de Morcerf's valet.

ÉTIENNE, valet to Danglars.

BARROIS, Noirtier's servant.

FANNY, Mademoiselle de Villefort's maid.

PÈRE PAMPHILE, of La Réserve Inn.

CAPTAIN LECLERC,
PENELON, a sailor,
CAPTAIN GAUMARD, } in the service of M. Morrel.

JOANNES, a jeweller.

THE

COUNT OF MONTE CRISTO

CHAPTER I

MARSEILLES—THE ARRIVAL

On the 28th of February, 1815, the watchman in the tower of Notre Dame de la Garde signalled the three-master, the *Pharaon*, from Smyrna, Trieste, and Naples. A pilot put off immediately, and rounding the Château d'If, got on board the vessel between Cape Morgion and the Isle of Rion.

The platform of Fort St. Jean was covered with spectators; it is always an event at Marseilles for a ship to come into port, especially when this ship, like the *Pharaon*, had been built, rigged, and laden at the wharves of the old Phocée, and belonged to an owner in the city.

The ship drew on; it had safely passed the strait which some volcanic shock has made between the Isle of Calasareigne and the Isle of Jaros, had doubled Pomègue, and approached the harbour under topsails, jib, and foresail, but so slowly and sedately that the idlers, with that instinct which misfortune sends before it, asked one another what misfortune could have happened on board. However, those experienced in navigation saw plainly that if any accident had occurred, it was not to the vessel herself, for as she approached she gave every indication of being under perfect control. Beside the pilot, who was steering the *Pharaon* through the narrow entrance of the port of Marseilles, was a young man, who, gesticulating rapidly, watched with a vigilant eye every motion of the ship, and repeated the orders of the pilot.

The vague disquietude which prevailed among the spectators had so much affected one of the crowd that he could not await the arrival of the vessel in harbour, but jumping into a small skiff, desired to be pulled alongside the *Pharaon*, which he reached as she came opposite the bay of La Réserve.

When the young man on board saw him coming, he left his station by the pilot, and came, hat in hand, to the side of the ship. He was a tall slim young fellow, nineteen or twenty years old, with black eyes, and hair as dark as the raven's wing; and his whole appearance bespoke that calmness and resolution peculiar to men accustomed from their cradle to contend with danger.

" Ah! is it you, Dantès? " cried the man in the skiff. " What's the matter? And why have you such an air of sadness aboard? "

" A great misfortune, M. Morrel! " replied the young man,— " a great misfortune, for me especially! Off Civita Vecchia we lost our brave Captain Leclere."

" And the cargo? " inquired the owner, eagerly.

" Is all safe, M. Morrel; and I think you will be satisfied on that head. But poor Captain Leclere—"

" What happened to him? " asked the owner, with an air of relief. " What happened to the worthy captain? "

" He is dead."

" Fell into the sea? "

" No, monsieur, he died of the brain fever, in dreadful agony." Then turning to the crew, he said, " Look out there! all ready to drop anchor! "

All hands obeyed. At the same moment the eight or ten seamen who composed the crew, sprang, some to the main-sheets, others to the braces, others to the halyards, others to the jib-ropes, and others to the topsail brails. The young sailor gave a look to see that his orders were promptly and accurately obeyed, and then turned again to the owner.

" And how did this misfortune occur? " inquired the latter, resuming the inquiry suspended for a moment.

" Alas, monsieur! in the most unexpected manner. After a long conversation with the harbour-master, Captain Leclere left Naples greatly disturbed in his mind. At the end of twenty-four hours he was attacked by a fever, and died three days afterwards. We performed the usual burial service, and he is at his rest, sewn up in his hammock with two bullets of thirty-six pounds each at his head and heels, off the island of El Giglio. We bring to his widow his sword and cross of honour. It was worth while, truly," added the young man with a melancholy smile, " to make war against the English for ten years, and to die in his bed at last, like everybody else."

" Why, you see, Edmond," replied the owner, who appeared more comforted every moment, " we are all mortal, and the old must make way for the young. If not, why, there would be no promotion; and as you have assured me that the cargo—"

" Is all safe and sound, M. Morrel, take my word for it; and I advise you not to take twenty-five thousand livres for the profits of the voyage."

Then, as they were just passing the Round Tower, the young man shouted out, " Ready, there, to lower topsails, foresail, and jib!"

The order was executed as promptly as if on board a man-of-war.

" Let go! and brail all!" At this last word all the sails were lowered, and the ship moved almost imperceptibly onwards.

" Now, if you will come on board, M. Morrel," said Dantès, observing the owner's impatience, " here is your supercargo, M. Danglars, coming out of his cabin, who will furnish you with every particular. As for me, I must look after the anchoring, and dress the ship in mourning."

The owner did not wait to be twice invited. He seized a rope which Dantès flung to him, and with an activity that would have done credit to a sailor, climbed up the side of the ship, while the young man, going to his task, left the conversation to the individual whom he had announced under the name of Danglars, who now came towards the owner. He was a man of twenty-five or twenty-six years of age, of unprepossessing countenance, obsequious to his superiors, insolent to his inferiors; and then aside from his position on board as responsible agent, which is always offensive to the sailors, he was personally as much disliked by the crew as Edmond Dantès was beloved by them.

" Well, M. Morrel," said Danglars, " you have heard of the misfortune that has befallen us? "

" Yes, yes! poor Captain Leclere! He was a brave and an honest man!"

" And a first-rate seaman, grown old between sky and ocean, —a proper man to be charged with the interests of a house so important as that of Morrel and Son," replied Danglars.

" But," replied the owner, following with his look Dantès, who was watching the anchoring of his vessel, " it seems to me that a sailor needs not to be so old as you say, Danglars, to understand his business, for our friend Edmond seems to understand it thoroughly, and not to require instruction from any one."

" Yes," said Danglars, casting towards Edmond a look in which gleamed a flash of hatred,—" yes, he is young, and youth is invariably self-confident. Scarcely was the captain's breath out of his body when he assumed the command without consulting any one, and he caused us to lose a day and a half at the Isle of Elba, instead of making for Marseilles direct."

"As to taking the command of the vessel," replied Morrel, "that was his duty as captain's mate; as to losing a day and a half off the Isle of Elba, he was wrong, unless the ship wanted some repair."

"The ship was as sound as I am, and as I hope you are, M. Morrel, and this day and a half was wasted through sheer caprice,—for the pleasure of going ashore, and nothing else."

"Dantès!" said the ship-owner, turning towards the young man, "come this way!"

"In a moment, sir," answered Dantès, "I shall be at your service." Then calling to the crew, he said, "Let go!"

The anchor was instantly dropped, and the chain ran rattling through the port-hole. Dantès continued at his post in spite of the presence of the pilot until this manœuvre was completed, and then he added, "Lower the pennant to half-mast; put the ensign in a weft, and slope the yards!"

"You see," said Danglars, "he fancies himself captain already, upon my word."

"And so, in fact, he is," said the owner.

"Yes, wanting your signature and your partner's, M. Morrel."

"And why should he not have it?" asked the owner; "he is young, it is true, but he seems to me a thorough seaman, and of full experience."

A cloud passed over Danglar's brow.

"Your pardon, M. Morrel," said Dantès, approaching; "the ship now rides at anchor, and I am at your service. You called me, did you not?"

Danglars retreated a step or two.

"I wished to inquire why you stopped at the Isle of Elba?"

"I do not know, sir; it was to fulfil a last instruction of Captain Leclere, who, when dying, gave me a packet for the Maréchal Bertrand."

"Did you see him, Edmond?"

"See whom?"

"The marshal."

"Yes."

Morrel looked around him, and then drawing Dantès on one side, he said suddenly, "And how is the emperor?"

"Very well, as far as I could judge from his appearance."

"You saw the emperor, then?"

"He entered the marshal's apartment while I was there."

"And you spoke to him?"

"Why, it was he who spoke to me, monsieur," said Dantès, with a smile.

" And what did he say to you? "

" Asked me questions about the ship,—when she would leave for Marseilles, the course she had taken, and what was her cargo. I believe, if she had not been laden, and I had been her master, he would have bought her. But I told him I was only mate, and that she belonged to the firm of Morrel and Son. ' Ah, ah! ' he said, ' I know them! The Morrels have been ship-owners from father to son; and there was a Morrel who served in the same regiment with me when I was in garrison at Valence.' "

" *Pardieu!* and that is true! " cried the owner, greatly delighted. " And that was Policar Morrel, my uncle, who was afterwards a captain. Dantès, you must tell my uncle that the emperor remembered him, and you will see it will bring tears into the old soldier's eyes. Come, come! " continued he, patting Edmond's shoulder kindly, " you did very right, Dantès, to follow Captain Leclere's instruction, and touch at the Isle of Elba,—although if it should become known that you had conveyed a packet to the marshal, and had conversed with the emperor, you might find yourself compromised."

" How could that compromise me, monsieur? " asked Dantès. " I did not even know of what I was the bearer; and the emperor merely made such inquiries as he would of the first comer. But, your pardon, here are the officers of health and the customs coming alongside! " and the young man went to the gangway.

As he departed, Danglars approached, and said,—

" Well, it appears that he has given you satisfactory reasons for his landing at Porto Ferrajo? "

" Yes, most satisfactory, my dear Danglars."

" Well, so much the better," said the supercargo; " for it is always painful to see a comrade who does not do his duty."

" Dantès has done his," replied the owner, " and that is not saying much. It was Captain Leclere who gave orders for this delay."

" Talking of Captain Leclere, has not Dantès given you a letter from him? "

" To me? No; was there one? "

" I believe that besides the packet Captain Leclere had confided a letter to his care."

" Of what packet are you speaking, Danglars? "

" Why, that which Dantès left at Porto Ferrajo."

" How do you know he had a packet to leave at Porto Ferrajo? "

Danglars turned very red. " I was passing close to the door

of the captain's cabin, which was half open, and I saw him give the packet and letter to Dantès."

"He did not speak to me of it," replied the ship-owner; "but if there be any letter he will give it to me."

Danglars reflected for a moment. "Then, M. Morrel, I beg of you," said he, "not to say a word to Dantès on the subject; I may have been mistaken."

At this moment the young man returned, and Danglars withdrew.

"Well, my dear Dantès, are you now free?" inquired the owner.

"Yes, monsieur."

"You have not been long detained."

"No. I gave the custom-house officers a copy of our bill of lading; and as to the other papers, they sent a man off with the pilot to whom I gave them."

"Then you have nothing more to do here?"

"No; all is arranged now."

"Then you can come and dine with me?"

"I beg you to excuse me, M. Morrel; but my first visit is due to my father. I am not the less grateful for the honour you have done me."

"Right, Dantès, quite right. I always knew you were a good son."

"And," inquired Dantès, with some hesitation, "do you know how my father is?"

"Well, I believe, my dear Edmond, though I have not seen him lately."

"Yes, he likes to keep himself shut up in his little room."

"That proves, at least, that he has wanted for nothing during your absence."

Dantès smiled. "My father is proud, sir; and if he had not a meal left, I doubt if he would have asked anything from any one, except God."

"Well, then, after this first visit has been made we rely on you."

"I must again excuse myself, M. Morrel,—for after this first visit has been paid I have another which I am most anxious to pay."

"True, Dantès, I forgot that there is at the Catalans some one who expects you no less impatiently than your father,— the lovely Mercédès."

Dantès blushed.

"Ah, ah!" said the ship-owner, "that does not astonish me,

for she has been to me three times, inquiring if there were any news of the *Pharaon*. *Peste!* Edmond, you have a very handsome mistress!"

"She is not my mistress," replied the young sailor, gravely; "she is my betrothed."

"Sometimes one and the same thing," said Morrel, with a smile.

"Not with us, monsieur," replied Dantès.

"Well, well, my dear Edmond," continued the owner, "do not let me detain you. You have managed my affairs so well that I ought to allow you all the time you require for your own. Do you want any money?"

"No, monsieur; I have all my pay to receive,—nearly three months' wages."

"You are a careful fellow, Edmond."

"Say that I have a poor father, monsieur."

"Yes, yes, I know that you are a good son. Go, then, to see your father. I have a son too, and I should be very wroth with any one who should keep him from me after a three months' voyage."

"Then I have your leave, monsieur?"

"Yes, if you have nothing more to say to me."

"Nothing."

"Captain Leclere did not, before he died, give you a letter for me?"

"He was unable to write, sir. But that reminds me that I must ask leave of absence for a fortnight."

"To get married?"

"Yes, first, and then to go to Paris."

"Very good; have what time you require, Dantès. It will take quite six weeks to unload the cargo, and we cannot get you ready for sea until three months after that; only be back again in three months,—for the *Pharaon*," added the owner, patting the young sailor on the back, "cannot sail without her captain."

"Without her captain!" cried Dantès, his eyes sparkling with animation; "pray mind what you say, for you are touching on the most secret wishes of my heart. Is it really your intention to make me captain of the *Pharaon*?"

"If I were sole owner I would appoint you this moment, my dear Dantès, and say it is settled; but I have a partner, and you know the Italian proverb,—*Chi ha compagno ha padrone,* 'He who has a partner has a master.' But the thing is at least half done, since of the two votes you have already secured one. Rely on me to procure you the other; I will do my best."

"Ah, M. Morrel," exclaimed the young seaman, with tears in his eyes, and grasping the owner's hand,—" M. Morrel, I thank you in the name of my father and of Mercédès."

"Good, good, Edmond! Devil take it, there's a God in heaven for good fellows! Go to your father; go and see Mercédès, and come to me afterwards."

"Shall I row you on shore?"

"No, I thank you; I shall remain and look over the accounts with Danglars. Have you been satisfied with him this voyage?"

"That is according to the sense you attach to the question, monsieur. Do you mean, is he a good comrade? No, for I think he never liked me since the day when I was silly enough, after a little quarrel we had, to propose to him to stop for ten minutes at the Isle of Monte Cristo to settle the dispute,—a proposition which I was wrong to suggest, and he quite right to refuse. If your question refers to his conduct as supercargo, I believe there is nothing to say against him, and that you will be content with the way in which he has performed his duty."

"But tell me, Dantès, if you had the command of the *Pharaon*, should you have pleasure in retaining Danglars?"

"Captain or mate, M. Morrel," replied Dantès, "I shall always have the greatest respect for those who possess our owner's confidence."

"Good, good, Dantès! I see you are at all points a good fellow. Let me detain you no longer. Go, for I see how impatient you are."

"Then I have leave?"

"Go, I tell you."

"May I have the use of your skiff?"

"Certainly."

"Then, for the present, M. Morrel, farewell, and a thousand thanks!"

"I hope soon to see you again, my dear Edmond. Good luck to you!"

The young sailor jumped into the skiff, and sat down in the stern, desiring to be put ashore at the Canebière. The two rowers bent to their work, and the little boat glided away as rapidly as possible in the midst of the thousand vessels which choke up the narrow way which leads between the two rows of ships from the mouth of the harbour to the Quai d'Orléans.

The ship-owner, smiling, followed him with his eyes until he saw him spring out on the quay and disappear in the midst of the throng which from five o'clock in the morning until nine o'clock at night chokes up this famous street of La Canebière, of which the modern Phocéens are so proud that they say with all the gravity in the world, and with that accent which gives so much character to what is said, "If Paris had La Canebière, Paris would be a second Marseilles." On turning round, the owner saw Danglars behind him, who apparently awaited his orders, but in reality followed, as he did, the young sailor with his eyes; but there was a great difference in the expression of the two men who thus watched the movements of Edmond Dantès.

CHAPTER II

FATHER AND SON

WE will leave Danglars struggling with the feelings of hatred, and endeavouring to insinuate in the ear of the ship-owner, Morrel, evil suspicions against his comrade, and follow Dantès, who, after having traversed the Canebière, took the Rue de Noailles, and entering into a small house situated on the left side of the Allées de Meillan, rapidly ascended four stories of a dark staircase, holding the baluster in one hand, while with the other he repressed the beatings of his heart; he paused before a half-opened door, which revealed the intèrior of a small apartment.

This apartment was occupied by Dantès's father. The news of the arrival of the *Pharaon* had not yet reached the old man, who, mounted on a chair, was amusing himself by staking with tremulous hand some nasturtiums, which, mingled with clematis, formed a kind of trellis at his window. Suddenly he felt an arm thrown round his body, and a well-known voice behind him exclaimed, "Father! dear father!"

The old man uttered a cry, and turned round; then, seeing his son, he fell into his arms, pale and trembling.

"What ails you, my dearest father? Are you ill?" inquired the young man, much alarmed.

"No, no, my dear Edmond—my boy—my son! no; but I did not expect you; and joy, the surprise of seeing you so suddenly—Ah! I really feel as if I were going to die."

"Come, come; cheer up, my dear father! 'Tis I,—really I! They say joy never hurts, and so I come to you without any warning. Come now, look cheerfully at me, instead of gazing as you do with wandering looks. Here I am back again, and we will now be happy."

"Yes, yes, my boy, so we will,—so we will," replied the old

man; "but how shall we be happy? Will you never leave me again? Come, tell me all the good fortune that has befallen you."

"God forgive me," said the young man, "for rejoicing at happiness derived from the misery of others; but Heaven knows I did not seek this good fortune. It has happened, and I really cannot affect to lament it. The good Captain Leclere is dead, father, and it is probable that, with the aid of M. Morrel, I shall have his place. Do you understand, father? Only imagine me a captain at twenty, with a hundred-louis pay, and a share in the profits! Is this not more than a poor sailor like me could have hoped for?"

"Yes, my dear boy," replied the old man,—"yes, it is very fortunate."

"Well, then, with the first money I touch, I mean that you shall have a small house, with a garden in which to plant your clematis, your nasturtiums, and your honeysuckles. But what ails you, father? Are you not well?"

"'Tis nothing, nothing; it will soon pass away;" and as he said so the old man's strength failed him, and he fell backwards.

"Come, come," said the young man, "a glass of wine, father, will revive you. Where do you keep your wine?"

"No, no, thank you. You need not look for it; I do not want it," said the old man.

"Yes, yes, father; tell me where it is," and Dantès opened two or three cupboards.

"It is of no use," said the old man; "there is no wine."

"What! no wine?" said Dantès, turning pale, and looking alternately at the hollow cheeks of the old man and the empty cupboards,—"what! no wine? Have you wanted money, father?"

"I want nothing since I see you," said the old man.

"Yet," stammered Dantès, wiping the perspiration from his brow,—"yet I gave you two hundred livres when I left, three months ago."

"Yes, yes, Edmond, that is true; but you forgot at that time a little debt to our neighbour Caderousse. He reminded me of it, telling me if I did not pay for you, he would apply to M. Morrel; and so, you see, lest he might do you an injury—"

"Well?"

"Why, I paid him."

"But," cried Dantès, "it was a hundred and forty livres I owed Caderousse."

"Yes," stammered the old man.

" And you paid him out of the two hundred livres I left you ? "
The old man made a sign in the affirmative.

" So that you have lived for three months on sixty livres ! "
muttered the young man.

" You know how little I require," said the old man.

" Heaven pardon me ! " cried Edmond, going on his knees
before the old man.

" What are you doing ? "

" You have wounded my very heart ! "

" Never mind it, for I see you once more," said the old man;
" and now all is forgotten, all is well again."

" Yes, here I am," said the young man, " with a happy
prospect and a little money. Here, father, here ! " he said,
" take this,—take it, and send for something immediately."
And he emptied his pockets on the table, whose contents consisted of a dozen pieces of gold, five or six crowns, and some
smaller coin. The countenance of old Dantès brightened.

" To whom does this belong ? " he inquired.

" To me ! to you ! to us ! Take it ; buy some provisions.
Be happy, and to-morrow we shall have more."

" Gently, gently," said the old man, with a smile ; " and by
your leave I will use your purse moderately,—for they would
say, if they saw me buy too many things at a time, that I
had been obliged to await your return in order to be able to
purchase them."

" Do as you please ; but first of all, pray have a servant,
father. I will not have you left alone so long. I have some
smuggled coffee and capital tobacco in a small chest in the
hold, which you shall have to-morrow. But hush ! here comes
somebody."

" 'Tis Caderousse, who has heard of your arrival, and no
doubt comes to congratulate you on your fortunate return."

" Ah ! lips that say one thing, while the heart thinks another,"
murmured Edmond. " But never mind, he is a neighbour who
has done us a service on a time, so he's welcome."

As Edmond finished his sentence in a low voice, there appeared
at the door the black and shock head of Caderousse. He was
a man of twenty-five or twenty-six years of age, and held in
his hand a piece of cloth, which in his capacity as a tailor he
was about to turn into the lining of a coat.

" What ! is it you, Edmond, returned ? " said he, with a
broad Marseillaise accent, and a grin that displayed his teeth
as white as ivory.

" Yes, as you see, neighbour Caderousse ; and ready to be

agreeable to you in any and every way," replied Dantès, hardly concealing his feelings under this appearance of civility.

"Thanks, thanks; but fortunately, I do not want for anything. It even happens sometimes that others have need of me." Dantès made a gesture. "I do not allude to you, my boy. No, no! I lent you money, and you returned it; that's like good neighbours, and we are quits."

"We are never quits with those who oblige us," was Dantès's reply,—"for when we do not owe them money, we owe them gratitude."

"What's the use of mentioning that? What is done is done. Let us talk of your happy return, my boy. I had gone on the quay to match a piece of mulberry cloth, when I met friend Danglars. 'What! you at Marseilles?' I exclaimed. 'Yes,' said he. 'I thought you were at Smyrna.' 'I was; but am now back again.' 'And where is the dear boy, our little Edmond?' 'Why, with his father, no doubt,' replied Danglars. And so I came," added Caderousse, "as fast as I could, to have the pleasure of shaking hands with a friend."

"Worthy Caderousse!" said the old man; "he is so much attached to us!"

"Yes, to be sure I am. I love and esteem you, because honest folks are so rare! But it seems you have come back rich, my boy," continued the tailor, looking askance at the handful of gold and silver which Dantès had thrown on the table.

The young man remarked the greedy glance which shone in the dark eyes of his neighbour. "Eh!" he said negligently, "this money is not mine; I was expressing to my father my fears that he had wanted many things in my absence, and to convince me he emptied his purse on the table. Come, father," added Dantès, "put this money back in your box,—unless neighbour Caderousse wants anything, and in that case it is at his service."

"No, my boy, no," said Caderousse. "I am not in any want, thank God! The state nourishes me. Keep your money,—keep it, I say. One never has too much; but I am as much obliged by your offer as if I took advantage of it."

"It was offered with good-will," said Dantès.

"No doubt, no doubt. Well, you stand well with M. Morrel, I hear, you insinuating dog, you!"

"M. Morrel has always been exceedingly kind to me," replied Dantès.

"Then you were wrong to refuse to dine with him."

"What! did you refuse to dine with him?" said old Dantès. "Did he invite you to dine?"

"Yes, my dear father," replied Edmond, smiling at his father's astonishment at the high honour paid to his son.

"And why did you refuse, my son?" inquired the old man.

"That I might the sooner see you again, my dear father," replied the young man. "I was most anxious to see you."

"But it must have vexed M. Morrel, good, worthy man," said Caderousse. "And when you are looking forward to be captain, it was wrong to annoy the owner."

"But I explained to him the cause of my refusal," replied Dantès; "and I hope he fully understood it."

"Yes, but to be captain one must give way a little to one's patrons."

"I hope to be captain without that," said Dantès.

"So much the better,—so much the better! Nothing will give greater pleasure to all your old friends; and I know one down there behind the citadel of St. Nicholas, who will not be sorry to hear it."

"Mercédès?" said the old man.

"Yes, my dear father, and with your permission, now that I have seen you and know you are well and have all you require, I will ask your permission to go and pay a visit to the Catalans."

"Go, my dear boy," said old Dantès; "and may God bless you in your wife as he has blessed me in my son!"

"His wife!" said Caderousse; "why, how fast you go on, Father Dantès; she is not his wife yet, it appears."

"No, but according to all probability she soon will be," replied Edmond.

"Yes, yes," said Caderousse; "but you were right to return as soon as possible, my boy."

"Why do you say that?"

"Because Mercédès is a very fine girl, and fine girls never lack lovers; she, particularly, has them by dozens."

"Really?" answered Edmond, with a smile which betrayed a slight uneasiness.

"Ay, yes," continued Caderousse, "and capital offers, too; but, you know, you will be captain, and who could refuse you then?"

"Meaning to say," replied Dantès, with a smile which did not hide his anxiety, "that if I were not a captain—"

"Eh, eh!" said Caderousse.

"Come, come," said the sailor, "I have a better opinion than you of women in general, and of Mercédès in particular; and I am certain that whether I am captain or not she will remain ever faithful to me."

"So much the better,—so much the better," said Caderousse. "When one is going to be married, there is nothing like implicit confidence. But never mind that, my boy; go and announce your arrival, and let her share your hopes."

"I will go directly," was Edmond's reply. He embraced his father, made a farewell gesture to Caderousse, and left the apartment.

Caderousse lingered for a moment, then taking leave of old Dantès, he went downstairs to rejoin Danglars, who awaited him at the corner of the Rue Senac.

"Well," said Danglars, "did you see him?"

"I have just left him," answered Caderousse.

"Did he allude to his hope of being captain?"

"He spoke of it as a thing already decided."

"Patience!" said Danglars, "he is in too much hurry, it appears to me."

"Why, it seems M. Morrel has promised him the thing."

"So that he is quite elated about it?"

"He is actually insolent on the matter, has already offered me his patronage as if he were a grand personage, and proffered me a loan of money as though he were a banker."

"Which you refused?"

"Most assuredly; although I might easily have accepted it, for it was I who put into his hands the first silver he ever touched. But now M. Dantès has no longer any occasion for assistance; he is about to become a captain."

"Pooh!" said Danglars, "he is not one yet."

"*Ma foi!* and it will be as well he never should be," answered Caderousse,—"for if he should be, there will be really no speaking to him."

"If we choose," replied Danglars, "he will remain what he is, perhaps become even less than he is."

"What do you mean?"

"Nothing; I was speaking to myself. And is he still in love with the beautiful Catalane?"

"Over head and ears; but unless I am much mistaken, there will be a storm in that quarter."

"Explain yourself."

"Why should I?"

"It is more important than you think, perhaps. You do not like Dantès?"

"I never like upstarts."

"Then tell me all you know relative to the Catalane."

"I know nothing for certain; only I have seen things which

induce me to believe, as I told you, that the future captain will find some annoyance in the environs of the Vieilles Infirmeries."

"What do you know? Come, tell me!"

"Well, every time I have seen Mercédès come into the city, she has been accompanied by a tall strapping black-eyed Catalan, with a red complexion, brown skin, and fierce air, whom she calls cousin."

"Really! and do you then think this cousin pays her attention?"

"I only suppose so. What else can a strapping chap of twenty-one mean with a fine wench of seventeen?"

"And you say Dantès has gone to the Catalans?"

"He started before I came down."

"Let us go the same way; we will stop at La Réserve, and while we drink a glass of La Malgue, we will wait for news."

"Come along," said Caderousse; "but mind you pay the shot."

"Certainly," replied Danglars; and going quickly to the spot alluded to, they called for a bottle of wine and two glasses.

Père Pamphile had seen Dantès pass not ten minutes before. Assured that he was at the Catalans, they sat down under the budding foliage of the planes and sycamores, in the branches of which a lively chorus of birds were celebrating one of the first fine days of spring.

CHAPTER III

THE CATALANS

ABOUT a hundred paces from the spot where the two friends, with their looks fixed on the distance and their ears attentive, imbibed the sparkling wine of La Malgue, behind a bare and weather-worn wall, was the village of the Catalans. One day a mysterious colony quitted Spain, and settled on the tongue of land on which it remains to this day. It arrived from no one knew where, and spoke an unknown tongue. One of its chiefs, who understood Provençal, begged the commune of Marseilles to give them this bare and barren promontory, on which, like the sailors of the ancient times, they had run their boats ashore. The request was granted; and three months afterwards, around the twelve or fifteen small vessels which had brought these gipsies of the sea, a small village sprang up. This village, constructed in a singular and picturesque manner, half Moorish, half Spanish, is that which we behold at the present day, inhabited by the descendants of those men, who speak the language of their fathers. For three or four centuries they have loyally clung to this small promontory, on which they had settled like a flight of sea-birds, without mixing with the Marseillaise population, intermarrying among themselves and preserving their original customs and the costume of their mother-country, as they have preserved its language.

Our readers will follow us along the only street of this little village, and enter with us one of the houses, on the outside of which the sun had stamped that beautiful colour of the dead leaf peculiar to the buildings of the country, and which, within, was coated with limewash, of that white tint which forms the only ornament of Spanish *posadas*. A young and beautiful girl, with hair as black as jet, her eyes as velvety as the gazelle's, was leaning with her back against the wainscot, rubbing in her slender fingers, moulded after the antique, a bunch of heath-blossoms, the flowers of which she was picking off and strewing on the floor; her arms, bare to the elbow, embrowned, and resembling those of the Venus at Arles, moved with a kind of restless impatience, and she tapped the earth with her pliant and well-formed foot so as to display the pure and full shape of her well-turned leg, in its red cotton stocking with grey and blue clocks. At three paces from her, seated in a chair which he balanced on two legs, leaning his elbow on an old worm-eaten table, was a tall young man of twenty or two-and-twenty, who was looking at her with an air in which vexation and uneasiness were mingled. He questioned her with his eyes, but the firm and steady gaze of the young girl controlled his look.

" You see, Mercédès," said the young man, " here is Easter come round again; tell me, is it not a good time for a wedding? "

" I have answered you a hundred times, Fernand; and really you must be your own enemy to ask me again."

" Well, repeat it,—repeat it, I beg of you, that I may at last believe it! Tell me for the hundredth time that you refuse my love, which had your mother's sanction. Make me fully comprehend that you are trifling with my happiness, that my life or death are immaterial to you. Ah! to have dreamed for ten years of being your husband, Mercédès, and to lose that hope, which was the sole aim of my existence! "

" At least it was not I who ever encouraged you in that hope, Fernand," replied Mercédès; " you cannot reproach me with the slightest coquetry. I have always said to you, ' I love you as a brother; but do not ask from me more than sisterly affection, for my heart is another's.' Have I not always told you that, Fernand?"

"Yes, I know it well, Mercédès," replied the young man. "Yes, you have been cruelly frank with me; but do you forget that it is among the Catalans a sacred law to intermarry?"

"You mistake, Fernand, it is not a law, but merely a custom; and, I pray of you, do not cite this custom in your favour. You are included in the conscription, Fernand, and are at liberty only on sufferance, liable at any moment to be called upon to take up arms. Once a soldier, what would you do with me,—a poor orphan, forlorn, without fortune, with nothing but a hut half in ruins, containing some ragged nets, a miserable inheritance left by my father to my mother, and by my mother to me? She has been dead a year, and you know, Fernand, I have subsisted almost entirely on public charity. Sometimes you pretend I am useful to you, and that is an excuse to share with me the produce of your fishing; and I accept it, Fernand, because you are the son of my father's brother, because we were brought up together, and still more because it would give you so much pain if I refused. But I feel very deeply that this fish which I go and sell, and with the produce of which I buy the flax I spin, —I feel very keenly, Fernand, that this is charity."

"And if it were, Mercédès, poor and lone as you are, you suit me as well as the daughter of the proudest ship-owner, or of the richest banker of Marseilles! What do such as we desire but an honest woman and careful housekeeper; and where can I find any one better than you in both these particulars?"

"Fernand," answered Mercédès, shaking her head, "a woman may become a bad manager; and who shall say she will remain an honest woman when she loves another man better than her husband? Rest content with my friendship, for I repeat to you that it is all I can promise, and I will promise no more than I can bestow."

"I understand," replied Fernand; "you can endure your own wretchedness patiently, but you are afraid of mine. Well, Mercédès, beloved by you, I would tempt fortune; you would bring me good luck, and I should become rich. I could extend my occupation as a fisherman, might get a place as clerk in a warehouse, and become myself a dealer in time."

"You could do no such thing, Fernand; you are a soldier, and if you remain at the Catalans it is because there is no war. Continue, then, to be a fisherman; don't cherish dreams which will make the reality still more intolerable. Be content with my friendship, since I cannot give you more."

"Well, you are right, Mercédès. I will be a sailor; instead of the costume of our fathers, which you despise, I will wear a varnished hat, a striped shirt, and a blue jacket, with an anchor on the buttons. Would not that dress please you?"

"What do you mean?" asked Mercédès, darting at him an angry glance,—"what do you mean? I do not understand you."

"I mean, Mercédès, that you are thus harsh and cruel with me because you are expecting some one who is thus attired; but perhaps he whom you await is inconstant, or if he is not, the sea is so to him."

"Fernand!" cried Mercédès, "I believed you were good-hearted, and I was mistaken! Fernand, you are wicked to call to your aid jealousy and the anger of God! Yes, I will not deny it, I do await, and I do love him to whom you allude; and if he does not return, instead of accusing him of the inconstancy which you insinuate, I shall maintain that he died loving me and me only."

The young Catalan made a gesture of rage.

"I understand you, Fernand: you would be revenged on him because I do not love you; you would cross your Catalan knife with his dirk. What end would that answer? You would lose my friendship if you were conquered, and would see that friendship changed into hate if you were conqueror. Believe me, to seek a quarrel with a man is a bad way to please the woman who loves that man. No, Fernand, you will not thus give way to evil thoughts. Unable to have me for your wife, you will content yourself with having me for your friend and sister; and besides," she added, her eyes troubled and moistened with tears, "wait, wait, Fernand! You said just now that the sea was treacherous, and he has been gone four months, and during these four months we have had some terrible storms."

Fernand made no reply, nor did he attempt to check the tears which flowed down the cheeks of Mercédès, although for each of these tears he would have shed his heart's blood; but these tears flowed for another. He arose, paced awhile up and down the hut, and then suddenly stopping before Mercédès, with his eyes glowing and his hands clinched, "Say, Mercédès," he said, "once for all, is this your final determination?"

"I love Edmond Dantès," the young girl calmly replied, "and none but Edmond shall be my husband."

"And you will always love him?"

"As long as I live."

Fernand lowered his head like a defeated man, heaved a sigh

which resembled a groan, and then suddenly looking her full in the face, with clinched teeth and expanded nostrils, said, " But if he is dead—"

" If he is dead, I shall die too."

" If he has forgotten you—"

" Mercédès!" cried a voice, joyously, outside the house, " Mercédès!"

" Ah!" exclaimed the young girl, blushing with delight, and springing up with love, " you see he has not forgotten me, for here he is!" And rushing towards the door, she opened it, saying, " Here, Edmond, here I am!"

Fernand, pale and trembling, fell back, like a traveller at the sight of a serpent, and stumbling against his chair, dropped into it. Edmond and Mercédès were clasped in each other's arms. The burning sun of Marseilles, which penetrated the room by the open door, covered them with a flood of light. At first they saw nothing around them. Their intense happiness isolated them from all the rest of the world, and they spoke only in broken words, which are the tokens of a joy so extreme that they seem rather the expression of sorrow. Suddenly Edmond saw the gloomy countenance of Fernand, as it was defined in the shadow, pale and threatening; and by a movement for which he could scarcely account to himself, the young Catalan placed his hand on the knife at his belt.

" Ah! your pardon!" said Dantès, frowning in his turn; " I did not perceive that there were three of us." Then, turning to Mercédès, he inquired, " Who is this gentleman?"

" One who will be your best friend, Dantès, for he is my friend, my cousin, my brother; it is Fernand,—the man whom, after you, Edmond, I love the best in the world. Do you not remember him?"

" Yes!" said Edmond, and without relinquishing Mercédès's hand, clasped in one of his own, he extended the other to the Catalan with a cordial air. But Fernand, instead of responding to this friendly gesture, remained silent and immovable as a statue. Edmond then cast his eyes scrutinisingly at Mercédès, agitated and embarrassed, and again on Fernand, gloomy and menacing. This look told him all, and his brow became suffused and angry.

" I did not know when I came with such haste to you that I was to meet an enemy here."

" An enemy!" cried Mercédès, with an angry look at her cousin. " An enemy in my house, do you say, Edmond? If I believed that, I would place my arm under yours and go with you to Marseilles, leaving the house to return to it no more."

Fernand's eye darted lightning.

" And should any misfortune occur to you, dear Edmond," she continued with the same calmness, which proved to Fernand that the young girl had read the very innermost depths of his sinister thought,—" if misfortune should occur to you, I would ascend the highest point of Cape Morgion, and cast myself headlong from it."

Fernand became deadly pale.

" But you are deceived, Edmond," she continued. " You have no enemy here—there is no one but Fernand, my brother, who will grasp your hand as a devoted friend."

And at these words the young girl fixed her imperious look on the Catalan, who, as if fascinated by it, came slowly towards Edmond, and offered him his hand. His hatred, like a powerless though furious wave, was broken against the strong ascendency which Mercédès exercised over him. Scarcely, however, had he touched Edmond's hand when he felt that he had done all he could do, and rushed hastily out of the house.

" Oh!" he exclaimed, running like a madman, and plunging his hands into his hair,—" oh! who will deliver me from this man? Wretched, wretched that I am!"

" Holloa, Catalan! Holloa, Fernand! where are you going? " exclaimed a voice.

The young man stopped suddenly, looked around him, and perceived Caderousse sitting at table with Danglars under an arbour.

" Well," said Caderousse, " why don't you come? Are you really in such a hurry that you have no time to say ' Good-day ' to your friends? "

" Particularly when they have still a full bottle before them," added Danglars.

Fernand looked at them both with a stupefied air, but did not say a word.

" He seems besotted," said Danglars, pushing Caderousse with his knee. " Are we mistaken, and is Dantès triumphant in spite of all we have believed? "

" Why, we must inquire into that," was Caderousse's reply; and turning towards the young man, he said, " Well, Catalan, can't you make up your mind? "

Fernand wiped away the perspiration streaming from his brow, and slowly entered the arbour, whose shade seemed to restore somewhat of calmness to his senses, and whose coolness refreshed his exhausted body.

"Good-day," said he. "You called me, didn't you?" And he fell, rather than sat down, on one of the seats which surrounded the table.

"I called you because you were running like a madman, and I was afraid you would throw yourself into the sea," said Caderousse, laughing. "The devil! when a man has friends, they are not only to offer him a glass of wine, but, moreover, to prevent his swallowing three or four pints of water unnecessarily!"

Fernand gave a groan which resembled a sob, and dropped his head into his hands, his elbows leaning on the table.

"Well, Fernand, I must say," said Caderousse, beginning the conversation with that brutality of the common people in which curiosity destroys all diplomacy, "you look uncommonly like a rejected lover; " and he burst into a hoarse laugh.

"Bah!" said Danglars, "a lad of his make was not born to be unhappy in love. You are laughing at him, Caderousse!"

"No," he replied, "only listen to his sighs! Come, come, Fernand!" said Caderousse, "hold up your head, and answer us. It's not polite not to reply to friends who ask news of your health."

"My health is well enough," said Fernand, clinching his hands without raising his head.

"Ah! you see, Danglars," said Caderousse, winking at his friend, "this it is: Fernand, whom you see here, is a good and brave Catalan, one of the best fishermen in Marseilles, and he is in love with a very fine girl named Mercédès; but it appears, unfortunately, that the fine girl is in love with the second in command on board the *Pharaon*, and as the *Pharaon* arrived to-day—why, you understand!"

"No, I do not understand," said Danglars.

"Poor Fernand has been dismissed," continued Caderousse.

"Well, and what then?" said Fernand, lifting up his head, and looking at Caderousse like a man who looks for some one on whom to vent his anger. "Mercédès is not accountable to any person, is she? Is she not free to love whomsoever she will?"

"Oh! if you take it in that sense," said Caderousse, "it is another thing! But I thought you were a Catalan, and they told me the Catalans were not men to allow themselves to be supplanted by a rival. It was even told me that Fernand, especially, was terrible in his vengeance."

Fernand smiled piteously. "A lover is never terrible," he said.

"Poor fellow!" remarked Danglars, affecting to pity the young man from the bottom of his heart. "Why, you see, he did not expect to see Dantès return so suddenly. He thought he was dead, perhaps; or perchance faithless! These things always come on us more severely when they come suddenly."

" Ah, *ma foi*, under any circumstances," said Caderousse, who drank as he spoke, and on whom the fumes of the wine of La Malgue began to take effect,—" under any circumstances Fernand is not the only person put out by the fortunate arrival of Dantès; is he, Danglars?"

" No, you are right; and I should say that would bring him ill luck."

" Well, never mind," answered Caderousse, pouring out a glass of wine for Fernand, and filling his own for the eighth or ninth time, while Danglars had merely sipped his. " Never mind; in the meantime he marries Mercédès, the lovely Mercédès,—at least, he returns to do that."

During this time Danglars fixed his piercing glance on the young man, on whose heart Caderousse's words fell like molten lead.

" And when is the wedding to be?" he asked.

" Oh, it is not yet fixed!" murmured Fernand.

" No, but it will be," said Caderousse, " as surely as that Dantès will be captain of the *Pharaon;* eh, Danglars?"

Danglars shuddered at this unexpected attack, and turned to Caderousse, whose countenance he scrutinised, to discover whether the blow was premeditated; but he read nothing but envy in a countenance already rendered brutal and stupid by drunkenness.

" Well," said he, filling the glasses, " let us drink to Capt. Edmond Dantès, husband of the beautiful Catalane!"

Caderousse raised his glass to his mouth with unsteady hand, and swallowed the contents at a gulp. Fernand dashed his on the ground.

" Eh, eh, eh!" stammered Caderousse. " What do I see down there by the wall in the direction of the Catalans? Look, Fernand! your eyes are better than mine. I believe I see double. You know wine is a deceiver; but I should say it was two lovers walking side by side, and hand in hand. Heaven forgive me! they do not know that we can see them, and they are actually embracing!"

Danglars did not lose one pang that Fernand endured.

" Do you know them, M. Fernand?" he said.

" Yes," was the reply, in a low voice. " It is M. Edmond and Mademoiselle Mercédès!"

" Ah! see there, now!" said Caderousse; " and I did

not recognise them! Holloa, Dantès! holloa, lovely damsel! Come this way, and let us know when the wedding is to be, for M. Fernand here is so obstinate he will not tell us!"

"Hold your tongue, will you?" said Danglars, pretending to restrain Caderousse, who, with the tenacity of drunkards, leaned out of the arbour. "Try to stand upright, and let the lovers make love without interruption. See, look at M. Fernand, and follow his example; he is well-behaved!"

Fernand, probably excited beyond bearing, pricked by Danglars, as the bull is by the *banderilleros*, was about to rush out; for he had risen from his seat, and seemed to be collecting himself to dash headlong upon his rival, when Mercédès, smiling and graceful, lifted up her lovely head and showed her clear, bright eyes. At this Fernand recollected her threat of dying if Edmond died, and dropped again heavily on his seat. Danglars looked at the two men, one after the other, the one brutalised by liquor, the other overwhelmed with love.

"I shall extract nothing from these fools," he muttered; "and I am very much afraid of being here between a drunkard and a coward. Yet this Catalan has eyes that glisten like the Spaniards, Sicilians, and Calabrians, who practise revenge so well. Unquestionably Edmond's star is in the ascendant, and he will marry the splendid girl; he will be captain, too, and laugh at us all, unless—" a sinister smile passed over Danglar's lips—"unless I mingle in the affair," he added.

"Holloa!" continued Caderousse, half rising, and with his fist on the table,—"holloa, Edmond! do you not see your friends, or are you too proud to speak to them?"

"No, my dear fellow," replied Dantès, "I am not proud, but I am happy; and happiness blinds, I think, more than pride."

"Ah! very well, that's an explanation!" said Caderousse. "Well, good-day, Madame Dantès!"

Mercédès bowed gravely, and said, "That is not my name; and in my country it bodes ill fortune, they say, to call a young girl by the name of her betrothed before he becomes her husband. Call me, then, Mercédès, if you please."

"We must excuse our worthy neighbour Caderousse," said Dantès, "he is so easily mistaken."

"So, then, the wedding is to take place immediately, M. Dantès," said Danglars, bowing to the young couple.

"As soon as possible, M. Danglars; to-day all preliminaries will be arranged at my father's, and to-morrow, or next day at latest, the wedding festival will take place here at La Réserve.

My friends will be there, I hope; that is to say, you are invited, M. Danglars, and you, Caderousse."

"And Fernand," said Caderousse, with a chuckle, "Fernand, too, is invited?"

"My wife's brother is my brother," said Edmond; "and we, Mercédès and I, should be very sorry if he were absent at such a time."

Fernand opened his mouth to reply, but his voice died on his lips, and he could not utter a word.

"To-day the preliminaries, to-morrow or next day the ceremony! you are in a hurry, captain!"

"Danglars," said Edmond, smiling, "I will say to you as Mercédès said just now to Caderousse, 'Do not give me a title which does not belong to me;' that may bring me bad luck."

"Your pardon," replied Danglars; "I merely said you seemed in a hurry. We have lots of time,—the *Pharaon* cannot be ready to sail in less than three months."

"We are always in a hurry to be happy, M. Danglars, for when we have suffered a long time, we have great difficulty in believing in good fortune. But it is not selfishness alone that makes me thus in haste; I must go to Paris."

"To Paris? really! and will it be your first visit there, Dantès?"

"Yes."

"Have you business there?"

"Not of my own; the last commission of poor Captain Leclere. You know to what I allude, Danglars; it is sacred. Besides, I shall only take the time to go and return."

"Yes, yes, I understand," said Danglars; and then in a low tone he added, "To Paris, no doubt, to deliver the letter which the grand-marshal gave him. Ah! this letter gives me an idea, a capital idea! Ah, Dantès, my friend, you are not yet registered Number One on the good ship *Pharaon;*" then turning towards Edmond, who was walking away, "*Bon voyage!*" he cried.

"Thank you," said Edmond, with a friendly nod; and the two lovers continued their route, calm and joyous.

CHAPTER IV

CONSPIRACY

Danglars followed Edmond and Mercédès with his eyes until the two lovers disappeared behind one of the angles of Fort St. Nicolas; then turning round, he perceived Fernand, who had fallen, pale and trembling, into his chair, while Caderousse stammered out the words of a drinking-song.

"Well, my dear sir," said Danglars to Fernand, "here is a marriage which does not appear to make everybody happy."

"It drives me to despair," said Fernand.

"Do you, then, love Mercédès?"

"I adore her!"

"Have you loved her long?"

"Ever since I have known her."

"And you sit there, tearing your hair, instead of seeking a remedy. The devil! I did not think that people of your race would act in this way."

"What would you have me do?" said Fernand.

"How do I know? Is it my affair? I am not in love with Mademoiselle Mercédès,—it is you. 'Seek,' says the Gospel, 'and you shall find.'"

"I have found already."

"What?"

"I would have stabbed the man, but the woman told me that if any misfortune happened to her betrothed she would kill herself."

"Pooh! women say those things, but never do them."

"You do not know Mercédès; what she threatens she will do."

"Idiot!" muttered Danglars; "whether she kill herself or not what matter, provided Dantès is not captain?"

"Rather than Mercédès should die," replied Fernand, with the accents of unshaken resolution, "I would die myself!"

"That's what I call love!" said Caderousse, with a voice more tipsy than ever. "That's love, or I don't know what love is."

"Come," said Danglars, "you appear to me a good sort of fellow, and the devil take me, I should like to help you, but—"

"Yes," said Caderousse, "but how?"

"My dear fellow," replied Danglars, "you are three parts drunk; finish the bottle, and you will be completely so. Drink, then, and do not meddle with what we are discussing, for that requires all one's wit and cool judgment."

"I drunk!" said Caderousse; "well, that's a good one! I could drink four more such bottles; they are no bigger than eau-de-cologne flasks. Père Pamphile, more wine!" and Caderousse rattled his glass upon the table.

"You were saying, monsieur?" said Fernand, awaiting with great anxiety the end of the interrupted remark.

"What was I saying? I forget. This drunken Caderousse has made me lose the thread of my thoughts."

"Drunk, if you like; so much the worse for those who fear wine, for it is because they have some evil thought which they are afraid the liquor will extract from their hearts;" and Caderousse began to sing the last two lines of a song very popular at the time—

> "All the wicked are drinkers of water;
> That is well proved by the Deluge."

"You said, monsieur, that you would like to help me, but—"

"Yes; but I was about to add, to help you it would be sufficient that Dantès did not marry her you love. And the marriage may easily be thwarted, methinks, and yet Dantès need not die."

"Death alone can separate them," remarked Fernand.

"You talk like a noodle, my friend," said Caderousse; "here is Danglars, who is a wide-awake, clever, deep fellow, who will prove to you that you are wrong. Prove it, Danglars. I have answered for you. Say there is no need that Dantès should die; it would, indeed, be a pity if he should. Dantès is a good fellow. I like Dantès; Dantès, your health!"

Fernand rose impatiently. "Let him run on," said Danglars, restraining the young man; "drunk as he is, he is not much out in what he says. Absence severs as well as death, and if the walls of a prison were between Edmond and Mercédès they would be as effectually separated as if he lay under a tombstone."

"Yes; but one gets out of prison," said Caderousse, who, with what sense was left him, listened eagerly to the conversation; "and when he gets out, if his name is Edmond Dantès, he revenges—"

"What matters that?" muttered Fernand.

"And why, I should like to know," persisted Caderousse, "should they put Dantès in prison? He has neither robbed nor killed nor murdered."

"Hold your tongue!" said Danglars.

"I won't hold my tongue!" replied Caderousse; "I say I want to know why they should put Dantès in prison. I like Dantès; Dantès, your health!" and he swallowed another glass of wine.

Danglars saw in the muddled look of the tailor the progress of his intoxication, and turning towards Fernand, said, "Well, you understand there is no need to kill him."

"Certainly not, if, as you said just now, you have the means of having Dantès arrested. Have you that means?"

"It is to be found for the searching. But what in the devil have I to do with it? It is no affair of mine."

"I know not whether it is your affair," said Fernand, seizing his arm; "but this I know, you have some motive of personal hatred against Dantès, for he who himself hates is never mistaken in the sentiments of others."

"I? motives of hatred against Dantès? None, on my word! I saw you were unhappy, and your unhappiness interested me; that's all. But since you believe I act for my own account, adieu, my dear friend, get out of the affair as best you may;" and Danglars rose as if he meant to depart.

"No, no;" said Fernand, restraining him, "stay! It is of very little consequence to me at the end of the matter whether you have any angry feeling or not against Dantès. I hate him! I declare it openly. Do you find the means, I will execute it, —provided it is not to kill the man, for Mercédès has declared she will kill herself if Dantès is killed."

Caderousse, who had let his head drop on the table, now raised it, and looking at Fernand with his dull and fishy eyes, he said, "Kill Dantès! who talks of killing Dantès? I won't have him killed,—I won't! He's my friend, and this morning offered to share his money with me, as I shared mine with him. I won't have Dantès killed,—I won't!"

"And who has said a word about killing him, muddle-head?" replied Danglars. "We were merely joking; drink to his health," he added, filling Caderousse's glass, "and do not interfere with us."

"Yes, yes, Dantès's good health!" said Caderousse, emptying his glass, "here's to his health! his health! hurrah!"

"But the means,—the means?" said Fernand.

"Have you not hit upon any?"

"No; you undertook to do so."

"True," replied Danglars; "the French have the superiority over the Spaniards, that the Spaniards ruminate, while the French invent."

"Do you invent, then!" said Fernand, impatiently.

"Waiter," said Danglars, "pen, ink, and paper."

"Pen, ink, and paper!" muttered Fernand.

"Yes; I am a supercargo. Pen, ink, and paper are my tools, and without my tools I am fit for nothing."

"Pen, ink, and paper!" called Fernand, loudly.

"All you require is on that table," said the waiter, pointing to the writing materials.

"Bring them here." The waiter did as he was desired.

"When one thinks," said Caderousse, letting his hand drop on the paper, "that here there is what will kill a man more surely than if we waited at the corner of a wood to assassinate him! I have always had more dread of a pen, a bottle of ink, and a sheet of paper than of a sword or pistol."

"The fellow is not so drunk as he appears to be," said Danglars. "Give him some more wine, Fernand."

Fernand filled Caderousse's glass, who, toper as he was, lifted his hand from the paper and seized the glass. The Catalan watched him until Caderousse, almost overcome by this fresh assault on his senses, rested, or rather allowed his glass to fall upon the table.

"Well!" resumed the Catalan, as he saw the final glimmer of Caderousse's reason vanishing before the last glass of wine.

"Well, then, I should say, for instance," resumed Danglars, "that if after a voyage such as Dantès has just made, and in which he touched the Isle of Elba, some one were to denounce him to the *procureur du roi* as a Bonapartist agent—"

"I will denounce him!" exclaimed the young man, hastily.

"Yes, but they will make you then sign your declaration, and confront you with him you have denounced; I will supply you with the means of supporting your accusation, for I know the fact well. But Dantès cannot remain forever in prison, and one day or other he will leave it; and the day when he comes out, woe betide him who was the cause of his incarceration!"

"Oh, I should wish nothing better than that he would come and seek a quarrel with me."

"Yes, and Mercédès,—Mercédès, who will detest you if you have only the misfortune to scratch the skin of her dearly beloved Edmond!"

"True!" said Fernand.

"No, no!" continued Danglars; "if we resolve on such a step, it would be much better to take, as I now do, this pen, dip it into this ink, and write with the left hand (that the writing may not be recognised) the denunciation we propose."

And Danglars, uniting practice with theory, wrote with his left hand and with a backward slant in a style wholly unlike his own, the following lines, which he handed to Fernand, and which Fernand read in an undertone:—

MONSIEUR,—The *procureur du roi* is informed by a friend of the throne and of religion, that one Edmond Dantès, mate of the ship *Pharaon*, who arrived this morning from Smyrna, after having touched at Naples and Porto Ferrajo, has been intrusted by Murat with a letter for the usurper, and by the usurper with a letter for the Bonapartist committee in Paris.

Proof of this crime will be found on arresting him, for the letter will be found upon him, or at his father's, or in his cabin on board the *Pharaon*.

"Very good," resumed Danglars; "now your revenge looks like common-sense, for in no way can it fall back on yourself, and the matter will work its own way. There is nothing to do now but fold the letter as I am doing, and write upon it, 'To M. le Procureur Royal,' and that's all settled. And Danglars wrote the address as he spoke.

"Yes, and that's all settled!" exclaimed Caderousse, who, by a last effort of intellect, had followed the reading of the letter, and instinctively comprehended all the misery which such a denunciation must entail. "Yes, and that's all settled; only it will be an infamous shame;" and he stretched out his hand to reach the letter.

"Yes," said Danglars, taking it from beyond his reach; "and as what I say and do is merely in jest, and I, among the first and foremost, should be sorry if anything happened to Dantès, the worthy Dantès, look here!" and taking the letter, he squeezed it up in his hands and threw it into a corner of the arbour.

"All right!" said Caderousse. "Dantès is my friend, and I won't have him ill-used."

"And who in the devil thinks of using him ill? Certainly neither I nor Fernand!" said Danglars, rising and looking at the young man, who still remained seated, but whose eye was fixed on the denunciatory sheet of paper flung into the corner.

"In that case," replied Caderousse, "let's have some more wine. I wish to drink to the health of Edmond and the lovely Mercédès."

"You have had too much already, drunkard," said Danglars; "and if you continue, you will be compelled to sleep here, because unable to stand on your legs."

"I?" said Caderousse, rising with all the offended dignity

of a drunken man, " I can't keep on my legs? Why, I'll bet a wager I go up into the belfry of the Accoules, and without staggering, too! "

" Well done! " said Danglars, " I'll take your bet; but to-morrow,—to-day it is time to return. Give me your arm, and let us go."

" Very well, let us go," said Caderousse; " but I don't want your arm at all. Come, Fernand, won't you return to Marseilles with us? "

" No," answered Fernand; " I shall return to the Catalans."

" You're wrong. Come with us to Marseilles; come along."

" I will not."

" What do you mean? You will not? Well, just as you like, my prince; there's liberty for all the world. Come along, Danglars, and let the young gentleman return to the Catalans if he chooses."

Danglars took advantage of Caderousse's temper at the moment to take him off towards Marseilles by the Porte St. Victor, staggering as he went.

When they had advanced about twenty yards, Danglars looked back and saw Fernand stoop, pick up the crumpled paper, and put it into his pocket, then rush out of the arbour towards Pillon.

" Well," said Caderousse, " why, what a lie he told! He said he was going to the Catalans, and he is going to the city. Holloa, Fernand! "

" Oh, you see wrong," said Danglars; " he's gone right enough."

" Well," said Caderousse, " I should have said not; how treacherous wine is! "

" Come, come," said Danglars to himself, " now I think the affair is well launched, and there is nothing to do but to let it go on."

CHAPTER V

THE MARRIAGE-FEAST

THE morning's sun rose clear and resplendent, gilding the heavens and even the foamy waves, with its bright refulgent beams.

The plenteous feast had been prepared at La Réserve, with whose arbour the reader is already acquainted. The apartment destined for the purpose was spacious and lighted by a number of windows, over each of which was written in golden letters the name of one of the principal cities of France; beneath these windows a wooden balcony extended the entire length of the house. Although the entertainment was appointed to begin at twelve o'clock, an hour previous to that time the balcony was filled with impatient and expectant guests, consisting of the favoured part of the crew of the *Pharaon*, and other personal friends of the bridegroom, all of whom had arrayed themselves in their choicest costumes, in order to do greater honour to the day. Various rumours were afloat to the effect that the owners of the *Pharaon* had promised to attend the nuptial feast; but all seemed unanimous in doubting that an act of such rare and exceeding condescension could possibly be intended.

Danglars, however, who now made his appearance, accompanied by Caderousse, confirmed the report, stating that he had recently conversed with M. Morrel, who had himself assured him that he intended joining the festive party upon the occasion of their second officer's marriage.

In fact, a moment later M. Morrel made his appearance in the chamber, and was greeted by the sailors with a unanimous burst of applause. The presence of the ship-owner was to them a sure indication that the man whose wedding-feast he thus delighted to honour would ere long be first in command of the *Pharaon*; and as Dantès was universally beloved on board his vessel, the sailors put no restraint on their tumultuous joy at finding the opinion and choice of their superiors so exactly coincide with their wishes.

This noisy though hearty welcome over, Danglars and Caderousse were despatched to the residence of the bridegroom to convey to him the intelligence of the arrival of the important personage who had recently joined them, and to desire he would hasten to receive his honourable guest.

The above-mentioned individuals started off upon their errand at full speed; but ere they had gone many steps they perceived a group advancing towards them, composed of the betrothed pair, and a party of young girls in attendance on the bride, by whose side walked Dantès's father. Behind them came Fernand, whose lips wore their usual sinister smile.

Neither Mercédès nor Edmond observed the strange expression of his countenance; they were so happy that they had eyes only for each other and for the clear, beautiful sky above them.

Having acquitted themselves of their errand and exchanged a hearty greeting with Edmond, Danglars walked by the side of Fernand, and Caderousse joined the elder Dantès, who was the centre of general attention. The old man was attired in a suit of black, trimmed with steel buttons, beautifully cut and polished. His thin but still powerful legs were arrayed in a pair of richly embroidered clocked stockings, evidently of English manufacture; from his three-cornered hat depended a long streaming knot of white and blue ribbons, and he supported himself on a curiously carved stick. By his side, as we have said, crept Caderousse, whose desire to partake of the good things provided for the wedding-party had induced him to become reconciled to the Dantès, father and son, and who still retained in his mind a faint and imperfect recollection of the events of the preceding night,—just as the brain retains on waking the dim and misty outline of a dream.

As Danglars approached the disappointed lover, he cast on him a look of deep meaning. Fernand, as he slowly paced behind the happy pair, who seemed in their own unmixed content to have entirely forgotten that such a being as himself existed, was pale and abstracted. Occasionally, however, a deep flush would overspread his countenance, and a nervous contraction distort his features, while with an agitated and restless gaze he would glance in the direction of Marseilles, like one who was expecting some striking event.

Dantès himself was simply though becomingly clad in the dress peculiar to the merchant service,—a costume somewhat between a military and a civil garb; and with his fine countenance, radiant with joy and happiness, a more perfect specimen of manly beauty could scarcely be imagined.

Lovely as the Greeks of Cyprus or Chios, Mercédès boasted the same bright flashing eyes of jet, and ripe round coral lips. She walked with the frank, free step of the Andalusians. One more practised in the arts of great cities would have hid her joy beneath a veil, or at least have cast down her thickly fringed lashes, so as to have concealed the liquid lustre of her animated eyes; but Mercédès looked around her with a smile that plainly said, "If you are my friends rejoice with me, for in truth I am very happy."

As soon as the bridal *cortége* came in sight of La Réserve, M. Morrel came forth to meet it, followed by the soldiers and sailors there assembled, to whom he had repeated the promise already given, that Dantès should be the successor of the late Captain Leclere. Edmond, at the approach of his patron, placed the arm of his affianced bride within that of M. Morrel, who forthwith conducting her up the flight of wooden steps leading to the chamber in which the feast was prepared, was gaily followed by the guests, beneath whose thronging numbers the slight structure creaked and groaned as though alarmed at the unusual pressure.

"Father," said Mercédès, stopping when she had reached the centre of the table, "sit, I pray you, on my right hand; on my left I will place him who has ever been as a brother to me," she added with a gentle tenderness that went to the heart of Fernand like the stroke of a dagger. His lips became pale, and even beneath the dark hue of his complexion the blood might be seen retreating as though some sudden pang drove it back to the heart.

Meanwhile Dantès, at the opposite side of the table, had been occupied in similarly placing his most honoured guests. M. Morrel was seated at his right hand, Danglars at his left; the rest of the company ranged themselves as they found it most agreeable.

And now began the work of devastation upon the many good things with which the table was loaded. Sausages of Arles, with their delicate seasoning and piquant flavour, lobsters in their dazzling red cuirasses, prawns of large size and brilliant colour, the echinus, with its prickly outside and dainty morsel within; the clovis, esteemed by the epicures of the South as more than rivalling the exquisite flavour of the oyster,—all these, in conjunction with the numerous delicacies cast up by the wash of waters on the sandy beach, and styled by the grateful fishermen "sea-fruits," served to furnish forth this marriage-table.

"A pretty silence truly!" said the old father of the bride-groom, as he carried to his lips a glass of wine of the hue and brightness of the topaz, and which had just been placed before Mercédès herself. "Now, would anybody think that there are here thirty persons who desire only to laugh?"

"Ah!" sighed Caderousse, "a husband is not always gay."

"The truth is," replied Dantès, "that I am too happy for noisy mirth; if that is what you meant by your observation, my worthy friend, you are right. Joy takes a strange effect at times; it seems to oppress us almost the same as sorrow."

Danglars looked towards Fernand, whose excitable nature received and betrayed each fresh impression.

"Why, what ails you?" asked he of Edmond. "Do you fear any approaching evil? I should say that you are the happiest man alive at this instant."

"And that is the very thing that alarms me," returned Dantès. "Man does not appear to me to be intended to enjoy felicity so unmixed. Happiness is like the enchanted palaces we read of in our childhood, where fierce fiery dragons defend the entrance and approach, and monsters of all shapes and kinds, requiring to be overcome ere victory is ours. I own that I am lost in wonder to find myself promoted to an honour of which I feel myself unworthy,—that of being the husband of Mercédès."

"The husband, the husband?" said Caderousse, laughing; "not yet, my captain. Attempt to play the husband a little, and see how you will be received."

Mercédès blushed. Fernand, restless and uneasy, started at the least noise, and from time to time wiped away large drops of sweat that appeared on his forehead, like the first drops of rain before a storm.

"Well, never mind that, neighbour Caderousse; it is not worth while to contradict me for such a trifle as that. 'Tis true that Mercédès is not actually my wife; but," added he, drawing out his watch, "in an hour and a half she will be."

Every one uttered a cry of surprise, with the exception of the elder Dantès, whose laugh displayed the still perfect beauty of his large white teeth. Mercédès smiled, and no longer blushed. Fernand grasped the handle of his knife with a convulsive clutch.

"In an hour?" inquired Danglars, turning pale. "How is that, my friend?"

"Yes, my friends," replied Dantès; "thanks to the influence of M. Morrel, to whom, next to my father, I owe all the blessings I enjoy, every difficulty has been removed. We have purchased permission to waive the usual delay; and at half-past two o'clock the Mayor of Marseilles will be waiting for us at the Hôtel de Ville. Now, as a quarter-past one has already struck, I do not consider I have asserted too much in saying that in another hour and thirty minutes Mercédès will have become Madame Dantès."

Fernand closed his eyes, a burning sensation passed across his brow, and he was compelled to support himself by the table to keep from falling; but in spite of all his efforts, he could not refrain from uttering a deep groan, which, however, was lost amid the noisy felicitations of the company.

"Upon my word," cried the old man, "you make short work of it. Arrived here only yesterday morning, and married to-day at three o'clock! Commend me to a sailor for going the quick way to work!"

"But," asked Danglars, in a timid tone, "how did you

manage about the other formalities,—the contract, the settlement?"

"Oh, bless you!" answered Dantès, laughingly, "our papers were soon drawn up. Mercédès has no fortune; I have none to settle on her. So, you see, our papers were quickly written out, and certainly do not come very expensive." This joke elicited a fresh burst of applause.

"So that what we presumed to be merely the betrothal feast turns out to be the actual wedding dinner?" said Danglars.

"No, no!" answered Dantès; "don't imagine I am going to put you off in that shabby manner. To-morrow morning I start for Paris. Four days to go, and the same to return, with one day to discharge the commission intrusted to me, and on the first of March I shall have returned; the next day I will give my real marriage-feast."

This prospect of fresh festivity redoubled the hilarity of the guests to such a degree that the elder Dantès, who, at the commencement of the repast had commented upon the silence that prevailed, now found it difficult amid the general din of voices to obtain a moment's tranquillity in which to drink to the health and prosperity of the bride and bridegroom.

Dantès, perceiving the affectionate eagerness of his father, responded by a look of grateful pleasure; while Mercédès, whose eyes had been constantly consulting the clock which adorned the chamber, made an expressive gesture to Edmond.

Around the festive board reigned that mirthful freedom from all restraint which is usually found at the termination of social meetings, among those, at least, whose inferior station in the world gives them a happy dispensation from the frigid rules of etiquette. Those who were dissatisfied with their places at the table had sought out other neighbours. All spoke at once; and no one troubled himself to reply to what his interlocutor was saying, but each spoke to his own thoughts.

The paleness of Fernand appeared to have communicated itself to Danglars. As for Fernand himself, he seemed as though undergoing the tortures of the damned. Unable to rest, he was among the first to quit the table, and as though seeking to avoid the hilarious mirth that rose in such deafening sounds, he continued in utter silence to pace the farther end of the salon.

Caderousse approached him just as Danglars, whom Fernand seemed most anxious to avoid, had joined him in a corner of the room.

"Upon my word," said Caderousse, from whose mind the

friendly treatment of Dantès, united with the effect of the excellent wine he had partaken of, had effaced every feeling of envy or jealousy at Dantès's good fortune,—" upon my word, Dantès is a downright good fellow, and when I see him sitting there beside his pretty wife that is so soon to be, I cannot help thinking it would have been a great pity to have served him that trick you were planning yesterday."

" Oh, there was no harm meant! " answered Danglars. " At first I certainly did feel somewhat uneasy as regarded what Fernand might be tempted to do; but when I saw how completely he had mastered his feelings, even so far as to be a groomsman at his rival's wedding, I knew there was no further cause for apprehension." Caderousse looked full at Fernand; he was ghastly pale.

" Certainly," continued Danglars, " the sacrifice was no trifling one, when the beauty of the bride is concerned. Upon my soul, that future captain of mine is a lucky dog! Gad! I only wish he would let me take his place."

" Shall we not set forth? " asked the sweet, silvery voice of Mercédès; " two o'clock has just struck, and you know we are expected at the Hôtel de Ville in a quarter of an hour."

" Yes, yes! " cried Dantès, eagerly quitting the table; " let us go directly! "

His words were re-echoed by the whole party, who rose with a simultaneous cheer, and began forming themselves into a procession.

At this moment Danglars, who had closely watched Fernand, saw him stagger and fall back with an almost convulsive spasm against a seat placed near one of the open windows. At the same instant was heard a noise on the stairs, followed by the measured tread of soldiery, with the clanking of swords and military accoutrements; then came a hum and buzz as of many voices, so as to deaden even the noisy mirth of the bridal party, which immediately gave place to an uneasy silence.

The noise approached. There were three knocks on the panel of the door. Every one looked at his neighbour with an air of astonishment.

" In the name of the law! " cried a resonant voice, to which there was no response. The door was opened, and a magistrate, wearing his official scarf, presented himself, followed by four soldiers and a corporal. Uneasiness now yielded to the most extreme dread on the part of those present.

" May I venture to inquire the reason of this unexpected visit? " said M. Morrel, addressing the magistrate, whom he evidently knew; "there is doubtless some mistake easily explained."

"If it be so, M. Morrel," replied the magistrate, "rely upon every reparation being made; meanwhile, I am the bearer of an order of arrest, and although I most reluctantly perform the task assigned me, it must nevertheless be fulfilled. Who among the persons here assembled answers to the name of Edmond Dantès?" Every eye was turned towards the young man, who, though much disturbed, advanced with dignity and said in a firm voice, "I am he; what is your pleasure with me?"

"Edmond Dantès," replied the magistrate, "I arrest you in the name of the law!"

"Me!" repeated Edmond, slightly changing colour, "and wherefore, I pray?"

"I do not know, but you will be informed at your first examination."

M. Morrel felt that further resistance or remonstrance was useless. A commissary girt with the official scarf is no longer a man; he is a statue of the law, cold and dumb. But the elder Dantès hastened to the officer,—for there are some things that the heart of a father or of a mother cannot comprehend. He prayed and supplicated; and though his prayers and tears could avail nothing, his despair was so great that the commissary was moved to sympathy. "Monsieur," he said, "calm your apprehensions. Your son has probably neglected some prescribed form relating to the customs or to quarantine; and it is more than probable he will be set at liberty after answering a few questions."

"What is the meaning of all this?" inquired Caderousse, frowningly, of Danglars, who had assumed an air of surprise.

"How can I tell you?" replied he; "I am, like yourself, utterly bewildered by all that is going on, not a word of which do I understand." Caderousse then looked around for Fernand, but he had disappeared.

The scene of the previous night now came back to his mind with startling accuracy. The catastrophe he had just witnessed appeared to have rent away the veil which the intoxication of the evening before had placed between himself and his memory.

"So! so!" said he, in a hoarse and choking voice, to Danglars, "this, then, I suppose, is a part of the trick you were concerting yesterday? In that case, cursed be the performer of it! It is a bad action."

"Nonsense!" returned Danglars; "you know very well that I tore the paper to pieces."

"No, you did not!" answered Caderousse, "you merely threw it by. I saw it lying in a corner."

"Hold your tongue! You saw nothing. You were drunk!"

"Where is Fernand?" inquired Caderousse.

"How do I know?" replied Danglars; "looking after his own affairs, most likely. Never mind where he is; let us go and see what is to be done for our poor friends in this their affliction."

During this conversation, Dantès, after shaking hands with all his friends, had surrendered himself to the officer, saying, "Make yourselves quite easy; there is some little mistake to clear up, and very likely I may not have to go so far as the prison to effect that."

"Oh, to be sure!" responded Danglars, who had now approached the group; "nothing more than a mistake, I feel quite certain."

Dantès descended the staircase, preceded by the magistrate, and followed by the soldiers. A carriage awaited him at the door; he got in, followed by two soldiers and the commissary, and the vehicle drove off towards Marseilles.

"Adieu, adieu, dearest Edmond!" cried Mercédès, stretching out her arms to him from the balcony.

The prisoner heard that last cry, which came like a sob from the lacerated heart of his betrothed; he leaned from the coach and cried, "*Au revoir*, Mercédès," and the coach disappeared round one of the corners of Fort St. Nicolas.

"Wait for me here, all of you!" cried M. Morrel; "I will take the first conveyance I find and hurry to Marseilles, whence I will bring you word how all is going on."

"That's right!" exclaimed a multitude of voices; "go, and return as quickly as you can!"

This second departure was followed by a moment of stupor on the part of those who were left behind. The old father and Mercédès remained for some time apart, each absorbed in their separate griefs; but at length the two poor victims of the same blow raised their eyes, and with a simultaneous burst of feeling rushed into each other's arms.

Meanwhile Fernand made his reappearance, poured out for himself a glass of water with a trembling hand, then hastily swallowing it, went to sit down on the first vacant chair he perceived. By chance this was placed next to the seat on which Mercédès had fallen half-fainting, when released from the embrace of the old man. Instinctively Fernand drew back his chair.

"It is he!" whispered Caderousse, who had never taken his eyes off Fernand, to Danglars.

"I do not think so," answered the other; "he is too stupid to imagine such a scheme. I only hope the mischief will fall upon the head of whoever wrought it."

"You don't speak of him who planned it," said Caderousse.

"Ah, surely," said Danglars, "one can't be held responsible for everything he may speak into the air!"

"Yes, when that which is spoken into the air falls back point first."

Meantime the subject of the arrest was being canvassed in every different form.

"What think you, Danglars," said one of the party, "of this event?"

"I think," said Danglars, "that it is just possible Dantès may have been detected with some trifling article on board ship considered here as contraband."

"But how could he have done so without your knowledge, Danglers, who was the ship's supercargo?"

"Why, as for that, I could only know what I was told respecting the merchandise with which the vessel was laden. I know she was loaded with cotton, and that she took in her freight at Alexandria from the warehouse of M. Pastret, and at Smyrna from M. Pascal's; that is all I was obliged to know, and I beg I may not be asked for any further particulars."

"Now I recollect!" said the afflicted old father; "my poor boy told me yesterday he had a small case of coffee and another of tobacco for me!"

"There, you see!" exclaimed Danglers. "Now the mischief is out; depend upon it the custom-house people went rummaging about the ship in our absence, and discovered poor Dantès's hidden treasures."

Mercédès, however, paid no heed to this explanation of her lover's arrest. Her grief, which she had hitherto tried to restrain, now burst out in a violent fit of hysterical sobbing.

"Come, come," said the old man, "be comforted, my poor child; there is still hope!"

"Hope!" repeated Danglars.

"Hope!" Fernand tried to say, but the word was stifled; his lips moved, but no sound came forth.

"Good news! good news!" shouted one of the party stationed in the balcony. "Here comes M. Morrel. No doubt now we shall hear that our friend is released!"

Mercédès and the old man rushed to meet the ship-owner, and met him at the door. M. Morrel was very pale.

" What news ? " exclaimed a general burst of voices.

" Alas, my friends," replied M. Morrel, with a mournful shake of his head, " the affair is more serious than we thought."

" Oh, indeed, indeed, sir, he is innocent ! " sobbed Mercédès.

" That I believe ! " answered M. Morrel ; " but still he is charged—"

" With what ? " inquired the elder Dantès.

" With being an agent of the Bonapartist faction ! "

Many of my readers may be able to recollect how formidable such an accusation became in the period at which our story is dated. A despairing cry escaped the pale lips of Mercédès, while the heart-stricken father fell listlessly into a chair.

" Ah, Danglars ! " whispered Caderousse, " you have deceived me,—the trick you spoke of last night has been played off, I see ; but I cannot suffer a poor old man or an innocent girl to die of grief through your fault. I am determined to tell them all about it."

" Be silent, you simpleton ! " cried Danglars, grasping him by the arm, " or I will not answer for your own safety. Who can tell whether Dantès be innocent or guilty ? The vessel did touch at Elba, where he quitted it, and passed a whole day in the island. Now, should any letters or other documents of a com-promising character be found upon him, it will be taken for granted that all who uphold him are his accomplices."

With the rapid instinct of selfishness, Caderousse perceived the solidity of this reasoning ; he looked at Danglars with eyes dulled by fear and grief, and then for one forward step he had taken, he took two in retreat.

" We will wait, then," he murmured.

" To be sure ! " answered Danglars. " Let us wait, by all means. If he be innocent, of course he will be set at liberty ; if guilty, why, it is of no use to involve ourselves in his conspiracy."

" Then let us go. I cannot remain here any longer."

" With all my heart ! " replied Danglars, but too pleased to find a partner in his retreat. " Let us take ourselves out of the way, and leave the rest to withdraw as they please."

After their departure, Fernand, who had now again become the protector of the young girl, took Mercédès by the hand and con-ducted her to the Catalans ; while some friends of Dantès con-veyed the heart-broken parent to his home.

The rumour of Edmond's arrest as a Bonapartist agent was not slow in circulating throughout the city.

"Could you ever have credited such a thing, my dear Danglars?" asked M. Morrel, as, on his return to the port for the purpose of gleaning fresh tidings of Dantès, he overtook his supercargo and Caderousse. "Could you have believed such a thing possible?"

"Why, you know I told you," replied Danglars, "that I considered the circumstance of his having anchored at the Isle of Elba to be very suspicious."

"And did you mention these suspicions to any person besides myself?"

"Certainly not!" returned Danglars, then added in a low whisper, "You understand that on account of your uncle, M. Policar Morrel, who served under the other government, and who does not altogether conceal what he thinks on the subject, you are strongly suspected of regretting the abdication of Napoleon. I should have feared to injure both Edmond and yourself, had I divulged my own apprehensions to a soul. I am well aware that though a subordinate, like myself, is bound to acquaint the ship-owner with everything that occurs, there are many things he ought most carefully to conceal from all others."

"'Tis well, Danglars; 'tis well!" replied M. Morrel. "You are a worthy fellow; and I had already thought of your interests in the event of poor Edmond having become captain of the *Pharaon*."

"In what way, monsieur?"

"Yes, I had previously inquired of Dantès what was his opinion of you, and if he should have any reluctance to continue you in your post,—for I have perceived a sort of coolness between you."

"And what was his reply?"

"That he certainly did think he had ground of complaint against you in an affair which he did not explain, but that whoever possessed the confidence of the ship's owners would have his also."

"The hypocrite!" murmured Danglars, between his teeth.

"Poor Dantès!" said Caderousse. "No one can deny his being a noble-hearted young fellow!"

"But in the midst of all our trouble," continued M. Morrel, "we must not forget that the *Pharaon* has at present no captain."

"Oh!" replied Danglars, "since we cannot leave this port for the next three months, let us hope that ere the expiration of that period Dantès will be set at liberty."

"Of that I entertain no doubt; but in the meantime what are we to do?"

"Well, until then I am here, M. Morrel," answered Danglars. "You know that I am as capable of managing a ship as the most experienced captain in the service; and it will be advantageous to you to accept my services, since upon Edmond's release from prison no further change will be requisite on board the *Pharaon* than for Dantès and myself each to resume our respective posts."

"Thanks, thanks! my good friend, for your excellent idea,— that will smooth all difficulties. I authorise you at once to assume the command of the *Pharaon* and to superintend the unloading of her freight. Business must not be allowed to suffer, whatever may happen to individuals."

"Depend upon my zeal and attention, M. Morrel; but when do you think it likely we may be permitted to visit our poor friend in his prison?"

"I will let you know that as soon as I have seen M. de Villefort, whom I shall endeavour to interest in Edmond's favour. I am aware he is a furious Royalist; but, in spite of that and of his being the *procureur du roi*, he is a man like ourselves, and I fancy not a bad one!"

"Perhaps not," replied Danglars; "but I have heard that he is extremely ambitious, and ambition is a sore hardener of the heart!"

"Well, well!" returned M. Morrel, "we shall see! But now hasten on board; I will join you there." So saying, the worthy ship-owner quitted the two friends, and proceeded in the direction of the Palais de Justice.

"You see," said Danglars, addressing Caderousse, "the turn things have taken. Do you still feel any desire to stand up in his defence?"

"Not the slightest; but yet it seems to me a shocking thing that a mere joke should lead to such frightful consequences."

"But who perpetrated that joke, let me ask? Neither you nor myself, but Fernand. You know very well that I threw the paper into a corner of the room,—indeed, I thought I had destroyed it."

"Oh, no!" replied Caderousse, "that I can answer for, you did not. I only wish I could see it now as plainly as I saw it lying all crushed and crumpled in a corner of the arbour."

"Well, then, if you did, depend upon it, Fernand picked it up, and either copied it or caused it to be copied; perhaps, even, he did not take the trouble of recopying it. And now I think of it, by Heaven! he has perhaps sent the letter itself! Fortunately for me, the handwriting was disguised."

"You knew, then, that Dantès was engaged in a conspiracy?"

"Not I. As I before said, I thought the whole thing was a joke, nothing more. It seems, however, that, like Harlequin, I have spoken the truth in jest."

"Still," argued Caderousse, "I would give a great deal if nothing of the kind had happened, or at least if I had had no hand in it. You will see, Danglars, that it will turn out an unlucky job for both of us."

"Nonsense! If any harm comes of it, it should fall on the guilty person; and that, you know, is Fernand. How can we be implicated in any way? All we have got to do is to keep our own counsel, and remain perfectly quiet, not breathing a word of all this; and you will see that the storm will pass away without in the least affecting us."

"Amen!" responded Caderousse, waving his hand in token of adieu to Danglars, and bending his steps towards the Allées de Meillan, moving his head to and fro, and muttering as he went, after the manner of those who are absorbed in thought.

"So far, then," said Danglars to himself, "all has gone as I would have it. I am temporarily commander of the *Pharaon*, with the certainty of being permanently so, if that fool of a Caderousse can be persuaded to hold his tongue. My only fear is that Dantès may be released. But, bah! he is in the hands of Justice; and," added he, with a smile, "she will take her own." So saying, he leaped into a boat, desiring to be rowed on board the *Pharaon*, where M. Morrel had appointed to meet him.

CHAPTER VI

THE DEPUTY PROCUREUR DU ROI

In one of the large, aristocratic mansions situated in the Rue du Grand Cours opposite the fountain of Medusa, a second marriage-feast was celebrated, almost at the same hour with the ill-fated nuptial repast given by Dantès. But instead of sailors, soldiers, and those belonging to the humblest grade of life, the present *réunion* was composed of the very flower and *élite* of Marseilles society,—magistrates who had resigned their office during the usurper's reign; officers who, scorning to fight under his banners, had offered their services to foreign powers; and younger persons who had been brought up to execrate the man whom five years of exile would have converted into a martyr, and fifteen of restoration elevated to the rank of a demigod.

The guests were still at table, and the heated and energetic conversation that prevailed betrayed the violent and vindictive passions that then agitated the inhabitants of the South, where for five hundred years religious strife had given increased bitterness to the violence of party feeling.

The emperor, now king of the Isle of Elba,—after having held sovereign sway over one half of the world, reigning over five or six thousand souls, after having been accustomed to hear the "Vive Napoléons!" of one hundred and twenty million subjects, and in ten different languages,—was regarded in that company as being for ever lost to France and to her throne.

The magistrates freely discussed their political views; the military part of the company talked of Moscow and Leipsic; the women, of the divorce of the Empress Josephine. That Royalist assembly, rejoicing and triumphing over, not the fall of a man, but the annihilation of a principle, believed that political prosperity was opening anew to them, and that they were leaving behind a painful dream.

An old man, decorated with the cross of Saint Louis, rose and proposed the health of King Louis XVIII. This aged individual was the Marquis de Saint-Méran. This toast, recalling at once the patient exile of Hartwell and the peace-loving King of France, excited universal enthusiasm; glasses were elevated in the air in the English manner, and the ladies, snatching bouquets from their fair bosoms, strewed the table with their floral treasures. In a word, an almost poetical fervour prevailed.

"Ah!" said the Marquise de Saint-Méran, a woman with a stern, forbidding eye, though still noble and elegant-looking, despite her having reached her fiftieth year,—"ah! these revolutionists, who have driven us from those very possessions they afterwards purchased for a mere trifle during the Reign of Terror, would be compelled to own, were they here, that all true devotion was on our side, since we were content to follow the fortunes of a falling monarch, while they, on the contrary, made their fortune by worshipping the rising sun; yes, yes, they could not help admitting that the king for whom we sacrificed rank, wealth, and station was truly our 'Louis the well-beloved,' while their wretched usurper has been and ever will be to them their evil genius, their 'Napoleon the accursed.' Am I not right, Villefort?"

"I beg your pardon, Madame. I really must pray you to

excuse me, but—in truth—I was not attending to the conversation."

"Marchioness, Marchioness!" interposed the same elderly personage who had proposed the toast, "let the young people alone; let me tell you, on one's wedding day there are more agreeable subjects of conversation than dry politics."

"Never mind, dearest mother," said a young and lovely girl, with a profusion of light brown hair, and eyes that seemed to float in liquid crystal, "'tis all my fault for seizing upon M. de Villefort, and preventing his listening to what you said. But there—now take him—he is your own for as long as you like. M. de Villefort, I beg to remind you that my mother speaks to you."

"If Madame the Marchioness will deign to repeat the words I but imperfectly caught, I shall be delighted to answer," said M. de Villefort.

"Never mind, Renée," replied the marchioness, with such a look of tenderness as all were astonished to see upon her harsh, dry features; but, however all other feelings may be withered in a woman's nature, there is always one bright smiling spot in the maternal breast,—it is that which God has consecrated to maternal love,—"I forgive you. What I was saying, Villefort, was, that the Bonapartists had neither our sincerity, enthusiasm, nor devotion."

"They had, however, what supplied the place of those fine qualities," replied the young man; "and that was fanaticism. Napoleon is the Mahomet of the West, and is worshipped by his commonplace but ambitious followers, not only as a leader and lawgiver, but also as the personification of equality."

"He!" cried the marchioness, "Napoleon the type of equality! For mercy's sake, then, what would you call Robespierre? Come, come, do not strip the latter of his just rights to bestow them on the Corsican; there has been usurpation enough, it seems to me."

"Nay, madame; I would place each of these heroes on his right pedestal,—that of Robespierre to be built where his scaffold was erected; that of Napoleon on the column of the Place Vendôme. The only difference consists in the opposite character of the equality supported by these two men,—the one advocates the equality that depresses, the other professes the equality that elevates; the one brings a king within reach of the guillotine, the other elevates the people to a level with the throne. Observe," said Villefort, smiling, "I do not mean to deny that both the individuals we have been referring to were revolutionary scoundrels, and that the 9th Thermidor and the 4th of April were lucky days for France, worthy of being grate-fully remembered by every friend to monarchy and civil order; but that explains how it comes to pass that, fallen, as I trust he is, for ever, Napoleon has still preserved a train of parasitical satellites. Still, marchioness, it has been so with other usurpers,—Cromwell, for instance, who was not half so bad as Napoleon, had his partisans and advocates."

" Do you know, Villefort, that you are talking in a most dreadfully revolutionary strain? But I excuse it; it is impos-sible to expect the son of a Girondin to be free from a small spice of the old leaven."

A deep crimson suffused the countenance of Villefort. " 'Tis true, madame," answered he, " that my father was a Girondin, but he was not among the number of those who voted for the king's death; he was an equal sufferer with yourself during the Reign of Terror, and had well-nigh lost his head on the same scaffold as your own father."

" True," replied the marchioness, without wincing in the slightest degree at the tragical remembrance thus called up; " but bear in mind, if you please, that our respective parents underwent persecution and proscription from diametrically opposite principles. In proof of which I may remark that while my family remained among the stanchest adherents of the exiled princes, your father lost no time in joining the new government; and that after the Citizen Noirtier had become a Girondin, the Comte Noirtier appeared as a senator and statesman."

" Dear mother," interposed Renée, " you know very well it was agreed that all these disagreeable reminiscences should for ever be laid aside."

" Madame," replied Villefort, " I unite with Mademoiselle de Saint-Méran in humbly requesting you to forget the past. What avails retrospection and recrimination touching circum-stances wholly beyond recall? For my own part, I have laid aside even the name of my father, and altogether disown his political principles. He was—nay, probably still is—a Bona-partist, and is called Noirtier; I, on the contrary, am a stanch Royalist, and style myself Villefort. Let what may remain of revolutionary sap exhaust itself and die away with the old trunk, and condescend only to regard the young shoot which has started up at a distance from the parent tree, without having the power, any more than the wish, to separate entirely from the stock from which it sprung."

" Bravo, Villefort!" cried the marquis; " excellently well said! Come, now, I have hopes of obtaining what I have been for years endeavouring to persuade the marchioness to promise; namely, a perfect amnesty and forgetfulness of the past."

" With all my heart," replied the marchioness; " let the past be for ever forgotten! I ask nothing better, and let it be so agreed; but at least, Villefort must be inflexible in the future. Remember, Villefort, that we have pledged ourselves to his Majesty for your fealty and strict loyalty, and that at our recommendation the king consented to forget the past [and here she extended to him her hand] as I now do at your entreaty. But bear in mind that should there fall in your way any one guilty of conspiring against the government, you will be the more bound to visit the offence with rigorous punishment, because it is known you belong to a suspected family."

" Alas, madame!" returned Villefort, " my profession, as well as the times in which we live, compel me to be severe. I shall be so. I have already successfully conducted several public prosecutions, and brought the offenders to merited punishment. Unhappily, we have not yet reached the end."

" Do you, indeed, think so? " inquired the marchioness.

" I am, at least, fearful of it. Napoleon, in the island of Elba, is too near France, and his proximity keeps up the hopes of his partisans. Marseilles is filled with half-pay officers, who are daily, under one frivolous pretext or other, getting up quarrels with the Royalists; hence arise duels in the higher classes, and assassinations in the lower."

" You have heard, perhaps," said the Comte de Salvieux, one of M. de Saint-Méran's oldest friends, and chamberlain to the Comte d'Artois, " that the Holy Alliance purpose removing him? "

" Yes; they were talking about it when we left Paris," said M. de Saint-Méran; " and where will they send him? "

" To St. Helena."

" To St. Helena? Where is that? " inquired the marchioness.

" An island situated on the other side of the equator, at least two thousand leagues from here," replied the count.

" So much the better! As Villefort observes, it is a great act of folly to have left such a man between Corsica, where he was born, and Naples, of which his brother-in-law is king, and opposite Italy, the sovereignty of which he coveted for his son."

" Unfortunately," said Villefort, " we have the treaties of 1814, and we cannot move against Napoleon without breaking those treaties."

"Very well, they will be broken," said M. de Salvieux. "Shall we be so very precise in obligations concerning him who caused the unhappy Duc d'Enghien to be shot?"

"Well," said the marchioness, "it seems probable that by the aid of the Holy Alliance we shall be rid of Napoleon; and we must trust to the vigilance of M. de Villefort to purify Marseilles of his partisans. The king is either a king or no king; if he be acknowledged as sovereign of France, he should be upheld in peace and tranquillity. And this can best be effected by employing the most inflexible agents to put down every attempt at conspiracy,—'tis the best and surest means of preventing mischief."

"Unfortunately, madame," answered Villefort, "the strong arm of the law is not called upon to interfere until the evil has taken place."

"Then all he has to do is to endeavour to repair it."

"Nay, madame, the law is frequently powerless to effect this; all it can do is to avenge the wrong done."

"Oh, M. de Villefort!" cried a beautiful young creature, daughter to Comte de Salvieux, and the cherished friend of Mademoiselle de Saint-Méran, "do try and get up some famous trial while we are at Marseilles. I never was in a law court; I am told it is so very amusing!"

"Amusing, certainly," replied the young man, "inasmuch as, instead of shedding tears as at the fictitious tale of woe produced at a theatre, you behold in a law court a case of real and genuine distress,—a drama of life. The prisoner whom you there see, pale, agitated, and alarmed, instead of—as is the case when the curtain falls on a tragedy—going home to sup peacefully with his family, and then retiring to rest that he may reassume his mimic woes on the morrow, is removed from your sight merely to be reconducted to his prison and delivered up to the executioner. I leave you to judge how far your nerves are calculated to bear you through such a scene. Of this, however, be assured, that should any favourable opportunity present itself, I will not fail to offer you the choice of being present at it."

"For shame, M. de Villefort!" said Renée, becoming quite pale; "don't you see how you are frightening us? and yet you laugh."

"What would you have? It is a duel. I have already recorded sentence of death five or six times for political or other offences; and who can say how many daggers may be ready sharpened, and only waiting a favourable opportunity to be buried in my heart?"

"Gracious heavens! M. de Villefort," said Renée, becoming more and more terrified; "you surely are not in earnest?"

"Indeed I am," replied the young magistrate, with a smile; "and in the interesting trial which that young lady desires to satisfy her curiosity, and which I myself desire to satisfy my ambition, the case would only be still more aggravated. Suppose, for instance, the prisoner to have served under Napoleon, —can you believe for an instant, that one accustomed at the word of his commander to rush fearlessly on the bayonets of his foe will scruple to drive a stiletto into the heart of one he knows to be his personal enemy, more than he would to kill a Russian, an Austrian, or a Hungarian, whom he had never before seen? And besides, that antagonism, you see, is essential to the situation; without it our business would be without excuse. For my own part, when I see gleaming in the eye of the accused the clear light of anger, I feel encouraged, I am exhilarated. It is no longer a trial; it is a combat. I struggle against him, he returns the attack; I redouble my energy, and the combat ends, like all combats, in victory or defeat. That is what pleading is; therein lies the danger of eloquence. If an accused person should smile upon my words I should think that I had spoken badly, that what I had said was pale, without force, inadequate. Imagine, then, the sensation of pride experienced by an advocate convinced that the accused is guilty, when he sees him blanch and bend under the thunders of his eloquence! That head is bowed, it will fall—"

Renée uttered a slight cry.

"Bravo!" cried one of the guests; "that is what I call talking to some purpose."

"Just the person we require at a time like the present," said a second.

"What a splendid business that last cause of yours was, my dear Villefort!" remarked a third; "I mean the trial of the man for murdering his father. Upon my word, you killed him ere the executioner had laid his hand upon him."

"Oh! as for parricides, and such dreadful people as that," interposed Renée, "it matters very little what is done to them; but as regards poor unfortunate creatures whose only crime consists in having mixed themselves up in political intrigues—"

"Why, that is the very worst offence they could possibly commit; for don't you see, Renée, the king is the father of his people, and he who shall plot or contrive aught against the life and safety of the parent of thirty-two million people is a parricide on a large scale?"

"I don't know anything about that," replied Renée, "but, M. de Villefort, you have promised me—have you not?—always to show mercy to those I plead for."

"Make yourself quite easy on that point," answered Villefort, with one of his sweetest smiles; "you and I will always consult upon our verdicts."

"My love," said the marchioness, "attend to your doves, your lap-dogs, and embroidery, but do not meddle with what you do not understand. Nowadays the military profession has rest, and the robe wins applause: there is a Latin saying about that, of profound depth."

"'Cedant arma togæ,'" said Villefort, bowing.

"I did not venture to speak Latin," replied the marchioness.

"Well," said Renée, "I cannot help regretting you had not chosen some other profession than your own,—that of a physician, for instance. The destroying angel, angel though he be, has always seemed terrible to me."

"Dear, good Renée!" whispered Villefort, as he gazed with unutterable tenderness on the lovely speaker.

"Let us hope, my child," cried the marquis, "that M. de Villefort may prove the moral and political physician of this province; if so, he will have achieved a noble work."

"And one which will go far to efface the recollection of his father's conduct," added the incorrigible marchioness.

"Madame," replied Villefort, with a mournful smile, "I have already had the honour to observe that my father has—at least I hope so—abjured his past errors, and that he is at the present moment a firm and zealous friend to religion and order,—a better Royalist, possibly, than his son; for he has to atone for past dereliction, while I have no other impulse than warm, decided preference and conviction." Having made this well-turned speech, Villefort looked carefully round to mark the effect of his oratory, much as he would have done had he been addressing the bench in open court.

"Do you know, my dear Villefort," cried the Comte de Salvieux, "that is as nearly as possible what I myself said the other day at the Tuileries, when questioned by his Majesty's principal chamberlain touching the singularity of an alliance between the son of a Girondin and the daughter of an officer in the army of Condé; and I assure you he seemed fully to comprehend that this mode of reconciling political differences was based upon sound and excellent principles. Then the king, who, without our suspecting it had overheard our conversation, interrupted us by saying 'Villefort'—observe that the king did not pronounce the word 'Noirtier,' but on the contrary placed considerable emphasis on that of 'Villefort'—'Villefort,' said his Majesty, 'is a young man of great judgment and discretion, who will be sure to make a figure in his profession; I like him much, and it gave me great pleasure to hear that he was about to become the son-in-law of M. le Marquis and Madame la Marquise de Saint-Méran. I should myself have recommended the match, had not the noble marquis anticipated my wishes by requesting my consent to it.'"

"Did the king say that, Count?" asked the enraptured Villefort.

"I give you his very words; and if the marquis chooses to be candid, he will confess that they perfectly agree with what his Majesty said to him, when he went six months ago to consult him upon the subject of your espousing his daughter."

"Certainly," answered the marquis; "you state but the truth."

"How much do I owe this gracious prince! What is there I would not do to evince my earnest gratitude!"

"That is right," cried the marchioness. "I love to see you thus. Now, then, were a conspirator to fall into your hands, he would be most welcome."

"For my part, dear mother," interposed Renée, "I pray God he will not hear you, and that he will only permit petty offenders, poor debtors, and miserable cheats, to fall into M. de Villefort's hands; then I shall be contented."

"Just the same," said Villefort, laughing, "as though you prayed that a physician might only be called upon to prescribe for headaches, measles, and the stings of wasps, or any other slight affection of the epidermis. If you wish to see me the *procureur du roi*, you must desire for me some of those violent and dangerous diseases from the cure of which so much honour redounds to the physician."

At this moment, and as though the utterance of Villefort's wish had sufficed to effect its accomplishment, a servant entered the room and whispered a few words in his ear. Villefort immediately rose from the table and quitted the room upon the plea of urgent business: he soon however returned, his whole face beaming with delight. Renée regarded him with fond affection; and certainly his handsome features, lit up as they then were with more than usual fire and animation, seemed formed to excite the innocent admiration with which she gazed on her graceful and intelligent lover.

"You were wishing just now," said Villefort, addressing her, "that I were a doctor instead of a lawyer. Well, I at least resemble the disciples of Æsculapius in one thing,—that of not being able to call a day my own, not even that of my betrothal."

"And wherefore were you called away just now?" asked Mademoiselle de Saint-Méran, with an air of slight uneasiness.

"Alas! for a patient who must be, if what is told me is true, in the last extremity. It is a serious case, and the malady touches the scaffold."

"How dreadful!" exclaimed Renée, her cheeks, that were before glowing with emotion, becoming pale as marble.

"Is it possible?" burst simultaneously from all who were near enough to the magistrate to hear his words.

"Why, if my information prove correct, a sort of Bonapartist conspiracy has just been discovered."

"Can I believe my ears?" cried the marchioness.

"I will read you the letter containing the accusation, at least," said Villefort:—

"The *procureur du roi* is informed by a friend of the throne and of religion, that one Edmond Dantès, mate of the ship *Pharaon*, who arrived this morning from Smyrna, after having touched at Naples and Porto Ferrajo, has been intrusted by Murat with a letter for the usurper, and by the usurper with a letter for the Bonapartist committee in Paris.

"Proof of this crime will be found on arresting him, for the letter will be found upon him, or at his father's, or in his cabin on board the *Pharaon*."

"But," said Renée, "this letter, which after all is but an anonymous scrawl, is not even addressed to you, but to the *procureur du roi*."

"True; but that gentleman being absent, his secretary, by his orders, opened his letters. Thinking this one of importance, he sent for me, but not finding me, took it upon himself to give the necessary orders for arresting the accused party."

"Then the guilty person is absolutely in custody?" said the marchioness.

"That is to say, the accused," said Renée.

"He is in safe custody," answered Villefort; "and as I had the honour of saying just now to Mademoiselle Renée, if the letter in question can be found, the patient is a very sick man indeed."

"And where is the unfortunate being?" asked Renée.

" He is at my house."

" Come, come, my friend," interrupted the marchioness, " do not neglect your duty to linger with us. You are the king's servant, and must go whithersoever that service calls you."

" Oh, M. de Villefort!" cried Renée, clasping her hands, " be merciful on this the day of our betrothal."

The young man passed round to the side of the table where the fair pleader sat, and leaning over her chair said tenderly,—

" To give you pleasure, my sweet Renée, I promise to show all the lenity in my power; but if the charges brought against this Bonapartist hero prove correct, why, then, you really must give me leave to order his head to be cut off."

Renée, with an almost convulsive shudder, turned away her head, as though the very mention of killing a fellow-creature in cold blood was more than her tender nature could endure.

" Never mind that foolish girl, Villefort," said the marchioness; " she will soon get over these things." So saying, Madame de Saint-Méran extended her dry bony hand to Villefort, which he kissed, while looking at Renée and saying with his eyes, " It is your hand that I kiss, or at least that I wish I were kissing, at this moment."

" These are mournful auspices to accompany a betrothal!" sighed poor Renée.

" Upon my word, child!" exclaimed the angry marchioness, " your folly exceeds all bounds. I should be glad to know what connection there can possibly be between your sickly sentimentality and the affairs of the state!"

" Oh, mother!" murmured Renée.

" Nay, madame, I pray you pardon this little traitor," said Villefort; " I promise you that to make up for her want of loyalty I will be most inflexibly severe." But while the magistrate addressed these words to the marchioness, the lover threw an expressive glance at his betrothed, which said, " Be tranquil, Renée; for the sake of your love I will be merciful." Renée answered that look with her sweetest smile, and Villefort went out with paradise in his heart.

CHAPTER VII

THE EXAMINATION

No sooner had Villefort left the salon than he assumed the grave air of a man who holds the balance of life and death in his hands. Now, in spite of the mobility of his features,—a mobility which the deputy had cultivated often before the mirror, as a professional speaker should,—at this moment it required an effort for him to wrinkle his brows and assume a dignified sobriety. Except for the recollection of the line of politics his father had adopted, and which might interfere, unless he acted with the greatest prudence, with his own career, Villefort was as happy as a man could be. Already rich, he held a high official situation, though only twenty-seven. He was about to marry a young and charming woman, whom he loved not passionately but reasonably, as a deputy *procureur du roi* is able to love. Besides her beauty, which was remarkable, Mademoiselle de Saint-Méran, his betrothed, belonged to one of the families in highest standing in the court of that period; and in addition to the political influence of her father and her mother, who having no other child could devote it entirely to their son-in-law, she brought to her husband a dowry of fifty thousand crowns, which might some day be increased to an inheritance of half a million. All these elements combined constituted for Villefort a ravishing sum of happiness; so that when with an inward view he contemplated steadily his interior life, it was as if he looked at spots on the sun.

At the door Villefort met the commissary of police, who was waiting for him. The sight of this officer recalled him from the third heaven to earth; he composed his face as we have before described, and said, " I have read the letter, monsieur, and you have acted rightly in arresting this man; now inform me what you have discovered concerning him and the conspiracy."

" We know nothing as yet of the conspiracy, monsieur; all the papers found have been sealed up and placed on your bureau. The prisoner himself is named Edmond Dantès, mate on board the three-master the *Pharaon*, trading in cotton with Alexandria and Smyrna, and belonging to Morrel and Son of Marseilles."

" Before he entered the navy, had he ever served in the marines?"

" Oh, no, monsieur; he is very young."

" How old ? "

" Nineteen or twenty at the most."

At this moment, as Villefort arrived at the corner of the Rue des Conseils, a man who seemed to have been waiting for him approached; it was M. Morrel.

" Ah, M. de Villefort," cried he, " I am delighted to see you! Some of your people have committed the strangest mistake,— they have just arrested Edmond Dantès, the mate of my ship."

" I know it, monsieur," replied Villefort, " and I am now going to examine him."

" Oh," said Morrel, carried away by his friendship for the young man, " you do not know him, and I do. He is the most estimable, the most trustworthy creature in the world, and I will venture to say there is not a better seaman in all the merchant-service. Oh, M. de Villefort, I beseech your indulgence for him! "

Villefort, as we have seen, belonged to the aristocratic party at Marseilles, Morrel to the plebeian; the first was a Royalist, the other suspected of Bonapartism. Villefort looked disdainfully at Morrel, and replied coolly,—

" You are aware, monsieur, that a man may be estimable and trustworthy in private life, and the best seaman in the merchant-service, and yet be, politically speaking, a great criminal. Is it not true? "

The magistrate laid emphasis on these words, as if he wished to apply them to the owner himself, while his eyes seemed to plunge into the heart of him who interceded for another when he ought to know that he himself had need of indulgence. Morrel reddened, for his own conscience was not quite clear in political matters; besides, what Dantès had told him of his interview with the grand-marshal, and what the emperor had said to him, embarrassed him. He replied, however, in tones of deep interest,—

" I entreat you, M. de Villefort, be, as you always are, kind and equitable, and give him back to us soon."

This " give us " sounded revolutionary in the sub-prefect's ears. " Ah, ah! " murmured he, " is Dantès then a member of some Carbonari society, that his protector thus employs the collective form? He was, if I recollect, arrested in a cabaret, in company with a great many others." Then he added, " Monsieur, you may rest assured I shall perform my duty impartially, and that if he be innocent you shall not have appealed to me in vain; should he, however, be guilty, in this present epoch impunity would furnish a dangerous example, and I must do my duty."

As he had now arrived at the door of his own house, which adjoined the Palais de Justice, he entered after having saluted the ship-owner with icy politeness, who stood as if petrified on the spot where Villefort had left him. The ante-chamber was full of agents of police and gendarmes, in the midst of whom, carefully watched but calm and smiling, stood the prisoner. Villefort traversed the ante-chamber, cast a side glance at Dantès, and taking a packet which a gendarme offered him, disappeared, saying, " Bring in the prisoner."

Rapid as had been Villefort's glance, it had served to give him an idea of the man he was about to interrogate. He had recognised intelligence in the high forehead, courage in the dark eye and bent brow, and frankness in the thick, half-open lips that showed a set of pearly teeth. Villefort's first impression was favourable; but he had been so often warned to mistrust first impulses that he applied the maxim to the impression, forgetting the difference between the two words. He stifled, therefore, the feelings of compassion that were rising, composed his features, and sat down at his bureau. An instant after Dantès entered. He was pale, but calm and smiling, and saluting his judge with easy politeness, looked round for a seat, as if he had been in the salon of M. Morrel. It was then that he encountered for the first time Villefort's look,—that look peculiar to justice, which while it seems to read the culprit's thoughts betrays nought of its own.

" Who and what are you? " demanded Villefort, turning over a pile of papers, containing information relative to the prisoner, that an agent of police had given to him on his entry.

" My name is Edmond Dantès," replied the young man, calmly; " I am mate of the *Pharaon*, belonging to MM. Morrel and Son."

" Your age? " continued Villefort.

" Nineteen," returned Dantès.

" What were you doing at the moment you were arrested? "

" I was at the festival of my marriage, monsieur," said the young man, his voice slightly tremulous, so great was the contrast between that happy moment and the painful ceremony he was now undergoing; so great was the contrast between the sombre aspect of M. de Villefort and the radiant face of Mercédès.

" You were at the festival of your marriage? " said the deputy, shuddering in spite of himself.

" Yes, monsieur, I am on the point of marrying a young girl I have been attached to for three years." Villefort, impassive as he was, was struck with this coincidence; and the tremulous voice of Dantès, surprised in the midst of his happiness, struck a sympathetic chord in his own bosom. He also was on the point of being married, and he was summoned from his own happiness to destroy that of another. "This philosophic reflection," thought he, "will make a great sensation at M. de Saint-Méran's;" and he arranged mentally, while Dantès awaited further questions, the antithesis by which orators often create a reputation for eloquence. When this speech was arranged, Villefort smiled at its probable effectiveness, and returned to Dantès.

"Continue, sir," said he.

"What would you have me continue?"

"To give all the information in your power."

"Tell me on which point you desire information, and I will tell all I know; only," added he, with a smile, "I warn you I know very little."

"Have you served under the usurper?"

"I was about to be incorporated in the royal marines when he fell."

"It is reported your political opinions are extreme," said Villefort, who had never heard anything of the kind, but was not sorry to make this inquiry as if it were an accusation.

"My political opinions! mine!" replied Dantès. "Alas, sir, I never had any opinions. I am hardly nineteen; I know nothing; I have no part to play. If I obtain the situation I desire, I shall owe it to M. Morrel. Thus all my opinions—I will not say political, but private—are confined to these three sentiments: I love my father, I respect M. Morrel, and I adore Mercédès. This, sir, is all I can tell you; and you see how uninteresting it is."

As Dantès spoke, Villefort gazed at his ingenuous and open countenance, and recollected the words of Renée, who without knowing who the culprit was, had besought his indulgence for him. With the deputy's knowledge of crime and criminals, every word the young man uttered convinced him more and more of his innocence. This lad,—for he was scarcely a man,—simple, natural, eloquent with that eloquence of the heart never found when sought for, full of affection for every-body because he was happy, and because happiness renders even the wicked good, extended his affection even to his judge, spite of Villefort's severe look and stern accent.

"*Pardieu!*" said Villefort, "he is a noble fellow! I hope I shall gain Renée's favour easily by obeying the first command she ever imposed on me. It will win me a pressure of the hand in public, and a sweet kiss in private." Full of this idea, Villefort's face became so joyous that when he turned to Dantès, the latter, who had watched the change on his physiognomy, was smiling also.

"Monsieur," said Villefort, "are you aware of having enemies?"

"I have enemies!" replied Dantès; "my position is not sufficiently elevated for that. As for my character, that is, perhaps, somewhat too hasty; but I have striven to repress it. I have ten or twelve sailors under me; and if you question them, they will tell you that they love and respect me, not as a father, for I am too young, but as an elder brother."

"But instead of enemies you may have excited jealousy. You are about to become captain at nineteen,—an elevated post for one in your condition; you are about to marry a pretty girl who loves you,—a happiness rare in all conditions in the world. And these two pieces of good fortune may have excited the envy of some one."

"You are right. You know men better than I do, and what you say may possibly be the case, I confess; but if these envious ones should be among my friends, I prefer not knowing them to being forced to hate them."

"You are wrong; you should always strive to see clearly around you. You seem a worthy young man; I will depart from the strict line of my duty to aid you in discovering the author of this accusation. Here is the paper; do you know the writing?" As he spoke, Villefort drew the letter from his pocket and presented it to Dantés. Dantès read it. A cloud passed over his brow as he said,—

"No, monsieur, I do not know the writing; it is disguised, and yet it is freely written. Whoever did it writes well. I am very fortunate," added he, looking gratefully at Villefort, "to be examined by such a man as you,—for this envious person is a real enemy." And by the rapid glance that the young man's eyes shot forth, Villefort saw how much energy lay hid beneath this mildness.

"Now," said the deputy, "answer me frankly,—not as a prisoner to a judge, but as a man in a false position to another who takes an interest in him,—what truth is there in the accusation contained in this anonymous letter?" And Villefort threw disdainfully on his bureau the letter Dantès had just given back to him.

"None at all. I will tell you the real facts. I swear by

my honour as a sailor, by my love for Mercédès, by the life of my father—"

"Speak, monsieur," said Villefort. Then, internally, "If Renée could see me, I hope she would be satisfied, and would no longer call me a decapitator."

"Well, when we quitted Naples, Captain Leclere was attacked with a brain fever. As we had no doctor on board, and he was so anxious to arrive at Elba that he would not touch at any other port, his disorder rose to such a height that at the end of the third day, feeling he was dying, he called me to him. 'My dear Dantès,' said he, 'swear to perform what I am going to tell you, for it is a matter of the deepest importance.'

"'I swear, captain,' replied I.

"'Well, as after my death the command devolves on you as mate, assume the command, and bear up for the Isle of Elba; disembark at Porto Ferrajo, ask for the grand-marshal, give him this letter; perhaps they will give you another letter, and charge you with a commission. You will accomplish what I was to have done, and derive all the honour and profit from it.'

"'I will do it, captain; but perhaps I shall not be admitted to the grand-marshal's presence as easily as you expect?'

"'Here is a ring that will obtain audience of him, and remove every difficulty,' said the captain. At these words he gave me a ring. It was time,—two hours after he was delirious, the next day he died."

"And what did you do then?"

"What I ought to have done, and what every one would have done in my place. Everywhere the last requests of a dying man are sacred; but with a sailor the last requests of his superior are commands. I sailed for the Isle of Elba, where I arrived the next day; I ordered everybody to remain on board, and went on shore alone. As I had expected, I found some difficulty in obtaining access to the grand-marshal; but I sent the ring I had received from the captain to him, and was instantly admitted. He questioned me concerning Captain Leclere's death, and, as the latter had told me, gave me a letter to carry on to a person in Paris. I undertook it because it was what my captain had bade me do. I landed here, regulated the affairs of the vessel, and hastened to visit my affianced bride, whom I found more lovely and more loving than ever. Thanks to M. Morrel, all the forms were got over; in a word, I was, as I told you, at my marriage-feast. And I should have been married in an hour, and to-morrow I intended to start for Paris, when upon that denunciation, which you now seem to despise as much as I do, I was arrested."

"Ah!" said Villefort, "this seems to me the truth. If you have been culpable, it was imprudence, and this imprudence was legitimised by the orders of your captain. Give up this letter you have brought from Elba, and pass your word you will appear should you be required, and go and rejoin your friends."

"I am free, then, sir?" cried Dantès, joyfully.

"Yes; but first give me this letter."

"You have it already; for it was taken from me with some others which I see in that packet."

"Stop a moment," said the deputy, as Dantès took his hat and gloves. "To whom is it addressed?"

"To M. Noirtier, Rue Coq-Héron, Paris."

Had a thunderbolt fallen into the room, Villefort could not have been more stupefied. He sank into his seat, and hastily turning over the packet, drew forth the fatal letter, at which he glanced with an expression of terror.

"M. Noirtier, Rue Coq-Héron, No. 13," murmured he, growing still paler.

"Yes," said Dantès, astonished; "do you, then, know him?"

"No," replied Villefort; "a faithful servant of the king does not know conspirators."

"It is a conspiracy, then?" asked Dantès, who, after believing himself free, now began to feel a greater alarm than at first. "I have already told you, however, monsieur, that I was ignorant of the contents of the letter."

"Yes, but you know the name of the person to whom it was addressed," said Villefort.

"I was obliged to read the address to know to whom to give it."

"Have you shown this letter to any one?" asked Villefort, becoming still more pale.

"To no one, on my honour."

"Everybody is ignorant that you are the bearer of a letter from the Isle of Elba, and addressed to M. Noirtier?"

"Everybody, except the person who gave it to me."

"This is too much," murmured Villefort. His brow darkened more and more; his white lips and set teeth filled Dantès with apprehension. After reading the letter, Villefort covered his face with his hands.

"Oh!" said Dantès, timidly, "what is the matter?" Villefort made no answer, but raised his head at the expiration of a few seconds, and again perused the letter.

"You give me your honour that you are ignorant of the contents of this letter?"

"I give you my honour, sir," said Dantès; "but what is the matter? You are ill. Shall I ring for assistance; shall I call?"

"No," said Villefort, rising hastily; "stay where you are. It is for me to give orders here, and not you."

"Monsieur," replied Dantès, proudly, "it was only to summon assistance for you."

"I want none; it was a temporary indisposition. Attend to yourself, and not to me; answer me."

Dantès waited, expecting a question, but in vain. Villefort fell back on his chair, passed his hand over his brow, moist with perspiration, and for the third time read the letter. "Oh, if he knows the contents of this," murmured he, "and that Noirtier is the father of Villefort, I am lost!" and he fixed his eyes upon Edmond as if he would have penetrated his thoughts.

"Oh! it is impossible to doubt it," cried he, suddenly.

"In Heaven's name," cried the unhappy young man, "if you doubt me, question me; I will answer you."

Villefort made a violent effort, and in a tone he strove to render firm, "Monsieur," said he, "very grave charges against you result from your examination. I am no longer able, as I had hoped, to restore you immediately to liberty. Before doing so, I must consult the judge of instruction; but you see how I behave towards you."

"Oh, monsieur," cried Dantès, "you have been rather a friend than a judge."

"Well, I must detain you some time longer, but I will make it as short as possible. The principal charge against you is this letter, and you see—" Villefort approached the fire, cast it in, and waited until it was entirely consumed.

"You see I destroy it."

"Oh!" exclaimed Dantès, "you are more than justice, you are goodness itself."

"Listen," continued Villefort; "you can now have confidence in me, after what I have done."

"Oh, order me, and I will obey!"

"Listen! this is not an order, but a counsel I give you."

"Speak, and I will follow your advice."

"I shall detain you until this evening in the Palais de Justice. Should any one else interrogate you, do not breathe a word of this letter."

"I promise."

It was Villefort who seemed to entreat, and the prisoner who reassured him. "You see," continued he, "the letter is destroyed; you and I alone know of its existence. Should you, therefore, be questioned, deny all knowledge of it."

"Fear nothing; I will deny it."

"It was the only letter you had?"

"It was."

"Swear it."

"I swear it."

Villefort rang. An agent of police entered. Villefort whispered some words in his ear, to which the officer replied by a motion of his head.

"Follow him," said Villefort to Dantès. Dantès saluted Villefort and retired. The door had hardly closed behind him when Villefort's strength gave way and he threw himself into a chair in a fainting condition.

Then, after a moment, "Oh, my God!" murmured he, "if the *procureur du roi* had been at Marseilles, if the judge of instruction had been called instead of me, I should have been ruined. This accursed letter would have plunged me into an abyss. Oh, my father, must your past career always interfere with my successes?" Suddenly a light passed over his face, a smile played round his mouth, his haggard eyes became fixed and seemed absorbed in the contemplation of an idea.

"This will do," said he; "and from this letter, which might have ruined me, I will make my fortune." And after having assured himself the prisoner was gone, the deputy *procureur* hastened to the house of his bride.

CHAPTER VIII

THE CHÂTEAU D'IF

THE commissary of police, as he crossed the ante-chamber, made a sign to two gendarmes, who placed themselves one on Dantès's right and the other on his left. A door that communicated with the Palais de Justice was opened, and they traversed a long range of gloomy corridors, whose appearance might have made even the boldest shudder. The Palais de Justice communicated with the prison,—a sombre edifice, that from its grated windows looks on the clock-tower of the Accoules. After numberless windings, Dantès saw an iron door. The commissary knocked thrice, every blow seeming to Dantès as if struck on his heart. The door opened, the two gendarmes gently pushed him forward, and the door closed with a loud sound behind him. The air he inhaled was no longer pure, but thick and mephitic,—he was in prison. He was conducted to a tolerably neat chamber, but grated and barred, and its appearance therefore did not greatly alarm him; besides, the words of Villefort, who seemed to interest himself so much, resounded still in his ears like a promise of freedom. It was four o'clock when Dantès was placed in this chamber. It was, as we have said, the 1st of March, and the prisoner was soon buried in darkness. The obscurity augmented the acuteness of his hearing. At the slightest sound he rose and hastened to the door, convinced that they were about to liberate him; but the sound died away, and Dantès sank again into his seat. At last, about ten o'clock, and just as Dantès began to despair, steps were heard in the corridor, a key turned in the lock, the bolts creaked, the massy oaken door flew open, and a flood of light from two torches pervaded the apartment. By the torchlight Dantès saw the glittering sabres and carbines of four gendarmes. He had advanced at first, but stopped at the sight of this fresh accession of force.

" Are you come to fetch me? " asked he.

" Yes," replied a gendarme.

" By the orders of the deputy of the *procureur du roi* ? "

" I believe so."

" Very well," said Dantès, " I am ready to follow you."

The conviction that they came from M. de Villefort relieved all Dantès's apprehensions; he advanced calmly, and placed himself in the centre of the escort. A carriage waited at the door, the coachman was on the box, and an exempt seated behind him.

" Is this carriage for me? " said Dantès.

" It is for you," replied a gendarme.

Dantès was about to speak; but feeling himself urged forward, and having neither the power nor the intention to resist, he mounted the steps, and was in an instant seated inside between two gendarmes; the two others took their places opposite, and the carriage rolled heavily over the stones.

The prisoner glanced at the windows; they were grated. He had changed his prison for another that was conveying him he knew not whither. Through the grating, however, Dantès saw they were passing through the Rue Caisserie, and by the Quai St. Laurent and the Rue Taramis, to the port. Presently he perceived, shining upon him through the grating of the windows, the light of the Consigne.

The carriage stopped, the exempt descended and approached the guard-house, a dozen soldiers came out and formed themselves in order; Dantès saw the reflection of their muskets by the light of the lamps on the quay.

"Can all this force be summoned on my account?" thought he.

The exempt opened the door, which was locked, and without speaking a word, answered Dantès's question,—for he saw between the ranks of the soldiers a passage formed from the carriage to the port. The two gendarmes who were opposite to him descended first, then he was ordered to alight, and the gendarmes on each side of him followed his example. They advanced towards a boat, which a custom-house officer held by a chain near the quay.

The soldiers looked at Dantès with an air of stupid curiosity. In an instant he was placed in the stern of the boat between the gendarmes, while the exempt stationed himself at the bow; a shove sent the boat adrift, and four sturdy oarsmen impelled it rapidly towards the Pilon. At a shout from the boat, the chain that closes the mouth of the port was lowered, and in a second they were outside the harbour.

The prisoner's first feeling was joy at again breathing the pure air,—for air is freedom; he inhaled with a full chest that lively breeze which bears upon its wings the unknown perfumes of the night and of the sea. But soon he breathed a sigh, for he passed before La Réserve, where he had that morning been so happy, and now through the open windows came the laughter and revelry of a ball. Dantès folded his hands, raised his eyes to heaven, and prayed.

The boat continued her voyage. They had passed the Tête de Mort, were now in front of the light-house, and about to double the battery. This manœuvre was incomprehensible to Dantès.

"Whither are you taking me?" asked he.

"You will soon know."

"But still—"

"We are forbidden to give you any explanation."

Dantès knew that nothing would be more absurd than to question subordinates who were forbidden to reply, and remained silent.

The most vague and wild thoughts passed through his mind. The boat they were in could not make a long voyage; there was no vessel at anchor outside the harbour; he thought perhaps they were going to leave him on some distant point. He was not bound, nor had they made any attempt to handcuff him; this seemed a good augury. Besides, had not the deputy, who had been so kind to him, told him that provided he did not pronounce the dreaded name of Noirtier he had nothing to apprehend? Had not Villefort in his presence destroyed the fatal letter, the only proof against him? He waited silently, striving to pierce through the darkness.

They had left the island of Ratonneau, where the light-house stood, on the right, and were now opposite the Point des Catalans. It seemed to the prisoner that he could distinguish a female form on the beach, for it was there Mercédès dwelt. How was it that a presentiment did not warn Mercédès that her lover was near her?

One light alone was visible, and Dantès recognised it as coming from the chamber of Mercédès. In all that little colony Mercédès alone was still awake. A loud cry could be heard by her. He did not utter it. What would his guards think if they heard him shout like a madman?

He remained silent, his eyes fixed upon the light; the boat went on, but the prisoner thought only of Mercédès. A rising ground hid the light. Dantès turned and perceived they had got out to sea. While he had been absorbed in thought, they had hoisted the sail.

In spite of his repugnance to address the guards, Dantès turned to the nearest gendarme, and taking his hand,—

"Comrade," said he, " I adjure you, as a Christian and a soldier, to tell me where we are going. I am Captain Dantès, a loyal Frenchman, though accused of treason; tell me where you are conducting me, and I promise you on my honour I will submit to my fate."

The gendarme looked irresolutely at his companion, who returned for answer a sigh that said, "I see no great harm in telling him now," and the gendarme replied,—

" You are a native of Marseilles and a sailor, and yet you do not know where you are going?"

" On my honour, I have no idea."

" That is impossible."

" I swear to you it is true. Tell me, I entreat."

" But my orders."

" Your orders do not forbid your telling me what I must know in ten minutes, in half an hour, or an hour. Spare me meanwhile ages of uncertainty. See, I ask it of you as if you were my friend. I have no wish to resist or to escape; besides, I am not able. Whither are we going?"

" Unless you are blind or have never been outside the harbour, you must know."

" I do not."

" Look round you, then."

Dantès rose and looked forward, when he saw rise within a hundred yards of him the black and frowning rock on which stands the Château d'If. This gloomy fortress, which has for more than three hundred years furnished food for so many wild legends, appearing thus suddenly to Dantès had upon him the effect which a view of the scaffold has upon one condemned to death.

" The Château d'If? " cried he; " what are we going there for? "

The gendarme smiled.

" I am not going there to be imprisoned," said Dantès; " it is only used for political prisoners. I have committed no crime. Are there any magistrates or judges at the Château d'If? "

" There are only," said the gendarme, " a governor, a garrison, turnkeys, and good thick walls. Come, come, do not look so astonished, or you will make me think you are laughing at me in return for my good-nature."

Dantès pressed the gendarme's hand as though he would crush it.

" You think, then," said he, " that I am conducted to the château to be imprisoned there? "

" It is probable; but there is no occasion to squeeze so hard."

" Without any formality? "

" All the formalities have been gone through."

" In spite of M. de Villefort's promises? "

" I do not know what M. de Villefort promised you," said the gendarme, " but I know we are taking you to the Château d'If. But what are you doing? Help, comrades, help! "

. By a rapid movement which the gendarme's practised eye had perceived, Dantès sprang forward to precipitate himself into the sea; but four vigorous arms seized him as his feet quitted the flooring of the boat. He fell back foaming with rage.

" Good! " said the gendarme, placing his knee on his chest; " this is how you keep the word of a sailor! Believe soft-spoken gentlemen again! Hark ye, my friend! I have disobeyed my first order, but I will not disobey the second; if you move, I will lodge a bullet in your brain." And he levelled his carbine at Dantès, who felt the muzzle touch his head.

For a moment he entertained the idea of making the forbidden movement, and so ending the evils that had suddenly overtaken him; but just because the evil was unexpected, Dantés thought that it could not be lasting. Then the remembrance of M. de Villefort's promises revived his hopes; and then death on the bottom of a boat at the hands of a gendarme seemed to him ugly and prosaic. He fell back, therefore, upon the seat, uttering a cry of rage and gnawing his hands with fury.

At this moment a violent shock made the bark tremble. One of the sailors leaped on shore, a cord creaked as it ran through a pulley, and Dantès understood that they were at the end of the voyage.

His guardians, taking hold of his arms, forced him to rise, and dragged him towards the steps that led to the gate of the fortress, while the exempt followed, armed with a carbine and bayonet.

Dantès made no resistance; he was like a man in a dream. He saw soldiers who stationed themselves on the sides; he was aware of stairs which obliged him to lift his feet; he perceived that he passed under a door, and that the door was closed behind him, but saw everything as in a mist, without distinguishing anything clearly. He no longer saw even the sea,—that spectacle so mournful to the captive, who looks into space with the painful reflection that he is powerless to traverse it.

They halted for a minute, during which he strove to collect his thoughts. He looked around; he was in a square court surrounded by high walls. He heard the measured tread of sentinels, and as they passed before the light he saw the barrels of their muskets shine.

They waited upwards of ten minutes. Certain that Dantès could not escape, the gendarmes released him. They seemed awaiting orders. The orders arrived.

" Where is the prisoner? " said a voice.

" Here," replied the gendarmes.

" Let him follow me; I am going to conduct him to his room."

" Go! " said the gendarmes, pushing Dantès.

The prisoner followed his conductor, who led him into a room almost underground, whose bare and reeking walls seemed as though impregnated with tears; a lamp placed on a stool illumined the apartment faintly, and showed Dantès the features of his conductor, an under-jailer, ill-clothed, and of sullen appearance.

" Here is your chamber for to-night," said he. " It is late,

and Monsieur the Governor is asleep. To-morrow, when he
awakes and is informed of the orders concerning you, he will
perhaps change your lodging. In the meantime there is bread,
water, and fresh straw; and that is all a prisoner can wish for.
Good-night." And before Dantès could open his mouth, before
he had noticed where the jailer placed his bread or the water,
before he had glanced towards the corner where the straw was,
the jailer had disappeared, taking with him the lamp.

Dantès was alone in the darkness and the silence, dumb and
still as those vaults whose icy atmosphere he felt upon his burning brow. With the first dawn of day the jailer returned with
orders to leave Dantès where he was. He found the prisoner
in the same position, as if fixed there, his eyes swollen with
weeping. He had passed the night standing, and without sleep.
The jailer advanced; Dantès appeared not to perceive him.
He touched him on the shoulder; Edmond started.

" Have you not slept? " said the jailer.

" I do not know," replied Dantès. The jailer stared.

" Are you hungry? " continued he.

" I do not know."

" Do you wish for anything? "

" I wish to see the governor."

The jailer shrugged his shoulders and left the chamber.

Dantès followed him with his eyes, and stretched forth his
hands towards the open door; but the door closed. All his
emotion then burst forth: he cast himself on the ground, weeping bitterly, and asking himself what crime he had committed
that he should be thus punished.

The day passed thus; he scarcely tasted food, but walked
round and round the cell like a wild beast in its cage. One
thought in particular tormented him; namely, that during his
journey hither when, not knowing whither they were conducting him, he had remained so calm and inactive, he might a
dozen times have plunged into the sea, and thanks to his powers
of swimming, for which he was famous, have gained the shore,
concealed himself until the arrival of a Genoese or Spanish
vessel, escaped to Spain or Italy, where Mercédès and his father
could have joined him. He had no fears as to how he should live;
good seamen are welcome everywhere. He spoke Italian like a
Tuscan, and Spanish like a Castilian. He would then have
been happy, whereas he was now confined in the Château d'If,
ignorant of the future destiny of his father and Mercédès; and
all this because he had trusted to Villefort's promise. The
thought was maddening, and Dantès threw himself furiously

down on his straw. The next morning the jailer made his appearance.

"Well," said the jailer, "are you more reasonable to-day?"

Dantès made no reply.

"Come, take courage; do you want anything in my power to do for you?"

"I wish to see the governor."

"Eh!" said the jailer, impatiently, "I have already told you it is impossible."

"Why so?"

"Because it is not allowed by the rules."

"What is allowed, then?"

"Better fare, if you pay for it; books, and leave to walk about."

"I do not want books, I am satisfied with my food, and I do not care to walk about; but I wish to see the governor."

"If you worry me by repeating the same thing, I will not bring you any more to eat."

"Well, then," said Edmond, "if you do not, I shall die of hunger,—that is all."

The tone in which Dantès uttered these words showed the jailer that his prisoner was quite willing to die; and therefore, since every prisoner is worth ten sous a day to his jailer, he replied in a more subdued tone, "What you ask is impossible; but if you are very well-behaved you will be allowed to walk about, and some day you will meet the governor; and if he chooses to reply, that is his affair."

"But," asked Dantès, "how long shall I have to wait?"

"Ah! a month—six months—a year."

"It is too long a time. I wish to see him at once."

"Ah," said the jailer, "do not brood always over what is impossible, or you will be mad in a fortnight."

"You think so?"

"Yes, mad; madness always begins in that way. We have an instance of it here. It was by offering continually a million of livres to the governor for his liberty that an abbé became mad who was in this chamber before you."

"How long since he left it?"

"Two years."

"Was he liberated then?"

"No; he was put in a dungeon."

"Listen," said Dantès: "I am not an abbé, I am not mad; perhaps I shall be, but at present unfortunately I am not. I will make you another proposition."

" What is that? "

" I do not offer you a million, because I haven't it to give; but I will give you a hundred crowns if the first time you go to Marseilles you will seek out a young girl named Mercédès, at the Catalans, and give her two lines from me."

" If I took them, and were detected, I should lose my place, which is worth two thousand livres a year; I should be a great fool to run such a risk for three hundred."

" Well," said Dantès, " mark this: if you refuse to carry two lines to Mercédès, or at least to tell her that I am here, I will some day hide myself behind the door, and when you enter I will dash out your brains with this stool."

" Threats! " cried the jailer, retreating and putting himself on the defensive; " you are certainly going mad. The abbé began like you, and in three days you will want a strait-waist-coat, like him; but fortunately there are dungeons here." Dantès seized the stool and whirled it round his head.

" Good! " said the jailer, " very good! Since you will have it so, I will go and notify the governor."

" That is right," returned Dantès, dropping the stool and sitting on it with drooping head and haggard eyes, as if he were indeed becoming insane. The jailer went out, and returned in an instant with a corporal and four soldiers.

" By the governor's orders," said he, " conduct the prisoner to the story beneath."

" To the dungeon, then," said the corporal.

" Yes; we must put the madman with the madmen." The soldiers seized Dantès, who fell into a sort of atony, and went with them without resistance.

He descended fifteen steps, the door of a dungeon was opened, and he entered, murmuring, " He is right; the mad should be placed with the mad." The door closed, and Dantès advanced with outstretched hands until he touched the wall; he then sat down in the corner until his eyes became accustomed to the darkness. The jailer was right; Dantès wanted but little of being utterly mad.

CHAPTER IX

THE EVENING OF THE BETROTHAL

VILLEFORT had, as we have said, hastened back to the Place du Grand Cours, and on entering the house found that the guests whom he had left at table had passed into the salon. Renée, with all the rest of the company, was anxiously awaiting him, and on his entrance he was greeted by a general exclamation.

"Well, decapitator, guardian of the State, Brutus, what is the matter?" said one.

"Are we threatened with a fresh Reign of Terror?" asked another.

"Has the Corsican ogre broken loose?" cried a third.

"Madame the Marchioness," said Villefort, approaching his future mother-in-law, "I request your pardon for thus leaving you. Monsieur the Marquis, honour me by a few moments' private conversation!"

"Ah! this affair is really serious, then?" asked the marquis, remarking the cloud on Villefort's brow.

"So serious that I must take leave of you for a few days; so," added he, turning to Renée, "judge for yourself if it be not important."

"You are going to leave us?" cried Renée, unable to hide her emotion.

"Alas!" returned Villefort, "I must."

"Where, then, are you going?" asked the marchioness.

"That, madame, is the secret of justice; but if you have any commissions for Paris, a friend of mine is going there to-night." The guests looked at each other.

"You wish to speak to me alone?" said the marquis.

"Yes, let us go into your cabinet." The marquis took his arm and left the salon.

"Well!" asked he, as soon as they were in his closet, "tell me, what is it?"

"An affair of the greatest importance, that demands my immediate presence in Paris. Now, excuse the indiscretion, marquis, but have you any property in state securities?"

"All my fortune is in the Funds,—seven or eight hundred thousand livres."

"Then sell out; sell out, marquis, as soon as you can."

"Eh! how can I sell out here?"

"You have a broker, have you not?"

"Yes."

"Then give me a letter to him, and tell him to sell out without an instant's delay; perhaps even now I shall arrive too late."

"The devil!" said the marquis, "let us lose no time, then!"

And, sitting down, he wrote a letter to his broker, ordering him to sell out at any price.

"Now, then," said Villefort, placing the letter in his pocket-book, "write another!"

" To whom? "

" To the king."

" I dare not write to his Majesty."

" I do not ask you to write to his Majesty; but ask M. de Salvieux to do so. I want a letter that will enable me to reach the king's presence without all the formalities of demanding an audience; that would occasion a loss of precious time."

" Address yourself to the keeper of the seals; he has the right of entry, and can procure you audience."

" Doubtless; but there is no occasion to divide the merit of my discovery with him. The keeper would leave me in the background, and take all the honour to himself. I tell you, marquis, my career is assured if I only reach the Tuileries the first, for I shall have rendered the king a service which he cannot forget."

" In that case make your preparations; I will call Salvieux and have him write the letter you require."

" Be as quick as possible, I must be *en route* in a quarter of an hour."

" Make your carriage stop at the door."

" You will present my excuses to the marchioness and Mademoiselle Renée, whom I leave on such a day with great regret."

" They are both in my room; you can say all this for yourself."

" A thousand thanks; busy yourself with the letter."

The marquis rang, a servant entered.

" Inform the Comte de Salvieux I am waiting for him."

" Now, then, go! " said the marquis.

" Yes, but I shall return immediately."

Villefort hastily quitted the apartment, but reflecting that the sight of the deputy *procureur* walking precipitately would be enough to throw the whole city into confusion, he resumed his ordinary pace, which was altogether magisterial. At his door he perceived a figure in the shadow that seemed to wait for him. It was Mercédès, who hearing no news of her lover, had come herself to learn the cause of his arrest.

As Villefort drew near, she advanced and stood before him. Dantès had spoken of his bride, and Villefort instantly recognised her. Her beauty and high bearing surprised him, and when she inquired what had become of her lover, it seemed to him that she was the judge, and he the accused.

" The young man you speak of," said Villefort, abruptly, " is a great criminal, and I can do nothing for him, mademoiselle."

Mercédès burst into tears, and as Villefort strove to pass her, again addressed him.

" But at least tell me where he is, that I may learn if he is alive or dead," said she.

" I do not know; he is no longer in my hands," replied Villefort.

And desirous of putting an end to the interview, he pushed by her and closed the door, as if to exclude the pain he felt. But remorse is not thus banished; like the fatal shaft of which Virgil speaks, the wounded man carried it with him. He entered and closed the door, but having reached his salon, his strength gave way; he gave vent to a sigh which was like a sob, and sunk into a chair.

Then, at the bottom of that diseased heart was produced the first germ of a mortal ulcer. The man he sacrificed to his ambition, that innocent victim he made pay the penalty of his father's faults, appeared to him pale and threatening, leading his affianced bride by the hand, pale like himself, and bringing with him remorse,—not such as the ancients figured, furious and terrible, but that slow and consuming agony whose pangs increase until the end of life. Then he had a moment's hesitation. He had frequently called for capital punishment on criminals, and owing to his irresistible eloquence they had been condemned; and yet the slightest shadow of remorse had never clouded Villefort's brow, because they were guilty,—at least, he believed so. But now the affair was very different. He had doomed an innocent man to the horrors of perpetual imprisonment,—an innocent man who was on the threshold of happiness; in this case he was not the judge, but the executioner.

As he thus reflected, he felt the sensation we have described, and which had hitherto been unknown to him, rise in his bosom, and it filled him with vague apprehensions. It is thus that a wounded man trembles instinctively at the approach of the finger to his wound until it be healed. But Villefort's was one of those that never close, or if they do, only close to reopen more agonising than ever. If at this moment the sweet voice of Renée had sounded in his ears pleading for mercy, or the fair Mercédès had entered and said, " In the name of God, I conjure you to restore me my affianced husband! " his cold and trembling hands would have signed his release, at the risk of whatever consequences might ensue. But no voice broke the stillness of the chamber, and the door was opened only by Villefort's valet, who came to tell him the travelling-carriage was in readiness.

Villefort rose, or rather sprang from his chair like a man who has triumphed in an internal struggle, hastily opened one of the drawers of his *secrétaire*, emptied all the gold it contained into his pocket, stood motionless an instant, his hand pressed to his head, muttered a few inarticulate sounds, and then perceiving that his servant had placed his cloak on his shoulders, he sprang into the carriage, ordering the postilions to go to Rue du Grand Cours, to the house of M. de Saint-Méran.

So the unhappy Dantès was condemned.

As the marquis had promised, Villefort found the marchioness and Renée in the cabinet. He started when he saw Renée, for he fancied she was again about to plead for Dantès. Alas! she was only thinking of Villefort's departure.

She loved Villefort, and he was leaving her at the moment he was about to become her husband. Villefort knew not when he should return, and Renée, far from pleading for Dantès, hated the man whose crime separated her from her lover.

What, then, had Mercédès to say? She had met Fernand at the corner of the Rue de la Loge; she had returned to the Catalans, and had despairingly cast herself on her couch. Fernand, kneeling by her side, took her hand, and covered it with kisses that Mercédès did not even feel. She passed the night thus. The oil in the lamp burned out, but she did not notice the darkness, and when the day returned she was not aware of its light. Grief had made her blind to all but one object; that was Edmond.

" Ah, you are there! " said she, at length.

" I have not quitted you since yesterday," returned Fernand, sorrowfully.

M. Morrel had not given up the battle. He had learned that Dantès had been conducted to prison, and he had gone to all his friends, and to the influential persons of the city; but the report was already in circulation that Dantès was arrested as a Bonapartist agent, and as the most sanguine looked upon any attempt of Napoleon to remount the throne as madness, he met with nothing but refusal, and had returned home in despair.

Caderousse also was restless and uneasy, but instead of seeking to aid Dantès, he had shut himself up with two bottles of wine, in the hope of drowning reflection. But he did not succeed, and became too intoxicated to fetch any more wine, and yet not so intoxicated as to forget what had happened.

Danglars alone was neither troubled nor uneasy; he was even joyous,—he had got rid of an enemy and preserved his situation on board the *Pharaon*. Danglars was one of those men of calculation who are born with a pen behind the ear, and an inkstand in place of a heart. Everything with him was multiplication or subtraction; and he estimated the life of a man as less precious than a figure, when that figure could increase, and that life would diminish, the total of the amount.

Villefort, after having received M. de Salvieux's letter, embraced Renée, kissed the marchioness's hand, and shaken hands with the marquis, started for Paris.

The father of Dantès was dying with grief and anxiety.

CHAPTER X

THE SMALL CABINET OF THE TUILERIES

WE will leave Villefort on the road to Paris, travelling with all speed, will cross two or three apartments, and enter the small cabinet of the Tuileries with the arched window, so well known as having been the favourite cabinet of Napoleon and of Louis XVIII.,—as it is also to-day that of Louis Philippe.

There, in this cabinet, seated before a walnut-tree table he had brought with him from Hartwell, and to which, through one of those fancies not uncommon to great people, he was particularly attached, the king, Louis XVIII., was carelessly listening to a man of fifty or fifty-two years of age, with gray hairs, aristocratic bearing, and exceedingly gentlemanly attire, while he was making a note in a volume of Horace, Gryphius's edition, which was much indebted to the sagacious philological observations of his Majesty.

" You say, sir—" said the king.

"That I am exceedingly disquieted, Sire."

" Really? Have you had a dream of the seven fat kine and seven lean kine? "

" No, Sire, for that would only betoken for us seven years of plenty and seven years of scarcity; and with a king as full of foresight as your Majesty, scarcity is not a thing to be feared."

" Then of what other scourge are you afraid, my dear Blacas?"

" Sire, I have every reason to believe that a storm is brewing in the South."

" Well, my dear duke," replied Louis XVIII., " I think you are wrongly informed, and I know positively that on the contrary it is very fine weather in that direction." Man of ability as he was, Louis XVIII. liked a pleasant jest.

"Sire," continued M. de Blacas, "if it only be to reassure a faithful servant, will your Majesty send into Languedoc, Provence, and Dauphiné, trusty men who will bring you back a faithful report as to the feeling in these three provinces?"

"*Canimus surdis*," replied the king, continuing the annotations in his Horace.

"Sire," replied the courtier, laughing, in order that he might seem to comprehend the quotation, "your Majesty may be perfectly right in relying on the good feeling of France, but I fear I am not altogether wrong in dreading some desperate attempt."

"By whom?"

"By Bonaparte, or at least his party."

"My dear Blacas," said the king, "you with your alarms prevent me from working."

"And you, Sire, with your security prevent me from sleeping."

"Wait, my dear sir, wait a moment,—for I have such a delightful note on the *Pastor quum traheret*,—wait, and I will listen to you afterwards."

There was a brief pause, during which Louis XVIII. wrote in a hand as small as possible another note on the margin of his Horace; and then, looking at the duke with the self-satisfied air of a man who thinks he has an idea of his own while he is but commenting upon the idea of another, he said,—

"Go on, my dear duke, go on; I listen."

"Sire," said Blacas, who had had for a moment the hope of confiscating Villefort to his own profit, "I am compelled to tell you that these are not mere rumours destitute of foundation which thus disquiet me; but a reflective man deserving all my confidence, and charged by me to watch over the South [the duke hesitated as he pronounced these words], has arrived in haste to tell me a great peril threatens the king, and then I hasten to you, Sire."

"*Mala ducis avi domum*," continued Louis XVIII., still annotating.

"Does your Majesty wish me not to continue this subject?"

"By no means, dear duke; but reach out your hand."

"Which?"

"Whichever you please; there, to the left."

"Here, Sire?"

"I tell you to the left, and you seek on the right. I mean on my left,—yes, there; you will find yesterday's report of the minister of police. But here is M. Dandré himself;" and M. Dandré, announced by the chamberlain-in-waiting, entered.

"Come in," said Louis XVIII., with an imperceptible smile, —" come in, Baron, and tell the duke all you know,—the latest news of M. de Bonaparte. Do not conceal anything, however serious; let us see, the island of Elba is a volcano, and we may expect to have issuing thence flaming and bristling war,—*bella, horrida bella.*" M. Dandré leaned very respectfully on the back of a chair with his two hands, and said,—

"Has your Majesty perused yesterday's report?"

"Yes, yes; but tell the duke himself, who cannot find it, what the report contains. Give him the particulars of what the usurper is doing in his islet."

"Monsieur," said the baron to the duke, "all the servants of his Majesty should be gratified by the latest intelligence which we have from the island of Elba. Bonaparte," M. Dandré looked at Louis XVIII., who, employed in writing a note, did not even raise his head,—" Bonaparte," continued the baron, " is mortally wearied, and passes whole days in watching his miners at work at Porto Longone."

"And scratches himself for amusement," added the king.

"Scratches himself?" inquired the duke, "what does your Majesty mean?"

"Yes, indeed, my dear duke. Do you forget that this great man, this hero, this demigod, is attacked with a malady of the skin which worries him to death, *prurigo?*"

"And moreover, Monsieur the Duke," continued the minister of police, "we are almost assured that in a very short time the usurper will be insane."

"Insane?"

"Insane to a degree; his head becomes weaker. Sometimes he weeps bitterly, sometimes laughs boisterously; at other times he passes hours on the sea-shore, flinging stones in the water, and when the flint makes 'duck-and-drake' five or six times, he appears as delighted as if he had gained another Marengo or Austerlitz. Now, you must agree these are indubitable symptoms of weakness."

"Or of wisdom, Monsieur the Baron,—or of wisdom," said Louis XVIII., laughing. "The greatest captains of antiquity amused themselves with casting pebbles into the ocean; see Plutarch's *Life of Scipio Africanus.*"

M. de Blacas pondered deeply on this blind repose of monarch and minister. Villefort, who did not choose to reveal the whole secret, lest another should reap all the benefit of the disclosure, had yet communicated enough to cause him the greatest uneasiness.

"Well, well, Dandré," said Louis XVIII., "Blacas is not yet convinced; proceed, therefore, to the usurper's conversion." The minister of police bowed.

"The usurper's conversion?" murmured the duke, looking at the king and Dandré, who spoke alternately, like Virgil's shepherds. "The usurper converted!"

"Decidedly, my dear duke."

"In what way converted?"

"To good principles. Explain it, Baron."

"Why, this it is, Monsieur the Duke," said the minister, with the gravest air in the world: "Napoleon lately had a review, and as two or three of his old veterans showed a desire to return to France, he gave them their dismissal, and exhorted them to 'serve their good king.' These were his own words, Monsieur the Duke, I am certain of that."

"Well, Blacas, what do you think of it?" inquired the king triumphantly, and neglecting for a moment the voluminous scholiast before him.

"I say, Sire, that Monsieur the Minister of Police is greatly deceived, or I am; and as it is impossible it can be the minister of police, since he has the guardianship of the safety and honour of your Majesty, it is probable I am in error. However, Sire, if I might advise, your Majesty will interrogate the person of whom I spoke to you, and I will urge your Majesty to do him this honour."

"Most willingly, duke; under your auspices I will receive any person you please, but with arms in hand. Monsieur the Minister, have you any report more recent than this? This is dated February 20, and we have reached the 3rd of March."

"No, Sire, but I am hourly expecting one; it may have arrived since I left my office this morning."

"Go thither, and if there be none—well, well," continued Louis XVIII., "make one; that is the usual way, is it not?" and the king laughed facetiously.

"Oh, Sire," replied the minister, "we have no occasion to invent any; every day our desks are loaded with most circumstantial denunciations coming from crowds of individuals who hope for some return for services which they do not render, but would like to. They trust to fortune, and hope that some unexpected event will give a kind of reality to their predictions."

"Well, sir, go," said Louis XVIII., "and remember that I am waiting for you."

"I will but go and return, Sire; I shall be back in ten minutes."

"And I, Sire," said M. de Blacas, "will go and find my messenger."

"Wait, sir, wait," said Louis XVIII. "Really, Blacas, I must change your armorial bearings; I will give you an eagle with outstretched wings, holding in its claws a prey which tries in vain to escape, and bearing this device,—*Tenax*."

"Sire, I listen," said M. de Blacas, biting his nails with impatience.

"I wish to consult you on this passage, '*Molli fugiens anhelitu;*' you know it refers to a stag flying from a wolf. Are you not a sportsman and a great wolf-hunter? Well, then, what do you think of the *molli anhelitu?*"

"Admirable, Sire; but my messenger is like the stag you refer to, for he has posted two hundred and twenty leagues in little more than three days."

"Which is undergoing great fatigue and anxiety, my dear duke, when we have a telegraph which takes only three or four hours, and that without putting it in the least in the world out of breath."

"Ah, Sire, you recompense but badly this poor young man, who has come so far, and with so much ardour, to give your Majesty useful information. If only for the sake of M. de Salvieux, who recommends him to me, I entreat your Majesty to receive him graciously."

"M. de Salvieux, my brother's chamberlain?"

"Yes, Sire."

"He is at Marseilles."

"And writes me thence."

"Does he speak to you of this conspiracy?"

"No; but strongly recommends M. de Villefort, and begs me to present him to your Majesty."

"M. de Villefort!" cried the king, "is the messenger's name M. de Villefort?"

"Yes, Sire."

"And he comes from Marseilles?"

"In person."

"Why did you not mention his name at once?" replied the king, betraying some uneasiness.

"Sire, I thought his name was unknown to your Majesty."

"No, no, Blacas; he is a man of strong and elevated understanding, ambitious too, and, *pardieu!* you know his father's name."

"His father?"

"Yes, Noirtier."

"Noirtier the Girondin? Noirtier the senator?"

"He himself."

"And your Majesty has employed the son of such a man?"

"Blacas, my friend, you have but limited comprehension. I told you Villefort was ambitious; to win success Villefort would sacrifice everything, even his father."

"Then, Sire, may I present him?"

"This instant, duke! Where is he?"

"Waiting below, in my carriage."

"Go for him at once."

"I will do so."

The duke left the royal presence with the speed of a young man; his really sincere royalism made him youthful again. Louis XVIII. remained alone, and turning his eyes on his half-opened Horace, muttered, "*Justum et tenacem propositi virum.*"

M. de Blacas returned with the same rapidity he had descended, but in the ante-chamber he was forced to appeal to the king's authority. Villefort's dusty garb, his costume, which was not of courtly cut, excited the susceptibility of M. de Brézé, who was all astonishment at finding that this young man had the pretension to enter before the king in such attire. The duke, however, removed all difficulties with a word,—his Majesty's order; and in spite of the observations which the master of the ceremonies made for the honour of his office and principles, Villefort was introduced.

The king was seated in the same place where the duke had left him. On opening the door, Villefort found himself facing him, and the young magistrate's first impulse was to pause.

"Come in, M. de Villefort," said the king, "come in." Villefort bowed, and advancing a few steps, waited until the king should interrogate him.

"M. de Villefort," said Louis XVIII., "the Duc de Blacas assures me you have some important information to communicate."

"Sire, the duke is right; and I believe your Majesty will recognise its importance."

"In the first place, and before everything else, sir, is the evil as great in your opinion as they wish to make me believe?"

"Sire, I believe the evil to be great, but I hope, thanks to the speed I have used, that it is not irreparable."

"Speak as fully as you please, sir," said the king, who began to give way to the emotion which had showed itself in Blacas's face and affected Villefort's voice. "Speak, sir, and pray begin at the beginning; I like order in everything."

"Sire," said Villefort, "I will render a faithful report to your Majesty, but I must entreat your forgiveness if my anxiety creates some obscurity in my language." A glance at the king after this discreet and subtle exordium assured Villefort of the benignity of his august auditor, and he continued,—

"Sire, I have come as rapidly to Paris as possible, to inform your Majesty that I have discovered in the exercise of my duties, not a commonplace and insignificant plot, such as is every day got up in the lower ranks of the people and in the army, but an actual conspiracy,—a storm which menaces even the throne of your Majesty. Sire, the usurper is arming three ships; he meditates some project, which, however mad, may yet be terrible. At this moment he will have left Elba, to go—whither? I know not, but assuredly to attempt a landing either at Naples, or on the coast of Tuscany, or perhaps on the shore of France. Your Majesty is well aware that the sovereign of the Isle of Elba has maintained his relations with Italy and France?"

"I am, monsieur," said the king, much agitated; "and recently we have had information of Bonapartist *réunions* in the Rue St. Jacques. But proceed, I beg of you. How did you obtain these details?"

"Sire, they are the results of an examination which I have made of a man of Marseilles, whom I have watched for some time, and arrested on the day of my departure. This person, a sailor of turbulent character, and whom I suspected of Bonapartism, has been secretly to the Isle of Elba. There he saw the grand-marshal, who charged him with a verbal mission to a Bonapartist in Paris, whose name I could not extract from him; but this mission was to prepare men's minds for a return (it is the man who says this, Sire),—a return which will soon occur."

"And where is this man?"

"In prison, Sire."

"And the matter seems serious to you!"

"So serious, Sire, that when this event surprised me in the midst of a family festival, on the very day of my betrothal, I left my bride and friends, postponing everything that I might hasten to lay to your Majesty's feet the fears which impressed me, and the assurance of my devotion."

"True," said Louis XVIII.; "was there not a marriage engagement between you and Mademoiselle de Saint-Méran?"

"Daughter of one of your Majesty's most faithful servants."

"Yes, yes; but let us talk of this plot, M. de Villefort."

"Sire, I fear it is more than a plot; I fear it is a conspiracy."

"A conspiracy in these times," said Louis XVIII., smiling,

" is a thing very easy to meditate, but more difficult to conduct to success, inasmuch as, re-established so recently on the throne of our ancestors, we have our eyes open at once upon the past, the present, and the future. For the last ten months my ministers have redoubled their vigilant watch of the shore of the Mediterranean, although it is well guarded. If Bonaparte landed at Naples, the whole coalition would be on foot before he could even reach Piombino; if he land in Tuscany, he will be in an unfriendly territory; if he land in France, it must be with a handful of men, and the result of that is easily foretold, execrated as he is by the population. Take courage, sir; but at the same time rely on our royal gratitude."

" Ah, here is M. Dandré!" cried Blacas. At this instant the minister of police appeared at the door, pale, trembling, and as if ready to faint. Villefort was about to retire, but M. de Blacas, taking his hand, restrained him.

CHAPTER XI

THE OGRE OF CORSICA

AT the sight of this agitation Louis XVIII. violently pushed away the table at which he was writing.

" What ails you, Monsieur the Baron?" he exclaimed. " You appear quite aghast. This trouble, this hesitation,—have they anything to do with what M. de Blacas has told me, and M. de Villefort has just confirmed?"

M. de Blacas moved suddenly towards the baron, but the fright of the courtier dominated the triumph of the statesman; and besides, as matters were, it was much more to his advantage that the prefect of police should triumph over him than that he should humiliate the prefect.

" Sire—" stammered the baron.

" Well, what is it?" asked Louis XVIII. The minister of police, giving way to an impulse of despair, was about to throw himself at the feet of Louis XVIII., who retreated a step and frowned.

" Will you speak?" he said.

" Oh, Sire, what a dreadful misfortune! I am indeed to be pitied. I can never forgive myself!"

" Monsieur," said Louis XVIII., " I command you to speak!"

" Well, Sire, the usurper left Elba on the 26th of February, and landed on the 1st of March."

" And where,—in Italy? " asked the king, eagerly.

" In France, Sire; at a small port, near Antibes, in the Gulf of Juan."

" The usurper landed in France near Antibes, in the Gulf of Juan, two hundred and fifty leagues from Paris, on the 1st of March, and you acquired this information only to-day, the 4th of March! Well, sir, what you tell me is impossible. You must have received a false report, or you have gone mad."

" Alas, Sire, it is but too true! "

Louis made a gesture of indescribable anger and alarm, and then drew himself up as if this sudden blow had struck him at the same moment in heart and countenance.

" In France! " he cried, " this usurper in France! Then they did not watch over this man. Who knows? they were perhaps in league with him! "

" Oh, Sire! " exclaimed the Duc de Blacas, " M. Dandré is not a man to be accused of treason! Sire, we have all been blind, and the minister of police has shared the general blindness, —that is all."

" But—" said Villefort, and then suddenly checked himself. " Your pardon, Sire," he said, bowing; " my zeal carried me away. Will your Majesty deign to excuse me? "

" Speak, sir, speak boldly," replied Louis. " You alone forewarned us of the evil; advise us now while we look for the remedy! "

" Sire," said Villefort, " the usurper is detested in the south; and it seems to me that if he ventures thither, it will be easy to raise Languedoc and Provence against him."

" Yes, assuredly," replied the minister; " but he is advancing by Gap and Sisteron."

" Advancing! he is advancing! " said Louis XVIII. " Is he then advancing on Paris? "

The minister of police kept a silence which was equivalent to a full admission.

" And Dauphiné, monsieur? " inquired the king, of Villefort. " Do you think it possible to rouse that as well as Provence? "

" Sire, I am sorry to tell your Majesty a cruel fact; but the feeling in Dauphiné is far from resembling that of Provence or Languedoc. The mountaineers are Bonapartists, Sire."

" Then," murmured Louis, " he was well informed. And how many men had he with him? "

" I do not know, Sire," answered the minister of police.

" What! you do not know? Have you neglected to obtain

information of this circumstance? It is true this is of small importance," he added with a withering smile.

"Sire, it was impossible to learn; the despatch simply stated the fact of the landing and the route taken by the usurper."

"And how did this despatch reach you?" inquired the king.

The minister bowed his head, and while a deep colour overspread his cheeks, he stammered out, "By the telegraph, Sire."

Louis XVIII. advanced a step, and folded his arms over his chest as Napoleon would have done. "So, then," he exclaimed, turning pale with anger, "seven allied armies overthrew that man. A miracle of Heaven replaced me on the throne of my fathers after twenty-five years of exile. I have, during those five-and-twenty years, studied, sounded, analysed the men and things of that France which was promised to me; and when I have attained the end of all my wishes, the power I hold in my hands bursts and shatters me to atoms!"

"Sire, it is fatality!" murmured the minister, feeling that such a pressure, however light for destiny, was sufficient to overwhelm a man.

"What our enemies say of us is then true: we have learned nothing, forgotten nothing! If I were betrayed as he was, I would console myself; but to be in the midst of persons elevated by myself to dignities, who ought to watch over me more carefully than over themselves,—for my fortune is theirs; before me they were nothing, after me they will be nothing,—and perish miserably from incapacity, ineptitude! Oh, yes, monsieur, you are right,—it is fatality!"

The minister was bowed beneath this crushing sarcasm. M. de Blacas wiped the moisture from his brow. Villefort smiled within himself, for he perceived his increased importance.

"To fall!" continued King Louis, who at the first glance had sounded the abyss over which the monarchy hung suspended,— "to fall, and learn that fall by telegraph! Oh! I would rather mount the scaffold of my brother, Louis XVI., than thus descend the staircase of the Tuileries driven away by ridicule. Ridicule, monsieur! why you know not its power in France, and yet you ought to know it!"

"Sire, Sire," murmured the minister, "for pity's—"

"Approach, M. de Villefort," resumed the king, addressing the young man, who, motionless and breathless, was listening to a conversation on which depended the destiny of a kingdom, —"approach, and tell monsieur that it was impossible to know beforehand all that he has not known."

"Sire, it was really impossible to learn secrets which that man concealed from all the world."

"Really impossible! Yes; that is a great word, monsieur. Unfortunately, there are great words, as there are great men; I have measured them. Really impossible for a minister who has an office, agents, spies, and fifteen hundred thousand francs for secret-service money, to know what is going on at sixty leagues from the coast of France! Well, then, see; here is a gentleman who had none of these resources at his disposal, —a gentleman, only a simple magistrate, who learned more than you with all your police, and who would have saved my crown, if, like you, he had the power of directing a telegraph."

The look of the minister of police was turned with an expression of concentrated hatred on Villefort, who bent his head with the modesty of triumph.

"I do not mean that for you, Blacas," continued Louis XVIII.; "for if you have discovered nothing, at least you have had the good sense to persevere in your suspicions. Any other than yourself would have considered the disclosure of M. de Villefort as insignificant, or else dictated by a venal ambition."

These words were meant to allude to those which the minister of police had uttered with so much confidence an hour before. Villefort understood the drift of the king's remarks. Any other person would perhaps have been too much overcome by the intoxication of praise; but he feared to make for himself a mortal enemy of the police minister, although he perceived that Dandré was irrevocably lost. In fact, the minister who in the plenitude of his power had been unable to penetrate Napoleon's secret, might in the convulsions of his dying throes penetrate his (Villefort's) secret, for which end he had but to interrogate Dantès. He therefore came to the rescue of the crestfallen minister, instead of aiding to crush him.

"Sire," said Villefort, "the rapidity of the event must prove to your Majesty that God alone can prevent it, by raising a tempest; what your Majesty is pleased to attribute to me as profound perspicacity is simply owing to chance, and I have profited by that chance like a good and devoted servant,— that's all. Do not attribute to me more than I deserve, Sire, that your Majesty may never have occasion to recall the first opinion you have been pleased to form of me."

The minister of police thanked the young man by an eloquent look, and Villefort understood that he had succeeded in his design; that is to say, that without forfeiting the gratitude of the king he had made a friend of one on whom, in case of necessity, he might rely.

" 'Tis well!" resumed the king. " And now, gentlemen," he continued, turning towards M. de Blacas and the minister of police, " I have no further occasion for you, and you may retire; what now remains to do must be done through the department of the minister of war."

" Fortunately, Sire," said M. de Blacas, " we can rely on the army; your Majesty knows how every report confirms their loyalty and attachment."

" Do not mention reports, monsieur, to me! for I know now what confidence to place in them. Yet, à propos of reports, Monsieur the Baron, what intelligence have you as to the affair in the Rue St. Jacques? "

" The affair in the Rue St. Jacques!" exclaimed Villefort, unable to repress an exclamation. Then, suddenly pausing, he added, " Your pardon, Sire, but my devotion to your Majesty has made me forget, not my respect towards you, for that is too deeply engraven in my heart, but the rules of etiquette."

" Say and act, sir!" replied the king; " you have acquired to-day the right to ask questions."

" Sire," replied the minister of police, " I came this moment to give your Majesty fresh information which I had obtained on this head, when your Majesty's attention was attracted by this terrible affair of the gulf; and now these facts will cease to interest your Majesty."

" On the contrary, monsieur,—on the contrary," said Louis XVIII., " this affair seems to me to have a decided connection with that which occupies our attention; and the death of General Quesnel will perhaps put us on the direct track of a great internal conspiracy."

At the name of General Quesnel, Villefort trembled.

" In fact, Sire," said the minister of police, " all evidence leads to the conclusion that this death is not the result of a suicide, as we at first believed, but of an assassination. General Quesnel had quitted, as it appears, a Bonapartist club when he disappeared. An unknown person had been with him that morning, and made an appointment with him in the Rue St. Jacques; unfortunately, the general's *valet-de-chambre*, who was dressing his hair at the moment when the stranger entered, though he heard the street mentioned, did not catch the number."

As the police minister related this to the king, Villefort, who followed the recital as if his very existence hung upon it, turned alternately red and pale. The king looked towards him.

" Do you not think with me, M. de Villefort, that General Quesnel, whom they believed attached to the usurper, but who was really entirely devoted to me, has perished the victim of a Bonapartist ambush? "

" It is probable, Sire," replied Villefort. " But is this all that is known? "

" They are on the traces of the man who appointed the meeting with him."

" On his traces? " said Villefort.

" Yes, the servant has given his description. He is a man of from fifty to fifty-two years of age, brown, with black eyes covered with shaggy eyebrows, and a thick mustache. He was dressed in a blue frock-coat, buttoned up to the chin, and wore at his button-hole the rosette of an officer of the Legion of Honour. Yesterday an individual was followed exactly corresponding with this description, but he was lost sight of at the corner of the Rue de la Jussienne and the Rue Coq-Héron."

Villefort leaned on the back of an armchair, for as the minister of police spoke he felt his legs bend under him; but when he learned that the unknown had escaped the vigilance of the agent who followed him, he breathed again.

" Continue to seek for this man, monsieur," said the king to the minister of police; " for if, as all conspires to convince me, General Quesnel, who would have been so useful to us at this moment, has been murdered, his assassins, Bonapartists or not, shall be cruelly punished."

It required all Villefort's *sang-froid* not to betray the terror with which this declaration of the king inspired him.

" How strange! " continued the king, with some asperity. " The police thinks all is said when it says, ' A murder has been committed;' and particularly when it adds, ' We are on the trace of the guilty persons.' "

" Sire, your Majesty will, I trust, be amply satisfied on this point at least."

" We shall see. I will no longer detain you, Baron. M. de Villefort, you must be fatigued after so long a journey; go and rest yourself. Of course you stopped at your father's? "

A faintness came over Villefort. " No, Sire," he replied; " I alighted at the Hôtel de Madrid, in the Rue de Tournon."

" But you have seen him? "

" Sire, I went straight to M. le Duc de Blacas."

" But you will see him, then? "

" I think not, Sire."

" Ah, I forgot," said Louis, smiling in a manner which proved that all these questions were not made without a motive; "I forgot you and M. Noirtier are not on the best terms possible; that is another sacrifice made to the royal cause, and for which you should be recompensed."

"Sire, the kindness your Majesty deigns to evince towards me is a recompense which so far surpasses my utmost ambition that I have nothing more to request."

"Never mind, monsieur, we will not forget you; make your mind easy. In the meanwhile [the king here detached the cross of the Legion of Honour which he usually wore over his blue coat near the cross of Saint Louis, above the order of Notre Dame du Mont Carmel and St. Lazare, and gave it to Villefort] —in the meanwhile take this cross."

"Sire," said Villefort, "your Majesty mistakes; this cross is that of an officer."

"*Ma foi !*" said Louis XVIII., "take it, such as it is, for I have not the time to procure you another. Blacas, let it be your care to see that the brevet is made out and sent to M. de Villefort."

Villefort's eyes were filled with tears of joy and pride; he took the cross and kissed it. "And now," he said, "may I inquire what are the orders with which your Majesty deigns to honour me?"

"Take what rest you require; and remember that, unable to serve me here in Paris, you may be of the greatest service to me at Marseilles."

"Sire," replied Villefort, bowing, "in an hour I shall have quitted Paris."

"Go, sir," said the king; "and should I forget you (kings' memories are short), do not be afraid to bring yourself to my recollection. Monsieur the Baron, send for the minister of war. Blacas, remain."

"Ah, sir," said the minister of police to Villefort, as they left the Tuileries, "you enter by the right door; your fortune is made."

"Will it continue?" muttered Villefort, saluting the minister, whose career was ended, and looking about him for a hackney-coach. One passed at the moment, which he hailed. He gave his address to the driver, and springing in, threw himself on the seat, and gave loose to dreams of ambition.

Ten minutes afterwards Villefort reached his hotel, ordered his horses in two hours, and desired to have his breakfast brought to him. He was about to commence his repast when the sound of the bell, rung by a free and firm hand, was heard.

The valet opened the door, and Villefort heard his name pronounced.

"Who could know that I was here already?" said the young man.

The valet entered.

"Well," said Villefort, "what is it? Who rang? Who asked for me?"

"A stranger, who will not send in his name."

"A stranger who will not send in his name! What can he want with me?"

"He wishes to speak to you."

"To me?"

"Yes."

"Did he mention my name?"

"Yes."

"What sort of person is he?"

"Why, sir, a man of about fifty."

"Short or tall?"

"About your own height, sir."

"Dark or fair?"

"Dark,—very dark; with black eyes, black hair, black eyebrows."

"And how dressed?" asked Villefort, quickly.

"In a blue frock-coat, buttoned up close, decorated with the Legion of Honour."

"It is he!" said Villefort, turning pale.

"Eh, *pardieu!*" said the individual whose description we have twice given, entering the door, "what a great deal of ceremony! Is it the custom in Marseilles for sons to keep their fathers waiting in their ante-rooms?"

"Father!" cried Villefort, "then I was not deceived; I felt sure it must be you."

"Well, then, if you felt so sure," replied the new-comer, putting his cane in a corner and his hat on a chair, "allow me to say, my dear Gérard, that it was not very filial of you to keep me waiting at the door."

"Leave us, Germain," said Villefort. The servant quitted the apartment with evident signs of astonishment.

CHAPTER XII

FATHER AND SON

M. NOIRTIER—for it was indeed he who entered—followed with his eyes the servant until he had closed the door, and then, fearing, no doubt, that he might be overheard in the ante-chamber, he opened the door again; nor was the precaution useless, as appeared from the rapid retreat of Germain, who proved that he was not exempt from the sin which ruined our first parents. M. Noirtier then took the trouble to close carefully the door of the ante-chamber, then that of the bed-chamber, and then extended his hand to Villefort, who had followed all his motions with a surprise from which he had not yet recovered.

"Well, now, my dear Gérard," said the visitor to the young man, with a very significant look, "do you know, you seem as if you were not very glad to see me?"

"My dear father," said Villefort, "I am, on the contrary, delighted; but I so little expected your visit that it has somewhat overcome me."

"But, my dear fellow," replied M. Noirtier, seating himself, "I might say the same thing to you, when you announce to me your wedding for the 28th of February, and on the 4th of March are here in Paris."

"And if I have come, my dear father," said Gérard, drawing closer to M. Noirtier, "do not complain, for it is for you that I came, and my journey will perhaps be your salvation."

"Ah, indeed!" said M. Noirtier, stretching himself out at his ease in the chair. "Really, pray tell me all about it, Monsieur the Magistrate, for it must be interesting."

"Father, you have heard of a certain club of Bonapartists held in the Rue St. Jacques?"

"No. 53; yes, I am its vice-president."

"Father, your coolness makes me shudder."

"Why, my dear boy, when a man has been proscribed by the mountaineers, has escaped from Paris in a hay-cart, been hunted in the wilderness of Bordeaux by M. Robespierre's bloodhounds, he becomes accustomed to most things. But go on, what about the club in the Rue St. Jacques?"

"Why, they induced General Quesnel to go there; and General Quesnel, who quitted his own house at nine o'clock in the evening, was found the next day in the Seine."

" And who told you this fine story ? "

" The king himself."

" Well, then, in return for your story," continued Noirtier, " I will tell you another."

" My dear father, I think I already know what you are about to tell me."

" Ah, you have heard of the landing of his Majesty the Emperor ? "

" Not so loud, father, I entreat of you,—for your own sake as well as mine. Yes, I heard this news, and knew it even before you could; for three days ago I posted from Marseilles to Paris with all possible speed, and half-desperate because I could not send with a wish two hundred leagues ahead of me the thought which was agitating my brain."

" Three days ago! You are crazy. Why, three days ago the emperor had not landed."

" No matter; I was aware of his project."

" How did you learn it ? "

" By a letter addressed to you from the Isle of Elba."

" To me ? "

" To you; and which I discovered in the pocket-book of the messenger. Had that letter fallen into the hands of another, you, my dear father, would probably ere this have been shot."

Villefort's father laughed. " Come, come," said he, " it appears that the Restoration has learned from the Empire the mode of settling affairs speedily. Shot, my dear boy! you go ahead with a vengeance. Where is this letter you talk about? I know you too well to suppose you would allow such a thing to pass you."

" I burned it, for fear that some fragment might remain, for that letter would have been your condemnation."

" And the destruction of your prospects," replied Noirtier; " yes, I can easily comprehend that. But I have nothing to fear while I have you to protect me."

" I do better than that, monsieur; I save you ! "

" You do? Why, really, the thing becomes more and more dramatic; explain yourself ! "

" I must refer again to the club in the Rue St. Jacques."

" It appears that this club is rather a bore to the police. Why didn't they search more vigilantly? They would have found—"

" They have not found; but they are on the track."

" Yes, that's the usual phrase; I know it well. When the

police is at fault it declares that it is on the track, and the Government patiently awaits the day when it comes to say with a sneaking air that the track is lost."

"Yes, but they have found a corpse; General Quesnel has been killed, and in all countries they call that a murder."

"A murder, do you say? Why, there is nothing to prove that the general was murdered. People are found every day in the Seine, having thrown themselves in, or been drowned through not knowing how to swim."

"Father, you know very well that the general was not a man to drown himself in despair; and people do not bathe in the Seine in the month of January. No, no! do not mistake; this death was clearly a murder."

"And who thus designated it?"

"The king himself."

"The king! I thought he was philosopher enough to allow that there was no murder in politics. In politics, my dear fellow, you know as well as I do there are no men, but ideas; no feelings, but interests; in politics we do not kill a man, we remove an obstacle. Would you like to know what has really happened? Well, I will tell you. It was thought that reliance might be placed on General Quesnel; he was recommended to us from the Isle of Elba. One of us went to him and invited him to the Rue St. Jacques, where he would find some friends. He came there, and the plan was unfolded to him,—the departure from Elba, the projected landing, etc. When he had heard and comprehended all to the fullest extent, he replied that he was a Royalist. Then all looked at each other,—he was made to take an oath, and did so, but with such an ill grace that it was really tempting Providence to swear thus! And yet in spite of that, the general was allowed to depart free,—perfectly free. Yet he did not return home. What could that mean? Why, my dear fellow, only that on leaving us he lost his way. A murder! really, Villefort, you surprise me. You, a deputy *procureur*, to found an accusation on such bad premises! Did I ever say to you, when you were fulfilling your character as a Royalist, and cut off the head of one of my party, 'My son, you have committed a murder'? No; I said, 'Very well, monsieur, you have gained the victory; to-morrow, perchance, it will be our turn.'"

"But, father, take care; when our turn comes, our revenge will be sweeping."

"I do not understand you."

"You rely on the usurper's return?"

" We do."

" You are mistaken; he will not advance two leagues into the interior of France without being followed, tracked, and caught like a wild beast."

" My dear fellow, the emperor is at this moment on the way to Grenoble; on the 10th or 12th he will be at Lyons, and on the 20th or 25th at Paris."

" The population will rise."

" Yes, to go to meet him."

" He has but a handful of men with him; and armies will be despatched against him."

" Yes, they will escort him into the capital. Really, my dear Gérard, you are but a child; you think yourself well informed because a telegraph has told you three days after the landing, ' The usurper has landed at Cannes with several men. He is pursued.' But where is he; what is he doing? You know nothing about it. He is pursued; that is all you know. Very well, in this way they will pursue him to Paris without drawing a trigger."

" Grenoble and Lyons are faithful cities, and will oppose to him an impassable barrier."

" Grenoble will open her gates to him with enthusiasm; all Lyons will hasten to welcome him. Believe me, we are as well informed as you; and our police is as good as your own. Would you like a proof of it? Well, you wished to conceal your journey from me; and yet I knew of your arrival half an hour after you had passed the barrier. You gave your direction to no one but your postilion; yet I have your address, and in proof I am here the very instant you are going to sit at table. Ring, then, if you please, for a second knife, fork, and plate, and we will dine together."

" Indeed! " replied Villefort, looking at his father with astonishment, " you really do seem very well informed."

" Eh! the thing is simple enough. You who are in power have only the means that money produces; we who are in expectation have those which devotion prompts."

" Devotion? " said Villefort, smiling.

" Yes, devotion; that is, I believe, the word for hopeful ambition." And Villefort's father extended his hand to the bell-rope to summon the servant whom his son had not called. Villefort arrested his arm.

" Wait, my dear father," said the young man; " one other word."

" Say it."

"However ill-conducted is the Royalist police, they yet know one terrible thing."

"What is that?"

"The description of the man who, on the morning of the day when General Quesnel disappeared, presented himself at his house."

"Oh, the admirable police have found that out, have they? And what may be that description?"

"Brown complexion; hair, eyebrows, and whiskers, black; blue frock-coat, buttoned up to the chin; rosette of an officer of the Legion of Honour in his button-hole; a hat with wide brim, and a Malacca cane."

"Ah, ah! they know that?" said Noirtier; "and why, then, have they not laid hands on the man?"

"Because yesterday, or the day before, they lost sight of him at the corner of the Rue Coq-Héron."

"Didn't I say your police was good for nothing?"

"Yes; but still it may lay hands on him."

"True," said Noirtier, looking carelessly around him,— "true, if this individual were not warned; but he is." And he added with a smile, "He will consequently change looks and costume." At these words he rose and put off his frock-coat and cravat, went towards a table on which lay his son's toilet articles, lathered his face, took a razor, and with a firm hand cut off the treacherous whiskers which gave the police so plain a mark of description. Villefort watched him with alarm not unmixed with admiration.

His whiskers cut off, Noirtier gave his hair a new turn, took, instead of his black cravat, a coloured neckerchief which lay at the top of an open portmanteau, put on, in lieu of his blue and high-buttoned frock-coat, a coat of Villefort's of dark brown and sloped away in front, tried on before the glass a narrow-brimmed hat of his son's which appeared to fit him perfectly; and leaving his cane in the corner where he had deposited it, he made to whistle in his powerful hand a small bamboo switch, which the dandy deputy used when he walked, and which aided in giving him that easy swagger which was one of his principal characteristics.

"Well," he said, turning towards his wondering son when this disguise was completed,—"well, do you think your police will recognise me now?"

"No, father," stammered Villefort; "at least, I hope not."

"And now, my dear boy," continued Noirtier, "I rely on

your prudence to remove all the things which I leave in your care."

" Oh, rely on me," said Villefort.

" Yes, yes! and now I believe you are right, and that you have really saved my life; but be assured I will return the obligation to you very soon."

Villefort shook his head.

" You are not convinced yet? "

" I hope, at least, that you may be mistaken."

" Shall you see the king again? "

" Perhaps."

" Would you pass in his eyes for a prophet? "

" Prophets of evil are not in favour at the court, father."

" True, but some day justice is done to them; and supposing a second restoration, you would then pass for a great man."

" Well, what should I say to the king? "

" Say this to him: 'Sire, you are deceived as to the feeling in France, as to the opinions of the towns and the prejudices of the army; he whom in Paris you call the ogre of Corsica, who at Nevers is styled the usurper, is already saluted as Bonaparte at Lyons, and emperor at Grenoble. You think he is tracked, pursued, captured; he is advancing as rapidly as his own eagles. The soldiers you believe dying with hunger, worn out with fatigue, ready to desert, increase like atoms of snow about the rolling ball which hastens onward. Sire, go! leave France to its real master,—to him who did not buy, but conquered it. Go, sire! not that you incur any risk,—for your adversary is powerful enough to show you mercy,—but because it would be humiliating for a grandson of Saint Louis to owe his life to the man of Arcola, Marengo, Austerlitz.' Tell him this, Gérard; or rather, tell him nothing. Keep your journey a secret; do not boast of what you have come to Paris to do, or have done. Return with all speed; enter Marseilles at night, and your house by the back door, and there remain, quiet, submissive, secret, and, above all, inoffensive, for this time, I swear to you, we shall act like powerful men who know their enemies. Go, my son; go, my dear Gérard; and through your obedience to my paternal orders—or, if you prefer it, friendly counsels—we shall be able to keep you in your place. This will be," added Noirtier, with a smile, " a means by which you may a second time save me if the political balance should one day place you high and me low. Adieu, my dear Gérard, and on your next journey alight at my door." Noirtier left the room when he had finished, with the same calmness that had characterised him during the whole of this remarkable and trying conversation. Villefort, pale and agitated, ran to the window, put aside the curtain, and saw him pass, cool and collected, by two or three ill-looking men at the corner of the street, who were there, perhaps, to arrest a man with black whiskers and a blue frock-coat and hat with broad brim.

Villefort stood watching, breathless, until his father had disappeared at the Rue Bussy. Then he turned to the various articles he had left behind him, put at the bottom of his portmanteau his black cravat and blue frock-coat, threw the hat into a dark closet, broke the cane into small bits and flung it in the fire, put on his travelling-cap, and calling his valet, checked with a look the thousand questions he was ready to ask, paid his bill, sprang into his carriage, which was ready, learned at Lyons that Bonaparte had entered Grenoble, and through the midst of the tumult which prevailed along the road, at length reached Marseilles, a prey to all the hopes and fears which enter into the heart of an ambitious man amid his first successes.

CHAPTER XIII

THE HUNDRED DAYS

M. Noirtier was a true prophet, and things progressed rapidly, as he had predicted. Every one knows the history of the famous return from Elba,—that strange and wonderful return, which, without example in the past, will probably remain without imitation in the future.

Louis XVIII. made but a faint attempt to parry this unexpected blow. The monarchy which he had scarcely reconstructed tottered on its precarious foundation, and it needed but a sign of the emperor to hurl to the ground all this edifice incongruously constructed of ancient prejudices and new ideas. Villefort therefore gained nothing save the king's gratitude (which was rather likely to injure him at the present time) and the cross of the Legion of Honour, which he had the prudence not to wear, although M. de Blacas had duly forwarded the brevet.

Napoleon would doubtless have deprived Villefort of his office had it not been for Noirtier, who was all-powerful at the court; and thus the Girondin of '93 and the senator of 1806 protected him who so lately had been his protector. All Villefort's power was devoted during that revival of the empire

—of which, however, it was easy to foresee the second fall—to stifling the secret which Dantès had so nearly divulged. The *procureur du roi* alone was deprived of his office, being suspected of royalism.

However, scarcely was the imperial power re-established,—that is, scarcely had the emperor re-entered the Tuileries and issued his numerous orders from that little cabinet into which we have introduced our readers, and on the table of which he found Louis XVIII.'s snuff-box half-full,—when Marseilles, notwithstanding the attitude of the magistrates, became aware that the embers of civil war (only partly extinguished in the south) were beginning to glow again; it would require but little to excite the populace to acts of more decided violence than the shouts and insults with which they assailed the Royalists whenever they ventured abroad.

Owing to this change, the worthy ship-owner became at that moment, we will not say all-powerful, because Morrel was a prudent and rather a timid man,—so much so that many of the most zealous partisans of Bonaparte accused him of "moderation,"—but sufficiently influential to make his voice heard in the utterance of a demand; and that demand, we may easily divine, had Dantès for its subject.

Villefort retained his place notwithstanding the fall of his chief, but his marriage was put off until a more favourable opportunity. If the emperor remained on the throne, Gérard would need a different alliance to aid his career, and his father had undertaken to procure one for him; if Louis XVIII. should return to the throne, the influence of M. de Saint-Méran would be much increased, as well as his own, and the marriage would be more desirable than ever.

The deputy *procureur* was, then, the first magistrate of Marseilles, when one morning his door opened, and M. Morrel was announced. Any one else would have hastened to receive him; but Villefort was a man of ability, and he knew this would be a sign of weakness. He made Morrel wait in the ante-chamber, although he had no one with him, for the simple reason that the *procureur du roi* always makes every one wait; and after a quarter of an hour passed in reading the papers, he ordered M. Morrel to be admitted.

Morrel expected Villefort would be dejected; he found him, as he had found him six weeks before, calm, firm, and full of that glacial politeness, the most insurmountable of all barriers, which separates the well-bred and the vulgar man. He had penetrated into Villefort's cabinet, convinced the magistrate would tremble at the sight of him; on the contrary, he felt a cold shudder all over him when he beheld Villefort seated, his elbow on his desk, and his head leaning on his hand. He stopped at the door. Villefort gazed at him as if he had some difficulty in recognising him; then, after a brief interval, during which the honest ship-owner turned his hat in his hands,—

"M. Morrel, I believe?" said Villefort.

"Yes, monsieur."

"Come nearer," said the magistrate, with a patronising wave of the hand, "and tell me to what circumstance I owe the honour of this visit."

"Do you not guess, monsieur?" asked Morrel.

"Not in the least; but if I can serve you in any way I shall be delighted."

"Everything depends on you."

"Explain yourself, pray."

"Monsieur," said Morrel, recovering his assurance as he proceeded, "you recollect that a few days before the landing of his Majesty the Emperor I came to intercede for a young man, the mate of my ship, who was accused of having relations with the Isle of Elba. Those relations, which were then a crime, are to-day titles to favour. You then served Louis XVIII., and you showed no favour,—it was your duty; to-day you serve Napoleon, and you ought to protect him,—it is equally your duty. I come, therefore, to ask what has become of that young man?"

Villefort made a violent effort over himself. "What is his name?" said he. "Tell me his name."

"Edmond Dantès."

Villefort would certainly have rather stood opposite the muzzle of a pistol at five-and-twenty paces than have heard this name pronounced; but he betrayed no emotion.

"Dantès?" repeated he, "Edmond Dantès?"

"Yes, monsieur."

Villefort opened a large register, then went to a table, from the table turned to his registers, and then turning to Morrel,—

"Are you quite sure you are not mistaken, monsieur?" said he, in the most natural tone in the world.

Had Morrel been a more quick-sighted man, or better versed in these matters, he would have been surprised at the *procureur du roi* answering him on such a subject, instead of referring him to the governors of the prison or the prefect of the department. But Morrel, disappointed in his expectations of exciting fear, saw in its place only condescension. Villefort had calculated rightly.

"No," said Morrel, "I am not mistaken. I have known him ten years, and the last four he has been in my service. I came about six weeks ago, as you may remember, to beseech your clemency, as I come to-day to beseech your justice. You received me very coldly. Oh, the Royalists were very severe with the Bonapartists in those days."

"Monsieur," returned Villefort, "I was then a Royalist, because I believed the Bourbons not only the heirs to the throne, but the chosen of the nation. The miraculous return of Napoleon has proved that I was mistaken; the legitimate monarch is he who is loved by his people."

"That's right!" cried Morrel. "I like to hear you speak thus, and I augur well for Edmond from it."

"Wait a moment," said Villefort, turning over the leaves of a register; "I have it,—a sailor, who was about to marry a young Catalan girl. I recollect now, it was a very serious charge."

"How so?"

"You know that when he left here he was taken to the prison of the Palais de Justice."

"Well?"

"I made my report to the authorities at Paris; I sent the papers found upon him. That was my duty, as you must admit. A week later he was carried off."

"Carried off!" said Morrel. "What can they have done with the poor lad?"

"Oh, he has been taken to Fenestrelle, to Pignerol, or to the island of Ste. Marguerite. Some fine morning he will return to assume the command of your vessel."

"Come when he will, it shall be kept for him. But how is it he is not already returned? It seems to me the first care of Bonapartist justice should be to set at liberty those who have been imprisoned by Royalist injustice."

"Do not be too hasty, M. Morrel," replied Villefort. "We must in all things proceed according to law. The order of imprisonment came from high authority, and the order for his liberation must proceed from the same source; and as Napoleon has scarcely been reinstated a fortnight, the letters have not yet been forwarded."

"But," said Morrel, "is there no way of expediting these formalities, now that we have triumphed? I have a few friends and some influence; I can obtain a withdrawal of his arrest."

" There has been no arrest."

" Of his enrolment, then, on the prison register."

" In political matters there is no prison registry. It is sometimes essential to government to cause a man's disappearance without leaving any traces. A registry might guide investigation."

" It was perhaps like that under the Bourbons, but at present—"

" It is always the same, my dear Morrel, since the reign of Louis XIV. The emperor is more strict in prison discipline than even Louis himself, and the number of prisoners whose names are not on the register is incalculable."

Had Morrel even any suspicions, so much kindness would have dispelled them. " Well, M. de Villefort, how would you advise me to act to hasten the return of poor Dantès? " asked he.

" Petition the minister."

" Oh, I know what that is; the minister receives two hundred every day, and does not read three."

" That is true; but he will read a petition countersigned and presented by me."

" And will you undertake to deliver it? "

" With the greatest pleasure. Dantès was then guilty, but now he is innocent; and it is as much my duty to free him as it was to condemn him."

In this way Villefort avoided the danger of an investigation —not very probable indeed, but possible—which would have ruined him.

" But how shall I address the minister? "

" Sit down there," said Villefort, giving up his place to Morrel, " and write what I dictate."

" Will you be so good? "

" Certainly. But lose no time; we have lost too much already."

" That is true. Let us remember that the poor young man is waiting, suffering, perhaps despairing."

Villefort shuddered at the idea of that prisoner cursing him in the silence and the darkness; but he had gone too far to recede,—Dantès must be crushed beneath the weight of Villefort's ambition.

Villefort dictated a petition in which with an excellent intention, no doubt, he exaggerated Dantès's patriotism and his services to the Bonapartist cause. In that petition Dantès appeared to have been one of the most active agents in the return of Napoleon. It was to be presumed that at the sight of this document the minister would instantly release him. The petition finished, Villefort read it aloud.

" That will do," said he; " leave the rest to me."

" Will the petition go soon? "

" To-day."

" Countersigned by you? "

" The best thing I can do will be to certify the truth of the contents of your petition." And sitting down, Villefort wrote the certificate at the bottom.

" What more is to be done? " asked Morrel.

" Wait," replied Villefort; " I will answer for everything."

This assurance charmed Morrel, who took leave of Villefort, and hastened to announce to old Dantès that he would soon see his son.

But Villefort, instead of sending it to Paris, carefully preserved the petition that so fearfully compromised Dantès, in case an event should occur that seemed not unlikely; that is, a second restoration.

So Dantès remained a prisoner lost in the depths of his dungeon; he heard nothing of the commotion attending the fall of Louis XVIII.'s throne, or of the disturbances even more terrible when the empire was overturned.

But Villefort had followed everything with a vigilant watchfulness, and had listened to everything with an attentive ear. Twice during the Hundred Days had Morrel renewed his demand, and twice had Villefort soothed him with promises. At last there was Waterloo, and Morrel came no more; he had done all that was in his power, and any fresh attempt would only compromise him uselessly.

Louis XVIII. remounted the throne; Villefort, to whom Marseilles suggested too many remorseful remembrances, demanded and obtained the situation of *procureur du roi* at Toulouse, and a fortnight afterwards married Renée, whose father stood better at court than ever. Thus is explained how Dantès during the Hundred Days and after Waterloo remained in prison forgotten by God, if not by men.

Danglars comprehended the full extent of the wretched fate that overwhelmed Dantès, and like all men of small abilities he termed this *a decree of Providence.* But when Napoleon returned to Paris, Danglars's heart failed him, and he feared at every instant to behold Dantès eager for vengeance; he therefore informed M. Morrel of his wish to quit the sea, and obtained a recommendation from him to a Spanish merchant, into whose service he entered at the end of March,—that is, ten or twelve days after Napoleon's return. He then left for Madrid, and was no more heard of.

Fernand understood nothing except that Dantès was absent. What had become of him he cared not to inquire. Only, during the respite the absence of his rival afforded him, he reflected, partly on the means of deceiving Mercédès as to the cause of that absence, partly on plans of emigration and abduction, as from time to time he sat sad and motionless on the summit of Cape Pharo, at the spot whence Marseilles and the village of the Catalans are visible, watching for the apparition of a young and handsome man, who was for him also the messenger of vengeance. Fernand's mind was made up: he would shoot Dantès, and then kill himself. But Fernand was mistaken; he would not have killed himself, for he still cherished certain hopes.

During this time the empire made a last appeal, and all the men in France capable of bearing arms rushed to obey the summons of their emperor. Fernand departed with the rest, bearing with him the terrible thought that perhaps his rival would come in his absence, and would marry Mercédès. Had Fernand really meant to kill himself, he would have done so when he parted from Mercédès. His devotion, and the compassion he showed for her misfortunes produced the effect they always produce on noble minds; Mercédès had always had a sincere regard for Fernand, and this was now strengthened by gratitude.

"My brother," said she, as she placed his knapsack on his shoulders, "be careful of yourself, for if you are killed, I shall be alone in the world." These words infused a ray of hope into Fernand's heart. Should Dantès not return, Mercédès might one day be his.

Mercédès was left alone to gaze on this vast plain that had never seemed so barren, and the sea that had never seemed so vast. Bathed in tears, she might be seen wandering continually about the little village of the Catalans. Sometimes she stood mute and motionless as a statue, gazing towards Marseilles; at other times sitting by the shore she listened to the groanings of the sea, eternal like her sorrow, and asked herself whether it were not better to cast herself into the abyss of ocean than thus to suffer the cruel vicissitudes of a waiting without hope. It was not want of courage that prevented her putting this idea into execution; but her religious feelings came to her aid and saved her.

Caderousse was, like Fernand, enrolled in the army, but being married and eight years older, he was merely sent to the frontier. Old Dantès, who was only sustained by hope, lost all hope at Napoleon's downfall. Five months after he had been separated from his son, and almost at the very hour at which he had been arrested, he breathed his last in Mercédès's arms. M. Morrel paid the expenses of his funeral and a few small debts the poor old man had contracted.

There was more than benevolence in this action; there was courage,—for to assist even on his death-bed the father of so dangerous a Bonapartist as Dantès, was stigmatised as a crime.

CHAPTER XIV

THE TWO PRISONERS

A YEAR after Louis XVIII.'s restoration, a visit was made to the Château d'If by the inspector-general of prisons. Dantès heard from the recesses of his cell the noises made by the preparations for receiving him,—sounds that at the depth where he lay would have been inaudible to any but the ear of a prisoner accustomed to hear in the silence of night the spider weave his web, and the periodic fall of the drop of water that formed every hour on the ceiling of his dungeon. He guessed something uncommon was passing among the living; he had so long ceased to have any intercourse with the world that he looked upon himself as dead.

The inspector visited the cells and dungeons, one after another, of several of the prisoners, whose good behaviour or stupidity recommended them to the clemency of the government; the inspector inquired how they were fed, and if they had anything to demand. The universal response was that the fare was detestable, and that they required their freedom. The inspector asked if they had anything else to demand. They shook their heads! What could they desire beyond their liberty? The inspector turned smilingly to the governor:—

"I do not know what reason government can assign for these useless visits; when you see one prisoner, you see all,—always the same thing, ill fed and innocent. Are there any others?"

"Yes; the dangerous and mad prisoners are in the dungeons."

"Let us visit them," said the inspector, with an air of fatigue. "I must fulfil my mission. Let us descend."

"Let us first send for two soldiers," said the governor. "The prisoners sometimes, through mere uneasiness of life, and in order to be sentenced to death, commit acts of useless violence, and you might fall a victim."

"Take all needful precautions," replied the inspector.

Two soldiers were accordingly sent for, and the inspector descended a stair so foul, so humid, so dark that the mere descent through such a place affected painfully the eye, the smell, and the respiration.

"Oh!" cried the inspector, stopping midway, "what devil can be lodged here?"

"A most dangerous conspirator, a man we are ordered to keep the most strict watch over, as he is daring and resolute."

"He is alone."

"Certainly."

"How long has he been here?"

"About a year."

"Was he placed here when he first arrived?"

"No, not until he attempted to kill the turnkey."

"To kill the turnkey?"

"Yes; the very one who is lighting us. Is it not true, Antoine?" asked the governor.

"True enough; he wanted to kill me!" replied the turnkey.

"He must be mad," said the inspector.

"He is worse than that,—he is a devil!" returned the turnkey.

"Shall I complain of him?" demanded the inspector.

"Oh, no; it is useless. He is sufficiently punished already. Besides, he is almost mad now, and in another year he will be quite so."

"So much the better for him,—he will suffer less," said the inspector. He was, as this remark shows, a man full of philanthropy, and in every way fit for his office.

"You are right, monsieur," replied the governor; "and this remark proves that you have deeply considered the subject. Now, we have in a dungeon about twenty feet distant, and to which you descend by another stair, an abbé, ancient leader of a party in Italy, who has been here since 1811, and in 1813 went mad, and who from that time has undergone an astonishing change. He used to weep; he now laughs. He grew thin, he now grows fat. You had better see him rather than the other, for his madness is amusing."

"I will see them both," returned the inspector; "I must conscientiously perform my duty." This was the inspector's first visit; he wished to display his authority. "Let us visit this one first," added he.

" Willingly," replied the governor; and he signed to the turnkey to open the door. At the sound of the key turning in the lock, and the creaking of the hinges, Dantès, who was crouched in a corner of the dungeon, where he received with unspeakable happiness the slight ray of light that pierced through his grating, raised his head. At the sight of a stranger, lighted by two turnkeys, accompanied by two soldiers, and to whom the governor spoke bareheaded, Dantès, who guessed the truth, and that the moment to address himself to the superior authorities was come, sprang forward with clasped hands.

The soldiers presented their bayonets, for they thought he was about to attack the inspector, and the latter recoiled two or three steps. Dantès saw that he was represented as a dangerous prisoner. Then, uniting in the expression of his features all that the heart of man can contain of gentleness and humility, and speaking with a sort of pious eloquence that astonished the attendants, he tried to touch the soul of the inspector.

The inspector listened attentively; then turning to the governor, observed, " He will become religious; he is already more gentle. He is afraid, and retreated before the bayonets; madmen are not afraid of anything. I made some curious observations on this at Charenton." Then turning to the prisoner, " What do you demand? " said he.

" I demand a knowledge of my crime; I demand to be brought to trial; I demand, in short, that I may be shot if I am guilty, and may be set at liberty if innocent."

" Are you well fed? " said the inspector.

" I believe so; I know not, but that matters little. What matters really, not only to me, an unhappy prisoner, but even more to the officers administering justice, and still more to the king who rules over us, is that an innocent man shall not be the victim of an infamous denunciation, and shall not die in prison cursing his executioners."

" You are very humble to-day," remarked the governor. " You are not so always; the other day, for instance, when you tried to kill the turnkey."

" It is true, sir, and I beg his pardon, for he has always been very good to me; but I was mad, I was furious."

" And you are not so any longer? "

" No; captivity has bent, broken, annihilated me. I have been here so long."

" So long? When were you arrested, then? " asked the inspector.

" The 28th of February, 1815, at half-past two in the afternoon."

" To-day is the 30th of July, 1816; why, it is but seventeen months."

" Only seventeen months!" replied Dantès. " Oh, you do not know what is seventeen months in prison! Seventeen ages rather, especially to a man who, like me, had arrived at the summit of his ambition; to a man who, like me, was on the point of marrying a woman he adored, who saw an honourable career open before him, and who loses all in an instant,—who from the enjoyment of a day the most beautiful falls into profoundest night; who sees his prospects destroyed, and is ignorant of the fate of his affianced wife, and whether his aged father be still living! Seventeen months' captivity to a man accustomed to the air of the sea, to the independence of a sailor's life, to space, to immensity, to infinity! Monsieur, seventeen months in prison is a greater punishment than is deserved by all the most odious crimes recognised in human speech. Have pity on me, then, and ask for me, not indulgence, but a trial. Monsieur, I ask only for judges; they cannot refuse judgment to one who is accused."

" We shall see," said the inspector; then turning to the governor, " On my word, the poor devil touches me. You must show me the register."

" Certainly; but you will find terrible notes against him."

" Monsieur," continued Dantès, " I know it is not in your power to release me, but you can plead for me, you can have me tried; and that is all I ask."

" Light me," said the inspector.

" Monsieur," cried Dantès, " I can tell by your voice you are touched with pity; tell me at least to hope."

" I cannot tell you that," replied the inspector; " I can only promise to examine into your case."

" Oh, I am free then! I am saved!"

" Who arrested you?"

" M. de Villefort. See him, and hear what he says."

" M. de Villefort is no longer at Marseilles; he is now at Toulouse."

" I am no longer surprised at my detention," murmured Dantès, " since my only protector is removed."

" Had he any cause of personal dislike to you?"

" None; on the contrary, he was very kind to me."

" I can, then, rely on the notes he has left concerning you, or which he may give me?"

" Entirely."

" That is well; wait patiently, then."

Dantès fell on his knees, and murmured a prayer in which he commended to God that man who had descended to his prison, like the Saviour going to deliver the souls in hell. The door closed; but now a new inmate was left with Dantès,— hope.

" Will you see the register at once," asked the governor, " or proceed to the other cell? "

" Let us visit them all," said the inspector. " If I once mounted the stairs, I should never have the courage to descend."

" Ah, this one is not like the other; and his madness is less affecting than the reason of his neighbour."

" What is his folly? "

" He fancies that he possesses an immense treasure. The first year he offered government a million livres for his release; the second, two; the third, three; and so on progressively. He is now in his fifth year of captivity; he will ask to speak to you in private, and offer you five millions."

" Ah, that is indeed quite interesting. And what is the name of this millionnaire? "

" The Abbé Faria."

" No. 27," said the inspector.

" It is here; unlock the door, Antoine."

The turnkey obeyed, and the inspector gazed curiously into the chamber of " the mad abbé." In the centre of the cell, in a circle traced upon the floor with a fragment of plaster detached from the wall, sat a man whose tattered garments scarcely covered him. He was drawing in this circle geometrical lines, and seemed as much absorbed in his problem as Archimedes when the soldier of Marcellus slew him. He did not move at the sound of the door, and continued his problem until the flash of the torches lighted up with an unwonted glare the sombre walls of his cell; then, raising his head, he perceived with astonishment the number of persons in his cell. He hastily seized the coverlid of his bed, and wrapped it round him.

" What do you demand? " said the inspector.

" I, monsieur! " replied the abbé, with an air of surprise, " I demand nothing."

" You do not understand," continued the inspector; " I am sent here by government to visit the prisons, and hear the requests of the prisoners."

" Oh, that is different," cried the abbé; " and we shall understand each other, I hope."

"There, now," whispered the governor, "he begins just as I told you he would."

"Monsieur," continued the prisoner, "I am the Abbé Faria, born at Rome. I was for twenty years Cardinal Spada's secretary; I was arrested—why I know not—in 1811; since then I have demanded my liberty from the Italian and French governments."

"Why from the French government?"

"Because I was arrested at Piombino; and I presume that, like Milan and Florence, Piombino has become the capital of some French department."

The inspector and the governor looked at each other with a smile.

"The devil! my good fellow," said the inspector, "your news from Italy is not fresh!"

"It dates from the day on which I was arrested," returned the Abbé Faria; "and as the emperor had created the kingdom of Rome for his infant son, I presume that he has realised the dream of Machiavel and Cæsar Borgia, which was to make Italy one solid kingdom."

"Monsieur," returned the inspector, "Providence has changed this gigantic plan which you advocate so warmly."

"It is the only means of rendering Italy happy and independent."

"Very possibly; but I have not come to take with you a course of ultramontane politics; I have come to ask you if you have any complaints to make in regard to food and lodging."

"The food is the same as in other prisons,—that is, very bad; the lodging is very unwholesome, but on the whole passable for a dungeon. No matter about that; what I would speak of is a secret which I have to reveal of the greatest importance."

"We are coming to the point," whispered the governor.

"It is for that reason I am delighted to see you," continued the abbé, "although you have disturbed me in a most important calculation, which if it succeeded would possibly change Newton's system. Could you allow me a few words in private?"

"What did I tell you?" said the governor.

"You knew him," returned the inspector.

"What you ask is impossible, monsieur," continued he, addressing Faria.

"But," said the abbé, "I would speak to you of a large sum, amounting to five millions."

"The very sum you named," whispered, in his turn, the inspector.

"However," continued Faria, perceiving the inspector was about to depart, "it is not absolutely necessary we should be alone; Monsieur the Governor can be present."

"Unfortunately," said the governor, "I know beforehand what you are about to say; it concerns your treasures, does it not?"

Faria fixed his eyes on him with an expression that would have convinced any one else of his sanity. "Doubtless," said he; "of what else should I speak?"

"Monsieur the Inspector," continued the governor, "I can tell you the story as well, for it has been dinned in my ears for the last four or five years."

"That proves," returned the abbé, "that you are like those of whom the Bible speaks, who have eyes and see not, who have ears and hear not."

"The government does not want your treasures," replied the inspector; "keep them until you are liberated."

The abbé's eyes glistened; he seized the inspector's hand. "But if I am not liberated," cried he, "if, contrary to all justice, I am kept in this dungeon, if I die here without having disclosed to any one my secret, that treasure will be lost! Would it not be better that the government should get some profit from it, and myself also? I will go as far as six millions, monsieur; yes, I will relinquish six millions, and content myself with what remains, if I may gain my liberty."

"On my word," said the inspector, in a low tone, "had I not been told beforehand this man was mad, I should believe what he says."

"I am not mad!" replied Faria, who, with that acuteness of hearing peculiar to prisoners, had not lost one of the inspector's words. "The treasure I speak of really exists; and I offer to sign a treaty with you in which I promise to lead you to the spot where you shall dig, and if I deceive you, bring me here again,—I ask no more."

The governor laughed. "Is the spot far from here?"

"A hundred leagues."

"It is not a bad idea," said the governor. "If every prisoner took it into his head to travel a hundred leagues, and their guardians consented to accompany them, they would have a capital chance of escaping."

"The scheme is well known," said the inspector; "and Monsieur the Abbé has not even the merit of its invention." Then turning to Faria, "I inquired if you are well fed?" said he.

" Swear to me," replied Faria, " to free me, if what I tell you prove true, and I will stay here while you go to the spot."

" Are you well fed ? " repeated the inspector.

" Monsieur, you run no risk, for, as I told you, I will stay here ; so there is no chance of my escaping."

" You do not reply to my question," replied the inspector, impatiently.

" Nor you to mine," cried the abbé. " A curse upon you, then ! as upon the other dolts who have refused to believe me. You will not accept my gold ; I will keep it for myself. You refuse me my liberty ; God will give it me. Go ! I have nothing more to say." And the abbé, casting away his coverlid, resumed his place, and continued his calculations.

" What is he doing there ? " said the inspector.

" Counting his treasures," replied the governor.

Faria replied to this sarcasm by a glance of profound contempt.

They went out, and the turnkey closed the door behind them.

" He has been wealthy once, perhaps," said the inspector.

" Or dreamed he was, and awoke mad."

" After all," said the inspector, with the naïveté of corruption, " if he had been rich, he would not have been here."

Thus ended the adventure for the Abbé Faria. He remained in his cell, and this visit only increased the belief of his insanity.

Caligula or Nero, those great treasure-seekers, those desirers of the impossible, would have accorded to the poor wretch in exchange for his wealth the liberty and the air he so earnestly prayed for. But the kings of modern ages, retained within the limits of probability, have no longer the courage of their desires. They fear the ear that hears their orders and the eye that scrutinises their actions. Formerly kings believed themselves, or at least called themselves, sons of Jupiter, and retained in some degree the manners of the god their father. What takes place beyond the clouds is not readily controlled ; but the kings of to-day hold themselves answerable to all persons.

It has always been against the policy of despotic governments to suffer the victims of their policy to reappear. As the Inquisition rarely suffered its victims to be seen with their limbs distorted and their flesh lacerated by torture, so madness is always concealed in its cell, or should it depart, it is conveyed to some gloomy hospital, where the doctor recognises neither man nor mind in the deformed remnant of a human being which the jailer delivers to him. The very madness of the Abbé Faria, gone mad in prison, condemned him to perpetual captivity.

The inspector kept his word with Dantès. He examined the register, and found the following note concerning him:

EDMOND DANTÈS.
{ Violent Bonapartist; took an active part in the return from Elba.
The greatest watchfulness and care to be exercised.

This note was in a different hand from the rest, which proved it had been added since his confinement. The inspector could not contend against this accusation; he simply wrote, "Nothing to be done."

That visit had, so to speak, recalled Dantès to life. Since he had entered the prison he had forgotten to count the days; but the inspector had given him a new date, and he had not forgotten it. He wrote on the wall with a piece of plaster broken from the ceiling, "July 30, 1816," and from that time he made a mark every day, in order not to lose his reckoning again. Days and weeks passed away, then months; Dantès still waited. He at first expected to be freed in a fortnight; this fortnight expired. He then reflected that the inspector would do nothing until his return to Paris, and that he would not reach there until his circuit was finished; he therefore fixed upon three months. Three months passed away, then six more. During all these months no favourable change had taken place; and Dantès began to fancy the inspector's visit was but a dream, an illusion of the brain.

At the expiration of a year the governor was removed; he had obtained the government of Ham. He took with him several of his subordinates, and among them Dantès's jailer. A new governor arrived. It would have been too tedious to acquire the names of the prisoners; he learned their numbers instead. This horrible place consisted of fifty chambers; their inhabitants were designated by the number of their chamber. And the unhappy young man was no longer called Edmond Dantès; he was now "No. 34."

CHAPTER XV

NO. 34 AND NO. 27

DANTÈS passed through all the degrees of misfortune that prisoners forgotten in their dungeon suffer. He commenced with pride,—a natural consequence of hope and a conscious-

ness of innocence; then he began to doubt his own innocence,
—a doubt which justified in some measure the governor's
belief in his mental alienation; and then he fell from the
height of his pride,—he prayed, not yet to God, but to men.
The unhappy man, who should begin by seeking the Lord, puts
trust in him only after exhausting all other hopes.

Dantès prayed, then, that he might be removed from his
present dungeon into another,—for a change, however disad-
vantageous, was still a change, and would afford him some
distraction. He entreated to be allowed to walk about, to have
books and instruments. Nothing was granted; no matter, he
asked all the same. He accustomed himself to speak to his
new jailer, although he was, if possible, more taciturn than the
former; but still, to speak to a man, even though mute, was
something. Dantès spoke for the sake of hearing his own voice;
he had tried to speak when alone, but the sound of his voice
terrified him. Often, before his captivity, Dantès's mind had
revolted at the idea of those assemblages of prisoners, composed
of thieves, vagabonds, and murderers. He now wished to be
among them, in order to see some other face besides that of his
jailer, who would not speak to him; he sighed for the galleys,
with their infamous costume, their chain, and the brand on the
shoulder. The galley-slaves breathed the fresh air of heaven,
and saw each other. They were very happy. He besought
the jailer one day to let him have a companion, were it even
the mad abbé.

The jailer, though rude and hardened by the constant sight
of so much suffering, was yet a man. At the bottom of his
heart he had often compassionated the unhappy young man
who suffered thus; and he laid the request of No. 34 before the
governor. But the latter, as prudent as if he had been a
politician, imagined that Dantès wished to conspire or attempt
an escape, and refused his request. Dantès had exhausted all
human resources; he then turned to God.

All the pious ideas that had been so long forgotten returned.
He recollected the prayers his mother had taught him, and
discovered in them a meaning until then unknown to him; for
in prosperity prayers seem but a mere assemblage of words,
until the day when misfortune comes to explain to the unhappy
sufferer the sublime language by which he invokes the pity of
Heaven! He prayed, not with fervour, but with rage. He
prayed aloud, no longer terrified at the sound of his voice.
Then he fell into a species of trance. He saw God listening to
every word he uttered; he laid every action of his life before

the Almighty, proposed tasks to accomplish, and at the end of every prayer introduced the entreaty oftener addressed to man than to God, "Forgive us our trespasses as we forgive them that trespass against us." Spite of his earnest prayers, Dantès remained a prisoner.

Then a gloomy feeling took possession of him. He was simple, and without education; he could not, therefore, in the solitude of his dungeon and of his own thoughts, reconstruct the ages that had passed, reanimate the nations that had perished, and rebuild the ancient cities that imagination renders so vast and stupendous, and that pass before our eyes, illuminated by the fires of heaven, as in Martinn's pictures. He could not do this, his past life was so short, his present so melancholy, and his future so doubtful. Nineteen years of light to reflect upon in eternal darkness! No distraction could come to his aid; his energetic spirit, that would have exulted in thus revisiting the past, was imprisoned like an eagle in a cage. He clung to one idea,—that of his happiness, destroyed without apparent cause by an unheard-of fatality; he considered and reconsidered this idea, devoured it (so to speak) as Ugolino devours the skull of the Archbishop Roger in the Inferno of Dante.

Rage succeeded to asceticism. Dantès uttered blasphemies that made his jailer recoil with horror, dashed himself furiously against the walls of his prison; he turned his fury against everything around him, and especially against himself, against the least thing that annoyed him,—a grain of sand, a straw, or a breath of air. Then the letter of denunciation which Villefort had showed to him recurred to his mind, and every line seemed visible in fiery letters on the wall, like the *Mene, Tekel, Upharsin* of Belshazzar. He said to himself that it was the enmity of man, and not the vengeance of Heaven, that had thus plunged him into the deepest misery. He devoted these unknown persecutors to the most horrible tortures he could imagine, and found them all insufficient, because after torture came death, and after death, if not repose, at least that insensibility that resembles it.

By dint of constantly dwelling on the idea that repose was death, and that in order to punish cruelly other tortures than death must be invented, he began to reflect on suicide. Unhappy he who on the brink of misfortune broods over these ideas! The idea of suicide is one of those dead seas that seem clear and smooth to the eye; but he who unwarily ventures within its embrace finds himself entangled in a quagmire that attracts and swallows him. Once thus ensnared, unless the protecting hand of God snatch him thence, all is over, and his struggles but tend to hasten his destruction. This state of mental anguish is, however, less terrible than the sufferings that precede and the punishment that perhaps awaits it; it is a sort of consolation that points to the yawning abyss, at the bottom of which is darkness.

Edmond found some solace in this idea. All his sorrows, all his sufferings, with their train of gloomy spectres, fled from his cell when the angel of death seemed about to enter. Dantès reviewed with composure his past life, and looking forward with terror to his future, chose that middle line that seemed to afford him a refuge.

"Sometimes," said he, "in my voyages, when I was still a man, free and powerful, and commanded other men, I have seen the heavens become overcast, the sea rage and foam, the storm arise, and like a monstrous bird cover the sky with its wings. Then I felt that my vessel was a vain refuge, for like a feather in the hand of a giant, it trembled and shook before the tempest. Soon the fury of the waves and the sight of the sharp rocks announced the approach of death, and death then terrified me; and I used all my skill and intelligence as a man and a sailor in a struggle against the Almighty! I did so because I was happy; because a return to life was a return to enjoyment; because I had not courted that death, had not chosen it; because this repose on a bed of rocks and seaweed seemed terrible; because I was unwilling that I, a creature made in the image of God, should serve for food to the gulls and ravens. But now it is different. I have lost all that bound me to life; death smiles and invites me to repose. I die after my own manner, I die exhausted and broken-spirited, as I fall asleep after one of those evenings of despair and rage when I have paced three thousand times round my cell."

No sooner had this idea taken possession of him than he became more composed; he arranged his couch to the best of his power, ate and slept little, and found this existence almost supportable, because he felt he could throw it off at pleasure, like a worn-out garment. He had two means of dying,—one was to hang himself with his handkerchief to the stanchions of the window; the other to refuse food and starve himself. But the former project was repugnant to him. Dantès had always entertained a horror of pirates, who are hung up to the yard-arm; he would not die by what seemed an infamous death. He resolved to adopt the second, and began that day to execute his resolve. Nearly four years had passed away; at the end of the second he had fallen again into ignorance of dates, from which the inspector had lifted him.

Dantès had said, " I wish to die," and had chosen the manner of his death; and fearful of changing his mind, he had taken an oath so to die. " When my morning and evening meals are brought," thought he, " I will cast them out of the window, and I shall be believed to have eaten them."

He kept his word; twice a day he cast out, by the barred aperture, the provisions his jailer brought him,—at first gaily, then with deliberation, and at last with regret. Nothing but the recollection of his oath gave him strength to proceed. Hunger rendered these viands, once so repugnant, appetising to the eye and exquisite to the sense of smell; sometimes he held the plate in his hand for an hour at a time, and gazed on the morsel of bad meat, of tainted fish, of black and mouldy bread. The deeper instincts of self-preservation yet strove within him, and occasionally vanquished his resolve; then his dungeon seemed less sombre, his condition less desperate. He was still young,—he was only four or five and twenty; he had nearly fifty years to live. In that vast space of time what unforeseen events might not open his prison door, and restore him to liberty? Then he raised to his lips the repast that, like a voluntary Tantalus, he had refused himself; but he thought of his oath, and that generous nature had too great fear of despising himself to be able to break his oath. He persisted, then, rigorous and pitiless, until at last he had not sufficient force to cast his supper out of the loophole. The next morning he could not see or hear; the jailer feared he was dangerously ill. Edmond hoped he was dying.

The day passed away thus. Edmond felt a species of stupor creeping over him; the gnawing pain at his stomach had ceased; his thirst had abated; when he closed his eyes he saw myriads of lights dancing before them, like the meteors that play about the marshes. It was the twilight of that mysterious country called Death!

Suddenly, about nine o'clock in the evening, Edmond heard a hollow sound in the wall against which he was lying.

So many loathsome animals inhabited the prison that their noise did not in general awake him; but now, whether abstinence had quickened his faculties, or whether the noise was really louder than usual, or whether in that supreme moment everything gained in significance, Edmond raised his head and listened. It was a continual scratching, as if made by a huge claw, a powerful tooth, or some iron instrument attacking the stones.

Although weakened, the young man's brain instantly recurred to the idea that haunts all prisoners,—liberty! It seemed to him that Heaven had at length taken pity on him, and had sent this noise to warn him on the very brink of the abyss. Perhaps one of those beloved ones he had so often thought of was thinking of him, and striving to diminish the distance that separated them.

No, no! doubtless he was deceived, and it was but one of those dreams that hover at the gate of death!

Edmond still heard the sound. It lasted about three hours; he then heard a noise of something falling, and all was silent.

Some hours afterwards it began nearer and more distinct; Edmond became already interested in that labour, which afforded him companionship. Suddenly the jailer entered.

During the week in which he was forming his resolution to die, and the four days since he began to put his resolve into execution, Edmond had not spoken to this man, had not answered him when he inquired what was the matter with him, and had turned his face to the wall when he looked too curiously at him; but now the jailer might hear this noise, and taking alarm, might put an end to it, thus destroying a ray of something like hope that soothed his last moments.

The jailer brought him his breakfast. Dantès raised himself up, and began to speak on all possible subjects,—on the bad quality of his food, on the coldness of his dungeon, grumbling and complaining in order to have an excuse for speaking louder, and wearying the patience of the jailer, who that very day had solicited some broth and white bread for his prisoner, and had brought it to him.

Fortunately the jailer fancied that Dantès was delirious; and placing his food on the rickety table, he withdrew. Free at last, Edmond again eagerly listened. The noise began again, and was now so distinct that he could hear it without effort.

"There can be no doubt," thought he; "it is some prisoner who is striving to obtain his freedom. Oh, if I were with him how I would help!"

Suddenly a cloud darkened that dawn of hope in a mind so used to misfortune that it could scarcely understand hope; the idea possessed him that the noise arose from the workmen the governor had ordered to repair the neighbouring dungeon.

It was easy to ascertain this; but how could he risk the question? It was easy to call his jailer's attention to the noise, and watch his countenance as he listened; but might he not by this means betray precious hopes for a short-lived satisfaction? Unfortunately, Edmond's brain was still so feeble that he could not bend his thoughts to anything in particular.

He saw but one means of restoring lucidity and clearness to his judgment. He turned his eyes towards the soup his jailer had brought him, rose, staggered towards it, raised the vessel to his lips, and drank off the contents with an indescribable sensation of comfort; then he had the courage to abstain. He had heard that shipwrecked persons had died through having eagerly devoured too much food. Edmond replaced on the table the bread he was about to devour, and returned to his couch; he no longer wished to die. He soon felt that his ideas became again collected; he could think, and strengthen his thoughts by reasoning. Then he said to himself, " I must put this to the test, but without compromising anybody. If it is a workman, I need but knock against the wall, and he will cease to work in order to find out who is knocking and why he does so; but as his occupation is sanctioned by the governor, he will soon resume it. If, on the contrary, it is a prisoner, the noise I make will alarm him; he will cease, and not resume until he thinks every one is asleep."

Edmond rose again, but this time his legs did not tremble, and his eyes were free from mists; he advanced to a corner of his dungeon, detached a stone loosened by the moisture, and with it knocked against the wall at the place where the noise was most audible. He struck thrice; at the first blow the sound ceased, as if by magic.

Edmond listened intently. An hour passed, two hours passed, and no sound was heard from the wall,—all was silent there.

Full of hope, Edmond swallowed a few mouthfuls of bread, drank some water, and thanks to the excellence of his constitution, found himself well-nigh recovered.

The day passed away in utter silence; night came without the noise having recommenced.

" It is a prisoner! " said Edmond, joyfully.

The night passed in unbroken silence. Edmond did not close his eyes.

In the morning the jailer brought his rations—he had already devoured those of the previous day; he ate these, listening anxiously for the sound, walking round and round his cell, shaking the iron bars of the loophole, restoring by exercise vigour and agility to his limbs, and preparing himself thus for what might lie before him.   At intervals he listened for a recurrence of the noise, and grew impatient at the prudence of the prisoner, who did not guess he had been disturbed by a captive as anxious for liberty as himself.

Three days passed,—seventy-two mortal hours, reckoned minute by minute!

At length, one evening just after the jailer's last visit, as for the hundredth time Dantès placed his ear against the wall, he fancied that he heard an almost imperceptible movement among the stones.   He recoiled from the wall, walked up and down his cell to collect his thoughts, and replaced his ear at the same spot.

There could be no doubt that something was taking place on the other side; the prisoner had discovered the danger, and to continue his work in greater security, had substituted the lever for the chisel.

Encouraged by this discovery, Edmond determined to assist the indefatigable labourer.   He began by moving his bed, behind which it seemed to him the work of deliverance was going on, and sought with his eyes for something with which he might pierce the wall, penetrate the cement, and displace a stone.

He saw nothing.   He had no knife or sharp instrument; the grating of his window alone was of iron, and he had too often assured himself of its solidity.   All his furniture consisted of a bed, a chair, a table, a pail, and a jug.   The bed had iron clamps; but they were screwed to the wood, and it would have required a screw-driver to take them off.   The table and chair had nothing that would serve; the pail had had a handle, but that had been removed.   There remained but one resource, which was to break the jug, and with one of the sharp fragments attack the wall.   He let the jug fall on the floor, and it broke in pieces. He concealed two or three of the sharpest fragments in his bed, leaving the rest on the floor.   The breaking of his jug was too natural an accident to excite suspicion.   He had all the night to work in, but in the darkness he could not do much, and he soon perceived that his instrument was blunted against something hard; he pushed back his bed, and awaited the day. With hope, patience had returned to him.

All night he heard the subterranean workman, who continued to mine his way.   The day came; the jailer entered. Dantès told him the jug had fallen from his hand in drinking, and the jailer went grumblingly to fetch another, without giving himself the trouble to remove the fragments of the broken one.   He returned speedily, recommended the prisoner to be more careful, and departed.

Dantès heard joyfully the key grate in the lock; he listened until the sound of steps died away, and then, hastily displacing his bed, saw by the faint light that penetrated into his cell that he had laboured uselessly the previous evening in attacking the stone instead of removing the plaster that surrounded it. The damp had rendered it friable, and he saw joyfully the plaster detach itself,—in small morsels, it is true; but at the end of half an hour he had scraped off a handful. A mathematician might have calculated that in two years, supposing that the rock was not encountered, a passage twenty feet long and two feet broad might be formed. The prisoner reproached himself with not having thus employed the hours which he had passed in prayers and despair. In the six years—as he reckoned—of his imprisonment, what might he not have accomplished?

In three days Dantès had succeeded, with the utmost precaution, in removing the cement and exposing the stone. The wall was formed of rough stones, to give solidity to which were imbedded at intervals blocks of hewn stone. It was one of these he had uncovered, and which he must remove from its socket. He strove to do so with his nails, but they were too weak; the fragments of the jug, inserted in the opening, broke, and after an hour of useless toil he paused. Was he to be thus stopped at the beginning, and was he to wait inactive until his neighbour, weary, perhaps, with toil, had accomplished everything? Suddenly an idea occurred to him; he smiled, and the perspiration dried on his forehead.

The jailer always brought Dantès's soup in an iron saucepan; this saucepan contained the soup of a second prisoner,—for Dantès had remarked that it was either quite full or half empty, according as the turnkey gave it to himself or his companion first. The handle of this saucepan was of iron; Dantès would have given ten years of his life in exchange for it.

The jailer poured the contents of this saucepan into Dantès's plate, who, after eating his soup with a wooden spoon, washed the plate, which thus served for every day. In the evening Dantès placed his plate on the ground near the door; the jailer, as he entered, stepped on it and broke it. This time he could not blame Dantès. He had done wrong in leaving it there, but the jailer was at fault in not noticing where he stepped.

The jailer therefore contented himself with grumbling. Then he looked about him for something to pour the soup into; Dantès's whole furniture consisted of one plate,—there was no alternative.

"Leave the saucepan," said Dantès; "you can take it away

when you bring me my breakfast." This advice was to the jailer's taste, as it spared him the necessity of ascending, descending, and ascending again. He left the saucepan.

Dantès was beside himself with joy. He rapidly devoured his food, and after waiting an hour, lest the jailer should change his mind and return, he removed his bed, took the handle of the saucepan, inserted the point between the hewn stone and rough stones of the wall, and employed it as a lever. A slight oscillation showed Dantès that his plan was a good one. At the end of an hour the stone was extricated from the wall, leaving a cavity of a foot and a half in diameter.

Dantès carefully collected the plaster, carried it into the corners of his cell, and covered it with earth. Then, wishing to make the best use of this night, in which chance, or rather his own stratagem, had placed so precious an instrument in his hands, he continued to work without ceasing. At the dawn of day he replaced the stone, pushed his bed against the wall, and lay down. The breakfast consisted of a piece of bread; the jailer entered and placed the bread on the table.

" Well, you do not bring me another plate," said Dantès.

" No," replied the turnkey, " you destroy everything. First you break your jug, then you make me break your plate; if all the prisoners followed your example the government would be ruined. I shall leave you the saucepan and pour your soup into that; under that arrangement you will perhaps avoid breaking dishes."

Dantès raised his eyes to heaven and clasped his hands beneath the coverlid. He felt more gratitude for the possession of this piece of iron than he had ever felt for anything. He had however remarked that the prisoner on the other side had ceased to labour. No matter, this was a greater reason for proceeding; if his neighbour would not come to him, he would go to him. All day he toiled on untiringly, and by the evening he had succeeded in extracting ten handfuls of plaster and fragments of stone. When the hour for his jailer's visit arrived, Dantès straightened the handle of the saucepan and put that receptacle in its accustomed place. The turnkey poured into it the customary ration of soup and meat, or rather of soup and fish, for it was a fast day; three times a week the prisoners were made to fast. This would have been a method of reckoning time, had not Dantès long ceased to do so. Having poured out the soup, the turnkey retired. Dantès wished to ascertain whether his neighbour had really ceased to work. He listened; all was silent, as it had been for the last three days. Dantès sighed; it was evident that his neighbour distrusted him. However, he toiled on all the night without being discouraged; but after two or three hours he encountered an obstacle. The iron made no impression, but glided on a smooth surface; Dantès touched it with his hands, and found it was a beam. This beam crossed, or rather blocked up, the hole Dantès had made; it was necessary, therefore, to dig above or under it. The unhappy young man had not expected this obstacle. "Oh, my God! my God!" murmured he, "I have so earnestly prayed to thee that I hoped my prayers had been heard. After having deprived me of my liberty, after having denied to me the repose of death, after having recalled me to existence,—my God! have pity on me, and do not let me die in despair!"

"Who talks of God and despair at the same time?" said a voice that seemed to come from beneath the earth, and deadened by the distance, sounded hollow and sepulchral in the young man's ears. Edmond's hair stood on end, and he recoiled on his knees.

"Ah!" said he, "I hear a human voice." He had not heard any one speak save his jailer for four or five years; and to a prisoner the jailer is not a man,—he is a living door added to his door of oak, a barrier of flesh and blood added to his barriers of iron.

"In the name of Heaven," cried Dantès, "speak again, though the sound of your voice terrifies me; who are you?"

"Who are you?" said the voice.

"An unhappy prisoner," replied Dantès, who made no hesitation in answering.

"Of what country?"

"A Frenchman."

"Your name?"

"Edmond Dantès."

"Your profession?"

"A sailor."

"How long have you been here?"

"Since the 28th of February, 1815."

"Your crime?"

"I am innocent."

"But of what are you accused?"

"Of having conspired to aid the emperor's return."

"What! the emperor's return! The emperor is no longer on the throne, then?"

"He abdicated at Fontainebleau in 1814, and was sent to

the island of Elba. But how long have you been here that you are ignorant of all this? "

" Since 1811."

Dantès shuddered; this man had been four years longer than himself in prison.

" Do not dig any more," said the voice; " only tell me how high up is your excavation? "

" On a level with the floor."

" How is it concealed? "

" Behind my bed."

" Has your bed been moved since you have been a prisoner? "

" No."

" What does your chamber open on? "

" A corridor."

" And the corridor? "

" On the court."

" Alas! " murmured the voice.

" Oh, what is the matter? " cried Dantès.

" I am deceived; and the imperfection of my plans has ruined all. An error of a line in the plan has been equivalent to fifteen feet in reality, and I took the wall you are mining for the wall of the fortress."

" But then you would be close to the sea? "

" That is what I hoped."

" And supposing you had succeeded? "

" I should have thrown myself into the sea, gained one of the islands near here,—the Isle de Daume or the Isle de Tiboulen, —and then I should have been safe."

" Could you have swum so far? "

" Heaven would have given me strength; and now all is lost! "

" All? "

" Yes; stop up your excavation carefully. Do not work any more; and wait until you hear from me."

" Tell me, at least, who you are."

" I am—I am No. 27."

" You mistrust me, then? " said Dantès. He fancied he heard a bitter laugh proceed from the unknown.

" Oh, I am a Christian," cried Dantès, guessing instinctively that this man meant to abandon him. " I swear to you by Christ that I will let them kill me rather than suffer your executioners and mine to get a glimpse of the truth; but in the name of Heaven, do not deprive me of your presence, do not withdraw your voice from me, or I swear to you—for I have reached the end of my endurance—that I will dash my brains out against the wall, and you will have my death to reproach yourself with."

"How old are you? Your voice is that of a young man?"

"I do not know my age, for I have not counted the years I have been here. All I know is that I was just nineteen when I was arrested, the 28th of February, 1815."

"Not quite twenty-six!" murmured the voice; "at that age one cannot be a traitor."

"Oh, no, no!" cried Dantès. "I swear to you again, rather than betray you I will let them hew me to pieces!"

"You have done well to speak to me and entreat me, for I was about to form another plan, and leave you; but your age reassures me. I will come again to you. Expect me."

"When?"

"I must calculate our chances; I will give you the signal."

"But you will not leave me; you will come to me, or you will let me go to you. We will escape together, and if we cannot escape we will talk,—you of those whom you love, and I of those whom I love. You must love somebody?"

"No, I am alone in the world."

"Then you will love me. If you are young, I will be your comrade; if you are old, I will be your son. I have a father, who is seventy, if he yet lives; I love only him and a young girl called Mercédès. My father has not yet forgotten me, I am sure; but God alone knows if she loves me still. I shall love you as I loved my father."

"It is well," returned the voice; "to-morrow."

These few words were uttered with an accent that left no doubt of his sincerity. Dantès rose, buried the fragments with the same precaution as before, and pushed back his bed against the wall. He then gave himself up to his happiness. He would no longer be alone; he was perhaps about to regain his liberty. At the worst, if he remained a prisoner, he would have a companion; and captivity that is shared is but half captivity.

All day Dantès walked up and down his cell, his heart bounding with joy. From time to time his joy stifled him; he sat down on his bed, pressing his hand on his breast. At the slightest noise he bounded towards the door. Once or twice the fear crossed his mind that he might be separated from this unknown, whom he loved already. In that case his resolution was formed; when the jailer moved his bed and stooped to examine the opening, he would kill him with his water-jug. He would be condemned to die, but he was already about to die of grief and despair when this miraculous noise recalled him to life.

The jailer came in the evening; Dantès was on his bed. It seemed to him that thus he better guarded the unfinished opening. Doubtless there was a strange expression in his eyes, for the jailer said, " Come, are you going mad again ? "

Dantès did not answer; he feared that the emotion of his voice would betray him. The jailer retired, shaking his head. The night came; Dantès hoped that his neighbour would profit by the silence to address him, but he was mistaken. The next morning, however, just as he removed his bed from the wall, he heard three knocks; he threw himself on his knees.

" Is it you ? " said he; " I am here."

" Is your jailer gone ? "

" Yes," said Dantès; " he will not return until the evening. We have twelve hours of liberty."

" I can work, then ? " said the voice.

" Oh, yes, yes; this instant, I entreat you ! "

In an instant the portion of the floor on which Dantès (half-buried in the opening) was leaning his two hands, began to yield under him; he cast himself back, while a mass of stones and earth disappeared in a hole that opened beneath the aperture he himself had formed. Then from the bottom of this passage, the depth of which it was impossible to measure, he saw appear, first the head, then the shoulders, and lastly the body of a man, who sprang lightly into his cell.

CHAPTER XVI

A LEARNED ITALIAN

DANTÈS received in his arms the friend so long and ardently desired, and drew him towards the window, in order to obtain a better view of his features by the aid of the imperfect light that struggled through the grating of the prison. He was a man of small stature, with hair blanched rather by suffering and sorrow than by years, with deep-set, penetrating eyes, almost buried beneath the thick grey eyebrows, and a long (and still black) beard reaching down to his breast. His worn countenance, deeply furrowed by care, joined to the bold outline of his strongly-marked features, announced a man more accustomed to exercise his moral faculties than his physical strength. Large drops of perspiration were now standing on his brow, while his garments hung about him in such rags as to render it useless to form a guess as to their primitive description.

The stranger might have numbered sixty or sixty-five years; but a certain vigour in his movements made it probable that he was aged more by long captivity than by mere lapse of years. He received the enthusiastic greeting of his young acquaintance with evident pleasure; his chilled affections seemed rekindled and invigorated by contact with that glowing soul. He thanked him with grateful cordiality for his kindly welcome, although his disappointment must have been severe on finding another dungeon where he had expected to find liberty.

"Let us first see," said he, "whether it is possible to remove the traces of my entrance here; all our security depends upon our jailers' being entirely ignorant of it." Advancing to the opening, he stooped and raised the stone as easily as though it had not weighed an ounce; then, fitting it into its place, he said,—

"You removed this stone very carelessly; but I suppose you had no tools to aid you."

"Why," exclaimed Dantès, with astonishment, "do you possess any?"

"I made myself some; and with the exception of a file, I have all that are necessary,—a chisel, pincers, and lever."

"Oh, I should like to see these products of your industry and patience!"

"Well, in the first place, here is my chisel." So saying, he displayed a sharp strong blade, with a handle made of beechwood.

"And with what did you contrive to make that?" inquired Dantès.

"With one of the clamps of my bedstead; and this very tool has sufficed me to hollow out the road by which I came hither, a distance of at least fifty feet."

"Fifty feet!" re-echoed Dantès, with a species of terror.

"Do not speak so loud, young man; don't speak so loud! It frequently occurs in a state prison like this that persons are stationed outside the doors of the cells purposely to overhear the conversation of the prisoners."

"But they believe I am shut up alone here."

"That makes no difference."

"And you say that you penetrated a length of fifty feet to arrive here?"

"I do; that is about the distance that separates your chamber from mine. Only, unfortunately I did not curve aright; for want of the necessary geometrical instruments to calculate my scale of proportion, instead of taking an ellipsis of forty feet, I have made fifty. I expected, as I told you, to reach the outer wall, pierce through it, and throw myself into the sea; I have, however, kept along the corridor, on which your chamber opens, instead of going beneath it. My labour is all in vain, for I find that the corridor looks into a courtyard filled with soldiers."

"That's true," said Dantès; "but the corridor you speak of bounds only *one* side of my cell; there are three others. Do you know anything of their situation?"

"This one is built against the solid rock; and it would take ten experienced miners, duly furnished with the requisite tools, as many years to penetrate it. This other wall adjoins the lower part of the governor's apartments, and were we to work our way through, we should only get into some lock-up cellars, where we must necessarily be recaptured. The fourth and last side of your cell faces — stop a minute; now what does it face?"

The side which thus excited curiosity was the one in which was fixed the loophole by which the light was admitted into the chamber. This loophole, which gradually diminished as it approached the outside, until there remained only an opening through which a child could not have passed, was for better security furnished with three iron bars, so as to quiet all apprehensions even in the mind of the most suspicious jailer as to the possibility of a prisoner's escape. As the stranger spoke, he dragged the table beneath the window. "Climb up," said he to Dantès.

The young man obeyed, mounted on the table, and divining the intentions of his companion, placed his back securely against the wall and held out both hands. The stranger, whom as yet Dantès knew only by the number of his cell, sprang up with an agility by no means to be expected in a person of his apparent age, and with the easy movement of a cat or a lizard, climbed from the table to the outstretched hands of Dantès, and from them to his shoulders; then, bending himself almost double,—for the ceiling of the dungeon prevented his holding himself erect,—he managed to slip his head through the top bar of the window, so as to be able to command an unobstructed view from top to bottom.

An instant afterwards he hastily drew back his head, saying, "I thought so!" and sliding from the shoulders of Dantès as dexterously as he had ascended, he nimbly leaped from the table to the ground.

" What did you expect to find? " asked the young man, in an anxious tone, in his turn descending from the table.

The elder prisoner appeared to meditate. " Yes," said he at length, " it is so. This side of your chamber looks out upon a kind of open gallery, where patrols are continually passing, and sentries keep watch day and night."

" Are you quite sure of that? "

" Certain. I saw the soldier's shako and the top of his musket; that made me draw in my head so quickly,—for I was fearful he might also see me."

" Well? " inquired Dantès.

" You perceive then the utter impossibility of escaping through your dungeon? "

" Then? " pursued the young man, with a questioning accent.

" Then," answered the elder prisoner, " the will of God be done! " and as the old man slowly pronounced those words, an air of profound resignation spread itself over his care-worn countenance. Dantès gazed on the individual who could thus philosophically resign hopes so long and ardently nourished, with an astonishment mingled with admiration.

" Tell me, I entreat you, who you are," said he, at length.

" Willingly," answered the stranger; " if indeed you feel any curiosity respecting me, now that I am powerless to aid you in any way."

" You can console and support me,—for you appear to me to be a strong man among the strong."

The stranger smiled sadly. " Then listen," said he, " I am the Abbé Faria, and have been imprisoned in this Château d'If since the year 1811; previously to which I had been confined for three years in the fortress of Fenestrelle. In the year 1811 I was transferred to Piedmont in France. At this period I learned that the destiny which seemed subservient to every wish formed by Napoleon had bestowed on him a son, named King of Rome even in his cradle. I was very far then from expecting the change of which you have just informed me; namely, that four years afterwards this colossus of power would be overthrown. Then who reigns in France at this moment,—Napoleon II.? "

" No, Louis XVIII."

" The brother of Louis XVI.! How inscrutable are the ways of Providence! For what great and mysterious purpose has it pleased Heaven to abase the man once so elevated, and raise up the individual so beaten down and depressed? "

Dantès whole attention was riveted on a man who could thus

forget his own misfortune while occupying himself with the destinies of others.

"But so it was," continued he, "in England. After Charles I. came Cromwell; to Cromwell succeeded Charles II., and then James II., who was succeeded by some son-in-law, some relative, some prince of Orange,—a stadtholder who made himself king; and then, new concessions to the people, then a constitution, then liberty! You will see that, young man," said he, turning towards Dantès with the kindling gaze of a prophet; "you are still young enough,—you will see it."

"Yes, if ever I get out of prison!"

"True," replied Faria, "we are prisoners; but I forget this sometimes, and there are even moments when my mental vision transports me beyond these walls, and I fancy myself at liberty."

"But wherefore are you here?"

"Because in 1807 I meditated the very scheme Napoleon wished to realise in 1811; because, like Machiavel, I desired to alter the political face of Italy, and instead of allowing it to be split up into a number of petty principalities, each held by some weak or tyrannical ruler, I sought to form one large, compact, and powerful empire; and lastly, because I fancied I had found my Cæsar Borgia in a crowned simpleton, who feigned to enter into my views only to betray me. It was projected equally by Alexander VI. and Clement VII.; but it will never succeed now, for they attempted it fruitlessly, and Napoleon was unable to complete his work. Italy seems fated to be unlucky." The old man uttered these last words in a tone of deep dejection, and his head fell listlessly on his breast.

To Dantès all this was incomprehensible; he did not understand how a man could risk his life for interests such as these. Napoleon, indeed, he knew something of, inasmuch as he had seen and spoken with him; but Clement VII. and Alexander VI. he had never heard of.

"Are you not," said Dantès, beginning to partake of the jailer's opinion touching the state of the abbé's brain, "the priest who is considered throughout the Château d'If to be—ill?"

"Mad, you mean, don't you?"

"I did not like to say so," answered Dantès, smiling.

"Well, then," resumed Faria, with a bitter smile, "let me answer your question in full, by acknowledging that I am the poor mad prisoner of the Château d'If, for many years permitted to amuse the different visitants to the prison with what is said to be my insanity; and in all probability I should be promoted to the honour of making sport for the children, if children could be found in an abode devoted like this to suffering and despair."

Dantès remained for a short time mute and motionless; at length he said, " Then you abandon all hope of flight?"

" I perceive its utter impossibility; and I consider it impious to attempt that which the Almighty evidently does not approve."

" Nay, be not discouraged. Would it not be expecting too much to hope to succeed in your first attempt? Why not try to find an opening in another direction?"

" But do you know what I have done, when you talk so lightly of beginning again? In the first place, I was four years making the tools I possess, and have been two years scraping and digging out earth, hard as granite itself; then I had to remove huge stones I should once have deemed impossible to loosen. Whole days have I passed in these titanic efforts, considering my labour well repaid if by night-time I had contrived to carry away a square inch of this hard-bound cement, changed by ages into a substance unyielding as the stones themselves. Then, to conceal the mass of earth and rubbish I dug up, I was compelled to break through a staircase, and throw the fruits of my labour into the hollow part of it; but the well is now so completely choked up that I scarcely think it would be possible to add another handful of dust without leading to a discovery. Consider also that I fully believed I had accomplished the end and aim of my undertaking, for which I had so exactly husbanded my strength as to make it just hold out to the termination of my enterprise; and just at the moment when I reckoned upon success, my hopes are for ever dashed from me. No, I repeat, nothing shall induce me to renew attempts evidently at variance with the Almighty's pleasure."

Dantès held down his head that his companion might not perceive how little of real regret at the failure of the scheme was expressed on his countenance; but in truth, the young man could entertain no other feeling than delight at finding his prison would be no longer solitary or uncheered by human participation.

The abbé rested upon Edmond's bed, while Edmond himself remained standing. Flight had never once occurred to him. There are indeed some things which appear so impossible that the mind does not dwell on them for an instant. To undermine the ground for fifty feet; to devote three years to a labour which if successful would conduct one to a precipice overhanging the sea; to plunge into the waves from a height of fifty or sixty or perhaps a hundred feet, at the risk of being dashed to pieces against the rocks, should the fugitive be fortunate enough to have escaped the balls from the sentinel's musket, and then, these perils past, to have to swim three miles,—these were difficulties so formidable that Dantès had never even dreamed of such a scheme, but had resigned himself to his fate. But the sight of an old man clinging to life with so desperate a courage gave a new direction to his ideas, and inspired him with courage and energy. Another man had attempted what he had not even thought of trying; another man, not so young nor so strong nor so adroit as he, by the exercise of skill and patience had provided himself with all the tools necessary for that astonishing work, which an erroneous measurement only had brought to nought. Another man had done all that; nothing, then, was impossible to Dantès! Faria had made his way through fifty feet of the prison; Dantès resolved to penetrate through double that distance. Faria, at the age of fifty, had devoted three years to the task; he, who was but half as old, would sacrifice six. Faria, a churchman and philosopher, had not shrunk from risking his life by trying to swim a distance of three miles to reach the isles of Daume, Ratonneau, or Lemaire; should a hardy sailor, an experienced diver, like himself, shrink from a similar task; should he, who had so often for mere amusement's sake plunged to the bottom of the sea to fetch up the bright coral-branch, hesitate to swim a distance of three miles? He could do it in an hour, and how many times had he for pure pastime continued in the water for more than twice as long! At once Dantès resolved to follow the brave example of his energetic companion, and to remember that what has once been done may be done again.

After continuing some time in profound meditation, the young man suddenly exclaimed, "I have found what you were in search of!"

Faria started. "Have you, indeed?" cried he, raising his head with quick anxiety; "pray let me know what it is you have discovered."

"The corridor through which you have bored your way from the cell you occupy extends in the same direction as the outer gallery, does it not?"

"It does."

"And is not above fifteen steps from it?"

"About that."

"Well, then, I will tell you what we must do. We must make a way through the middle of the corridor, like the arm of a cross. This time you will make your measurements more accurately; we shall get out into the gallery you have described, kill the sentinel who guards it, and make our escape. All we require to insure success is courage, which you possess, and strength, in which I am not deficient; as for patience, you have abundantly proved yours,—you shall now see me prove mine."

"One instant, my dear friend," replied the abbé; "it is clear you do not understand the nature of the courage with which I am endowed, and what use I intend making of my strength. As for patience, I think I have abundantly exercised that in taking up again every morning the task of the previous night, and every night beginning again the task of the day. But then, young man,—listen to me,—then I thought I could not be doing anything displeasing to the Almighty in trying to set an innocent being at liberty,—one who had committed no offence and merited no condemnation."

"And have your notions changed?" asked Dantès. "Do you think yourself guilty since you have encountered me?"

"No; but I do not wish to become so. Hitherto I have fancied myself merely waging war against circumstances; now you propose an enterprise against men. I have been able to bore through a wall, or destroy a staircase; but I will not pierce a heart or take away a life."

A slight movement of surprise escaped Dantès. "Is it possible," said he, "that where your liberty is at stake you can be restrained by a scruple such as that?"

"Tell me," replied Faria, "what has hindered you from knocking down your jailer with a piece of wood torn from your bedstead, dressing yourself in his clothes, and endeavouring to escape?"

"Simply that I never thought of such a scheme," answered Dantès.

"Because," said the old man, "the natural repugnance to the commission of such a crime prevented its bare idea from occurring to you. In all simple and allowable things our natural instincts keep us from deviating from the strict line of duty. The tiger, whose nature teaches him to delight in shedding blood, needs but the organ of smelling to know when his prey is within his reach; he springs upon his victim and tears it to pieces. That is his instinct, and he obeys it; man, on the contrary, shrinks from blood. Not social law only, but natural law is opposed to murder."

Dantès remained confused and silent by this explanation of the thoughts which had unconsciously been working in his mind, or rather soul; for there are thoughts that proceed from the head, and thoughts that emanate from the heart.

"Since my imprisonment," said Faria, "I have gone over in my mind all the most celebrated instances of escape from prison. Attempted escapes have succeeded but rarely. Those that have been crowned with full success have been long meditated upon and carefully arranged,—for instance, the escape of the Duc de Beaufort from the Château de Vincennes, that of the Abbé Dubuquoi from For l'Evêque, and Latude's from the Bastille. Chance frequently affords opportunities we should never ourselves have thought of. Let us, therefore, wait patiently for some favourable moment; rely upon it, you will not find me more backward than yourself in seizing it."

"Ah!" said Dantès, "you might well endure the tedious delay; you were constantly employed in the task you set yourself, and when weary with toil, you had your hopes to refresh and encourage you."

"I assure you," replied the old man, "I did not turn to that source for recreation or support."

"What did you do, then?"

"I wrote or studied."

"Were you then permitted the use of pens, ink, and paper?"

"Oh, no!" answered the abbé; "I had none but what I made for myself."

"Do you mean to tell me," exclaimed Dantès, "that you have made paper, pens, and ink?"

"Yes."

Dantès looked upon him with admiration; some doubt, however, still lingered in his mind, which was quickly perceived by the penetrating eye of the abbé.

"When you pay me a visit in my cell," said he, "I will show you an entire work, the fruits of the thoughts and reflections of my whole life,—formed in the ruins of the Coliseum of Rome, at the foot of St. Mark's column at Venice, and on the borders of the Arno at Florence. I did not anticipate that some time my jailers would give me leisure to write them out within the walls of the Château d'If. The work I speak of is called *A Treatise on the Practicability of forming Italy into one General Monarchy*, and will make one large quarto volume."

"And on what have you written all this?"

"On two of my shirts. I invented a preparation that makes linen as smooth and as easy to write on as parchment."

"You are, then, a chemist?"

"Somewhat; I knew Lavoisier, and was the intimate friend of Cabanis."

"But for such a work you must have needed books; had you any?"

"I possessed nearly five thousand volumes in my library at Rome; but after reading them over many times, I found out that with one hundred and fifty well-chosen books a man possesses a complete analysis of all human knowledge, or at least all that is either useful or desirable to be acquainted with. I devoted three years of my life to reading and studying these one hundred and fifty volumes, till I knew them nearly by heart; so that since I have been in prison, a very slight effort of memory has enabled me to recall their contents as readily as though the pages were open before me. I could recite to you the whole of Thucydides, Xenophon, Plutarch, Titus Livius, Tacitus, Strada, Jornandès, Dante, Montaigne, Shakspeare, Spinosa, Machiavel, and Bossuet. I name only the most important writers."

"You must be acquainted, then, with several languages?"

"Yes, I speak five of the modern tongues; that is to say, German, French, Italian, English, and Spanish. By the aid of ancient Greek I learned modern Greek; I don't speak it so well as I could wish, but I am now studying it."

"You are studying it?" repeated Dantès.

"Yes, I made a vocabulary of the words I knew, turned, re-turned, and arranged them, so as to enable me to express my thoughts with them. I know about one thousand words, all that are absolutely necessary, although I believe there are nearly one hundred thousand in the dictionaries. I cannot hope to be very fluent, but I shall be able to make myself understood, and that is enough."

Stronger grew the wonder of Dantès, who almost fancied he had to do with one gifted with supernatural powers; still, hoping to find some imperfection which might bring him down to a level with human beings, he added, "But if you were not furnished with pens, how did you manage to write the work you speak of?"

"I made myself some excellent ones, which would be universally preferred to all others if once known. You are aware what huge whitings are served to us on fast-days. Well, I selected the cartilages of the heads of these fishes, and you can scarcely imagine the delight with which I welcomed the arrival of each Wednesday, Friday, and Saturday, as affording me the means of increasing my stock of pens,—for I will freely confess that my historical labours have been my greatest solace and relief. While retracing the past, I forget the present; and while coursing through history, free and independent, I remember no longer that I am a prisoner."

" But the ink," said Dantès, " how have you procured that? "

" I will tell you," replied Faria. " There was formerly a fireplace in my dungeon, but closed up long ere I became an occupant of this prison. Still, it must have been many years in use, for it was thickly covered with a coating of soot; this soot I dissolved in a portion of the wine brought to me every Sunday, and I assure you a better ink cannot be desired. For very important notes, intended to attract special observation, I have pricked one of my fingers, and written with my blood."

" And when," asked Dantès, " will you show me all this? "

" Whenever you please," replied the abbé.

" Oh, then let it be directly! " exclaimed the young man.

" Follow me, then," said the abbé, as he re-entered the subterranean passage, in which he soon disappeared. Dantès followed him.

CHAPTER XVII

THE ABBÉ'S CHAMBER

AFTER having passed with tolerable ease through the subterranean passage, which, however, did not admit of their holding themselves erect, the two friends reached the farther end of the corridor, into which the cell of the abbé opened; from that point the opening became much narrower, barely permitting one to creep through on his hands and knees. The floor of the abbé's cell was paved, and it had been by raising one of the stones in the most obscure corner that Faria had been able to commence the laborious task of which Dantès had witnessed the completion. As he entered the chamber of his friend, Dantès cast around one eager and searching glance in quest of the expected marvels, but nothing more than common met his view.

" It is well," said the abbé; " we have some hours before us,—it is now just a quarter past twelve o'clock."

Instinctively Dantès turned round to observe by what watch or clock the abbé had been able so accurately to specify the hour.

" Look at this ray of light which enters by my window," said the abbé, " and then observe the lines traced on the wall. Well, by means of these lines, which are in accordance with the double motion of the earth, as well as the ellipse it describes round the sun, I am enabled to ascertain the precise hour with more minuteness than if I possessed a watch; for that might be broken or deranged in its movements, while the sun and earth are never out of order."

This last explanation was wholly lost upon Dantès, who had always imagined, from seeing the sun rise from behind the mountains and set in the Mediterranean, that it moved, and not the earth. A double movement in the globe he inhabited, and of which he could feel nothing, appeared to him almost impossible; still, though unable to comprehend the full meaning of his companion's allusions, each word that fell from his lips seemed fraught with the wonders of science, as admirably deserving of being brought fully to light as were the glittering treasures he could just recollect having visited during his earliest youth in a voyage he made to Guzerat and Golconda.

"Come," said he to the abbé, "show me the wonderful inventions you told me of; I am all impatience to behold them."

The abbé smiled, and proceeding to the disused fireplace, raised by the help of his chisel a long stone, which had doubtless been the hearth, beneath which was a cavity of considerable depth, serving as a safe depository of the articles mentioned to Dantès.

"What do you wish to see first?" asked the abbé.

"Show me your great work on monarchy in Italy."

Faria then drew forth from his hiding-place three or four rolls of linen, laid one over the other, like the folds of papyrus found in mummy-cases. These rolls consisted of slips of cloth about four inches wide and eighteen long; they were all carefully numbered and closely covered with writing, so legible that Dantès could easily read it, as well as make out the sense,—it being in Italian, a language which he, as a Provençal, perfectly understood.

"There!" said he, "there is the work complete; I wrote the word 'finis' at the end of the sixty-eighth strip about a week ago. I have torn up two of my shirts and all my handkerchiefs to complete the precious pages. Should I ever get out of prison and find a printer courageous enough to publish what I have composed, my reputation is made."

"I see," answered Dantès. "Now let me behold the pens with which you have written your work."

"Look!" said Faria, showing to the young man a slender stick about six inches long, and much resembling in size the handle of a fine painting-brush, to the end of which was tied by a piece of thread one of those cartilages of which the abbé had before spoken to Dantès; it was pointed and divided at the nib like an ordinary pen. Dantès examined it and looked around for the instrument with which it had been shaped so correctly into form.

"Ah, yes," said Faria, "you are wondering where I found my penknife? It is my masterpiece; I made it, as well as this knife, out of an old iron candlestick." The penknife was sharp and keen as a razor; as for the other knife, it possessed the double advantage of being capable of serving either as a dagger or a knife.

Dantès examined the various articles shown to him with the same attention he had bestowed on the curiosities and strange tools exhibited in the shops at Marseilles as the works of the savages in the South Seas, whence they had been brought by the sea-captains.

"As for the ink," said Faria, "I told you how I managed to obtain that; I make it from time to time, as I require it."

"There is one thing that puzzles me still," observed Dantès, "and that is how you managed to do all this by daylight."

"I worked at night also," replied Faria.

"Night! are your eyes like cats', that you can see to work in the dark?"

"Indeed they are not; but God has supplied man with intelligence to supplement the poverty of the senses; I provided myself with light."

"You did? Pray tell me how!"

"I separated the fat from the meat served to me, melted it, and made a most capital oil; here is my lamp." So saying, the abbé exhibited a sort of vessel very similar to those employed upon the occasion of public illuminations.

"But how do you procure a light?"

"Oh, here are two flints and a morsel of burnt linen."

"And your matches?"

"Were easily prepared. I feigned a disorder of the skin, and asked for a little sulphur, which was readily supplied."

Dantès laid gently on the table the different things he had been looking at, and stood with his head drooping on his breast, overwhelmed by such perseverance and energy of character.

"You have not seen all yet," continued Faria, "for I did not think it wise to trust all my treasures in the same hiding-place. Let us close this."

Dantès helped him to replace the stone as they first found it; the abbé sprinkled a little dust over it to conceal the traces of its removal, rubbed his foot well on it to make it assume the same appearance as the other, and then going towards his bed, he removed it from the spot where it stood. Behind the head of the bed, and concealed by a stone fitting in so closely as to defy all suspicion, was a hollow space, and in this space a ladder of cords, between twenty-five and thirty feet in length. Dantès closely and eagerly examined it. He found it firm, solid, and compact enough to bear any weight.

" Who supplied you with the cord you needed in making this wonderful work? " asked Dantès.

" No one but myself. I tore up several of my shirts and unravelled the sheets of my bed during my three years' imprisonment at Fenestrelle; and when I was removed to the Château d'If, I managed to bring the ravellings with me, so that I have been able to finish my work here."

" And was it not discovered that your sheets were unhemmed? "

" Oh, no! for when I had taken out the thread I required, I hemmed the edges over again."

" With what? "

" With this needle," said the abbé, as opening his ragged vestments he showed Dantès a long sharp fishbone, with a small perforated eye for the thread, a small portion of which still remained in it. " I once thought," continued Faria, " of removing these iron bars, and letting myself down from the window, which, as you see, is somewhat wider than yours, although I should have enlarged it still more preparatory to my flight; however, I discovered that I should merely have dropped into a sort of inner court, and I therefore renounced the project altogether as too full of risk and danger. Nevertheless, I carefully preserved my ladder against one of those unforeseen opportunities of which I spoke just now, and which sudden chance frequently brings about."

While affecting to be deeply engaged in examining the ladder, the mind of Dantès was in fact busily occupied by the idea that a person so intelligent, ingenious, and clear-sighted as the abbé might perhaps be able to clear up the mystery of his own misfortunes, which he had in vain endeavoured to penetrate.

" What are you thinking of? " asked the abbé, smilingly imputing the deep abstraction in which his visitor was plunged to the excess of his awe and wonder.

" I was reflecting, in the first place," replied Dantès, " upon the enormous degree of intelligence and ability you must have employed to attain to these achievements. What would you not have accomplished had you been free? "

"Nothing, perhaps; the overflow of my brain would have evaporated in futilities. Trouble is needed to develop the mines of human intelligence. Pressure is required to ignite powder; captivity has collected into one single focus all the floating faculties of my mind. They have come into close contact in a narrow space; and, you know, from the collision of clouds comes electricity; from electricity, lightning; from lightning, illumination."

"No, I know nothing," said Dantès, humiliated by his ignorance. "Some of the words you have used are to me words without sense. You must be very happy in knowing so much."

The abbé smiled. "Well," said he, "but you had another subject for your thoughts besides admiration for me; did you not say so just now?"

"I did."

"You have told me as yet but one of them; let me hear the other."

"It was this: that while you have related to me your history, you are unacquainted with mine."

"Your life, my young friend, has not been of sufficient length to include any very important events."

"It includes an immense calamity," said Dantès,—"a calamity which I have not deserved; and that I may no longer curse God, as I sometimes have, I wish to refer my wretchedness to the men who are responsible for it."

"Then you profess to be innocent of the crime with which you are charged?"

"Entirely innocent; I swear by the two beings most dear to me upon earth,—my father and Mercédès."

"Come," said the abbé, closing his hiding-place and pushing the bed back to its original situation, "let me hear your story."

Dantès obeyed, and commenced what he called his history, which consisted only of the account of a voyage to India, and two or three in the Levant, until he arrived at the recital of his last cruise; the death of Captain Leclere; the receipt of a packet to be delivered by himself to the grand-marshal; his interview with that personage, and his receiving, in place of the packet brought, a letter addressed to M. Noirtier; his arrival at Marseilles and interview with his father; his love for Mercédès and their nuptial fête; his arrest and subsequent examination in the temporary prison of the Palais de Justice; and finally, his imprisonment in the Château d'If. From the period of his arrival all was a blank to Dantès; he knew nothing, not even the length of time he had been imprisoned. His recital finished, the abbé reflected long and earnestly.

"There is," said he, at the end of his meditations, "a clever maxim, which bears upon what I was saying to you a little while ago, and that is, that save where wickedness originates in a distorted organisation, human nature revolts at crime. Still, from an artificial civilisation have sprung wants, vices, and false tastes, which occasionally become so powerful as to stifle within us all good feelings, and ultimately to lead us into guilt and wickedness. Hence the maxim: If you wish to discover the author of any bad action, seek first to discover the person to whom the perpetration of that bad action might be profitable. To whom could your disappearance have been serviceable?"

"My God! to no one. I was so insignificant."

"Do not speak thus, for your reply lacks at the same time logic and philosophy. Everything is relative, my dear friend, from the king who is in the way of his successor to the employee who is in the way of his substitute. If the king dies, his successor inherits a crown; if the employee dies, the substitute steps into his shoes, and receives his salary of twelve thousand livres. Well, these twelve thousand livres are his civil list, and are as essential to him as the twelve millions to a king. Every individual, from the highest to the lowest degree, has his place in the ladder of social life, and around him are grouped a little world of interests, composed of vortices and hooked atoms, like the worlds of Descartes. But these worlds are always larger in proportion to their elevation. They constitute an inverted spiral, which rests on its point by a trick of equilibrium. But let us return to your world. You say you were on the point of being appointed captain of the *Pharaon*?"

"I was."

"And about to become the husband of a young and lovely girl?"

"True."

"Now, could any one have had any interest in preventing the accomplishment of these two events? Was it for any one's interest that you should not be captain of the *Pharaon*?"

"No; I was generally liked on board, and had the sailors possessed the right of selecting a captain themselves, I am sure they would have chosen me. There was only one man who had any feeling of ill-will towards me. I had quarrelled with him some time previously, and had even challenged him to fight me; but he had refused."

"Now we are getting on. And what was this man's name?"

" Danglars."

" What rank did he hold on board? "

" He was supercargo."

" And had you been captain, should you have retained him in his employment? "

" Not if the choice had remained with me, for I had frequently observed inaccuracies in his accounts."

" Good again! Now then, tell me, was any person present during your last conversation with Captain Leclere? "

" No, we were quite alone."

" Could your conversation be overheard by any one? "

" It might, for the cabin door was open, and—stay; now I recollect—Danglars himself passed by just as Captain Leclere was giving me the packet for the grand-marshal."

" That will do," cried the abbé; " now we are on the right scent. Did you take anybody ashore with you when you put into the port of Elba? "

" Nobody."

" Somebody there gave you a letter? "

" Yes; the grand-marshal did."

" And what did you do with that letter? "

" Put it into my pocket-book."

" You had your pocket-book with you, then? Now, how could a pocket-book, large enough to contain an official letter, find sufficient room in the pockets of a sailor? "

" You are right: my pocket-book was left on board."

" Then it was only on your return to the ship that you placed the letter in the pocket-book? "

" Yes."

" And what did you do with this letter while returning from Porto Ferrajo to your vessel? "

" I carried it in my hand."

" So that when you went on board the *Pharaon*, everybody could perceive you held a letter in your hand? "

" To be sure they could."

" Danglars, as well as the rest? "

" Yes; he as well as others."

" Now, listen to me, and try to recall every circumstance attending your arrest. Do you recollect the words in which the information against you was couched? "

" Oh, yes! I read it over three times, and the words sank deeply into my memory."

" Repeat it to me."

Dantès paused a few instants, as though collecting his ideas, then said, " This is it, word for word: ' The *procureur du roi* is informed by a friend of the throne and of religion, that one Edmond Dantès, mate of the ship *Pharaon*, who arrived this morning from Smyrna, after having touched at Naples and Porto Ferrajo, has been intrusted by Murat with a letter for the usurper, and by the usurper with a letter for the Bonapartist committee in Paris. Proof of this crime will be found on arresting him, for the letter will be found upon him, or at his father's, or in his cabin on board the *Pharaon*.' "

The abbé shrugged his shoulders. " The thing is clear as day," said he; " and you must have had a very unsuspecting nature, as well as a good heart, not to have suspected the origin of the whole affair."

" Do you really think so? Ah, that would indeed be the treachery of a villain."

" How did Danglars usually write? "

" A handsome running hand."

" And how was the anonymous letter written? "

" With a backward slant."

Again the abbé smiled. " In fact, it was a disguised hand? "

" I don't know; it was very boldly written, if disguised."

" Stop a bit," said the abbé. He took up what he called his pen and after dipping it into the ink, wrote on a morsel of prepared linen with his left hand the first two or three words of the accusation. Dantès drew back, and gazed on the abbé with a sensation almost amounting to terror.

" How very astonishing! " cried he, at length. " Why, your writing exactly resembles that of the accusation! "

" Simply because that accusation had been written with the left hand; and I have always remarked one thing—"

" What is that? "

" That whereas all writings done with the right hand are dissimilar, those performed with the left hand invariably resemble each other."

" You have evidently seen and observed everything."

" Let us proceed."

" Oh, yes, yes! let us go on."

" Now as regards the second question. Was there any person who might be interested in preventing your marriage with Mercédés? "

" Yes, a young man who loved her "

" And his name was— "

" Fernand."

" That is a Spanish name."

" He was a Catalan."

" Do you think that he was capable of writing the letter? "

" Oh, no! he would more likely have got rid of me by sticking a knife into me."

" That is in strict accordance with the Spanish character; an assassination they will unhesitatingly commit, but an act of cowardice, never."

" Besides," said Dantès, " the various circumstances mentioned in the letter were wholly unknown to him."

" You had never spoken of them yourself to any one? "

" To no person whatever."

" Not even to your mistress? "

" No, not even to my betrothed bride."

" Then it is Danglars, beyond a doubt."

" I feel quite sure of it now."

" Wait a little. Was Danglars at all acquainted with Fernand? "

" No; yes, he was. Now I recollect—"

" What? "—

" I saw them both sitting at table together beneath an arbour at Père Pamphile's the evening before the day fixed for my wedding. They were in earnest conversation. Danglars was joking in a friendly way, but Fernand looked pale and agitated."

" Were they alone? "

" There was a third person with them whom I knew well, and who had in all probability made their acquaintance,—a tailor named Caderousse; but he was already quite intoxicated. Stay! stay! How strange that it should not have occurred to me before! On the table round which they were sitting were pens, ink, and paper. Oh, the heartless, treacherous scoundrels!" exclaimed Dantès, pressing his hand to his throbbing brows.

" Is there anything else you would like to know? " asked the abbé, smiling.

" Yes, yes," replied Dantès, eagerly; " I would beg of you, who see so completely to the depths of things, and to whom the greatest mystery seems but an easy riddle, to explain to me why I had no second examination, why I was never brought to trial, and, above all, why I was condemned without process? "

" That is altogether a different and more serious matter," responded the abbé. " The ways of justice are frequently too dark and mysterious to be easily penetrated. All we have hitherto done in the matter has been child's play. If you wish me to enter upon the more difficult part of the business, you must assist me by the most minute information on every point."

" That I will gladly. So pray begin, my dear abbé, and ask me whatever questions you please; for in good truth you see more clearly into my life than I do myself."

" In the first place, then, who examined you,—the *procureur du roi*, his deputy, or a magistrate? "

" The deputy."

" Was he young or old? "

" About twenty-seven or twenty-eight years of age, I should say."

" To be sure," answered the abbé,—" not yet corrupt, but already ambitious. And how did he treat you? "

" With more of mildness than severity."

" Did you tell him your whole story? "

" I did."

" And did his conduct change at all in the course of your examination? "

" Yes; certainly he did appear much disturbed when he read the letter that had brought me into this scrape. He seemed quite overcome at the thoughts of the danger I was in."

" *You* were in? "

" Yes."

" Then you feel very sure that it was your misfortune that he regretted? "

" Why, he gave me one great proof of his sympathy, at least."

" And what was that? "

" He burned the sole proof that could at all have criminated me."

" Do you mean the letter of accusation? "

" Oh, no! the letter that I was intrusted to convey to Paris."

" Are you sure he burned it? "

" He did so before my eyes."

" Ay, indeed! that alters the case. That man might be a greater scoundrel than you think."

" Upon my word," said Dantès, " you make me shudder. Is the world indeed peopled by tigers and crocodiles? "

" Yes, but the two-legged tigers and crocodiles are more dangerous than others."

" Let us go on."

" With all my heart! You tell me he burned the letter in your presence? "

" He did,—saying at the same time, ' You see I thus destroy the only proof existing against you.' "

" This action is somewhat too sublime to be natural."

" You think so? "

" I am sure of it. To whom was this letter addressed? "

" To M. Noirtier, No. 13 Rue Coq-Héron, Paris."

" Now can you think of any interest that your deputy *procureur* could have had in the destruction of that letter? "

" Why, it is not altogether impossible he might have had, for he made me promise several times never to speak of that letter to any one, assuring me that he so advised me for my own interest; and more than this, he insisted on my taking a solemn oath never to utter the name written in the address."

" Noirtier! " repeated the abbé,—" Noirtier! I knew a person of that name at the court of the Queen of Etruria,—a Noirtier who had been a Girondin during the Revolution! What was the name of your deputy? "

" Villefort! "

The abbé burst into a fit of laughter, while Dantès gazed on him in utter astonishment.

" What ails you? " said he, at length.

" Do you see this ray of light? "

" I do."

" Well! I see my way into the full meaning of all the proceedings against you more clearly than you even discern that sunbeam. Poor fellow! poor young man! And you tell me this magistrate expressed great sympathy and commiseration for you? "

" He did."

" And the worthy man destroyed your compromising letter? "

" He burned it before me."

" That honest purveyor for the scaffold made you swear never to utter the name of Noirtier? "

" Certainly."

" Why, you poor short-sighted simpleton, do you know who this Noirtier was? "

" Indeed, I do not! "

" That Noirtier was his father! "

Had a thunderbolt fallen at the feet of Dantès, or hell opened its yawning gulf before him, he could not have been more completely transfixed with horror than at the sound of words so wholly unexpected, revealing as they did the fiendish perfidy which had consigned him to wear out his days in the dark cell of a prison that was to him as a living grave. Starting up, he clasped his hands around his head as though to prevent his very brain from bursting, as in a choked and almost inarticulate voice he exclaimed, " His father! his father! "

"His own father," replied the abbé, "whose name is Noirtier de Villefort."

At this instant, a bright light shot through the mind of Dantès, and cleared up all that had been dark and obscure before. The change that had come over Villefort during the examination, the destruction of the letter, the exacted promise, the almost supplicating tones of the magistrate, who seemed rather to implore mercy than denounce punishment,—all returned to his memory. A cry of mental agony escaped his lips, and he staggered against the wall almost like a drunken man; then, as the paroxysm passed away, he hurried to the opening conducting from the abbé's cell to his own, and said, "Oh! I must be alone to think over all this."

When he regained his dungeon, he threw himself on his bed, where the turnkey found him at his evening visit, sitting with fixed gaze and contracted features, still and motionless as a statue. During those hours of meditation, which to him had seemed but as minutes, he had formed a fearful resolution, and bound himself to its fulfilment by a solemn oath. Dantès was at length roused from his reverie by the voice of Faria, who, having also been visited by his jailer, had come to invite his fellow-sufferer to share his supper. In his character as mad-man, and especially as an amusing madman, the abbé enjoyed certain privileges. He was supplied with bread of a finer, whiter description than the usual prison fare, and even regaled each Sunday with a small quantity of wine. The present day chanced to be Sunday; and the abbé came to invite his young companion to share his bread and wine. Dantès followed him with a firm and assured step. His features had lost their almost spasmodic contraction, and now wore their usual expression; but he had acquired a certain rigidity and sternness which announced the forming of a deep and settled purpose. Faria bent on him his penetrating eye. "I regret now," said he, "having helped you in your late inquiries, or having given you the information I did."

"Why so?" inquired Dantès.

"Because it has instilled a new passion in your heart,—that of vengeance."

A bitter smile played over the features of the young man. "Let us talk of something else," said he.

Again the abbé looked at him, then mournfully shook his head; but in accordance with Dantès's request, he began to speak of other matters. The elder prisoner was one of those persons whose conversation, like that of all who have experienced many trials, contained many useful and important hints as well as sound information; but it was never egotistical, for the unfortunate man never alluded to his own sorrows. Dantès listened with admiring attention to all he said. Some of his remarks corresponded with what he already knew, or applied to the sort of knowledge his nautical life had enabled him to acquire; others related to things unknown to him, but like those auroræ boreales which serve to light the navigators in northern latitudes, they sufficed to open fresh views to the inquiring mind of the listener, and to give a glimpse of new horizons illumined by the wild meteoric flash. He justly estimated the delight an intelligent mind would have in following that lofty spirit along the moral, philosophical, or social heights where it found exercise.

"You must teach me a small part of what you know," said Dantès, "if only to prevent your growing weary of me. I can well believe that so learned a person as yourself would prefer absolute solitude to being tormented with the company of one as ignorant and uninformed as myself. If you will only agree to my request, I promise you never to mention another word about escaping."

The abbé smiled. "Alas, my child!" said he, "human knowledge is confined within very narrow limits; and when I have taught you mathematics, physics, history, and the three or four modern languages with which I am acquainted, you will know as much as I do myself. Now, it will scarcely require two years for me to communicate to you the stock of learning I possess."

"Two years!" exclaimed Dantès; "do you really believe I can acquire all these things in so short a time?"

"Not their application, certainly, but their principles you may; to learn is not to know. There are the learned and the knowing. Memory makes the one, philosophy the other."

"But cannot one learn philosophy?"

"Philosophy is not to be learned; it is the combination of sciences acquired by the genius which applies them. Philosophy—it is the dazzling cloud on which Christ placed his foot to mount into the heavens."

"Well, then," said Dantès, "what will you teach me first? I am eager to begin; I thirst for knowledge."

"Good!" said the abbé.

That very evening the prisoners sketched a plan of education to be entered upon the following day. Dantès possessed a prodigious memory combined with an astonishing quickness and readiness of conception. The mathematical turn of his mind rendered him apt at all kinds of calculation, while his imagination imbued with interest the dry reality of arithmetical computation or the rigid severity of lines. He already knew Italian, and had also picked up a little of the Romaic dialect on his voyages to the East; and by the aid of these two languages he easily comprehended the construction of all the others, so that at the end of six months he began to speak Spanish, English, and German. In strict accordance with the promise made to the abbé, Dantès never even alluded to flight. It might have been that the delight his studies afforded him supplied the place of liberty, or that the recollection of his pledged word (a point, as we have already seen, to which he paid a rigid attention) kept him from reverting to any plan for escape. The instructive days passed rapidly, and at the end of a year Dantès was a new man.

As to the Abbé Faria, Dantès remarked that, spite of the relief his society afforded, he daily grew sadder; one thought seemed incessantly to harass and distract his mind. Sometimes he would fall into long reveries, sigh heavily and involuntarily, then suddenly rise, and with folded arms begin pacing the confined space of his dungeon. One day he stopped all at once in the midst of these so often-repeated promenades, and exclaimed, " Ah, if there were no sentinel! "

" There shall not be one a minute longer than you please," said Dantès, who had followed his thought through the covering of his brain as if through a crystal.

" Ah! I have already told you," answered the abbé, " that I revolt at murder."

" But this murder, if committed, will be for our safety, prompted by the instinct of self-defence."

" No matter; I could never agree to it."

" Still, you have thought of it? "

" Incessantly, alas! " cried the abbé.

" And you have discovered a means of regaining our freedom, have you not? " asked Dantès, eagerly.

" I have; if they should happen to place a blind and deaf sentinel in the gallery beyond us."

" He shall be blind, he shall be deaf! " replied the young man, with an air of determined resolution that made his companion shudder.

" No, no! " cried the abbé; " it is impossible! " In vain did Dantès endeavour to renew the subject; the abbé shook his head and refused any further conversation respecting it.

Three months passed away.

"Do you feel yourself strong?" inquired the abbé of Dantès. The young man, in reply, took up the chisel, bent it into the form of a horseshoe, and then as readily straightened it.

"And will you engage not to do any harm to the sentry, except in the last extremity?"

"Yes, upon honour."

"Then," said the abbé, "we may hope to put our design into execution."

"And how long shall we be in accomplishing the necessary work?"

"At least a year."

"And shall we begin at once?"

"Directly."

"We have lost a year to no purpose!" cried Dantès.

"Do you consider the last twelve months as wasted?" asked the abbé, in a tone of mild reproach.

"Forgive me!" cried Edmond, blushing.

"Tut, tut!" answered the abbé; "man is but man at last, and you are about the best specimen of the genus I have ever known. Come, let me show you my plan." The abbé then showed Dantès a design which he had drawn. It consisted of a plan of his own cell and that of Dantès, with the corridor which united them. In this passage he proposed to form a tunnel, such as is employed in mines; this tunnel would conduct the two prisoners immediately beneath the gallery where the sentry kept watch. Once there, a large excavation would be made, and one of the flag-stones with which the gallery was paved be so completely loosened that at the desired moment it would give way beneath the soldier's feet, who, falling into the excavation below, would be immediately bound and gagged ere, stunned by the effects of his fall, he had power to offer any resistance. The prisoners were then to make their way through one of the gallery windows, and to let themselves down from the outer walls by means of the abbé's ladder of cords. The eyes of Dantès sparkled with joy, and he rubbed his hands with delight at the idea of a plan so simple, yet apparently so certain to succeed.

That very day the miners commenced their labour, and with the more ardour because it succeeded to a long rest from fatigue, and was destined, in all probability, to fulfil their dearest wish. Nothing interrupted the progress of their work except the necessity of returning to their respective cells against the hour in which their jailer was in the habit of visiting them; they had learned to distinguish the almost imperceptible sound of his footsteps as he descended towards their dungeons, and happily, never failed being prepared for his coming. The fresh earth excavated during their present work, and which would have entirely blocked up the old passage, was thrown by degrees and with the utmost precaution, out of the window in either Faria's or Dantès's cell, the rubbish being first pulverised so finely that the night wind carried it far away without permitting the smallest trace to remain.

More than a year had been consumed in this undertaking, the only tools for which had been a chisel, a knife, and a wooden lever,—Faria still continuing to instruct Dantès by conversing with him, sometimes in one language, sometimes in another; at others, relating to him the history of nations and of the great men who from time to time have left behind them one of those bright tracks called glory. The abbé was a man of the world, and had moreover mixed in the first society of the day; his appearance was impressed with that air of melancholy dignity which Dantès, thanks to the imitative powers bestowed on him by nature, easily acquired, as well as that elegant politeness which he had previously lacked, and which is seldom possessed except by those who have been placed in constant intercourse with persons of high birth and breeding.

At the end of fifteen months the tunnel was made and the excavation completed beneath the gallery, and the two workmen could distinctly hear the measured tread of the sentinel as he paced to and fro over their heads. Compelled as they were to await a night sufficiently dark to favour their flight, they were obliged to defer their final attempt till that auspicious moment should arrive. Their greatest dread now was lest the stone through which the sentry was doomed to fall should give way before its right time, and this they had in some measure provided against by placing under it, as a kind of a prop, a sort of bearer they had discovered among the foundations through which they had worked their way. Dantès was occupied in arranging this piece of wood when he heard Faria, who had remained in Edmond's cell for the purpose of cutting a peg to secure their rope-ladder, call to him in accents of distress. Dantès hastened to his dungeon, where he found him standing in the middle of the room, pale, his forehead streaming with perspiration, and his hands clinched tightly together.

"Gracious heavens!" exclaimed Dantès, "what is the matter? what has happened?"

"Quick! quick!" returned the abbé, "listen to me!"

Dantès looked in fear and wonder at the livid countenance of Faria, his eyes circled by a halo of a bluish cast, his white lips, his disordered hair, and terrified, let fall to the ground the chisel he was holding in his hand. " What, then, is it ? " he cried.

" I am lost ! " said the abbé. " Listen to me. I am seized with a terrible, perhaps mortal illness; I can feel that the paroxysm is fast approaching. I had a similar attack the year previous to my imprisonment. This malady admits of but one remedy; I will tell you what that is. Go into my cell as quickly as you can; lift one of the feet that support the bed. You will find it has been hollowed out for the purpose of containing a small phial you will see there half-filled with a red fluid. Bring it to me—or rather, no, no ! I may be found here —help me back to my room while I have still some strength. Who knows what may happen while the fit continues ? "

Spite of the magnitude of the misfortune which thus suddenly frustrated his hopes, Dantès did not lose his presence of mind, but descended into the corridor, dragging his unfortunate companion with him; then, half-carrying, half-supporting him, he managed to reach the abbé's chamber, when he immediately laid the sufferer on his bed.

" Thanks ! " said the poor abbé, shivering as though his veins were filled with ice. " I am seized with a fit of catalepsy; when it comes to its height, I shall perhaps lie still and motionless as though dead, uttering neither sigh nor groan. On the other hand, the symptoms may be much more violent, and cause me to fall into fearful convulsions, cover my lips with foaming, and force from me the most piercing shrieks. This last evil you must carefully guard against, for were my cries to be heard, it is more than probable I should be removed to another part of the prison, and we should be separated for ever. When I become quite motionless, cold, and rigid as a corpse, then, and not before, you understand, force open my teeth with a chisel, pour from eight to ten drops of the liquor contained in the phial down my throat, and perhaps I shall revive."

" Perhaps ? " exclaimed Dantès, in grief-stricken tones.

" Help ! help ! " cried the abbé, " I—I—die—I—"

So sudden and violent was the fit that the unfortunate prisoner was unable to complete the sentence begun; a violent convulsion shook his whole frame, his eyes started from their sockets, his mouth was drawn on one side, his cheeks became purple, he struggled, foamed, dashed himself about, and uttered the most dreadful cries, which, however, Dantès prevented from being heard by covering his head with the blanket. The fit lasted two hours; then, more helpless than an infant, and colder and paler than marble, more crushed and broken than a reed trampled underfoot, he stretched himself out in a last convulsion and became livid.

Edmond waited till life seemed extinct in the body of his friend, then, taking up the chisel, he with difficulty forced open the closely-fixed jaws, carefully poured the appointed number of drops down the rigid throat, and anxiously awaited the result. An hour passed away without the old man's giving the least sign of returning animation. Dantès began to fear he had too long delayed administering the remedy, and thrusting his hands into his hair, continued gazing on the lifeless features of his friend in an agony of despair. At length a slight colour tinged the livid cheeks, consciousness returned to the dull, open eyeballs, a faint sigh issued from the lips, and the sufferer made a feeble effort to move.

"He is saved! he is saved!" cried Dantès, in a paroxysm of delight.

The sick man was not yet able to speak, but he pointed with evident anxiety towards the door. Dantès listened, and plainly distinguished the approaching steps of the jailer. It was therefore near seven o'clock; but Edmond's anxiety had put all thoughts of time out of his head. The young man sprang to the entrance, darted through it, carefully drawing the stone over the opening, and hurried to his cell. He had scarcely done so when the door opened, and disclosed to the jailer's inquisitorial gaze the prisoner seated as usual on the side of his bed. Almost before the key had turned in the lock, and before the departing steps of the jailer had died away in the long corridor he had to traverse, Dantès, whose restless anxiety concerning his friend left him no desire to touch the food brought him, hurried back to the abbé's chamber, and raising the stone by pressing his head against it, was soon beside the sick man's couch. Faria had now fully regained consciousness, but he still lay helpless and exhausted on his miserable bed.

"I did not expect to see you again," said he, feebly, to Dantès.

"And why not?" asked the young man. "Did you expect, then, to die?"

"No, but all is ready for flight; and I thought you would escape."

The deep glow of indignation suffused the cheeks of Dantès. "And did you really think so meanly of me," cried he, "as to believe I would depart without you?"

"At least," said the abbé, "I now see that I was mistaken. Alas, alas! I am fearfully exhausted and debilitated by this attack."

"Be of good cheer," replied Dantès; "your strength will return." And as he spoke he seated himself on the bed beside Faria, and tenderly chafed his chilled hands.

The abbé shook his head. "The former of these fits," said he, "lasted but half an hour, at the termination of which I experienced no other feeling than a great sensation of hunger, and I rose from my bed without help; now I can neither move my right arm nor leg, and my head is confused, which indicates a rush of blood to the brain. The next of these fits will either carry me off or leave me paralysed for life."

"No, no!" cried Dantès; "you are mistaken; you will not die! And your third attack (if indeed you should have another) will find you at liberty. We shall save you another time, as we have done this, only with a better chance, because we shall be able to command every requisite assistance."

"My good Edmond," answered the abbé, "be not deceived. The attack which has just passed away condemns me to perpetual imprisonment. None can escape but those who can walk."

"Well, we will wait a week, a month, two months, if necessary. In the meantime your strength will return; and as it only remains with us to fix the hour and minute, we will choose the first instant that you feel able to swim to execute our project."

"I shall never swim again," replied Faria. "This arm is paralysed; not for a time, but for ever. Lift it, and judge by its weight if I am mistaken."

The young man raised the arm, which fell back by its own weight, inanimate and helpless. A sigh escaped him.

"You are convinced now, Edmond, are you not?" asked the abbé. "Depend upon it, I know what I say. Since the first attack I experienced of this malady, I have continually reflected on it. Indeed, I expected it, for it is a family inheritance; both my father and grandfather were taken off by it. The physician who prepared for me the remedy I have twice successfully taken was no other than the celebrated Cabanis; and he predicted a similar end for me."

"The physician may be mistaken!" exclaimed Dantès. "And as for your poor arm, what difference will that make in our escape? Never mind if you cannot swim; I can take you on my shoulders, and swim for both of us."

"My son," said the abbé, "you, who are a sailor and a

swimmer, must know as well as I do that a man so loaded would sink ere he had advanced fifty yards in the sea. Cease, then, to deceive yourself with vain hopes that even your own excellent heart refuses to believe in. Here I shall remain till the hour of my deliverance arrives; and that, in all human probability, will be the hour of my death. As for you, who are young and active, delay not on my account, but fly—go! I give you back your promise."

"It is well," said Dantès. "And now hear my determination also." Then rising and extending his hand with an air of solemnity over the old man's head, he slowly added, "By the blood of Christ I swear that I will not leave you while you live!"

Faria looked at that young man, so noble, so simple, of so lofty a spirit, and read in his honest open countenance ample confirmation of truthfulness, as well as sincere, affectionate, and faithful devotion.

"Thanks," murmured the invalid, extending the one hand of which he still retained the use. "Thanks for your generous offer, which I accept as frankly as it was made." Then, after a short pause he added, "You may one of these days reap the reward of your disinterested devotion. But as I cannot, and you will not, quit this place, it becomes necessary to fill up the excavation beneath the soldier's gallery; he might, by chance, notice a hollow sound produced by his footsteps over the excavated ground, and call the attention of his officer to the circumstance. That would bring about a discovery which would inevitably lead to our being separated. Go, then, and set about this work, in which unhappily I can offer you no assistance; keep at it all night, if necessary, and do not return here tomorrow till after the jailer has visited me. I shall have something important to communicate to you."

Dantès took the hand of the abbé in his, and affectionately pressed it. Faria smiled encouragingly on him, and the young man retired to his task, filled with a religious determination faithfully and unflinchingly to discharge the vow which bound him to his afflicted friend.

CHAPTER XVIII

THE TREASURE

WHEN Dantès returned next morning to the chamber of his companion in captivity, he found Faria seated and looking composed. In the ray of light which entered by the narrow window of his cell, he held open in his left hand, of which alone, it will be recollected, he retained the use, a morsel of paper, which from being constantly rolled into a small compass, had the form of a cylinder, and was not easily kept open. He did not speak, but showed the paper to Dantès.

" What is that? " inquired the latter.

" Look at it," said the abbé, with a smile.

" I have looked at it with all possible attention," said Dantès, " and I only see a half-burned paper, on which are traces of Gothic characters, traced with a peculiar kind of ink."

" This paper, my friend," said Faria, " I may now avow to you, since I have proved you,—this paper is my treasure, of which, from this day forth, one half belongs to you."

A cold damp started to Dantès's brow. Until this day— through what a period of time!—he had avoided talking to the abbé of this treasure, the source of the imputation of madness against him. With his instinctive delicacy Edmond had preferred avoiding any touch on this painful chord, and Faria had been equally silent. He had taken the silence of the old man for a return to reason, and now these few words, uttered by Faria after so painful a crisis, seemed to announce a serious relapse of mental alienation.

" Your treasure? " stammered Dantès. Faria smiled.

" Yes," said he. " You are indeed a noble heart, Edmond; and I see by your paleness and your shudder what is passing in your heart at this moment. No, be assured; I am not mad. This treasure exists, Dantès; and if I have not been allowed to possess it, you will. Yes; you. No one would listen to me or believe me, because they thought me mad; but you, who must know that I am not, listen to me, and believe me afterwards if you will."

" Alas! murmured Edmond to himself, " this is a terrible relapse! There was only this blow wanting." Then he said aloud, " My dear friend, your attack has perhaps fatigued you; had you not better repose a while? To-morrow, if you will, I will hear your narrative; but to-day I wish to nurse you carefully. Besides," he said, "a treasure is not a matter very urgent for us."

"It is very urgent, Edmond!" replied the old man. "Who knows if to-morrow, or the next day after, the third attack may not come on? Remember that then all will be over. I have often thought with a bitter joy that these riches, which would make the wealth of a dozen families, will be for ever lost to those men who persecute me. This idea was revenge to me, and I tasted it slowly in the night of my dungeon and the despair of my captivity. But now that I have forgiven the world for the love of you; now that I see you young and full of hope and prospect; now that I think of all that may result to you in the good fortune of such a disclosure,—I shudder at any delay, and tremble lest I should not assure to one as worthy as yourself the possession of so vast an amount of hidden treasure."

Edmond turned away his head with a sigh.

"You persist in your incredulity, Edmond," continued Faria. "My words have not convinced you. I see you require proofs. Well, then, read this paper, which I have never shown to any one."

"To-morrow, my dear friend," said Edmond, unwilling to yield to the old man's madness. "I thought it was understood that we should not talk of that until to-morrow."

"Then we will not talk of it until to-morrow; but read this paper to-day."

"I will not irritate him," thought Edmond, and taking the paper, of which half was wanting, having been burned, no doubt, by some accident, he read,—

This treasure, which may amount to two
of Roman crowns in the most distant a
of the second opening wh
declare to belong to him alo
heir.
25th April, 149

"Well!" said Faria, when the young man had finished reading it.

"Why," replied Dantès, "I see nothing but broken lines and unconnected words, which are rendered illegible by fire."

"Yes, to you, my friend, who read them for the first time; but not for me, who have grown pale over them by many nights' study, and have reconstructed every phrase, completed every thought."

"And do you believe you have discovered the concealed sense?"

" I am sure I have, and you shall judge for yourself; but first listen to the history of this paper."

" Silence!" exclaimed Dantès. " Steps approach—I go—adieu."

And Dantès, happy to escape the history and explanation which could not fail to confirm his apprehensions, glided like a snake along the narrow passage, while Faria, restored by his alarm to a kind of activity, pushed with his foot the stone into its place, and covered it with a mat in order the more effectually to avoid discovery.

It was the governor, who, hearing of Faria's accident from the jailer, had come in person to see him.

Faria sat up to receive him, avoided every movement that might betray his condition, and continued to conceal from the governor the paralysis that had already stricken with death one half of his body. His fear was lest the governor, touched with pity, might order him to be removed to a prison more wholesome, and thus separate him from his young companion. But fortunately this did not happen, and the governor left him, convinced that the poor madman, for whom in his heart he felt a kind of affection, was only affected with a slight indisposition.

During this time Edmond, seated on his bed with his head in his hands, tried to collect his scattered thoughts. All was so rational, so grand, so logical, with Faria since he had known him, that he could not understand how so much wisdom on all other points could be allied to madness in any one. Was Faria deceived as to his treasure, or was all the world deceived as to Faria?

Dantès remained in his cell all day, not daring to return to his friend, thinking thus to defer the moment when he should acquire the certainty that the abbé was mad,—that conviction would be so terrible to him!

But towards the evening, after the usual visitation, Faria, not seeing the young man appear, tried to get over the distance which separated them. Edmond shuddered when he heard the painful efforts which the old man made to drag himself along; his leg was inert, and he could no longer make use of one arm. Edmond was compelled to draw him towards himself, for otherwise he could not enter by the small aperture which led to Dantès's chamber.

" Here I am, pursuing you remorselessly," he said with a benignant smile. " You thought to escape my munificence, but it is in vain. Listen to me."

Edmond saw there was no escape, and placing the old man on his bed, he seated himself on the stool beside him.

" You know," said the abbé, " that I was the secretary and intimate friend of Cardinal Spada, the last of the princes of that name. I owe to this worthy lord all the happiness I ever knew. He was not rich, although the wealth of his family had passed into a proverb, and I heard the phrase very often, ' As rich as a Spada.' But he, like public rumour, lived on this reputation for wealth. His palace was my paradise. I instructed his nephews, who are dead; and when he was alone in the world, I returned to him, by an absolute devotion to his will, all he had done for me during ten years. The house of the cardinal had no secrets for me. I had often seen my noble patron annotating ancient volumes, and eagerly searching among dusty family manuscripts. One day when I was reproaching him for his unavailing searches, and the kind of prostration of mind that followed them, he looked at me, and smiling bitterly, opened a volume relating to the history of the city of Rome. There, in the twenty-ninth chapter of the *Life of Pope Alexander VI.*, were the following lines, which I can never forget:—

" ' The great wars of Romagna had ended; Cæsar Borgia, who had completed his conquest, had need of money to purchase all Italy. The pope had also need of money to make a final settlement with Louis, the twelfth king of France, formidable still in spite of his recent reverses. It was necessary, therefore, to have recourse to some profitable speculation, which was a matter of great difficulty in the impoverished condition of exhausted Italy. His Holiness had an idea; he determined to make two cardinals.'

" In choosing two of the greatest personages of Rome, especially rich men, the holy father looked for the following profits from his speculation. In the first place he had to sell the great appointments and splendid offices which these two cardinals held; and then he had the two hats to sell besides. There was a third profit in the speculation, which will appear hereafter. The pope and Cæsar Borgia first found the two future cardinals; they were Jean Rospigliosi, who held four of the highest dignities of the holy seat, and Cæsar Spada, one of the noblest and richest of the Roman nobility. Both felt the high honour of such a favour from the pope. They were ambitious. These having been selected, Cæsar Borgia soon found purchasers for their appointments. The result was that Rospigliosi and Spada paid for being cardinals, and eight other persons paid for the offices the cardinals held before their elevation, and thus eight hundred thousand crowns entered into the coffers of the speculators.

" It is time now to proceed to the last part of the speculation. The pope having almost smothered Rospigliosi and Spada with caresses, having bestowed upon them the insignia of cardinals and induced them to realise their fortunes and fix themselves at Rome,—the pope and Cæsar Borgia invited the two cardinals to dinner. This was a matter of contest between the holy father and his son. Cæsar thought they could make use of one of the means which he always had ready for his friends; that is to say, in the first place the famous key with which they requested certain persons to go and open a particular cupboard. This key was furnished with a small iron point,—a negligence on the part of the locksmith. When this was pressed to effect the opening of the cupboard, the lock of which was difficult, the person was pricked by this small point, and the next day he died. Then there was the ring with the lion's head, which Cæsar wore when he meant to give certain squeezes of the hand. The lion bit the hand thus favoured, and at the end of twenty-four hours the bite was mortal. Cæsar, then, proposed to his father either to ask the cardinals to open the cupboard, or to give each a cordial squeeze of the hand; but Alexander VI. replied to him : ' While we are thinking of these worthy cardinals, Spada and Rospigliosi, let us ask both of them to a dinner. Something tells me that we shall regain this money. Besides, you forget, Cæsar, an indigestion declares itself immediately, but a prick or a bite only after one or two days.' Cæsar gave way before such cogent reasoning; and the cardinals were consequently invited to dinner.

" The table was laid in a vineyard belonging to the pope, near St. Pierre ès Liens,—a charming retreat which the cardinals knew very well by report. Rospigliosi, quite giddy with his dignity, prepared his stomach and assumed his best looks. Spada, a prudent man, and greatly attached to his only nephew, a young captain of highest promise, took paper and pen and made his will. He then sent to his nephew to await him in the vicinity of the vineyard; but it appeared the servant did not find him.

" Spada knew the meaning of these invitations; since Christianity, so eminently civilising, had made progress in Rome, it was no longer a centurion who came from the tyrant with a message, ' Cæsar wills that you die,' but it was a legate *a latere* who came with a smile on his lips to say from the pope, ' His Holiness requests you will dine with him.'

"Spada set out about two o'clock to St. Pierre ès Liens. The pope awaited him. The first figure that struck the eyes of Spada was that of his nephew in full costume, and Cæsar Borgia paying him most marked attentions. Spada turned pale, as Cæsar looked at him with an ironical air, which proved that he had anticipated all, and that the snare was well spread. They began dinner, and Spada was only able to inquire of his nephew if he had received his message. The nephew replied no,—perfectly comprehending the meaning of the question. It was too late, for he had already drunk a glass of excellent wine, placed for him expressly by the pope's butler. Spada at the same moment saw another bottle approach him, from which he was liberally supplied. An hour afterwards a physician declared they were both poisoned through eating mushrooms. Spada died on the threshold of the vineyard; the nephew expired at his own door, making signs which his wife could not comprehend.

"Then Cæsar and the pope hastened to lay hands on the heritage, under pretence of seeking for the papers of the dead man. But the inheritance consisted in this only,—a scrap of paper on which Spada had written: ' I bequeath to my beloved nephew my coffers, my books, and, among them, my breviary with the gold corners, which I beg he will preserve in remembrance of his affectionate uncle.'

"The heirs sought everywhere, admired the breviary, laid hands on the furniture, and were greatly astonished that Spada, the rich uncle, was really the most miserable of uncles. There were no treasures, except those of science, comprised in the library and laboratories. This was all: Cæsar and his father searched, examined, scrutinised, but found nothing, or at least, very little,—not exceeding a few thousand crowns in plate, and about the same in ready money; but the nephew had time to say to his wife before he expired: ' Look well among my uncle's papers; there is a will.'

"They sought even more thoroughly than the august heirs had done, but it was fruitless. There were two palaces and a vineyard behind the Palatine Hill; but in these days landed property had not much value, and the two palaces and the vineyard remained to the family as beneath the rapacity of the pope and his son. Months and years rolled on. Alexander VI. died, poisoned,—you know by what mistake. Cæsar, poisoned at the same time, escaped with his skin coloured like that of a snake, and assumed a new cuticle, on which the poison left spots, like those we see on the skin of a tiger; then, compelled to quit Rome, he went and killed himself in obscurity in a night skirmish scarcely noticed in history. After the pope's death and his son's exile, it was supposed the Spada family would again make the splendid figure they had before the cardinal's time; but this was not the case. The Spadas remained in doubtful ease; a mystery hung over this dark affair; and the public rumour was that Cæsar, a better politician than his father, had carried off from the pope the fortune of the two cardinals. I say the two because Cardinal Rospigliosi, who had not taken any precaution, was completely despoiled.

"Up to this time," said Faria, interrupting the thread of his narrative, "this seems to you very ridiculous, no doubt?"

"Oh, my friend," cried Dantès, "on the contrary, it seems as if I were reading a most interesting narrative; go on, I pray of you."

"I continue: The family began to feel accustomed to this obscurity. Years rolled on, and among the descendants some were soldiers, others diplomatists; some churchmen, some bankers; some grew rich, and some were ruined. I come now to the last of the family, whose secretary I was,—the Comte de Spada. I had often heard him complain of the disproportion of his rank with his fortune; and I advised him to sink all he had in an annuity. He did so, and thus doubled his income. The celebrated breviary remained in the family, and was in the count's possession. It had been handed down from father to son,—for the singular clause of the only will that had been found, had rendered it a real *relique*, preserved in the family with superstitious veneration. It was an illuminated book, with beautiful Gothic characters, and so weighty with gold that a servant always carried it before the cardinal on days of great solemnity.

"At the sight of papers of all sorts,—titles, contracts, parchments, which were kept in the archives of the family all descending from the poisoned cardinal,—I, like twenty servitors, stewards, secretaries before me, in my turn examined the immense bundles of documents; but in spite of the most accurate researches, I found—nothing. Yet I had read, I had even written a precise history of the Borgia family, for the sole purpose of assuring myself whether any increase of fortune had occurred to them on the death of the Cardinal Cæsar Spada; but could trace only the acquisition of the property of the Cardinal Rospigliosi, his companion in misfortune.

"I was then almost assured that the inheritance had profited neither the Borgias nor the family, but had remained without an owner, like the treasures of the Arabian Nights, which slept in the bosom of the earth under the eyes of a genie. I searched, ransacked, counted, calculated a thousand and a thousand times the income and expenditure of the family for three hundred years; it was useless. I remained in my ignorance, and the Comte de Spada in his poverty. My patron died. He had reserved from his annuity his family papers, his library composed of five thousand volumes, and his famous breviary. All these he bequeathed to me, with a thousand Roman crowns which he had in ready money, on condition that I would have anniversary masses said for the repose of his soul, and that I would draw up a genealogical tree and history of his house. All this I did scrupulously. Be easy, my dear Edmond, we are near the conclusion.

"In 1807, a month before I was arrested, and fifteen days after the death of Comte de Spada, on the 25th of December (you will see presently how the date became fixed in my memory), I was reading for the thousandth time the papers I was arranging,—for the palace was sold to a stranger, and I was going to leave Rome and settle in Florence, intending to take with me twelve thousand livres I possessed, my library and famous breviary,—when tired with my constant labour at the same thing and overcome by a heavy dinner I had eaten, my head dropped on my hands and I fell asleep; it was about three o'clock in the afternoon. I woke as the clock was striking six. I raised my head; all was in darkness. I rang for a light, but as no one came, I determined to find one for myself. It was indeed a philosophical habit which I should soon be under the necessity of adopting. I took a wax candle in one hand and with the other groped about for a piece of paper (my match-box being empty), with which I proposed to procure a light from the small flame still playing on the embers. Fearing, however, that in the darkness I might use some valuable paper, I hesitated for a moment, then recollected that I had seen in the famous breviary, which was on the table beside me, an old paper quite yellow with age, and which had served as a marker for centuries, kept in its place by the veneration of the heirs. I felt for it, found it, twisted it, and putting it into the expiring flame, set light to it.

"'But beneath my fingers, as if by magic, as the fire ascended I saw yellowish characters appear on the paper. Then terror seized upon me. I grasped the paper in my hand, put out the flame as quickly as I could, lighted my taper in the fire itself, and opened the crumpled paper with inexpressible emotion. I found that these characters had been traced in mysterious and sympathetic ink, visible only when exposed to the fire. A little more than one-third of the paper had been consumed by the flame. It was that paper you read this morning; read it again, Dantès, and then I will complete for you the broken phrases and unconnected sense."

Faria with an air of triumph offered the paper to Dantès, who this time read the following words, traced with a rust-coloured ink:—

> This 25th day of April, 1498, be
> Alexander VI. and fearing that not
> he may desire to become my heir and re
> and Bentivoglio, who were poisoned,
> my sole heir, that I have bu
> and has visited with me (that is, in
> island of Monte Cristo) all I poss
> jewels, diamonds, gems; that I alone
> may amount to nearly two mil
> will find on raising the twentieth ro
> creek to the east in a right line.   Two open
> in these caves; the treasure is in the farthest a
> which treasure I bequeath and leave en
> as my sole heir.
>
> CÆS
>
> 25th April, 1498.

" And now," said the abbé, " read this other paper; " and he presented to Dantès a second leaf with fragments of lines written on it, which Edmond read as follows:—

> ing invited to dine by his Holiness
> content with making me pay for my hat,
> serves for me the fate of Cardinals Caprara
> I declare to my nephew, Guido Spada,
> ried in a place he knows
> the caves of the small
> essed of ingots, gold, money,
> know of the existence of this treasure, which
> lions of Roman crowns, and which he
> ck from the small
> ings have been made
> ngle in the second;
> tire to him
>
> AR † SPADA.

Faria followed him with excited look. " And now," he said when he saw that Dantès had read the last line, " put the two fragments together, and judge for yourself." Dantès obeyed; and the conjoined pieces gave the following:—

> This 25th day of April, 1498, be— ing invited to dine by his
> Holiness Alexander VI., and fearing that not— content with making

me pay for my hat, he may desire to become my heir and re— serves
for me the fate of Cardinals Caprara and Bentivoglio, who were
poisoned,— I declare to my nephew, Guido Spada, my sole heir, that
I have bu— ried in a place he knows and has visited with me (that
is, in— the caves of the small island of Monte Cristo) all I poss—
essed of ingots, gold, money, jewels, diamonds, gems; that I alone—
know of the existence of this treasure, which may amount to nearly
two mil— lions of Roman crowns, and which he will find on raising
the twentieth ro— ck from the small creek to the east in a right line.
Two open— ings have been made in these caves; the treasure is in
the farthest a— ngle in the second; which treasure I bequeath and
leave en— tire to him as my sole heir.

CÆS—AR † SPADA.

25th April, 1498.

" Well, do you comprehend now? " inquired Faria.

" It is the declaration of Cardinal Spada, and the will so long
sought for? " replied Edmond, still incredulous.

" Yes! a thousand times yes! "

" And who completed it as it now is? "

" I did. Aided by the remaining fragment, I guessed the
rest,—measuring the length of the lines by that of the paper,
and divining the hidden meaning by means of what was in part
revealed, as we are guided in a cavern by the small ray of light
above us."

" And what did you do when you arrived at this conclusion? "

" I resolved to set out, and did set out that very instant,
carrying with me the beginning of my great work on the unity
of Italy; but for some time the imperial police,—who at this
period, quite contrary to what Napoleon desired so soon as he
had a son born to him, wished for a partition of provinces,—
had their eyes on me. And my hasty departure, the cause of
which they were unable to guess, having aroused their suspicions, I was arrested at the very moment I was leaving Piombino. Now," continued Faria, addressing Dantès with an
almost paternal expression,—" now, my dear fellow, you know
as much as I do myself. If we ever escape together, half this
treasure is yours; if I die here, and you escape alone, the whole
belongs to you."

" But," inquired Dantès, hesitating, " has this treasure no
more legitimate possessor in this world than ourselves? "

" No, no, be easy on that score; the family is extinct. The
last Comte de Spada, moreover, made me his heir; bequeathing
to me this symbolic breviary, he bequeathed to me all it contained. No, no, be assured; if we lay hands on this fortune,
we may enjoy it without remorse."

" And you say this treasure amounts to—"

"Two millions of Roman crowns,—about thirteen millions of our money."

"Impossible!" said Dantès, staggered at the enormous amount.

"Impossible! and why?" asked the old man. "The Spada family was one of the oldest and most powerful families of the fifteenth century; and in those times when all speculative and industrial enterprises were wanting, those accumulations of gold and jewels were by no means rare. There are at this day Roman families perishing of hunger, though possessed of nearly a million in diamonds and jewels handed down as heirlooms, which they cannot touch."

Edmond thought he was in a dream; he wavered between incredulity and joy.

"I have only kept this secret so long from you," continued Faria, "that I might prove you and then surprise you. Had we escaped before my attack of catalepsy, I should have conducted you to Monte Cristo; now," he added with a sigh, "it is you who will conduct me thither. Well! Dantès, you do not thank me."

"This treasure belongs to you, my dear friend," replied Dantès; "and to you only. I have no right to it. I am no relative of yours."

"You are my son, Dantès!" exclaimed the old man. "You are the child of my captivity. My profession condemns me to celibacy. God has sent you to me to console, at one and the same time, the man who could not be a father and the prisoner who could not get free." And Faria extended the arm which he still could use to the young man, who threw himself on his neck and wept.

CHAPTER XIX

THE THIRD ATTACK

Now that this treasure which had so long been the object of the abbé's meditations could insure the future happiness of him whom Faria really loved as a son, it had doubled its value in his eyes, and every day he expatiated on the amount, explaining to Dantès all the good which with thirteen or fourteen millions of livres a man could do in these days to his friends; and then Dantès's countenance became gloomy, for the oath of vengeance he had taken recurred to his memory, and he reflected how much ill in these times a man with thirteen or fourteen millions could do to his enemies.

The abbé did not know the Isle of Monte Cristo; but Dantès knew it and had often passed it, situated twenty-five miles from Pianosa, between Corsica and the Isle of Elba, and had once touched at it. This island was, always had been, and still is, completely deserted. It is a rock of almost conical form, which seems as though projected by some volcanic effort from the depth to the surface of the ocean. Dantès traced a plan of the island for Faria, and Faria gave Dantès advice as to the means he should employ to recover the treasure. But Dantès was far from being as enthusiastic and confident as the old man. It was certain indeed that Faria was not a lunatic, and the way in which he had achieved the discovery which had given rise to the suspicion of his madness increased Dantès's admiration of him; but at the same time he could not believe that that deposit, supposing it had ever existed, still existed; and though he considered the treasure as by no means chimerical, he yet believed it was no longer there.

However, as if fate resolved on depriving the prisoners of their last chance, and making them understand that they were condemned to perpetual imprisonment, a new misfortune befell them; the gallery on the sea side, which had long been in ruins, was rebuilt. They repaired it completely, and stopped up with vast masses of stone the hole Dantès had partly filled in. But for this precaution, which it will be remembered had been suggested to Edmond by the abbé, the misfortune would have been still greater,—for their attempt to escape would have been discovered, and they would undoubtedly have been separated. Thus a new and even stronger door was closed upon them.

"You see," said the young man, with an air of sorrowful resignation, to Faria, " that God deems it right to take from me even what you call my devotion to you. I have promised to remain for ever with you, and now I could not break my promise if I would. I shall no more have the treasure than you; and neither of us will quit this prison. But my real treasure is not that, my dear friend, which awaits me beneath the sombre rocks of Monte Cristo, but it is your presence,—our living together five or six hours a day, in spite of our jailers; it is those rays of intelligence you have elicited from my brain, the languages you have implanted in my memory, and which spring there with all their philological ramifications. These different sciences that you have made so easy to me by the depth of the knowledge you possess of them and the clearness of the principles to which you have reduced them,—this is my treasure, my beloved friend, and with this you have made me rich and happy. Believe me, and take comfort; this is better for me than tons of gold and cases of diamonds, even were they not perhaps delusive,—like the clouds we see in the morning floating over the sea, which we take for *terra firma*, and which evaporate and vanish as we draw near to them. To have you as long as possible near me; to hear your eloquent voice enriching my mind, strengthening my soul, and making my whole frame capable of great and terrible things if I should ever be free, so filling my soul that the despair to which I was just on the point of yielding when I knew you has no longer any hold over me,—this is my fortune, and there is nothing uncertain about it. I owe it all to you; and all the sovereigns of the earth, were they Cæsar Borgias, could not take it from me."

Thus the days which these two unfortunates passed together, if they were not happy days, at least went as quickly as the days that followed. Faria, who for so long a time had kept silence as to the treasure, now perpetually talked of it. As he had foreseen, he remained paralysed in the right arm and the left leg, and had given up all hope of ever enjoying it himself. But he was continually thinking over some means of escape for his young companion, and he enjoyed it for him. For for the letter might be some day lost or abstracted, he compelled Dantès to learn it by heart; and he thus knew it from one end to the other. Then he destroyed the second portion, assured that if the first were seized, no one would be able to penetrate its real meaning. Whole hours sometimes passed while Faria was giving instructions to Dantès,—instructions which were to serve him when he was at liberty. Then, once free, from the day and hour and moment when he was so, he could have but one only thought, which was to gain Monte Cristo by some means and remain there alone under some pretext which would give no suspicions; and once there, to endeavour to find the wonderful cavern and search in the appointed spot,—the appointed spot, be it remembered, being the farthest angle in the second opening.

In the meanwhile the hours passed, if not rapidly, at least tolerably. Faria, as we have said, without having recovered the use of his hand and foot, had resumed all the clearness of his understanding, and had gradually, besides the moral instructions we have detailed, taught his youthful companion the patient and sublime duty of a prisoner, who learns to make something from nothing. They were thus perpetually employed,

—Faria, that he might not see himself grow old; Dantès, for fear of recalling the almost extinct past which now floated in his memory like a distant light wandering in the night. So the days passed by as in lives which have not been disordered by calamity and which glide on mechanically and tranquilly beneath the eye of Providence.

But beneath this superficial calm there were in the heart of the young man, and perhaps in that of the old man, many repressed desires, many stifled sighs which found vent when Faria was left alone, and when Edmond returned to his cell. One night Edmond awoke suddenly, believing he heard some one calling him. He opened his eyes and tried to pierce through the gloom. His name, or rather a plaintive voice which essayed to pronounce his name, reached him. "Great God!" murmured Edmond, "what does it mean?"

He moved his bed, drew up the stone, rushed into the passage, and reached the opposite extremity; the secret entrance was open. By the light of the wretched and wavering lamp of which we have spoken, Dantès saw the old man, pale but yet erect, clinging to the bedstead. His features were writhing with those horrible symptoms which Dantès already knew, and which had so seriously alarmed him when he saw them for the first time.

"Well, my friend," said Faria, in a resigned tone, "you understand, do you not; and I need not attempt to explain to you?"

Edmond uttered a cry of agony, and quite out of his senses, rushed towards the door, exclaiming, "Help! help!" Faria had just sufficient strength to retain him.

"Silence!" he said, "or you are lost. Think now of yourself,—of making your captivity supportable or your flight possible. It would require years to renew only what I have done here, and which would be instantly destroyed if our jailers knew we had communicated with each other. Besides, be assured, my dear Edmond, the dungeon I am about to leave will not long remain empty; some other unfortunate being will soon take my place, and to him you will appear like an angel of salvation. Perhaps he will be young, strong, and enduring, like yourself, and will aid you in your escape; while I should only hinder it. You will no longer have a half-dead body tied to you to paralyse all your movements. At length Providence has done something for you; he restores to you more than he takes away, and it is time for me to die."

Edmond could only clasp his hands and exclaim, "Oh, my friend! my friend! speak not thus!" And then resuming all his presence of mind, which had for a moment staggered under this blow, and his strength, which had failed at the words of the old man, he said, " Oh, I have saved you once, and I will save you again ! " And raising the foot of the bed, he drew out the phial, still containing some of the red liquor.

" See ! " he exclaimed ; " there remains still some of this saving draught. Quick, quick ! tell me what I must do this time ; are there any fresh instructions ? Speak, my friend ; I listen."

" There is no hope," replied Faria, shaking his head ; " but no matter. God wills it that man, whom he has created and in whose heart he has so profoundly rooted the love of life, should do all in his power to preserve that existence, which however painful it may be is yet always so dear."

" Oh, yes, yes ! " exclaimed Dantès, " and I tell you you shall yet be saved ! "

" Well, then, try. The cold gains upon me. I feel the blood flowing towards my brain. This horrible trembling which makes my teeth chatter and seems to dislocate my bones, begins to pervade my whole frame ; in five minutes the malady will reach its height, and in a quarter of an hour there will be nothing left of me but a dead body."

" Oh ! " exclaimed Dantès, his heart wrung with anguish.

" Do as you did before, only do not wait so long. All the springs of life are now exhausted in me, and death," he continued, looking at his paralysed arm and leg, " has but half its work to do. If after having made me swallow twelve drops instead of ten, you see that I do not recover, then pour the rest down my throat. Now lift me on my bed, for I can no longer support myself."

Edmond took the old man in his arms, and laid him on the bed.

" And now, friend," said Faria, " sole consolation of my wretched existence,—you whom Heaven gave me somewhat late, but still gave me, a priceless gift, and for which I am most grateful,—at the moment of separating from you for ever, I wish you all the happiness and all the prosperity you so well deserve. My son, I bless thee ! "

The young man cast himself on his knees, leaning his head against the old man's bed.

" Listen now to what I say in this my dying moment. The treasure of the Spadas exists. By the grace of God there is no longer for me either distance or obstacle. I see it in the depths of the inner cavern. My eyes pierce the inmost recesses of the earth and are dazzled at the sight of so much riches. If you do escape, remember that the poor abbé whom all the world called mad was not so. Hasten to Monte Cristo; avail yourself of the fortune,—for you have indeed suffered long enough."

A violent shock interrupted the old man. Dantès raised his head and saw Faria's eyes injected with blood. It seemed as if a wave of blood had ascended from the chest to the head.

"Adieu! adieu!" murmured the old man, clasping Edmond's hand convulsively; "adieu!"

"Oh, no, no! not yet!" he cried; "do not forsake me! Oh, help him! Help! help!"

"Hush! hush!" murmured the dying man, "that they may not separate us if you save me!"

"You are right. Oh, yes, yes! be assured I shall save you! Besides, although you suffer much, you do not seem in such agony as before."

"Do not mistake! I suffer less because there is in me less strength to endure. At your age we have faith in life; it is the privilege of youth to believe and hope, but old men see death more clearly. Oh! 'tis here—'tis here—'tis over—my sight is gone—my reason escapes! Your hand, Dantès! Adieu! —adieu!" And raising himself by a final effort in which he united all his faculties, he said, "Monte Cristo! forget not Monte Cristo!" and he fell back on his bed. The crisis was terrible; on that bed of pain were twisted limbs, swollen eyelids, bloody foam, and a body without motion,—instead of the intelligent being who, a moment before, was lying there.

Dantès took the lamp, and placed it on a projecting stone above the bed, whence its tremulous light fell with strange and fantastic ray on this discomposed countenance and this motionless and stiffened body. With fixed eyes he awaited boldly the moment for administering the saving remedy.

When he believed the instant had arrived, he took the knife, unclosed the teeth, which offered less resistance than before, counted one after the other twelve drops, and watched. The phial contained, perhaps, twice as much more. He waited ten minutes, a quarter of an hour, half an hour; nothing moved. Trembling, his hair erect, his brow bathed with perspiration, he counted the seconds by the beatings of his heart. Then he thought it was time to make the last trial, and he put the phial to the violet lips of Faria; and without having occasion to force open his jaws, which had remained extended, he poured the whole of the liquid down his throat.

The draught produced a galvanic effect; a violent trembling pervaded the old man's limbs; his eyes opened until it was fearful to gaze upon them; he heaved a sigh which resembled a shriek; and then all this vibrating frame returned gradually to its state of immobility, the eyes remaining open.

Half an hour, an hour, an hour and a half elapsed; and during this time of anguish Edmond leaned over his friend, his hand applied to his heart, and felt the body gradually grow cold, and the heart's pulsation become more and more deep and dull, until at length all stopped. The last movement of the heart ceased; the face became livid; the eyes remained open, but the look was glazed. It was six o'clock in the morning; the dawn was just breaking, and its weak ray came into the dungeon and paled the dying light of the lamp. Singular shadows passed over the countenance of the dead man, which at times gave it the appearance of life. While this struggle between day and night lasted, Dantès still doubted; but as soon as the daylight gained the pre-eminence he saw that he was alone with a corpse. Then an invincible and extreme terror seized upon him, and he dared not again press the hand that hung out of bed; he dared no longer to gaze on those fixed and vacant eyes which he tried many times to close, but in vain,— they opened again always. He extinguished the lamp, carefully concealed it, and then went away, closing as well as he could the entrance to the secret passage by the large stone as he descended.

It was time, for the jailer was coming. On this occasion he began his rounds at Dantès's cell, and on leaving him he went on to Faria's dungeon, where he was taking breakfast and some linen. Nothing indicated that the man knew anything of what had occurred. He went on his way.

Dantès was then seized with an indescribable desire to know what was going on in the dungeon of his unfortunate friend. He therefore returned by the subterranean gallery, and arrived in time to hear the exclamations of the turnkey, who called out for help. Other turnkeys came, and then was heard the regular tramp habitual to soldiers even when not on duty; behind them came the governor.

Edmond heard the noise of the bed, on which they were moving the corpse, heard the voice of the governor, who desired them to throw water on the face, and seeing that in spite of this application the prisoner did not recover, sent for the doctor. The governor then went out, and some words of pity fell on Dantès's listening ears, mingled with brutal laughter.

"Well, well!" said one, "the madman has gone to look after his treasure. Good journey to him!"

"With all his millions, he will not have enough to pay for his shroud!" said another.

"Oh!" added a third voice, "the shrouds of the Château d'If are not dear!"

"Perhaps," said one of the previous speakers, "as he was a priest, they may go to some expense in his behalf."

"They may give him the honours of the sack."

Edmond did not lose a word, but comprehended very little of what was said. The voices soon ceased; and it seemed to him as if the persons had all left the cell. Still he dared not to enter, as they might have left some turnkey to watch the dead. He remained, therefore, mute and motionless, restraining even his respiration. At the end of an hour he heard a faint noise, which increased. It was the governor, who returned, followed by the doctor and other attendants. There was a moment's silence; it was evident that the doctor was examining the dead body. The inquiries soon commenced.

The doctor analysed the symptoms of the malady under which the prisoner had sunk, and declared he was dead. Questions and answers followed in a careless tone that made Dantès indignant, for he felt that all the world should experience for the poor abbé the love he bore him.

"I am very sorry for what you tell me," said the governor, replying to the assurance of the doctor that the old man was really dead; "for he was a quiet, inoffensive prisoner, happy in his folly, and required no watching."

"Ah!" added the turnkey, "there was no occasion for watching him; he would have stayed here fifty years, I'll answer for it, without any attempt to escape."

"Still," said the governor, "I believe it will be requisite, notwithstanding your certainty, and not that I doubt your science, but for my own responsibility's sake, that we should be perfectly assured that the prisoner is dead."

There was a moment of complete silence, during which Dantès, still listening, conjectured that the doctor was examining and touching the corpse a second time.

"You may make your mind easy," said the doctor; "he is dead. I will answer for that."

"You know, monsieur," said the governor, persisting, "that we are not content in such cases as this with a simple examination. In spite of all appearances, be so kind therefore as to finish your duty by fulfilling the formalities prescribed by law."

"Let the irons be heated," said the doctor; "but really it is a useless precaution."

This order to heat the irons made Dantès shudder. He heard hasty steps, the creaking of a door, people going and coming; and some minutes afterwards a turnkey entered, saying, "Here is the brazier, lighted."

There was a moment's silence, and then was heard the noise made by burning flesh, of which the peculiar and nauseous smell penetrated even behind the wall where Dantès was listening horrified. At this smell of human flesh carbonised, the damp came over the young man's brow, and he felt as if he should faint.

"You see, monsieur, he is really dead," said the doctor; "this burn in the heel is decisive. The poor fool is cured of his folly, and delivered from his captivity."

"Wasn't his name Faria?" inquired one of the officers who accompanied the governor.

"Yes, sir; and according to his pretension, it was an ancient name. He was, too, very learned, and rational enough on all points which did not relate to his treasure; but on that indeed he was obstinate."

"It is the sort of malady which we call monomania," said the doctor.

"You never found anything in him to complain of?" said the governor to the jailer who had charge of the abbé.

"Never, sir," replied the jailer, "never; on the contrary, he sometimes amused me very much by telling me stories. One day too when my wife was ill, he gave me a prescription which cured her."

"Ah, ah!" said the doctor, "I was ignorant that I had a competitor; but I hope, Monsieur the Governor, that you will show him all proper respect in consequence."

"Yes, yes, make your mind easy; he shall be decently interred in the newest sack we can find. Will that satisfy you?"

"Must we perform that last ceremony in your presence, sir?" inquired a turnkey.

"Certainly. But make haste! I cannot stay here all day." There was a renewed sound of footsteps; and a moment afterwards the noise of rustling cloth reached Dantès ears, the bed creaked on its hinges, and the heavy foot of a man who lifts a weight resounded on the floor; then the bed again creaked under the weight deposited upon it.

"This evening," said the governor.

"Will there be mass?" asked one of the attendants.

"That is impossible," replied the governor. "The chaplain of the château came to me yesterday to beg for leave of absence, in order to take a trip to Hyères for a week. I told him I would attend to the prisoners in his absence. If the poor abbé had not been in such a hurry, he might have had his requiem."

"Pooh, pooh!" said the doctor, with the accustomed impiety of persons of his profession, "he is a churchman. God will respect his profession, and not give the devil a wicked pleasure by sending him a priest." A shout of laughter followed this brutal jest. During this time the operation of shrouding the body was continued.

"This evening," said the governor, when the task was ended.

"At what o'clock?" inquired a turnkey.

"Why, about ten or eleven o'clock."

"Shall we watch by the corpse?"

"Of what use would it be? Shut the dungeon as if he were alive; that is all."

Then the steps retreated, and the voices died away in the distance. The noise of the door, with its creaking hinges and bolts, ceased; and a silence duller than any solitude ensued,— the silence of death, which embraced everything, even to the young man's frozen soul. Then he raised the flag-stone cautiously with his head, and looked carefully round the chamber. It was empty; and Dantès, quitting the passage, entered it.

CHAPTER XX

THE CEMETERY OF THE CHÂTEAU D'IF

On the bed, at full length, and faintly lighted by the pale ray that penetrated the window, was visible a sack of coarse cloth, under the large folds of which were stretched a long and stiffened form; it was Faria's last winding-sheet,—that winding-sheet which, as the turnkey said, cost so little. All, then, was completed. A material separation had taken place between Dantès and his old friend; he could no longer see those eyes which had remained open as if to look even beyond death; he could no longer clasp that hand of industry which had lifted for him the veil that had concealed hidden and obscure things. Faria, the useful and the good companion with whom he was accustomed to live so intimately, no longer breathed. He seated himself on the edge of that terrible bed, and fell into a melancholy and gloomy reverie.

Alone! he was alone again!—fallen back into silence! He found himself once again in the presence of nothingness! Alone, —no longer to see, no longer to hear the voice of the only human being who attached him to life! Was it not better, like Faria, to go and ask of God the meaning of life's enigma at the risk of passing through the mournful gate of suffering? The idea of suicide, driven away by his friend and forgotten in his presence while living, arose like a phantom before him in presence of his dead body. "If I could die," he said, "I should go where he goes, and should assuredly find him again. But how to die? It is very easy," he continued with a smile of bitterness; "I will remain here; I will rush on the first person who opens the door; I will strangle him, and then they will guillotine me."

But as it happens that in excessive griefs, as in great tempests, the abyss is found between the tops of the loftiest waves, Dantès recoiled from the idea of this infamous death and passed suddenly from despair to an ardent desire for life and liberty.

"Die! oh, no!" he exclaimed; "not die now, after having lived so long, and suffered so much! It might have been good to die when I formed the purpose to do so, years ago; but now it would be indeed to give way to my bitter destiny. No, I will live; I will struggle to the very last; I will reconquer the happiness of which I have been deprived. Before I die I must not forget that I have my executioners to punish, and perhaps too, who knows, some friends to reward. But here I am, forgotten; and I shall go out from my dungeon only as Faria goes." As he said this he remained motionless, his eyes fixed like a man struck with a sudden idea, but whom this idea fills with amazement. Sudenly he rose, lifted his hand to his brow as if his brain were giddy, paced twice or thrice round his chamber, and then paused abruptly at the bed. "Ah! ah!" he muttered, "who inspires me with this thought? Is it thou, gracious God? Since none but the dead pass freely from this dungeon, let me assume the place of the dead!"

Without giving himself time to reconsider his decision, and indeed that he might allow his thoughts to be distracted from his desperate resolution, he bent over the appalling sack, opened it with the knife which Faria had made, drew the corpse from the sack, and carried it to his cell, laid it on his couch, passed round its head the strip of cloth he wore at night round his own, covered it with his counterpane, once again kissed the ice-cold brow and tried vainly to close the resisting eyes, which remained open, turned the head towards the wall, so that the jailer might, when he brought his evening meal, believe that he was asleep, as was his frequent custom, returned along the gallery, drew the bed against the wall, returned to the other cell, took from the hiding-place the needle and thread, flung off his rags, that they might feel naked flesh only beneath the coarse sackcloth, and getting inside the sack, placed himself in the posture in which the dead body had been laid, and sewed up the mouth of the sack on the inside.

The beating of his heart might have been heard if by any mischance the jailers had entered at that moment. He might have waited until the evening visit was over, but he was afraid the governor might change his resolution and order the dead body to be removed earlier; in that case his last hope would have been destroyed. Now his project was settled under any circumstances, and he hoped thus to carry it into effect. If on the way out the grave-diggers should discover that they were conveying a live instead of a dead body, Dantès did not intend to give them time to recognise him, but with a sudden cut of the knife he meant to open the sack from top to bottom and profiting by their alarm, escape; if they tried to catch him, he would use his knife. If they conducted him to the cemetery and laid him in the grave, he would allow himself to be covered with earth; and then, as it was night, the grave-diggers could scarcely have turned their backs ere he would work his way through the soft soil and escape. He hoped that the weight would not be too heavy for him to support. If he was deceived in this, and the earth proved too heavy, he would be stifled, and then so much the better; all would be over. Dantès had not eaten since the previous evening, but he had not thought of hunger or thirst, nor did he now think of it. His position was too precarious to allow him time to think of anything else.

The first risk that Dantès ran was that the jailer, when he brought his supper at seven o'clock, might perceive the substitution he had effected; fortunately, twenty times at least, from misanthropy or fatigue, Dantès had received his jailer in bed; and then the man placed his bread and soup on the table, and went away without saying a word. This time the jailer might not be silent as usual, but speak to Dantès, and seeing that he received no reply, go to the bed and thus discover all.

When seven o'clock came, Dantès agony really commenced. His hand placed upon his heart was unable to repress its throbbings, while with the other he wiped the perspiration from his temples. From time to time shudderings ran through his whole frame and oppressed his heart as if it were seized in an icy grasp. Then he thought he was going to die. Yet the hours passed on without any stir in the château, and Dantès perceived that he had escaped this first danger; it was a good augury. At length, about the hour the governor had appointed, footsteps were heard on the stairs. Edmond understood that the moment had arrived, and summoning up all his courage, held his breath; he would have been glad to repress at the same time the rapid pulsations of his arteries.

The steps paused at the door; there were steps of two persons, and Dantès guessed it was the two grave-diggers who came to seek him. This idea was soon converted into certainty when he heard the noise they made in putting down the hand-bier. The door opened, and a dim light reached Dantès's eyes through the coarse sack that covered him; he saw two shadows approach his bed, a third remaining at the door with a torch in his hand. Each of these two men, approaching the ends of the bed, took the sack by its extremities.

" He's heavy, though, for an old and thin man," said one, as he raised the head.

" They say every year adds half a pound to the weight of the bones," said another, lifting the feet.

" Have you tied the knot? " inquired the first speaker.

" What would be the use of carrying so much more weight? " was the reply; " I can do that when we get there."

" Yes, you're right," replied the companion.

" What's the knot for? " thought Dantès.

They deposited the supposed corpse on the bier. Edmond stiffened himself in order to play his part of a dead man, and then the party, lighted by the man with the torch, who went first, ascended the stairs. Suddenly Dantès felt the fresh and sharp night air, and he recognised the *mistral*. It was a sudden sensation, at the same time replete with delight and agony. The bearers advanced twenty paces, then stopped, putting their bier down on the ground. One of them went away, and Dantès heard his shoes on the pavement.

" Where am I, then? " he asked himself.

" Really, he is by no means a light load! " said the other bearer, sitting on the edge of the hand-barrow. Dantès's first impulse was to escape, but fortunately he did not attempt it.

" Light me, stupid," said the other bearer, " or I shall not find what I am looking for." The man with the torch complied, although n)t asked in the most polite terms.

" What can he be looking for? " thought Edmond. " The spade, perhaps."

An exclamation of satisfaction indicated that the grave-digger had found the object of his search. "Here it is at last," he said, "not without some trouble, though."

"Yes," was the answer; "but it has lost nothing by waiting."

As he said this, the man came towards Edmond, who heard a heavy and sounding substance laid down beside him, and at the same moment a cord was fastened round his feet with sudden and painful violence.

"Well, have you tied the knot?" inquired the grave-digger who was looking on.

"Yes, and pretty tight too, I can tell you," was the answer.

"Move on, then." And the bier was lifted once more, and they proceeded. They advanced fifty paces farther, and then stopped to open a door, then went forward again. The noise of the waves dashing against the rocks on which the château is built, reached Dantès's ear distinctly as they proceeded.

"Bad weather!" observed one of the bearers; "not a pleasant night for a dip in the sea."

"Why, yes, the abbé runs a chance of being wet," said the other; and then there was a burst of laughter. Dantès did not comprehend the jest, but his hair stood erect on his head.

"Well, here we are at last," said one of them.

"A little farther! a little farther!" said the other. "You know very well that the last was stopped on his way, dashed on the rocks, and the governor told us next day that we were careless fellows."

They ascended five or six more steps, and then Dantès felt that they took him, one by the head and the other by the heels, and swung him to and fro. "One!" said the grave-diggers, "two! three, and away!" And at the same instant Dantès felt himself flung into the vast void, passing through the air like a wounded bird,—falling, falling with a rapidity that made his blood curdle. Although drawn downwards by some heavy weight which hastened his rapid descent, it seemed to him that the fall continued through a hundred years. At last, with a terrific dash he entered the ice-cold water; and as he did so he uttered a shrill cry, stifled in a moment by his immersion beneath the waves.

Dantès had been flung into the sea, into whose depths he was dragged by a thirty-six pound shot tied to his feet. The sea is the cemetery of Château d'If.

CHAPTER XXI

THE ISLE OF TIBOULEN

DANTÈS, although giddy and almost suffocated, had yet sufficient presence of mind to hold his breath; and as his right hand (prepared as he was for every chance) held his knife open, he rapidly ripped up the sack and extricated his arm and then his body; but in spite of all his efforts to free himself from the ball, he continued to sink. He then bent his body and by a desperate effort severed the cord that bound his legs, at the moment he was suffocating. With a vigorous spring he rose to the surface of the sea, while the bullet bore to its depths the sack that had so nearly become his shroud.

Dantès merely paused to breathe, and then dived again, in order to avoid being seen. When he rose a second time, he was fifty paces from where he had first sunk. He saw overhead a black and tempestuous sky, over which the wind was driving the fleeting vapours that occasionally suffered a twinkling star to appear; before him was the vast expanse of waters, sombre and terrible, whose waves foamed and roared as if before the approach of a storm. Behind him, blacker than the sea, blacker than the sky, rose like a phantom the giant of granite, whose projecting crags seemed like arms extended to seize their prey; and on the highest rock was a torch that lighted two figures. He fancied these two forms were looking at the sea; doubtless these strange grave-diggers had heard his cry. Dantès dived again, and remained a long time beneath the water. This manœuvre was already familiar to him, and usually attracted a crown of spectators in the bay before the lighthouse at Marseilles when he swam there, who with one accord pronounced him the best swimmer in the port. When he reappeared the light had disappeared.

It was necessary to strike out to sea. Ratonneau and Pomègue are the nearest isles of all those that surround the Château d'If; but Ratonneau and Pomègue are inhabited, and so is the little island of Daume. Tiboulen or Lemaire were the most secure. These islands are a league from the Château d'If; Dantès nevertheless determined to make for them. But how could he find his way in the darkness of the night? At this moment he saw before him, like a brilliant star, the lighthouse of Planier. By leaving this light on the right, he kept the Isle of Tiboulen a little on the left; by turning to the left, therefore, he would find it. But as we have said, it was at least a league from the Château d'If to this island. Often in prison Faria had said to him when he saw him idle and inactive, "Dantès, you must not give way to this listlessness; you will be drowned if you seek to escape and your strength has not been properly exercised and prepared for exertion." These words sounded in Dantès's ears, even beneath the waves; he hastened to cleave his way through them to see if he had not lost his strength. He found with pleasure that his captivity had taken away nothing of his power, and that he was still master of that element on whose bosom he had so often sported as a boy.

Fear, that relentless pursuer, doubled Dantès's efforts. He listened to ascertain if any noise was audible; each time that he rose over the waves his looks scanned the horizon and strove to penetrate the darkness. Every wave a little higher than others seemed a boat in his pursuit, and then he redoubled exertions that increased his distance from the château, but the repetition of which reduced his strength. He swam on still, and already the terrible château had disappeared in the darkness. He could not see it, but he felt its presence.

An hour passed, during which Dantès, excited by the feeling of freedom, continued to cleave the waves. "Let us see," said he, "I have swum above an hour, but as the wind is against me that has retarded my speed; however, if I am not mistaken, I must be close to the Isle of Tiboulen. But what if I were mistaken?" A shudder passed over him. He sought to float on the water, in order to rest himself; but the sea was too violent, and he saw that he could not make use of this means of repose.

"Well," said he, "I will swim on until I am worn out, or the cramp seizes me, and then I shall sink." And he struck out with the energy of despair.

Suddenly the sky seemed to him to become still darker and more dense, and compact clouds lowered towards him; at the same time he felt a violent pain in his knee. His imagination told him a ball had struck him, and that in a moment he would hear the report; but he heard nothing. He put out his hand and felt resistance; he then extended his leg and felt the land; he saw then what the object was which he had taken for a cloud.

Before him rose a mass of strangely-formed rocks that resembled nothing so much as a vast fire petrified at the moment of its most fervent combustion. It was the Isle of Tiboulen. Dantès rose, advanced a few steps, and with a fervent prayer of gratitude stretched himself on the granite, which seemed to him softer than down. Then, in spite of the wind and rain, he fell into the deep, sweet sleep of those worn out by fatigue. At the expiration of an hour Edmond was awakened by the roar of the thunder. The tempest was unchained and let loose in all its fury; from time to time a flash of lightning ran across the heavens like a fiery serpent, lighting up the clouds that rolled on like the waves of an immense chaos.

Dantès had not been deceived; he had reached the first of the two isles, which is in fact Tiboulen. He knew that it was barren and without shelter; but when the sea should become more calm, he would plunge into its waves again and swim to Lemaire, equally arid, but larger and consequently better adapted for concealment.

An overhanging rock offered him a temporary shelter, and scarcely had he availed himself of it when the tempest burst in all its fury. Edmond felt the rock beneath which he lay tremble; the waves, dashing themselves against the granite rock, wet him with their spray. In safety as he was, he felt himself become giddy in the midst of this war of the elements and the dazzling brightness of the lightning. It seemed to him that the island trembled to its base, and that it would like a vessel at anchor break its moorings and bear him off into the centre of the storm. He then recollected that he had not eaten or drunk for four-and-twenty hours. He extended his hands and drank greedily of the rain-water that had lodged in a hollow of the rock.

As he rose, a flash of lightning, that seemed to open the sky even to the foot of the dazzling throne of God, illumined the darkness. By its light, between the island of Lemaire and Cape Croiselle, a quarter of a league distant, Dantès saw, like a spectre, a fishing-boat driven rapidly on by the force of the winds and waves. A second after, he saw it again, approaching nearer. Dantès cried at the top of his voice to warn them of their danger, but they saw it themselves. Another flash showed him four men clinging to the shattered mast and the rigging, while a fifth clung to the broken rudder.

The men he beheld saw him doubtless, for their cries were carried to his ears by the wind. Above the splintered mast a sail rent to tatters was waving; suddenly the ropes that still held it gave way, and it disappeared in the darkness of the night like a great sea-bird. At the same moment a violent crash was heard, and cries of distress reached his ears. Perched on the summit of the rock, Dantès saw, by the lightning, the vessel in pieces; and among the fragments were visible heads with despairing faces, and arms stretched towards the sky.

Then all became dark again; the terrible spectacle had been brief as the lightning.

Dantès ran down the rocks at the risk of being himself dashed to pieces. He listened, he strove to examine; but he heard and saw nothing. All human cries had ceased, and the tempest alone continued to rage. By degrees the wind abated, vast grey clouds rolled towards the west, and the blue firmament appeared, studded with bright stars. Soon a red streak became visible in the horizon; the waves whitened, a light played over them and gilded their foaming crests with gold. It was day.

Dantès stood silent and motionless before this grand spectacle, for since his captivity he had forgotten it. He turned towards the fortress and looked both at the sea and the land. The gloomy building rose from the bosom of the ocean with that imposing majesty of things immovable, which seem at once to watch and to command. It was about five o'clock. The sea continued to grow calmer.

"In two or three hours," thought Dantès, "the turnkey will enter my chamber, find the body of my poor friend, recognise it, seek for me in vain, and give the alarm. Then the passage will be discovered; the men who cast me into the sea, and who must have heard the cry I uttered, will be questioned. Then boats filled with armed soldiers will pursue the wretched fugitive. The cannon will warn every one to refuse shelter to a man wandering about naked and famished. The police of Marseilles will be on the alert by land while the governor pursues me by sea. I am cold, I am hungry; I have lost even the knife that saved me. Oh, my God, I have suffered enough surely! Have pity on me, and do for me what I am unable to do for myself!"

As Dantès (his eyes turned in the direction of the Château d'If) uttered this prayer in a sort of delirium brought on by exhaustion, he saw appear at the extremity of the Isle of Pomègue, like a bird skimming over the sea, a small vessel that the eye of a sailor alone could recognise as a Genoese tartan. She was coming out of Marseilles harbour, and was standing out to sea rapidly, her sharp prow cleaving through the waves. "Oh!" cried Edmond, "to think that in half an hour I could join her, did I not fear being questioned, detected, and conveyed back to Marseilles! What can I do? What story can I invent? Under pretext of trading along the coast, these men, who are in reality smugglers, will prefer selling me to doing a good action. I must wait. But I cannot; I am starving. In a few hours my strength will be utterly exhausted; besides, perhaps I have not been missed at the fortress. I can pass as one of the sailors wrecked last night. This story will pass current, for there is no one left to contradict me."

As he spoke Dantès looked towards the spot where the fishing-vessel had been wrecked, and started. The red cap of one of the sailors hung to a point of the rock, and some fragments of the vessel's keel floated at the foot of the crags. In an instant Dantès's plan was formed. He swam to the cap, placed it on his head, seized one of the fragments of the keel, and struck out so as to cross the line the vessel was taking. "I am saved!" murmured he. And this conviction restored his strength.

Edmond soon perceived the vessel, which, having the wind right ahead, was tacking between the Château d'If and the tower of Planier. For an instant he feared that instead of keeping in shore she would stand out to sea; but he soon saw by her manœuvres that she wished to pass, like most vessels bound for Italy, between the islands of Jaros and Calaseraigne. However, the vessel and the swimmer insensibly neared one another, and in one of its tacks the vessel approached within a quarter of a mile of him. He rose on the waves, making signs of distress; but no one on board perceived him and the vessel stood on another tack. Dantès would have cried out, but he reflected that the wind would drown his voice. Then he rejoiced at his precaution in taking the beam, for without it he would have been unable perhaps to reach the vessel,—certainly to return to shore, should he be unsuccessful in attracting attention.

Dantès, although almost sure as to what course the bark would take, had yet watched it anxiously until it tacked and stood towards him. Then he advanced; but before they had met, the vessel again changed her direction. By a violent effort he rose half out of the water, waving his cap and uttering a loud shout peculiar to sailors. This time he was both seen and heard, and the tartan instantly steered towards him. At the same time he saw they were about to lower the boat. An instant after the boat, rowed by two men, advanced rapidly towards him. Dantès abandoned the beam, which he thought now useless, and swam vigorously to meet them. But he had reckoned too much upon his strength, and then he felt how serviceable the beam had been to him. His arms grew stiff, his legs had lost their flexibility, and he was almost breathless.

He uttered a second cry. The two sailors redoubled their efforts, and one of them cried in Italian, "Courage!"

The word reached his ear as a wave which he no longer had the strength to surmount passed over his head. He rose again to the surface, supporting himself by one of those desperate efforts a drowning man makes, uttered a third cry, and felt himself sink again, as if the fatal bullet were again tied to his feet. The water passed over his head, and through the water he saw a pale sky and black clouds. A violent effort again brought him to the surface. He felt as if something seized him by the hair; but he saw and heard nothing. He had fainted.

When he opened his eyes Dantès found himself on the deck of the tartan. His first care was to see what direction they were pursuing. They were rapidly leaving the Château d'If behind. Dantès was so exhausted that the exclamation of joy he uttered was mistaken for a sigh of pain.

As we have said, he was lying on the deck. A sailor was rubbing his limbs with a woollen cloth; another, whom he recognised as the one who had cried out "Courage!" held a gourd full of rum to his mouth; while the third, an old sailor, at once the pilot and captain, looked on with that egotistical pity men feel for a misfortune that they have escaped yesterday and which may overtake them to-morrow. A few drops of the rum reanimated the young man's failing heart, while the friction applied to his limbs restored their elasticity.

"Who are you?" said the captain, in bad French.

"I am," replied Dantès, in bad Italian, "a Maltese sailor. We were coming from Syracuse laden with grain. The storm of last night overtook us at Cape Morgion, and we were wrecked on these rocks."

"Where do you come from?"

"From these rocks that I had the good luck to cling to while our captain and the rest of the crew were all lost. I saw your ship, and fearful of being left to perish on the desolate island, I swam off on a fragment of the vessel, trying to reach you. You have saved my life, and I thank you," continued Dantès; "I was lost when one of your sailors caught hold of my hair."

"It was I," said a sailor of a frank and manly appearance; "and it was time, for you were sinking."

"Yes," returned Dantès, holding out his hand, "I thank you again."

"I almost hesitated, though," replied the sailor; "you looked more like a brigand than an honest man, with your beard of six inches and your hair a foot long." Dantès recollected that his hair and beard had not been cut all the time he was at the Château d'If.

"Yes," said he, "I made a vow to our Lady of the Grotto

not to cut my hair or beard for ten years if I were saved in a
moment of danger; but to-day the vow expires."

"Now what are we to do with you?" said the captain.

"Alas! anything you please. My captain is dead. I have
barely escaped; but I am a good sailor. Leave me at the first
port you make; I shall be sure to find employment on some
merchant-vessel."

"Do you know the Mediterranean?"

"I have sailed over it since my childhood."

"You know the best harbours?"

"There are few ports that I could not enter or leave with my
eyes shut."

"I say, captain," said the sailor who had cried "Courage!"
to Dantès, "if what he says is true, what hinders his staying
with us?"

"If he says true," said the captain, doubtingly. "But in
the condition of this poor devil, one promises much and does
what he can."

"I will do more than I promise," said Dantès.

"We shall see," returned the other, smiling.

"Where are you going?" asked Dantès.

"To Leghorn."

"Then why, instead of tacking so frequently, do you not sail
nearer the wind?"

"Because we should run straight on to the island of Rion."

"You will pass it more than twenty fathoms from the shore."

"Take the helm, and let us see what you know."

The young man took the helm, ascertained by a slight pressure
that the vessel answered the rudder, and seeing that without
being a first-rate sailer, she yet was tolerably manageable, he
cried out, "To the braces!"

The four seamen who composed the crew obeyed, while the
captain looked on.

"Haul taut!" Dantès continued.

The sailors promptly obeyed.

"Belay!"

This order was also executed; and the vessel passed, as
Dantès had predicted, twenty fathoms to the right.

"Bravo!" said the captain.

"Bravo!" repeated the sailors. And they all regarded with
astonishment this man, whose eye had recovered an intelligence
and his body a vigour they were far from suspecting.

"You see," said Dantès, quitting the helm, "I shall be of
some use to you, at least during the voyage. If you do not want

me at Leghorn, you can leave me there; and I will pay you out of the first wages I get for my food and the clothes you lend me."

"Ah," said the captain, "we can agree very well, if you are reasonable."

"Give me what you give the others, and all will be arranged," returned Dantès.

"That's not fair," said the seaman who had saved Dantès; "for you know more than we do."

"What in the devil is that to you, Jacopo?" returned the captain. "Every one is free to ask what he pleases."

"That's true," replied Jacopo; "I only made a remark."

"Well, you would do much better to lend him a jacket and a pair of trousers, if you have them to spare."

"No," said Jacopo; "but I have a shirt and a pair of trousers."

"That is all I want," interrupted Dantès. "Thank you, my friend."

Jacopo dived into the hold and soon returned with the two garments, which Dantès assumed with unspeakable pleasure.

"Now, then, do you wish for anything else?" said the captain.

"A piece of bread and another glass of the capital rum I tasted; for I have not eaten or drunk for a long time." He had not tasted food for forty hours. A piece of bread was brought, and Jacopo offered him the gourd.

"Larboard your helm!" cried the captain to the steersman. Dantès glanced to the same side as he lifted the gourd to his mouth; but his hand stopped.

"Holloa! what's the matter at the Château d'If?" said the captain.

A small white cloud, which had attracted Dantès's attention, crowned the summit of the bastion of the Château d'If. At the same moment the faint report of a gun was heard. The sailors looked at one another.

"What does that mean?" asked the captain.

"A prisoner has escaped from the Château d'If, and they are firing the alarm gun," replied Dantès. The captain glanced at him; but he had lifted the rum to his lips and was drinking it with so much composure that his suspicions, if he had any, died away.

"This rum is devilish strong," said Dantès, wiping the perspiration from his brow with his shirt-sleeve.

"At any rate," murmured the captain, watching him, "if it is he, so much the better, for I have made a rare acquisition."

Under pretence of being fatigued, Dantès asked that he might

take the helm; the steersman, enchanted to be relieved, looked
at the captain, and the latter by a sign indicated that he might
abandon it to his new comrade. Dantès could thus keep his
eyes on Marseilles.

"What is the day of the month?" asked he of Jacopo, who
sat down beside him.

"The 28th of February."

"In what year?"

"In what year! you ask me in what year?"

"Yes," replied the young man; "I ask you in what year."

"You have forgotten it, then?"

"I was so frightened last night," replied Dantès, smiling,
"that I have almost lost my memory. I ask you what year
is it?"

"The year 1829," returned Jacopo. It was fourteen years
day for day since Dantès's arrest. He was nineteen when he
entered the Château d'If; he was thirty-three when he escaped.
A sorrowful smile passed over his face; he asked himself what
had become of Mercédès, who must believe him dead. Then his
eyes lighted up with hatred as he thought of the three men who
had caused him so long and wretched a captivity. He renewed
against Danglars, Fernand, and Villefort the oath of implacable
vengeance he had made in his dungeon. This oath was no longer
a vain menace; for the fastest sailer in the Mediterranean would
have been unable to overtake the little tartan, that with every
stitch of canvas set was flying before the wind to Leghorn.

CHAPTER XXII

THE SMUGGLERS

DANTÈS had not been a day on board before he was well acquainted with the persons with whom he sailed. Without
having been in the school of the Abbé Faria, the worthy master
of *La Jeune Amélie* (the name of the Genoese tartan) had a
smattering of all the tongues spoken on the shores of that large
lake called the Mediterranean, from the Arabic to the Provençal;
and this, while it spared him the necessity of employing inter-
preters,—persons always troublesome and frequently indiscreet,
—gave him great facility in communication, either with the
vessels he met at sea, with the small barks sailing along the
coast, or with those persons without name, country, or apparent
calling, who are always seen on the quays of seaports, and who

live by those hidden and mysterious means which we must suppose come straight from Providence, as they have no visible resources. We may conclude that Dantès was on board a smuggling lugger.

For the reason given above, the captain had received Dantès on board wth a certain degree of mistrust. He was very well known to the custom-house officers of the coast; and as there was between these worthies and himself a competition in strategy, he had at first thought that Dantès might be an emissary of the revenue department, who employed this ingenious means of penetrating some of the secrets of his trade. But the skilful manner in which Dantès had manœuvred the little bark had entirely reassured him; and then when he saw the light smoke floating like a plume above the bastion of the Château d'If and heard the distant explosion, he was instantly struck with the idea that he had on board his vessel one for whom they accord salutes of cannons as for kings. This made him less uneasy, it must be owned, than if the new-comer had proved a custom-house officer; but this latter supposition also disappeared like the first, when he beheld the perfect tranquillity of his recruit.

Edmond thus had the advantage of knowing what the owner was, without the owner knowing what he was; and in whatever manner the old sailor and his crew attacked him, he held firm and betrayed nothing, giving accurate descriptions of Naples and Malta, which he knew as well as Marseilles, and persisting stoutly in his first statement. Thus the Genoese, subtle as he was, was duped by Edmond, who was aided by his mild demeanour and his nautical skill. Moreover, it is possible that the Genoese was one of those shrewd persons who know nothing but what they should know, and believe nothing but what it is for their interest to believe.

It was thus, in this reciprocal position, that they reached Leghorn. Here Edmond was to undergo another trial; it was to see if he should recognise himself after fourteen years in which he had not seen his own features. He had preserved a tolerably good remembrance of what the youth had been, and was now to find what the man had become. His comrades believed that his vow was fulfilled. He had previously touched twenty times at Leghorn; he remembered a barber in the Rue St. Ferdinand, and went there to have his beard and hair cut. The barber gazed in amazement at this man with the long hair and thick and black beard, who resembled one of Titian's glorious heads. At this period it was not the fashion to wear so large a beard and hair so long; now a barber would only be surprised if a man gifted with such advantages should consent voluntarily to deprive himself of them. The Leghorn barber went to work without a single observation.

When the operation was concluded, when Edmond felt his chin was completely smooth and his hair reduced to its usual length, he called for a looking-glass in which he might see himself. He was now, as we have said, three-and-thirty years of age, and his fourteen years' imprisonment had produced a great moral change, so to speak, in his appearance. Dantès had entered the Château d'If with the round open smiling face of a young and happy man with whom the early paths of life have been smooth, and who expects the future to be a natural sequence of the past. This was now all changed. His oval face was lengthened; his smiling mouth had assumed the firm and marked lines which betoken resolution; above his arched eyebrows appeared a solitary wrinkle, expressing thoughtfulness; his eyes were full of melancholy, and from their depths occasionally sparkled gloomy fires of misanthropy and hatred; his complexion, so long kept from the sun, had now that pale colour which produces when the features are encircled with black hair the aristocratic beauty of the man of the North; the deep learning he had acquired had besides diffused over his features the light of calm intelligence; naturally tall, he had acquired also the vigour possessed by a frame which has so long concentrated all its force within itself.

To the elegance of a nervous and slight form had succeeded the solidity of a rounded and muscular figure. As to his voice, his prayers, sobs, and imprecations had changed it, now into a soft and singularly touching tone, and now into a sound rude and almost hoarse. Moreover, being perpetually in twilight or darkness, his eyes had acquired that singular faculty of distinguishing objects in the night common to the hyena and the wolf. Edmond smiled when he beheld himself; it was impossible that his best friend—if indeed he had any friend left—should recognise him; he could not recognise himself.

The captain of *La Jeune Amélie*, who was very desirous of retaining in his crew a man of Edmond's value, had offered to him some advances out of his future profits which Edmond had accepted. His next care on leaving the barber's who had achieved his first metamorphosis was to enter a shop and buy a complete sailor's suit,—a garb, as we all know, very simple, and consisting of white trousers, a striped shirt, and a cap. It was in this costume, when bringing back to Jacopo the shirt and trousers he had lent him, that Edmond reappeared before the captain of *La Jeune Amélie*, who had made him tell his story again. The captain could not recognise in the neat and trim sailor the man with thick and matted beard, his hair tangled with sea-weed, and his body soaking in sea brine, whom he had picked up naked and nearly drowned. Attracted by his prepossessing appearance, he renewed his offers of an engagement to Dantès; but Dantès, who had his own projects, would not agree for a longer time than three months.

La Jeune Amélie had a very active crew, very obedient to their captain, who was accustomed to lose as little time as possible. He had scarcely been a week at Leghorn before the hold of his vessel was filled with painted muslins, prohibited cottons, English powder, and tobacco on which the crown had forgotten to put its mark. The master was to get all this out of Leghorn free of duties and land it on the shores of Corsica, where certain speculators undertook to forward the cargo to France. They sailed; Edmond was again cleaving the azure sea which had been the first horizon of his youth, and of which he had so often dreamed in prison. He left Gorgone on his right and La Pianosa on his left, and went towards the country of Paoli and Napoleon. The next morning, going on deck, which he always did at an early hour, the captain found Dantès leaning against the bulwarks gazing with intense earnestness at a pile of granite rocks which the rising sun tinged with rosy light. It was the Isle of Monte Cristo. *La Jeune Amélie* left it three quarters of a league to the larboard, and kept on for Corsica.

Dantès thought as they passed thus closely the island whose name was so interesting to him that he had only to leap into the sea and in half an hour he would be on the promised land. But then what could he do without instruments to discover his treasure, without arms to defend himself? Besides, what would the sailors say; what would the captain think? He must wait. Fortunately, he had learned how to wait; he had waited fourteen years for his liberty, and now that he was free he could wait at least six months or a year for wealth. Would he not have accepted liberty without riches if it had been offered to him? Besides, were not those riches chimerical; offspring of the brain of the poor Abbé Faria, had they not died with him? It is true that letter of the Cardinal Spada was singularly circumstantial, and Dantès repeated to himself from one end to the other the letter, of which he had not forgotten a word.

The evening came on, and Edmond saw the island pass, covered with the tints that twilight brings, and disappear in the darkness from all eyes except his own; but he, with his gaze accustomed to the gloom of a prison, continued to see it after all the others, and he remained last upon deck. When the morning broke they were off the coast of Aleria; all day they coasted, and in the evening saw the fires lighted on land. By the arrangement of these fires they were probably informed that it was practicable to land,—for a ship's lantern was hung up at the mast-head instead of the streamer, and they neared the shore within gunshot. Dantès remarked that the captain of *La Jeune Amélie* had as he neared the land mounted two small culverines, which without making much noise can throw a ball of four to the pound a thousand paces or so.

But on this occasion the precaution was superfluous, and everything proceeded with the utmost smoothness. Four shallops came off with very little noise alongside the bark, which, no doubt in acknowledgment of the compliment, lowered her own shallop into the sea; and the five boats worked so well that by two o'clock in the morning all the cargo was out of *La Jeune Amélie* and on *terra firma*. The same night, so systematic was the captain of *La Jeune Amélie*, the profits were divided; and each man had a hundred Tuscan livres,—that is to say, about eighty livres of our money. But the voyage was not ended; they turned the bowsprit towards Sardinia, where they intended to take in a cargo, which was to replace what had been discharged. The second operation was as successful as the first; *La Jeune Amélie* was in luck. This new cargo was destined for the coast of the Duchy of Lucca, and consisted almost entirely of Havana cigars, sherry, and Malaga wines.

There, in going out, they had a bit of a skirmish with the revenue police, that relentless enemy to the captain of *La Jeune Amélie*. A custom-house officer was laid low and two sailors were wounded; Dantès was one of the latter, a ball having touched him in the left shoulder. Dantès was almost glad of this affray and almost pleased at being wounded; they were rude lessons which taught him with what eye he could view danger, and with what endurance he could bear suffering. He had contemplated danger with a smile, and when wounded had exclaimed with the great philosopher, "Pain, thou art not an evil!" He had moreover looked upon the custom-house officer wounded to death, and whether from heat of blood produced by the rencontre, or the dulness of his humane sentiments, this sight had made but slight impression upon him. Dantès was on the way he desired to follow, and was moving towards the end he wished to achieve,—his heart was in a fair way of becoming petrified. Jacopo, seeing him fall, had believed him killed, and rushing towards him raised him up, and then attended to him with all the kindness of an attached comrade.

This world was not then so good as Doctor Pangloss believed it to be, neither was it so wicked as Dantès had considered it, since this man, who had nothing to expect from his comrade but the inheritance of his share of the prize-money, testified so much sorrow when he saw him fall. Fortunately, as we have said, Edmond was only wounded; and with certain herbs gathered at certain seasons, and sold to the smugglers by the old Sardinian women, the wound soon closed. Edmond, wishing to test Jacopo, offered him in return for his attention a share of his prize-money; but Jacopo refused it indignantly.

It resulted therefore from this kind of sympathetic devotion, which Jacopo had bestowed on Edmond from the first time he saw him, that Edmond felt for Jacopo a certain degree of affection; it was sufficient for Jacopo, who already instinctively perceived Edmond's superior rank,—a superiority concealed from all others; and with that measure of regard which Edmond bestowed upon him the brave sailor was content.

Then in the long days on board ship when the vessel, gliding on with security over the azure sea, required nothing, thanks to the favourable wind that swelled her sails, but the hand of the helmsman, Edmond with a chart in his hand became the instructor of Jacopo, as the poor Abbé Faria had been his instructor. He pointed out to him the bearings of the coast, explained to him the variations of the compass, and taught him to read in that vast book opened over our heads, called " the heavens," where God has written upon the azure with letters of diamond. And when Jacopo asked him, " What is the use of teaching all these things to a poor sailor like me ? " Edmond replied, " Who knows ? You may one day be the captain of a vessel. Your fellow-countryman, Bonaparte, became emperor." We have forgotten to say that Jacopo was a Corsican.

Two months and a half elapsed in these trips, and Edmond had become as skilful a coaster as he had been a hardy seaman; he had formed an acquaintance with all the smugglers on the coast, and learned all the masonic signs by which these half-pirates recognise each other. He had passed and repassed his Isle of Monte Cristo twenty times, but not once had he found an opportunity of landing there. He then formed a resolution: as soon as his engagement with the captain of *La Jeune Amélie* ended, he would hire a small bark on his own account,—for in his several voyages he had amassed a hundred piastres,—and under some pretext land at the Isle of Monte Cristo. Then he would be free to make his researches,—not perhaps entirely free, for he would be doubtless watched by those who accompanied him; but in this world we must risk something. Prison had made Edmond prudent, and he was desirous of running no risk whatever. But in vain did he rack his imagination; fertile as it was, he could not devise any plan for reaching the wished-for isle without being accompanied thither.

Dantès was tossed about on these doubts and wishes when the captain, who had great confidence in him and was very desirous of retaining him in his service, took him by the arm one evening and led him to a tavern on the Via del' Oglio, where the leading smugglers of Leghorn used to congregate. It was here they discussed the affairs of the coast. Already Dantès had visited this maritime Bourse two or three times, and seeing all these hardy free-traders, who supplied the whole coast for nearly two hundred leagues, he had asked himself what power might not that man attain who should give the impulse of his will to all these contrary and diverging links. This time it was a great matter that was under discussion,—connected with a vessel laden with Turkey carpets, stuffs of the Levant, and cashmeres. It was necessary to agree upon some neutral ground on which an exchange could be made, and then to try and land these goods on the coast of France. If successful, the profit would be enormous; there would be a gain of fifty or sixty piastres each for the crew.

The captain of *La Jeune Amélie* proposed as a place of landing the island of Monte Cristo, which being completely deserted and having neither soldiers nor revenue officers seemed to have been placed in the midst of the ocean since the time of the heathen Olympus by Mercury, the god of merchants and robbers,—classes which we in modern times have separated, if not made distinct, but which antiquity appears to have included in the same category. At the mention of Monte Cristo Dantès started with joy; he rose to conceal his emotion, and took a turn round the smoky tavern, where all the languages of the known world were jumbled in a *lingua franca.* When he again joined the two persons who had been discussing, it had been decided that they should touch at Monte Cristo, and set out on the following night. Edmond, being consulted, was of opinion that the island offered every possible security, and that great enterprises, to be well done, should be done quickly. Nothing, then, was altered in the plan arranged, and it was agreed that they should get under way next night, and wind and weather permitting, try to gain on the evening of the following day the waters of the neutral isle.

CHAPTER XXIII

THE ISLE OF MONTE CRISTO

THUS, at length, by one of those pieces of unlooked-for good fortune which sometimes occur to those on whom misfortune has for a long time spent itself, Dantès was about to arrive at his wished-for opportunity by simple and natural means, and and on the island without incurring any suspicion. One night only separated him from his expedition so ardently wished for.

That night was one of the most feverish that Dantès had ever passed, and during its progress all the possibilities, favourable and unfavourable, passed through his brain. If he closed his eyes, he saw the letter of Cardinal Spada written on the wall in characters of flame; if he slept for a moment, the wildest dreams haunted his brain. He descended into grottos paved with emeralds, with walls of rubies, and the roof glowing with diamond stalactites. Pearls fell drop by drop, as subterranean moisture is wont to drop. Edmond, amazed, wonderstruck, filled his pockets with the radiant gems and then returned to daylight, when his prizes were all converted into common pebbles. He then endeavoured to re-enter these marvellous grottos, but now the way serpentined into countless paths, and the entrance had become invisible. In vain did he tax his memory for the magic and mysterious word which opened the splendid caverns of Ali Baba to the Arabian fisherman. All was useless; the treasure had disappeared, and had again reverted to the genii from whom for a moment he had hoped to carry it off.

The day came at length, and was almost as feverish as the night had been; but it brought reason to the aid of imagination, and Dantès was then enabled to arrange a plan which had hitherto been vague and unsettled in his brain. The appointed evening arrived, and preparations were made for setting out. These preparations served to conceal Dantès's agitation. He had by degrees assumed such authority over his companions that he was almost like a commander on board; and as his orders were always clear, distinct, and easy of execution, his comrades obeyed him with celerity and pleasure.

The old captain did not interfere, for he too had recognised the superiority of Dantès over the crew and himself. He saw in the young man his natural successor, and regretted that he had not a daughter, that he might have bound Edmond to him by a distinguished alliance. At seven o'clock in the evening all was ready, and at ten minutes past seven they doubled the lighthouse just as the light was kindled. The sea was calm, and with a fresh breeze from the south-east they sailed beneath a bright blue sky in which God also lighted up in turn his beacon-lights, each of which is a world. Dantès told them that all hands might turn in, and he would take the helm. When the Maltese (for so they called Dantès) had said this, it was sufficient, and all went to their cots contentedly. This frequently happened. Dantès, rejected by all the world, sometimes felt an imperious desire for solitude; and what solitude is at the same time so complete and so poetical as that of a vessel floating isolated on the sea in the obscurity of night, in the silence of immensity, and under the eye of Heaven?

At this time the solitude was peopled with his thoughts, the night lighted up by his illusions, and the silence animated by his anticipations. When the captain awoke, the vessel was hurrying on with every sail set and every inch of cloth blown upon by the wind. They were making nearly ten knots an hour. The island of Monte Cristo loomed large in the horizon. Edmond resigned the vessel to the master's care and went and lay down in his hammock; but in spite of his previous night without sleep, he could not close his eyes for a moment. Two hours afterwards he came on deck as the boat was about to double the island of Elba. They were just abreast of Mareciana, and beyond the flat but verdant Isle of La Pianosa. The peak of Monte Cristo, reddened by the burning sun, was seen against the azure sky. Dantès desired the helmsman to port the helm, in order to leave La Pianosa on the right hand, expecting thus to decrease the distance by two or three knots. At about five o'clock in the evening the view of the island was quite distinct and everything on it was plainly perceptible, owing to that atmospheric brightness which is peculiar to the light which the rays of the sun cast at its setting.

Edmond gazed most earnestly at the mass of rocks which gave out all the variety of twilight colours from the brightest pink to the deepest blue; and from time to time his cheeks flushed, his brow became purple, and a mist passed over his eyes. Never did gamester whose whole fortune is staked on one cast of the die experience the anguish which Edmond felt in his paroxysms of hope. Night came; and at ten o'clock they anchored. *La Jeune Amélie* was the first at the rendezvous. In spite of his usual command over himself, Dantès could not restrain his impetuosity. He was the first who jumped on shore; and had he dared, he would, like Lucius Brutus, have " kissed his mother earth." It was dark; but at eleven o'clock the moon rose in the midst of the ocean, whose every wave she silvered, and then, as she ascended, played in floods of pale light on the rocky hills of this second Pelion.

The island was familiar to the crew of *La Jeune Amélie;* it was one of her halting-places. As to Dantès, he had passed it on his voyages to and from the Levant, but never touched at it. He questioned Jacopo. "Where shall we pass the night?" he inquired.

"Why, on board the tartan," replied the sailor.

"Should we not be better in the grottos?"

"What grottos?"

"Why, the grottos of the island."

"I do not know of any grottos," replied Jacopo.

A cold damp sprang to Dantès brow. "What! are there no grottos at Monte Cristo?" he asked.

"None."

For a moment Dantès was speechless; then he remembered that these caves might have been filled up by some accident, or even stopped up for the sake of greater security, by Cardinal Spada. The point was, then, to discover the lost opening. It was useless to search at night, and Dantès therefore delayed all investigation until the morning. Besides, a signal made half a league out at sea, and to which *La Jeune Amélie* also replied by a similar signal, indicated that the moment was arrived for business. The vessel waiting outside, assured by the answering signal that all was as it should be, soon came in sight, white and silent as a phantom, and cast anchor within a cable's length of shore.

Then the landing began. Dantès reflected as he worked on the shout of joy which with a single word he could produce from among all these men if he gave utterance to the one unchanging thought that filled his heart; but far from disclosing this precious secret, he almost feared that he had already said too much, and that by his restlessness and continual questions, his minute observations and evident preoccupation, he had aroused suspicions. Fortunately, as regarded this circumstance at least, with him the painful past reflected on his countenance an indelible sadness; and the glimmerings of gaiety seen beneath this cloud were indeed but transitory.

No one had the slightest suspicion; and when next day, taking a fowling-piece, powder, and shot, Dantès testified a desire to go and kill some of the wild goats that were seen springing from rock to rock, his wish was construed into a love of sport or a desire for solitude. However, Jacopo insisted on following him; and Dantès did not oppose this, fearing if he did so that he might arouse distrust. Scarcely, however, had he gone a quarter of a league than having killed a kid, he begged Jacopo to take it to his comrades and request them to cook it, and when ready to let him know by firing a gun. Some dried fruits and a flask of the wine of Monte Pulciano would complete the repast. Dantès went forwards, looking behind and round about him from time to time. Having reached the summit of a rock, he saw, a thousand feet beneath him, his companions whom Jacopo had rejoined, and who were all busy preparing the repast which Edmond's skill as a marksman had augmented with a capital dish.

Edmond looked at them for a moment with the sad and soft smile of a man superior to his fellows. " In two hours' time," said he, " these persons will depart richer by fifty piastres each, to go and risk their lives again by endeavouring to gain fifty more such pieces; then they will return with a fortune of six hundred livres and waste this treasure in some city with the pride of sultans and the insolence of nabobs. At this moment hope makes me despise their riches, which seem to me contemptible. Yet perchance to-morrow disillusion will so act on me that I shall be compelled to consider such a contemptible possession as the utmost happiness. Oh, no! " he exclaimed, " that will not be. The wise, unerring Faria could not be mistaken in this one thing. Besides, it were better to die than to continue to lead this low and wretched life." Thus Dantès, who but three months before had no desire but liberty, had now not liberty enough, and panted for wealth. The cause was not in Dantès, but in Providence, who while limiting the power of man has filled him with boundless desires.

Meanwhile, by a way hidden between two walls of rock, following a path worn by a torrent, and which in all human probability human foot had never before trod, Dantès approached the spot where he supposed the grottos must have existed. Keeping along the coast, and examining the smallest object with serious attention, he thought he could trace on certain rocks marks made by the hand of man.

Time, which incrusts all physical substances with its mossy mantle, as it invests all things moral with its mantle of forgetfulness, seemed to have respected these signs, traced with certain regularity, and probably with design. Occasionally these marks disappeared beneath tufts of myrtle, which spread into large bushes laden with blossoms, or beneath parasitica lichen. It was thus requisite that Edmond should remove branches or remove the mosses in order to perceive the indicating marks which were to be his guides in this labyrinth. These signs had renewed hope in his mind. Why should it not have been the cardinal who had first traced them, in order that they might, in the event of a catastrophe which he could not foresee would have been so complete, serve as a guide for his nephew? This solitary place was clearly one likely to be selected by a man desirous of burying a treasure. Only, might not these betraying marks have attracted other eyes than those for whom they were made; and had the dark and wondrous isle indeed faithfully guarded its precious secret?

It seemed however to Edmond, who was hidden from his comrades by the inequalities of the ground, that at sixty paces from the harbour the marks ceased; nor did they terminate at any grotto. A large round rock, placed solidly on its base, was the only spot to which they seemed to lead. Edmond reflected that perhaps instead of having reached the end, he had only touched on the beginning, and he therefore turned round and retraced his steps.

During this time his comrades had prepared the repast, had got some water from a spring, spread out the fruit and bread, and cooked the kid. Just at the moment when they were taking the dainty animal from the spit, they saw Edmond, who, light and daring as a chamois, was springing from rock to rock, and they fired the signal agreed upon. The sportsman instantly changed his direction and ran quickly towards them. But at the moment when they were all following with their eyes his agile bounds, the boldness of which alarmed them, Edmond's foot slipped, and they saw him stagger on the edge of a rock and disappear. They all rushed towards him, for all loved Edmond in spite of his superiority; but Jacopo reached him first.

He found Edmond stretched bleeding and almost senseless. He had rolled down a height of twelve or fifteen feet. They poured some drops of rum down his throat, and this remedy, which had before been so beneficial to him, produced the same effect as formerly. He opened his eyes, complained of great pain in his knee, a feeling of heaviness in his head, and severe pains in his loins. They wished to carry him to the shore, but when they touched him, although under Jacopo's directions, he declared with heavy groans that he could not bear to be moved

It may be supposed that Dantès did not now think of his dinner, but he insisted that his comrades, who had not his reasons for fasting, should have their meal. As for himself, he declared that he had only need of a little rest, and that when they returned he should be easier. The sailors did not require much urging. They were hungry, and the smell of the roasted kid was very savoury, and your tars are not very ceremonious. An hour afterwards they returned. All that Edmond had been able to do was to drag himself about a dozen paces forward to lean against a moss-covered rock.

But, far from being easier, Dantès's pains had appeared to increase in violence. The old captain, who was obliged to sail in the morning in order to land his cargo on the frontiers of Piedmont and France, between Nice and Frejus, urged Dantès to try and rise. Edmond made great exertions in order to comply; but at each effort he fell back, moaning and turning pale.

"He has broken his ribs," said the captain, in a low voice. "No matter; he is an excellent fellow, and we must not leave him. We will try to carry him on board the tartan." Dantès declared however that he would rather die where he was than undergo the agony caused by the slightest movement he made.

"Well," said the captain, "let what may happen, it shall never be said that we deserted a good comrade like you. We will not go till evening."

This very much astonished the sailors, although not one opposed it. The captain was so strict that this was the first time they had ever seen him give up an enterprise, or even delay an arrangement. Dantès would not allow that any such infraction of regular and proper rules should be made in his favour. "No, no," he said to the captain, "I was awkward, and it is just that I should pay the penalty of my clumsiness. Leave me a small supply of biscuit, a gun, powder, and balls, to kill the kids or defend myself at need, and a pickaxe, to build me something like a shed if you delay in coming back for me."

"But you'll die of hunger," said the captain.

"I would rather do so," was Edmond's reply, "than suffer the inexpressible agonies which the slightest motion brings on."

The captain turned towards his vessel, which was lying in the small harbour with her sails partly set, and nearly ready for sea.

"What are we to do, Maltese?" asked the captain. "We cannot leave you here in this condition, and yet we cannot stay."

"Go, go!" exclaimed Dantès.

"We shall be absent at least a week," said the captain, "and then we must run out of our course to come here and take you up again."

"Why," said Dantès, "if in two or three days you hail any fishing-boat, desire them to come here to me. I will pay twenty-five piastres for my passage back to Leghorn. If you do not come across one, return for me."

The captain shook his head.

"Listen, Captain Baldi; there's one way of settling this," said Jacopo. "Do you go, and I will stay and take care of the wounded man."

"And give up your share of the venture," said Edmond, "to remain with me?"

"Yes," said Jacopo, "and without any hesitation."

"You are a good fellow and a kind-hearted messmate," replied Edmond, "and Heaven will recompense you for your generous intentions; but I do not wish any one to stay with me. A rest of one or two days will set me up, and I hope I shall find among the rocks certain herbs most excellent for contusions;" and a singular smile passed over his lips. He squeezed Jacopo's hand warmly; but nothing could shake his determination to remain,—and remain alone.

The smugglers left with Edmond what he had requested and departed, but not without turning about several times, and each time making signs of a cordial leave-taking, to which Edmond replied with his hand only, as if he could not move the rest of his body. Then, when they had disappeared, he said with a smile, "'Tis strange that it should be among such men that we find proofs of friendship and devotion." Then he dragged himself cautiously to the top of a rock from which he had a full view of the sea, and thence he saw the tartan complete her preparations for sailing, weigh anchor, and balancing herself as gracefully as a water-fowl ere it takes to the wing, set sail. At the end of an hour she was completely out of sight; at least, it was impossible for the wounded man to see her any longer from the spot where he was. Then Dantès rose, more agile and light than the kid among the myrtles and shrubs of these wild rocks, took his gun in one hand, his pickaxe in the other, and hastened towards the rock on which the marks he had noted terminated. "And now," he exclaimed, remembering the tale of the Arabian fisherman which Faria had related to him,— "now, open sesame!"

CHAPTER XXIV

THE SECRET CAVE

THE sun had nearly reached the meridian, and his scorching rays fell full on the rocks, which seemed themselves sensible of the heat. Thousands of grasshoppers, hidden in the bushes, chirped with a monotonous and dull note; the leaves of the myrtle and olive trees waved and rustled in the wind. At every step that Edmond took he disturbed the lizards glittering with the hues of the emerald; afar off he saw the wild goats bounding from crag to crag. In a word, the isle was inhabited, yet Edmond felt himself alone, guided by the hand of God. He felt an indescribable sensation somewhat akin to dread,—that dread of the daylight which even in the desert makes us fear that we are observed. This feeling was so strong that at the moment when Edmond was about to commence his labour, he stopped, laid down his pickaxe, seized his gun, mounted to the summit of the highest rock, and from thence gazed round in every direction.

But it was not upon Corsica, the very houses of which he could distinguish, nor on Sardinia, nor on the Isle of Elba with its historical associations, nor upon the almost imperceptible line that to the experienced eye of a sailor alone revealed the coast of Genoa the proud and Leghorn the commercial, that he gazed. It was upon the brigantine that had left in the morning and the tartan that had just set sail, that Edmond fixed his eyes. The first was just disappearing in the straits of Bonifacio; the other, following an opposite direction, was about to round the island of Corsica. This sight reassured him. He then looked at the objects near him. He saw himself on the highest point of the isle, a statue on this vast pedestal of granite, nothing human in sight; while the blue ocean beat against the base of the island and covered it with a fringe of foam. Then he descended with cautious and slow step, for he dreaded lest an accident similar to that he had so adroitly feigned should happen in reality.

Dantès, as we have said, had traced back the marks in the rock; and he had noticed that they led to a small creek, hidden like the bath of some ancient nymph. This creek was sufficiently wide at its mouth and deep in the centre to admit of the entrance of a small vessel of the *spéronare* class, which would be perfectly concealed from observation.

Then following the clue that in the hands of the Abbé Faria had been so skilfully used to guide him through the Dædalian labyrinth of probabilities, he thought that Cardinal Spada, anxious not to be watched, had entered the creek, concealed his little vessel, followed the line marked by the notches in the rock, and at the end of it had buried his treasure. It was this idea that had brought Dantès back to the circular rock. One thing only perplexed Edmond and went against his theory. How could this rock, which weighed several tons, have been lifted to this spot without the aid of many men? Suddenly an idea flashed across his mind. "Instead of raising it," thought he, "they lowered it." And he sprang from the rock in order to inspect the base on which it had formerly stood. He soon perceived that a slope had been formed, and the rock had slid along this until it stopped at the spot it now occupied. A large stone had served as a wedge; flints and pebbles had been inserted around it so as to conceal the orifice; this species of masonry had been covered with earth, and grass and weed had grown there, moss had clung to the stones, myrtle-bushes had taken root, and the old rock seemed fixed to the earth.

Dantès raised the earth carefully, and detected, or fancied he detected, the ingenious artifice. He attacked this wall, cemented by the hand of Time, with his pickaxe. After ten minutes' labour the wall gave way, and a hole large enough to insert the arm was opened. Dantès went and cut the strongest olive-tree he could find, stripped off its branches, inserted it in the hole, and used it as a lever. But the rock was too heavy and too firmly wedged to be moved by any one man, were he Hercules himself. Dantès saw that he must attack this wedge; but how? He cast his eyes around, and saw the horn full of powder which his friend Jacopo had left him. He smiled; the infernal invention would serve him for this purpose. With the aid of his pickaxe Dantès dug between the upper rock and the one that supported it a mine similar to those formed by pioneers when they wish to spare human labour, filled it with powder, then made a match by rolling his handkerchief in saltpetre. He lighted it and retired. The explosion was instantaneous; the upper rock was lifted from its base by the terrific force of the powder; the lower one flew into pieces; thousands of insects escaped from the aperture Dantès had previously formed, and a huge snake, like the guardian demon of the treasure, rolled himself along with a sinuous motion and disappeared.

Dantès approached the upper rock, which now without any support leaned towards the sea. The intrepid treasure-seeker walked round it, and selecting the spot where it seemed most open to attack, placed his lever in one of the crevices, and strained every nerve to move the mass. The rock, already shaken by the explosion, tottered on its base. Dantès redoubled his efforts; he seemed like one of the ancient Titans, who uprooted the mountains to hurl them against the father of the gods. The rock yielded, rolled, bounded, and finally disappeared in the ocean.

On the spot it had occupied were visible a circular place and an iron ring let into a square flag-stone. Dantès uttered a cry of joy and surprise; never had a first attempt been crowned with more perfect success. He would fain have continued, but his knees trembled, his heart beat so violently, and his eyes became so dim that he was forced to pause. This feeling lasted but for a moment. Edmond inserted his lever in the ring and exerted all his strength; the flag-stone yielded and disclosed a kind of stair that descended until it was lost in the obscurity of a subterranean grotto. Any one else would have rushed on with a cry of joy. Dantès turned pale, hesitated, and reflected. "Come," said he to himself, "I will be a man. I am accustomed to adversity; I must not be cast down by disappointment. What, then, would be the use of all I have suffered? The heart breaks when after having been elated by flattering hopes, it sees all these illusions destroyed. Faria has dreamed this; Cardinal Spada buried no treasure here. Perhaps he never came here; or if he did, Cæsar Borgia, the intrepid adventurer, the stealthy and indefatigable plunderer, has followed him, discovered his traces, pursued them as I have done, like me raised the stone, and descending before me, has left me nothing." He remained motionless and pensive, his eyes fixed on the sombre aperture that was open at his feet, and said, "Now that I expect nothing, now that I have said to myself that it would be folly to entertain any hope, the end of this adventure becomes a simple matter of curiosity." And he still remained motionless and thoughtful.

"Yes, yes; this is an adventure worthy a place in the lights and shades of the life of this royal bandit. This fabulous event has formed but a link of a vast chain. Yes, Borgia has been here, a torch in one hand, a sword in the other, and within twenty paces, at the foot of this rock perhaps, two guards kept watch on land and sea while their master descended as I am about to descend, dispelling the darkness before his terrible advance."

"But what was the fate of these guards who thus possessed his secret?" asked Dantès of himself.

"The fate," replied he, smiling, "of those who buried Alaric."

"Yet had he come," thought Dantès, "he would have found the treasure; and Borgia, he who compared Italy to an artichoke which he could devour leaf by leaf, knew too well the value of time to waste it in replacing this rock. I will go down."

Then he descended with a smile of doubt on his lips, and murmuring that last word of human philosophy, " Perhaps!" But instead of the darkness and the thick and mephitic atmosphere he had expected to find, Dantès saw a dim and bluish light which, as well as the air, entered, not merely by the aperture he had just formed, but by interstices and crevices of the rock which were invisible from without, and through which he could distinguish the blue sky and the waving branches of the evergreen oaks and the tendrils of the creepers that grew from the rocks. After having stood a few minutes in the cavern, the atmosphere of which was rather warm than damp, Dantès's eye, habituated as it was to darkness, could pierce even to the remotest angles of the cavern, which was of granite that sparkled like diamonds. "Alas!" said Edmond, smiling, "these are the treasures the cardinal has left; and the good abbé, seeing in a dream these glittering walls, has indulged in fallacious hopes."

But he called to mind the words of the will, which he knew by heart. "In the farthest angle of the second opening," said the cardinal's will. He had found only the first grotto; he had now to seek the second. Dantès began his search. He reflected that this second grotto would naturally penetrate deeper into the island; he examined the stones and sounded one part of the wall where he fancied the opening existed, masked for precaution's sake. The pickaxe sounded for a moment with a dull sound that covered Dantès's forehead with large drops of perspiration. At last it seemed to him that one part of the wall gave forth a more hollow and deeper echo; he eagerly advanced, and with the quickness of perception that no one but a prisoner possesses, saw that it was there in all probability the opening must be.

However, he, like Cæsar Borgia, knew the value of time; and in order to avoid a fruitless toil, he sounded all the other walls with his pickaxe, struck the earth with the butt of his gun, and finding nothing that appeared suspicious, returned to that part of the wall whence issued the encouraging sound he had before heard. He again struck it, and with greater force. Then a singular sight presented itself. As he struck the wall, a species of stucco similar to that used as the ground of arabesques detached itself, and fell to the ground in flakes, exposing a large white stone. The aperture of the rock had been closed with stones, then this stucco had been applied, and painted to imitate granite. Dantès struck with the sharp end of his pickaxe, which entered some way between the interstices of the stone. It was there he must dig. But by some strange phenomenon of the human organisation, in proportion as the proofs that Faria had not been deceived became stronger, so did his heart give way and a feeling of discouragement steal over him. This last proof instead of giving him fresh strength deprived him of it. The pickaxe fell, almost dropping out of his hands; he placed it on the ground, passed his hand over his brow, and remounted the stairs, alleging to himself as an excuse a desire to be assured that no one was watching him, but in reality because he felt he was ready to faint. The isle was deserted, and the sun seemed to cover it with its fiery glance; afar off a few small fishing-boats studded the bosom of the blue ocean.

Dantès had tasted nothing, but he thought not of hunger at such a moment; he hastily swallowed a few drops of rum and again entered the cavern. The pickaxe that had seemed so heavy was now like a feather in his grasp; he seized it and attacked the wall. After several blows he perceived that the stones were not cemented, but merely placed one upon the other and covered with stucco; he inserted the point of his pickaxe, and using the handle as a lever, soon saw with joy the stone turn as if on hinges and fall at his feet. He had nothing more to do now but with the iron tooth of the pickaxe to draw the stones towards him by one one. The first aperture was sufficiently large to enter, but by waiting, he could still cling to hope and retard the certainty of deception. At last, after fresh hesitation Dantès entered the second grotto. The second grotto was lower and more gloomy than the other; the air, that could enter only by the newly-formed opening, had that mephitic smell Dantès was surprised not to find in the first. He waited in order to allow pure air to displace the foul atmosphere, and then entered. At the left of the opening was a dark and deep angle. But to Dantès's eye there was no darkness. He glanced round this second grotto; it was, like the first, empty.

The treasure, if it existed, was buried in that dark corner. The time had at length arrived; two feet of earth removed, and Dantès's fate would be decided. He advanced towards the angle, and summoning all his resolution, attacked the ground with the pickaxe. At the fifth or sixth blow the pickaxe struck against an iron substance. Never did funeral knell, never did alarm-bell produce a greater effect on the hearer. Had Dantès found nothing, he could not have become more ghastly pale. He again struck his pickaxe into the earth, and encountered the same resistance, but not the same sound. " It is a casket of wood bound with iron," thought he. At this moment a shadow passed rapidly before the opening; Dantès seized his gun, sprang through the opening, and mounted the stair. A wild goat had passed before the mouth of the cave, and was feeding at a little distance. This would have been a favourable opportunity to secure his dinner; but Dantès feared lest the report of his gun should attract attention.

He reflected an instant, cut a branch of a resinous tree, lighted it at the fire at which the smugglers had prepared their breakfast, and descended with this torch. He wished to see all. He approached with the torch the hole he had formed, and saw that his pickaxe had in reality struck against iron and wood. He planted his torch in the ground and resumed his labour. In an instant a space three feet long by two feet broad was cleared, and Dantès could see an oaken coffer, bound with cut steel; in the midst of the lid he saw engraved on a silver plate, which was still untarnished, the arms of the Spada family; namely, a sword, pale, on an oval shield, like all the Italian armorial bearings, and surmounted by a cardinal's hat. Dantès easily recognised them, Faria had so often drawn them for him. There was no longer any doubt,—the treasure was there; no one would have been at such pains to conceal an empty casket. In an instant he had cleared every obstacle away, and he saw successively the lock, placed between two padlocks, and the two handles at each end, all carved as things were carved at that epoch, when art rendered the commonest metals precious. Dantès seized the handles, and strove to lift the coffer; it was impossible. He sought to open it; lock and padlock were closed,—these faithful guardians seemed unwilling to surrender their trust. Dantès inserted the sharp end of the pickaxe between the coffer and the lid, and pressing with all his force on the handle, burst open the fastenings. The hinges yielded in their turn and fell, still holding in their grasp fragments of the planks, and all was open.

A vertigo seized Edmond; he cocked his gun and laid it beside him. He then closed his eyes as children do in order to perceive in the shining night of their own imagination more stars than are visible in the firmament; then he reopened them and stood motionless with amazement. Three compartments divided the coffer. In the first, blazed piles of golden coin; in the second, bars of unpolished gold, which possessed nothing attractive save their value, were ranged; in the third, Edmond grasped handfuls of diamonds, pearls, and rubies, which as they fell on one another sounded like hail against glass. After having touched, felt, examined these treasures, Edmond rushed through the caverns like a man seized with frenzy; he leaped on a rock whence he could behold the sea. He was alone,—alone with these countless, these unheard-of treasures! Was he awake, or was it but a dream?

He would fain have gazed upon his gold, and yet he had not strength enough. For an instant he leaned his head in his hands as if to prevent his senses from leaving him, and then rushed madly about the rocks of Monte Cristo, terrifying the wild goats and scaring the sea-fowls with his wild cries and gestures; then he returned, and still unable to believe the evidence of his senses, rushed into the grotto and found himself before this mine of gold and jewels. This time he fell on his knees, and clasping his hands convulsively, uttered a prayer intelligible to God alone. He soon felt himself calmer and more happy, for now only he began to credit his felicity. He then set himself to work to count his fortune. There were a thousand ingots of gold, each weighing from two to three pounds; then he piled up twenty-five thousand crowns, each worth about eighty livres of our money and bearing the effigies of Alexander VI. and his predecessors, and he saw that the compartment was only half empty. Then he measured ten double handfuls of precious stones, many of which, mounted by the most famous workman of that period, exhibited in their artistic setting a value that was remarkable even by the side of their intrinsic value. Dantès saw the light gradually disappear, and fearing to be surprised in the cavern, left it, his gun in his hand. A piece of biscuit and a small quantity of rum formed his supper, and he snatched a few hours' sleep, lying across the mouth of the cave.

This night was a delicious and yet terrible one, like two or three others which that man of strong emotion had already experienced in his previous life.

CHAPTER XXV

THE UNKNOWN

Daylight, for which Dantès had so eagerly and impatiently waited, again dawned upon the desert shores of Monte Cristo. In the earliest light Dantès rose, climbed the rocky height he had ascended the previous evening, and strained his view to catch every peculiarity of the landscape; but it wore the same wild, barren aspect when seen by the rays of the morning sun which it had done when surveyed by the fading glimmer of eve. Returning to the cave, he raised the stone, filled his pockets with precious stones, put the box together as well and securely as he could, sprinkled fresh sand over the spot from which it had been taken, and carefully trod down the ground to give it everywhere a similar appearance; then, quitting the grotto, he replaced the stone, heaped on it broken masses of rocks and rough fragments of crumbling granite, filling the intervals with earth, planted myrtle and flowering thorn in these intervals, watered the new plants so that they should seem of long standing, effaced the traces of his footsteps around the place, and awaited with impatience the return of his companions. He had no desire to spend his days looking at that gold and those diamonds, or to remain at Monte Cristo like a dragon watching over useless treasures. It was now necessary for him to return to life, to be among men, and to assume in society the rank, influence, and power which in this world wealth alone can give, —the first and grandest of the forces at the disposal of man.

On the sixth day the smugglers returned. From a distance Dantès recognised *La Jeune Amélie*, and dragging himself with affected difficulty towards the landing-place, he met his companions with an assurance that although considerably better than when they quitted him, he still suffered acutely from his late accident. He then inquired how they had fared in their trip. To this question the smugglers replied that although successful in landing their cargo in safety, they had scarcely done so when they received intelligence that a guard-ship had just quitted the port of Toulon and was crowding all sail towards them; this obliged them to make all the speed they could to evade the enemy,—lamenting the absence of Dantès, whose superior skill in the management of a vessel would have availed them so materially. In fact, the chasing vessel had almost overtaken them when fortunately night came on, and enabled them to double the Cape of Corsica, and so elude all further pursuit. Upon the whole, however, the trip had been sufficiently successful to satisfy all concerned; the crew, and particularly Jacopo, expressed great regret that Dantès had not been with them, so that he might have been an equal sharer with themselves in the profits, amounting to no less a sum than fifty piastres each.

Edmond remained impenetrable,—not even smiling at the enumeration of all the benefits he would have reaped had he been able to quit the isle; but as *La Jeune Amélie* had merely come to Monte Cristo to fetch him away, he embarked that same evening and proceeded with the captain to Leghorn. Arrived at Leghorn, he repaired to the house of a Jew, a dealer in precious stones, to whom he disposed of four of his smallest diamonds for five thousand livres each. Dantès half feared that such valuable jewels in the hands of a poor sailor like himself might excite suspicion; but the cunning purchaser asked no troublesome questions concerning a bargain by which he gained at least four thousand livres.

The following day Dantès presented Jacopo with an entirely new vessel, accompanying the gift by a donation of one hundred piastres, that he might provide himself with a suitable crew and other requisites for his outfit,—upon condition that he should go direct to Marseilles and inquire after an old man named Louis Dantès, residing in the Allées de Meillan, and also a young woman called Mercédès, an inhabitant of the Catalan village.

It was Jacopo's turn to think that he was dreaming. Dantès told him that he had been a sailor merely from whim and a desire to spite his friends, who did not allow him as much money as he liked to spend; but that on his arrival at Leghorn he had come into possession of a large fortune, left him by an uncle, whose sole heir he was. The superior education of Dantès gave an air of such extreme probability to this statement that it never once occurred to Jacopo to doubt its accuracy. The term for which Edmond had engaged to serve on board *La Jeune Amélie* having expired, Dantès took leave of the captain, who at first tried all his powers of persuasion to induce him to remain one of the crew, but having been told the history of the legacy, he ceased to importune him further. The succeeding morning Jacopo set sail for Marseilles, with directions from Dantès to join him at the island of Monte Cristo.

Having seen Jacopo fairly out of the harbour, Dantès proceeded to make his final adieux on board *La Jeune Amélie*, distributing so liberal a gratuity among her crew as procured him the unanimous good wishes and expressions of cordial interest in all that concerned him. To the captain he promised to write when he had made up his mind as to his future plans. This leave-taking over, Dantès departed for Genoa. At the moment of his arrival a small yacht was making its trial trip in the bay; it had been built by order of an Englishman, who, having heard that the Genoese excelled all other builders along the shores of the Mediterranean in the construction of fast-sailing vessels, was desirous of possessing a specimen of their skill. The price agreed upon between the Englishman and the Genoese builder was forty thousand livres. Dantès offered sixty thousand livres for it upon condition that it should be delivered to him immediately. The person for whom the yacht was intended had gone upon a tour through Switzerland, and was not expected back in less than three weeks or a month, by which time the builder reckoned upon being able to complete another. A bargain was therefore struck. Dantès led the owner of the yacht to the dwelling of a Jew, retired with the latter individual for a few minutes to a small back parlour, and upon their return the Jew counted out to the ship-builder the sum of sixty thousand livres.

The builder then offered his services in providing a suitable crew for the little vessel, but this Dantès declined with thanks, saying he was accustomed to cruise about quite alone, and his principal pleasure consisted in managing his yacht himself; the only thing he wished was that the builder would contrive a sort of secret closet in the cabin at his bed's head, which should contain three secret compartments. He gave the measure of these compartments, which were completed on the following day.

Two hours afterwards Dantès sailed from the port of Genoa, under the gaze of an immense crowd of the curious who wished to see the rich Spanish nobleman who preferred managing his vessel himself. Dantès handled his vessel admirably; and by aid of the helm, and without having occasion to leave it, he made his yacht perform all the movements he wished. It seemed, indeed, to be inspired by intelligence, so promptly did it obey the slightest impulse given; and Dantès required but a short trial of his beautiful craft to convince himself that the Genoese deserved their high reputation in the art of ship-building. The spectators followed the little vessel with their eyes so long as it remained visible; they then turned their conjectures upon her probable destination. Some insisted she was making for Corsica, others for the island of Elba; bets were offered that she was bound for Spain, while some maintained that she was going to Africa; but no one thought of Monte Cristo.

Nevertheless it was to Monte Cristo that Dantès went. He arrived at the close of the second day; his yacht had proved herself a first-class sailer, and had come the distance from Genoa in thirty-five hours. Dantès had carefully noted the general appearance of the shore, and instead of landing at the usual place, he dropped anchor in the little creek. The isle was utterly deserted, nor did it seem as though human foot had trodden on it since he quitted it. His treasure was just as he had left it. Early on the following morning he began the removal of his riches, and ere nightfall the whole of his immense wealth was safely deposited in the secret compartments of his hidden closet.

A week passed by. Dantès employed it in trying the sailing qualities of his yacht,—studying it as a skilful horseman would the animal he destined for some important service,—till at the end of that time he was perfectly conversant with its good and bad qualities. The former he proposed to augment, the latter to remedy.

Upon the eighth day he discerned a small vessel crowding all sail towards Monte Cristo. As it neared, he recognised it as the vessel which he had given to Jacopo. He immediately signalled it. His signal was returned, and in two hours afterward the bark lay at anchor near the yacht. A mournful answer awaited each of Edmond's eager inquiries. Old Dantès was dead; Mercédès had disappeared. Dantès listened to these melancholy tidings with outward calmness; but when he went ashore he signified his desire to be quite alone. In a couple of hours he returned. Two of the men from Jacopo's bark came on board the yacht to assist in navigating it, and he commanded that she should be steered direct to Marseilles. For his father's death he was in some manner prepared; but what had become of Mercédès?

Without divulging his secret, Dantès could not give sufficiently clear instructions to an agent. There were, besides, other particulars he was desirous of ascertaining, and those were of a nature he alone could investigate in a manner satisfactory to himself. His looking-glass had assured him during his stay at Leghorn that he ran no risk of recognition; and besides, he had now the means of adopting any disguise he thought proper. One fine morning, then, his yacht, followed by the little vessel, boldly entered the port of Marseilles, and anchored exactly opposite the memorable spot whence, on the

never-to-be-forgotten night of his departure for the Château
d'If, he had been put on board the vessel destined to convey
him thither. Dantès could not view without a shudder the
approach of a gendarme in the quarantine boat; but with that
self-possession which he had acquired during his acquaintance
with Faria, Dantès coolly presented an English passport he had
purchased at Leghorn, and by means of that foreign passport,
much more respected in France than our own, Dantès was able
to land without difficulty.

The first object that attracted the attention of Dantès as he
landed on the Canebière was one of the crew of the *Pharaon*.
Edmond hailed the appearance of this man, who had served
under himself, as a sure test of the changes which had been
wrought in his own appearance. Going straight towards him,
he began a variety of questions on different subjects, carefully
watching the man's countenance as he did so; but not a word
or look implied his having the slightest idea of ever having seen
before the individual with whom he was then conversing.
Giving the sailor a piece of money in return for his civility,
Dantès proceeded onwards; but ere he had gone many steps he
heard the man running after him. Dantès instantly turned to
meet him. "I beg your pardon, monsieur," said the honest
fellow, in almost breathless haste, "but I believe you made a
mistake; you intended to give me a two-franc piece, and you
gave me a double napoleon."

"Thank you, my good friend. I see that I have made a
trifling mistake, as you say; but by way of rewarding your
honest spirit I give you another double napoleon, that you may
drink to my health with your comrades."

So extreme was the surprise of the sailor that he was unable
even to thank Edmond, whose receding figure he continued to
gaze after in speechless astonishment. At length, when Dantès
had wholly disappeared, he drew a deep breath, and with
another look at his gold, he returned to the quay, saying to
himself, "It is some nabob arrived from India."

Dantès meanwhile continued his route. Each step he trod
oppressed his heart with fresh emotion. His first and most
indelible recollections were of that place; not a tree, not a street
that he passed failed to awaken dear and cherished reminiscences. When he reached the end of the Rue de Noailles and
perceived the Allées de Meillan, his knees tottered under him
and he nearly fell under the wheels of a carriage. At length he
came to the house in which his father had lived.

The nasturtiums and other plants which the good man had

delighted to train before his window, had all disappeared from the upper part of the house. Leaning against a tree, Dantès remained a long time gazing at that poor little house; then he advanced to the door, and inquired whether there were any chambers to be let in the house. Though answered in the negative, he begged so earnestly to be permitted to visit those on the fifth floor that the *concierge* went up and asked the occupants of the two rooms to allow a stranger to inspect them. The tenants were a young couple married only a week previously; upon seeing them Dantès breathed a deep sigh.

Nothing in the two small chambers forming the apartment remained as it had been in the time of the elder Dantès; the very paper was different. The old furniture, familiar to his childhood, present in all their details to his remembrance, had disappeared; the walls alone remained the same. The bed belonging to the present occupants was placed as the former tenant of the chamber had been accustomed to have his; and in spite of his efforts to prevent it, the eyes of Edmond were suffused with tears as he reflected that on that spot the aged man had expired, vainly calling for his son. The young couple beheld with astonishment this man with a stern countenance, on whose cheeks tears were flowing down; but they felt the sacredness of his grief, and refrained from questioning him. They left him to indulge his sorrow alone. When he withdrew, they both accompanied him downstairs, expressing their hope that he would come again whenever he pleased, and assuring him that their poor dwelling should ever be open to him. As Edmond passed the doors on the fourth floor, he paused at one of them to inquire whether Caderousse the tailor still dwelt there; but he was informed that the individual in question had got into difficulties, and at the present time kept a small inn on the route from Bellegarde to Beaucaire.

Having obtained the address of the person to whom the house in the Allées de Meillan belonged, Dantès next proceeded thither, and under the name of Lord Wilmore (the name and title given in his passport), purchased the small dwelling for the sum of twenty-five thousand livres, at least ten thousand more than it was worth; but had its owner asked ten times the sum he did, it would unhesitatingly have been given. The very same day, the occupants of the apartments on the fifth floor of the house, now become the property of Dantès, were duly informed by the notary who had arranged the necessary transfer of deeds that the new landlord gave them their choice among the rooms in the house without any increase of rent, upon condition of their giving up to him the two small chambers they at present inhabited.

This strange event furnished food for wonder and curiosity in the neighbourhood of the Allées de Meillan, and gave rise to a thousand conjectures, not one of which was correct. But that which raised public astonishment to a climax and set all speculations at defiance was the circumstance that the same stranger who had in the morning visited the Allées de Meillan had been seen in the evening walking in the little village of the Catalans, and afterwards had entered a poor fisherman's hut and spent more than an hour in inquiring after persons who had either been dead or gone away for more than fifteen or sixteen years. On the following day the family from whom all these particulars had been asked received a handsome present, consisting of an entirely new fishing-boat, with a full supply of excellent nets. The delighted recipients of these munificent gifts would gladly have poured out their thanks to their generous benefactor; but they had seen him, upon quitting the hut, merely give some orders to a sailor, and then, springing lightly on horseback, quit Marseilles by the Porte d'Aix.

CHAPTER XXVI

THE INN OF PONT DU GARD

SUCH of my readers as have made a pedestrian excursion to the south of France may perchance have noticed, midway between the town of Beaucaire and the village of Bellegarde, a small roadside inn, from the front of which hangs, creaking and flapping in the wind, a sheet of tin covered with a caricature resemblance of the Pont du Gard. This little inn, if we take our direction from the course of the Rhone, is situated on the left-hand side of the road, with its back to the river. Attached to it is what in Languedoc is styled a garden, consisting of a small plot of ground, a full view of which might be obtained from a door immediately opposite the grand portal by which travellers were ushered in to partake of the hospitality of mine host of the Pont du Gard. In this plaisance, or garden, scorched beneath the ardent sun of a latitude of thirty degrees, a few dingy olives and stunted fig-trees struggle hard for existence, but their withered, dusty foliage abundantly proves how unequal is the conflict. Between these sickly shrubs, grows a scanty supply of garlic, tomatoes, and eschalots; while lone and solitary, like a forgotten sentinel, a tall pine raises its melancholy head in one of the corners of this unattractive spot and displays its flexible stem and fan-shaped summit, dried and cracked by the withering influence of the *mistral*, that scourge of Provence.

In the surrounding plain, which more resembles a dusty lake than solid ground, are scattered a few miserable stalks of wheat, the effect, no doubt, of a curious desire on the part of the agriculturists of the country to see whether the raising of grain in those parched regions is practicable. The scanty stalks, however, serve to accommodate the numerous grasshoppers who follow the unfortunate invader of this bare soil with untiring persecution, resting themselves after their chase upon the stunted specimens of horticulture, while they fill the ear with their sharp, shrill cry.

For about eight years this little inn was kept by a man and his wife, with two servants: one, who was called Trinette, officiated in the capacity of chamber-maid; while the other, named Pacaud, took charge of the stable. But, alas! the occupation of each domestic was but nominal, for a canal recently made between Beaucaire and Aiguemortes had led to the substitution of canal-boats for waggons and barges for the diligence. And as though to add to the daily misery which this prosperous canal inflicted on the unfortunate innkeeper, whose utter ruin it was fast accomplishing, it was situated not a hundred steps from the forsaken inn, of which we have given a brief but faithful description.

The innkeeper was a man of from forty to forty-five years of age, tall, strong, and bony, a good specimen of the natives of those southern latitudes; he had dark, sparkling, and deep-set eyes, curved nose, and teeth white as those of a carnivorous animal; his hair, which in spite of the light touch time had as yet left on it seemed reluctant to whiten, was like his beard, which he wore under his chin, thick and curly, and but slightly mingled with a few silvery threads. His naturally murky complexion had assumed a still further shade of brown from the habit the poor devil had acquired of stationing himself from morning to night at the threshold of his door, in eager hope that some traveller, either equestrian or pedestrian, might bless his eyes, and give him the delight of once more seeing a guest enter his doors. His patience and his expectations were alike useless; yet there he stood, day after day, exposed to the meridional rays of a burning sun, with no other protection for his head than a red handkerchief twisted around it after the manner of the Spanish muleteers. This man was our former acquaintance Caderousse. His wife, on the contrary, whose maiden name had been Madeleine Radelle, was pale, meagre, and sickly-looking. Born in the neighbourhood of Arles, she had shared in the beauty for which its women are proverbial; but that beauty had gradually withered beneath the devastating influence of one of those slow fevers so prevalent in the vicinity of the waters of the Aiguemortes and the marshes of Camargue. She remained nearly always in her chamber, situated on the first floor, sitting shivering in her chair, or extended languid and feeble on her bed, while her husband kept his daily watch at the door,—a duty he performed with the greater willingness, as it saved him the necessity of listening to the endless plaints and murmurs of his helpmate, who never saw him without breaking out into bitter invectives against fate and the unmerited hardships she was called upon to endure; to all of which her husband would calmly return an unvarying reply, couched in these philosophic words: " Be silent, La Carconte; it is God who has arranged these matters."

The sobriquet of La Carconte had been bestowed on Madeleine Radelle on account of her birth in a village so called, situated between Salon and Lambesc; and as a custom existed among the inhabitants of that part of France where Caderousse lived of styling every person by some particular and distinctive appellation, her husband had bestowed on her the name of La Carconte instead of Madeleine, which perhaps was too smooth and euphonious for his rough tongue. Still, let it not be supposed that in spite of his affected resignation to the will of Providence, the unfortunate innkeeper was not profoundly aware of the misery to which he had been reduced by that wretched canal of Beaucaire, or that he was invulnerable to the incessant complaints of his wife, did not writhe under the double misery of seeing the hateful canal carry off alike his customers and profits, and the daily implication of his peevish partner's murmurs and lamentations. Like other dwellers in the South, he was a man of sober habits and moderate desires, but fond of external show, vain, and addicted to display. During the days of his prosperity, not a fête, festivity, or ceremonial took place without himself and wife being among the spectators. He dressed in the picturesque costume worn upon grand occasions by the inhabitants of the south of France, bearing equal resemblance to the style adopted both by the Catalans and Andalusians; while La Carconte displayed the charming fashion prevalent among the women of Arles, a mode of attire borrowed equally from Greece and Arabia. But by degrees, watch-chains, necklaces, many-coloured scarfs, embroidered bodices, velvet vests, elegantly-worked stockings, striped gaiters, and silver buckles for the shoes, all disappeared; and Gaspard Caderousse, unable to appear abroad in his pristine splendour, had given up any further participation in these pomps and vanities, both for himself and his wife, although a bitter feeling of envious discontent filled his mind as the sound of mirth and merry music from the joyous revellers reached even the miserable hostelry to which he still clung,—more for the shelter than the profit it afforded.

Caderousse was, as usual, at his place of observation before the door, his eyes glancing listlessly from a piece of closely-shaven grass, on which some fowls were industriously though fruitlessly endeavouring to turn up some grain or insect suited to their taste, to the deserted road, the two extremities of which pointed respectively north and south, when he was roused from his daily speculations as to the possibility of the inn of the Pont du Gard ever again being called upon to exercise its hospitable capabilities to any chance visitant, by the shrill voice of his wife summoning him to her presence with all speed. Murmuring at the disagreeable interruption to his not very agreeable thoughts, he however proceeded to the story on which was situated the chamber of his better half,—taking care however, preparatory to so doing, to set the entrance-door wide open, as if to invite travellers not to forget him in passing.

At the moment Caderousse quitted his sentry-like watch before the door, the road on which he so eagerly strained his sight was void and lonely as a desert at midday. There it lay stretched out, one interminable line of dust and sand, with its sides bordered by tall, meagre trees, altogether presenting so uninviting an appearance that no one in their senses could have imagined that any traveller at liberty to regulate his hours for journeying would choose to expose himself to the scorch of a meridian sun in that formidable Sahara. Nevertheless, had Caderousse but retained his post a few minutes longer, he might have caught a dim outline of something approaching from the direction of Bellegarde. As the moving object drew nearer, he would easily have perceived it consisted of a man and horse, between whom the kindest and most amiable understanding appeared to exist. The horse was of Hungarian breed, and ambled along with the easy pace peculiar to that race of animals. His rider was a priest, dressed in black, and wearing a three-cornered hat; and spite of the ardent rays of a noonday sun, the pair came on at a tolerably smart trot.

Having arrived before the inn of the Pont du Gard, the horse stopped, but whether for his own pleasure or that of his rider it would have been difficult to say. However that might have been, the priest, dismounting, led his steed by the bridle in search of some place to which he could secure him. Availing himself of a handle that projected from a half-fallen door, he tied the animal safely, patted him kindly, and having drawn a red cotton handkerchief from his pocket, wiped away the perspiration that streamed from his brow; then advancing to the door, he struck thrice with the end of his iron-shod stick. At this unusual sound, a huge black dog came rushing to meet the daring assailant of his ordinarily tranquil abode, snarling and displaying his sharp white teeth with a determined hostility that abundantly proved how little he was accustomed to society. At that moment a heavy footstep was heard descending the wooden staircase that led from the upper floor, and with many bows and courteous smiles appeared the landlord of that small inn, at the door of which the priest was waiting.

"Here I am!" said the astonished Caderousse. "Here I am! Be quiet, Margotin! Don't be afraid, monsieur; he barks, but he never bites. I make no doubt a glass of good wine would be acceptable this dreadfully hot day!" Then perceiving for the first time the description of traveller he had to entertain, Caderousse hastily exclaimed: "A thousand pardons, your Reverence! I did not observe whom I had the honour to receive under my poor roof. What would you please to have, Monsieur the Abbé? What refreshment can I offer you? All I have is at your service."

The priest gazed on the individual addressing him with a long and searching gaze; he even appeared to court a similar scrutiny on the part of the innkeeper. Then, remarking in the countenance of the latter no other expression than extreme surprise at his own want of attention to an inquiry so courteously worded, he deemed it as well to terminate this dumb show, and therefore said, speaking with a strong Italian accent, "You are, I presume, M. Caderousse?"

"Your Reverence is quite correct," answered the host, even more surprised at the question than he had been by the silence which had preceded it; "I am Gaspard Caderousse, at your service."

"Gaspard Caderousse!" rejoined the priest. "Yes, that agrees both with the baptismal appellation and surname of the individual I allude to. You formerly lived, I believe, in the Allées de Meillan, on the fourth floor of a small house situated there?"

"I did."

"Where you followed the business of a tailor?"

"Yes, I was a tailor, till the trade fell off so as not to afford me a living. Then, it is so very hot at Marseilles that really I could bear it no longer; and it is my idea that all the respectable inhabitants will be obliged to follow my example and quit it. But talking of heat, is there nothing I can offer you by way of refreshment?"

"Yes; let me have a bottle of your best wine, and then, with your permission, we will resume our conversation where we leave it."

"As you please, Monsieur the Abbé," said Caderousse, who, anxious not to lose the present opportunity of finding a customer for one of the few bottles of the wine of Cahors still remaining in his possession, hastily raised a trap-door in the floor of the room they were in, which served both as parlour and kitchen. Upon issuing forth from his subterranean retreat at the expiration of five minutes, he found the abbé seated on a species of stool, leaning his elbow on a table, while Margotin, whose animosity seemed to have been appeased by the unusual order for refreshments, had crept up to him, and had established himself very comfortably between his knees, his long skinny neck resting on his lap, while his dim eye was fixed earnestly on the traveller's face.

"Are you quite alone?" inquired the guest, as Caderousse placed before him the bottle of wine and a glass.

"Quite, quite alone," replied the man, "or at least, very near it, Monsieur the Abbé; for my poor wife is laid up with illness, and unable to render me the least assistance, poor thing!"

"You are married, then?" said the priest, with a species of interest, glancing round as he spoke at the scanty style of the accommodation and humble furnishing of the room.

"Ah, Monsieur the Abbé," said Caderousse, with a sigh, "you perceive that I am not a rich man; but to thrive in this world it is not enough to be an honest man."

The abbé fixed on him a penetrating glance.

"Yes, honest man,—I can certainly say that much for myself," continued the innkeeper, fairly sustaining the scrutiny of the abbé; "and," continued he, significantly nodding his head, "that is more than every one can say nowadays."

"So much the better for you, if what you assert be true,"

said the abbé; "for I am firmly persuaded that sooner or later the good will be rewarded and the wicked punished."

"Such words as those belong to your profession, Monsieur the Abbé," answered Caderousse, "and you do well to repeat them; but," added he, with a bitter expression of countenance, "any one is privileged not to believe them."

"You are wrong to speak thus," said the abbé; "and perhaps I may in my own person be able to prove to you the truth of what I have said."

"What do you mean?" inquired Caderousse, with a look of surprise.

"In the first place, I must be satisfied that you are the person I am in search of."

"What proofs do you require?"

"Did you, in the year 1814 or 1815, know anything of a young sailor named Dantès?"

"Dantès! Did I know him, that poor Edmond? I should think I did. He was even one of my best friends!" exclaimed Caderousse, whose countenance assumed an almost purple hue, while the clear calm eye of the questioner seemed to dilate until it completely covered him.

"You remind me," said the priest, "that the young man concerning whom I asked you was said to bear the name of Edmond."

"Said to bear the name!" repeated Caderousse, becoming excited and eager. "Why, he was so called as truly as I myself am called Gaspard Caderousse. But, Monsieur the Abbé, tell me, I pray, what has become of poor Edmond. Did you know him? Is he alive and at liberty? Is he prosperous and happy?"

"He died a prisoner, more wretched, hopeless, heart-broken than the felons who pay the penalty of their crimes at the galleys of Toulon."

A deadly paleness succeeded the deep suffusion which had before spread itself over the countenance of Caderousse. He turned away, and the priest saw him wipe away a tear with the corner of the red handkerchief twisted round his head.

"Poor fellow!" murmured Caderousse. "Well, there, Monsieur the Abbé, is another proof of what I told you,—that the good God is good only to the wicked. Ah," continued Caderousse, speaking in the highly-coloured language of the South, "the world grows worse and worse. Why does not God, if he really hates the wicked, as he is said to do, send down brimstone and fire, and consume them altogether?"

" You speak as though you had loved this young Dantès," observed the abbé.

" And so I did," replied Caderousse; " though once, I confess, I envied him his good fortune. But I swear to you, Monsieur the Abbé, that I have since then deeply and sincerely lamented his unhappy fate."

There was a brief silence, during which the searching gaze of the abbé questioned the mobile features of the innkeeper.

" You knew the poor lad, then? " continued Caderousse.

" I was called to his dying bed that I might administer to him the consolations of religion."

" And of what did he die?" asked Caderousse, in a choking voice.

" Of what does one die in prison at the age of thirty years, if not of the prison itself? "

Caderousse wiped away the large beads of perspiration that gathered on his brow.

" But the strangest part of the story is," resumed the abbé, " that Dantès, even in his dying moments, swore by the Christ whose feet he kissed that he did not know the cause of his imprisonment."

" It is true, it is true! " murmured Caderousse, " he could not know it. Ah, Monsieur the Abbé, the poor fellow told you the truth."

" And he besought me to try and clear up a mystery he had never been able to penetrate, and to clear his memory, should any stain have fallen on it." And here the look of the abbé, becoming more and more fixed, devoured the expression, almost gloomy, which appeared on the face of Caderousse.

" A rich Englishman," continued the abbé, " who had been his companion in misfortune, but was released from prison upon the second restoration, was possessed of a diamond of immense value. On leaving prison he gave this diamond to Dantès as a mark of his gratitude for the kindness and brotherly care with which Dantès had nursed him through a severe illness. Instead of employing this diamond in attempting to bribe his jailers, who indeed might have taken it and then betrayed him to the governor, Dantès carefully preserved it, that in the event of his getting out of prison he might have wherewithal to live; for by selling the diamond he could make his fortune."

" Then, I suppose," asked Caderousse, with eager looks, " that it was a stone of immense value? "

" Why, everything is relative," answered the abbé. " To one in Edmond's position the diamond certainly was of great value. It was estimated at fifty thousand livres."

" Bless me ! " exclaimed Caderousse; " what a sum! Fifty thousand livres ! it must have been as large as a nut ! "

" No," replied the abbé. " it was not of such a size as that. But you shall judge for yourself; I have it with me."

The sharp gaze of Caderousse was instantly directed towards the priest's garments, as though hoping to discover the treasure. Calmly drawing forth from his pocket a small box covered with black shagreen, the abbé opened it and displayed to the delighted eyes of Caderousse the sparkling jewel it contained, set in a ring of admirable workmanship. " And that diamond," cried Caderousse, almost breathless with eager admiration, " you say is worth fifty thousand livres ? "

" It is, without the setting, which is also valuable," replied the abbé, as he closed the box and returned it to his pocket, while its brilliant hues seemed still to dance before the eyes of the fascinated innkeeper.

" But how comes this diamond in your possession, Monsieur the Abbé? Did Edmond make you his heir ? "

" No, but his testamentary executor. When dying, the unfortunate youth said to me, ' I once possessed four dear and faithful friends, besides the maiden to whom I was betrothed; and I feel convinced they have all unfeignedly grieved over my loss. The name of one of the four friends I allude to is Caderousse.' "

The innkeeper shivered.

" ' Another of the number,' " continued the abbé, without seeming to notice the emotion of Caderousse, " ' is called Danglars; and the third, although my rival, entertained a very sincere affection for me.' "

A sinister smile played over the features of Caderousse, who was about to break in upon the abbé's speech when the latter, waving his hand, said, " Allow me to finish first, and then if you have any observations to make, you can do so afterwards. ' The third of my friends, although my rival, was much attached to me; his name was Fernand; that of my betrothed was—' Stay, stay," continued the abbé, " I have forgotten what he called her."

" Mercédès," cried Caderousse, eagerly.

" True," said the abbé, with a stifled sigh, " Mercédès it was."

" Go on," urged Caderousse.

" Bring me a *carafe* of water," said the abbé.

Caderousse quickly performed the stranger's bidding; and after pouring some into a glass and slowly swallowing its contents, the abbé, resuming his usual placidity of manner, said, as he placed his empty glass on the table, " Where were we? "

" The betrothed of Edmond was called Mercédès."

" To be sure. ' You will go to Marseilles,'—it is Dantès who speaks, you understand? "

" Perfectly."

" ' For the purpose of selling this diamond, the proceeds of which you will divide into five equal parts, and give an equal portion to the only persons who have loved me upon earth.'"

" But why into five parts? " asked Caderousse; " you mentioned only four persons."

" Because the fifth is dead, as I hear. The fifth sharer in Edmond's bequest was his own father."

" Too true, too true! " ejaculated Caderousse, almost suffocated by the contending passions which assailed him, " the poor old man is dead."

" I learned so much at Marseilles," replied the abbé, making a strong effort to appear indifferent; " but from the length of time that has elapsed since the death of the elder Dantès, I was unable to obtain any particulars of his end. Do you know anything about the last days of that old man? "

" Eh! " said Caderousse, " who should know better than I? Why, I lived almost on the same floor with the poor old man. Ah, yes! it was hardly a year after the disappearance of his son when the poor old man died."

" Of what did he die? "

" Why, the doctors called his complaint an internal inflammation, I believe. His acquaintances say he died of grief; but I, who almost saw him die, I say he died of—"

" Of what? " asked the priest, eagerly.

" Why, of starvation."

" Starvation! " exclaimed the abbé, springing from his seat. " Why, the vilest animals are not suffered to die of starvation. The very dogs that wander houseless and homeless in the streets find some pitying hand to cast them a mouthful of bread; and that a man, a Christian, should be allowed to perish of hunger, surrounded by other men who call themselves Christian! impossible! Oh, it is impossible! "

" What I have said, I have said," answered Caderousse.

" And you are wrong," said a voice from the top of the stairs. " Why should you meddle with what does not concern you? "

The two men turned and perceived the sickly countenance of La Carconte leaning over the rail of the staircase. Attracted by the sound of voices, she had feebly dragged herself down the stairs, and seated on the lower step, she had listened to the foregoing conversation.

"Why do you meddle yourself, wife?" replied Caderousse. "This gentleman asks me for information which common politeness will not permit me to refuse."

"Yes, but which prudence requires you to refuse. How do you know the motives that person may have for making you speak, simpleton?"

"I pledge you my sacred word, madame," said the abbé, "that my intentions are free from all sorts of harm or injury to you or yours; and that your husband has nothing to fear, provided he answers me candidly."

"Nothing to fear, yes! You begin with fine promises, then come down to 'nothing to fear,' then go away and forget what you have said; and some fine morning down comes misfortune on the heads of the poor wretches, who do not even know whence it comes."

"Nay, nay, my good woman, calm your anxiety; no misfortune will ever come to you through me, I assure you."

Some inarticulate sounds escaped La Carconte, then letting her head, which she had raised during the excitement of conversation, again droop on to her lap, she continued her feverish trembling, and left the two speakers to resume the conversation, but still remaining where she could hear every word they uttered. Again the abbé had been obliged to swallow a draught of water to calm the emotions that threatened to overpower him. When he had sufficiently recovered himself, he said, "It appears, then, that the miserable old man you were telling me of was forsaken by every one, since he died in that way?"

"Why, he was not altogether forsaken," replied Caderousse; "for Mercédès the Catalane and M. Morrel were very kind to him; but somehow the poor old man had contracted a profound antipathy to Fernand,—the very person," added Caderousse, with a bitter smile, "that you named just now as being one of Dantès's faithful and attached friends."

"And was he not so?" asked the abbé.

"Gaspard! Gaspard!" murmured the woman from her seat on the stairs, "mind what you are saying!"

Caderousse made no reply to these words, though evidently irritated and annoyed by the interruption, but addressing the abbé, said, "Can a man be faithful to another whose wife he desires for himself? Dantès, who was a heart of gold, believed everybody's professions of friendship. Poor Edmond! but it is well that he never found them out; it would have been too difficult to pardon them in the hour of death. And whatever people may say," continued Caderousse, in his native language, which was not altogether devoid of rude poetry, " I cannot help fearing more the malediction of the dead than the hatred of the living."

" Simpleton! " exclaimed La Carconte.

" Do you, then, know in what manner Fernand injured Dantès? " inquired the abbé of Caderousse.

" Do I? No one better."

" Speak out, then; say what it was! "

" Gaspard! " cried La Carconte, " do as you please,—you are the master; but if you are guided by me, you will have nothing to say on this subject."

" Well, well, wife," replied Caderousse, " I believe you are right. I shall follow your advice."

" Then you are determined not to reveal the circumstances you alluded to? " said the abbé.

" Why, what good would it do? " asked Caderousse. " If the poor lad were living, and came to me to beg that I would candidly tell him who were his true and who his false friends, why perhaps I should not hesitate. But you tell me he is no more; he can have nothing to do with hatred or revenge, so let all such feelings be buried with him."

" You are willing, then," said the abbé, " that I should bestow on men who you say are false and treacherous the reward intended for faithful friendship? "

" That is true enough," returned Caderousse. " You say truly, the gift of poor Edmond was not meant for such traitors as Fernand and Danglars; besides, what would it be to them? —no more than a drop of water in the ocean."

" Without considering," said the woman, " that those two men can crush you with a single movement."

" How so? " inquired the abbé. " Are these persons, then, so rich and powerful? "

" Do you not know their history? "

" I do not. Pray relate it to me! "

Caderousse seemed to reflect an instant, then said, " No, truly, it would take up too much time."

" Well, my good friend," returned the abbé, in a tone that indicated utter indifference on his part, " you are at liberty either to speak or be silent, just as you please; for my own part, I respect your scruples and admire your sentiments, so let the matter end. I shall do my duty as conscientiously as I can, and fulfil my promise to the dying man. My first business will be to dispose of this diamond." So saying, the abbé again drew the small box from his pocket, opened it, and contrived to hold it in such a light that a bright flash of brilliant hues passed before the dazzled gaze of Caderousse.

"Wife, wife!" cried he, in a voice almost hoarse with eager emotion, "come hither and behold this rich diamond!"

"Diamond!" exclaimed La Carconte, rising and descending to the chamber with a tolerably firm step; "what diamond are you talking about?"

"Why, did you not hear all we said?" inquired Caderousse. "It is a diamond left by poor Edmond Dantès to be sold, and the money divided among his father, Mercédès, his betrothed bride, Fernand, Danglars, and myself. The jewel is worth at least fifty thousand livres."

"Oh, what a splendid diamond!" cried the woman.

"The fifth part of the proceeds of this stone belongs to us, then, does it not?" asked Caderousse, still devouring the glittering gem with his eyes.

"It does," replied the abbé; "with the addition of a share in the part intended for the elder Dantès, which I conceive myself at liberty to share equally with the four surviving persons."

"And wherefore among us four?" inquired Caderousse.

"Because you were the four friends of Edmond."

"I don't call those friends who betray and ruin you," murmured the wife, in a low, muttering voice.

"Of course not!" rejoined Caderousse, quickly; "no more do I. And that was what I was observing to this gentleman just now. I said I looked upon it as a sacrilegious profanation to reward treachery, perhaps crime."

"Remember," answered the abbé, calmly, as he replaced the jewel and its case in the pocket of his cassock, "it is your fault, not mine, that I do so. You will have the goodness to furnish me with the address of Edmond's friends, in order that I may execute his last wishes."

The agitation of Caderousse became extreme, and large drops of perspiration rolled from his heated brow. As he saw the abbé rise from his seat and go towards the door, as though to ascertain if his horse were sufficiently refreshed to continue his journey, Caderousse and his wife exchanged looks of deep meaning with each other.

"This splendid diamond might be all our own," said Caderousse.

"Do you believe it?"

"Why, surely a man of his holy profession would not deceive us!"

"Well," replied La Carconte, "do as you like. For my part, I wash my hands of the affair." So saying, she once more climbed the staircase leading to her chamber, her frame shuddering with aguish chills, and her teeth rattling in her head, notwithstanding the intense heat of the weather. Arrived at the top stair, she turned round, and called out in a warning tone to her husband, "Gaspard, consider well what you are about to do!"

"I have decided," answered Caderousse.

La Carconte then entered her chamber, the flooring of which creaked beneath her heavy, uncertain tread, as she proceeded towards her armchair, into which she fell as though exhausted.

"What have you decided?" asked the abbé.

"To tell you all I know," was the reply.

"I certainly think you act wisely in so doing," said the priest. "Not because I have the least desire to learn anything you may desire to conceal from me, but simply because if you can assist me to distribute the legacy according to the wishes of the testator, why, so much the better."

"I hope I can," replied Caderousse, his face flushed with hope and cupidity.

"Now, then, begin if you please," said the abbé; "I am waiting."

"Stop a minute," answered Caderousse; "we might be interrupted in the most interesting part of my recital, which would be a pity; and it is as well that your visit hither should be known only to ourselves." With these words he went stealthily to the door, which he closed, and by way of still greater precaution bolted and barred it as he was accustomed to do at night. During this time the abbè had chosen his place for listening at his ease. He removed his seat into a corner of the room where he himself would be in deep shadow, while the light would be fully thrown on the narrator; then with head bent down and hands clasped, or rather clinched together, he prepared to give his whole attention to Caderousse, who seated himself on a little stool opposite to him.

"Remember, I did not urge you to this," said the trembling voice of La Carconte, as though through the flooring of her chamber she could see what was taking place below.

"Enough, enough!" replied Caderousse; "say no more about it. I will take all the consequences upon myself." And he began his story.

CHAPTER XXVII

THE RECITAL

"First," said Caderousse, "I must beg you, monsieur, to promise me one thing."

"What is that?" inquired the abbé.

"It is that if you ever make use of the details I am about to give you, you will never let any one know that it was I who supplied them; for the persons of whom I am about to talk are rich and powerful, and if they only laid the tips of their fingers on me, I should break to pieces like glass."

"Make yourself easy, my friend," replied the abbé. "I am a priest, and confessions die in my breast. Recollect, our only desire is to carry out in a fitting manner the last wishes of our friend. Speak, then, without reserve, as without hatred; tell the truth, the whole truth. I do not know, never may know, the persons of whom you are about to speak. Besides, I am an Italian and not a Frenchman, and belong to God and not to man; and I retire to my convent, which I have only quitted to fulfil the last wishes of a dying man."

This last assurance seemed to give Caderousse courage. "Well, then, under these circumstances," said he, "I will, indeed I must, undeceive you as to the friendship which poor Edmond believed so sincere and unquestionable."

"Begin with his father, if you please," said the abbé; "Edmond talked to me a great deal about the old man, for whom he had the deepest love."

"The history is a sad one, sir," said Caderousse, shaking his head; "perhaps you know all the earlier part of it?"

"Yes," answered the abbé; "Edmond related to me everything until the moment when he was arrested in a small cabaret close to Marseilles."

"At La Réserve! Oh, yes! I can see it all before me this moment."

"Was it not his betrothal feast?"

"It was; and the feast that began so gaily had a very sorrowful ending: a commissary of police, followed by four soldiers, entered, and Dantès was arrested."

"Yes; and up to this point I know all," said the priest. "Dantès himself knew only what had happened to him personally, for he never beheld again any of the five persons I have named to you, nor heard them mentioned."

"Well, when Dantès was arrested, M. Morrel hastened to

obtain the particulars, and they were very sad. The old man returned alone to his home, folded up his wedding suit with tears in his eyes, and paced up and down his chamber the whole day, and would not go to bed at all,—for I was underneath him and heard him walking the whole night; and for myself, I assure you I could not sleep either, for the grief of the poor father gave me great uneasiness, and every step he took went to my heart as really as if his foot had pressed against my breast. The next day Mercédès came to Marseilles to implore the protection of M. de Villefort; she obtained nothing. She then went to visit the old man. When she saw him so miserable and heart-broken, and learned that he had not been in bed nor tasted food since the previous day, she wished him to go with her that she might take care of him; but the old man would not consent. ' No,' was his reply, ' I will not leave this house, —for my poor dear boy loves me better than anything in the world, and if he gets out of prison he will come to see me the first thing; and what would he think if I did not wait here for him?' I heard all this from the window, for I was anxious that Mercédès should persuade the old man to accompany her; his footsteps over my head night and day did not leave me a moment's repose."

" But did you not go upstairs and try to console the poor old man? " asked the abbé.

" Ah, sir," replied Caderousse, " we cannot console those who will not be consoled, and he was one of these; besides, I know not why, but he seemed to dislike seeing me. One night, however, I heard his sobs, and I could not resist my desire to go up to him; but when I reached his door he was no longer weeping, he was praying. I cannot now repeat to you, sir, all the eloquent words and imploring language he made use of. It was more than piety, it was more than grief; and I, who am no canter, and hate the Jesuits, said then to myself, ' It is really fortunate that I am alone, and that the good God has not sent me children; for if I were a father, and if I should suffer a grief like that of this poor old man, not finding in my memory or in my heart all that he is saying to the good God, I should throw myself into the sea at once, to escape from my grief.' "

" Poor father! " murmured the priest.

" From day to day he lived on alone, and more and more solitary. M. Morrel and Mercédès came often to see him, but his door was closed; and although I was certain he was at home, he would not make any answer. One day, when contrary to his custom he had admitted Mercédès, and the poor girl, in spite of her own grief and despair, endeavoured to console him, he said to her, ' Be assured, my dear daughter, he is dead; and instead of our awaiting him, he is awaiting us. I am quite happy, for I am the oldest, and of course shall see him first.' However well disposed we may be, we soon cease visiting those who make us sad. And so at last old Dantès was left all to himself, and I only saw from time to time strangers go up to him and come down again with some bundle which they tried to hide; but I guessed what these bundles were: he was selling piece by piece all that he had, to get money for food. At length the poor old fellow reached the end of his possessions; he owed three quarters' rent, and they threatened to turn him out. He begged for another week, which was granted to him. I know this, because the landlord came into my apartment when he left his. For the first three days I heard him walking about as usual, but on the fourth I heard him no longer. I then resolved to go up to him at all risks. The door was closed; but I looked though the keyhole, and saw him so pale and haggard that believing him very ill I went and told M. Morrel, and then ran on to Mercédès. They both came immediately, M. Morrel bringing a doctor; and the doctor said it was an affection of the stomach, and ordered him a limited diet. I was there too, and I never shall forget the old man's smile at this prescription. From that time he opened his door; he had an excuse for not eating any more, as the doctor had put him on a diet."

The abbé uttered a kind of groan.

" The story interests you, does it not, sir? " inquired Caderousse.

" Yes," replied the abbé; " it is very affecting."

" Mercédès came again, and she found him so altered that she was even more anxious than before to have him taken to her own abode. This was M. Morrel's wish also, who would fain have conveyed the old man against his consent; but the old man resisted, and cried so that they were afraid to persevere. Mercédès remained therefore by his bedside, and M. Morrel went away, making a sign to her that he had left his purse on the chimney-piece. But availing himself of the doctor's order, the old man would not take any sustenance. At length (after nine days' despair and fasting) the old man died, cursing those who had caused his misery, and saying to Mercédès, ' If you ever see my Edmond again, tell him I die blessing him.' "

The abbé rose from his chair, made two turns round the chamber, and pressed his trembling hand against his parched throat. " And you believe he died—"

"Of hunger, sir, of hunger," said Caderousse. "I am as certain of it as that we two are Christians."

The abbé with a shaking hand seized a glass of water that was standing by him half-full, emptied it at one gulp, and then resumed his seat with red eyes and pale cheeks. "This was indeed a horrible event," said he, in a hoarse voice.

"The more so, sir, as it was men's and not God's doing."

"Tell me of those men," said the abbé; "and remember," he added in a voice that was nearly menacing in its tone, "you have promised to tell me everything. Tell me therefore who are these men who have killed the son with despair, and the father with famine?"

"Two men jealous of him, monsieur, one through love, and the other through ambition,—Fernand and Danglars."

"Tell me, how was this jealousy manifested?"

"They denounced Edmond as a Bonapartist agent."

"Which of the two denounced him? Which was the real delinquent?"

"Both, sir; one wrote the letter, and the other put it in the post."

"And where was this letter written?"

"At La Réserve, the day before the festival of the betrothing."

"'Twas so, then; 'twas so, then," murmured the abbé. "Oh, Faria, Faria! how well did you judge men and things!"

"What did you please to say, sir?" asked Caderousse.

"Nothing, nothing," replied the priest; "go on."

"It was Danglars who wrote the denunciation with his left hand, that his writing might not be recognised, and Fernand who put it in the post."

"But," exclaimed the abbé, suddenly, "you were there yourself!"

"I!" said Caderousse, astonished; "who told you I was there?"

The abbé saw that he had gone too far, and he added quickly, "No one; but in order to have known everything so well, you must have been an eye-witness."

"True, true!" said Caderousse, in a choking voice, "I was there."

"And did you not remonstrate against such infamy?" asked the abbé; "if not, you were an accomplice."

"Monsieur," replied Caderousse, "they had made me drink to such an excess that I nearly lost all perception. I had only an indistinct understanding of what was passing around me. I said all that a man in such a state could say; but they both assured me that it was a jest they were carrying on, and perfectly harmless."

"Next day, monsieur, next day, you must have seen plainly enough what they had been doing; yet you said nothing, though you were present when Dantès was arrested."

"Yes, sir, I was there, and very anxious to speak; but Danglars restrained me. 'If he should really be guilty,' said he, 'and did really land on the island of Elba; if he is really charged with a letter for the Bonapartist committee at Paris, and if they find this letter upon him,—those who have supported him will be regarded as his accomplices.' I was afraid,—the political condition being full of hidden dangers,—and I held my tongue. It was cowardly, I confess, but it was not criminal."

"I comprehend,—you allowed matters to take their course, that was all."

"Yes, monsieur," answered Caderousse, "and I think of it with remorse night and day. I often ask pardon of God for it, I swear to you, and with the more reason because I believe that this action, the only one with which I have seriously to reproach myself in all my life, is the cause of my abject condition. I am expiating a moment of selfishness; and thus it is I always say to Carconte when she complains, 'Hold your tongue, woman! it is the will of God.'" And Caderousse bowed his head with every sign of real repentance.

"Well, sir," said the abbé, "you have spoken frankly; thus to accuse yourself is to deserve pardon."

"Unfortunately, Edmond is dead, and has not pardoned me."

"He did not know about it," said the abbé.

"But he knows it all now," interrupted Caderousse; "they say the dead know everything."

There was a brief silence; the abbé rose and paced up and down pensively, and then resumed his seat. "You have two or three times mentioned a M. Morrel," he said; "who was he?"

"The owner of the *Pharaon* and the patron of Dantès."

"And what part did he play in this sad drama?" inquired the abbé.

"The part of an honest man, full of courage and affection. Twenty times he interceded for Edmond. When the emperor returned, he wrote, implored, threatened, and so energetically that on the second restoration he was persecuted as a Bonapartist. Ten times, as I told you, he came to see Dantès's father, and offered to receive him in his own house; and the night or two before his death, as I have already said, he left his purse on the mantel-piece, with the contents of which they paid the old man's debts and buried him decently. So that Edmond's father died as he had lived, without doing harm to any one. I have the purse still by me,—a large one, made of red silk."

" And," asked the abbé, " is M. Morrel still alive? "

" Yes," replied Caderousse.

" In that case," replied the abbé, " he should be a man favoured of God. Is he rich, happy? "

Caderousse smiled bitterly. "Yes, happy,—like me," said he.

" What, M. Morrel unhappy! " exclaimed the abbé.

" He is reduced almost to the last extremity,—nay, he is almost at the point of dishonour."

" Is it as bad as that? "

" Yes," continued Caderousse, " it is as bad as that. After twenty-five years of labour, after having acquired a most honourable name in the trade of Marseilles, M. Morrel is utterly ruined. He has lost five ships in two years, has suffered by the bankruptcy of three large houses, and his only hope now is in that very *Pharaon* which poor Dantès commanded, and which is expected from the Indies with a cargo of cochineal and indigo. If this ship founders like the others, he is a ruined man."

" And has the unfortunate man wife or children? " inquired the abbé.

" Yes, he has a wife, who in all this has behaved like an angel; he has a daughter who was about to marry the man she loved, but whose family now will not allow him to wed the daughter of a ruined man; he has besides a son, a lieutenant in the army; and as you may suppose, all this, instead of soothing, doubles his grief. If he were alone in the world he would blow out his brains, and there would be an end."

" Horrible! " ejaculated the priest.

" And it is thus that Heaven recompenses virtue, monsieur," added Caderousse. " You see I, who never did a bad action but that I have told you of, am in destitution; after having seen my poor wife die of a fever, unable to do anything in the world for her, I shall die of hunger as old Dantès did, while Fernand and Danglars are rolling in wealth."

" And how has that happened? "

" Because with them everything turns out well, while with those who are honest everything goes wrong."

" What has become of Danglars, the instigator, and therefore the most guilty? "

" What has become of him? Why, he left Marseilles, and was taken on the recommendation of M. Morrel, who did not know his crime, into a Spanish bank as cashier. During the war with Spain he was employed in the commissariat of the French army and made a fortune; then with that money he speculated in the funds and trebled or quadrupled his capital, and having first married his banker's daughter, who left him a widower, has married a second time, a widow, a Madame de Nargonne, daughter of M. de Servieux, the king's chamberlain, who is in high favour at court. He is a millionaire, and they have made him a count; and now he is the Comte Danglars, with a hotel in the Rue de Mont Blanc, with ten horses in his stables, six footmen in his ante-chamber, and I know not how many hundreds of thousands in his strong-box."

"Ah!" said the abbé, with a peculiar tone; "and is he happy?"

"Happy! Who can answer for that? Happiness or unhappiness is the secret known but to one's self and the walls; walls have ears but no tongue. If a large fortune produces happiness, Danglars is happy."

"And Fernand?"

"Fernand! Why, that is still another history."

"But how could a poor Catalan fisher-boy, without education or resources, make a fortune? I confess this surprises me."

"And it has surprised everybody. There must have been in his life some strange secret no one knows."

"But by what visible steps has he attained this high fortune or high position?"

"Both, monsieur; he has both fortune and position."

"You are giving me a tale of fiction!"

"It would seem so; but listen, and you will understand. Some days before the return of the emperor, Fernand was drawn in the conscription. The Bourbons left him quietly enough at the Catalans; but Napoleon returned, an extraordinary muster was determined on, and Fernand was compelled to join. I went too; but as I was older than Fernand, and had just married my poor wife, I was sent only to the coast. Fernand was enrolled in the active forces, went to the frontier with his regiment, and was at the battle of Ligny. The night after that battle he was sentry at the door of a general who carried on a secret correspondence with the enemy. That same night the general was to go over to the English. He proposed to Fernand to accompany him; Fernand agreed to do so, deserted his post, and followed the general. That which would have brought Fernand to a court-martial if Napoleon had remained on the throne, served for his recommendation to the Bourbons. He returned to France with the epaulette of sub-lieutenant, and as the protection of the general, who is in the highest favour, was accorded to him, he was a captain in 1823 during the Spanish war; that is to say, at the time when Danglars made his early speculations. Fernand was a Spaniard; and being sent to Spain to ascertain the feeling of his fellow-countrymen, found Danglars there, became on very intimate terms with him, procured for his general support from the Royalists of the capital and the provinces, received promises and made pledges on his own part, guided his regiment by paths known to himself alone in gorges of the mountains held by the Royalists, and in fact rendered such services in this brief campaign that after the taking of Trocadero he was made colonel, and received the title of count and the cross of an officer of the Legion of Honour."

" Destiny! destiny!" murmured the abbé.

"Yes, but listen; this was not all. The war with Spain being ended, Fernand's career was checked by the long peace which seemed likely to continue throughout Europe. Greece only had risen against Turkey and had begun her war of independence; all eyes were turned towards Athens,—it was the fashion to pity and support the Greeks. The French government, without protecting them openly, as you know, tolerated partial migrations. Fernand sought and obtained leave to go and serve in Greece, still having his name kept in the ranks of the army. Some time after it was stated that the Comte de Morcerf—this was the name he bore—had entered the service of Ali Pacha, with the rank of instructor-general. Ali Pacha was killed, as you know; but before he died he recompensed the services of Fernand by leaving him a considerable sum, with which he returned to France, when his rank of lieutenant-general was confirmed."

" So that now—" inquired the abbé.

"So that now," continued Caderousse, "he possesses a magnificent hotel,—No. 27 Rue du Helder, Paris."

The abbé opened his mouth, remained for a moment like a man who hesitates, then, making an effort over himself, he said, "And Mercédès,—they tell me that she has disappeared?"

"Disappeared," said Caderousse, "yes, as the sun disappears, to rise the next day with still more splendour."

"Has she also made a fortune?" inquired the abbé, with an ironical smile.

"Mercédès is at this moment one of the greatest ladies in Paris," replied Caderousse.

"Go on," said the abbé; "it seems as if I were hearing the

recital of a dream. But I have seen things so extraordinary that those you mention to me seem less astonishing."

"Mercédès was at first in the deepest despair at the blow which deprived her of Edmond. I have told you of her attempts to propitiate M. de Villefort, her devotion to the father of Dantès. In the midst of her despair, a fresh trouble overtook her. This was the departure of Fernand,—of Fernand, whose crime she did not know, and whom she regarded as her brother. Fernand went, and Mercédès remained alone. Three months she spent in weeping; no news of Edmond, no news of Fernand, nothing before her but an old man who was dying with despair. One evening, after having been seated, as was her custom, all day at the angle of two roads that lead to Marseilles from the Catalans, she returned to her home more depressed than ever; neither her lover nor her friend returned by either of these roads, and she had no intelligence of either. Suddenly she heard a step she knew, turned round anxiously, the door opened, and Fernand, dressed in the uniform of a sub-lieutenant, stood before her. It was not the half of her life for which she mourned; but it was still a portion of her past which was thus returned to her. Mercédès seized Fernand's hands with a transport which he took for love, but which was only joy at being no longer alone in the world, and seeing at last a friend, after long hours of solitary sorrow. And then, it must be confessed, Fernand had never been an object of dislike to her; only she had not loved him. Another possessed all Mercédès heart; that other was absent, had disappeared, perhaps was dead. At this last idea Mercédès burst into a flood of tears and wrung her hands in agony; but this idea, which she had always repelled before when it was suggested to her by another, came now in full force upon her mind; and then too old Dantès incessantly said to her, ' Our Edmond is dead; if he were not he would return to us.' The old man died, as I have told you; had he lived, Mercédès, perchance, had not become the wife of another, for he would have been there to reproach her infidelity. Fernand saw this, and when he learned the old man's death he returned. He was now a lieutenant. At his first coming he had not said a word of love to Mercédès; at the second he reminded her that he loved her. Mercédès begged for six months more to expect and bewail Edmond."

"So that," said the abbé, with a bitter smile, "that makes eighteen months in all. What more could the most devoted lover desire?" Then he murmured the words of the English poet, "' Frailty, thy name is woman.'"

"Six months afterwards," continued Caderousse, "the marriage took place in the church of Accoules."

"The very church in which she was to have married Edmond," murmured the priest; "there was only a change of bridegroom."

"Well, Mercédès was married," proceeded Caderousse; "but although in the eyes of the world she appeared calm, she nearly fainted as she passed La Réserve, where eighteen months before, the betrothal had been celebrated with him whom she would have seen she still loved had she dared to search her heart. Fernand, more happy, but not more at his ease,—for I saw at this time he was in constant dread of Edmond's return,—was very anxious to get his wife away and to depart himself. There were too many dangers and recollections associated with the Catalans, and eight days after the wedding they left Marseilles."

"Did you ever see Mercédès again?" inquired the priest.

"Yes, during the war of Spain, at Perpignan, where Fernand had left her; she was attending to the education of her son."

The abbé started. "Her son?" said he.

"Yes," replied Caderousse; "little Albert."

"But, then, to be able to instruct her child," continued the abbé, "she must have received an education herself. I understood from Edmond that she was the daughter of a simple fisherman, beautiful but uneducated."

"Oh!" replied Caderousse, "did he know so little of his betrothed? Mercédès might have been a queen, monsieur, if the crown were to be placed on the heads of the loveliest and most intelligent. Her fortune had increased, and she became greater with her fortune. She learned drawing, music,—everything. Besides, I believe, between ourselves, she did this in order to distract her mind, that she might forget; and she only filled her head to alleviate the weight on her heart. But now everything must be told," continued Caderousse; "no doubt fortune and honours have comforted her. She is rich, a countess, and yet—"

"And yet what?" asked the abbé.

"Yet I am sure she is not happy," said Caderousse.

"What makes you believe this?"

"Why, when I found myself very wretched, I have thought my old friends would perhaps assist me. So I went to Danglars, who would not even receive me; I called on Fernand, who sent me a hundred livres by his *valet de chambre*."

"Then you did not see either of them?"

"No; but Madame de Morcerf saw me."

"How was that?"

"As I went away a purse fell at my feet; it contained five-and-twenty louis. I raised my head quickly and saw Mercédès, who shut the blind directly."

"And M. de Villefort?" asked the abbé.

"Oh, he never was a friend of mine; I did not know him, and I had nothing to ask of him."

"Do you not know what became of him, and the share he had in Edmond's misfortunes?"

"No; I only know that some time after having arrested him, he married Mademoiselle de Saint-Méran, and soon after left Marseilles. No doubt but he has been as lucky as the rest; no doubt he is as rich as Danglars, as high in station as Fernand. I only, as you see, have remained poor, wretched, and forgotten."

"You are mistaken, my friend," replied the abbé. "God may seem sometimes to forget for a while, while his justice reposes, but there always comes a moment when he remembers—and behold a proof." As he spoke, the abbé took the diamond from his pocket, and giving it to Caderousse, said, "Here, my friend, take this diamond, it is yours."

"What! for me only?" cried Caderousse. "Ah, monsieur, do not jest with me!"

"This diamond was to have been shared among his friends. Edmond had one friend only, and thus it cannot be divided. Take the diamond, then, and sell it. It is, as I have said, worth fifty thousand livres; and I trust that this sum may suffice to release you from your wretchedness."

"Oh, monsieur," said Caderousse, putting out one hand timidly, and with the other wiping away the perspiration which bedewed his brow,—"oh, monsieur, do not make a jest of a man's happiness or despair!"

"I know what happiness and what despair are, and I never make a jest of such feelings. Take it, then, but in exchange—"

Caderousse, who touched the diamond, withdrew his hand. The abbé smiled. "In exchange," he continued, "give me the red silk purse that M. Morrel left on old Dantès's chimney-piece, and which you tell me is still in your hands."

Caderousse, more and more astonished, went to a large oaken cupboard, opened it, and gave the abbé a long purse of faded red silk, round which were two copper runners that had once been gilt. The abbé took it, and in return gave Caderousse the diamond.

"Oh! you are a man of God, sir," cried Caderousse; "for no one knew that Edmond had given you this diamond, and you might have kept it."

" Which," said the abbé to himself, " you would have done, it appears." He rose and took his hat and gloves. " Well," he said, " all that you have told me is perfectly true, then, and I may believe it in every particular? "

" See, Monsieur the Abbé," replied Caderousse, " in this corner is a crucifix of holy wood; here on this shelf is my wife's Bible. Open this book, and I will swear upon it with my hand on the crucifix, by my soul's salvation, my faith as a Christian, that I have told everything to you as it occurred, and as the angel of men will tell it to the ear of God at the day of the last judgment! "

" 'Tis well," said the abbé, convinced by his manner and tone that Caderousse spoke the truth. " 'Tis well, and may this money profit you! Adieu! I return to my place apart from men who thus do evil to one another."

The abbé with difficulty got away from the enthusiastic thanks of Caderousse, opened the door himself, got out and mounted his horse, once more saluted the innkeeper, who kept uttering his loud farewells, and then returned by the road he had travelled in coming. When Caderousse turned round, he saw behind him La Carconte, paler, and trembling more than ever.

" Is, then, all that I have heard really true? " she inquired.

" What! that he has given the diamond to us only? " inquired Caderousse, half-bewildered with joy.

" Yes."

" Nothing more true! See! here it is."

The woman gazed at it a moment, and then said in a gloomy voice, " Suppose it's false? "

Caderousse started and turned pale. " False! " he muttered. " False! why should that man give me a false diamond? "

" To possess your secret without paying for it, you block-head! "

Caderousse remained for a moment aghast under the weight of such an idea. " Oh! " he said, taking up his hat, which he placed on the red handkerchief tied round his head, " we will soon learn that."

" In what way? "

" Why, it is the fair of Beaucaire; there are always jewellers from Paris there, and I will show it to them. Take care of the house, wife, and I will be back in two hours." Caderousse left the house in haste, and ran rapidly in a direction contrary to that which the unknown had taken.

" Fifty thousand livres! " muttered La Carconte, when left alone; " it is a large sum of money, but it is not a fortune."

CHAPTER XXVIII

THE PRISON REGISTER

THE day after that on which occurred the interview described above, a man about thirty or thirty-two years of age, dressed in a bright blue frock-coat, nankeen trousers, and a white waistcoat, having the appearance and accent of an Englishman, presented himself before the mayor of Marseilles. " Monsieur," said he, " I am chief clerk of the house of Thomson and French, of Rome. We are, and have been these ten years, connected with the house of Morrel and Son, of Marseilles. We have a hundred thousand livres or thereabouts engaged in speculation with them, and we are a little uneasy at reports that have reached us that the firm is on the eve of ruin. I have come, therefore, express from Rome, to ask you for information as to this house."

" Monsieur," replied the mayor, " I know very well that during the last four or five years, misfortune seems to pursue M. Morrel. He has lost four or five vessels, and suffered by three or four bankruptcies; but it is not for me, although I am a creditor myself to the amount of ten thousand livres, to give any information as to the state of his finances. If you ask of me, as mayor, what is my opinion of M. Morrel, I shall say he is a man honourable to the last degree, who has up to this time fulfilled every engagement with scrupulous punctuality. This is all I can say, monsieur; if you wish to learn more, address yourself to M. de Boville, the inspector of prisons, No. 15 Rue de Nouailles. He has, I believe, two hundred thousand livres placed in the hands of Morrel; and if there be any grounds for apprehension, as this is a greater amount than mine, you will most probably find him better informed than myself."

The Englishman seemed to appreciate this extreme delicacy, made his bow, and went away, walking with that step peculiar to the sons of Great Britain towards the street mentioned. M. de Boville was in his private room, and the Englishman on perceiving him made a gesture of surprise which seemed to indicate that it was not the first time he had been in his presence. As to M. de Boville, he was in such a state of despair that it was evident that all the faculties of his mind were absorbed in the thought which occupied him at the moment, and that neither his memory nor his imagination had leisure for recurring to the past. The Englishman, with the coolness of his nation, addressed him in terms nearly similar to those with which he had accosted the mayor of Marseilles.

"Oh, monsieur," exclaimed M. de Boville, "your fears are unfortunately but too well founded, and you see before you a man in despair. I had two hundred thousand livres placed in the hands of Morrel and Son; these two hundred thousand livres were my daughter's dowry, who was to be married in a fortnight, and they were payable, half on the 15th of this month, and the other half on the 15th of next month. I had informed M. Morrel of my desire to have these payments punctually; and he has been here within the last half-hour to tell me that if his ship, the *Pharaon*, did not come into port on the 15th, he would be wholly unable to make this payment."

"But," said the Englishman, "this looks very much like a suspension of payments!"

"Say, monsieur, that it resembles a bankruptcy!" exclaimed M. de Boville, despairingly.

The Englishman appeared to reflect a moment, and then said, "So, monsieur, this credit inspires you with considerable apprehension?"

"To say truth, I consider it lost."

"Well, then, I will buy it of you."

"You?"

"Yes, I."

"But at a tremendous discount, of course?"

"No, for two hundred thousand livres. Our house," added the Englishman, with a laugh, "does not do things in that way."

"And you will pay—"

"Ready money." And the Englishman drew from his pocket a bundle of bank-notes, which might have been twice the sum M. de Boville feared to lose.

A ray of joy passed across M. de Boville's countenance, yet he made an effort over himself and said, "Monsieur, I ought to tell you that in all probability you will not have six per cent. of this sum."

"That's no affair of mine," replied the Englishman; "that is the affair of the house of Thomson and French, in whose name I act. They have perhaps some motive to serve in hastening the ruin of a rival firm. But all I know, monsieur, is that I am ready to hand you over this sum in exchange for your assignment of the debt. I only ask a brokerage."

"Of course that is perfectly just," cried M. de Boville. "The commission is usually one and a half; will you have two, three five per cent., or even more? Speak!"

"Monsieur," replied the Englishman, laughing, "I am like my house, and do not do such things; no, the commission I ask is quite different."

"Name it, monsieur, I beg."

"You are the inspector of prisons?"

"I have been so these fourteen years."

"You keep the registers of entries and departures?"

"I do."

"To these registers there are added notes relative to the prisoners?"

"There are special reports on every prisoner."

"Well, monsieur, I was educated at Rome by a poor devil of an abbé, who disappeared suddenly. I have since learned that he was confined in the Château d'If, and I should like to learn some particulars of his death."

"What was his name?"

"The Abbé Faria."

"Oh, I recollect him perfectly," cried M. de Boville, "he was crazy."

"So they said."

"Oh, he was, decidedly."

"Very possibly; but what sort of madness was it?"

"He pretended to know of an immense treasure, and offered vast sums to government if they would liberate him."

"Poor devil! and he is dead?"

"Yes, sir; five or six months ago last February."

"You have a good memory, sir, to recollect dates so well."

"I recollect this because the poor devil's death was accompanied by a singular circumstance."

"May I ask what that was?" asked the Englishman, with an expression of curiosity which a close observer would have been astonished at discovering in his phlegmatic countenance.

"Oh, dear, yes, monsieur; the abbé's dungeon was forty or fifty feet distant from that of an old agent of Bonaparte, one of those who had contributed most actively to the return of the usurper in 1815,—a very resolute and very dangerous man."

"Indeed!" said the Englishman.

"Yes," replied M. de Boville; "I myself had occasion to see this man in 1816 or 1817, and we could go into his dungeon only with a file of soldiers. That man made a deep impression on me. I shall never forget his countenance!"

The Englishman smiled imperceptibly. "And you say, monsieur," he said, "that the two dungeons—"

" —Were separated by a distance of fifty feet; but it appears that this Edmond Dantès—"

" This dangerous man's name was—"

" Edmond Dantès. It appears, monsieur, that this Edmond Dantès had procured tools, or made them, for they found a passage by which the prisoners communicated."

" This passage was formed, no doubt, with an intention of escape? "

" No doubt; but unfortunately for the prisoners, the Abbé Faria had an attack of catalepsy and died."

" I see; that would naturally cut short the projects of escape."

" For the dead man, yes," replied M. de Boville; " but not for the survivor. On the contrary, this Dantès saw a means of accelerating his escape. He no doubt thought that prisoners who died in the Château d'If were interred in a burial-ground as usual; and he conveyed the dead man into his own cell, assumed his place in the sack in which they had sewn up the defunct, and awaited the moment of interment."

" It was a bold step, and one that indicated some courage," remarked the Englishman.

" As I have already told you, monsieur, he was a very dangerous man; and fortunately by his own act disembarrassed the government of the fears it had on his account."

" How was that? "

" How? do you not comprehend? "

" No."

" The Château d'If has no cemetery; and they simply throw the dead into the sea, after having fastened a thirty-six pound bullet to their feet."

" Well? " observed the Englishman, as if he were slow of comprehension.

" Well, they fastened a thirty-six pound bullet to his feet and threw him into the sea."

" Really? " exclaimed the Englishman.

" Yes, monsieur," continued the inspector of prisons. " You may imagine the amazement of the fugitive when he found himself flung headlong down towards the rocks. I should like to have seen his face at that moment."

" That would have been difficult."

" No matter," replied M. de Boville in supreme good-humour at the certainty of recovering his two hundred thousand livres —" no matter; I can fancy it." And he shouted with laughter

" So can I," said the Englishman, and he laughed too; but

he laughed as the English do, at the end of his teeth. "And so," continued the Englishman, who first gained his composure, "he was drowned?"

"Unquestionably."

"So that the governor got rid of the fierce and the crazy prisoner at the same time?"

"Precisely."

"But some official document was drawn up as to this affair, I suppose?" inquired the Englishman.

"Yes, yes; the mortuary deposition. You understand that Dantès's relatives, if he had any, might have some interest in knowing if he were dead or alive."

"So that now, if there were anything to inherit from him, they may do so with easy conscience. He is dead, and no mistake about it?"

"Oh, yes; and they may have the fact attested whenever they please."

"So be it," said the Englishman. "But to return to these registers."

"True, this story has diverted our attention from them. Excuse me."

"Excuse you for what,—for the story? By no means; it really seems to me very curious."

"Yes, indeed. So, monsieur, you wish to see all relating to the poor abbé, who really was gentleness itself?"

"Yes, you will much oblige me."

"Go into my study here, and I will show it to you;" and they both entered M. de Boville's study. All was here arranged in perfect order; each register had its number, each file of paper its place. The inspector begged the Englishman to seat himself in an armchair, and placed before him the register and documents relative to the Château d'If, giving him all the time he desired to examine it, while he seated himself in a corner and began to read his newspaper. The Englishman easily found the entries relative to the Abbé Faria; but it seemed that the history which the inspector had related interested him greatly, for after having perused the first documents he turned over the leaves until he reached the deposition respecting Edmond Dantès. There he found everything in its place,—the denunciation, examination, Morrel's petition, M. de Villefort's marginal notes. He folded up the denunciation quietly and put it as quietly in his pocket, read the examination and saw that the name of Noirtier was not mentioned in it, perused too the application, dated April 10, 1815, in which Morrel, by the deputy *procureur's* advice, exaggerated with the best intentions (for Napoleon was then on the throne) the services Dantès had rendered to the imperial cause,—services which Villefort's certificates rendered indisputable. Then he understood the matter. This petition to Napoleon, kept back by Villefort, had become under the second restoration a terrible weapon against him in the hands of the *procureur du roi*. He was no longer astonished when he searched on to find in the register this note, placed in a bracket against his name:—

EDMOND DANTÈS. { Violent Bonapartist; took an active part in the return from Elba.
The greatest watchfulness and care to be exercised.

Beneath these lines was written in another hand: " See note above,—nothing can be done." He compared the writing in the bracket with the writing of the certificate placed beneath Morrel's petition, and discovered that the note in the bracket was in the same writing as the certificate,—that is to say, was in Villefort's handwriting. As to the note which accompanied this, the Englishman understood that it might have been added by some inspector who had taken a momentary interest in Dantès's situation, but who had, on account of the records we have given, found it impossible to give any effect to the interest he experienced.

As we have said, the inspector, from discretion, and that he might not disturb the Abbé Faria's pupil in his researches, had seated himself in a corner and was reading *Le Drapeau Blanc*. He did not see the Englishman fold up and place in his pocket the denunciation written by Danglars under the arbour of La Réserve, and which had the post-mark of Marseilles, March 2, delivery six o'clock P.M. But it must be said that if he had seen it, he attached so small importance to this scrap of paper, and so great importance to his two hundred thousand livres, that he would not have opposed what the Englishman did, however irregular it might be.

" Thanks ! " said the latter, closing the register with a noise, " I have all I want; now it is for me to perform my promise. Give me a simple assignment of your debt, acknowledge therein the receipt of the cash, and I will hand you over the money." He rose, gave his seat to M. de Boville, who took it without ceremony and quickly drew up the required assignment, while the Englishman was counting out the bank-notes on the other side of the desk.

CHAPTER XXIX

THE HOUSE OF MORREL AND SON

ANY one who had quitted Marseilles a few years previously, well acquainted with the house of Morrel and Son, and had returned at this date, would have found a great change in it. Instead of that air of life, of comfort, and of happiness that exhales from a flourishing and prosperous house; instead of the merry faces seen at the windows; instead of the busy clerks hurrying to and fro in the long corridors; instead of the court filled with bales of goods, re-echoing the cries and the jokes of the porters,—he would have at once perceived an air of sadness and gloom. In the deserted corridor and the empty office, out of all the numerous clerks who used to fill the office but two remained. One was a young man of three or four and twenty, named Emmanuel Herbaut, who was in love with M. Morrel's daughter, and had remained with him against the efforts of his friends to induce him to withdraw; the other was an old one-eyed cashier, named Coclès, a nickname given him by the young men who used to inhabit this vast bee-hive, now almost deserted, and which had so completely replaced his real name that he would not in all probability have replied to any one who addressed him by it.

Coclès remained in M. Morrel's service, and a most singular change had taken place in his situation; he had at the same time risen to the rank of cashier and sunk to the rank of a servant. He was, however, the same Coclès, good, patient, devoted, but inflexible on the subject of arithmetic, the only point on which he would have stood firm against the world, even against M. Morrel, and strong in the multiplication table, which he had at his fingers' ends, no matter what scheme or what trap was laid to catch him. In the midst of the distress of the house, Coclès was the only one unmoved. This did not arise from a want of affection, but on the contrary from a firm conviction. Like rats that leave by degrees the vessel doomed to perish at sea, until all these egotistical guests have completely abandoned the ship at the moment when the vessel weighs anchor, so all these numerous clerks had by degrees deserted the bureaux and warehouse. Coclès had seen them go without thinking of inquiring the cause of their departure. Everything was, as we have said, a question of arithmetic to Coclès; and during twenty years he had always seen all payments made with such exactitude that it seemed as impossible to him that the house should stop payment as it would to a miller that the river that had so long turned his mill should cease to flow.

Nothing had as yet occurred to shake Coclès's belief; the last month's payments had been made with the most scrupulous exactitude. Coclès had detected an error of fourteen sous to the prejudice of Morrel, and the same evening he had brought them to M. Morrel, who with a melancholy smile threw them into an almost empty drawer, saying, "Thanks, Coclès; you are the pearl of cashiers."

Coclès retired perfectly happy, for by this eulogium of M. Morrel, himself the pearl of the honest men of Marseilles, he was more pleased than he would have been by a present of fifty pounds. But since the end of the month M. Morrel had passed many an anxious hour. In order to meet the end of the month, he had collected all his resources; and fearing lest the report of his distress should get bruited abroad at Marseilles when he was known to have recourse to such measures, he went to the fair of Beaucaire to sell his wife's and daughter's jewels, and a portion of his plate. By this means the honour of the house was still maintained; but his resources were now exhausted. Credit, owing to the reports afloat, was no longer to be had; and to meet the one hundred thousand livres due on the 15th of the present month to M. de Boville, and the one hundred thousand due on the 15th of the next month, M. Morrel had in reality no hope but the return of the *Pharaon*, whose departure he had learned from a vessel which had weighed anchor at the same time, and which had already arrived in harbour. But this vessel, which like the *Pharaon* came from Calcutta, had arrived a fortnight before, while no intelligence had been received of the *Pharaon*.

Such was the state of things when, the day after his interview with M. de Boville, the confidential clerk of the house of Thomson and French, of Rome, presented himself at M. Morrel's. Emmanuel received him; the young man—whom every new face alarmed, for each new face announced a new creditor coming in alarm to question the head of the house—wished to spare his employer the pain of this interview, and questioned the new-comer; but the stranger declared he had nothing to say to Emmanuel, and that his business was with M. Morrel in person. Emmanuel sighed, and summoned Coclès. Coclès appeared; and the young man bade him conduct the stranger to M. Morrel's apartment. Coclès went first, and the stranger followed him. On the staircase they met a beautiful girl of sixteen or seventeen, who looked with anxiety at the stranger.

"M. Morrel is in his office, is he not, Mademoiselle Julie?" said the cashier.

"Yes; I think so, at least," said the young girl, hesitatingly. "Go and see, Coclès; and if my father is there announce this gentleman."

"It will be useless to announce me, mademoiselle," returned the Englishman. "M. Morrel does not know my name; this worthy gentleman has only to announce the confidential clerk of the house of Thomson and French, of Rome, with whom your father does business."

The young girl turned pale, and continued to descend, while the stranger and Coclès continued to mount the staircase. She entered the office where Emmanuel was, while Coclès, by the aid of a key he possessed, opened a door in the corner of a landing-place on the second staircase, conducted the stranger into an ante-chamber, opened a second door, which he closed behind him, and after having left the clerk of the house of Thomson and French alone for a moment, returned and signed to him that he could enter. The Englishman entered, and found Morrel seated at a table, turning over the formidable columns of his ledger, which contained the list of his liabilities. At the sight of the stranger, M. Morrel closed the ledger, rose, and offered a seat to the stranger; and when he had seen him seated, resumed his own chair. Fourteen years had changed the worthy merchant, who, in his thirty-sixth year at the opening of this history, was now in his fiftieth. His hair had turned white; time and sorrow had ploughed deep furrows on his brow; and his look, once so firm and penetrating, was now irresolute and wandering, as if he feared being forced to fix his attention on an idea or a man. The Englishman looked at him with an air of curiosity evidently mingled with interest. "Monsieur," said Morrel, whose uneasiness was increased by this examination, "you wish to speak to me?"

"Yes, monsieur; you are aware from whom I come?"

"The house of Thomson and French; at least so my cashier tells me."

"He has told you rightly. The house of Thomson and French had three or four hundred thousand livres to pay this month in France, and knowing your strict punctuality, have collected all the bills bearing your signature, and charged me as they became due to present them, and to make use of the money." Morrel sighed deeply and passed his hand over his forehead, which was covered with perspiration.

"So, then, sir," said Morrel, "you hold bills of mine?"

"Yes, and for a considerable sum."

"What is the amount?" asked Morrel, with a voice he strove to render firm.

"Here is," said the Englishman, taking a quantity of papers from his pocket, "an assignment of two hundred thousand livres to our house by M. de Boville, the inspector of prisons, to whom they are due. You acknowledge, of course, that you owe this sum to him?"

"Yes; he placed the money in my hands at four and a half per cent. nearly five years ago."

"When are you to pay?"

"Half the 15th of this month, half the 15th of next."

"Just so; and now here are 32,500 livres payable shortly. They are all signed by you and assigned to our house by the holders."

"I recognise them," said M. Morrel, whose face was suffused as he thought that for the first time in his life he would be unable to honour his own signature. "Is this all?"

"No; I have for the end of the month these bills, which have been assigned to us by the house of Pascal, and the house of Wild and Turner, of Marseilles, amounting to nearly fifty-five thousand livres,—in all, 287,500 livres."

It is impossible to describe what Morrel suffered during this enumeration. "287,500 livres!" repeated he.

"Yes, monsieur," replied the Englishman. "I will not," continued he, after a moment's silence, "conceal from you that while your probity and exactitude up to this moment are universally acknowledged, yet the report is current in Marseilles that you are not able to meet your engagements."

At this almost brutal speech Morrel turned deathly pale. "Monsieur," said he, "up to this time—and it is now more than four-and-twenty years since I received the direction of this house from my father, who had himself conducted it for five-and-thirty years—never has anything bearing the signature of Morrel and Son been dishonoured."

"I know that," replied the Englishman. "But as a man of honour should answer another, tell me fairly, shall you pay these with the same punctuality?"

Morrel shuddered, and looked at the man who had spoken thus with more assurance than he had hitherto shown. "To questions frankly put," said he, "a straightforward answer should be given. Yes, I shall pay if, as I hope, my vessel arrives safely,—for its arrival will again procure me the credit which the numerous accidents of which I have been the victim have deprived me; but if the *Pharaon* should be lost, and this last resource be gone—" The poor man's eyes filled with tears.

"Well," said the other, "if this last resource fail you?"

"Well," returned Morrel, "it is a cruel thing to be forced to say, but already used to misfortune, I must habituate myself to shame. I fear I shall be forced to suspend my payments."

"Have you no friends who could assist you?"

Morrel smiled mournfully. "In business, monsieur," said he, "one has no friends, only correspondents."

"It is true," murmured the Englishman; "then you have but one hope?"

"But one."

"The last?"

"The last."

"So that if this fail—"

"I am ruined, completely ruined!"

"As I came here, a vessel was entering the port."

"I know it, monsieur; a young man who still adheres to my fallen fortunes passes a part of his time in a cupola at the top of the house, in hopes of being the first to announce good news to me. He has informed me of the entrance of this ship."

"And it is not yours?"

"No, it is a vessel of Bordeaux, *La Gironde ;* it comes from India also, but it is not mine."

"Perhaps it has spoken the *Pharaon*, and brings you some tidings of it."

"Shall I tell you plainly one thing, monsieur? I dread almost as much to receive any tidings of my vessel as to remain in doubt. Incertitude is still hope." Then in a low voice Morrel added, "This delay is not natural. The *Pharaon* left Calcutta on the 5th of February; it ought to have been here a month ago."

"What is that?" asked the Englishman. "What is the meaning of this noise?"

"Oh, oh!" cried Morrel, turning pale, "what is this?" A loud noise was heard on the stairs, of people moving hastily, and half-stifled sobs. Morrel rose and advanced to the door; but his strength failed him and he sank into a chair. The two men remained opposite one another,—Morrel trembling in every limb, the stranger gazing at him with an air of profound pity. The noise had ceased; but it seemed that Morrel expected something: something had occasioned the noise, and something must follow. The stranger fancied he heard footsteps on the stairs, and that the steps, which were those of several persons, stopped at the door. A key was inserted in the lock of the first door, and the creaking of hinges was audible.

" There are only two persons who have the key of the door," murmured Morrel,—" Coclès and Julie." At this instant the second door opened, and the young girl, her eyes bathed with tears, appeared. Morrel rose tremblingly, supporting himself by the arm of the chair. He would have spoken; but his voice failed him. " Oh, father!" said she, clasping her hands, " forgive your child for being the messenger of ill."

Morrel again changed colour. Julie threw herself into his arms. " Oh, father, father!" murmured she, " courage!"

" The *Pharaon* has then perished?" said Morrel, in a hoarse voice. The young girl did not speak; but she made an affirmative sign with her head as she lay on her father's breast.

" And the crew?" asked Morrel.

" Saved," said the girl; " saved by the crew of the vessel that has just entered the harbour."

Morrel raised his two hands to heaven with an expression of resignation and sublime gratitude. " Thanks, my God," said he; " at least thou strikest but me alone!"

Notwithstanding his habitual impassiveness, a tear moistened the eye of the Englishman.

" Come in, come in!" said Morrel; " for I presume you are all at the door."

Scarcely had he uttered those words when Madame Morrel entered, weeping bitterly; Emmanuel followed her, and in the ante-chamber were visible the rough faces of seven or eight half-naked sailors. At the sight of these men the Englishman started and advanced a step, then restrained himself and retired into the farthest and most obscure corner of the room. Madame Morrel sat down by her husband and took one of his hands in hers; Julie still lay with her head on his shoulder; Emmanuel stood in the centre of the chamber and seemed to serve as a link between Morrel's family and the sailors at the door.

" How did it happen?" said Morrel.

" Draw nearer, Penelon," said the young man, " and relate all."

An old seaman bronzed by the tropical sun advanced, twirling the remains of a hat between his hands. " Good-day, M. Morrel," said he, as if he had quitted Marseilles the previous evening, and had just returned from Aix or Toulon.

"Good-day, Penelon!" returned Morrel, who could not refrain from smiling through his tears; "where is the captain?"

"The captain, M. Morrel,—he has stayed behind sick at Palma; but please God, it won't be much, and you will see him in a few days all alive and hearty."

"Well, now tell your story, Penelon."

Penelon rolled his quid in his cheek, placed his hand before his mouth, turned his head, sent a long jet of tobacco-juice into the ante-chamber, advanced his foot, and began: "You see, M. Morrel," said he, "we were somewhere between Cape Blanc and Cape Bogador, sailing with a fair breeze south-southwest after a week's calm, when Captain Gaumard comes up to me,— I was at the helm I should tell you,—and says, 'Penelon, what do you think of those clouds that are rising there?' I was just then looking at them myself. 'What do I think, captain? why, I think that they are rising faster than they have any business to, and that they would not be so black if they did not mean mischief.' 'That's my opinion, too,' said the captain, 'and I'll take precautions accordingly. We are carrying too much canvas. Holloa! all hands to slacken sail and lower the flying jib!' It was time; the squall was on us, and the vessel began to heel. 'Ah,' said the captain, 'we have still too much canvas set; all hands to lower the mainsail!' Five minutes after, it was down; and we sailed under mizzen-topsails and topgallant-sails. 'Well, Penelon,' said the captain, 'what makes you shake your head?' 'Why,' I says, 'I don't think that we shall stop here.' 'I think you are right,' answered he; 'we shall have a gale.' 'A gale! more than that; we shall have a tempest, or I know nothing about it.' You could see the wind coming like the dust at Montredon; luckily the captain understood his business. 'All hands take in two reefs in the topsails!' cried the captain; 'let go the bowlines, brace to, lower the topgallant-sails, haul out the reef-tackles on the yards!'"

"That was not enough for those latitudes," said the Englishman; "I should have taken four reefs in the topsails and lowered the mizzen."

His firm, sonorous, and unexpected voice made every one start. Penelon put his hand over his eyes, and then stared at the man who thus criticised the manœuvres of his captain. "We did better than that, sir," said the old sailor, with a certain show of respect; "we put the helm to the wind to run before the tempest. Ten minutes after, we struck our topsail, and scudded under bare poles."

" The vessel was very old to risk that," said the Englishman.

" Eh, it was that that wrecked us; after having been tossed about for twelve hours we sprang a leak. ' Penelon,' said the captain, ' I think we are sinking; give me the helm and go down into the hold.' I gave him the helm and descended; there was already three feet of water. I cried, ' All hands to the pumps! ' but it was too late, and it seemed the more we pumped the more came in. ' Ah,' said I, after four hours' work, ' since we are sinking, let us sink; we can die but once.' ' Is that the example you set, Penelon? ' cries the captain; ' very well, wait a minute.' He went into his cabin and came back with a brace of pistols. ' I will blow the brains out of the first man who leaves the pump,' said he."

" Well done! " said the Englishman.

" There's nothing gives you so much courage as good reasons," continued the sailor. " During that time the wind had abated, and the sea had gone down; but the water kept rising,—not much, only two inches an hour, but still it rose. Two inches an hour does not seem much, but in twelve hours that makes two feet; and two feet with the three we had before makes five. ' Come,' said the captain, ' we have done all in our power, and M. Morrel will have nothing to reproach us with; we have tried to save the ship, let us now save ourselves. To the boats, my lads, as quick as you can! ' Now," continued Penelon, " you see, M. Morrel, a sailor is attached to his ship, but still more to his life; so we did not wait to be told twice. The more so that the ship was sinking under us, and seemed to say, ' Get along; save yourselves! ' We soon launched the boat, and all eight of us got into it. The captain descended the last, or rather he did not descend, he would not leave the vessel; so I took him round the waist and threw him into the boat, and then I jumped after him. It was time, for just as I jumped, the deck burst with a noise like the broadside of a man-of-war. Ten minutes after she pitched forward, then the other way, spun round and round, and then good-bye to the *Pharaon*. As for us, we were three days without anything to eat or drink, so that we began to think of drawing lots who should feed the rest, when we saw *La Gironde ;* we made signals of distress, she perceived us, made for us, and took us all on board. There now, M. Morrel, that's the whole truth, on the honour of a sailor; is not it true, you fellows there? "

A general murmur of approbation showed that the narrator had faithfully detailed their misfortunes and sufferings.

" Well, well," said M. Morrel, " I know there was no one in

fault but destiny. It was the will of God that this should happen; blessed be his name! What wages are due to you?"

"Oh, don't let us talk of that, M. Morrel."

"On the contrary, let us speak of it."

"Well, then, for three months," said Penelon.

"Coclès! pay two hundred livres to each of these good fellows," said Morrel. "At another time," added he, "I should have said, Give them, besides, two hundred livres over as a present; but times are changed, and the little money that remains to me is not my own."

Penelon turned to his companions, and exchanged a few words with them.

"As for that, M. Morrel," said he, again turning his quid,— "as for that—"

"As for what?"

"The money."

"Well?"

"Well, we all say that fifty livres will be enough for us at present, and that we will wait for the rest."

"Thanks, my friends, thanks!" cried Morrel, touched to the heart. "Take it, take it! and if you can find another employer, enter his service. You are free to do so."

These last words produced a prodigious effect on the seamen; Penelon nearly swallowed his quid; fortunately he recovered. "What! M. Morrel," said he, in a low voice, "you send us away? you are then angry with us!"

"No, no!" said M. Morrel, "I am not angry. I do not send you away; but I have no more ships, and therefore I do not want any sailors."

"No more ships!" returned Penelon; "well, then, you'll build some. We'll wait for you."

"I have no money to build ships with, Penelon," said the owner, with a sad smile, "so that I cannot accept your kind offer."

"No more money! then you must not pay us. We can go, like the *Pharaon*, under bare poles."

"Enough! enough, my friends!" cried Morrel, almost overpowered. "Leave me, I pray you; we shall meet again in a happier time. Emmanuel, accompany them, and see that my orders are executed."

"At least, we shall see each other again, M. Morrel?" asked Penelon.

"Yes, my friends; I hope so, at least. Now go." He made a sign to Coclès, who marched first; the seamen followed him, and Emmanuel brought up the rear. "Now," said the owner to his wife and daughter, "leave me; I wish to speak to this gentleman." And he glanced towards the clerk of Thomson and French, who had remained motionless in the corner during this scene, in which he had taken no part except the few words we have mentioned. The two women looked at this person, whose presence they had entirely forgotten, and retired; but as she left the room, Julie gave the stranger a supplicating glance, to which he replied by a smile that an indifferent spectator would have been surprised to see on his stern features. The two men were left alone. "Well, sir," said Morrel, sinking into a chair, "you have heard all; and I have nothing further to tell you."

"I see," returned the Englishman, "that a new and unmerited misfortune has overwhelmed you; and this only increases my desire to serve you."

"Oh, monsieur!" cried Morrel.

"Let me see," continued the stranger, "I am one of your largest creditors, am I not?"

"Your bills, at least, are the first that will fall due."

"Do you wish for time to pay?"

"A delay would save my honour, and consequently my life."

"How long a delay do you wish for?"

Morrel reflected. "Two months," said he.

"I will give you three," replied the stranger.

"But," asked Morrel, "will the house of Thomson and French consent?"

"Oh, I take everything on myself. To-day is the 5th of June."

"Yes."

"Well, renew these bills up to the 5th of September; and on the 5th of September, at eleven o'clock [the hand of the clock pointed to eleven], I shall come to receive the money."

"I shall expect you," returned Morrel; "and I will pay you —or I shall be dead." These last words were uttered in so low a tone that the stranger could not hear them. The bills were renewed, the old ones destroyed; and the poor ship-owner found himself with three months before him to collect his resources. The Englishman received his thanks with the calmness peculiar to his race; and Morrel, overwhelming him with grateful blessings, conducted him to the staircase. The stranger met Julie on the stairs; she affected to be descending, but in reality she was waiting for him. "Oh, monsieur!" said she, clasping her hands.

"Mademoiselle," said the stranger, "one day you will receive a letter signed 'Sinbad the Sailor.' Do exactly what the letter bids you, however strange it may appear to you."

"Yes, sir," returned Julie.

"Do you promise?"

"I swear to you I will!"

"It is well. Adieu, mademoiselle! Remain as pure and virtuous as you are at present, and I have great hopes that heaven will reward you by giving you Emmanuel for a husband."

Julie uttered a faint cry, blushed like a rose, and leaned against the baluster. The stranger waved his hand, and continued to descend. In the court he found Penelon, who, with a *rouleau* of a hundred livres in either hand, seemed unable to make up his mind to retain them.

"Come with me, my friend," said the Englishman; "I wish to speak to you."

CHAPTER XXX

THE FIFTH OF SEPTEMBER

The delay afforded by the agent of the house of Thomson and French, at the moment when Morrel expected it least, appeared to the poor ship-owner one of those returns of good fortune which announce to a man that Fate is at length weary of wasting her spite upon him. The same day he related to his wife, to Emmanuel, and his daughter, what had occurred to him; and a ray of hope, if not tranquillity, returned to the family. Unfortunately, however, Morrel had engagements not alone with the house of Thomson and French, who had shown themselves so considerate towards him; and as he had said, in business one has correspondents, and not friends. When he reflected deeply, he could by no means account for this generous conduct on the part of Thomson and French towards him, and could only attribute it to the selfish reflection which that house might have made: "We had better support a man who owes us nearly three hundred thousand livres, and have those three hundred thousand livres at the end of three months, than hasten his ruin, and get but six or eight per cent. of the debt." Unfortunately, whether from hate or blindness, all Morrel's correspondents did not reflect similarly; and some made even a contrary reflection. The bills signed by Morrel were therefore presented at his office with scrupulous exactitude, and thanks to the delay granted by the Englishman, were paid by Coclès with equal punctuality. Coclès thus remained in his accustomed tranquillity. It was Morrel alone who remembered with alarm that if he had to repay on the 15th the fifty thousand livres of M. de Boville, and on the 30th the 32,500 livres of bills, for which, as well as the debt due to the inspector of prisons, he had time granted, he must be a ruined man.

The opinion of all the commercial men was that under the reverses which had successively weighed down Morrel, it was impossible for him to stand secure. Great therefore was the astonishment when they saw the end of the month come, and that he fulfilled all his engagements with his usual punctuality. Still, confidence was not restored to all minds, and the general voice postponed only until the end of the month following, the complete ruin of the unfortunate ship-owner. The month passed amid unheard-of efforts on the part of Morrel to get in all his resources. Formerly his paper, at any date, was taken with confidence, and was even in request. Morrel now tried to negotiate bills at ninety days only, and found all the banks closed. Fortunately Morrel had some moneys coming in on which he could rely; and as they reached him, he found himself in a condition to meet his engagements when the end of July came. The agent of Thomson and French had not been again seen at Marseilles. The day after, or two days after, his visit to Morrel, he had disappeared; and as in that city he had had no intercourse but with the mayor, the inspector of prisons, and M. Morrel, his appearance left no other trace than the different remembrances of him which these three persons retained. As to the sailors of the *Pharaon*, it seemed that they must have found some engagement, for they had disappeared also.

Captain Gaumard, recovered from his illness, had returned from Palma. He hesitated to present himself at Morrel's, but the owner, hearing of his arrival, went to him. The worthy ship-owner knew from Penelon's recital of the captain's brave conduct during the storm, and tried to console him. He brought him also the amount of his wages, which Captain Gaumard had not dared to apply for. As he descended the staircase, Morrel met Penelon, who was going up. Penelon had, it would seem, made good use of his money, for he was newly clad. When he saw his employer, the worthy tar seemed much embarrassed, drew on one side into the corner of the landing-place, passed his quid from one cheek to the other, stared stupidly with his great eyes, and only acknowledged the

squeeze of the hand which Morrel as usual gave him by a slight
pressure in return. Morrel attributed Penelon's embarrassment to the elegance of his attire; it was evident that the good
fellow had not gone to such an expense on his own account. He
was no doubt engaged on board some other vessel, and thus his
bashfulness arose from the fact of his not having, if we may
so express ourselves, worn mourning for the *Pharaon* longer.
Perhaps he had come to tell Captain Gaumard of his good luck,
and to offer him employment from his new master. " Worthy
fellows ! " said Morrel, as he went away, " may your new master
love you as I loved you, and be more fortunate than I have
been ! "

August rolled by in unceasing efforts on the part of Morrel to
renew his credit or open new accounts. On the 20th of August
it was known at Marseilles that he had taken a place in the *malle-
poste*, and then it was said that it was at the end of the month
the docket was to be struck; and Morrel had gone away that
he might not be present at this cruel act, but had left his chief
clerk, Emmanuel, and his cashier Coclès to meet it. But contrary to all expectation, when the 31st of August came the house
opened as usual, and Coclès appeared behind the grating of the
counter, examined all bills presented with the same scrutiny,
and from first to last, paid all with the same precision. There
came in, moreover, two indorsed notes which M. Morrel had
discounted, and which Coclès paid as punctually as those bills
on which the ship-owner was directly liable. All this was incomprehensible; and then, with the tenacity peculiar to
prophets of evil, the failure was fixed to take place at the end
of September. On the 1st, Morrel returned; he was awaited by
his family with extreme anxiety, for on this journey to Paris
they had rested their last hopes. Morrel had thought of
Danglars, who was now immensely rich, and had been under
great obligations to Morrel in former days, since to him it was
owing that Danglars entered the service of the Spanish banker
with whom his immense fortune had its beginning. It was
said at this moment that Danglars was worth from six million
to eight million livres, and had unlimited credit. Danglars
then, without taking a crown from his pocket, could save
Morrel; he had but to pass his word for a loan, and Morrel was
saved. Morrel had long thought of Danglars; but there are
instinctive revoltings impossible to control, and Morrel had
delayed as long as possible before he had recourse to this last
resource. And Morrel was right, for he returned home borne
down by all the humiliation of a refusal. Yet on his arrival

Morrel did not utter a complaint, nor say one harsh word; he embraced his weeping wife and daughter, pressed Emmanuel's hand with friendly warmth, and then going to his private room on the second floor, had sent for Coclès.

"Then," said the two women to Emmanuel, "we are indeed ruined."

It was agreed in a brief council held among them that Julie should write to her brother, who was in garrison at Nismes, to come to them as speedily as possible. The poor women felt instinctively that they would need all their strength to support the blow that impended. Besides, Maximilian Morrel, though hardly two-and-twenty, had great influence over his father. He was a strong-minded, upright young man. At the time when he decided on his profession his father had no desire to choose for him, but had consulted young Maximilian's taste. He had at once declared for a military life; he had afterwards studied hard, passed brilliantly through the Ecole Polytechnique, and left it as sub-lieutenant of the Fifty-third of the line. For a year he had held this rank, and expected promotion on the first vacancy. In his regiment Maximilian Morrel was noted as a most rigid observer, not only of the obligations imposed on a soldier, but also of the duties of a man; and he thus gained the name of "the Stoic." We need hardly say that many of those who gave him this epithet repeated it because they had heard it, and did not even know what it meant.

This was the young man whom his mother and sister called to their aid to sustain them under the grave circumstances which they felt they would soon have to endure. They had not mistaken the gravity of this event, for the moment after Morrel had entered his office with Coclès, Julie saw the latter leave it, pale, trembling, and his features betraying the utmost consternation. She would have questioned him as he passed by her, but the worthy creature hastened down the staircase with unusual precipitation, and only raised his hands to heaven and exclaimed, "Oh, mademoiselle, mademoiselle! what a dreadful misfortune! Who could ever have believed it!" A moment afterwards Julie saw him go upstairs carrying two or three heavy ledgers, a pocket-book, and a bag of money.

Morrel examined the ledgers, opened the pocket-book, and counted the money. All his funds amounted to six thousand or eight thousand livres, his expectancies up to the 5th to four thousand or five thousand, which, making the best of everything, gave him fourteen thousand livres to meet bills amounting to 287,500 livres. He could not make such a proposal.

However, when Morrel went down to his dinner, he appeared very composed. This calmness was more alarming to the two women than the deepest dejection would have been. After dinner Morrel usually went out, and used to take his coffee at the club of the Phocéens, and read the *Semaphore ;* but this day he did not leave the house, he returned to his office.

As to Coclès, he seemed completely bewildered. For part of the day he went into the courtyard, seated himself on a stone with his head bare, and exposed to a sun of thirty degrees. Emmanuel tried to comfort the women; but his eloquence faltered. The young man was too well acquainted with the business of the house not to feel that a great catastrophe hung over the Morrel family. Night came. The two women had watched, hoping that when he left his room Morrel would come to them; but they heard him pass before their door, trying to conceal the noise of his footsteps. They listened; he went into his sleeping-room and fastened the door inside. Madame Morrel sent her daughter to bed; and half an hour after Julie had retired she rose, took off her shoes, and went stealthily along the passage to see through the keyhole what her husband was doing. In the passage she saw a retreating shadow; it was Julie, who, uneasy herself, had anticipated her mother. The young lady went towards Madame Morrel. " He is writing," she said. They had understood each other without speaking. Madame Morrel looked again through the keyhole. Morrel was writing; but Madame Morrel remarked what her daughter had not observed, that her husband was writing on stamped paper. The terrible idea that he was writing his will flashed across her; she shuddered, and yet had not strength to utter a word. Next day M. Morrel seemed as calm as ever, went into his office as usual, and came to his breakfast punctually; but after dinner he placed his daughter beside him, took her head in his arms, and held her for a long time against his bosom. In the evening Julie told her mother that although he was so calm in appearance, she had remarked that her father's heart beat violently. The next two days passed in the same manner. On the evening of the 4th of September, M. Morrel asked his daughter for the key of his office. Julie trembled at this request, which seemed to her of bad omen. Why did her father ask for this key which she always kept, and which was only taken from her in childhood as a punishment? The young girl looked at Morrel. " What have I done wrong, father," she said, " that you should take this key from me ? "

" Nothing, my dear," replied the unhappy man, the tears

starting to his eyes at this simple question; "nothing, only I want it."

Julie made a pretence to feel for the key. "I must have left it in my room," she said. And she went out; but instead of going to her apartment she hastened to consult Emmanuel. "Do not give this key to your father," said he; "and to-morrow morning, if possible, do not quit him for a moment." She questioned Emmanuel, but he knew nothing, or would not say anything. During the night between the 4th and 5th of September Madame Morrel remained listening for every sound, and until three o'clock in the morning she heard her husband pacing the room in great agitation. It was three o'clock when he threw himself on the bed. The mother and daughter passed the night together. They had expected Maximilian since the previous evening. At eight o'clock in the morning Morrel entered their chamber. He was calm; but the agitation of the night was legible in his pale and careworn visage. They did not dare to ask him how he had slept. Morrel was kinder to his wife, more affectionate to his daughter, than he had ever been. He could not cease gazing at and kissing the sweet girl. Julie, mindful of Emmanuel's request, was following her father when he quitted the room, but he said to her quickly, "Remain with your mother." Julie wished to accompany him. "I wish it," he said.

This was the first time Morrel had said to his daughter, "I wish it;" but he said it in a tone of paternal kindness, and Julie did not dare refuse compliance. She remained on the same spot, standing mute and motionless. An instant afterward the door opened, she felt two arms encircle her, and lips were pressed upon her forehead. She looked up and uttered an exclamation of joy. "Maximilian! my brother!" she cried. At these words Madame Morrel rose and threw herself into her son's arms.

"Mother," said the young man, looking alternately at Madame Morrel and her daughter, "what has happened? Your letter has frightened me, and I have come hither with all speed."

"Julie," said Madame Morrel, making a sign to the young man, "go and tell your father that Maximilian has just arrived." The young lady rushed out of the apartment, but on the first step of the staircase she found a man holding a letter in his hand.

"Are you not Mademoiselle Julie Morrel?" inquired the man, with a strong Italian accent.

"Yes, sir," replied Julie, with hesitation; "what is your pleasure? I do not know you."

"Read this letter," he said, handing it to her. Julie hesitated. "It concerns the best interests of your father," said the messenger.

The young girl hastily took the letter from him. She opened it quickly and read:—

Go this moment to the Allées de Meillan; enter the house No. 15; ask the porter for the key of the room on the fifth floor; enter the apartment, take from the corner of the mantel-piece a purse netted in red silk, and give it to your father. It is important that he should receive it before eleven o'clock. You promised to obey me implicitly. Remember your promise.

SINBAD THE SAILOR.

The young girl uttered a joyful cry, raised her eyes, looked round to question the messenger, but he had disappeared. She cast her eyes again over the note to peruse it a second time, and saw there was a postscript. She read:—

It is important that you should fulfil this mission in person and alone. If you go accompanied by any other person, or should any one else present himself, the porter will reply that he does not know anything about it.

This postscript was a great check to the young girl's joy. Was there nothing to fear; was there not some snare laid for her? Her innocence had kept her in ignorance of the dangers that might assail a young girl of her age. But there is no need to know danger in order to fear it; indeed, it may be observed that it is usually unknown perils that inspire the greatest terror.

Julie hesitated, and resolved to take counsel. Yet, by a singular feeling, it was neither to her mother nor her brother that she applied, but to Emmanuel. She hastened down and told him what had occurred on the day when the agent of the house of Thomson and French had come to her father's, related the scene on the staircase, repeated the promise she had made, and showed him the letter.

"You must go, then, mademoiselle," said Emmanuel.

"Go there?" murmured Julie.

"Yes; I will accompany you."

"But did you not read that I must be alone?" said Julie.

"And you shall be alone," replied the young man. "I will await you at the corner of the Rue du Musée; and if you are so long absent as to make me uneasy, I will hasten to rejoin you, and woe to him of whom you shall have cause to complain to me!"

"Then, Emmanuel," said the young girl, with hesitation, "it is your opinion that I should obey this injunction."

" Yes; did not the messenger say that it concerns your father's safety? "

" But what danger threatens him, then, Emmanuel? " she asked.

Emmanuel hesitated a moment; but his desire to make Julie decide immediately urged him on.

" Listen," he said; " to-day is the 5th of September, is it not? "

" Yes."

" To-day, then, at eleven o'clock, your father has nearly three hundred thousand livres to pay."

" Yes, we know that."

" Well," continued Emmanuel, " we have not fifteeen thousand livres in the house."

" What will happen then? "

" Why, if to-day before eleven o'clock your father has not found some one who will come to his aid, he will be compelled at twelve o'clock to declare himself a bankrupt."

" Oh, come, come! " cried she, hastening away with the young man.

During this time, Madame Morrel had told her son everything. The young man knew quite well that after the succession of misfortunes which had befallen his father, great changes had taken place in the style of living and housekeeping; but he did not know that matters had reached such a point. He was thunderstruck. Then, rushing hastily out of the apartment, he ran up the stairs, expecting to find his father in his office, but he rapped there in vain. While he was yet at the door of the office he heard the bedroom door open, turned, and saw his father. Instead of going direct to his office, M. Morrel had returned to his bed-chamber, which he was only this moment quitting. Morrel uttered a cry of surprise at the sight of his son, of whose arrival he was ignorant. He remained motionless on the spot, pressing with his left hand something he had concealed under his coat. Maximilian sprang down the staircase and threw his arms round his father's neck; but suddenly he recoiled and placed his right hand on Morrel's breast. " Father! " he exclaimed, turning pale as death, " what are you going to do with the brace of pistols under your coat? "

" Oh, this is what I feared! " said Morrel.

" Father, father! in Heaven's name," exclaimed the young man, " what are these weapons for? "

" Maximilian," replied Morrell, looking fixedly at his son, " you are a man, and a man of honour. Come, and I will explain to you."

And with a firm step Morrel went up to his office, while Maximilian followed him, trembling as he went. Morrel opened the door, and closed it behind his son, then, crossing the ante-room, went to his desk, on which he placed the pistols, and pointed with his finger to an open ledger. In this ledger was made out an exact balance-sheet of affairs. Morrel had to pay, within half an hour, 287,500 livres. All he possessed was 15,257 livres. " Read! " said Morrel.

The young man was overwhelmed as he read. Morrel said not a word. What could he say? What need he add to such a desperate proof in figures?

" And have you done all that is possible, father, to meet this disastrous result? " asked the young man, after a moment's pause.

" I have," replied Morrel.

" You have no money coming in on which you can rely? "

" None."

" You have exhausted every resource? "

" All."

" And in half an hour," said Maximilian, in a gloomy voice, " our name is dishonoured! "

" Blood washes out dishonour," said Morrel.

" You are right, father; I understand you." Then extending his hand towards one of the pistols, he said, " There is one for you and one for me; thanks! "

Morrel checked his hand. " Your mother! your sister! Who will support them? "

A shudder ran through the young man's frame.

" Father," he said, " do you reflect that you are bidding me to live? "

" Yes, I do bid you," answered Morrel; " it is your duty. You have a calm, strong mind, Maximilian. Maximilian, you are no ordinary man. I desire nothing; I command nothing; I only say to you, examine my position as if it were your own, and then judge for yourself."

The young man reflected an instant; then an expression of sublime resignation appeared in his eyes, and with a slow and sad gesture he took off his two epaulettes, the marks of his rank. " Be it so, then, my father," he said, extending his hand to Morrel; " die in peace, my father. I will live."

Morrel was about to cast himself on his knees before his son, but Maximilian caught him in his arms, and those two noble hearts were pressed against each other for a moment. " You know it is not my fault," said Morrel.

Maximilian smiled. " I know, father, you are the most honourable man I have ever known."

" Good, my son. And now all is said; go now and rejoin your mother and sister."

" My father," said the young man, bending his knee, " bless me ! "

Morrel took his head between his two hands, drew him towards him, and kissing his forehead several times, said, " Oh, yes, yes; I bless you in my own name and in the name of three generations of irreproachable men, who say by my voice, ' The edifice which misfortune has destroyed, Providence may build up again.' On seeing me die such a death the most inexorable will have pity on you. To you, perhaps, they will accord the time they have refused to me. Try that the word of disgrace be never pronounced. Go to work, labour, young man; struggle ardently and courageously; live, yourself, your mother and sister, with the most rigid economy, so that from day to day the property of those to whom I am indebted may augment and fructify in your hands. Reflect how glorious a day it will be, how grand, how solemn, that day of complete restoration on which you will say in this very office, ' My father died because he could not do what I have this day done; but he died calmly and peaceably, because in dying he knew what I should do.' "

" My father ! my father ! " cried the young man, " why should you not live ? "

" If I live, all would be changed; if I live, interest would be converted into doubt, pity into hostility. If I live, I am only a man who has broken his word, failed in his engagements,—in fact, only a bankrupt. If on the contrary I die, remember, Maximilian, my corpse is that of an honest but unfortunate man. Living, my best friends would avoid my house; dead, all Marseilles will follow me in tears to my last home. Living, you would feel shame at my name; dead, you may raise your head and say, ' I am the son of him who killed himself because for the first time he has been compelled to fail in his word.' "

The young man uttered a groan, but appeared resigned. For the second time conviction entered, not his heart, but his mind.

" And now," said Morrel, " leave me alone, and endeavour to keep your mother and sister away."

" Will you not see my sister once more ? " asked Maximilian. A last dull hope was concealed by the young man in the effect of this interview, and he had suggested it for that reason.

Morrel shook his head. "I saw her this morning," he said, "and bade her adieu."

"Have you no particular commands to leave with me, my father?" inquired Maximilian, in a faltering voice.

"Yes, my son, and a sacred command."

"Say it, my father."

"The house of Thomson and French is the only one who from humanity, or it may be selfishness,—it is not for me to read men's hearts,—has had any pity for me. Its agent, who will in ten minutes present himself to receive the amount of a bill of 287,500 livres, I will not say granted, but offered me three months. Let this house be the first repaid, my son, and let that man be sacred to you."

"Father, I will," said Maximilian.

"And now once more, adieu," said Morrel. "Go! leave me. I would be alone. You will find my will in the secretary in my bedroom."

The young man remained standing and motionless, having only the force to will but not the power to execute.

"Hear me, Maximilian," said his father. "Suppose I were a soldier like you, and ordered to carry a certain redoubt, and you knew I must be killed in the assault, would you not say to me, as you said just now, 'Go, father; for you are dishonoured by delay, and death is preferable to shame'?"

"Yes, yes!" said the young man, "yes!" and once again embracing his father with convulsive pressure, he said, "Be it so, my father." And he rushed out of the cabinet.

When his son had left him, Morrel remained an instant standing with his eyes fixed on the door; then putting forth his arm, he pulled the bell. After a moment's interval, Coclès appeared.

He was no longer the same man; the fearful convictions of the last three days had crushed him. This thought—the house of Morrel and Son is about to stop payment—bent him to the earth more than twenty years would otherwise have done.

"My worthy Coclès," said Morrel, in a tone impossible to describe, "do you remain in the ante-chamber. When the gentleman who came three months ago—the agent of the house of Thomson and French—arrives, announce his arrival to me." Coclès made no reply; he made a sign with his head, went into the anteroom, and seated himself. Morrel fell back in his chair, his eyes fixed on the clock; there were seven minutes left, that was all. The hand moved on with incredible rapidity; it seemed to him as if he saw it move.

What then passed at this final moment of time in the mind

of this man, who, still young, by a course of reasoning, false perhaps, but at least specious, was about to separate himself from all he loved in the world, and quit life, which possessed for him all domestic delights, it is impossible to express. To form any idea of his feelings, he must have been seen with his brow bathed in perspiration, yet resigned, his eyes moistened with tears and yet raised to heaven. The clock-hand moved on. The pistols were cocked; he stretched forth his hand, took one up, and murmured his daughter's name. Then he laid down the mortal weapon, took up his pen, and wrote a few words. It seemed to him as if he had not taken a sufficient farewell of his beloved daughter. Then he turned again to the clock; he no longer counted by minutes, but by seconds. He took up the deadly weapon again, his mouth half-opened and his eyes fixed on the clock, and then shuddered at the click of the trigger as he cocked the pistol. At this moment a colder perspiration moistened his brow; a more mortal agony clutched at his heart-strings. He heard the door of the staircase creak on its hinges; the clock gave its warning to strike eleven; the door of his cabinet opened. Morrel did not turn round; he expected these words of Coclès, "The agent of Thomson and French." He placed the muzzle of the pistol between his teeth. Suddenly he heard a cry,—it was his daughter's voice. He turned and saw Julie. The pistol fell from his hands.

"My father!" cried the young girl, out of breath and half dead with joy; "saved! you are saved!" And she threw herself into his arms, holding in her extended hand a red netted silk purse.

"Saved, my child!" said Morrel; "what do you mean?"

"Yes, saved—saved! see, see!" said the young girl.

Morrel took the purse, and started as he did so, for a vague remembrance reminded him that it once belonged to himself. At one end was the bill for the 287,500 livres. The bill was receipted. At the other end was a diamond as large as a hazel-nut, with these words on a small slip of parchment: "Julie's Dowry."

Morrel passed his hand over his brow; it seemed to him a dream. At this moment the clock struck eleven. The sound vibrated through him as if each stroke of the hammer struck on his heart. "Explain, my child," he said, "explain! where did you find this purse?"

"In a house in the Allées de Meillan, No. 15, on the corner of a mantel-piece in a small room on the fifth floor."

"But," cried Morrel, "this purse is not yours!"

Julie handed to her father the letter she had received in the morning.

" And did you go alone? " asked Morrel, after he had read it.

" Emmanuel accompanied me, father. He was to have waited for me at the corner of the Rue du Musée, but strange to say, he was not there when I returned."

" M. Morrel! " exclaimed a voice on the stairs,—" M. Morrel!"

" It is his voice! " said Julie. At this moment Emmanuel entered, his countenance full of animation and joy. " The *Pharaon!* " he cried; " the *Pharaon!* "

" What!—what! the *Pharaon!* Are you mad, Emmanuel? You know the vessel is lost."

" The *Pharaon*, sir! they signal the *Pharaon!* The *Pharaon* is entering the harbour! "

Morrel fell back in his chair. His strength was failing him; his understanding refused to comprehend such incredible, unheard-of, fabulous events. But his son came in.

" Father! " cried Maximilian, " how could you say the *Pharaon* was lost? She has been signalled from the watch-tower, and they say she is now coming into port."

" My dear friends! " said Morrel, " if this were so, it must be a miracle of Heaven! Impossible! impossible! "

But what was real and not less incredible was the purse he held in his hand, the acceptance receipted, the splended diamond.

" Ah, monsieur! " exclaimed Coclès, " what can it mean,— the *Pharaon?* "

" Come, my dear," said Morrel, rising from his seat, " let us go and see, and Heaven have pity upon us if it be false intelligence! "

They all went out, and on the stairs met Madame Morrel, who had been afraid to go up into the office. In an instant they were at the Canebière. There was a crowd on the pier. All the crowd gave way before Morrel. " The *Pharaon!* the *Pharaon!* " said every voice.

And wonderful to say, in front of the tower of St. Jean was a vessel bearing on her stern these words, printed in white letters, " The *Pharaon*, Morrel and Son, of Marseilles." It precisely resembled the other *Pharaon*, and was loaded, as that had been, with cochineal and indigo. It cast anchor, brailed all sails, and on the deck was Captain Gaumard giving orders, and Maître Penelon making signals to M. Morrel. To doubt any longer was impossible! there was the evidence of the senses, and ten thousand persons who came to corroborate the testimony. As Morrel and his son embraced on the pier-head in the presence and amid the applause of the whole city witnessing this prodigy, a man with his face half-covered by a black beard, and who, concealed behind the sentry-box, watched the scene with delight, uttered these words in a low tone, " Be happy, noble heart! be blessed for all the good thou hast done and wilt do hereafter, and let my gratitude rest in the shade with your kindness! "

And with a smile in which joy and happiness were revealed, he left his hiding-place, and without being observed descended one of those flights of steps which serve for debarkation, and hailing three times, shouted " Jacopo! Jacopo! Jacopo! " Then a shallop came to shore, took him on board, and conveyed him to a yacht splendidly fitted up, on whose deck he sprang with the activity of a sailor; thence he once again looked towards Morrel, who weeping with joy was shaking hands most cordially with all the crowd around him, and thanking with a look the unknown benefactor whom he seemed to be seeking in the skies.

" And now," said the unknown, "farewell kindness, humanity, and gratitude! Farewell to all the feelings that expand the heart! I have been Heaven's substitute to recompense the good; now the god of vengeance yields to me his power to punish the wicked! " At these words he gave a signal, and as if only awaiting this signal, the yacht instantly put out to sea.

CHAPTER XXXI

ITALY: SINBAD THE SAILOR

TOWARDS the beginning of the year 1838, two young men belonging to the first society of Paris, the Vicomte Albert de Morcerf and the Baron Franz d'Epinay, were at Florence. They had agreed to see the Carnival at Rome that year, and that Franz, who for the last three or four years had inhabited Italy, should act as *cicerone* to Albert. As it is no slight affair to spend the Carnival at Rome, especially when you have no great desire to sleep on the Place du Peuple, or the Campo Vaccino, they wrote to Maître Pastrini, the proprietor of the Hôtel de Londres, Place d'Espagne, to reserve comfortable apartments for them. Maître Pastrini replied that he had only two rooms and a cabinet *al secondo piano*, which he offered at the low charge of a louis *per diem*. They accepted his offer; but wishing to make the best use of the time that was left, Albert started for Naples. As for Franz, he remained at Florence. After having passed several days here, when he had walked in the Eden called the Casines, when he had passed two or three evenings at the houses of the nobles of Florence, he took a fancy into his head after having already visited Corsica, the cradle of Bonaparte, to visit Elba, the halting-place of Napoleon.

One evening he loosened a boat from the iron ring that secured it to the port of Leghorn, laid himself down, wrapped in his cloak, at the bottom, and said to the crew, "To the Isle of Elba!" The boat shot out of the harbour like a bird, and the next morning Franz disembarked at Porto Ferrajo. He traversed the island after having followed the traces which the footsteps of the giant have left, and re-embarked for Marciana. Two hours after he landed at Pianosa, where he was assured that red partridges abounded. The sport was bad; Franz succeeded in killing only a few partridges, and like every unsuccessful sportsman, he returned to the boat very much out of temper.

"Ah, if your excellency chose," said the captain, "you might have capital sport."

"Where?"

"Do you see that island?" continued the captain, pointing to a conical pile that rose from the blue sea.

"Well; what is this island?"

"The island of Monte Cristo."

"But I have no permission to shoot over this island."

"Your excellency does not require a permission, for the island is uninhabited."

"Ah, indeed!" said the young man. "A desert island in the midst of the Mediterranean must be a curiosity."

"It is very natural; this isle is a mass of rocks, and does not contain an acre of land capable of cultivation."

"To whom does this island belong?"

"To Tuscany."

"What game shall I find there?"

"Thousands of wild goats."

"Who live by licking the stones, I suppose," said Franz, with an incredulous smile.

"No; but by browsing the shrubs and trees that grow out of the crevices of the rocks."

"Where can I sleep?"

"On shore, in the grottos, or on board in your cloak; besides, if your excellency pleases, we can leave as soon as the chase is finished. We can sail as well by night as by day, and if the wind drops we can use our oars."

As Franz had sufficient time before rejoining his companion, and had no further occasion to trouble himself about his apartment in Rome, he accepted the proposition. Upon his answer in the affirmative, the sailors exchanged a few words together in a low tone. "Well," he asked; "what? is there any difficulty to be surmounted?"

"No," replied the captain, "but we must warn your excellency that the island is contumacious."

"What do you mean?"

"That Monte Cristo, although uninhabited, yet serves occasionally as a refuge for the smugglers and pirates who come from Corsica, Sardinia, and Africa; and that if anything betrays that we have been there, we shall have to perform quarantine for six days on our return to Leghorn."

"The devil! that is quite another thing! Six days! just the time which God required to create the world. It is somewhat long, my children."

"But who will say that your excellency has been to Monte Cristo?"

"Oh, I shall not," cried Franz.

"Nor I! nor I!" chorused the sailors.

"Then steer for Monte Cristo."

The captain gave his orders; the bow was turned towards the island; and the boat was soon sailing in that direction. Franz waited until all was finished; and when the sail was filled and the four sailors had taken their places, three forward and one at the helm, he resumed the conversation. "Gaetano," said he to the captain, "you tell me Monte Cristo serves as a refuge for pirates, who are, it seems to me, a very different kind of game from the goats."

"Yes, your excellency; and it is true."

"I knew there were smugglers; but I thought that since the capture of Algiers and the destruction of the regency, pirates existed only in the romances of Cooper and Captain Marryat."

"Your excellency is mistaken; there are pirates, just as there are bandits,—who were believed to have been exterminated by Pope Leo XII., and who yet every day rob travellers at the gates of Rome. Has not your excellency heard that the French *chargé d'affaires* was robbed six months ago within five hundred paces of Velletri?"

"Oh, yes, I heard that."

"Well, then, if like us your excellency lived at Leghorn, you would hear from time to time that a little merchant vessel, or an English yacht that was expected at Bastia, at Porto

Ferrajo, or at Civita Vecchia, has not arrived; that no one knows what has become of it, and that doubtless it has struck on a rock and foundered. Now, this rock it has met is a long and narrow boat manned by six or eight men, who have surprised and plundered it some dark and stormy night near some desert and gloomy isle, as bandits plunder a carriage at the corner of a wood."

"But," asked Franz, who lay wrapped in his cloak at the bottom of the bark, "why do not those who have been plundered complain to the French, Sardinian, or Tuscan governments?"

"Why?" said Gaetano, with a smile.

"Yes, why?"

"Because in the first place they transfer from the vessel to their own boat whatever they think worth taking, then they bind the crew hand and foot; they attach to every one's neck a four-and-twenty pound ball; a large hole is pierced in the vessel's bottom, and then they leave her. At the end of ten minutes the vessel begins to roll, labour, and then sink; then one of the sides plunges and then the other. It rises and sinks again; suddenly a noise like the report of a cannon is heard, —it is the air breaking the deck. Soon the water rushes out of the scupper-holes like a whale spouting; the vessel gives a last groan, spins round and round and disappears, forming a vast whirlpool in the ocean, and then all is over. So that in five minutes nothing but the eye of God can see the vessel where she lies at the bottom of the sea. Do you understand now," said the captain, laughing, "why no complaints are made to the government, and why the vessel does not arrive at the port?"

It is probable that if Gaetano had related this previously to proposing the expedition, Franz would have hesitated ere he accepted it; but now that they had started, he thought it would be cowardly to draw back. He was one of those men who do not rashly court danger, but if danger presents itself, encounter it with imperturbable coolness. He was one of those calm and resolute men who look upon a danger as an adversary in a duel; who calculate its movements and study its attacks; who retreat sufficiently to take breath, but not to appear cowardly; who, understanding all their advantages, kill at a single blow. "Bah!" said he, "I have travelled through Sicily and Calabria, I have sailed two months in the Archipelago; and yet I never saw even the shadow of a bandit or a pirate."

"I did not tell your excellency this to deter you from your project," replied Gaetano; "but you questioned me, and I have answered,—that's all."

"Yes, my dear Gaetano, and your conversation is most interesting; and as I wish to enjoy it as long as possible, steer for Monte Cristo."

The wind blew strongly; the boat sailed six or seven knots an hour; and they were rapidly nearing the end of their voyage. As they approached, the island seemed to rise a huge mass from the bosom of the sea; and through the clear atmosphere in the light of closing day, they could distinguish the rocks heaped on one another like bullets in an arsenal, in whose crevices they could see the green bushes and trees that were growing. As for the sailors, although they appeared perfectly tranquil, yet it was evident that they were on the alert, and that they very carefully watched the glassy surface over which they were sailing, and on which a few fishing-boats with their white sails were alone visible. They were within fifteen miles of Monte Cristo when the sun began to set behind Corsica, whose mountains appeared against the sky, and showing their rugged peaks in bold relief; this mass of stones, like the giant Adamastor, rose threateningly before the boat, from which it hid the sun that gilded its higher peaks. By degrees the shadow rose from the sea and seemed to drive before it the last rays of the expiring day. At last the reflection rested on the summit of the mountain, where it paused an instant, like the fiery crest of a volcano; then the shadow gradually covered the summit as it had covered the base, and the island now appeared to be a grey mountain that grew continually darker. Half an hour later, and the night was quite dark.

Fortunately the mariners were used to these latitudes and knew every rock in the Tuscan archipelago, for in the midst of this obscurity Franz was not without uneasiness. Corsica had long since disappeared, and Monte Cristo itself was invisible; but the sailors seemed, like the lynx, to see in the dark, and the pilot who steered did not evince the slightest hesitation. An hour had passed since the sun had set, when Franz fancied he saw, at a quarter of a mile to the left, a dark mass; but it was impossible to make out what it was, and fearing to excite the mirth of the sailors by mistaking a floating cloud for land, he remained silent. Suddenly a great light appeared on the strand; land might resemble a cloud, but the fire was not a meteor. "What is this light?" he asked.

"Silence!" said the captain; "it is a fire."

"But you told me the island was uninhabited!"

"I said there were no fixed habitations on it; but I said also that it served sometimes as a harbour for smugglers."

" And for pirates ? "

" And for pirates," returned Gaetano, repeating Franz's words. " It is for that reason I have given orders to pass the isle, for, as you see, the fire is behind us."

" But this fire," continued Franz, " seems to me a thing that should rather assure than alarm us; men who did not wish to be seen would not light a fire."

" Oh, that goes for nothing," said Gaetano. " If you can guess the position of the island in the darkness, you will see that the fire cannot be seen from the side, or from Pianoso, but only from the sea."

" You think, then, that this fire announces unwelcome neighbours ? "

" That is what we must ascertain," returned Gaetano, fixing his eyes on this terrestrial star.

" How can you ascertain ? "

" You shall see."

Gaetano consulted with his companions; and after five minutes' discussion a manœuvre was executed which caused the boat to tack about. They returned in the direction from which they had come, and in a few minutes the fire disappeared, hidden by a rise in the land. The pilot again changed the course of the little vessel, which rapidly approached the island, and was soon within fifty paces of it. Gaetano lowered the sail, and the boat remained stationary. All this was done in silence, and since their course had been changed not a word was spoken.

Gaetano, who had proposed the expedition, had taken all the responsibility on himself; the four sailors fixed their eyes on him, while they prepared their oars and held themselves in readiness to row away, which, thanks to the darkness, would not be difficult. As for Franz, he examined his arms with the utmost coolness. He had two double-barrelled guns and a rifle; he loaded them, looked at the locks, and waited quietly. During this time the captain had thrown off his vest and shirt, and secured his trousers round his waist; his feet were naked, so he had no shoes and stockings to take off. After these preparations he placed his finger on his lips, and lowering himself noiselessly into the sea, swam towards the shore with such precaution that it was impossible to hear the slightest sound; he could be traced only by the phosphorescent line in his wake. This track soon disappeared; it was evident that he had touched the shore. Every one on board remained motionless during half an hour, when the same luminous track was again observed, and in two strokes he had regained the boat.

"Well?" exclaimed Franz and the sailors all together.

"They are Spanish smugglers," said he; "they have with them two Corsican bandits."

"And what are these Corsican bandits doing here with Spanish smugglers?"

"Alas!" returned the captain, with an accent of profound Christian charity, "we ought always to help one another. Very often the bandits are hard pressed by gendarmes or carbineers; well, they see a boat, and good fellows like us on board. They come and demand hospitality of us. How can you refuse help to a poor hunted devil? We receive them, and for greater security we stand out to sea. This costs us nothing, and saves the life, or at least the liberty, of a fellow-creature, who on the first occasion returns the service by pointing out some safe spot where we can land our goods without interruption."

"Ah!" said Franz, "then you are a smuggler occasionally, Gaetano?"

"Your excellency, one does a little of everything; we must live somehow," returned the other, smiling in a way impossible to describe.

"Then you know the men who are now on Monte Cristo?"

"Oh, yes, we sailors are like freemasons, and recognise each other by certain signs."

"And do you think we have nothing to fear if we land?"

"Nothing at all! smugglers are not thieves."

"But these two Corsican bandits?" said Franz, calculating the chances of peril.

"Eh!" said Gaetano, "it is not their fault that they are bandits; it is that of the authorities."

"How so?"

"Because they are pursued for having made a *peau*, as if it was not in a Corsican's nature to revenge himself."

"What do you mean by having made a *peau*,—having assassinated a man?" said Franz, continuing his investigation.

"I mean that they have killed an enemy, which is a very different thing," returned the captain.

"Well," said the young man, "let us demand hospitality of these smugglers and bandits. Do you think they will grant it?"

"Without doubt."

"How many are they?"

"Four, and the two bandits make six."

"Just our number, so that if they prove troublesome we shall be able to check them; so for the last time steer to Monte Cristo."

"Yes; but your excellency will permit us to take some precautions."

"By all means; be as wise as Nestor and as prudent as Ulysses. I do more than permit, I exhort you."

"Silence, then!" said Gaetano.

Every one obeyed. For a man who, like Franz, viewed his position in its true light, it was a grave one. He was alone in the darkness with sailors whom he did not know and who had no reason to be devoted to him; who knew that he had in his belt several thousand livres; and who had often examined his arms, which were very beautiful, if not with envy, at least with curiosity. On the other hand, he was about to land without any other escort than these men, on an island which bore a very religious name, but which did not seem to offer Franz any other hospitality than that of Calvary to Christ, thanks to the smugglers and bandits. The history of the scuttled vessels, which had appeared improbable during the day, seemed very probable at night. Placed as he was between two imaginary dangers, he did not quit the crew with his eyes, or his gun with his hand.

However, the sailors had again hoisted the sail, and the vessel was once more cleaving the waves. Through the darkness Franz, whose eyes were now more accustomed to it, distinguished the granite giant by which the boat was sailing; and then, turning an angle of the rock, he saw the fire more brilliant than ever, round which five or six persons were seated. The blaze illumined the sea for a hundred paces round. Gaetano skirted the light, carefully keeping the boat out of its rays; then, when they were opposite the fire, he entered into the centre of the circle, singing a fishing-song, of which his companions sang the chorus. At the first words of the song, the men seated round the fire rose and approached the landing-place, their eyes fixed on the boat, of which they evidently sought to judge the force and divine the intention. They soon appeared satisfied and returned (with the exception of one, who remained at the shore) to their fire, at which a whole goat was roasting. When the boat was within twenty paces of the shore, the man on the beach made with his carbine the movement of a sentinel who sees a patrol, and cried, "Who goes there?" in Sardinian. Franz coolly cocked both barrels. Gaetano then exchanged a few words with this man, which the traveller did not understand, but which evidently concerned him.

"Will your excellency give your name, or remain *incognito?*" asked the captain.

"My name must rest unknown; merely say I am a French-man travelling for pleasure."

As soon as Gaetano had transmitted this answer, the sentinel gave an order to one of the men seated round the fire, who rose and disappeared among the rocks. Not a word was spoken, every one seemed occupied,—Franz with his disembarkment, the sailors with their sails, the smugglers with their goat,—but in the midst of all this carelessness it was evident that they mutually observed each other. The man who had disappeared returned suddenly on the opposite side to that by which he had left; he made a sign with his head to the sentinel, who, turning to the boat uttered these words, "*S'accommodi*." The Italian *s'accommodi* is untranslatable; it means at once: "Come; enter; you are welcome; make yourself at home; you are the master." It is like that Turkish phrase of Molière's that so astonished *le bourgeois gentilhomme* by the number of things it contained. The sailors did not wait for a second invitation; four strokes of the oar brought them to the land. Gaetano sprang to shore, exchanged a few words with the sentinel; then his comrades disembarked, and lastly came Franz's turn. One of his guns was swung over his shoulder, Gaetano had the other, and a sailor held his rifle; his dress, half artist, half dandy, excited no suspicion, and consequently no disquietude. The boat was moored to the shore, and they advanced a few paces to find a comfortable bivouac; but doubtless the spot they chose did not suit the smuggler who filled the post of sentinel, for he cried out, "Not that way, if you please."

Gaetano faltered an excuse, and advanced to the opposite side, while two sailors kindled torches at the fire to light them on their way. They advanced about thirty paces, and then stopped at a small esplanade surrounded with rocks, in which seats had been cut, not unlike sentry-boxes. Around in the crevices of the rocks grew a few dwarf oaks and thick bushes of myrtles. Franz lowered a torch and saw by the light of a mass of cinders that he was not the first to discover this retreat, which was doubtless one of the halting-places of the wandering visitors of Monte Cristo. As for his anticipation of events, once on *terra firma*, once that he had seen the indifferent if not friendly appear-ance of his hosts, his preoccupation had disappeared, or rather at sight of the goat had turned to appetite. He mentioned this to Gaetano, who replied that nothing could be more easy than to prepare a supper, since they had in their boat bread, wine, half a dozen partridges, and a good fire to roast them by. "Besides,' added he, " if the smell of their roast meat tempts you, I will go and offer them two of our birds for a slice."

" You seem born for negotiation," returned Franz; " go and try."

During this time the sailors had collected dried sticks and branches, with which they made a fire. Franz waited impatiently, smelling the odour of the goat, when the captain returned with a mysterious air.

" Well," inquired Franz, " anything new? Do they refuse? "

" On the contrary," returned Gaetano, " the chief, who was told you were a young Frenchman, invites you to sup with him."

" Well," observed Franz, " this chief is very polite; and I see no objection,—especially as I bring my share of the supper."

" Oh, it is not that,—he has plenty and to spare for supper; but he attaches a singular condition to your presentation at his house."

" His house! has he built one here, then? "

" No, but he has a very comfortable one all the same, so they say."

" You know this chief, then? "

" I have heard him spoken of."

" Ill or well? "

" Both."

" The devil! and what is this condition? "

" That you are blindfolded, and do not take off the bandage until he himself bids you." Franz looked at Gaetano, to see, if possible, what he thought of this proposal. " Ah," replied he, guessing Franz's thought, " I know this merits reflection."

" What should you do in my place? "

" I, who have nothing to lose,—I should go."

" You would accept? "

" Yes, were it only out of curiosity."

" There is something very curious about this chief, then? "

" Listen," said Gaetano, lowering his voice; " I do not know if what they say is true—" He stopped to see if any one was near.

" What do they say? "

" That this chief inhabits a cavern to which the Pitti Palace is nothing."

" What nonsense! " said Franz, reseating himself.

" It is no nonsense; it is quite true. Cama, the pilot of the *St. Ferdinand*, went in once, and he came back amazed, vowing that such treasures were only heard of in fairy tales."

" Do you know," observed Franz, " that with such stories

you would make me enter the enchanted cavern of Ali Baba?"

"I tell you what I have been told."

"Then you advise me to accept?"

"Oh, I don't say that; your excellency will do as you please. I should be sorry to advise you in the matter."

Franz reflected a few moments, felt that a man so rich could not have any intention of plundering him of what little he had; and seeing only the prospect of a good supper, he accepted. Gaetano departed with the reply. Franz was prudent, and wished to learn all he possibly could concerning his host. He turned towards the sailor who during this dialogue had sat gravely plucking the partridges with the air of a man proud of his office, and asked him how these men had landed, as no vessel of any kind was visible.

"Never mind that," returned the sailor; "I know their vessel."

"Is it a very beautiful vessel?"

"I would not wish for a better to sail round the world."

"Of what burden is she?"

"About a hundred tons; but she is built to stand any weather. She is what the English call a yacht."

"Where was she built?"

"I do not know; but my own opinion is she is a Genoese."

"And how did a leader of smugglers," continued Franz, "venture to build a vessel designed for such a purpose at Genoa?"

"I did not say that the owner was a smuggler," replied the sailor.

"No; but Gaetano did, I thought."

"Gaetano had only seen the vessel from a distance; he had not then spoken to any one."

"And if this person be not a smuggler, who is he?"

"A wealthy signor, who travels for his pleasure."

"Come," thought Franz, "he is still more mysterious, since the two accounts do not agree. What is his name?"

"If you ask him he says Sinbad the Sailor; but I doubt its being his real name."

"Sinbad the Sailor?"

"Yes."

"And where does he reside?"

"On the sea."

"What country does he come from?"

"I do not know."

" Have you ever seen him? "

" Sometimes."

" What sort of a man is he? "

" Your excellency will judge for yourself."

" Where will he receive me? "

" No doubt in the subterranean palace Gaetano told you of."

" Have you never had the curiosity, when you have landed and found this island deserted, to seek for this enchanted palace? "

" Oh, yes, more than once, but always in vain; we examined the grotto all over, but we never could find the slightest trace of any opening. They say that the door is not opened by a key, but by a magic word."

" Decidedly," muttered Franz, " this is an adventure of the *Arabian Nights*."

" His excellency waits for you," said a voice which Franz recognised as that of the sentinel. He was accompanied by two of the yacht's crew. Franz drew his handkerchief from his pocket and presented it to the man who had spoken to him. Without uttering a word they bandaged his eyes with a care that showed their apprehension of his committing some indiscretion. Afterwards he was made to promise that he would not make any attempt to raise the bandage. Then his two guides took his arms, and he advanced, guided by them and preceded by the sentinel. After advancing about thirty paces he perceived the appetising odour of the kid that was roasting, and knew thus that he was passing the bivouac; they then led him on about fifty paces farther, evidently advancing in the direction forbidden to Gaetano,—a prohibition which he could now comprehend. Presently, by a change in the atmosphere he perceived that they were entering a cave; after going on for a few seconds more he heard a crackling, and it seemed to him as though the atmosphere again changed, and became balmy and perfumed. At length his feet touched on a thick and soft carpet, and his guides let go their hold of him.

There was a moment's silence, and then a voice, in excellent French, although with a foreign accent, said, " Welcome, monsieur! I beg you will remove your bandage." As may be easily imagined, Franz did not wait for a repetition of this permission, but took off the handkerchief and found himself in the presence of a man from thirty-eight to forty years of age, dressed in a Tunisian costume,—that is to say, a red cap with a long blue silk tassel, a vest of black cloth embroidered with gold, pantaloons of deep red, large and full gaiters of the same colour, embroidered with gold like the vest, and yellow slippers; he had a splendid cashmere round his waist, and a small cimeter, sharp and curved, was passed through his girdle. Although of a paleness that was almost livid, this man had a remarkably handsome face; his eyes were penetrating and sparkling; his nose, straight and almost in line with his brow, exhibited the Greek type in all its purity, while his teeth, as white as pearls, were well set off by the black mustache that covered them.

But that paleness was striking; it might be imagined that he had been imprisoned for a long time in a tomb, and was unable to recover the healthy glow and hue of the living. He was not particularly tall, but extremely well made, and like the men of the South, had small hands and feet. But what astonished Franz, who had treated Gaetano's description as a fable, was the splendour of the apartment in which he found himself. The entire chamber was lined with crimson brocade worked with flowers of gold. In a recess was a kind of divan, surmounted by a stand of Arabian swords in silver scabbards, the handles resplendent with gems; from the ceiling hung a lamp of Venetian glass, of beautiful shape and colour, while the feet rested on a Turkey carpet, in which they sunk to the instep; tapestry was suspended before the door by which Franz had entered, and also in front of another door, leading into a second apartment, which seemed to be brilliantly lighted up.

The host left Franz for a moment absorbed in his surprise, and moreover rendered him look for look, not taking his eyes off him. "Monsieur," he said at length, "a thousand excuses for the precaution taken in your introduction hither; but as during the greater portion of the year this island is deserted, if the secret of this abode were discovered, I should doubtless on my return hither find my temporary retirement in a state of great disorder, which would be exceedingly annoying, not for the loss it might occasion, but because I should not have the certainty I now possess of being able to separate myself at pleasure from all the rest of mankind. Let me now endeavour to make you forget this temporary unpleasantness, and offer you what no doubt you did not expect to find here,—that is to say, a tolerable supper and pretty comfortable beds."

"*Ma foi!* my dear host," replied Franz, "make no apologies. I have always observed that they bandage the eyes of those who penetrate enchanted palaces,—for instance, those of Raoul in *The Huguenots;* and really I have nothing to complain of, for what I see is a sequel to the wonders of the *Arabian Nights.*"

"Alas! I may say with Lucullus, 'If I could have anticipated the honour of your visit, I would have prepared for it.' But such as is my hermitage, it is at your disposal; such as is my supper, it is yours to share if you will. Ali, is the supper ready ? "

At this moment the tapestry was moved aside, and a Nubian, black as ebony, and dressed in a plain white tunic, made a sign to his master that all was prepared in the dining-hall.

" Now," said the unknown to Franz, " I do not know if you are of my opinion, but I think nothing is more annoying than for two persons to remain two or three hours face to face without knowing by what name or title to address one another. Pray observe that I too much respect the laws of hospitality to ask your name or title. I only request you to give me one by which I may have the pleasure of addressing you. As for myself, that I may put you at your ease, I tell you that I am generally called ' Sinbad the Sailor.' "

" And I," replied Franz, " will tell you, as I only require his wonderful lamp to make me precisely like Aladdin, that I see no reason why at this moment I should not be called Aladdin. That will keep us from going away from the East, whither I am tempted to think I have been conveyed by some good genius."

" Well, then, Signor Aladdin," replied the singular amphitryon, " you heard our repast announced; will you now take the trouble to enter the dining-hall, your humble servant going first to show the way ? " At these words, moving aside the tapestry, Sinbad preceded his guest. Franz proceeded from one enchantment to another; the table was splendidly covered, and once convinced of this important point, he cast his eyes around him. The dining-hall was scarcely less striking than the boudoir he had just left; it was entirely of marble, with antique bas-reliefs of priceless value, and at the two ends of the hall, which was oblong, were two magnificent statues having baskets in their hands. These baskets contained four pyramids of magnificent fruit; there were the pine-apples of Sicily, pomegranates from Malaga, oranges from the Balearic Isles, peaches from France, and dates from Tunis. The supper consisted of a roast pheasant garnished with Corsican blackbirds; a boar's ham, *à la gelée*, a quarter of a kid, *à la tartare*, a glorious turbot, and a gigantic lobster. Between these large dishes were smaller ones containing various dainties. The dishes were of silver and the plates of Japanese porcelain.

Franz rubbed his eyes to assure himself that this was not a dream. Ali alone was present to wait at table, and acquitted himself so admirably that the guest complimented his host thereupon.

"Yes," he replied, while he did the honours of the supper with much ease and grace,—"yes, he is a poor devil who is much devoted to me, and does all he can to prove it. He remembers that I saved his life, and as he has a regard for his head, he feels some gratitude towards me for having kept it on his shoulders."

Ali approached his master, took his hand, and kissed it.

"Would it be impertinent, Signor Sinbad," said Franz, "to ask you under what circumstances you performed that excellent deed?"

"Oh! it is a simple matter," replied the host. "It seems the fellow had been caught wandering nearer to the harem of the Bey of Tunis than etiquette permits to one of his colour; and he was condemned by the bey to have his tongue cut out, and his hand and head cut off,—the tongue the first day, the hand the second, and the head the third. I always had a desire to have a mute in my service. I waited until his tongue had been cut out, and then proposed to the bey that he should sell me Ali for a splendid double-barrelled gun which I knew he was very eager to possess. He hesitated a moment, so intent was he on finishing up with the poor devil. But when I added to the gun an English cutlass with which I had shivered his Highness's yataghan, the bey yielded, and agreed to forgive the hand and head, but on condition that he would never again set foot in Tunis. This was a useless clause in the bargain, for whenever the coward sees the first glimpse of the shores of Africa, he runs down below, and can be induced to appear again only when we are out of sight of the third part of the globe."

Franz remained a moment mute and pensive, hardly knowing what to think of the cruel *bonhomie* with which his host had related this incident. "And like the celebrated sailor whose name you have assumed," he said, by way of changing the conversation, "you pass your life in travelling?"

"Yes. It is in fulfilment of a vow which I made at a time when I little thought I should ever be able to accomplish it," said the unknown, with a singular smile. "I made some others also, which I hope I may fulfil in due season."

Although Sinbad pronounced these words with much calmness, his eyes darted gleams of singular ferocity.

"You have suffered a great deal, monsieur?" said Franz, inquiringly.

Sinbad started and looked fixedly at him, as he replied, " What makes you suppose so? "

"Everything!" answered Franz, "your voice, your look, your pallid complexion, and even the life you lead."

"I! I live the happiest life I know,—the real life of a pacha. I am king of all creation. I am pleased with one place, and stay there; I get tired of it, and leave it. I am free as a bird, and have wings like one. My attendants obey me at a signal. Sometimes I amuse myself by carrying off from human justice some bandit it is in quest of, some criminal whom it pursues. Then I have my mode of dispensing justice, silent and sure, without respite or appeal, which condemns or pardons, and which no one sees. Ah! if you had tasted my life, you would not desire any other, and would never return to the world unless you had some great project to accomplish there."

"A vengeance, for instance!" observed Franz.

The unknown fixed on the young man one of those looks which penetrate into the depth of the heart and of the thoughts. "And why a vengeance? " he asked.

"Because," replied Franz, "you seem to me like a man who, persecuted by society, has a fearful account to settle with it."

"Ah!" responded Sinbad, laughing with his singular laugh, which displayed his white and sharp teeth. "You have not guessed rightly. Such as you see me, I am a sort of philosopher; and one day perhaps I shall go to Paris to rival M. Appert and the man in the Little Blue Cloak."

"And will that be the first time you will have made that journey? "

"Yes, it will. I must seem to you by no means curious, but I assure you that it is not my fault I have delayed it so long; I shall get around to it some day."

"And do you propose to make this journey soon? "

"I do not know; it depends on circumstances which are subject to uncertain contingencies."

"I should like to be there at the time you come, and I will endeavour to repay you as far as lies in my power for your liberal hospitality at Monte Cristo."

"I should avail myself of your offer with pleasure," replied the host; "but unfortunately, if I go there, I shall perhaps prefer to remain unknown."

Meantime they were proceeding with the supper, which however appeared to have been supplied solely for Franz, for the unknown scarcely touched one or two dishes of the splendid banquet to which his unexpected guest did ample justice. Then Ali brought on the dessert, or rather took the baskets from the hands of the statues and placed them on the table. Between the two baskets he placed a small silver cup, closed with a lid of the same metal. The care with which Ali placed this cup on the table roused Franz's curiosity. He raised the lid and saw a kind of greenish paste, something like preserved angelica, but which was entirely unknown to him. He replaced the lid, as ignorant of what the cup contained as he was before he had looked at it, and then casting his eyes towards his host he saw him smile at his disappointment.

" You cannot divine what sort of confection is contained in that little vase; and it perplexes you, does it not? "

" I confess it."

" Well, then, that green confection is nothing less than the ambrosia which Hebe served at the table of Jupiter."

" But," replied Franz, " this ambrosia, no doubt, in passing through mortal hands has lost its heavenly appellation and assumed a human name; in vulgar phrase, what may you term this composition?—for which, to say the truth, I do not feel any particular desire."

" Ah! thus it is that our material origin is revealed," cried Sinbad: " we frequently pass so near to happiness without seeing, without regarding it; or if we do see and regard it, yet without recognising it. Are you a man for the substantials, and is gold your god? taste this, and the mines of Peru, Guzerat, and Golconda are opened to you. Are you a man of imagination,—a poet? taste this, and the boundaries of possibility disappear; the fields of infinite space open to you; you advance free in heart, free in mind, into the boundless realms of unfettered revelry. Are you ambitious, and do you seek to reach the high places of the earth? taste this, and in an hour you will be a king,—not a king of a petty kingdom hidden in some corner of Europe, like France, Spain, or England, but king of the world, king of the universe, king of creation; your throne will be established on the mountain to which Jesus was taken by Satan, and without being obliged to do homage to Satan, without being compelled to kiss his claw, you will be sovereign lord of all the kingdoms of the earth. Is it not tempting? And is it not an easy thing, since it is only to do thus? look!" At these words he uncovered the small cup which contained the substance so lauded, took a teaspoonful of the magic sweetmeat, raised it to his lips, and swallowed it slowly, with his eyes half shut and his head bent backward. Franz did not disturb him while he absorbed his favourite *bonne bouche*, but when he had finished, he inquired,—

"What, then, is this precious stuff?"

"Did you ever hear," asked the host, "of the Old Man of the Mountain, who attempted to assassinate Philippe Augustus?"

"Of course I have."

"Well, you know he reigned over a rich valley which was overhung by the mountain whence he derived his picturesque name. In this valley were magnificent gardens planted by Hassen-ben-Sabah, and in these gardens isolated pavilions. Into these pavilions he admitted the elect; and there, says Marco Polo, he gave them a certain herb to eat, which transported them to Paradise to the midst of ever blooming shrubs, ever ripe fruit, and ever lovely virgins. Now, what these happy persons took for reality was but a dream, but it was a dream so soft, so voluptuous, so enthralling, that they sold themselves body and soul to him who gave it to them. They were as obedient to his orders as to those of God; they went to the ends of the earth to strike down the victim indicated to them; and they died in torture without a murmur,—believing that death was but a quick transition to that life of delights of which the holy herb now before you had given them a slight foretaste."

"Then," cried Franz, "it is hashish! I know that—by name at least."

"That is it precisely, Signor Aladdin; it is hashish,—the best and purest hashish of Alexandria; the hashish of Abou-Gor, the celebrated maker, the unique man, the man to whom there should be built a palace inscribed with these words, 'A grateful world to the dealer in happiness.'"

"Do you know," said Franz, "I have a very great inclination to judge for myself of the truth or exaggeration of your eulogies."

"Judge for yourself, Signor Aladdin; judge, but do not confine yourself to one trial. As in everything else, we must habituate the senses to any new impression, gentle or violent, sad or joyous. There is a struggle in nature against this divine substance,—in nature, which is not made for joy, and clings to pain. Nature, subdued, must yield in the combat; reality must succeed to the dream; and then the dream reigns supreme. Then the dream becomes life, and life becomes the dream. But what a change is wrought by that transfiguration, on comparing the pains of actual being with the joys of the fictitious existence! you desire to live no longer, but to dream thus for ever. When you return to this mundane sphere from your visionary world, you seem to leave a Neapolitan spring for a Lapland winter,—to quit paradise for earth, heaven for hell! Taste the hashish, guest of mine,—taste the hashish!"

Franz's only reply was to take a teaspoonful of the marvellous preparation, about as much in quantity as his host had eaten, and lift it to his mouth. "The devil!" he said after having swallowed the divine confection, "I do not know if the result will be as agreeable as you describe, but the thing does not appear to me as succulent as you say."

"Because your palate has not yet attained the sublimity of the substance it tastes. Tell me, the first time you tasted oysters, tea, porter, truffles, and sundry other dainties which you now adore, did you like them? Can you comprehend how the Romans stuffed their pheasants with assafœtida, and the Chinese eat swallows' nests? Eh, no! Well, it is the same with hashish; only eat for a week, and nothing in the world will seem to you to equal the delicacy of its flavour, which now appears to you tasteless and nauseating. Let us now go into the side-chamber,—that is, into your chamber,—and Ali will bring us coffee and pipes."

They both arose, and while he who called himself Sinbad—and whom we have occasionally so named, that we might like his guest have some title by which to distinguish him—gave some orders to the servant, Franz entered the adjoining chamber. It was simply yet richly furnished. It was round, and a large divan completely encircled it. Divan, walls, ceiling, floor, were all covered with magnificent skins, as soft and downy as the richest carpets; there were skins of the lions of Atlas, with their large manes; skins of the Bengal tigers, with their striped hides; skins of the panthers of the Cape, spotted beautifully like those that appeared to Dante; skins of the bears of Siberia, and of the foxes of Norway; and all these skins were strewn in profusion one on the other, so that it seemed like walking over the most mossy turf, or reclining on the most luxurious bed. Both laid themselves down on the divan; chibouques with jasmine tubes and amber mouthpieces were within reach, and all prepared so that there was no need to smoke the same pipe twice. Each of them took one, which Ali lighted; Ali then retired to prepare the coffee. There was a moment's silence, during which Sinbad gave himself up to thoughts that seemed to occupy him incessantly, even in the midst of his conversation; and Franz abandoned himself to that mute reverie into which we always sink when smoking excellent tobacco, which seems to remove with its smoke all the troubles of the mind, and to give the smoker in exchange all the visions of the soul.

Ali brought in the coffee.

"How do you take it?" inquired the unknown; "*à la française* or *à la turque*, strong or weak, with sugar or without, cool or boiling? As you please; it is ready in all ways."

"I will take it *à la turque*," replied Franz.

"And you are right," said his host; "it shows you have a taste for Oriental life. Ah! those Orientals,—they are the only men who know how to live. As for me," he added with one of those singular smiles which did not escape the young man, "when I have completed my affairs in Paris, I shall go and die in the East; and should you wish to see me again, you must seek me at Cairo, Bagdad, or Ispahan."

"*Ma foi!*" said Franz, "it would be the easiest thing in the world,—for I feel eagle's wings springing out at my shoulders, and with these wings I could make a tour of the world in four-and-twenty hours."

"Ah, ah! it is the hashish that is operating. Well, unfurl your wings, and fly into superhuman regions. Fear nothing,— there is a watch over you; and if your wings, like those of Icarus, melt before the sun, we are here to receive you."

He then said some Arabian words to Ali, who made a sign of obedience and withdrew, but remained near. As to Franz, a strange transformation had taken place in him. All the bodily fatigue of the day, all the preoccupation of mind which the events of the evening had brought on, disappeared, as they do in the early moments of repose, when we are still sufficiently conscious to be aware of the coming of slumber. His body seemed to acquire an airy lightness; his perception brightened in a remarkable manner; his senses seemed to redouble their power. The horizon continued to expand; it was not that gloomy horizon over which hovers a vague terror, and which he had seen before he slept, but a blue, transparent, unbounded horizon, with all the blue of the ocean, all the spangles of the sun, all the perfumes of the summer breeze. Then, in the midst of the songs of his sailors,—songs so clear and sounding that they would have made a divine harmony had their notes been taken down,—he saw the island of Monte Cristo, no longer as a threatening rock in the midst of the waves, but as an oasis lost in the desert. Then, as the boat approached, the songs became louder,—for an enchanting and mysterious harmony rose to heaven from this island, as if some fay-like Loreley or

some enchanter like Amphion had wished to attract thither a
soul or build there a city.

At length the boat touched the shore, but without effort,
without shock, as lips touch lips; and he entered the grotto
amid continued strains of most delicious melody. He descended,
or rather seemed to descend, several steps, inhaling the fresh
and balmy air, like that which may be supposed to reign around
the grotto of Circe, formed from such perfumes as set the mind
a-dreaming, and such fires as burn the very senses; and he saw
again all he had seen before his sleep, from Sinbad, his singular
host, to Ali, the mute attendant. Then all seemed to fade away
and become confused before his eyes, like the last shadows of
the magic lantern before it is extinguished; and he was again
in the chamber of statues, lighted only by one of those pale and
antique lamps which watch in the dead of the night over sleep
or pleasure. They were the same statues, rich in form, in
attraction, and poesy, with eyes of fascination, smiles of love,
and flowing hair. They were Phryne, Cleopatra, Messalina,
those three celebrated courtesans. Then among them glided
like a pure ray, like a Christian angel in the midst of Olympus,
a chaste figure, a calm shadow, a soft vision, which seemed to
veil its virgin brow before these marble wantons. Then these
three statues advanced towards him with looks of love, and
approached the couch on which he was reposing,—their feet
hidden in their long tunics, their throats bare, hair flowing like
waves, and assuming attitudes which the gods could not resist,
but which saints withstood, and looks inflexible and ardent like
the serpent's on the bird; and then he gave way before these
looks, as painful as a powerful grasp and as delightful as a kiss.
It seemed to Franz that he closed his eyes, and that in his last
look around he saw the modest statue completely veiled; and
then his eyes being closed to all reality, his senses were opened
to receive strange impressions.

CHAPTER XXXII

THE WAKING

WHEN Franz returned to himself exterior objects seemed a
second portion of his dream. He thought himself in a sepulchre
into which scarcely penetrated, like a look of pity, a ray of the
sun. He stretched forth his hand and touched stone; he rose
to a sitting posture, and found himself on his burnoose in a bed

of dry heather, very soft and odoriferous. The vision had entirely
fled; and as if the statues had been but shadows coming from
their tomb during his dream, they had vanished at his waking.
He advanced several paces towards the point whence the light
came, and to all the excitement of his dream succeeded the calmness of reality. He found that he was in a grotto, went towards
the opening, and through an arched doorway saw a blue sea
and an azure sky. The air and water were shining in the beams
of the morning sun; on the shore the sailors were sitting, chat-
ting and laughing; and at ten yards from them the boat was
gracefully riding at anchor. There for some time he enjoyed the
fresh breeze which played on his brow, and listened to the gentle
noise of the waves, which came up on the beach and left on the
rocks a lace of foam as white as silver. He abandoned himself
for some time without reflection or thought to the divine charm
which is in the things of nature, especially after a fantastic
dream; then gradually this outward life, so calm, so pure, so
grand, showed him the unreality of his dream, and remembrances
began to return to him. He recalled his arrival on the island,
his presentation to a smuggler chief, a subterranean palace full
of splendour, an excellent supper, and a spoonful of hashish.
It seemed however, even in the face of open day, that at least
a year had elapsed since all these things had happened, so deep
was the impression made in his mind by the dream, and so
strong a hold had it taken of his imagination. Thus every now
and then his fancy placed amid the sailors, seated on a rock,
or saw on the boat, moving with its motion, one of those shadows
which had shared his dreams with their looks and their kisses.
Otherwise, his head was perfectly clear and his body completely
rested. There was no dulness in his brain; on the contrary,
he felt a certain degree of lightness, a faculty of absorbing the
pure air and enjoying the bright sunshine more vividly than ever.

He went gaily up to the sailors, who rose as soon as they
perceived him; and the captain, accosting him, said, "The
Signor Sinbad has left his compliments for your excellency, and
desires us to express the regret he feels at not being able to take
his leave in person; but he trusts you will excuse him, as very
important business calls him to Malaga."

"So then, Gaetano," said Franz, "this is, then, all reality;
there exists a man who has received me on this island, entertained me right royally, and has departed while I was asleep?"

"He exists so really that you may see his little yacht with
all her sails spread; and if you will use your glass, you will in
all probability recognise your host in the midst of his crew."

So saying, Gaetano pointed in a direction in which a small vessel was making sail towards the southern point of Corsica. Franz adjusted his telescope and directed it towards the place indicated. Gaetano was not mistaken. At the stern the mysterious stranger was standing up, looking towards the shore, and holding a spy-glass in his hand. He was attired as he had been on the previous evening, and waved his pocket-handkerchief to his guest in token of adieu. Franz returned the salute by shaking his handkerchief in like manner. After a second a slight cloud of smoke was seen at the stern of the vessel, which rose gracefully as it expanded in the air, and then Franz heard a light report. "There, do you hear?" observed Gaetano; "he is bidding you adieu." The young man took his carbine and fired it in the air, but without any idea that the noise could be heard at the distance which separated the yacht from the shore.

"What are your excellency's orders?" inquired Gaetano.

"In the first place, light me a torch."

"Ah, yes, I understand," replied the captain; "to find the entrance to the enchanted apartment. With much pleasure, your excellency, if it would amuse you; and I will get you the torch you ask for. I too have had the idea you have, and two or three times the same fancy has come over me; but I have always given it up. Giovanni, light a torch," he added, "and give it to his excellency."

Giovanni obeyed. Franz took the lamp and entered the subterranean grotto, followed by Gaetano. He recognised the place where he had slept by the bed of heather that was there; but it was in vain that he carried his torch all over the exterior surface of the grotto. He saw nothing except, by traces of smoke, that others had before him attempted the same thing, and like him, in vain. Yet he did not leave a foot of this granite wall, as impenetrable as futurity, without strict scrutiny; he did not see a fissure without introducing the blade of his hunting-sword into it, nor a projecting point on which he did not lean and press, in the hope that it would give way. All was vain; and he lost two hours in that examination without results. At the end of this time he gave up his research; Gaetano was triumphant.

When Franz appeared again on the shore, the yacht seemed like a small white speck on the horizon. He looked again through his glass, but even then he could not distinguish anything. Gaetano reminded him that he had come for the purpose of shooting goats,—which he had utterly forgotten.

He took his fowling-piece and began to hunt over the island with the air of a man who is fulfilling a duty rather than enjoying a pleasure; and at the end of a quarter of an hour he had killed a goat and two kids. These animals, though wild and agile as chamois, were too much like domestic goats, and Franz could not consider them as game. Moreover, other ideas, much more powerful, occupied his mind. Since the evening before, he had really been the hero of one of the tales of the *Thousand and One Nights*, and he was irresistibly attracted towards the grotto. Then, in spite of the failure of his first search, he began a second, after having told Gaetano to roast one of the two kids. The second visit was a long one, and when he returned the kid was roasted and the repast ready. Franz was sitting on the spot where he was on the previous evening when his mysterious host had invited him to supper; and he saw the little yacht, now like a sea-gull on the wave, continuing her flight towards Corsica.

"Why," he remarked to Gaetano, "you told me that Signor Sinbad was going to Malaga; but it seems to me that he is going straight to Porto Vecchio."

"Don't you remember," said the captain, "I told you that among the crew there were two Corsican brigands?"

"True! and he is going to land them?" added Franz.

"Precisely so," replied Gaetano. "Ah! he is a man who fears neither God nor devil, they say, and would at any time run fifty leagues out of his course to do a poor devil a service."

"But such services as these might involve him with the authorities of the country in which he practises this kind of philanthropy," said Franz.

"Ah, well," replied Gaetano, with a laugh, "what does he care for the authorities? He smiles at them. Let them try to pursue him! why, in the first place, his yacht is not a ship but a bird, and he would beat any frigate three knots in every twelve; and if he were to throw himself on the coast, why, isn't he certain of finding friends everywhere?"

It was evident from all this that the Signor Sinbad, Franz's host, had the honour of being on excellent terms with the smugglers and bandits along the whole coast of the Mediterranean,—which placed him in a position singular enough. As to Franz, he had no longer any inducement to remain at Monte Cristo. He had lost all hope of detecting the secret of the grotto. He consequently despatched his breakfast, and his boat being ready, he hastened on board, and they were soon under way. At the moment the boat began her course they lost sight of the yacht, as it disappeared in the gulf of Porto

Vecchio. With it was effaced the last trace of the preceding night; supper, Sinbad, hàshish, statues,—all became buried in the same dream. The boat went on all day and all night, and next morning when the sun rose, they had lost sight of Monte Cristo. When Franz had once again set foot on shore, he forgot, for the moment at least, the events which had just passed, while he finished his affairs of pleasure at Florence, and then thought of nothing but how he should rejoin his companion, who was waiting him at Rome. He set out therefore, and on the Saturday evening reached the Place de la Douane by the *malle-poste*. Apartments, as we have said, had been retained beforehand, and thus he had but to go to the hotel of Maître Pastrini. But this was not so easy a matter, for the streets were thronged with people, and Rome was already a prey to that low and feverish murmur which precedes all great events. At Rome there are four great events in every year,—the Carnival, the Holy Week, the Fête Dieu, and the St. Peter. All the rest of the year the city is in that state of dull apathy, between life and death, which renders it similar to a kind of station between this world and the next,—a sublime spot, a resting-place full of poetry and character, at which Franz had already halted five or six times, and at each time found it more marvellous and striking. At last he made his way through this mob, which was continually increasing and becoming more agitated, and reached the hotel. On his first inquiry he was told, with the impertinence peculiar to coachmen who have plenty of employment, and innkeepers whose houses are filled, that there was no room for him at the Hôtel de Londres. Then he sent his card to Maître Pastrini, and demanded Albert de Morcerf. This plan succeeded; and Maître Pastrini himself ran to him, excusing himself for having made his excellency wait, scolding the waiters, taking the candlestick in his hand from the *cicerone*, who was ready to pounce on the traveller, and was about to lead him to Albert, when Morcerf himself appeared.

The apartments consisted of two small rooms and a closet. The two rooms looked on to the street,—a fact which Maître Pastrini commented upon as an inappreciable advantage. The remainder of the story was hired by a very rich gentleman, who was supposed to be a Sicilian or Maltese; but the host was unable to decide to which of the two nations the traveller belonged.

"Very good, Maître Pastrini," said Franz; "but we must have some supper instantly, and a carriage for to-morrow and the following days."

The Waking 293

"As to supper," replied the landlord, "you shall be served immediately; but as for the carriage—"

"What as to the carriage?" exclaimed Albert. "Come, come, Maître Pastrini, no joking; we must have a carriage."

"Monsieur," replied the host, "we will do all in our power to procure you one; that is all I can say."

"And when shall we know?" inquired Franz.

"To-morrow morning," answered the innkeeper.

"Oh, the devil!" said Albert, "then we shall pay the more, that's all. I see plainly enough. At Drake and Aaron's one pays twenty-five livres for common days, and thirty or thirty-five livres for Sundays and fêtes; add five livres for extras,— that will make forty,—and there's an end of it."

"I fear," said the landlord, "that those gentlemen, even if you offer them twice that amount, will not be able to procure you a carriage."

"Then they must put horses to mine," said Albert. "It is a little worse for the journey, but that's no matter."

"There are no horses."

Albert looked at Franz like a man who hears a reply he does not understand. "Do you understand that, my dear Franz? —no horses!" he said; "but can't we have post-horses?"

"They have been all hired this fortnight, and there are none left but those absolutely necessary to the service."

"What do you say to that?" asked Franz.

"I say that when a thing completely surpasses my comprehension, I am accustomed not to dwell on that thing, but to pass to another. Is supper ready, Maître Pastrini?"

"Yes, your excellency."

"Well, then, let us sup."

"But the carriages and horses?" said Franz.

"Be easy, my dear boy; they will come in due season. It is only a question of how much shall be charged for them."

Morcerf then, with that admirable philosophy which believes that nothing is impossible to a full purse or a well-lined pocketbook, supped, went to bed, slept soundly, and dreamed that he rode through the Carnival in a coach with six horses.

CHAPTER XXXIII

ROMAN BANDITS

THE next morning Franz woke first, and instantly rang the bell. The sound had not yet died away when Maître Pastrini himself entered.

"Well, excellency," said the landlord, triumphantly, and without waiting for Franz to question him, "I feared yesterday, when I would not promise you anything, that you were too late; there is not a single carriage to be had—that is, for the last three days."

"Yes," returned Franz; "that is, for those on which it is absolutely necessary."

"What is the matter?" said Albert, entering; "no carriage to be had?"

"Precisely, my dear fellow," said Franz; "you have hit it the first time."

"Well! your Eternal City is a devilish nice city."

"That is to say, excellency," replied Pastrini, who was desirous to keep up the dignity of the capital of the Christian world in the eyes of his guest, "there are no carriages to be had from Sunday to Tuesday evening, but from now till Sunday you can have fifty if you please."

"Ah! that is something," said Albert; "to-day is Thursday, and who knows what may arrive between this and Sunday?"

"Ten or twelve thousand travellers will arrive," replied Franz, "which will make it still more difficult."

"My friend," said Morcerf, "let us enjoy the present without gloomy forebodings."

"At least," asked Franz, "we can have a window?"

"Where?"

"Looking on the Rue du Cours, to be sure."

"Ah, a window!" exclaimed Maître Pastrini,—"utterly impossible; there was only one left on the fifth floor of the Doria Palace, and that has been let to a Russian Prince for twenty sequins a day."

The two young men looked at each other with an air of stupefaction.

"Well," said Franz to Albert, "do you know what is the best thing we can do? It is to pass the Carnival at Venice; there we are sure of obtaining gondolas if we cannot have carriages."

"Ah, the devil! no," cried Albert; "I came to Rome to see the Carnival, and I will, though I see it on stilts."

"Bravo! an excellent idea! We will disguise ourselves as monster Punchinellos or shepherds of the Landes, and we shall have complete success."

"Do your excellencies still wish for a carriage from now to Sunday morning?"

"*Parbleu!*" said Albert, "do you think we are going to run about on foot in the streets of Rome like lawyer's clerks?"

"I hasten to comply with your excellencies' wishes; only I tell you beforehand the carriage will cost you six piastres a day."

"And as I am not a millionaire like our neighbour," said Franz, "I warn you that as I have been four times before at Rome, I know the prices of all the carriages. We will give you twelve piastres for to-day, to-morrow, and the day after, and then you will make a good profit."

"But, excellency——" said Pastrini, still striving to gain his point.

"Now go," returned Franz, "or I shall go myself and bargain with your *affettatore*, who is mine also. He is an old friend of mine, who has plundered me pretty well already; and in the hope of making more out of me he will fix upon a price smaller than I am now offering you. You will then lose the difference, and that will be your fault."

"Do not give yourself the trouble, excellency," returned Maître Pastrini, with that smile of the Italian speculator who avows himself defeated; "I will do all I can, and I hope you will be satisfied."

"And now we understand each other."

"When do you wish the carriage to be here?"

"In an hour."

"In an hour it will be at the door."

An hour later, the carriage was in fact awaiting the two young men. It was a modest *fiacre*, which was elevated to the rank of a private carriage in honour of the occasion; but in spite of its humble exterior, the young men would have thought themselves happy had they been able to procure such a carriage for the last three days of the Carnival.

"Excellency," cried the *cicerone*, seeing Franz approach the window, "shall I bring the carriage nearer to the palace?"

Accustomed as Franz was to the Italian phraseology, his first impulse was to look round him, but these words were addressed to him. Franz was the "excellency," the vehicle was the "carriage," and the Hôtel de Londres was the "palace." The laudatory habit of the people was well exhibited in that single sentence.

Franz and Albert descended; the carriage approached the palace; their excellencies stretched their legs along the seats; the *cicerone* sprang into the seat behind. " Where do your excellencies wish to go? " asked he.

" To St. Peter's first, and then to the Colosseum," returned Albert.

But Albert did not know that it takes a day to see St. Peter's, and a month to study it. The day was passed at St. Peter's alone. Suddenly the daylight began to fade away. Franz took out his watch; it was half-past four. They returned to the hotel; at the door Franz ordered the coachman to be ready at eight. He wished to show Albert the Colosseum by moonlight, as he had shown him St. Peter's by daylight. When we show to a friend a city we have already visited, we feel the same pride as when we point out a woman whose lover we have been. He was to leave the city by the Porta del Popolo, skirt the outer wall, and re-enter by the Porta San Giovanni; thus they would behold the Colosseum without being in some measure prepared by the sight of the Capitol, the Forum, the Arch of Septimius Severus, the Temple of Antoninus and Faustina, and the Via Sacra.

They sat down to dinner. Maître Pastrini had promised them a banquet; he gave them a tolerable repast. At the end of the dinner he entered in person. Franz concluded he came to hear his dinner praised, and began accordingly; but at the first words the landlord interrupted him. " Excellency," said he, " I am delighted to have your approbation; but it was not for that I came."

" Did you come to tell us you have procured a carriage? " asked Albert, lighting his cigar.

" No; and your excellencies will do well not to think of that any longer. At Rome things can or cannot be done; when you are told anything cannot be done, there is an end of it."

" It is much more convenient at Paris,—when anything cannot be done, you pay double and it is done directly."

" That is what all the French say," returned Maître Pastrini, somewhat piqued; " for that reason I do not understand why they travel."

" But," said Albert, emitting a volume of smoke and balancing his chair on its hind legs, " only madmen, or blockheads such as we are, travel. Men in their senses do not quit their hotel in the Rue du Helder, their walk on the Boulevard de Gand, and the Café de Paris."

It is of course understood that Albert resided in the street mentioned, appeared every day on the fashionable walk, and dined frequently at the only *café* where you can really dine,— that is, if you are on good terms with the waiters. Maître Pastrini remained silent a short time; it was evident that he was musing over this answer, which did not seem very clear.

"But," said Franz, in his turn interrupting his host's meditations, "you had some motive for coming here; may I beg to know what it was?"

"Ah, yes; you have ordered your carriage for eight o'clock?"

"I have."

"You intend visiting *il Colosseo*."

"That is to say, *le Colisée*?"

"It is the same thing. You have told your coachman to leave the city by the Porta del Popolo, to drive round the walls, and re-enter by the Porta San Giovanni?"

"These are my words exactly."

"Well, this route is impossible."

"Impossible!"

"Very dangerous, to say the least."

"Dangerous! and why?"

"On account of the famous Luigi Vampa."

"Pray who may this famous Luigi Vampa be?" inquired Albert; "he may be very famous at Rome, but I can assure you he is quite unknown at Paris."

"What! do you not know him?"

"I have not that honour."

"You have never heard his name?"

"Never."

"Well, then, he is a bandit compared to whom the Decesaris and the Gasparones were mere children."

"Now, then, Albert," cried Franz, "here is a bandit for you at last!"

"I forewarn you, Maître Pastrini, that I shall not believe one word of what you are going to tell us. That point being settled between us, you may say all you wish; I will listen. Once upon a time,—well, go ahead!"

Maître Pastrini turned round to Franz, who seemed to him the more reasonable of the two. We must do him justice; he had had a great many Frenchmen in his house, but had never been able to comprehend them. "Excellency," said he, gravely, addressing Franz, " if you look upon me as a liar, it is useless for me to say anything; it was for your interest I—"

" Albert does not say you are a liar, Maître Pastrini," said Franz; " he says he will not believe you,—that's all. But I will believe all you say; so proceed."

" But your excellency well understands that if any one doubts my veracity—"

" Maître Pastrini," returned Franz, " you are more susceptible than Cassandra, who was a prophetess, and yet no one believed her, while you at least are sure of the credence of half your auditory. Come, make an effort, and tell us who this M. Vampa is."

" I have told your excellency; he is the most famous bandit we have had since the days of Mastrilla."

" Well, what has this bandit to do with the order I have given the coachman to leave the city by the Porta del Popolo, and to re-enter by the Porta San Giovanni? "

" This," replied Maître Pastrini,—" that you will go out by one, but I very much doubt your returning by the other."

" Why? " asked Franz.

" Because after nightfall you are not safe fifty yards from the gates."

" On your honour, is that true? " cried Albert.

" Monsieur the Viscount," returned Maître Pastrini, hurt at Albert's repeated doubts of the truth of his assertions, " I do not say this to you, but to your companion, who knows Rome, and knows too that these things are not to be laughed at."

" My dear fellow," said Albert, turning to Franz, " here is an admirable adventure; we will fill our carriage with pistols, blunderbusses, and double-barrelled guns. Luigi Vampa comes to take us, and we take him; we bring him back to Rome and present him to his Holiness the Pope, who asks how he can recompense so great a service; then we merely ask for a carriage and a pair of horses, and we see the Carnival in a carriage, and doubtless the Roman people will crown us at the Capitol, and proclaim us, like Curtius and Horatius Cocles, the preservers of the country."

While Albert proposed this scheme, Maître Pastrini's face assumed an expression impossible to describe.

" And pray," asked Franz, " where are these pistols, blunderbusses, and other deadly weapons with which you intend filling the carriage? "

" Not in my armoury, for at Terracina I was plundered even of my hunting-knife."

" I shared the same fate at Aquapendente."

"Do you know, Maître Pastrini," said Albert, lighting a second cigar at the first, " that this practice is very convenient for robbers, and that it has the appearance of a plan for sharing with them? "

Doubtless Maître Pastrini found this pleasantry compromising, for he answered only half the questions, addressing himself to Franz, as the only one likely to listen with attention: " Your excellency knows that it is not customary to offer defence when attacked by bandits."

" What! " cried Albert, whose courage revolted at the idea of being plundered tamely, " not make any resistance! "

" No, for it would be useless. What can you do against a dozen bandits who spring out of some pit, ruin, or aqueduct, and attack you all at once? "

" Eh, *parbleu!* I will make them kill me."

The innkeeper turned to Franz with an air that seemed to say, " Your friend is decidedly mad."

" My dear Albert," returned Franz, " your answer is sublime, and worthy the ' Let him die,' of Corneille. But when Horace made that answer the safety of Rome was concerned, while here there is only the question of gratifying a caprice; and it would be ridiculous to risk our lives for a caprice."

" Ah, *per Bacco!* " cried Maître Pastrini, " that is good! that is speaking to some purpose! "

Albert poured himself out a glass of *lacryma Christi,* which he sipped at intervals, muttering some unintelligible words.

" Well, Maître Pastrini," said Franz, " now that my companion is quieted, and you have seen how peaceful my intentions are, tell me who is this Luigi Vampa. Is he a shepherd or a nobleman; young or old; tall or short? Describe him, in order that if we meet him by chance, like Jean Sbogar or Lara, we may recognise him."

" You could not apply to any one better able to inform you on all these points; for I knew him when he was a child, and one day when I fell into his hands going from Ferentino to Alatri, he, fortunately for me, recollected me, and not only set me free without ransom, but made me a present of a very splendid watch, and related his history to me."

" Let us see the watch," said Albert.

Maître Pastrini drew from his fob a magnificent Breguet, bearing the name of its maker, the Parisian stamp, and a count's coronet.

" Here it is," said he.

"*Peste!*" returned Albert, "I compliment you on it; I have its fellow,"—he took his watch from his waistcoat pocket,—"and it cost me three thousand livres."

"Let us hear the history," said Franz, drawing up an easy-chair and making a sign to Maître Pastrini to seat himself.

"Your excellencies permit it?" asked the host.

"*Pardieu!*" cried Albert, "you are not a preacher, to speak standing!"

The host sat down, after having made each of them a respectful bow, which meant to say he was ready to tell them all they wished to know concerning Luigi Vampa. "You tell me," said Franz, at the moment Maître Pastrini was about to open his mouth, "that you knew Luigi Vampa when he was a child; he is still a young man, then?"

"A young man! he is hardly two-and-twenty. Oh, he is a rattling blade, who will have a career, you may be sure."

"What do you think of that, Albert,—at two-and-twenty to be thus famous?"

"Yes, at his age Alexander, Cæsar, and Napoleon, who have all made some noise in the world, were not so advanced."

"So," continued Franz, "the hero of this history is only two-and-twenty?"

"Scarcely so much, as I have had the honour to tell you."

"Is he tall or short?"

"Of the middle height,—about the same stature as his excellency," returned the host, pointing to Albert.

"Thanks for the comparison," said Albert, with a bow.

"Go on, Maître Pastrini," continued Franz, smiling at his friend's susceptibility. "To what class of society does he belong?"

"He was a shepherd-boy attached to the farm of the Comte de San Felice, situated between Palestrina and the Lake of Gabri. He was born at Pampinara, and entered the count's service when he was five years old; his father was also a shepherd, who owned a small flock and lived by the wool and the milk which he sold at Rome. When quite a child, the little Vampa was of a most extraordinary disposition. One day, when he was seven years old, he came to the curé of Palestrina, and prayed him to teach him to read. It was somewhat difficult, for he could not quit his flock; but the good curé went every day to say mass at a little hamlet too poor to pay a priest, and which having no other name was called Borgo. He told Luigi that he might meet him on his return, and that then he would give him a lesson, warning him that it would be short, and that he must profit as much as possible by it. The child accepted joyfully. Every day Luigi led his flock to graze on the road that leads from Palestrina to Borgo; every day, at nine o'clock in the morning, the priest and the boy sat down on a bank by the wayside, and the little shepherd took his lesson out of the priest's breviary. At the end of three months he had learned to read. This was not enough,—he must now learn to write. The priest procured from a teacher of writing at Rome three alphabets,—one in large letters, one in letters of medium size, and one in small letters,—and showed him how by the help of a sharp instrument he could trace the letters on a slate, and thus learn to write. The same evening, when the flock was safe at the farm, the little Luigi hastened to the smith at Palestrina, took a large nail, forged it, sharpened it, and formed a sort of antique stylus. The next morning, having collected a quantity of slates, he began his lessons. At the end of three months he had learned to write. The curé, astonished at his quickness and intelligence, made him a present of pens, paper, and a penknife. This involved new study, but nothing compared to the first; at the end of a week he wrote as well with the pen as with the stylus. The curé related this anecdote to the Comte de San Felice, who sent for the little shepherd, made him read and write before him, ordered his attendant to let him eat with the domestics, and to give him two piastres a month. With this Luigi purchased books and pencils. He applied to everything his imitative powers, and like Giotto, when young, he drew on his slate sheep, houses, and trees. Then, with his knife, he began to carve all sorts of objects in wood; it was thus that Pinelli, the famous sculptor, had commenced.

"A girl of six or seven—that is, a little younger than Vampa —tended sheep on a farm near Palestrina; she was an orphan, born at Valmontone, and was named Teresa. The two children met, sat down near each other, let their flocks mingle together, played, laughed, and conversed together; in the evening they separated the flock of the Comte de San Felice from those of the Baron de Cervetri, and the children returned to their respective farms, promising to meet the next morning, and the next day they kept their word. Thus they grew, side by side, until Vampa was twelve and Teresa eleven. Meantime, their natural dispositions revealed themselves. While he still followed his inclination for the fine arts, which Luigi had carried as far as he could in his solitude, he was sad by fits, ardent by starts, angry by caprice, and always sarcastic. None of the lads of Pampinara, of Palestrina, or of Valmontone had been able to gain any influence over him, or even to become his companion. His disposition (always inclined to exact concessions rather than to make them) kept him aloof from all friendships. Teresa alone ruled by a look, a word, a gesture, this impetuous character, which was pliant under the hand of a woman, but under the hand of any man whatever would have resisted until it broke.

" Teresa was, on the contrary, lively and gay, but coquettish to excess. The two piastres that Luigi received every month from the Comte de San Felice's steward, and the price of all the little carvings in wood he sold at Rome, were expended in ear-rings, necklaces, and gold hair-pins; so that thanks to her friend's generosity, Teresa was the most beautiful and the best attired peasant near Rome.

" The two children continued to grow up together, passing all their time with each other, and giving themselves up to the wild ideas of their different characters. Thus in all their dreams, their wishes, and their conversations, Vampa saw himself the captain of a vessel, general of an army, or governor of a province. Teresa saw herself rich, superbly attired, and attended by a train of liveried domestics. Then, when they had thus passed the day in building castles in the air, they separated their flocks and descended from the elevation of their dreams to the reality of their humble position.

" One day the young shepherd told the count's steward that he had seen a wolf come out of the Sabine Mountains and prowl around his flock. The steward gave him a gun; this was what Vampa longed for. This gun had an excellent barrel, made at Breschia, and carrying a ball with the precision of an English rifle; but one day the count broke the stock, and had then cast the gun aside. This, however, was nothing to a sculptor like Vampa. He examined the ancient stock, calculated what change it would require to adapt the gun to his shoulder, and made a fresh stock, so beautifully carved that it would have brought fifteen or twenty piastres, had he chosen to sell it; but nothing could be farther from his thoughts. For a long time a gun had been the young man's greatest ambition. In every country where independence has taken the place of liberty, the first desire of a manly heart is to possess a weapon, which at once renders him capable of defence or attack, and by rendering its owner terrible often makes him feared. From this moment Vampa devoted all his leisure time to perfecting himself in the use of this precious weapon; he purchased powder and ball, and everything served him for a mark,—the trunk of some old and moss-grown olive-tree that grew on the Sabine Mountains; the fox, as he quitted his earth on some marauding excursion; the eagle that soared above their heads. And thus he soon became so expert that Teresa overcame the terror she at first felt at the report, and amused herself by watching him while he directed the ball wherever he pleased, with as much accuracy as if placed by the hand.

"One evening a wolf emerged from a pine wood near which they were usually stationed, but had scarcely advanced ten yards ere he was dead. Proud of this exploit, Vampa took the dead animal on his shoulders, and carried him to the farm. All these circumstances had gained Luigi considerable reputation. The man of superior abilities always finds admirers, go where he will. He was spoken of as the most adroit, the strongest, and the most courageous *contadino* for ten leagues round; and although Teresa was universally allowed to be the most beautiful girl of the Sabines, no one had ever spoken to her of love, because it was known that she was beloved by Vampa. And yet these two had never confessed their love to one another; they had grown up side by side, like two trees which intertwine their roots in the ground and their branches in the air, and whose perfume rises together to the heavens. Only their wish to see each other had become a necessity, and they would have preferred death to a day's separation. Teresa was sixteen and Vampa eighteen. About this time a band of brigands that had established itself in the Lepini Mountains began to be much spoken of. The brigands had never been really extirpated from the neighbourhood of Rome. Sometimes a chief is wanted, but when a chief presents himself he rarely wants a band.

"The celebrated Cucumetto, pursued in the Abruzzo, driven out of the kingdom of Naples, where he had carried on a regular war, had crossed the Garigliano, like Manfred, and had come between Sonnino and Juperno to take refuge on the banks of the Amasine. He strove to reorganise a band, and followed in the footsteps of Decesaris and Gasperone, whom he hoped to surpass. Many young men of Palestrina, Frascati, and Pampinara disappeared. Their disappearance at first caused much inquietude; but it was soon known that they had joined the band of Cucumetto. After some time Cucumetto became the object of universal attention; the most extraordinary traits of ferocious daring and brutality were related of him. One day he carried off a young girl, the daughter of a surveyor of Frosinone. The bandits' laws are positive: a young girl belongs first to him who carries her off; then the rest draw lots for her, and she is abandoned to their brutality until death relieves her sufferings. When her parents are sufficiently rich to pay a ransom, a messenger is sent to treat concerning it. The prisoner is hostage for the security of the messenger; should the ransom be refused, the prisoner is irrevocably lost. The young girl's lover was in Cucumetto's troop; his name was Carlini. When she recognised her lover, the poor girl extended her arms to him and believed herself safe; but Carlini felt his heart sink, for he but too well knew the fate that awaited her. However, as he was a favourite with Cucumetto; as he had for three years faithfully served him; and as he had saved his life by shooting a dragoon who was about to cut him down,—he hoped he would have pity on him. He took him apart, while the young girl, seated at the foot of a huge pine that stood in the centre of the forest, formed with her picturesque head-dress a veil to hide her face from the lascivious gaze of the bandits. There he told him all,—his affection for the prisoner, their promises of mutual fidelity, and how every night since he had been near they had met in a ruin.

" It so happened that night that Cucumetto had sent Carlini to a neighbouring village, so that he had been unable to go to the place of meeting. Cucumetto had been there, however,— by accident, as he said,—and had carried the maiden off. Carlini besought his chief to make an exception in Rita's favour, as her father was rich, and could pay a large ransom. Cucumetto seemed to yield to his friend's entreaties, and bade him find a shepherd to send to Rita's father at Frosinone. Carlini flew joyfully to Rita, telling her she was saved, and bidding her write to her father to inform him what had occurred, and that her ransom was fixed at three hundred piastres. Twelve hours' delay was all that was granted,—that is, until nine the next morning. The instant the letter was written Carlini seized it, and hastened to the plain to find a messenger. He found a young shepherd watching his flock. The natural messengers of the bandits are the shepherds, who live between the city and the mountains, between civilised and savage life. The boy undertook the commission, promising to be in Frosinone in less than an hour. Carlini returned, eager to see his mistress, and announce the joyful intelligence. He found the troop in the glade, supping off the provisions exacted as contributions from the peasants; but his eye vainly sought Rita and Cucumetto among them. He inquired where they were, and was answered by a burst of laughter. A cold perspiration burst from every pore, and his hair stood on end. He repeated his question. One of the bandits rose and offered him a glass filled with wine of Orvietto, saying, 'To the health of the brave Cucumetto and the fair Rita!' At this moment Carlini heard the cry of a woman; he divined the truth, seized the glass, broke it across the face of him who presented it, and rushed towards the spot whence the cry came. After going a hundred yards he turned the corner of the thicket; he found Rita senseless in the arms of Cucumetto. At the sight of Carlini, Cucumetto rose, a pistol in each hand. The two brigands looked at each other for a moment,—the one with a smile of lasciviousness on his lips, the other with the pallor of death on his brow. It seemed that something terrible was about to pass between these two men; but by degrees Carlini's features relaxed. His hand, which had grasped one of the pistols in his belt, fell to his side. Rita lay between them. The moon lighted the group.

"'Well,' said Cucumetto, 'have you executed your commission?' 'Yes, captain,' returned Carlini. 'At nine o'clock to-morrow, Rita's father will be here with the money.' 'It is well; in the meantime, we will have a merry night. This young girl is charming, and does credit to your taste. Now, as I am not selfish, we will return to our comrades and draw lots for her.' 'You have determined, then, to abandon her to the common law?' said Carlini. 'Why should an exception be made in her favour?' 'I thought that my entreaties—' 'What right have you, any more than the rest, to ask for an exception?' 'It is true.' 'But never mind,' continued Cucumetto, laughing, 'sooner or later your turn will come.' Carlini's teeth clinched convulsively. 'Now, then,' said Cucumetto, advancing towards the other bandits, 'are you coming?' 'I follow you.' Cucumetto departed without losing sight of Carlini, for doubtless he feared lest he should strike him unawares; but nothing betrayed a hostile design on Carlini's part. He was standing, his arms folded, near Rita, who was still insensible. Cucumetto fancied for a moment the young man was about to take her in his arms and fly; but this mattered little to him now Rita had been his, and as for the money, three hundred piastres distributed among the band was so small a sum that he cared little about it. He continued to follow the path to the glade; but to his great surprise, Carlini arrived almost as soon as himself. 'Let us draw lots! let us draw lots!' cried all the brigands, when they saw the chief.

"Their demand was fair; and the chief inclined his head in sign of acquiescence. The eyes of all shone fiercely as they made their demand, and the red light of the fire made them look like demons. The names of all, including Carlini, were placed in a hat, and the youngest of the band drew forth a ticket; the ticket bore the name of Diavolaccio. He was the man who had proposed to Carlini the health of their chief, and to whom Carlini had replied by breaking the glass across his face. A large wound, extending from the temple to the mouth, was bleeding profusely. Diavolaccio, seeing himself thus favoured by fortune, burst into a loud laugh. 'Captain,' said he, 'just now Carlini would not drink your health when I proposed it to him; propose mine to him, and let us see if he will be more condescending to you than to me.' Every one expected an explosion on Carlini's part; but to their great surprise, he took a glass in one hand and a flask in the other, and filling it, 'Your health, Diavolaccio,' said he, calmly, and he drank it off without his hand trembling in the least. Then sitting down by the fire, 'My supper,' said he; 'my expedition has given me an appetite.' 'Well done, Carlini!' cried the brigands; 'that is acting like a good fellow;' and they all formed a circle round the fire, while Diavolaccio disappeared. Carlini ate and drank as if nothing had happened. The bandits looked at him with astonishment, not understanding his strange impassiveness, when upon the ground behind them they heard a heavy footstep. They turned round and saw Diavolaccio bearing the young girl in his arms. Her head hung back, and her long hair swept the ground. As they entered the circle, the bandits could perceive by the firelight the unearthly pallor of the young girl and of Diavolaccio. This apparition was so strange and so solemn that every one rose with the exception of Carlini, who remained seated, and ate and drank calmly. Diavolaccio advanced amid the most profound silence and laid Rita at the captain's feet. Then every one could understand the cause of that pallor of the young girl and of the bandit. A knife was plunged up to the hilt in Rita's left breast. Every one looked at Carlini; the sheath at his belt was empty. 'Ah, ah!' said the chief, 'I now understand why Carlini stayed behind.'

"All savage natures appreciate a desperate deed. No other of the bandits would perhaps have done the same; but they all understood what Carlini had done. 'Now, then,' cried Carlini, rising in his turn and approaching the corpse, his hand on the butt of one of his pistols, 'does any one dispute the possession of this woman with me?' 'No,' returned the chief, 'she is thine.' Carlini raised her in his arms and carried her out of the circle of light around the fire. Cucumetto placed his sentinels for the night, and the bandits wrapped themselves in their cloaks and lay down before the fire. At midnight the sentinel gave the alarm, and in an instant all were on the alert. It was Rita's father, who brought his daughter's ransom in person. 'Here,' said he to Cucumetto,—'here are three hundred piastres; give me back my child.' But the chief, without taking the money, made a sign to him to follow him. The old man obeyed. They both advanced beneath the trees, through whose branches streamed the moonlight. Cucumetto stopped at last and pointed to two persons grouped at the foot of a tree. 'There,' said he, 'demand thy child of Carlini; he will tell thee what has become of her;' and he returned to his companions.

"The old man remained motionless; he felt that some great and unforeseen misfortune hung over his head. At length he advanced towards the group, which he could not comprehend. As he approached, Carlini raised his head, and the forms of two persons became visible to the old man's eyes. A female lay on the ground, her head resting on the knees of a man who was seated by her; as he raised his head the female's face became visible. The old man recognised his child, and Carlini recognised the old man. 'I expected thee,' said the bandit to Rita's father. 'Wretch!' returned the old man, 'what hast thou done?' and he gazed with terror on Rita, pale and bloody, a knife buried in her bosom. A ray of moonlight poured through the trees and lighted up the face of the dead. 'Cucumetto had violated thy daughter,' said the bandit; 'I loved her, therefore I slew her,—for she would have served as the sport of the whole band.' The old man spoke not, and grew pale as death. 'Now,' continued Carlini, 'if I have done wrongly, avenge her;' and withdrawing the knife from the wound in Rita's bosom, he held it out to the old man with one hand, while with the other he tore open his vest. 'Thou hast done well!' returned the old man, in a hoarse voice; 'embrace me, my son.' Carlini threw himself, sobbing like a child, into the arms of his mistress's father. These were the first tears the man of blood had ever wept. 'Now,' said the old man, 'aid me to bury my child.' Carlini fetched two pickaxes, and the father and the lover began to dig at the foot of a huge oak, beneath which the young girl was to repose. When the grave was formed, the father embraced her first, and then the lover; afterwards, one taking the head, the other the feet, they placed her in the grave. Then they knelt on each side of the grave and said the prayers of the dead. Then, when they had finished, they cast the earth over the corpse until the grave was filled. Then, extending his hand, the old man said, ' I thank you, my son; and now leave me alone.' ' Yet—' replied Carlini. ' Leave me, I command you.' Carlini obeyed, rejoined his comrades, folded himself in his cloak, and soon appeared as deep asleep as the rest.

" It had been resolved the night before to change their encampment. An hour before daybreak Cucumetto aroused his men and gave the word to march. But Carlini would not quit the forest without knowing what had become of Rita's father. He went towards the place where he had left him. He found the old man suspended from one of the branches of the oak which shaded his daughter's grave. He then took an oath of bitter vengeance over the dead body of the one and the tomb of the other. But he was unable to complete this oath, for two days afterwards, in a rencontre with the Roman carbineers, Carlini was killed. There was some surprise, however, that as he was with his face to the enemy he should have received a ball between his shoulders. That astonishment ceased when one of the brigands remarked to his comrades that Cucumetto was stationed ten paces in Carlini's rear when he fell. On the morning of the departure from the forest of Frosinone he had followed Carlini in the darkness, had heard his oath of vengeance, and like a wise man had prevented its fulfilment.

" They told ten other stories of this bandit chief not less strange than this. Thus, from Fondi to Perouse, every one trembled at the name of Cucumetto. These narratives were frequently the themes of conversation between Luigi and Teresa. The young girl trembled very much at all these tales. But Vampa reassured her with a smile, tapping the butt of his good fowling-piece, which threw its ball so well; and if that did not restore her courage, he pointed to a crow perched on some dead branch, took an aim, touched the trigger, and the bird fell dead at the foot of the tree. Time passed on; and the two young persons had agreed to be married when Vampa should be twenty and Teresa nineteen years of age. They were both orphans, and had only their employer's leave to ask, which had been already sought and obtained. One day when they were talking over their plans for the future, they heard two or three reports of fire-arms, and then suddenly a man came out of the wood near which the two young persons used to graze their flocks, and hurried towards them. When he came within hearing, he exclaimed, ' I am pursued; can you conceal me?' They knew full well that this fugitive must be a bandit; but there is a natural sympathy between the Roman brigand and the Roman peasant, and the latter is always ready to aid the former.

Vampa, without saying a word, hastened to the stone that closed up the entrance to their grotto, drew it away, made a sign to the fugitive to take refuge there in a retreat unknown to every one, closed the stone upon him, and then went and resumed his seat by Teresa. Instantly afterwards four carbineers on horseback appeared on the edge of the wood; three of them appeared to be looking for the fugitive, while the fourth dragged a brigand prisoner by the neck. The three carbineers looked around them on all sides, saw the young peasants, and galloping up, interrogated them. They had seen no one. 'That is very annoying,' said the brigadier; 'for the man we are looking for is the chief.' 'Cucumetto?' cried Luigi and Teresa at the same moment. 'Yes,' replied the brigadier; 'and as his head is valued at a thousand Roman crowns, there would have been five hundred for you if you had helped us to catch him.' The two young persons exchanged looks. The brigadier had a moment's hope. Five hundred Roman crowns are three thousand livres, and three thousand livres are a fortune for two poor orphans who are going to be married. 'Yes, it is very annoying,' said Vampa; 'but we have not seen him.'

"Then the carbineers scoured the country in different directions, but in vain; then after a time they disappeared. Vampa then removed the stone, and Cucumetto came out. He had seen, through the crevices in the granite, the two young peasants talking with the carbineers, and guessed the subject of their parley. He had read in the countenances of Luigi and Teresa their steadfast resolution not to surrender him, and he drew from his pocket a purse full of gold, which he offered to them. But Vampa raised his head proudly; as to Teresa, her eyes sparkled when she thought of all the fine gowns and gay jewellery she could buy with this purse of gold.

"Cucumetto was a cunning fiend who had assumed the form of a brigand instead of a serpent; and this look of Teresa revealed to him that she was a worthy daughter of Eve. He returned to the forest, pausing several times on his way under the pretext of saluting his protectors. Several days elapsed, and they neither saw nor heard of Cucumetto. The time of the Carnival was at hand. The Comte de San Felice announced a grand masked ball, to which all that were distinguished in Rome were invited. Teresa had a great desire to see this ball. Luigi asked permission of his protector, the steward, that she and he might be present among the servants of the house. This was granted. The ball was given by the count for the particular pleasure of his daughter Carmela, whom he adored. Carmela was precisely the age and figure of Teresa, and Teresa was as handsome as Carmela. On the evening of the ball Teresa was attired in her best,—her most brilliant hair ornaments and gayest glass beads; she was in the costume of the women of Frascati. Luigi wore the very picturesque garb of the Roman peasant at holiday time. They both mingled, as they had leave to do, with the servants and peasants.

" The fête was magnificent,—not only was the villa brilliantly illuminated, but thousands of coloured lanterns were suspended from the trees in the garden; and very soon the palace overflowed to the terraces, and the terraces to the garden-walks. At each cross-path were an orchestra, and tables spread with refreshments; the guests stopped, formed quadrilles, and danced in every part of the grounds they pleased. Carmela was attired like a woman of Sonnino. Her cap was embroidered with pearls, the pins in her hair were of gold and diamonds, her girdle was of Turkey silk with large embroidered flowers, her bodice and skirt were of cashmere, her apron of Indian muslin, and the buttons of her corset were of jewels. Two of her companions were dressed, the one as a woman of Nettuno, and the other as a woman of La Riccia. Four young men of the richest and noblest families of Rome accompanied them with Italian freedom, which has not its parallel in any other country of the world. They were attired as peasants of Albano, Velletri, Civita Castellana, and Sora. I need not tell you that these peasant costumes, like those of the women, were brilliant with gold and jewels.

" Carmela wished to make a uniform quadrille, but there was one woman wanting. She looked all around her, but not one of the guests had a costume similar to her own or those of her companions. The Comte de San Felice pointed out to her, in the group of peasants, Teresa, who was hanging on Luigi's arm. ' Will you allow me, father? ' said Carmela. ' Certainly,' replied the count; ' are we not in Carnival time? ' Carmela turned towards the young man who was talking with her, and saying a few words to him, pointed with her finger to Teresa. The young man followed with his eyes the lovely hand which made this indication, bowed in obedience, and then went to Teresa and invited her to dance in a quadrille directed by the count's daughter. Teresa felt something like a flame pass over her face; she looked at Luigi, who could not refuse his assent. Luigi slowly relinquished Teresa's arm, which he had held beneath his own, and Teresa, accompanied by her elegant cavalier, took her appointed place with much agitation in the aristocratic quadrille. Certainly, in the eyes of an artist the exact and severe costume of Teresa had a very different character from that of Carmela and her companions; but Teresa was frivolous and coquettish, and thus the embroidery and muslins, the cashmere waist-girdles, all dazzled her, and the reflection of sapphires and diamonds almost turned her giddy brain.

"Luigi felt a sensation hitherto unknown arising in his mind. It was like an acute pain which gnawed at his heart, and then passed thrillingly throughout his frame, chasing through his veins, and pervading his entire body. He followed with his eyes each movement of Teresa and her cavalier. When their hands touched, he felt as though he should swoon; every pulse beat with violence, and it seemed as though a bell were ringing in his ears. When they spoke, although Teresa listened timidly and with downcast eyes to the conversation of her cavalier, as Luigi could read in the ardent looks of the good-looking young man that his language was that of praise, it seemed as if the whole world was turning round with him, and all the voices of hell were whispering in his ears ideas of murder and assassination. Then fearing that his paroxysm might get the better of him, he clutched with one hand the branch of a tree against which he was leaning, and with the other convulsively grasped the dagger with a carved handle which was in his belt, and which, unwittingly, he drew from the scabbard from time to time. Luigi was jealous! He felt that, influenced by her ambition and coquettish disposition, Teresa might escape him.

"The young peasant girl, at first timid and almost frightened, soon recovered herself. I have said that Teresa was handsome, but this is not all; Teresa had the fascination of those wild graces which are so much more potent than our affected and studied elegancies. She had almost all the honours of the quadrille, and if she was envious of the Comte de San Felice's daughter, I will not undertake to say that Carmela was not jealous of her; and with overpowering compliments her handsome cavalier led her back to the place whence he had taken her and where Luigi awaited her. Twice or thrice during the dance the young girl glanced at Luigi, and each time she saw that he was pale and that his features were agitated; once even the blade of his knife, half drawn from its sheath, had dazzled her eyes with its sinister gleam. Thus she was almost trembling when she resumed her lover's arm. The quadrille had been very successful; and it was evident there was a great demand for a repetition of it. Carmela alone objected to it; but the Comte de San Felice begged his daughter so earnestly that she acceded. One of the cavaliers then hastened to invite Teresa, without whom it was impossible to form the quadrille, but the young girl had disappeared. In fact, Luigi had not the strength to support another such trial, and half by persuasion and half by force, he had removed Teresa to another part of the garden. Teresa had yielded in spite of herself; but when she looked at the agitated countenance of the young man, she understood by his silence and trembling voice that something strange was passing within him. She herself was not free from internal emotion, and without having done anything wrong, yet fully comprehended that Luigi would be in the right if he should reproach her. Why, she did not know, but she did not the less feel that she had somehow deserved to be blamed. However, to Teresa's great astonishment Luigi remained mute, and not a word escaped his lips the rest of the evening. But when the chill of the night had driven away the guests from the gardens, and the gates of the villa were closed for the fête indoors, he took Teresa away; and as he left her at her home, he said, ' Teresa, what were you thinking of as you danced opposite the young Comtesse de San Felice?' ' I thought,' replied the young girl, with all the frankness of her nature, ' that I would give half my life for a costume such as she wore.' ' And what said your cavalier to you?' ' He said it only depended on myself to have it, and I had only one word to say.' ' He was right,' said Luigi; ' do you desire it as ardently as you say?' ' Yes.' ' Well, then, you shall have it!'

" The young girl, much astonished, raised her head to look at him; but his face was so gloomy and terrible that her words froze to her lips. As Luigi spoke thus, he left her. Teresa followed him with her eyes into the darkness as long as she could, and when he had quite disappeared she entered her apartment with a sigh.

" That night a great accident happened, no doubt from the imprudence of some servant who had neglected to extinguish the lights. The Villa de San Felice took fire in the rooms adjoining the very apartment of the lovely Carmela. Wakened in the night by the light of the flames, she had sprung out of bed, wrapped herself in a dressing-gown, and attempted to escape by the door; but the corridor by which she hoped to fly was already a prey to the flames. She had then returned to her room, calling for help as loudly as she could, when suddenly her window, which was twenty feet from the ground, was opened; a young peasant jumped into the chamber, seized her in his arms, and with superhuman skill and strength conveyed her to the turf of the grass-plot, where she fainted. When she recovered, her father was by her side. All the servants surrounded her, offering her assistance. An entire wing of the villa was burned down; but what was that, since Carmela was safe and uninjured? Her preserver was everywhere sought for, but did not appear; he was inquired for everywhere, but no one had seen him. Carmela was greatly troubled that she had not recognised him. As the count was immensely rich, setting aside the peril to Carmela,—which in view of her miraculous escape seemed to him rather a new favour of Providence than an actual misfortune, —the loss occasioned by the conflagration was to him but a trifle.

"The next day at the usual hour the two young peasants were on the borders of the forest. Luigi arrived first. He came towards Teresa in high spirits, and seemed to have completely forgotten the events of the previous evening. The young girl was visibly thoughtful; but seeing Luigi so cheerful, she on her part assumed a smiling air, which was natural to her when no excitement of passion came to disturb her. Luigi took her arm beneath his own, and led her to the door of the grotto. There he paused. The young girl, perceiving that there was something extraordinary, looked at him steadfastly. 'Teresa,' said Luigi, 'yesterday evening you told me you would give all the world to have a costume similar to that of the count's daughter.' 'Yes,' replied Teresa, with astonishment; 'but I was mad to utter such a wish.' 'And I replied, "Very well, you shall have it."' 'Yes,' replied the young girl, whose astonishment increased at every word uttered by Luigi, 'but of course your reply was only to please me.' 'I have promised no more than I have given you, Teresa,' said Luigi, proudly. 'Go into the grotto and dress yourself.' At these words he drew away the stone and showed Teresa the grotto, lighted up by two wax lights, which burned on each side of a splendid mirror; on a rustic table, made by Luigi, were spread out the pearl necklace and the diamond pins, and on a chair at the side was laid the rest of the costume.

"Teresa uttered a cry of joy, and without inquiring whence this attire came, or even thanking Luigi, darted into the grotto, transformed into a dressing-room. Luigi pushed the stone behind her, for he saw on the crest of a small adjacent hill between him and Palestrina, a traveller on horseback, who stopped a moment as if uncertain of his road, and was thus visible against the azure sky with that distinctness of outline peculiar to the perspective of southern countries. When he saw Luigi, he put his horse into a gallop and advanced towards him. Luigi was not mistaken. The traveller, who was going from Palestrina to Tivoli, had mistaken his way. The young man directed him; but as at the distance of a quarter of a mile the road again divided into three ways, and on reaching these the traveller might again stray from his route, he begged Luigi to be his guide. Luigi threw his cloak on the ground, placed his carbine on his shoulder, and freed from his heavy covering, preceded the traveller with the rapid step of a mountaineer, which a horse can scarcely keep up with. In ten minutes Luigi and the traveller reached the cross-roads alluded to by the young shepherd. On arriving there, with an air as majestic as that of an emperor he stretched his hand towards that one of the roads which the traveller was to follow. 'That is your road, excellency; and now you cannot again mistake.' 'And here is your recompense,' said the traveller, offering the young herdsman some pieces of small money. 'Thank you,' said Luigi, drawing back his hand; 'I render a service, I do not sell it.' 'Well,' replied the traveller, who seemed used to this difference between the servility of a man of the cities and the pride of the mountaineer, 'if you refuse pay, you will perhaps accept a present.' 'Ah, yes, that is another thing.' 'Then,' said the traveller, 'take these two Venetian sequins and give them to your bride, to make herself a pair of ear-rings.' 'And then do you take this poniard,' said the young herdsman; 'you will not find one better carved between Albana and Civita Castellana.' 'I accept it,' answered the traveller; 'but then the obligation will be on my side, for this poniard is worth more than two sequins.' 'For a dealer, perhaps; but for me, who engraved it myself, it is hardly worth a piastre.' 'What is your name?' inquired the traveller. 'Luigi Vampa,' replied the shepherd, in the same manner in which he would have said, 'Alexander, King of Macedon;' 'and yours?' 'I,' said the traveller, 'am called Sinbad the Sailor.'"

Franz d'Epinay started with surprise. "Sinbad the Sailor?" he said.

"Yes," replied the narrator; "that was the name which the traveller gave to Vampa as his own."

"Well, and what may you have to say against this name?" inquired Albert. "It is a very pretty name; and the adventures of the gentleman of that name amused me very much in my youth, I must confess."

Franz said no more. The name of Sinbad the Sailor, as may well be supposed, awakened in him a world of recollections. "Proceed!" said he to the host.

"Vampa put the two sequins haughtily into his pocket, and

slowly returned by the way he had gone. As he came within two or three hundred paces of the grotto, he thought he heard a cry. He listened to know whence this sound could proceed. A moment afterwards and he heard his own name pronounced distinctly. The cry proceeded from the grotto. He bounded like a chamois, cocking his carbine as he went, and in a moment reached the summit of a hill opposite to that on which he had perceived the traveller. There the cries for help came to him more distinctly. He cast his eyes around him, and saw a man carrying off Teresa, as the Centaur Nessus carried Dejanira. This man, who was hastening towards the wood, was already three-quarters of the way on the road from the grotto to the forest. Vampa measured the distance; the man was at least two hundred paces in advance of him, and there was not a chance of overtaking him. The young shepherd stopped as if his feet had been rooted to the ground; then he put the butt of his carbine to his shoulder, took aim at the ravisher, followed him for a second in his track, and then fired. The ravisher stopped suddenly, his knees bent under him, and he fell with Teresa in his arms. The young girl rose instantly; but the man lay on the earth struggling in the agonies of death. Vampa then rushed towards Teresa,—for at ten paces from the dying man her legs had failed her and she had dropped on her knees; so that the young man feared that the ball that had brought down his enemy had also wounded his betrothed. Fortunately, she was unscathed; and it was fright alone that had overcome Teresa. When Luigi had assured himself that she was safe and unharmed, he turned towards the wounded man. He had just expired, with clinched hands, his mouth in a spasm of agony, and his hair on end in the sweat of death. His eyes remained open and menacing. Vampa approached the body and recognised Cucumetto.

"From the day on which the bandit had been saved by the two young peasants, he had been enamoured of Teresa, and had sworn she should be his. From that time he had watched them, and profiting by the moment when her lover had left her alone while he guided the traveller on his way, had carried her off, and believed he at length had her in his power, when the ball, directed by the unerring skill of the young herdsman, had pierced his heart. Vampa gazed on him for a moment without betraying the slightest emotion; while on the contrary Teresa, shuddering in every limb, dared not approach the slain ruffian but by degrees, and threw a hesitating glance at the dead body over the shoulder of her lover. Suddenly Vampa turned towards his mistress; 'Ah, ah!' said he, 'good, good! you are attired; it is now my turn to dress myself.'

"Teresa was clothed from head to foot in the garb of the Comte de San Felice's daughter. Vampa took Cucumetto's body in his arms and conveyed it to the grotto, while in her turn Teresa remained outside. If a second traveller had passed he would have seen a strange thing,—a shepherdess watching her flock, clad in a cashmere gown, with ear-rings and necklace of pearls, diamond pins, and buttons of sapphires, emeralds, and rubies. He would no doubt have believed that he had returned to the times of Florian, and would have declared on reaching Paris that he had met a shepherdess of the Alps seated at the foot of the Sabine Hill. At the end of a quarter of an hour Vampa quitted the grotto; his costume was no less elegant than that of Teresa. He wore a vest of garnet-coloured velvet, with buttons of cut gold; a silk waistcoat covered with embroidery; a Roman scarf tied round his neck; a cartouche-box worked with gold and red and green silk; sky-blue velvet breeches fastened above the knee with diamond buckles; garters of deer-skin worked with a thousand arabesques; and a hat whereon hung ribbons of all colours. Two watches hung from his girdle, and a splendid poniard was in his belt. Teresa uttered a cry of admiration. Vampa in this attire resembled a painting by Léopold Robert or by Schnetz. He had assumed the entire costume of Cucumetto. The young man saw the effect produced on his betrothed, and a smile of pride passed over his lips. 'Now,' he said to Teresa, 'are you ready to share my fortune, whatever it may be?' 'Oh, yes!' exclaimed the young girl, enthusiastically. 'And follow me wherever I go?' 'To the world's end.' 'Then take my arm and let us go on; we have no time to lose.' The young girl took her lover's arm without asking him whither he was conducting her, —for he appeared to her at this moment as handsome, proud, and powerful as a god. They went towards the forest and soon entered it. All the paths of the mountain were of course well known to Vampa. He therefore went forward without a moment's hesitation, although there was no beaten track; but he knew his path by looking at the trees and bushes, and thus they kept on advancing for nearly an hour and a half. At the end of this time they had reached the thickest of the forest. A torrent, whose bed was dry, led into a deep gorge. Vampa took this wild road, which, enclosed between two ridges and shadowed by the tufted umbrage of the pines, seemed, but for the difficulties of its descent, that path to Avernus of which

Virgil speaks. Teresa had become alarmed at the wild and deserted look of the plain around her, and pressed closely against her guide, not uttering a syllable; but as she saw him advance with even step and composed countenance, she endeavoured to repress her emotion. Suddenly, about ten paces from them, a man advanced from behind a tree and aimed at Vampa. 'Not another step,' he said, 'or you are a dead man!' 'What, then!' said Vampa, raising his hand with a gesture of disdain, while Teresa, no longer able to restrain her alarm, clung closely to him; 'do wolves rend each other?' 'Who are you?' inquired the sentinel. 'I am Luigi Vampa, shepherd of the farm of San Felice.' 'What do you want?' 'I would speak with your companions who are in the recess at Rocca Bianca.' 'Follow me, then,' said the sentinel; 'or as you know your way, go first.' Vampa smiled disdainfully at this precaution of the bandit, went before Teresa, and continued to advance with the same firm and easy step as before. At the end of ten minutes the bandit made them a sign to stop. The two young persons obeyed. Then the bandit thrice imitated the cry of a crow; a croak answered this signal. 'Good!' said the sentry; 'you may now advance.' Luigi and Teresa again set forward; as they advanced, Teresa clung tremblingly to her lover as she saw through the trees arms appear and the barrels of carbines shine. The retreat of Rocca Bianca was at the top of a small mountain, which no doubt in former days had been a volcano, —a volcano extinct before the days when Remus and Romulus had deserted Alba to come and found the city of Rome. Teresa and Luigi reached the summit, and all at once found themselves in the presence of twenty bandits. 'Here is a young man who seeks and wishes to speak to you,' said the sentinel. 'What has he to say?' inquired the young man who was in command in the chief's absence. 'I wish to say that I am tired of a shepherd's life,' was Vampa's reply. 'Ah, I understand,' said the lieutenant; 'and you seek admittance into our ranks?' 'Welcome!' cried several bandits of Ferrusino, Pampinara, and Anagni, who had recognised Luigi Vampa. 'Yes, but I come to ask something more than to be your companion.' 'And what may that be?' inquired the bandits, with astonishment. 'I come to ask to be your captain,' said the young man. The bandits shouted with laughter. 'And what have you done to aspire to this honour?' demanded the lieutenant. 'I have killed your chief, Cucumetto, whose dress I now wear; and I set fire to the Villa de San Felice to procure a wedding-dress for my betrothed.' An hour afterwards Luigi Vampa was chosen captain, *vice* Cucumetto deceased."

"Well, my dear Albert," said Franz, turning towards his friend, "what think you of citizen Luigi Vampa?"

"I say he is a myth," replied Albert, "and never had an existence."

"And what may a myth be?" inquired Pastrini.

"The explanation would be too long, my dear landlord," replied Franz. "And you say that Maître Vampa exercises his profession at this moment in the environs of Rome?"

"Yes, with a boldness of which no bandit before him ever gave an example."

"Then the police have vainly tried to lay hands on him?"

"Why, you see, he has a good understanding with the shepherds in the plains, the fishermen of the Tiber, and the smugglers of the coast. They seek for him in the mountains, and he is on the waters; they follow him on the waters, and he is on the open sea. Then they pursue him, and he has suddenly taken refuge in the Isle of Giglio, of Guanouti, or Monte Cristo; and when they hunt for him there, he reappears suddenly at Albano, Tivoli, or La Riccia."

"And how does he behave towards travellers?"

"Alas! his plan is very simple. It depends on the distance he may be from the city whether he gives eight hours, twelve hours, or a day wherein to pay their ransom; and when that time has elapsed he allows another hour's grace. At the sixtieth minute of this hour, if the money is not forthcoming he blows out the prisoner's brains with a pistol-shot, or plants his dagger in his heart, and that settles the account."

"Well, Albert," inquired Franz of his companion, "are you still disposed to go to the Colosseum by the outer boulevards?"

"Certainly," said Albert, "if the way be picturesque."

The clock struck nine as the door opened, and a coachman appeared. "Excellencies," said he, "the coach is ready."

"Well, then," said Franz, "let us to the Colosseum."

"By the Porta del Popolo, or by the streets, your excellencies?"

"By the streets, *morbleu!* by the streets!" cried Franz.

"Ah, my dear fellow," said Albert, rising and lighting his third cigar, "really, I thought you had more courage." So saying, the two young men went down the staircase, and got into the carriage.

CHAPTER XXXIV

AN APPARITION

FRANZ had so appointed his route that during the ride to the Colosseum they passed not a single ancient ruin; so that no gradual preparation was made on the mind for the colossal proportions of the gigantic building they came to admire. The road selected was a continuation of the Via Sistina; then, by cutting off the right angle of the street in which stands Santa Maria Maggiore, and proceeding by the Via Urbana and San Pietro in Vincoli, the travellers would find themselves directly opposite the Colosseum. This itinerary possessed another great advantage,—that of leaving Franz at full liberty to indulge his deep reverie upon the subject of the story recounted by Maître Pastrini, in which his mysterious host of the Isle of Monte Cristo was so strangely mixed up. Seated with folded arms in a corner of the carriage, he continued to ponder over the singular history he had so lately listened to, and to ask himself an interminable number of questions touching its various circumstances, without, however, arriving at a satisfactory reply to any of them. One fact more than the rest brought his friend " Sinbad the Sailor " back to his recollection, and that was the mysterious sort of intimacy that seemed to exist between the brigands and the sailors; and Pastrini's account of Vampa's having found refuge on board the vessels of smugglers and fishermen, reminded Franz of the two Corsican bandits he had found supping so amicably with the crew of the little yacht, which had even deviated from its course and touched at Porto Vecchio for the sole purpose of landing them. The very name assumed by his host of Monte Cristo, and repeated by the landlord of the Hôtel de Londres, proved to him that his island friend was playing the same philan-thropic part on the shores of Piombino, Civita Vecchia, Ostia, and Gaëta, as on those of Corsica, Tuscany, and Spain; and further, Franz remembered that he had spoken of Tunis and Palermo, which showed how far his circle of acquaintances extended.

But however the mind of the young man might be absorbed in these reflections, they were at once dispersed at the sight of the dark frowning ruins of the stupendous Colosseum, through the various openings of which the pale moonlight played and flickered like the unearthly gleam from the eyes of the wandering dead. The carriage stopped near the Mesa Sudans; the door was opened; and the young men, eagerly alighting, found themselves opposite a *cicerone*, who appeared to have sprung up from the ground.

The usual guide from the hotel having followed them, they had two of them; nor is it possible at Rome to avoid this superfluity of guides. Besides the ordinary *cicerone* who seizes upon you when you set foot in your hotel and never quits you while you remain in the city, there is also a special *cicerone* belonging to each monument,—nay, almost to each part of a monument. It may therefore be easily imagined that there is no scarcity of guides at the Colosseum,—that wonder of all ages, which Martial thus eulogises: " Let Memphis cease to boast the barbarous miracles of her pyramids, and let the wonders of Babylon be talked of no more among us; all other works must give place to the immense amphitheatre of the Cæsars, and all voices of Fame should unite to celebrate that monument."

As for Albert and Franz, they essayed not to escape from their ciceronian tyrants; and indeed it would have been especially difficult to do so, since the guides alone are permitted to visit these monuments with torches in their hands. The young men made no resistance, but surrendered themselves unreservedly to their conductors. Franz had already made ten similar excursions to the Colosseum, while his companion trod for the first time the classic memorial of Flavius Vespasian; and to his credit be it spoken, his mind, even amid the glib loquacity of the guides, was strongly impressed. In fact, without seeing it no one can form any idea of the majesty of such a ruin, all whose proportions appear twice as large in the mysterious light of that southern moon, whose rays have the effect of a twilight in the east. Scarcely therefore had the reflective Franz walked a hundred steps beneath the interior porticos of the ruin, when, abandoning Albert to the guides, who would by no means yield their prescriptive right to exhibit to him the Den of Lions, the Gladiators' Chamber, and the Gallery of the Cæsars, he ascended a dilapidated staircase, and leaving them to their prescribed course of sight-seeing, went quietly to sit in the shadow of a column and opposite a large chasm, which permitted him to enjoy a full and undisturbed view of the gigantic dimensions of this majestic ruin.

Franz had remained nearly a quarter of an hour hidden by the shadow of a column, whence his eyes followed the motions of Albert and his guides, who, holding torches in their hands, had emerged from a vomitarium placed at the opposite extremity of the Colosseum, and then again disappeared down the steps conducting to the seats reserved for the Vestal Virgins, resembling, as they glided along, some restless shades following the flickering glare of so many ignes-fatui, when all at once his ear caught a sound resembling that of a stone rolling down the staircase opposite the one by which he had himself ascended. There was nothing remarkable in the circumstance of a piece of granite giving way and falling heavily below; but it seemed to him that the substance that fell gave way beneath the pressure of a foot, and also that some one who endeavoured as much as possible to prevent his footsteps from being heard, was approaching the spot where he sat. Conjecture soon became certainty,—for the figure of a man appeared, gradually emerging from the darkness as he ascended the staircase, the summit of which was lighted by the moon, while its steps descended into obscurity. He might be a traveller who like Franz preferred the enjoyment of solitude and his own thoughts to the frivolous gabble of the guides,—so that his appearance there was not surprising; but the hesitation with which he proceeded onwards, stopping and listening with anxious attention at every step he took, convinced Franz that he had come with a definite purpose, and that he was expecting some one. By an instinctive impulse Franz withdrew as much as possible behind his pillar. About ten feet from the spot where himself and the stranger were placed, the roof had given way, leaving a large round aperture through which might be seen the blue vault of heaven thickly studded with stars. Around this opening, which had possibly for ages permitted a free entrance to the moonlight, grew a quantity of creeping plants, whose delicate green branches stood out in bold relief against the clear azure of the firmament, while large masses of thick strong fibrous shoots forced their way through the chasm and hung floating to and fro like so many waving strings. The person whose mysterious arrival had attracted the attention of Franz stood in a kind of half-light that rendered it impossible to distinguish his features, although his dress was easily made out. He wore a large brown mantle, one fold of which thrown over his left shoulder served likewise to mask the lower part of his countenance, while the upper part was completely hidden by his broad-brimmed hat. The lower part of his dress was more distinctly visible by the bright rays of the moon, which entering through the broken ceiling showed that he wore boots of polished leather, over which descended trousers of black cloth. Evidently he belonged to high society, if not to the aristocracy.

After a few moments the stranger began to show signs of impatience, when a slight noise was heard outside the aperture in the roof, and almost immediately a dark shadow seemed to obstruct the light, and the figure of a man was clearly seen gazing with eager scrutiny on the immense space beneath him; then, as he perceived the man in the mantle, he grasped a floating mass of thickly-matted boughs and glided down by their help to within three or four feet of the ground, and then leaped lightly on his feet. He wore the costume of a Transteverian.

"I beg your excellency's pardon for keeping you waiting," said the man, in the Roman dialect; "but I don't think I'm many minutes after my time. Ten o'clock has just struck by the clock of St. Jean de Latran."

"Say not a word about being late," replied the stranger, in purest Tuscan; "'tis I who am too soon. But even if you had caused me to wait a little while, I should have felt quite sure that the delay was not occasioned by any fault of yours."

"Your excellency is right," said the man; "I came here direct from the Château St. Ange, and I had an immense deal of trouble before I could get to speak to Beppo."

"And who is Beppo?"

"Oh, Beppo is employed in the prison; and I give him so much a year to let me know what is going on within his Holiness's château."

"Indeed! You are a provident person, I see."

"Why, you see, no one knows what may happen. Perhaps some of these days I may be entrapped like poor Peppino, and may be very glad to have some little nibbling mouse to gnaw the meshes of my net."

"Briefly, what did you learn?"

"That two executions of considerable interest will take place on Tuesday, at two o'clock, as is customary at Rome at the commencement of all great festivals. One of the culprits will be *mazzolato*; he is an atrocious villain, who murdered the priest who brought him up, and deserves not the smallest pity. The other sufferer is sentenced to be *decapitato*; and he, your excellency, is poor Peppino."

"What can you expect? You have inspired not only the pontifical government, but also the neighbouring states, with such fear that they are glad of an opportunity to make an example."

"But Peppino did not even belong to my band; he was merely a poor shepherd, whose only crime consisted in furnishing us with provisions."

"Which makes him your accomplice to all intents and purposes. But mark the distinction with which he is treated:

instead of being knocked on the head as you would be if once they caught hold of you, he is simply sentenced to be guillotined. In that way the amusements of the day are diversified, and there is a spectacle to please every spectator."

"Without reckoning the wholly unexpected one I am preparing to surprise them with."

"My good friend," said the man in the cloak, "excuse me for saying that you seem to me precisely in the mood to commit some act of folly."

"I am in the mood to prevent the execution of the poor devil who has got into this scrape solely through having served me. By the Madonna! I should despise myself as a coward did I desert the brave fellow in his present extremity."

"And what do you mean to do?"

"To surround the scaffold with twenty of my best men, who at a signal from me will rush forward when Peppino is brought for execution, and by the assistance of their stilettos drive back the guard and carry off the prisoner."

"That seems to me as hazardous as uncertain, and I am quite sure that my scheme is far better than yours."

"And what is your excellency's project?"

"Just this: I will so advantageously bestow ten thousand piastres that the person receiving them shall obtain a respite till next year for Peppino; and during that year I will so bestow one thousand additional piastres that he will escape from prison."

"And do you feel sure of succeeding?"

"*Pardieu!*" exclaimed in French the man in the cloak.

"What did your excellency say?" inquired the other.

"I say, my good fellow, that I will do more single-handed with my gold than you and all your band could effect with stilettos, pistols, carbines, and blunderbusses included. Leave me, then, to act, and have no fears for the result."

"Very good! but if you fail, we shall be ready."

"Take what precautions you please, but rely upon my obtaining the reprieve."

"Remember the execution is fixed for the day after tomorrow, and that you have but one day to work in."

"And what then? Is not a day divided into twenty-four hours, each hour into sixty minutes, and every minute subdivided into sixty seconds? Now, in 86,400 seconds very many things can be done."

"And how shall I know whether your excellency has succeeded or not?"

"Oh! that is very easily arranged. I have engaged the three lower windows at the Café Rospoli; should I have obtained the requisite pardon for Peppino, the two outside windows will be hung with yellow damask, and the centre with white having a large cross in red marked on it."

"And whom will you employ to carry the reprieve to the officer directing the execution?"

"Send one of your men disguised as a penitent friar, and I will give it to him; in that dress he can approach the scaffold itself and deliver the official order to the officer who in his turn will hand it to the executioner. In the meantime, acquaint Peppino with what we have determined on, to prevent his dying of fear or losing his senses; in either case a useless expense will have been incurred for him."

"Your excellency," said the man, "you are fully persuaded of my entire devotion to you, are you not?"

"Nay, I flatter myself that there can be no doubt of it," replied the cavalier in the cloak.

"Well, then, if you save Peppino, henceforward you shall receive not only devotedness, but obedience."

"Have a care how far you pledge yourself, my good friend, for I may remind you of your promise at some perhaps not very distant period, when I, in my turn, may require your aid and influence."

"Let that day come sooner or later, your excellency will find me what I have found you in this my heavy trouble; and if from the other end of the world you but write me word to do such or such a thing, conclude it done, for done it shall be, on the word and faith of——"

"Hush!" interrupted the stranger; "I hear a noise."

"'Tis some travellers who are visiting the Colosseum by torch-light."

"'Twere better we should not be seen together. Those guides are nothing but spies, and might possibly recognise you; and however I may be honoured by your friendship, my worthy friend, if once the extent of our intimacy were known, I am afraid my reputation would suffer thereby."

"Well, then, if you obtain the reprieve?"

"The middle window at the Café Rospoli will be hung with white damask bearing on it a red cross."

"And if you fail?"

"Then all three windows will have yellow draperies."

"And then?"

"And then, my good fellow, use your daggers in any way

you please; and I further promise you to be there as a spectator of your prowess."

" All is then understood between us. Adieu, your excellency; depend upon me as firmly as I do upon you."

Saying these words, the Transteverian disappeared down the staircase; while his companion, muffling his features more closely than before in the folds of his mantle, passed almost close to Franz, and descended to the arena by an outward flight of steps. The next minute Franz heard himself called by Albert, who made the lofty building re-echo with the sound of his friend's name. Franz, however, did not obey the summons till he had satisfied himself the two men had gone,—not wishing them to learn that there had been a witness of their interview who, if unable to recognise their faces, had at least heard every word that passed. Ten minutes later Franz was on the road to the Hôtel d'Espagne, listening with indifference to the learned dissertation delivered by Albert, after the manner of Pliny and Calpurnius, touching the iron-pointed nets used to prevent the ferocious beasts from springing on the spectators. Franz let him proceed without interruption; he longed to be alone that he might without interruption ponder over all that had occurred. One of those two men was an entire stranger to him, but not so the other; and though Franz had been unable to distinguish his features, wrapped in his mantle or obscured by the shadow, the tones of his voice had made too powerful an impression on him the first time he heard them for him ever to forget them. There was especially in his tones of raillery a certain metallic vibration which had startled him among the ruins of the Colosseum as in the grotto of Monte Cristo. He was therefore well satisfied that this man was no other than " Sinbad the Sailor."

Now, under any other circumstances, so great was his curiosity about this strange being, Franz would have made himself known to him; but in the present instance, the confidential nature of the conversation he had overheard suggested to him the reasonable apprehension that his appearance at such a time would be anything but agreeable. As we have seen, therefore, he had allowed the man to depart without addressing him,—promising himself that if he should meet him again he would not allow him to escape a second time. In vain did Franz endeavour to forget the many perplexing thoughts which assailed him; in vain did he court the refreshment of sleep. Slumber refused to visit his eyelids, and his night was passed in feverish contemplation of the chain of circumstances tending to prove the identity of the mysterious visitant to the Colosseum and the inhabitant of the grotto of Monte Cristo; and the more he thought, the firmer grew his opinion on the subject. Worn out at length, he fell asleep at daybreak and did not awake till late. Like a genuine Frenchman, Albert had employed his time in arranging for the evening's diversion. He had sent to engage a box at the Teatro Argentino; and Franz, having a number of letters to write, relinquished the carriage to Albert for the whole of the day. At five o'clock Albert returned; he had delivered his letters of introduction, had received invitations for all his evenings, and had seen Rome. A day had sufficed Albert for all that; and he had also had time enough to ascertain the name of the piece to be played that night at the Teatro Argentino, and also what performers appeared in it.

The opera of "Parisina" was announced for representation, and the principal actors were Coselli, Moriani, and La Spech. The young men had reason to consider themselves fortunate in having the opportunity of hearing one of the best works by the composer of "Lucia di Lammermoor," supported by three of the most renowned vocalists of Italy. Albert had never been able to endure the Italian theatres, which have orchestras from which it is impossible to see, and no balconies or open boxes; these defects pressed hard on a man who had his stall at the Bouffes, and his share in the omnibus-box at the opera. Nevertheless, Albert displayed his most dazzling and effective costume whenever he visited the theatres. It was wasted splendour,— for it must be confessed that one of the most worthy representatives of Parisian fashion had overrun Italy for four months without meeting with a single adventure.

Sometimes Albert would affect to make a joke of his want of success, but internally he was deeply mortified that he, Albert de Morcerf, one of the young men most sought after, should still have only his labour for his pains. And the thing was the more annoying because, with the characteristic modesty of a Frenchman, Albert had quitted Paris with the full conviction that he had only to show himself in Italy to carry all before him, and that upon his return he should astonish the Parisian world with the recital of his numerous love affairs. Alas! none of those interesting adventures fell in his way. The lovely countesses— Genoese, Florentine, and Neapolitan—were all faithful, if not to their husbands, at least to their lovers; and Albert had gained the painful conviction that the women of Italy have at least this advantage over those of France, that they are faithful to their infidelity. I would not venture to deny that in Italy, as every-where else, there are exceptions. Albert, besides being an elegant, well-looking young man, was also possessed of considerable talent and ability; moreover, he was a viscount,—a recently created one, certainly, but in the present day it is of no consequence whether one dates from 1399 or from 1815. But to crown all these advantages, Albert de Morcerf commanded an income of fifty thousand livres, a more than sufficient sum to render him a personage of considerable importance in Paris. It was therefore no small mortification to him not to have been seriously regarded by any one in any of the cities which he had visited. He hoped, however, to recover himself at Rome,—the Carnival being, in all the countries of the earth which celebrate that excellent institution, a period of liberty in which even the wisest and gravest throw off the usual rigidity of their lives, and suffer themselves to be drawn into acts of folly.

The Carnival was to commence on the morrow; therefore Albert had not an instant to lose in setting forth the programme of his hopes, expectations, and claims to notice. With this design he had engaged a box in the most conspicuous part of the theatre, and exerted himself to set off his personal attractions by the aid of an elaborate toilet. The box taken by Albert was in the first circle, which with us is the gallery. The first three tiers of boxes are equally aristocratic, and are called for that reason " the boxes of the nobility." The box engaged, which would contain a dozen persons easily, had cost the two friends a little less than a box for four would cost at the Ambigu. Albert had still another hope. If he could engage the affection of some fair Roman, that would lead naturally to a seat in a carriage, or a place in a princely balcony from which he might behold the gaieties of the Carnival. These united considerations made Albert more lively and anxious to please than he had hitherto been. Totally disregarding the business of the stage, he leaned from his box and began attentively scrutinising the beauty of each pretty woman, aided by a powerful *lorgnette*. But alas! this attempt to attract similar notice wholly failed,— not even curiosity had been excited; and it was but too apparent that the lovely creatures into whose good graces he was desirous of stealing were all so much engrossed with themselves, their lovers, or their own thoughts, that they had not so much as remarked him or the pointing of his glass.

The truth was that the anticipated pleasures of the Carnival, with the " Holy Week," that was to succeed it, so filled every fair breast as to prevent the least attention being bestowed even on the business of the stage; the actors made their entries and exits unobserved or unthought of. At certain conventional moments the spectators would suddenly cease their conversation, or rouse themselves from their musings to listen to some brilliant effort of Moriani's, a well-executed recitative by Coselli, or to join in loud applause at the wonderful powers of La Spech; but that momentary excitement over, they quickly relapsed into their former state of preoccupation or interesting conversation. Towards the close of the first act the door of a box which had been hitherto vacant was opened; a lady entered to whom Franz had been introduced in Paris, where indeed he had imagined she still was. The quick eye of Albert caught the involuntary start with which his friend beheld the new arrival, and turning to him, he said hastily, "Do you know that woman?"

"Yes; what do you think of her?"

"She is supremely beautiful; what a complexion! And such magnificent hair! Is she French?"

"No; a Venetian."

"And her name is—"

"Comtesse G——"

"Ah! I know her by name," exclaimed Albert; "she is said to possess as much wit and cleverness as beauty! Ah! when I think that I might have been presented to her at the last ball of Madame de Villefort, where she was present, and neglected the opportunity,—what a ninny I was!"

"Shall I assist you in repairing your negligence?" asked Franz.

"My dear fellow, are you really on such good terms with her as to venture to take me to her box?"

"Why, I have had the honour of speaking to her three or four times in my life; but you know that even such an acquaintance as that might warrant my doing what you ask."

At this instant the countess perceived Franz and graciously waved her hand to him, to which he replied by a respectful inclination of the head.

"Upon my word," said Albert, "you seem to be on excellent terms with the beautiful countess!"

"You are mistaken in thinking so," returned Franz, calmly; "but you fall into the same error which leads so many of our countrymen to commit the most egregious blunders,—I mean that of judging the habits and customs of Italy and Spain by our Parisian notions. Believe me, nothing is more fallacious than to form an estimate of the degree of intimacy existing among persons by the familiar manner of their intercourse;

there is a similarity of feeling at this instant between ourselves and the countess,—nothing more."

" Is there, indeed, my good fellow? Pray tell me, is it sympathy of heart? "

" No; of taste! " continued Franz, gravely.

" And what is the cause of it? "

" A visit to the Colosseum, like that which we made together."

" By moonlight? "

" Yes."

" Alone? "

" Very nearly so."

" And you talked of—"

" The dead."

" Ah! " cried Albert, " that must have been exhilarating. Well, I promise you that if I have the good fortune to attend the beautiful countess on such a promenade, I shall talk to her of the living."

" And you will make a mistake."

" In the meantime you will present me to her, as you have promised? "

" As soon as the curtain falls."

" The first act is devilish long."

" Hear the end; it is very fine, and Coselli sings admirably."

" Yes; but what a figure! "

" La Spech, then; it is impossible to be more dramatic."

" But you must understand that when one has heard Sontag and Malibran—"

" At least you must admire Moriani's style and execution."

" I never fancied men of his dark, ponderous appearance singing with a voice like a woman's."

" My good friend," said Franz, turning to him, while Albert continued to point his glass at every box in the theatre, " you seem determined not to approve; you are really too difficult to please."

The curtain at length fell on the performances, to the infinite satisfaction of the Vicomte de Morcerf, who seized his hat, rapidly passed his fingers through his hair, arranged his cravat and wristbands, and signified to Franz that he was waiting for him to lead the way. Franz, who had mutely interrogated the countess and received from her a gracious smile in token that he would be welcome, did not delay the gratification of Albert's eager impatience, but began at once the tour of the house closely followed by Albert, who availed himself of the few minutes required to reach the opposite side of the theatre to adjust his collar and to arrange the lappets of his coat; this important task was just completed as they arrived at the countess's box. The young man who was seated beside the countess in the front of the *loge* instantly rose, in obedience to the Italian custom, and surrendered his place to the strangers, who, in turn, would be expected to retire upon the arrival of other visitors.

Franz presented Albert as one of the most distinguished young men of the day, both as regarded his position in society and extraordinary talents; nor did he say more than the truth, for in Paris and the circle in which the viscount moved, he was looked upon and cited as a model of perfection. Franz added that his companion, deeply grieved because he had not been presented to the countess during her sojourn in Paris, had requested him (Franz) to remedy that misfortune by conducting him to her box, and concluded by asking pardon for his presumption in doing so. The countess replied by a charming bow to Albert, and extended her hand with cordial kindness to Franz. Albert, being invited by her, took the vacant place by her side, and Franz sat in the second row behind her. Albert was soon deeply engrossed in discoursing upon Paris and Paris matters, speaking to the countess of the various persons they both knew there. Franz perceived how completely he was in his element, and unwilling to interfere with the pleasure he so evidently felt, took up Albert's *lorgnette*, and began in his turn to survey the audience. Sitting alone, in the front of a box immediately opposite, but situated in the third tier, was a woman of exquisite beauty, dressed in a Greek costume, which it was evident from the ease and grace with which she wore it was her national attire. Behind her, but in deep shadow, was the outline of a male figure; but the features of this latter personage it was not possible to distinguish. Franz could not forbear breaking in upon the apparently interesting conversation passing between the countess and Albert, to inquire of the former if she knew who was the fair Albanian opposite, since beauty such as hers was well worthy of being remarked by either sex.

" All I can tell you about her," replied the countess, " is that she has been at Rome since the beginning of the season,—for I saw her where she now sits the very first night of the theatre's opening; and since then she has never missed a performance. Sometimes she is accompanied by the individual who is with her, and at others merely attended by a black servant."

" And what do you think of her personal appearance? "

" Oh, I consider her perfectly lovely,—she is just my idea of what Medora must have been."

Franz and the countess exchanged a smile; and then the latter resumed her conversation with Albert, while Franz returned to his previous survey of the house and company. The curtain rose on the ballet, which was one of those excellent specimens of the Italian school, arranged and put on the stage by Henri, who has established for himself a great reputation throughout Italy for his taste and skill in the chorographic art, —one of those masterly productions of grace, method, and elegance in which the whole *corps de ballet,* from the principal dancers to the humblest supernumerary, are all engaged on the stage at the same time; and a hundred and fifty persons may be seen exhibiting the same attitude, or elevating the same arm or leg with a simultaneous movement. The ballet was called " Poliska." However much the ballet might have claimed his attention, Franz was too deeply occupied with the beautiful Greek to take any note of it, while she seemed to experience an almost childlike delight in watching it; her eager, animated looks contrasted strongly with the utter indifference of her companion, who during the whole time the piece lasted never even moved, spite of the furious crashing din produced by the trumpets, cymbals, and Chinese bells, made to produce their loudest sound from the orchestra. The apathetic companion of the fair Greek took no heed of the deafening sounds that prevailed, but was apparently enjoying soft repose and bright celestial dreams. The ballet at length came to a close; and the curtain fell amid the frenzied plaudits of an enthusiastic audience.

Owing to the very judicious plan of dividing the two acts of the opera with a ballet, the pauses between the performances are very short in Italy,—the singers in the opera having time to rest themselves and change their costume when necessary, while the dancers are executing their pirouettes and exhibiting their graceful steps. The overture to the second act began; and at the first sound of the leader's bow across his violin, Franz observed the sleeper slowly arise and approach the Greek girl, who turned round to say a few words to him, and then leaning forward again on the railing, became as absorbed as before in what was going on. The countenance of the person who h_ addressed her remained so completely in the shade that F_ could not distinguish his features. The curtain was raise_ the attention of Franz was attracted by the actors; _ wandered for a moment from the box containing the _ Greek to watch the scene on the stage.

Most of my readers are aware that the second act o_

opens with the celebrated and effective duet in which Parisina, while sleeping, betrays to Azzo the secret of her love for Ugo. The injured husband goes through all the workings of jealousy until conviction seizes on his mind; and then in a frenzy of rage and indignation, he awakens his guilty wife to tell her he knows her guilt, and to threaten her with his vengeance.   This duet is one of the most beautiful, expressive, and terrible that have emanated from the fruitful pen of Donizetti.   Franz now listened to it for the third time; and though he was not especially susceptible to the power of music, it produced upon him a profound effect.   He rose with the audience and was about to join in the loud, enthusiastic applause that followed, but suddenly his purpose was arrested, his hands fell by his sides, and the half-uttered " bravos " expired on his lips.   The occupant of the box in which the Greek girl sat appeared to share the universal admiration that prevailed, for he left his seat to stand up in the front; so that his countenance being fully revealed, Franz had no difficulty in recognising him as the mysterious inhabitant of Monte Cristo, and the man whose voice and figure he had thought he recognised the preceding evening in the ruins of the Colosseum. All doubt of his identity was now at an end; the mysterious traveller evidently resided at Rome.   The surprise and agitation occasioned by this full confirmation of Franz's former suspicion had no doubt imparted a corresponding expression to his features, —for the countess, after gazing with a puzzled look on his speaking countenance, burst into a fit of laughter, and begged to know what had happened.

" Madame the Countess," returned Franz, " I asked you a short time since if you knew any particulars respecting the Albanian lady opposite; I ask now if you know her husband? "

" Nay," answered the countess, " I know no more of him than of her."

" Perhaps you never before remarked him ? "

" What a question,—so truly French! Do you not know that we Italians have eyes only for the man we love? "

" True," replied Franz.

" All I can say," continued the countess, taking up the *lorgnette*, and directing it to the box in question, " is that the gentleman seems to me as though he had just been dug up; he looks more like a corpse permitted by some friendly grave-digger to quit his tomb for a while and revisit this earth of ours than anything human.   How ghastly pale he is!"

" Oh, he is always as colourless as you now see him," said Franz.

" Then you know him? " asked the countess. " Then I will inquire of you who he is."

" I fancy I have seen him before; and I even think he recognises me."

" And I can well understand," said the countess, shrugging up her beautiful shoulders, as though an involuntary shudder passed through her veins, " that those who have once seen that man will never be likely to forget him."

The sensation experienced by Franz was evidently not peculiar to himself; another, and wholly uninterested person, felt the same unaccountable awe and misgiving. " Well," he inquired after the countess had a second time directed her *lorgnette* at the *loge* of their mysterious *vis-à-vis*, " what do you think of that man? "

" Why, that he is no other than Lord Ruthven himself in a living form."

This fresh allusion to Byron interested Franz. If any man could lead him to believe in the existence of vampires, it was the man before him.

" I must find out who and what he is," said Franz, rising from his seat.

" No, no! " cried the countess; " you must not leave me! I depend upon you to escort me home. Oh, indeed, I cannot permit you to go! "

" Is it possible," whispered Franz, " that you entertain any fear? "

" I'll tell you," answered the countess. " Byron swore to me that he believed in the existence of vampires, and even assured me that he had seen them. He described to me their appearance; it is precisely like his,—the coal black hair, large bright glittering eyes in which a wild, unearthly fire seems burning, that ghastly paleness. Then observe, too, that the very woman he has with him is altogether unlike all others of her sex. She is a foreigner—a Greek—a heretic—probably a magician like himself. I entreat of you not to go near him,— at least to-night. And if to-morrow your curiosity still continues as great, pursue your researches if you will; but now I mean to keep you."

Franz protested that he could not defer his pursuit till the following day for many reasons.

" Listen to me," said the countess; " I am going home. I have a party at my house to-night, and therefore cannot possibly remain till the conclusion of the opera. Will you be so discourteous as to refuse me your company? "

There was nothing left for Franz to do but to take up his hat, open the door of the *loge*, and offer the countess his arm. It was quite evident from the countess's manner that her uneasiness was not feigned; and Franz himself could not resist a species of superstitious dread,—the stronger in him, as it arose from a variety of corroborating recollections, while the terror of the countess sprang from an instinctive feeling. Franz could even feel her arm tremble as he assisted her into the carriage. He conducted her to her home. No company was there; and she was not expected. He reproached her about it.

" In very truth," she said, " I am not well, and I need to be alone; the sight of that man has completely upset me."

Franz began to laugh.

" Do not laugh," she said; " you really do not feel like laughing. Now make me a promise."

" What is it? "

" Promise me."

" I will do anything you desire except relinquish my determination of finding out who this man is. I have more reasons than you can imagine for desiring to know who he is, whence he came, and whither he is going."

" Where he comes from I don't know; but I can tell you where he is going,—he is going to hell, without the least doubt."

" Let us return to the promise you wished me to make," said Franz.

" Well, then, you must give me your word to return immediately to your hotel, and make no attempt to follow this man to-night. There are certain affinities between the persons we quit and those we meet afterwards. For Heaven's sake, do not serve as a conductor between that man and me! Pursue him to-morrow as eagerly as you please; but never bring him near me if you would not see me die of terror. And now good-night; retire to your apartment and try to sleep away all recollections of this evening. For my own part, I am quite sure I shall not be able to close my eyes." So saying, the countess quitted Franz, leaving him unable to decide whether she was merely amusing herself at his expense or was disturbed by actual apprehensions.

Upon his return to the hotel, Franz found Albert in his dressing-gown and slippers, listlessly extended on a sofa, smoking a cigar. " My dear fellow! " cried he, springing up, " is it really you? Why, I did not expect to see you before to-morrow."

" My dear Albert! " replied Franz, " I am glad of this opportunity to tell you, once and for ever, that you entertain a most erroneous notion concerning Italian women. I should have thought the continual failures you have met with in all your own love affairs might have taught you better by this time."

"Upon my soul! these women would puzzle the very devil to read them aright. Why, here,—they give you their hand, they press yours in return, they keep up a whispering conversation, permit you to accompany them home! Why, if a Parisian were to do one quarter as much she would lose her reputation!"

"And the very reason why the women of this fine country put so little restraint on their words and actions is that they live so much in public, and have really nothing to conceal. Besides, you must have perceived that the countess was really alarmed."

"At what,—at the sight of that respectable gentleman sitting opposite to us with the lovely Greek? Now, for my part, I met them in the lobby after the conclusion of the piece; and hang me, if I can guess where you got your notions of the other world! He is a fine-looking fellow, well dressed, with the air of one who clothes himself in France, with Blin or with Humann, —a trifle pale, indeed, but you know that paleness is a mark of distinction."

Franz smiled,—for he well remembered that Albert particularly prided himself on the entire absence of colour in his own complexion. "Well, that tends to confirm my own ideas," said he, "that the countess's suspicions were destitute alike of sense and reason. Did he speak in your hearing; and did you catch any of his words?"

"I did; but they were uttered in the Romaic dialect. I knew that from the mixture of broken Greek words. I must tell you, my boy, that when I was at college I was rather strong in Greek."

"He spoke the Romaic language, did he?"

"I think so."

"That settles it," murmured Franz. "'Tis he, past all doubt."

"What do you say?"

"Nothing, nothing! But tell me, what were you doing here?"

"Oh, I was arranging a little surprise."

"Indeed! Of what nature?"

"Why, you know it is quite impossible to procure a carriage."

"I should think so, when we have in vain made every possible endeavour."

"Well, I have had a marvellous idea."

Franz looked at Albert as though he had not much confidence in the suggestions of his imagination.

" My dear fellow," said Albert, " you honour me with a look which well deserves that I should demand satisfaction of you."

" And I promise to give you the satisfaction of a gentleman if your scheme turns out as ingenious as you say it is."

" Well, then, listen."

" I listen."

" You agree, do you not, that obtaining a carriage is out of the question? "

" I do."

" Neither can we procure horses? "

" True."

" But we might procure a cart? "

" Perhaps."

" And a pair of oxen? "

" Probably."

" Then you see, my good fellow, with a cart and a couple of oxen our business can be managed. The cart must be tastefully ornamented; and if you and I dress ourselves as Neapolitan reapers, we may get up a striking tableau, after the manner of that splendid picture by Léopold Robert. It would add greatly to the effect if the countess would join us in the costume of a peasant from Puzzoli or Sorrento. Our group would then be quite complete, more especially as the countess is quite beautiful enough to be taken for the original of ' The Mother of the Child.' "

" Well," said Franz, " this time, M. Albert, I am bound to give you credit for having hit upon a capital idea."

" And quite a national one, too," replied Albert, with gratified pride. " A mere mask borrowed from our own festivities. Ha, ha! Messieurs the Romans; you thought to make us unhappy strangers trot at the heels of your processions, like so many lazzaroni, because no carriages or horses are to be had in your beggarly city. Very well; we have invented them."

" And have you communicated your triumphant idea to any person? "

" Only to our host. Upon my return home I sent for him and explained to him my wishes. He assured me that nothing would be easier. I wanted him to have the horns of the oxen gilded, but he told me there would not be time, as it would require three days to effect that; so you see we must do without that little superfluity."

" And where is he now? "

" Who? "

" Our host."

" Gone out in search of our equipage; by to-morrow it might be too late."

" Then he will be able to give us an answer to-night? "

" Oh, I expect him every minute."

At this instant the door opened, and the head of Maître Pastrini appeared. " *Permesso ?* " inquired he.

" Certainly, certainly ! " cried Franz.

" Now then," asked Albert, eagerly, " have you found the desired cart and oxen? "

" Better than that ! " replied the Maître Pastrini, with the air of a man perfectly well satisfied with himself.

" Take care, my worthy host," said Albert; " *better* is a sure enemy to *well*."

" Let your excellencies only leave the matter to me," returned Maître Pastrini, in a tone indicative of unbounded self-confidence.

" But what have you done? " asked Franz.

" Your excellencies are aware," responded the landlord, swelling with importance, " that the Count of Monte Cristo is living on the same floor with yourselves ! "

" I should think we did know it," exclaimed Albert, " since it is owing to that circumstance that we are packed into these small rooms like two poor students in the back streets of Paris."

" Well, then, the Count of Monte Cristo, hearing of the dilemma in which you are placed, has sent to offer you seats in his carriage and two places at his windows in the Palace Rospoli."

Albert and Franz looked at each other. " But do you think," asked Albert, " that we ought to accept such offers from a stranger? "

" What sort of person is this Count of Monte Cristo? " asked Franz of his host.

" A very great nobleman, but whether Maltese or Sicilian I cannot exactly say; but this I know, that he is noble as a Borghese and rich as a gold mine."

" It seems to me," said Franz, speaking in an undertone to Albert, " that if this man merited the high panegyrics of our landlord, he would have conveyed his invitation through another channel, and not permitted it to be brought to us in this unceremonious way. He would have written, or—"

At this instant some one knocked at the door. " Come in ! " said Franz. A servant, wearing a livery of peculiar elegance, appeared at the threshold; and placing two cards in the landlord's hands, who forthwith presented them to the two young men, he said, 'From M. le Comte de Monte Cristo to M. le Vicomte Albert de Morcerf and M. Franz Epinay. M. le Comte de Monte Cristo," continued the servant, "begs these gentlemen's permission to wait upon them as their neighbour to-morrow morning, and he desires to know at what time they will please to receive him."

"Faith, Franz," whispered Albert, "there is not much to find fault with here."

"Tell the count," replied Franz, "that we will do ourselves the pleasure of calling on him." The servant bowed and retired.

"That is what I call an elegant mode of attack," said Albert. "You were quite correct in what you stated, Maître Pastrini. The Count of Monte Cristo is unquestionably a man of good breeding."

"Then you accept his offer?" said the host.

"Of course we do," replied Albert. "Still, I must own I am sorry to be obliged to give up the cart and the group of reapers; it would have produced such an effect! And were it not for the windows at the Palace Rospoli, by way of recompense for the loss of our beautiful scheme, I don't know but what I should have held on by my original plan. What say you, Franz?"

"Oh, I agree with you; the windows in the Palace Rospoli alone decided me."

The mention of two places in the Palace Rospoli had recalled to Franz's mind the conversation he had overheard the preceding evening in the ruins of the Colosseum between the mysterious unknown and the Transteverian, in which the stranger in the cloak had engaged himself to obtain the freedom of a condemned criminal. Now, if the man with the cloak was, as everything led Franz to believe, the same as the person he had just seen in the Teatro Argentino, he would clearly recognise him; and then nothing would prevent his satisfying his curiosity concerning him. Franz passed the night in dreaming of those two apparitions and longing for the morrow. The next day must clear up every doubt; and unless his host of Monte Cristo possessed the ring of Gyges, and by its power were able to render himself invisible, it was very certain he could not escape this time. Eight o'clock found Franz up and dressed, while Albert, who had not the same motives for early rising, was still profoundly asleep. The first act of Franz was to summon his landlord, who presented himself with his accustomed obsequiousness.

"Pray, Maître Pastrini," asked Franz, "is not some execution appointed to take place to-day?"

"Yes, your excellency; but if your reason for inquiry is that you may procure a window, you are much too late."

"Oh, no!" answered Franz, "I had no such intention; and even if I had felt a wish to witness the spectacle, I might have done so from Monte Pincio, could I not?"

"Oh! I thought your excellency would not wish to mingle with the rabble, to whom that hill is a sort of natural amphitheatre."

"Very possibly I may not go," answered Franz; "but give me some particulars."

"What particulars would your excellency like to hear?"

"Why, the number of persons condemned to suffer, their names, and description of the death they are to die."

"That happens well, your excellency! Only a few minutes ago they brought me the *tavolettas*."

"What are they?"

"Wooden tablets hung up at the corners of streets the evening before an execution, on which is pasted a paper containing the names of the condemned persons, their crimes, and mode of punishment. The purpose of this notification is to summon the faithful to pray that God will grant to the culprits a sincere repentance."

"And these tablets are brought to you that you may add your prayers to those of the faithful, are they?" asked Franz, somewhat incredulously.

"Oh, dear no, your excellency; I have an agreement with the man who pastes up the papers, and he brings them to me as he would the play-bills; so that in case any person staying at my hotel should like to witness an execution, he may obtain every requisite information in season."

"Upon my word, that is most delicate attention on your part, Maître Pastrini," cried Franz.

"Why, your excellency," returned the landlord, smiling, "I think I may take upon myself to say that I neglect nothing to deserve the support and patronage of the noble visitors to this poor hotel."

"I see that plainly enough, my most excellent host, and you may rely upon my repeating so striking a proof of your attention to your guests wherever I go. Meanwhile, oblige me by a sight of one of these *tavolettas*."

"Nothing can be easier than to comply with your excellency's wish," said the landlord, opening the door of the chamber;

" I have caused one to be placed on the landing, close by your apartments." Then, taking the tablet from the wall, he handed it to Franz, who read as follows:—

" The public is informed that on Wednesday, February 23, being the first day of the Carnival, two executions will take place in the Place del Popolo, by order of the Tribunal de la Rota, of two individuals, named Andrea Rondola, and Peppino, otherwise called Rocca Priori; the former found guilty of the murder of a venerable and exemplary priest, named Don César Torlini, canon of the church of St. Jean de Latran; and the latter convicted of being an accomplice of the atrocious and sanguinary bandit, Luigi Vampa, and his band. The first-named malefactor will be *mazzolato*, the second culprit *decapitato*. The prayers of all charitable souls are entreated for these unfortunate men, that it may please God to awaken them to a sense of their guilt, and to grant them a hearty and sincere repentance for their crimes."

This was precisely what Franz had heard the evening before in the ruins of the Colosseum. No part of the programme differed. The names of the condemned persons, their crimes, and mode of punishment, all agreed with his previous information. In all probability, therefore, the Transteverian was no other than the bandit Luigi Vampa himself, and the man shrouded in the mantle " Sinbad the Sailor," who no doubt was still pursuing his philanthropic undertakings in Rome as he had already done at Porto Vecchio and Tunis. Time was getting on, however; it was nine o'clock, and Franz was going to awaken Albert, when to his great astonishment he saw him come out of his chamber fully dressed. The anticipated delights of the Carnival had so run in Albert's head as to make him leave his pillow earlier than his friend had expected.

" Now, my excellent Maître Pastrini," said Franz, addressing his landlord, " since we are both ready, do you think we may proceed at once to visit the Count of Monte Cristo? "

" Most assuredly," replied he.   " The Count of Monte Cristo is always an early riser; and I can answer for his having been up these two hours."

" Then you really think that we shall commit no impropriety if we pay our respects to him immediately? "

" Not the least."

" In that case, Albert, if you are ready—"

" Entirely ready," said Albert.

" Let us go and thank our neighbour for his courtesy."

" Come on."

The landlord preceded the friends across the landing, which was all that separated them from the apartments of the count.

rang at the bell, and upon the door being opened by a servant, said, " *I Signori Francesi.*"

The domestic bowed respectfully and invited them to enter. They passed through two rooms furnished with a style and luxury they had not expected to find under the roof of Maître Pastrini, and were shown into an elegantly-fitted-up salon. The richest Turkey carpets covered the floor, and the softest and most inviting couches, *bergères*, and sofas offered their high-piled and yielding cushions to such as desired repose or refreshment. Splendid paintings by the first masters were ranged against the walls, intermingled with magnificent trophies of war, while heavy curtains of costly tapestry were suspended before the different doors of the room. " If your excellencies will please to be seated," said the man, " I will let Monsieur the Count know that you are here."

And with these words he disappeared behind one of the tapestried *portières*. As the door opened the sound of a *guzla* reached the ears of the young men, but was almost immediately lost, for the rapid closing of the door merely allowed one rich swell of harmony to enter the salon. Franz and Albert looked inquiringly at each other, then at the gorgeous furniture of the apartment. All seemed even more splendid on a second view than it had at first.

" Well," said Franz to his friend, " what do you think of all this ? "

" Why, upon my soul, my dear fellow, it strikes me our neighbour must either be some successful stock-jobber who has speculated in the fall of the Spanish funds, or some prince travelling *incognito.*"

" Hush ! " replied Franz, " that is what we shall soon discover, —for here he comes."

As Franz spoke, he heard the sound of a door turning on its hinges; and almost immediately afterwards the tapestry was drawn aside, and the owner of all these riches stood before the two young men. Albert instantly rose to meet him; but Franz remained spell-bound on his chair. He who entered was the mysterious visitant to the Colosseum, the occupant of the box at the theatre, and the mysterious host of Monte Cristo.

CHAPTER XXXV

LA MAZZOLATA

"Gentlemen," said the Count of Monte Cristo as he entered, "I pray you to excuse me for suffering my visit to be anticipated; but I feared to disturb you by presenting myself earlier at your apartments. Besides, you sent me word you would come to me; and I have held myself at your disposal."

"Franz and I have to thank you a thousand times, Monsieur the Count," returned Albert. "You extricated us from a great dilemma; and we were on the point of inventing some very fantastic vehicle when your friendly invitation reached us."

"Indeed!" returned the count, motioning the two young men to sit down. "It was the fault of that blockhead Pastrini that I did not sooner assist you in your distress. He did not mention your embarrassment to me, who, alone and isolated as I am, seek every opportunity of making the acquaintance of my neighbours. As soon as I heard I could in any way assist you, I eagerly seized the opportunity of offering my services."

The two young men bowed. Franz had as yet found nothing to say. He had formed no plan of action; and as nothing in the count's manner manifested the wish that he should recognise him, he did not know whether to make any allusion to the past, or to wait until he had more proof. Besides, although sure it was he who had been in the box the previous evening, he could not be equally positive that he was the man he had seen at the Colosseum. He resolved, therefore, to let things take their course without making any direct overture to the count. Besides, he had this advantage over him,—he was master of his secret, while he had no hold on Franz, who had nothing to conceal. However, he resolved to lead the conversation to a subject which might possibly clear up his doubts.

"Monsieur the Count," said he, "you have offered us places in your carriage, and at your windows of the Rospoli Palace. Can you tell us where we can obtain a sight of the Place del Popolo?"

"Ah!" said the count, negligently, looking attentively at Morcerf, "is there not something like an execution upon the Place del Popolo?"

"Yes," returned Franz, finding that the count was coming to the point he wished.

"Stay, I think I told my steward yesterday to attend to this;

perhaps I can render you this slight service also." He extended his hand, and rang the bell thrice. "Did you ever occupy yourself," said he to Franz, "with the employment of time and the means of simplifying the summoning your servants? I have: when I ring once, it is for my valet; twice, for my *maître d'hôtel*; thrice, for my steward. Thus I do not waste a minute or a word. Here he is!"

A man from forty-five to fifty years old entered, who exactly resembled the smuggler who had introduced Franz into the cavern; but he did not appear to recognise him. It was evident he had his orders.

"M. Bertuccio," said the count, "have you procured me a window looking on the Place del Popolo, as I ordered you yesterday?"

"Yes, excellency," returned the steward; "but it was very late."

"Did I not tell you I wished for one?" replied the count, frowning.

"And your excellency has one, which had been let to Prince Lobanieff; but I was obliged to pay a hundred—"

"That will do,—that will do, M. Bertuccio; spare these gentlemen all such domestic arrangements. You have the window; that is sufficient. Give orders to the coachman; and be in readiness on the stairs to conduct us to it." The steward bowed, and was about to quit the room. "Ah!" continued the count, "be good enough to ask Pastrini if he has received the *tavoletta*, and if he can send us an account of the execution."

"There is no need to do that," said Franz, taking out his tablets; "for I saw the account, and copied it down."

"Very well, you can retire, M. Bertuccio; let us know when breakfast is ready. These gentlemen," added he, turning to the two friends, "will, I trust, do me the honour to breakfast with me?"

"But, Monsieur the Count," said Albert, "we shall abuse your kindness."

"Not at all; on the contrary, you will give me great pleasure. You will, one or the other of you, perhaps both, return it to me at Paris. M. Bertuccio, lay covers for three." He took Franz's tablets out of his hand.

"'The public is informed,'" he read in the same tone with which he would have read a newspaper, "'that on Wednesday, February 23, being the first day of the Carnival, two executions will take place in the Place del Popolo, by order of the Tribunal de la Rota, of two individuals, named Andrea Rondola, and Peppino, otherwise called Rocca Priori; the former found guilty of the murder of a venerable and exemplary priest, named Don César Torlini, canon of the church of St. Jean de Latran; and the latter convicted of being an accomplice of the atrocious and sanguinary bandit, Luigi Vampa, and his band.' Hum! ' The first-named malefactor will be *mazzolato*, the second culprit *decapitato*.'

" Yes," continued the count, " it was at first arranged in this way; but I think since yesterday some change has taken place in the order of the ceremony."

" Really! " said Franz.

" Yes; I passed the evening at the Cardinal Rospigliosi's, and there mention was made of something like a pardon for one of the two men."

" For Andrea Rondolo? " asked Franz.

" No," replied the count, carelessly; "for the other [he glanced at the tablets as if to recall the name], for Peppino, called Rocca Priori. You are thus deprived of seeing a man guillotined; but the *mazzolato* still remains, which is a very curious punishment when seen for the first time, and even the second, while the other, as you must know, is very simple. The *mandaïa* never fails, never trembles, never strikes thirty times ineffectually, like the soldier who beheaded the Comte de Chalais, and to whose tender mercy Richelieu had doubtless recommended the sufferer. Ah! " added the count, in a contemptuous tone, " do not tell me of European punishments; they are in the infancy, or rather the old age, of cruelty."

" Really, Monsieur the Count," replied Franz, " one would think that you had studied the different tortures of all the nations of the world."

" There are, at least, few that I have not seen," said the count, coldly.

" And you took pleasure in beholding these dreadful spectacles? "

" My first sentiment was horror; the second indifference; the third curiosity."

" Curiosity! that is a terrible word."

" Why so? In life, our greatest preoccupation is death. Is it not, then, curious to study the different ways by which the soul and body can part; and how, according to their different characters, temperaments, and even the different customs of their countries, individuals bear the transition from life to death, from existence to annihilation? As for myself, I can assure you of one thing,—the more men you see die, the easier it becomes to die; and in my opinion, death may be a torture, but it is not an expiation."

" I do not quite understand you," replied Franz; " pray

explain your meaning, for you excite my curiosity to the highest pitch."

"Listen," said the count, and deep hatred mounted to his face as the blood would to the face of any other. " If a man had by unheard-of and excruciating tortures destroyed your father, your mother, your mistress,—in a word, one of those beings who when they are torn from you leave a desolation, a wound that never closes, in your breast,—do you consider sufficient the reparation that society gives you by causing the knife of the guillotine to pass between the base of the occiput and the trapezal muscles of the murderer, and by inflicting a few seconds' physical pain upon him who has caused you years of moral sufferings? "

" Yes, I know," said Franz, " that human justice is insufficient to console us. She can give blood in return for blood,—that is all; but you must demand from her only what it is in her power to grant."

" I will put another case to you," continued the count: " that where society, attacked by the death of a person, avenges death by death. But are there not a thousand tortures by which a man may be made to suffer without society taking the least cognisance of them, or offering him even the insufficient means of vengeance of which we have just spoken? Are there not crimes for which the impalement of the Turks, the augers of the Persians, the stake and the brand of the Iroquois Indians, would be inadequate punishment, and which nevertheless society, indifferent, leaves unpunished? Answer me, do not these crimes exist? "

" Yes," answered Franz; " and it is to punish them that duelling is tolerated."

" Ah, duelling ! " cried the count,—" a pleasant manner, upon my soul, of arriving at your end when that end is vengeance! A man has carried off your mistress; a man has seduced your wife; a man has dishonoured your daughter,—he has rendered the whole life of one who had the right to expect from Heaven that portion of happiness God has promised to every one of his creatures an existence of misery and infamy; and you think you are avenged because you send a ball through the head, or pass a sword through the breast of that man who has planted madness in your brain and despair in your heart,—without considering that it is often he who comes off victorious from the strife, cleared in the eyes of the world, and in a manner absolved by God! No, no," continued the count; " had I to avenge myself, it is not thus I would take revenge."

"Then you disapprove of duelling; you would not fight a duel?" asked Albert, in his turn, astonished at this strange theory.

"Oh, yes!" replied the count; "understand me, I would fight a duel for a trifle, for an insult, for a blow; and the more readily because, thanks to my skill in all bodily exercises and the indifference to danger I have gradually acquired, I should be almost certain to kill my man. Oh, I would fight for such a cause; but in return for a slow, profound, eternal torture, I would give back the same, were it possible: an eye for an eye, a tooth for a tooth, as the Orientalists say,—our masters in everything; those favoured creatures who have formed for themselves a life of dreams and a paradise of realities."

"But," said Franz to the count, "with this theory, which renders you at once judge and executioner of your own cause, it would be difficult to adopt a course in which you would always avoid falling under the power of the law. Hatred is blind; rage carries you away; and he who pours out vengeance runs the risk of tasting a bitter draught."

"Yes, if he be poor and inexperienced; not if he be rich and skilful. Besides, the worse that could happen to him would be the punishment of which we have already spoken, and which the philanthropic French Revolution has substituted for being torn to pieces by horses, or broken on the wheel. What matters this punishment, as long as he is avenged? On my word, I almost regret that in all probability this miserable Peppino will not be *decapitato*, as you might have had an opportunity then of seeing how short a time the punishment lasts, and whether it is worth even mentioning—but really this is a most singular conversation for the Carnival, gentlemen; how did it arise? Ah, I recollect! you asked for a place at my window. You shall have it; but let us first sit down to table, for here comes the servant to inform us that breakfast is ready." As he spoke, a servant opened one of the four doors of the salon, saying, "*Al suo commodo!*" The two young men rose and entered the breakfast-room.

During the meal, which was excellent, and admirably served, Franz looked repeatedly at Albert, in order to remark the impression which he doubted not had been made on him by the words of their entertainer; but whether with his usual carelessness he had paid but little attention to him; whether the explanation of the Count of Monte Cristo with regard to duelling had satisfied him; or whether the events which Franz knew of had redoubled for him alone the effect of the count's theories,

—he remarked that his companion was not at all preoccupied, but on the contrary ate like a man who for the last four or five months had been condemned to partake of Italian cookery, —that is, the worst in the world. As for the count, he just touched the dishes; it seemed as if he fulfilled the duties of an entertainer by sitting down with his guests, and awaited their departure to be served with some strange or more delicate food. This brought back to Franz, in spite of himself, the recollection of the terror with which the count had inspired the Comtesse G——, and her firm conviction that the man in the opposite box was a vampire. At the end of the breakfast Franz took out his watch.

"Well," said the count, "what are you doing?"

"You must excuse us, Monsieur the Count," returned Franz; "but we have still much to do."

"What may that be?"

"We have no disguises; and it is absolutely necessary to procure them."

"Do not concern yourself about that; we have, I think, a private room in the Place del Popolo. I will have whatever costumes you choose brought to us, and you can dress there."

"After the execution?" cried Franz.

"Before or after, as you please."

"Opposite the scaffold?"

"The scaffold forms part of the fête."

"Monsieur the Count, I have reflected on the matter," said Franz. "I thank you for your courtesy, but I shall content myself with accepting a place in your carriage and at your window at the Rospoli Palace; and I leave you at liberty to dispose of my place at the Place del Popolo."

"But I warn you, you will lose a very curious sight," returned the count.

"You will relate it to me," replied Franz; "and the recital from your lips will make as great an impression on me as if I had witnessed it. I have more than once intended witnessing an execution, but I have never been able to make up my mind; and you, Albert?"

"I," replied the viscount,—"I saw Castaing executed; but I think I was rather intoxicated that day, for I had quitted college the same morning, and we had passed the previous night at a tavern."

"Besides, the fact that you have not done a thing in Paris is no reason for your not doing it abroad; when you travel, it is to see everything. Think what a figure you will make when you are asked, 'How do they execute at Rome?' and you reply 'I do not know'! And they say that the culprit is an infamous scoundrel, who killed with a log of wood a worthy canon who had brought him up like his own son. The devil! when a churchman is killed, it should be with a different weapon than a log, especially when he has behaved like a father. If you went to Spain, would you not see the bull-fights? Well, suppose it is a bull-fight that we were going to see. Recollect the ancient Romans of the Circus, and the sports where they killed three hundred lions and a hundred men. Think of the eighty thousand applauding spectators, the sage matrons who took their daughters, and the charming Vestals who made with the thumb of their white hands the fatal sign that said, 'Come, no idling! kill me that man, already nearly dead.'"

"Shall you go, then, Albert?" asked Franz.

"*Ma foi!* yes. Like you, I hesitated, but the count's eloquence decides me!"

"Let us go, then," said Franz, "since you wish it; but on our way to the Place del Popolo, I wish to pass through the Rue du Cours. Is this possible, Monsieur the Count?"

"On foot, yes; in a carriage, no!"

"I will go on foot, then!"

"Is it important that you should pass through this street?"

"Yes, there is something I wish to see."

"Well, we will pass by the Rue du Cours. We will send the carriage to wait for us on the Place del Popolo, by the Strada del Babuino, for I shall be glad to pass, myself, through the Rue du Cours, to see if some orders I have given have been executed."

"Excellency," said a servant, opening the door, "a man in the dress of a penitent wishes to speak to you."

"Ah, yes!" returned the count; "I know who he is, gentlemen. Will you return to the salon? You will find on the centretable some excellent Havana cigars. I will be with you directly."

The young men rose and returned into the salon, while the count, again apologising, left by another door. Albert, who was a great smoker, and who had considered it no small sacrifice to be deprived of the cigars of the Café de Paris, approached the table, and uttered a cry of joy at perceiving some veritable *puros*.

"Well," asked Franz, "what do you think of the Count of Monte Cristo?"

"What do I think?" said Albert, evidently surprised at such a question from his companion. "I think that he is a delightful fellow, who does the honours of his table admirably; who has travelled much, read much, is, like Brutus, of the Stoic school;

and moreover," added he, sending a volume of smoke up towards the ceiling, "that he has excellent cigars."

Such was Albert's opinion of the count; and as Franz well knew that Albert professed never to form an opinion except upon long reflection, he made no attempt to change it. "But," said he, "did you remark one very singular thing?"

"What?"

"How attentively he looked at you."

"At me?"

"Yes."

Albert reflected. "Ah!" replied he, sighing, "that is not very surprising. I have been more than a year absent from Paris, and my clothes are of a most antiquated cut; the count takes me for a provincial. The first opportunity you have, undeceive him, I beg, and tell him I am nothing of the kind."

Franz smiled; an instant after, the count entered. "I am now quite at your service, gentlemen," said he. "The carriage is going one way to the Place del Popolo, and we will go another; and if you please, by the Rue du Cours. Take some of these cigars, M. de Morcerf."

"With all my heart," returned Albert; "these Italian cigars are horrible. When you come to Paris, I will return all this."

"I will not refuse. I intend going there soon; and since you allow me, I will pay you a visit. Come; we have not any time to lose, it is half-past twelve,—let us set off!"

All three descended; the coachman received his master's orders, and drove down the Via del Babuino, while the three gentlemen walked towards the Place d'Espagne and the Via Frattina, which led directly between the Fiano and Rospoli Palaces. All Franz's attention was directed towards the windows of the palace last named, for he had not forgotten the signal agreed between the man in the mantle and the Transteverian peasant. "Which are your windows?" asked he of the count, with as much indifference as he could assume.

"The last three," returned he, with a negligence evidently unaffected,—for he could not imagine with what intention the question was put. Franz glanced rapidly towards the three windows. The side windows were hung with yellow damask, and the centre one with white damask and a red cross. The man in the mantle had kept his promise to the Transteverian, and there could now be no doubt that he was the count. The three windows were still untenanted. Preparations were making on every side; chairs were placed, scaffolds were raised, and windows were hung with flags. The masks could not appear;

the carriages could not move about until the striking of the clock; but the masks were visible behind the windows, the carriages behind all the gates.

Franz, Albert, and the count continued to descend the Rue du Cours. As they approached the Place del Popolo the crowd became more dense, and above the heads of the multitude two objects were visible,—the obelisk, surmounted by a cross, which marks the centre of the place; and before the obelisk at the point where the three streets, del Babuino, del Corso, and di Ripetta meet, the two uprights of the scaffold, between which glittered the curved knife of the *mandaïa*. At the corner of the street they met the count's steward, who was awaiting his master. The window, hired doubtless at an exorbitant price, which the count had wished to conceal from his guests, was on the second floor of the great palace, situated between the Rue del Babuino and the Monte Pincio. It belonged, as we have said, to a small dressing-room, opening into a bedroom; and when the door of communication was shut, the inmates were quite alone. On the chairs were laid elegant costumes of *paillasse*, in blue and white satin.

"As you left the choice of your costumes to me," said the count to the two friends, "I have had these brought, as they will be the most worn this year; and they are most suitable, on account of the *confetti*, as they do not show the flour."

Franz heard the words of the count but imperfectly, and he perhaps did not fully appreciate this new attention, for he was wholly absorbed by the spectacle that the Place del Popolo presented, and by the terrible instrument which at that moment was its principal ornament. It was the first time Franz had ever seen a guillotine,—we say guillotine because the Roman *mandaïa* is formed on almost the same model as the French instrument; the knife, which is shaped like a crescent, that cuts with the convex side, falls from a less height, and that is all the difference. Two men, seated on the movable plank on which the culprit is laid, were eating their breakfast while waiting for the criminal. Their repast consisted apparently of bread and sausages. One of them lifted the plank, took thence a flask of wine, drank some and then passed it to his companion. These two men were the executioner's assistants. At this sight Franz felt the perspiration start forth upon his brow.

The prisoners, transported the previous evening from the Carceri Nuovo to the little church of Santa Maria del Popolo, had passed the night, each accompanied by two priests, in a chapel closed by a grating before which were two sentinels, relieved at intervals. A double line of carbineers, placed on each side of the door of the church, reached to the scaffold and formed a circle round it, leaving a path about ten feet wide, and around the guillotine a space of nearly a hundred feet. All the rest of the place was paved with heads of men and women. Many women held their infants on their shoulders, and thus the children had the best view. The Monte Pincio seemed a vast amphitheatre filled with spectators. The balconies of the two churches at the corner of the Rue del Babuino and the Rue di Ripetta were crammed; the steps even seemed a parti-coloured sea, that was impelled towards the portico; every niche in the wall held its living statue. What the count said was true,—the most curious spectacle in life is that of death.

And yet, instead of the silence which the solemnity of the spectacle would seem to demand, a great noise arose from that crowd,—a noise composed of laughter and joyous shouts; it was evident that this execution was in the eyes of the people only the commencement of the Carnival. Suddenly the tumult ceased as if by magic; the doors of the church opened. A brotherhood of penitents clothed from head to foot in robes of grey sackcloth, with holes for the eyes alone, and holding in their hands lighted tapers, appeared first; the chief marched at the head. Behind the penitents came a man of lofty stature. He was naked, with the exception of cloth drawers, at the left side of which hung a large knife in a sheath, and he bore on his right shoulder a heavy mace. This man was the executioner. He had, moreover, sandals bound on his feet by cords. Behind the executioner came, in the order in which they were to die, first Peppino, and then Andrea. Each was accompanied by two priests. Neither had his eyes bandaged. Peppino walked with a firm step, doubtless aware of what awaited him. Andrea was supported by two priests. Each of them kissed from time to time the crucifix a confessor held out to them. At this sight alone Franz felt his legs tremble under him. He looked at Albert; he was white as his shirt, and mechanically cast away his cigar, although he had not half smoked it. The count alone seemed unmoved,—nay, more, a slight colour seemed striving to rise in his pale cheeks. His nostril dilated like that of a wild beast that scents its prey; and his lips, half-opened, disclosed his white teeth, small and sharp like those of a jackal. And yet his features wore an expression of smiling tenderness, such as Franz had never before witnessed in them; his black eyes especially were full of kindness and pity. However, the two culprits advanced, and as they approached, their faces became visible. Peppino was a handsome young man, twenty-four or twenty-five years old, bronzed by the sun; he carried his head erect, and seemed to sniff the air to ascertain on which side his liberator would appear. Andrea was short and fat; his visage, marked with brutal cruelty, did not indicate age; he might be thirty. In prison he had suffered his beard to grow; his head fell on his shoulder, his legs bent beneath him, and he seemed to obey a mechanical movement of which he was unconscious.

"I thought," said Franz to the count, "that you told me there would be but one execution."

"I told you the truth," replied he, coldly.

"However, here are two culprits."

"Yes; but only one of these two is about to die. The other has long years to live."

"If the pardon is to come, there is no time to lose."

"And see, here it comes!" said the count.

At the moment when Peppino arrived at the foot of the *mandaia*, a penitent, who seemed to arrive late, forced his way through the soldiers, and advancing to the chief of the brother hood, gave him a folded paper. The piercing eye of Peppino had noticed all. The chief took the paper, unfolded it, and raising his hand, "Heaven be praised! and his Holiness also!" said he, in a loud voice. "Here is a pardon for one of the prisoners!"

"A pardon!" cried the people, with one voice,—"a pardon!"

At this cry Andrea raised his head. "Pardon for whom?" cried he. Peppino remained breathless.

"A pardon for Peppino, called Rocca Priori," said the principal friar; and he passed the paper to the officer commanding the carbineers, who read and returned it to him.

"For Peppino!" cried Andrea, who seemed aroused from the torpor in which he had been plunged. "Why for him and not for me? We ought to die together. I was promised he should die with me. You have no right to put me to death alone. I will not die alone! I will not!" And he broke from the priests, struggling and raving like a wild beast, and striving desperately to break the cords that bound his hands. The executioner made a sign, and his assistants leaped from the scaffold and seized him.

"What is the matter with him?" asked Franz of the count, for as all had been spoken in the Roman dialect, he had not perfectly comprehended it.

"Do you not see?" returned the count. "This human creature who is about to die is furious that his fellow-sufferer does not perish with him; and were he able, he would rather tear him to pieces with his teeth and nails than let him enjoy the life he himself is about to be deprived of. Oh, man, man! race of crocodiles!" cried the count, extending his clinched hands towards the crowd, "I recognise you well in that. At all times you are worthy of yourselves!"

All this time Andrea and the two executioners were struggling on the ground; and he kept exclaiming, "He ought to die! he shall die! I will not die alone!"

"Look, look!" cried the count, seizing the young men's hands,—"look! for on my soul, it is curious. Here is a man who had resigned himself to his fate, who was going to the scaffold to die,—like a coward, it is true, but he was about to die without resistance. Do you know what gave him strength; do you know what consoled him? It was that another partook of his punishment; that another partook of his anguish; that another was to die before him! Lead two sheep to the butcher's, two oxen to the slaughter-house, and make one of them understand his companion will not die,—the sheep will bleat for pleasure, the ox will bellow with joy. But man,—man, whom God created in his own image; man, upon whom God has laid his first, his supreme commandment, to love his neighbour; man, to whom God has given a voice to express his thoughts, —what is his first cry when he hears his fellow-man is saved? A blasphemy! Honour to man, this masterpiece of nature, this king of the creation!" And the count burst into a laugh, but a terrible laugh, that showed he must have suffered horribly.

In the meantime the struggle continued, and it was dreadful to witness. The people all took part against Andrea, and twenty thousand voices cried, "Kill him! Kill him!" Franz sprang back; but the count seized his arm and held him before the window. "What are you doing?" said he. "Do you pity him? If you heard the cry of 'Mad dog!' you would take your gun, you would unhesitatingly shoot the poor beast, who after all would be guilty only of having been bitten by another dog. And yet you pity a man who, without being bitten by one of his race, has yet murdered his benefactor; and who, now unable to kill any one because his hands are bound, wishes to see his companion in captivity perish. No, no; look, look!"

This recommendation was needless. Franz was fascinated by the horrible spectacle. The two assistants had borne Andrea to the scaffold, and there, in spite of his struggles, his bites, and his cries, had forced him to his knees. Meanwhile the executioner had put himself in position by his side, and lifting his mace, he signed to them to get out of the way; the criminal strove to rise, but ere he had time, the mace fell on his left temple. A dull and heavy sound was heard, and the man dropped like an ox, with his face to the ground, and then turned over on his back. The executioner let fall his mace, drew his knife, and with one stroke opened his throat, and mounting on his stomach, stamped violently on it with his feet. At every stroke a jet of blood sprang from the wound.

Franz could sustain himself no longer, but sank half-fainting into a seat. Albert, with his eyes closed, was standing grasping the window-curtains. The count was erect and triumphant, like the avenging angel.

CHAPTER XXXVI

THE CARNIVAL AT ROME

WHEN Franz recovered his senses, he saw Albert drinking a glass of water, of which his paleness showed he stood in great need, and the count assuming his costume of *paillasse*. He glanced mechanically towards the place. All had disappeared, —scaffold, executioners, victims; nought remained but the people, full of noise and excitement. The bell of Monte Citorio, which sounds only on the pope's decease and the opening of the Carnival, was ringing a joyous peal. "Well," asked he of the count, "what has then happened?"

"Nothing," replied the count; "only, as you see, the Carnival had commenced. Make haste and dress yourself."

"In reality," said Franz, "this horrible scene has passed away like a dream."

"It is indeed nothing but a dream,—a nightmare that has disturbed you."

"Yes, as to myself; but the culprit?"

"That is a dream also. Only he has remained asleep, while you have awakened; and who knows which of you is the most fortunate?"

"But Peppino,—what has become of him?"

"Peppino is a lad of sense who unlike most men, who are furious if they pass unnoticed, was delighted to see that the general attention was directed towards his companion. He profited by this distraction to slip away among the crowd, without even thanking the worthy priests who had accompanied him. Decidedly, man is an ungrateful and egotistical animal. But dress yourself; see, M. de Morcerf sets you the example."

Albert was in fact drawing on the satin trousers over his black trousers and varnished boots. "Well, Albert," said Franz, "do you feel much inclined to join the revels? Come; answer frankly."

"*Ma foi!* no," returned Albert. "But I am really glad to have seen such a sight; and I understand what Monsieur the Count said,—that when you have once habituated yourself to such a spectacle, it is the only one that causes you any emotion."

"Without reflecting that it is the only moment in which you can study characters," said the count. "On the steps of the scaffold death tears off the mask that has been worn through life, and the real visage is disclosed. It must be allowed Andrea was not very handsome,—the hideous scoundrel! Come, dress yourselves, gentlemen; dress yourselves!"

Franz felt that it would be ridiculous not to follow his two companions' example. He assumed his costume and fastened on his mask, which certainly was not paler than his own face. Their toilet finished, they descended; the carriage awaited them at the door, filled with *confetti* and bouquets. They fell into the line of carriages. It is difficult to form an idea of the perfect change that had taken place. Instead of the spectacle of gloomy and silent death, the Place del Popolo presented a spectacle of gay and noisy revelry. A crowd of masks flowed in from all sides, escaping from the doors, descending from the windows. From every street and every turn drove carriages filled with *pierrots*, harlequins, dominos, marchionesses, Transteverians, knights, and peasants, screaming, fighting, gesticulating, whirling eggs filled with flour, *confetti*, bouquets, attacking with their sarcasms and missiles friends and foes, companions and strangers, indiscriminately, without any one taking offence, or doing anything else than laugh.

Franz and Albert were like men who to drive away a violent sorrow have recourse to wine, and who, as they drink and become intoxicated, feel a thick veil drawn between the past and the present. They saw always, or rather they continued to perceive within themselves the reflection of what they had witnessed; but little by little the general excitement gained upon them, and they felt themselves obliged to take part in the noise and confusion. A handful of *confetti* that came from a neighbouring carriage, and which, while it covered Morcerf and his two companions with dust, pricked his neck and that portion of his face uncovered by his mask like a hundred pins, plunged him into the general combat, in which all the masks around him were engaged. He rose in his turn, and seizing handfuls of *confetti*, with which the carriage was filled, cast them at his neighbours with all the force and address he was master of. The strife had fairly commenced; and the recollection of what they had seen half an hour before was gradually effaced from the young men's minds, so much were they occupied by the gay and glittering procession they now beheld. As for the Count of Monte Cristo, he had never for an instant shown any appearance of having been moved.

Imagine the large and splendid Rue du Cours bordered from one end to the other with lofty palaces, with their balconies hung with carpets, and their windows with flags; at these balconies and windows, three hundred thousand spectators,—Romans, Italians, strangers from all parts of the world; the united aristocracy of birth, wealth, and genius; lovely women who, yielding to the influence of the scene, bend over their balconies or lean from their windows and shower down upon the passing carriages *confetti*, which are returned by bouquets; the air seems darkened with falling *confetti* and ascending flowers; in the streets the lively crowd, dressed in the most fantastic costumes,—gigantic cabbages walk gravely about, buffaloes' heads bellow from men's shoulders, dogs walk on their hind legs; in the midst of all this a mask is lifted, and as in Callot's "Temptation of Saint Anthony," a lovely face is exhibited which we would fain follow, but from which we are separated by troops of fiends,—this will give a faint idea of the Carnival at Rome.

At the second turn the count stopped the carriage and asked of his companions permission to quit them, leaving the vehicle at their disposal. Franz looked up; they were opposite the Rospoli Palace. At the centre window, the one hung with white damask with a red cross, was a blue domino, beneath which Franz's imagination easily pictured the beautiful Greek of the theatre.

"Gentlemen," said the count, springing out, "when you are tired of being actors, and wish to become spectators of this scene, you know you have places at my windows. In the meantime, dispose of my coachman, my carriage, and my servants."

We have forgotten to mention that the count's coachman was attired in a bear-skin exactly resembling Odry's in "The Bear and the Pacha"; and the two footmen behind were dressed up as green monkeys, with spring masks with which they made grimaces at every one who passed.

Franz thanked the count for his attention. As for Albert, he was busily occupied throwing bouquets at a carriage full of Roman peasants that had halted near him. Unfortunately for him, the line of carriages moved on again, and while he descended towards the Place del Popolo, the other ascended towards the Palais de Venise. "Ah! my dear fellow!" said he to Franz; "you did not see?"

"What?"

"There,—that *calèche* filled with Roman peasants."

"No."

"Well, I am convinced they are charming women."

"How unfortunate you were masked, Albert!" said Franz; "here was an opportunity of making up for past disappointments."

"Oh!" replied he, half laughing, half serious; "I hope the Carnival will not pass without bringing me some compensation."

But in spite of Albert's hope, the day passed unmarked by any incident, excepting meeting two or three times the *calèche* with the Roman peasants. At one of these encounters, accidentally or by Albert's intention, his mask fell off. He instantly rose and cast the remainder of the bouquets into the carriage. Doubtless one of the charming women Albert had divined beneath their coquettish disguise was touched by his gallantry, —for in her turn, as the carriage of the two friends passed her, she threw a bunch of violets into it. Albert seized it; and as Franz had no reason to suppose it was sent to him, he suffered Albert to retain it. Albert placed it in his button-hole, and the carriage went triumphantly on.

"Well," said Franz to him, "here is the commencement of an adventure."

"Laugh if you please; I really think so. So I will not abandon this bouquet."

"*Pardieu!*" returned Franz, laughing, "I believe you; it is a sign of recognition."

The jest, however, soon appeared to become earnest,—for when Albert and Franz again encountered the carriage with the *contadini*, the one who had thrown the violets to Albert clapped her hands when she beheld them in his button-hole.

"Bravo! bravo!" said Franz; "things go wonderfully. Shall I leave you? Perhaps you would prefer being alone?"

"No," replied he; "I will not be caught like a fool at a

first demonstration, by a rendezvous under the clock, as they say at the opera-balls. If the fair peasant wishes to carry matters any farther, we shall find her, or rather she will find us to-morrow; then she will give me some sign, and I shall know what I have to do."

"On my word," said Franz, "you are wise as Nestor and prudent as Ulysses; and your fair Circe must be very skilful or very powerful if she succeed in changing you into a beast of any kind."

Albert was right; the fair unknown had resolved, doubtless, to carry the intrigue no farther on that day; for although the young men made several more turns, they did not again see the *calèche*, which had turned up one of the neighbouring streets. Then they returned to the Rospoli Palace; but the count and the blue domino had also disappeared. The two windows, hung with yellow damask, were still occupied by persons whom probably the count had invited. At this moment the same bell that had proclaimed the opening of the Carnival sounded the retreat. The file on the Corso broke the line, and in a second all the carriages had disappeared. Franz and Albert were opposite the Via delle Maratte; the coachman, without saying a word, drove up it, passed along the Place d'Espagne and the Rospoli Palace and stopped at the door of the hôtel. Maître Pastrini came to the door to receive his guests. Franz's first care was to inquire after the count, and to express his regret that he had not returned in time to take him; but Pastrini reassured him by saying that the Count of Monte Cristo had ordered a second carriage for himself, and that it had gone at four o'clock to fetch him from the Rospoli Palace. The count had moreover charged him to offer the two friends the key of his box at the Argentina. Franz questioned Albert as to his intentions; but Albert had great projects to put into execution before going to the theatre, and instead of making any answer, he inquired if Maître Pastrini could procure him a tailor.

"A tailor!" said the host; "and for what?"

"To make us between now and to-morrow two costumes of Roman peasants," returned Albert.

The host shook his head. "To make you two costumes between now and to-morrow? I ask your excellencies' pardon, but this is a demand quite French; for the next week you will not find a single tailor who would consent to sew six buttons on a waistcoat if you paid him a crown for each button."

"Then I must give up the idea?"

"No; we have them ready-made. Leave all to me; and

to-morrow, when you wake, you shall find a collection of costumes with which you will be satisfied."

"My dear Albert," said Franz, "leave all to our host; he has already proved himself full of resources. Let us dine quietly, and afterwards go and see the 'Italienne à Alger.'"

"Agreed," returned Albert; "but recollect, Maître Pastrini, that both my friend and myself attach the greatest importance to having to-morrow the costumes we have asked for."

The host again assured them they might rely on him, and that their wishes should be attended to; upon which Franz and Albert mounted to their apartments, and proceeded to disencumber themselves of their costumes. Albert, as he took off his dress, carefully preserved the bunch of violets; it was his sign of recognition for the morrow. The two friends sat down to table. Albert could not refrain from remarking the difference between the table of the Count of Monte Cristo and that of Maître Pastrini; and Franz, notwithstanding the dislike he seemed to have taken to the count, was obliged to confess that the advantage was not on Pastrini's side. During dessert the servant inquired at what time they wished for the carriage. Albert and Franz looked at each other, fearing indeed to abuse the count's kindness. The servant understood them. "His excellency the Count of Monte Cristo," he said, "has given positive orders that the carriage shall remain at their lordships' orders all the day; and their lordships therefore can use it without fear of indiscretion."

They resolved to profit by the count's courtesy, and ordered the horses to be harnessed, while they substituted an evening costume for that which they had on, and which was somewhat the worse for the numerous combats they had sustained. This precaution taken, they went to the theatre, and installed themselves in the count's box. During the first act the Comtesse G—— entered hers. Her first look was at the *loge* where she had seen the count the previous evening, so that she perceived Franz and Albert in the box of the very person concerning whom she had expressed so strange an opinion to Franz. Her opera-glass was so fixedly directed towards them that Franz saw it would be cruel not to satisfy her curiosity; and availing himself of one of the privileges of the spectators of the Italian theatres, which consists in using their boxes as reception-rooms, the two friends quitted their box to pay their respects to the countess. Scarcely had they entered the *loge* when she motioned to Franz to assume the seat of honour. Albert in his turn sat behind.

"Well," said she, hardly giving Franz time to sit down, "it seems you have nothing better to do than to make the acquaintance of this new Lord Ruthven; and here you are, the best friends in the world."

"Without being so far advanced as that, Madame the Countess," returned Franz, "I cannot deny that we have abused his good nature all day."

"All day?"

"Yes; this morning we breakfasted with him; we rode in his carriage all day, and now we have taken possession of his box."

"You know him, then?"

"Yes, and no."

"How so?"

"It is a long story."

"Relate it to me."

"It would frighten you too much."

"Another reason."

"At least wait until the story has a conclusion."

"Very well. I prefer complete histories; but tell me how you made his acquaintance? Did any one introduce you to him?"

"No; it was he who introduced himself to us."

"When?"

"Last night, after we left you."

"Through what medium?"

"The very prosaic one of our landlord."

"He is staying, then, at the Hôtel des Londres with you?"

"Not only in the same hotel, but on the same floor."

"What is his name,—for of course you know?"

"The Count of Monte Cristo."

"What kind of a name is that? it is not a family name."

"No, it is the name of an island he has purchased."

"And he is a count?"

"A Tuscan count."

"Well, we must put up with that," said the countess, who was herself of one of the oldest families of Venice. "What sort of a man is he?"

"Ask the Vicomte de Morcerf."

"You hear, M. de Morcerf; I am referred to you," said the countess.

"We should be very hard to please, madame," returned Albert, "did we not think him delightful; a friend of ten years' standing could not have done more for us,—and that with a grace, a delicacy, a courtesy which indicate clearly a man of society."

"Come," observed the countess, smiling, "I see that my vampire is only some millionaire, who has taken the appearance of Lara in order to avoid being confounded with M. de Rothschild. And you have seen her?"

"Her?"

"The beautiful Greek of yesterday."

"No; we heard, I think, the sound of her *guzla*, but she remained invisible."

"When you say invisible," interrupted Albert, "it is only to keep up the mystery; for whom do you take the blue domino at the window with the white curtains?"

"Where was this window with white hangings?" said the countess.

"At the Rospoli Palace."

"The count had three windows at the Rospoli Palace?"

"Yes. Did you pass through the Rue du Cours?"

"Yes."

"Well, did you remark two windows hung with yellow damask, and one with white damask with a red cross? Those were the count's windows."

"Why, he must be a nabob! Do you know what those three windows were worth?"

"Two or three hundred Roman crowns?"

"Two or three thousand!"

"The devil!"

"Does his island produce him such a revenue?"

"It does not bring him a penny."

"Then why did he purchase it?"

"For a whim."

"He is an original, then?"

"In fact," observed Albert, "he seemed to me somewhat eccentric; were he at Paris, and a frequenter of the theatres, I should say that he was a malicious joker playing a part, or that he was a poor devil whom literature had ruined,—in fact, this morning he made two or three exits worthy of Didier or Anthony."

At this moment a new visitor entered, and according to custom, Franz gave up his seat to him. This circumstance had moreover the effect of changing the conversation; an hour afterwards the two friends returned to their hotel. Maître Pastrini had already set about procuring their disguises for the morrow; and he assured them they would be perfectly satisfied.

The next morning, at nine o'clock, the host entered Franz's room, followed by a tailor, who had eight or ten costumes of Roman peasants on his arm; they selected two exactly alike, and charged the tailor to sew on each of their hats about twenty yards of ribbon, and to procure them two of those long silken sashes of different colours with which the lower orders decorate themselves on fête days. Albert was impatient to see how he looked in his new costume; it was a jacket and breeches of blue velvet, silk stockings with clocks, shoes with buckles, and a silk waistcoat. This picturesque attire set him off to great advantage; and when he had bound the scarf around his waist, and his hat, placed coquettishly on one side, let fall on his shoulder a stream of ribbons, Franz was forced to confess that costume has much to do with the physical superiority we accord to certain nations. The Turks, who used to be so picturesque with their long and flowing robes,—are they not now hideous with their blue frocks buttoned up to the chin, and their red caps, which make them look like a bottle of wine with a red seal? Franz complimented Albert, who looked at himself in the glass with an unequivocal smile of satisfaction. They were thus engaged when the Count of Monte Cristo entered.

"Gentlemen," said he, "although a companion is agreeable, perfect freedom is sometimes still more agreeable. I come to say that to-day and during the remainder of the Carnival, I leave the carriage entirely at your disposal. The host will tell you that I have three or four more, so that you do not deprive me in taking it. Employ it, I pray you, for your pleasure or your business."

The young men wished to decline, but they could find no good reason for refusing an offer which was so agreeable to them. The Count of Monte Cristo remained a quarter of an hour with them, conversing on all subjects with the greatest ease. He was, as we have already said, well acquainted with the literature of all countries. A glance at the walls of his salon proved to Franz and Albert that he was a lover of pictures. A few words he let fall showed them he was no stranger to the sciences, and he seemed especially interested in chemistry. The two friends did not venture to return to the count the breakfast he had given them; it would have been too absurd to offer him in exchange for his excellent table the very inferior one of Maître Pastrini. They told him so frankly, and he received their excuses with the air of a man who appreciated their delicacy. Albert was charmed with the count's manners, and he was only prevented from recognising him for a veritable gentleman by his scientific knowledge. The permission to do what he liked with the carriage pleased him above all,—for the fair peasants had appeared in a very elegant carriage the preceding evening, and Albert was not sorry to be upon an equal footing with them. At half-past one they descended; the coachman and footman had put on their livery over their disguises, which gave them a more ridiculous appearance than ever, and which gained them the applause of Franz and Albert. Albert had fastened the faded bunch of violets to his button-hole. At the first sound of the bell they hastened into the Rue du Cours by the Via Vittoria. At the second turn, a bunch of fresh violets, thrown from a carriage filled with *paillassines*, indicated to Albert that, like himself and his friend, the peasants had changed their costume also; and whether it was the result of chance, or whether a similar feeling had possessed both parties, while he had taken their costume, they had taken his.

Albert placed the fresh bouquet in his button-hole, but he kept the faded one in his hand; and when he again met the *calèche* he raised it expressively to his lips,—an action which seemed greatly to amuse not only the fair lady who had thrown it, but her joyous companions also. The day was as gay as the preceding one, perhaps even more animated and noisy; they saw the count for an instant at his window, but when they again passed he had disappeared. It is needless to say that the flirtation between Albert and the fair peasant continued all day. In the evening, on his return, Franz found a letter from the embassy, to inform him he would have the honour of being received by his Holiness the next day. At each previous visit he had made to Rome he had solicited and obtained the same favour; and incited as much by a religious feeling as by gratitude, he was unwilling to quit the capital of the Christian world without laying his respectful homage at the feet of one of Saint Peter's successors, who has set a rare example of all virtues. For that day, then, he was not in a mood to think much of the Carnival,—for in spite of his condescension and touching kindness, one cannot incline one's self without awe before the venerable and noble old man called Gregory XVI.

On his return from the Vatican, Franz carefully avoided the Rue du Cours; he brought away with him a treasure of pious thoughts, to which the mad gaiety of the Carnival would have been profanation. At ten minutes past five Albert entered. He was at the summit of joy. The *paillassine* had reassumed her peasant's costume, and as she passed she had raised her mask. She was charming. Franz congratulated Albert, who received his congratulations with the air of a man conscious they are merited. He had recognised by certain unmistakable signs that the beautiful unknown belonged to the aristocracy. He had made up his mind to write to her the next day. Franz remarked, while he gave these details, that Albert seemed to have something to ask of him, but that he was unwilling to ask it. He insisted upon it, declaring beforehand that he was willing to make any sacrifice he required. Albert let himself be pressed just as long as friendship required, and then avowed to Franz that he would do him a great favour by allowing him to occupy the carriage alone the next day. Albert attributed to Franz's absence the extreme kindness of the fair peasant in raising her mask. Franz was of course not selfish enough to stop Albert in the middle of an adventure that promised to prove so agreeable to his curiosity and so flattering to his vanity. He felt assured that the complete unreserve of his friend would duly inform him of all that happened; and as during two or three years that he had travelled in Italy he had found no opportunity to start such an intrigue on his own account, Franz was by no means sorry to learn how to act on such an occasion. He therefore promised Albert that he would content himself on the morrow with witnessing the Carnival from the windows of the Rospoli Palace.

The next morning he saw Albert pass and repass. He held an enormous bouquet, which he doubtless meant to make the bearer of his amorous epistle. This belief was changed into certainty when Franz saw the bouquet (remarkable by a circle of white camellias) in the hand of a charming *paillassine* dressed in rose-coloured satin. And so when evening came Albert was elated, not with joy, but with delirium; he had no doubt that the fair unknown would reply in the same manner. Franz anticipated his wishes by telling him that the noise fatigued him, and that he should pass the next day in writing and looking over his journal.

Albert was not wrong in his expectations, for the next evening Franz saw him enter shaking triumphantly a folded paper he held by one corner. "Well," said he, "was I mistaken?"

"She has answered you!" cried Franz.

"Read!" This word was pronounced in a manner impossible to describe. Franz took the letter, and read:—

Tuesday evening, at seven o'clock, descend from your carriage opposite the Via dei Pontefici, and follow the Roman peasant who snatches your *moccoletto* from you. When you arrive at the first step of the church of San Giacomo, be sure to fasten a knot of rose coloured ribbons to the shoulder of your costume of *paillasse*, in order that you may be recognised. Until then you will not see me.

CONSTANCY AND DISCRETION.

"Well," asked he, when Franz had finished, "what do you think of that?"

"I think that the adventure is assuming a very agreeable appearance."

"I think so too," replied Albert; "and I very much fear you will go alone to the Duc de Bracciano's ball."

Franz and Albert had received that morning an invitation from the celebrated Roman banker. "Take care, Albert," said Franz. "All the nobility of Rome will be present; and if your fair unknown belongs to the higher class of society, she must go there."

"Whether she goes there or not, my opinion is still the same," returned Albert.

"You have read the letter?"

"Yes."

"You know how imperfectly the women of the middle class are educated in Italy?"

"Yes."

"Well; read the letter again. Look at the writing, and find a fault in the language or orthography." The writing was in fact charming, and the orthography irreproachable.

"You are born to good fortune," said Franz, as he returned the letter.

"Laugh as much as you will," replied Albert, "I am in love."

"You alarm me," cried Franz. "I see that I shall not only go alone to the Duc de Bracciano's, but also return to Florence alone."

"If my unknown be as amiable as she is beautiful," said Albert, "I shall fix myself at Rome for six weeks at least. I adore Rome, and I have always had a great taste for archæology."

"Come, two or three more such adventures, and I do not despair of seeing you a member of the academy."

Doubtless Albert was about to discuss seriously his right to the academic chair when they were informed that dinner was ready. Albert's love had not taken away his appetite. He hastened with Franz to seat himself, intending to resume the discussion after dinner. After dinner the Count of Monte Cristo was announced. They had not seen him for two days. Maître Pastrini informed them that business had called him to Civita Vecchia. He had started the previous evening, and had returned only an hour since. He was charming. Whether he kept a watch over himself, or whether accident did not sound the acrimonious chords that certain circumstances had already touched, he was like everybody else. This man was an enigma to Franz. The count must feel sure he recognised him, and yet had not let fall a single word that indicated he had seen him anywhere. On his side, however great Franz's desire was to allude to their former interview, the fear of its being disagreeable to the man who had loaded himself and his friend with kindness prevented him from mentioning it. The count had learned that the two friends had sent to secure a box at the Argentina Theatre, and were told they were all let. In consequence, he brought them the key of his own; at least such was the apparent motive of his visit. Franz and Albert made some difficulty, alleging their fear of depriving him of it; but the count replied that as he was going to the Palli Theatre, the box at the Argentina Theatre would not be used if they did not occupy it. This assurance determined the two friends to accept it.

Franz had become by degrees accustomed to the count's paleness, which had so forcibly struck him the first time he saw him. He could not refrain from admiring the severe beauty of his features, the only defect, or rather the principal quality of which was the pallor. Veritable hero of Byron! Franz could not, we will not say see him, but even think of him without representing his stern head on the shoulders of Manfred, or beneath the casque of Lara. His forehead was marked by the line that indicates the constant presence of a bitter thought; he had those fiery eyes that seem to penetrate to the heart, and the haughty and disdainful upper lip that gives to the words it utters a peculiar character that impresses them on the minds of those to whom they are addressed. The count was no longer young. He was at least forty; and yet it was easy to understand that he was formed to rule the young men with whom he was now associated. In reality, to complete his resemblance with the fantastic heroes of the English poet, the count seemed to have the power of fascination. Albert was constantly expatiating on their good fortune in meeting such a man. Franz was less enthusiastic; but the count exercised over him also the ascendency a strong mind always acquires. He thought several times of the project the count had of visiting Paris; and he had no doubt but that with his eccentric character, his characteristic face, and his colossal fortune, he would produce a great effect there. And yet he did not wish to be at Paris when the count was there.

The evenings passed as evenings mostly pass at Italian theatres; that is, not in listening to the music, but in paying visits and conversing. The Comtesse G—— wished to revive the subject of the count, but Franz announced he had something far newer to tell her; and in spite of Albert's demonstrations of affected modesty, he informed the countess of the great event which had preoccupied them for the last three days. As similar intrigues are not uncommon in Italy, if we may credit travellers, the countess did not manifest the least incredulity, but congratulated Albert on his success. They promised, upon separating, to meet at the Duc de Bracciano's ball, to which all Rome was invited. The heroine of the bouquet kept her word; neither on the morrow nor on the day following did she give Albert any sign of her existence.

At length arrived the Tuesday, the last and most tumultuous day of the Carnival. On Tuesday the theatres open at ten o'clock in the morning, as Lent begins at eight at night. On Tuesday all those who through want of money, time, or enthusiasm have not been to see the Carnival before, mingle in the gaiety, and contribute to the noise and excitement. From two o'clock till five Franz and Albert followed in the procession, exchanging handfuls of *confetti* with the other carriages and the pedestrians, who crowded among the horses' feet and the carriage-wheels without a single accident, a single dispute, or a single fight. The fêtes are veritable days of pleasure to the Italians. The author of this history, who has resided five or six years in Italy, does not recollect to have ever seen a ceremony interrupted by one of those events which so often accompany celebrations among ourselves. Albert was triumphant in his costume of *paillasse*. A knot of rose-coloured ribbons fell from his shoulder almost to the ground. In order that there might be no confusion, Franz wore his peasant's costume.

As the day advanced, the tumult became greater. There was not on the pavement, in the carriages, at the windows, a single tongue that was silent, a single arm that did not move. It was a human storm, composed of a thunder of cries, and a hail of confectionery, flowers, eggs, oranges, and bouquets. At three o'clock the sound of fireworks, let off on the Place del Popolo and the Palais de Venise, heard with difficulty amid the din and confusion, announced that the races were about to begin. The races, like the *moccoli*, are one of the episodes peculiar to the last days of the Carnival. At the sound of the fireworks the carriages instantly broke the ranks, and retired by the adjacent streets. All these evolutions are executed with an inconceivable address and marvellous rapidity, without the police interfering in the matter. The pedestrians ranged themselves against the walls; then the trampling of horses and the clashing of steel were heard. A detachment of carbineers, fifteen abreast, galloped up the Rue du Cours in order to clear it for the *barberi*. When the detachment arrived at the Palais de Venise, a second volley of fireworks was discharged, to announce that the street was clear. Almost instantly, in the midst of a tremendous and general outcry, seven or eight horses, excited by the shouts of three hundred thousand spectators, passed by like lightning. Then the Castle of St. Angelo fired three cannons to indicate that Number Three had won. Immediately, without any other signal, the carriages moved on, flowing on towards the Corso, down all the streets, like torrents pent up for a while, which again flow into the parent river; and the immense stream again continued its course between its two banks of granite.

A new source of noise and movement was added to the crowd. The sellers of *moccoletti* entered on the scene. The *moccoli*, or *moccoletti*, are candles which vary in size from the paschal tape to the rushlight, and which stimulate the actors in the great scene which terminates the Carnival to two diverse enterprises: (1) to preserve their *moccoletti* alight; (2) to extinguish the *moccoletti* of others. The *moccoletto* is like life: man has found but one means of transmitting it, and that one comes from God, but he has discovered a thousand means of taking it away, although the Devil has somewhat aided him. The *moccoletto* is kindled by approaching it to a light. But who can describe the thousand means of extinguishing the *moccoletto* ?—the gigantic bellows, the monstrous extinguishers, the superhuman fans. Every one hastened to purchase *moccoletti*,—Franz and Albert among the rest.

The night was rapidly approaching; and already, at the cry of "*Moccoli!*" repeated by the shrill voices of a thousand venders, two or three stars began to burn among the crowd. It was a signal. At the end of ten minutes fifty thousand lights glittered, descending from the Palais de Venise to the Place del Popolo, and mounting from the Place del Popolo to the Palais de Venise. It seemed the fête of Jack-o'-lanterns. It is impossible to form any idea of it without having seen it. Suppose all the stars had descended from the sky and mingled in a wild dance on the face of the earth,—the whole accompanied by cries that were never heard in any other part of the world. The *facchino* follows the prince, the Transteverian the citizen, every one blowing, extinguishing, relighting. Had old Æolus appeared at this moment, he would have been proclaimed king of the *moccoli*, and Aquilo the heir-presumptive to the throne. This flaming race continued for two hours; the Rue du Cours was light as day; the features of the spectators on the third and fourth stories were visible. Every five minutes Albert took out his watch; at length it pointed to seven. The two friends were in the Via dei Pontefici. Albert sprang out, bearing his *moccoletto* in his hand. Two or three masks strove to knock his *moccoletto* out of his hand; but Albert, a first-rate pugilist, sent them rolling in the street, one after the other, and continued his course towards the church of San Giacomo. The steps were crowded with masks, who strove to snatch each other's torches. Franz followed Albert with his eyes, and saw him mount the first step. Instantly a mask, wearing the well-known costume of a female peasant, snatched his *moccoletto* from him without his offering any resistance. Franz was too far off to hear what they said, but without doubt, nothing hostile passed, for he saw Albert disappear arm-in-arm with the peasant girl. He watched them pass through the crowd some time, but at length he lost sight of them in the Via Macello. Suddenly the bell that gives the signal for the end of the Carnival sounded, and at the same instant all the *moccoletti* were extinguished as if by enchantment. It seemed as though one immense blast of the wind had extinguished every one. Franz found himself in utter darkness. No sound was audible save that of the carriages that conveyed the masks home; nothing was visible save a few lights that burned behind the windows. The Carnival was over.

CHAPTER XXXVII

THE CATACOMBS OF ST. SEBASTIAN

IN his whole life perhaps Franz had never experienced so sudden an impression, so rapid a transition from gaiety to sadness as in this moment. It seemed as though Rome, under the magic breath of some demon of the night, had suddenly been changed into a vast tomb. By a chance, which added yet more to the intensity of the darkness, the moon, which was on the wane, would not rise until eleven o'clock, and the streets which the young man traversed were plunged in the deepest obscurity. The distance was short; and at the end of ten minutes his carriage, or rather the count's, stopped before the Hôtel de Londres. Dinner was waiting; but as Albert had told him that he should not return so soon, Franz sat down without him. Maître Pastrini, who had been accustomed to see them dine together, inquired into the cause of his absence, and Franz replied that Albert had received on the previous evening an invitation which he had accepted. The sudden extinction of the *moccoletti*, the darkness which had replaced the light, and the silence which had succeeded the turmoil had left in Franz's mind a certain depression which was not free from uneasiness. He therefore dined very silently, in spite of the officious attention of his host, who presented himself two or three times to inquire if he wanted anything.

Franz resolved to wait for Albert as late as possible. He ordered the carriage, therefore, for eleven o'clock, desiring Maître Pastrini to inform him the moment Albert returned to the hotel. At eleven o'clock Albert had not come back. Franz dressed himself and went out, telling his host that he was going to pass the night at the Duc de Bracciano's. The house of the Duc de Bracciano is one of the most delightful in Rome; his lady, one of the last heiresses of the Colonnas, does its honours with the most consummate grace, and thus their fêtes have a European celebrity. Franz and Albert had brought to Rome letters of introduction to them; and the first question on Franz's arrival was, where was his travelling companion. Franz replied that he had left him at the moment they were about to extinguish the *moccoli*, and that he had lost sight of him in the Via Macello.

" Then he has not returned? " said the duke.

" I waited for him until this hour," replied Franz.

" And do you know whither he went? "

" No, not precisely; however, I think it was something very like an assignation."

" The devil!" said the duke, " this is a bad day, or rather a bad night, to be out late; is it not, countess? " These words were addressed to the Comtesse G——, who had just arrived, and was leaing on the arm of M. Torlonia, the duke's brother.

" I think, on the contrary, that it is a charming night," replied the countess; " and those who are here will complain of only one thing,—its too rapid flight."

" I am not speaking," said the duke, with a smile, " of the persons who are here. The only danger here is,—for the men, that of falling in love with you; and for the women, that of falling ill of jealousy at seeing you so lovely. I allude to those who are out in the streets of Rome."

" Ah!" asked the countess, " who is out in the streets of Rome at this hour, unless it be to go to a ball? "

" Our friend, Albert de Morcerf, countess, whom I left in pursuit of his unknown about seven o'clock this evening," said Franz, " and whom I have not seen since."

" And don't you know where he is ? "

" Not at all."

" Is he armed ? "

" He is *en paillasse*."

" You should not have allowed him to go," said the duke to Franz,—" you, who know Rome better than he does."

" You might as well have tried to stop Number Three of the *barberi*, who gained the prize in the race to-day," replied Franz; " and besides, what could happen to him ? "

" Who can tell? The night is gloomy, and the Tiber is very near the Via Macello."

Franz felt a shudder run through his veins at observing the feeling of the duke and the countess so much in unison with his own anxiety. " I informed them at the hotel that I had the honour of passing the night here, duke," said Franz, " and desired them to come and inform me of his return."

" Ah ! " replied the duke, " here, I think, is one of my servants who is seeking you."

The duke was not mistaken; when he saw Franz the servant came up to him. " Your excellency," he said, " the master of the Hôtel de Londres has sent to let you know that a man is waiting for you with a letter from the Vicomte de Morcerf."

" A letter from the viscount ! " exclaimed Franz.

" Yes."

" And who is the man ? "

" I do not know."

" Why did he not bring it to me here ? "

" The messenger did not say."

" And where is the messenger ? "

" He went away as soon as he saw me enter the ball-room to find you."

" Oh ! " said the countess to Franz, " go with all speed ! Poor young man ! perhaps some accident has happened to him."

" I will hasten," replied Franz.

" Shall you return to give us any information ? " inquired the countess.

" Yes, if it is not any serious affair; otherwise I cannot answer as to what I may do myself."

" Be prudent, in any event," said the countess.

" Oh ! be assured of that."

Franz took his hat and went away in haste. He had sent

away his carriage with orders for it to fetch him at two o'clock: fortunately the Palace Bracciano, which is on one side in the Rue du Cours and on the other in the Place des Saints Apôtres, is hardly ten minutes' walk from the Hôtel de Londres. As he came near the hotel Franz saw a man in the middle of the street. He had no doubt that it was the messenger from Albert. The man was wrapped up in a large cloak. He went up to him, but to his extreme astonishment, the man first addressed him. "What does your excellency want of me?" he asked, retreating a step, as if to keep on his guard.

"Are not you the person who brought me a letter," inquired Franz, "from the Vicomte de Morcerf?"

"Your excellency lodges at Pastrini's hotel?"

"I do."

"Your excellency is the travelling companion of the viscount?"

"I am."

"Your excellency's name—"

"Is the Baron Franz d'Epinay."

"Then it is to your excellency that this letter is addressed."

"Is there any answer?" inquired Franz, taking the letter from him.

"Yes; your friend at least hopes so."

"Come upstairs with me and I will give it to you."

"I prefer waiting here," said the messenger, with a smile.

"And why?"

"Your excellency will know when you have read the letter."

"Shall I find you, then, here?"

"Certainly."

Franz entered the hotel. On the staircase he met Maître Pastrini. "Well?" said the landlord.

"Well, what?" responded Franz.

"You have seen the man who desired to speak with you from your friend?" he asked of Franz.

"Yes, I have seen him," he replied, "and he has handed this letter to me. Light the candle in my apartment, if you please."

The innkeeper gave orders to a servant to go before Franz with a candle. The young man had found Maître Pastrini looking very much alarmed, and this had only made him the more anxious to read Albert's letter; and thus he went instantly towards the waxlight, and unfolded the letter. It was written and signed by Albert. Franz read it twice before he could comprehend what it contained. It was thus conceived:—

MY DEAR FELLOW,—The moment you have received this, have

the kindness to take from my pocket-book, which you will find in the square drawer of the secretary, the letter of credit; add your own to it, if it be not sufficient. Run to Torlonia, draw from him instantly four thousand piastres, and give them to the bearer. It is urgent that I should have this money without delay. I do not say more, relying on you as you may rely on me.—Your friend,

ALBERT DE MORCERF.

P.S.—I now believe in Italian banditti.

Below these lines were written in a strange hand the following in Italian:—

Se alle sei della mattina le quattro mila piastre non sono nelle mie mani, alle sette il Conte Alberto avrà cessato di vivere.[1]—LUIGI VAMPA.

This second signature explained all to Franz, who now understood the objection of the messenger to coming up into the apartment: the street was safer for him. Albert, then, had fallen into the hands of the famous chief of banditti in whose existence he had for so long a time refused to believe. There was no time to lose. He hastened to open the secretary, and found the pocket-book in the drawer, and in it the letter of credit. It was for six thousand piastres in all; but of these six thousand Albert had already expended three thousand. As to Franz, he had no letter of credit, as he lived at Florence, and had come to Rome to pass only seven or eight days; he had brought but a hundred louis, and of these he had not more than fifty left. Thus seven or eight hundred piastres were wanting to them both to make up the sum that Albert required. True, he might in such a case rely on the kindness of M. Torlonia. He was therefore about to return to the Palace Bracciano without loss of time, when suddenly a luminous idea crossed his mind. He remembered the Count of Monte Cristo. Franz was about to ring for Maître Pastrini, when that worthy presented himself. " My dear sir," he said hastily, " do you know if the count is within? "

" Yes, your excellency; he has this moment returned."

" Is he in bed? "

" I should say no."

" Then ring at his door, if you please, and request him to be so kind as to give me an audience."

Maître Pastrini did as he was desired, and returning five minutes after, he said, " The count awaits your excellency."

Franz went along the corridor, and a servant introduced him

---

[1] If by six in the morning the four thousand piastres are not in my hands, by seven o'clock the Vicomte Albert de Morcerf will have ceased to live.

to the count. He was in a small cabinet which Franz had not yet seen, and which was surrounded with divans. The count came towards him. "Well, what good wind blows you hither at this hour?" said he; "have you come to sup with me? It would be very kind of you."

"No; I have come to speak to you of a very serious matter."

"A serious matter!" said the count, looking at Franz with the earnestness usual to him; "and what may it be?"

"Are we alone?"

"Yes," replied the count, going to the door, and returning. Franz gave him Albert's letter.

"Read that," he said.

The count read it. "Ah, ah!" said he.

"Did you see the postscript?"

"I did, indeed,—

Se alle sei della mattina le quattro mila piastre non sono nelle mie mani, alle sette il Conte Alberto avrà cessato di vivere.—LUIGI VAMPA.

"What do you think of that?" inquired Franz.

"Have you the money he demands?"

"Yes, all but eight hundred piastres."

The count went to his secretary, opened it, and pulling out a drawer filled with gold, said to Franz, "I hope you will not offend me by applying to any one but myself."

"You see, on the contrary, I come to you first and instantly," replied Franz.

"And I thank you; help yourself;" and he made a sign to Franz to take what he pleased.

"Is it absolutely necessary, then, to send the money to Luigi Vampa?" asked the young man, looking fixedly in his turn at the count.

"Judge for yourself," replied he; "the postscript is explicit."

"I think that if you would take the trouble of reflecting, you could find a way of simplifying the negotiation," said Franz.

"How so?" returned the count, with surprise.

"If we were to go together to Luigi Vampa, I am sure he would not refuse you Albert's freedom."

"What influence can I possibly have over a bandit?"

"Have you not just rendered him one of those services that are never forgotten?"

"What is that?"

"Have you not saved Peppino's life?"

"Ah, ah!" said the count, "who told you that?"

" No matter; I know it."

The count knit his brows and remained silent an instant. " And if I went to seek Vampa, would you accompany me? "

" If my society would not be disagreeable."

" Be it so. It is a lovely night; and a walk in the suburbs of Rome will do us both good."

" Shall I take any arms? "

" For what purpose? "

" Any money? "

" It is useless. Where is the man who brought the letter? "

" In the street."

" He awaits the answer? "

" Yes."

" I must learn where we are going. I will summon him hither."

" It is useless; he would not come up."

" To your apartments, perhaps; but he will not make any difficulty in entering mine."

The count went to the window of the apartment that looked on to the street, and whistled in a peculiar manner. The man in the mantle quitted the wall and advanced into the centre of the street. " *Salite !* " said the count, in the same tone in which he would have given an order to his servant. The messenger obeyed without the least hesitation, but rather with alacrity, and mounting the steps of the passage at a bound, entered the hotel; five seconds afterwards he was at the door of the cabinet. " Ah, it is you, Peppino," said the count. But Peppino, instead of answering, threw himself on his knees, seized the count's hand and covered it with kisses.

" Ah," said the count, " you have then not forgotten that I saved your life; that is strange, for it is a week ago ! "

" No, excellency; and never shall I forget it," returned Peppino, with an accent of profound gratitude.

" Never! That is a long time; but it is something that you believe so. Rise and answer." Peppino glanced anxiously at Franz. " Oh, you may speak before his excellency," said the count; " he is one of my friends. You allow me to give you this title? " continued the count, in French; " it is necessary in order to gain this man's confidence."

" You can speak before me," said Franz; " I am a friend of the count's."

" Good! " returned Peppino. " I am ready to answer any questions your excellency may address to me."

" How did the Vicomte Albert fall into Luigi's hands? "

" Excellency, the Frenchman's carriage passed several times the one in which was Teresa."

" The chief's mistress? "

" Yes. The Frenchman threw her a bouquet; Teresa returned it,—with the consent of the chief, who was in the carriage."

" What ! " cried Franz; " was Luigi Vampa in the carriage with the Roman peasants? "

" It was he who drove, disguised as the coachman," replied Peppino.

" Well? " said the count.

" Well, then, the Frenchman took off his mask; Teresa, with the chief's consent, did the same. The Frenchman asked for a rendezvous; Teresa gave him one,—only, instead of Teresa, it was Beppo who was on the steps of the church of San Giacomo."

" What ! " exclaimed Franz, " the peasant girl who snatched his *moccoletto* from him—"

" Was a lad of fifteen," replied Peppino. " But it was no disgrace to your friend to have been deceived; Beppo has taken in plenty of others."

" And Beppo led him outside the walls? " said the count.

" Exactly so; a carriage was waiting at the end of Via Macello. Beppo got in, inviting the Frenchman to follow him, and he did not wait to be asked twice. He gallantly offered the right-hand seat to Beppo, and sat by him. Beppo told him he was going to take him to a villa a league from Rome; the Frenchman assured him he would follow him to the end of the world. The coachman went up the Rue di Ripetta and out by the Porta San Paolo. When they were two hundred yards outside, as the Frenchman became somewhat too forward, Beppo put a brace of pistols to his head; the coachman pulled up and did the same. At the same time four of the band, who were concealed on the banks of the Almo, surrounded the carriage. The Frenchman made some resistance and nearly strangled Beppo; but he could not resist five armed men, and was forced to yield. They made him get out, walk along the banks of the river, and then brought him to Teresa and Luigi, who were waiting for him in the catacombs of St. Sebastian."

" Well," said the count, turning towards Franz, " it seems to me that is a very pretty story. What do you say to it? "

" Why, that I should think it very amusing," replied Franz, " if it had concerned any one but poor Albert."

" And in truth, if you had not found me here," said the count, " it might have proved a gallant adventure which would have cost your friend dear; but now, be assured, his alarm will be the only serious consequence."

" And shall we go and find him? " inquired Franz.

" Oh, decidedly. He is in a very picturesque place; do you know the catacombs of St. Sebastian? "

" I was never in them, but I have often resolved to visit them."

" Well, here is an opportunity made to your hand, and it would be difficult to contrive a better. Have you a carriage? "

" No."

" That is of no consequence; I always have one ready, day and night."

" Always ready? "

" Yes. I am a very capricious being; and I should tell you that sometimes when I rise, or after my dinner, or in the middle of the night, I resolve on starting for some particular point, and away I go." The count rang, and a footman appeared. " Order out the carriage," he said, " and remove the pistols which are in the holsters. You need not awaken the coachman; Ali will drive."

In a moment the noise of wheels was heard, and the carriage stopped at the door. The count took out his watch. " Half-past twelve," he said. " We might start at five o'clock and be in time; but the delay may cause your friend to pass an uneasy night, and therefore we had better go with all speed to extricate him from the hands of the infidels. Are you still resolved to accompany me? "

" More determined than ever."

" Well, then, come along."

Franz and the count went downstairs, accompanied by Peppino. At the door they found the carriage. Ali was on the box, in whom Franz recognised the dumb slave of the grotto of Monte Cristo. Franz and the count got into the carriage. Peppino placed himself beside Ali, and they set off at a rapid pace. Ali had received his instructions, and went down the Rue du Cours, crossed the Campo Vaccino, went up the Strada San Gregorio, and reached the gates of St. Sebastian. There the porter raised some difficulties, but the Count of Monte Cristo produced an authority from the governor of Rome to quit or enter the city at any and all hours of the day or night; the portcullis was therefore raised, the porter had a louis for his trouble, and they went on their way. The road which the carriage now traversed was the ancient Appian Way, and bordered with tombs. From time to time, by the light of the moon, which began to rise, Franz imagined that he saw a sentinel stand out from the ruin, and suddenly retreat into the darkness on a signal from Peppino. A short time before they reached the circus of Caracalla the carriage stopped, Peppino opened the door, and the count and Franz alighted.

"In ten minutes," said the count to his companion, "we shall arrive there."

He then took Peppino aside, gave him some order in a low voice, and Peppino went away, taking with him a torch, brought with them in the carriage. Five minutes elapsed, during which Franz saw the shepherd advance along a narrow path in the midst of the irregular ground formed by upheavals in the plain of Rome, and disappear in the midst of the high red herbage, which seemed like the bristling mane of some enormous lion. "Now," said the count, "let us follow him." Franz and the count in their turn then advanced along the same path, which at the end of a hundred paces led them by a declivity to the bottom of a small valley. They then perceived two men conversing in the shade.

"Ought we to advance?" asked Franz of the count; "or should we pause?"

"Let us go on; Peppino will have warned the sentry of our coming."

One of these two men was Peppino, and the other a bandit on the lookout. Franz and the count advanced, and the bandit saluted them.

"Your excellency," said Peppino, addressing the count, "if you will follow me, the opening of the catacombs is close at hand."

"Go on, then," replied the count.

They came to an opening behind a clump of bushes, and in the midst of a pile of rocks by which a man could scarcely pass. Peppino glided first into this crevice; but after advancing a few paces the passage widened. Then he paused, lighted his torch, and turned round to see if they came after him. The count first reached a kind of square space, and Franz followed him closely. The path sloped in a gentle descent, and widened as they proceeded; still Franz and the count were compelled to advance stooping, and scarcely able to proceed two abreast. They went on a hundred and fifty paces thus, and then were stopped by "Who goes there?" At the same time they saw the reflection of their torch on the barrel of a carbine.

"A friend!" responded Peppino; and advancing alone towards the sentry, he said a few words to him in a low tone, and then he, like the first, saluted the nocturnal visitors, making a sign that they might proceed.

Behind the sentinel was a staircase with twenty steps. Franz and the count descended these, and found themselves in a kind of cross-roads, forming a burial-ground. Five roads diverged like the rays of a star, and the walls, dug into niches in the shape of coffins, showed that they were at last in the catacombs. In one of the cavities whose extent it was impossible to determine some rays of light were visible. The count laid his hand on Franz's shoulder. " Would you like to see a camp of bandits in repose? " he inquired.

" Certainly," replied Franz.

" Come with me, then. Peppino, extinguish the torch."

Peppino obeyed, and Franz and the count were suddenly in utter darkness; but fifty paces in advance of them there played along the wall some reddish beams of light, more visible since Peppino had put out his torch. They advanced silently, the count guiding Franz as if he had the singular faculty of seeing in the dark. Franz himself, however, distinguished his way more plainly in proportion as he advanced towards the rays of light, which served them as a guide. Three arcades, of which the middle served as a door, gave them passage. These arcades opened on one side into the corridor in which were the count and Franz, and on the other into a large square chamber entirely surrounded by niches similar to those of which we have spoken. In the midst of this chamber were four stones, which had formerly served as an altar, as was evident from the cross which still surmounted them. A lamp, placed at the base of a pillar, lighted up with its pale and flickering flame the singular scene which presented itself to the eyes of the two visitors concealed in the shadow. A man was seated with his elbow leaning on the column, and was reading with his back turned to the arcades, through the openings of which the new-comers contemplated him. This was the chief of the band, Luigi Vampa. Around him and in groups, according to their fancy, lying in their mantles, or with their backs against a kind of stone bench which went all around the Columbarium, were to be seen twenty brigands or more, each having his carbine within reach. At the farther end, silent, scarcely visible, and like a shadow, was a sentinel, who was walking up and down before a kind of opening, which was distinguishable only as in that spot the darkness seemed thicker. When the count thought Franz had gazed sufficiently on this picturesque tableau, he raised his finger to his lips, to warn him to be silent, and ascending the three steps which led to the corridor of the Columbarium, entered the chamber by the centre arcade, and advanced towards Vampa, who was so intent on the book before him that he did not hear the noise of his footsteps.

"Who goes there?" cried the sentinel, less occupied, and who saw by the lamp's light a shadow which approached his chief. At this sound, Vampa rose quickly, drawing at the same moment a pistol from his girdle. In a moment all the bandits were on their feet, and twenty carbines were levelled at the count. "Well," said he, in a voice perfectly calm, and no muscle of his countenance disturbed,—"well, my dear Vampa, it appears to me that you receive a friend with a great deal of ceremony!"

"Ground arms!" exclaimed the chief, with an imperative sign of the hand, while with the other he took off his hat respectfully; then turning to the singular personage who had caused this scene, he said, "Your pardon, Monsieur the Count, but I was so far from expecting the honour of a visit that I did not recognise you."

"It seems that your memory is equally short in everything, Vampa," said the count, "and that not only do you forget people's faces, but also the agreements you make with them."

"What agreements have I forgotten, Monsieur the Count?" inquired the bandit, with the air of a man who having committed an error is anxious to repair it.

"Was it not agreed," asked the count, "that not only my person, but also that of my friends, should be respected by you?"

"And how have I broken that treaty, your excellency?"

"You have this evening carried off and conveyed hither the Vicomte Albert de Morcerf. Well," continued the count, in a tone that made Franz shudder, "this young gentleman is one of *my friends ;* this young gentleman lodges in the same hotel as myself; this young gentleman has been up and down the Corso for eight hours in my private carriage,—and yet, I repeat to you, you have carried him off and conveyed him hither, and," added the count, taking the letter from his pocket, "you have set a ransom on him, as if he were an indifferent person."

"Why did you not tell me all this,—you?" inquired the brigand chief, turning towards his men, who all retreated before his look. "Why have you exposed me thus to fail in my word towards a gentleman like the count, who has all our lives in his hands? By the blood of Christ! if I thought that any one of you knew that the young gentleman was the friend of his excellency, I would blow his brains out with my own hand!"

" Well," said the count, turning towards Franz, " I told you there was some mistake in this."

" Are you not alone? " asked Vampa, with uneasiness.

" I am with the person to whom this letter was addressed, and to whom I desired to prove that Luigi Vampa was a man of his word.   Come, your excellency, here is Luigi Vampa, who will himself express to you his deep regret at the mistake he has committed."

Franz approached, the chief advancing several steps to meet him.   " Welcome among us, your excellency! " he said to him; " you heard what the count just said, and also my reply.   Let me add that I would not have such a thing as this happen for the four thousand piastres at which I had fixed your friend's ransom."

" But," said Franz, looking round him uneasily, " where is the viscount?   I do not see him."

" Nothing has happened to him, I hope? " said the count, frowning.

" The prisoner is there," replied Vampa, pointing to the hollow space in front of which the bandit was on guard; " and I will go myself and tell him that he is free."   The chief went towards the place he had pointed out as Albert's prison, and Franz and the count followed him.   " What is the prisoner doing? " inquired Vampa of the sentinel.

" *Ma foi!* captain," replied the sentry, " I do not know; for the last hour I have not heard him stir."

" Come in, your excellency," said Vampa.

The count and Franz ascended seven or eight steps after the chief, who drew back a bolt, and opened a door.   Then, by the gleam of a lamp similar to that which lighted the Columbarium, Albert was to be seen wrapped up in a cloak which one of the bandits had lent him, lying in a corner in profound slumber.

" Come! " said the count, smiling with his own peculiar smile, " not so bad for a man who is to be shot at seven o'clock to-morrow morning! "

Vampa looked at Albert with a kind of admiration; he was not insensible to such a proof of courage.

" You are right, Monsieur the Count," he said; " this must be one of your friends."   Then, going to Albert, he touched him on the shoulder, saying, " Will your excellency please to awaken? "

Albert stretched out his arms, rubbed his eyelids, and opened his eyes.   " Ah, ah! " said he, " is it you, captain?   You should have allowed me to sleep.   I had such a delightful dream: I was dancing the galop at Torlonia's with the Comtesse G——." Then he drew from his pocket his watch, which he had kept that he might see how time sped.

"Half-past one only!" said he. "Why the devil do you rouse me at this hour?"

"To tell you that you are free, your excellency."

"My dear fellow," replied Albert, with perfect ease of mind, "remember for the future Napoleon's maxim, 'Never awaken me but for bad news;' if you had let me sleep on I should have finished my galop, and have been grateful to you all my life. So, then, they have paid my ransom?"

"No, your excellency."

"Well, then, how am I free?"

"Some one to whom I can refuse nothing has come to demand you."

"Come hither?"

"Yes, hither."

"Really! that some one is a most amiable person." Albert looked round, and perceived Franz. "What!" said he, "is it you, my dear Franz, whose devotion and friendship are thus displayed?"

"No, not I," replied Franz; "but our neighbour, the Count of Monte Cristo."

"Ah, ah! Monsieur the Count," said Albert, gaily, and arranging his cravat and wristbands, "you are really most kind, and I hope you will consider me as eternally obliged to you,— in the first place for the carriage, and in the next for this;" and he put out his hand to the count, who shuddered as he gave his own, but who nevertheless did give it. The bandit gazed on this scene with amazement; he was evidently accustomed to see his prisoners tremble before him, and yet here was one whose gay humour was not for a moment altered. As for Franz, he was enchanted at the way in which Albert had sustained the national honour in the presence of the bandit. "My dear Albert," he said, "if you will make haste, we shall yet have time to finish the night at Torlonia's. You may conclude your interrupted galop, so that you will owe no ill-will to Signor Luigi, who has indeed throughout this whole affair acted like a gentleman."

"You are decidedly right; and we may reach the palace by two o'clock. Signor Luigi," continued Albert, "is there any formality to fulfil before I take leave of your excellency?"

"None, sir," replied the bandit; "you are as free as air."

"Well, then, a happy and merry life to you! Come, gentlemen, come."

And Albert, followed by Franz and the count, descended the staircase, crossed the square chamber, where stood all the bandits, hat in hand. "Peppino," said the brigand chief, "give me the torch."

"What are you going to do, then?" inquired the count.

"I will show you the way back myself," said the captain; "that is the least honour I can testify to your excellency." And taking the lighted torch from the hands of the herdsman, he preceded his guests, not as a servant who performs an act of civility, but like a king who precedes ambassadors. On reaching the door he bowed. "And now, Monsieur the Count," added he, "allow me to repeat my apologies; and I hope you will not entertain any resentment at what has occurred."

"No, my dear Vampa," replied the count; "besides, you redeem your errors so politely that one almost feels obliged to you for having committed them."

"Gentlemen," added the chief, turning towards the young men, "perhaps the offer may not appear very tempting to you; but if you should ever feel inclined to pay me a second visit, wherever I may be, you shall be welcome."

Franz and Albert bowed. The count went out first, then Albert. Franz paused for a moment. "Has your excellency anything to ask me?" said Vampa, with a smile.

"Yes, I have," replied Franz; "I am curious to know what work you were perusing with so much attention as we entered?"

"*Cæsar's Commentaries,*" said the bandit; "it is my favourite work."

"Well, are you coming?" asked Albert.

"Yes," replied Franz, "here I am!" and he in his turn left the caves.

They advanced to the plain. "Ah, your pardon!" said Albert, turning round; "will you allow me, captain?" And he lighted his cigar at Vampa's torch. "Now, Monsieur the Count," he said, "let us on with all the speed we may. I am enormously anxious to finish my night at the Duc de Bracciano's."

They found the carriage where they had left it. The count said a word in Arabic to Ali, and the horses went off at great speed. It was just two o'clock by Albert's watch when the two friends entered into the dancing-room. Their return was quite an event; but as they entered together, all uneasiness on Albert's account ceased instantly.

" Madame," said the Vicomte de Morcerf, advancing towards the countess, " yesterday you were so condescending as to promise me a galop; I am rather late in claiming this gracious promise, but here is my friend, whose character for veracity you well know, and he will assure you the delay arose from no fault of mine." And as at this moment the music gave the warning for the waltz, Albert put his arm round the waist of the countess, and disappeared with her in the whirl of dancers. In the meanwhile Franz was considering the singular shudder that had pervaded the Count of Monte Cristo's frame at the moment when he had been, in some sort, forced to give his hand to Albert.

CHAPTER XXXVIII

THE RENDEZVOUS

ALBERT'S first words to his friend on the following morning contained a request that he would accompany him to visit the count. True, he had warmly and energetically thanked him the previous evening; but services such as he had rendered were worthy of a twofold acknowledgment. Franz, who was attracted by some invisible influence towards the count, in which terror was strangely mingled, felt an extreme reluctance to permit his friend to be exposed alone to the singular fascination which the mysterious count seemed to exercise over him, and therefore made no objection to Albert's request, but at once accompanied him; they were ushered into the salon, and five minutes later the count appeared.

" Monsieur the Count," said Albert, advancing to meet him, " permit me to repeat the poor thanks I offered last night, and to assure you that the remembrance of all I owe to you will never be effaced from my memory; I shall always remember the important service you have rendered me, and that to you I am indebted even for my life."

" My dear neighbour," replied the count, with a smile, " you exaggerate your obligations to me. You owe me nothing but the saving of some twenty thousand livres in your travelling expenses. Permit me to congratulate you on the ease and unconcern with which you resigned yourself to your fate."

" Upon my word," said Albert, " I deserve no credit for what I could not help; namely, a determination to take everything as I found it, and to let those bandits see that although men get into troublesome scrapes all over the world, there is no nation but the French can smile even in the face of grim Death himself. All that, however, has nothing to do with my obligations to you; and I now come to ask you whether in my own person, my family, or connections, I can in any way serve you. My father, the Comte de Morcerf, although of Spanish origin, possesses considerable influence both at the court of France and Madrid, and I unhesitatingly place the best services of myself and all to whom my life is dear, at your disposal."

"M. de Morcerf," replied the count, "your offer, far from surprising me, is precisely what I expected from you; and I accept it in the same spirit of hearty sincerity with which it is made. I had already made up my mind to ask a great favour at your hands."

"What is it?"

"I am wholly a stranger to Paris; it is a city I have never yet seen."

"Is it possible," exclaimed Albert, "that you have reached your present age without visiting Paris? I can scarcely credit it."

"Nevertheless, it is quite true; still, I agree with you in thinking that my present ignorance of the first city in Europe is a reproach to me in every way, and calls for immediate correction. Probably I should have made that important journey long ago had I known any one who could introduce me into that world with which I have no connection."

"Oh! a man like you!" cried Albert.

"You are most kind; but since I find in myself no other merit than the ability to compete as millionaire with M. Aguado or with M. Rothschild, and since I do not go to Paris to speculate, that trifling circumstance has withheld me. Now your offer decides me. Let us see; you undertake, my dear M. de Morcerf" (these words were accompanied by a most peculiar smile), "upon my arrival in France, to open to me the doors of that fashionable world of which I know no more than a Huron or a native of Cochin China."

"Oh, that I do, and with infinite pleasure!" answered Albert; "and so much the more readily as a letter received this morning from my father summons me to Paris in consequence of a treaty for my alliance (my dear Franz, do not smile, I beg of you) with a family of high standing and connected with the very *élite* of Parisian society."

"Alliance by marriage?" said Franz, laughing.

"Good Lord, yes!" answered Albert; "so when you return

to Paris you will find me settled down, and perhaps father of a family. That will agree well with my natural gravity, will it not? In any case, count, I repeat that I and mine are devoted to you, body and soul."

"I accept," said the count, "for I give you my solemn assurance that I only waited an opportunity like the present to realise schemes I have long meditated."

Franz doubted not that these schemes were the same concerning which he had dropped some words in the grotto of Monte Cristo; and while the count spoke, the young man closely examined him in the hope of reading in his face some revelation of the plans which drew him to Paris. But it was very difficult to penetrate to the soul of that man, especially when he veiled it with a smile.

"But tell me now, count," exclaimed Albert, delighted at the idea of having to introduce so distinguished a person as Monte Cristo,—"tell me truly whether you are in earnest, or if this project of visiting Paris is merely one of those chimerical and uncertain things of which we make so many in the course of our lives, but which, like a house built on the sand, is liable to be blown over by the first puff of wind?"

"I pledge you my honour," returned the count, "that I mean to do as I have said; both inclination and positive necessity compel me to visit Paris."

"When do you propose going thither?"

"Have you made up your mind when you shall be there yourself?"

"Certainly I have,—in a fortnight or three weeks' time; that is to say, as fast as I can get there!"

"Well," said the count, "I will give you three months; you see I make an ample allowance for all delays and difficulties."

"And in three months' time," said Albert, "you will be at my house?"

"Shall we make a positive appointment for a particular day and hour?" inquired the count; "only let me warn you that I am desperately punctual."

"The very thing!" exclaimed Albert; "an exact appointment,—that suits me to a dot."

"So be it, then," replied the count; and extending his hand towards a calendar suspended near the chimney-piece, he said, "to-day is the 21st of February," and drawing out his watch, added, "it is exactly half-past ten o'clock. Now promise me to remember this, and expect me on the 21st of May at half-past ten in the forenoon."

" Capital! " exclaimed Albert; " breakfast will be ready."

" Where do you live? "

" No. 27 Rue du Helder."

" Have you bachelor's apartments there? I hope my coming will not put you to any inconvenience."

" I reside in my father's hotel, but occupy a pavilion at the farther side of the courtyard, entirely separated from the main building."

" Good," replied the count, as taking out his tablets, he wrote down, " No. 27 Rue du Helder, 21st May, half-past ten in the morning." " Now then," said he, returning his tablets to his pocket, " make yourself perfectly easy; the hand of your time-piece will not be more punctual than I shall be."

" Shall I see you again before my departure? " asked Albert.

" That will be according to circumstances; when do you set off? "

" To-morrow evening, at five o'clock."

" In that case I must say adieu to you, as I am compelled to go to Naples, and shall not return hither before Saturday evening or Sunday morning. And you, Monsieur the Baron," pursued the count, addressing Franz, " do you also depart to-morrow? "

" Yes."

" To France? "

" No, to Venice; I shall remain in Italy for another year or two."

" Then we shall not meet in Paris? "

" I fear I shall not have that honour."

" Well, since we must part," said the count, holding out a hand to each of the young men, " allow me to wish you both a safe and pleasant journey."

It was the first time the hand of Franz had come in contact with that of this mysterious man, and unconsciously he shuddered at its touch, for it felt cold and icy as that of a corpse.

" Let us understand each other," said Albert; " it is agreed— is it not?—that you are to be in the Rue du Helder on the 21st of May, at half-past ten in the morning, and your word of honour is passed for your punctuality? "

" All that is settled and arranged upon honour," replied the count; " rely upon seeing me at the time and place agreed on."

The young men then rose, bowed to the count, and quitted the room.

" What is the matter? " asked Albert of Franz, when they

had returned to their own apartments; "you seem more than commonly thoughtful."

"I will confess to you, Albert," replied Franz, "that I am deeply puzzled to unravel the real career of this strange count; and the appointment you have made to meet him in Paris fills me with a thousand apprehensions."

"My dear fellow," exclaimed Albert, "what can there possibly be in that to excite uneasiness? Why, you are mad!"

"As you please," said Franz; "mad or not, so it is."

"Listen to me, Franz," said Albert; "and I am glad of the opportunity to tell you that I have noticed a marked coldness in your manner towards the count, who on the other hand has been simply perfect in his manner towards us. Have you anything against him?"

"Possibly."

"Did you ever meet him previously to coming hither?"

"I have."

"And where?"

"Will you promise me not to repeat a single word of what I am about to tell you?"

"I promise."

"Upon honour?"

"Upon honour."

"That is satisfactory; listen, then."

Franz then related to his friend the history of his excursion to the island of Monte Cristo, and of his finding a party of smugglers there, with whom were two Corsican bandits. He dwelt with considerable force and energy on the almost magical hospitality he had received from the count, and the magnificence of his entertainment in the grotto of the "Thousand and One Nights." He recounted all the particulars of the supper,—the hashish, the statues, the dream, and the reality; and how at his awakening there remained no proof or trace of all these events, save the small yacht seen in the distant horizon sailing towards Porto Vecchio. Then he detailed the conversation overheard by him at the Colosseum between the count and Vampa, in which the count had promised to obtain the release of the bandit Peppino,—an engagement which as our readers are aware, he most faithfully fulfilled. At last he arrived at the adventure of the preceding night, and the embarrassment in which he found himself placed by not having six hundred or seven hundred piastres, and his idea of applying to the count,—an idea which had led to results so picturesque and satisfactory.

Albert listened with the most profound attention. "Well,"

said he, when Franz had concluded, "what do you find to object to in all you have related? The count is fond of travelling, and being rich possesses a vessel of his own. Go to Portsmouth or Southampton, and you will find the harbours crowded with the yachts belonging to wealthy Englishmen who have the same fancy. To have a resting-place in his travels; to escape the frightful cooking which has poisoned us,—me for four months, you for four years; to avoid lying on these abominable beds on which no one can sleep,—he furnishes a place at Monte Cristo. Then, when his place is furnished he fears that the Tuscan government will drive him away, and that his expenses will be lost money; he therefore buys the island and takes its name. Just ask yourself, my good fellow, whether there are not many persons of our acquaintance who assume the names of lands and properties they never in their lives were master of."

"But," said Franz, "how do you account for the circumstance of the Corsican bandits being among the crew of his vessel?"

"Well, what is there surprising in that? Nobody knows better than yourself that the bandits of Corsica are not rogues or thieves, but purely and simply fugitives driven by some vendetta from their native town or village, and that their fellowship involves no disgrace or stigma; for my own part I protest that should I ever visit Corsica, my first visit, ere even I presented myself to the governor or prefect, should be to the bandits of Colomba, if I could only manage to meet them. I find them charming."

"Still," persisted Franz, "I suppose you will allow that such men as Vampa and his band are villains who have no other motive than plunder when they seize your person. How do you explain the influence of the count over those ruffians?"

"My good friend, as in all probability I owe my present safety to that influence, it would ill become me to search too closely into its source. Therefore, instead of condemning him for his intimacy with outlaws, you must give me leave to excuse any little irregularity there may be in such a connection,—not altogether for preserving my life, for my own idea was that it never was in such danger; but certainly for saving me four thousand piastres, which, being translated, means neither more nor less than twenty-four thousand livres of our money,—a sum at which, most assuredly, I should never have been estimated in France; proving most indisputably," added Albert, with a laugh, "that no prophet is honoured in his own country."

"Talking of countries," replied Franz, "of what country is

the count; what is his native tongue; what are his means of existence; whence does he derive his immense fortune; what were those events of his early life—a life as marvellous as unknown—that have tinctured his succeeding years with so dark and gloomy a misanthropy? Certainly these are questions that in your place I should like to have answered."

" My dear Franz," replied Albert, " when upon receipt of my letter you found the necessity of asking the count's assistance, you promptly went to him, saying, ' My friend Albert de Morcerf is in danger; help me to deliver him.' Was not that nearly what you said? "

" It was."

" Well, then, did he ask you, ' Who is M. Albert de Morcerf; how does he come by his name, his fortune; what are his means of existence; what is his birth-place; of what country is he a native? Tell me, did he put all these questions to you? "

" I confess he asked me none."

" No; he merely came and freed me from the hands of M. Vampa, where, I can assure you, in spite of all my appearance of ease and unconcern, I did not very particularly care to remain. Now then, Franz, when in return for services so promptly and unhesitatingly rendered, he but asks me to do for him what is done daily for any Russian prince or Italian noble who may pass through Paris,—merely to introduce him into society,—would you have me refuse? My good fellow, you must have lost your senses to think it possible I could act with such cold-blooded policy." And this time it must be confessed that contrary to custom, all the good arguments were on Albert's side.

" Well," said Franz, with a sigh, " do as you please, my dear viscount, for your arguments are beyond my powers of refutation. But it is none the less true that this Count of Monte Cristo is a strange man."

" He is a philanthropist," answered the other; " and no doubt his motive in visiting Paris is to compete for the Monthyon prize. If my vote and interest can obtain it for him, I will readily give him the one and promise the other. And now, my dear Franz, let us talk of something else. Come, shall we take our luncheon, and then pay a last visit to St. Peter's? " Franz silently assented; and the following afternoon at half-past five o'clock, the young men parted,—Albert de Morcerf to return to Paris, and Franz d'Epinay to pass a fortnight at Venice. But ere he entered his travelling-carriage, Albert, fearing that his expected guest might forget the engagement he had entered into, placed in the care of the waiter of the hotel a card to be delivered to the Count of Monte Cristo, on which, beneath the name of Albert de Morcerf, he had written in pencil, " 27 Rue du Helder, May 21, half-past ten, A.M."

CHAPTER XXXIX

THE GUESTS

IN the house in the Rue du Helder, to which Albert had invited the Count of Monte Cristo, preparation was made on the morning of the 21st of May to honour the young man's invitation. Albert de Morcerf inhabited a pavilion situated at a corner of a large court, and directly opposite another building in which were the servants' apartments. Two windows only of the pavilion faced the street; three other windows looked into the court, and two at the back into the garden. Between the court and the garden, built in the heavy style of the imperial architecture, was the large and fashionable dwelling of the Comte and Comtesse de Morcerf. A high wall surrounded the whole of the hotel, surmounted at intervals by vases filled with flowers, and broken in the centre by a large gate of gilded iron which served as the carriage entrance. A small door close to the lodge of the *concierge* gave ingress and egress to the servants or to the masters when they were on foot.

In this choice of the pavilion as Albert's residence it was easy to discern the delicate care of a mother unwilling to part from her son, and yet aware that he required the full exercise of his liberty; also, it must be admitted, the intelligent egotism of the young man himself, captivated by that free and idle life. Through these two windows looking into the street, Albert could see all that passed; the sight of what is going on is so necessary to young men, who wish always to see the world traverse their horizon, be that horizon but the street only. Then should anything appear to merit a more minute examination, Albert de Morcerf could follow up his researches by going out at a small gate, similar to that close to the *concierge's* door, and which merits a particular description. It was a little entrance that seemed never to have been opened since the house was built, so entirely was it covered with dust and dirt; but the well-oiled hinges and locks announced a frequent and mysterious employment. This door laughed at the *concierge,* from whose vigilance jurisdiction it escaped, opening, like the door in the *Arabian Nights,* the " Sesame " of Ali Baba, by a cabalistic word, or a concerted tap without, from the sweetest voices or whitest fingers in the world. At the end of a long corridor with which the door communicated, and which formed the ante-chamber, was, on the right, Albert's breakfast-room looking into the court, and on the left the salon looking into the garden. Shrubs and creeping plants covered the windows and hid from the garden and court these two rooms,—the only rooms into which, as they were on the ground-floor, the prying eyes of the curious could penetrate. On the first floor were corresponding rooms, with the addition of a third formed out of the ante-chamber; these three rooms were a salon, a boudoir, and a bedroom. The salon downstairs was only an Algerian divan for the use of smokers. The boudoir upstairs communicated with the bed-chamber by an invisible door on the staircase; it was evident that every precaution had been taken. Above this floor was a large studio, which had been increased in size by pulling down the partitions,—a pandemonium, in which the artist and the dandy strove for pre-eminence. There were collected and piled up all Albert's successive caprices,—hunting-horns, bass-viols, flutes,—a whole orchestra, for Albert had had, not a taste, but the whim for music; easels, palettes, brushes, pencils,—for the whim for music had been succeeded by a fatuous passion for painting; foils, boxing-gloves, broad-swords, and single-sticks,—for following the example of the fashionable young men of the time, Albert de Morcerf cultivated with far more perseverance than music and drawing the three arts that complete a dandy's education, namely, fencing, boxing, and single-stick; and it was in this room that he received Grisier, Cook, and Charles Lecour. The rest of the furniture of this privileged chamber consisted of old cabinets of the time of Francis I., filled with China and Japan vases, earthenware from Lucca or Robbia, plates of Bernard de Palissy; of old armchairs, which perhaps Henry IV. or Sully, Louis XIII. or Richelieu had occupied,—for two of these armchairs, adorned with a carved shield on which were engraved the *fleur-de-lis* of France on an azure field, evidently came from the Louvre, or at least some royal residence. On these dark and sombre chairs were thrown splendid stuffs, dyed beneath Persia's sun or woven by the fingers of the women of Calcutta or of Chandernagor. What these stuffs were there for it was impossible to say. They awaited, while gratifying the eyes, a destination unknown to their owner himself; in the meantime they filled the room with their golden and silky reflections. In the centre of the room was a piano in rosewood, of Roller and Blanchet, of small dimensions, but containing an orchestra in its narrow and sonorous cavity, and groaning beneath the weight of the *chefs-d'œuvre* of Beethoven, Weber, Mozart, Haydn, Grétry, and Porpora. On the walls, over the doors, on the ceiling, were swords, daggers, Malay creeses, maces, battle-axes, suits of armour gilded, damaskeened, and inlaid, dried plants, minerals, and stuffed birds, opening their flame-coloured wings as if for flight, and their beaks that never close. This was the favourite sitting-room of Albert.

However, on the day of the appointed rendezvous the young man had established himself in the small salon downstairs. There, on a table surrounded at some distance by a large and luxurious divan, every species of tobacco known, from the yellow tobacco of Petersburg to the black tobacco of Sinai, the Maryland, the Porto Rico, and the Latakia, was exposed in those pots of crackled earthenware of which the Dutch are so fond. Beside them in boxes of fragrant wood were ranged, according to their size and quality, *puros*, regalias, havanas, and manillas; and in an open cabinet a collection of German pipes, of chibouques with their amber mouth-pieces ornamented with coral, and of nargiles with their long tubes of morocco, awaited the caprice or the desire of the smokers. Albert had himself presided at the arrangement, or rather the symmetrical derangement which after coffee the guests at a breakfast of modern days like to contemplate through the vapour that escapes from their mouths, and ascends in long and fanciful wreaths to the ceiling. At a quarter to ten a valet entered; he composed, with a little groom named John and who spoke English only, all Albert's establishment, although the cook of the hotel was always at his service, and on great occasions the count's *chasseur* also. This valet, whose name was Germain, and who enjoyed the entire confidence of his young master, held in one hand a number of papers, and in the other a packet of letters which he gave to Albert. Albert glanced carelessly at the different missives, selected two written in a small and delicate hand and enclosed in scented envelopes, opened them, and perused their contents with some attention. " How did these letters come ? " said he.

" One by the post; Madame Danglars's footman left the other."

" Let Madame Danglars know that I accept the place she offers me in her box. Wait; then, during the day, tell Rosa that when I leave the opera I will sup with her as she wishes. Take to her six bottles of assorted wines,—Cyprus, sherry, and Malaga,—and a keg of Ostend oysters; get the oysters at Borel's, and be sure you say they are for me."

" At what o'clock, monsieur, do you breakfast? "

" What time is it now? "

" A quarter to ten."

" Very well; at half-past ten. Debray will perhaps be obliged to go to his office; and besides [Albert looked at his tablets], it is the hour I appointed with the count,—May 21, at half-past ten,—and though I do not much rely upon his promise, I wish to be punctual. Is Madame the Countess up yet? "

" If Monsieur the Viscount wishes, I will inquire."

" Yes; ask her for one of her *liqueur* cellarets,—mine is incomplete; and tell her I shall have the honour of seeing her about three o'clock, and that I request permission to introduce some one to her."

The valet left the room. Albert threw himself on the divan, tore off the cover of two or three of the papers, looked at the playbills, made a face at perceiving they played an opera and not a ballet, hunted vainly among the advertisements for a new tooth-powder of which he had heard, and threw down, one after the other, the three leading papers of Paris, muttering, " These papers become more and more stupid every day." A moment after, a carriage stopped before the door, and the servant announced M. Lucien Debray. A tall young man, with light hair, clear grey eyes, and thin, compressed lips, dressed in a blue coat with buttons of gold beautifully carved, a white neckcloth, and a tortoise-shell eye-glass suspended by a silken thread, and which by an effort of the superciliary and zygomatic nerves he fixed in his eye, entered with a half-official air, without smiling or speaking.

" Good-morning, Lucien! good-morning! " said Albert; " your punctuality really alarms me. What do I say? Punctuality! You, whom I expected last, you arrive at five minutes to ten, when the time fixed was half-past! It is wonderful! Has the ministry fallen? "

" No, my dear fellow," returned the young man, seating himself on the divan; " reassure yourself. We are tottering always, but we never fall; and I begin to believe that we shall pass comfortably into a state of permanence,—without reckoning that the affairs of the Peninsula will completely consolidate us."

" Ah, true! you drive Don Carlos out of Spain."

" No, no, my dear fellow; do not confound our plans. We take him to the other side of the French frontier, and offer him hospitality at Bourges."

" At Bourges? "

" Yes, he has not much to complain of; Bourges is the capital of Charles VII. What! You didn't know that? All Paris knew it yesterday; and the day before it had already transpired on the Bourse, and M. Danglars (I do not know by what means that man contrives to obtain intelligence as soon as we do) speculated for a rise, and won a million! "

" And you another order apparently, for I see you have a blue ribbon at your button-hole."

" Yes, they sent me the order of Charles III.," returned Debray, carelessly.

" Come, do not affect indifference, but confess you were pleased to have it. "

" Oh, it is very well as a finish to the toilet. It looks very neat on a black coat buttoned up."

" And makes you resemble the Prince of Wales or the Duc de Reichstadt."

" It is for that reason you see me so early."

" Because you have the order of Charles III., and you wish to announce the good news to me? "

" No, because I passed the night writing letters,—five-and-twenty despatches. I returned home at day-break and strove to sleep; but my head ached, and I got up to ride for an hour. At the Bois de Boulogne, *ennui* and hunger attacked me at once,—two enemies who rarely accompany each other, and who are yet leagued against me, a sort of Carlo-republican alliance. I then recollected that you were to give a breakfast this morning, and here I am. I am hungry; feed me. I am bored; amuse me."

" It is my duty as your host," returned Albert, ringing the bell, while Lucien turned over with his gold-mounted cane the papers that lay on the table. " Germain, a glass of sherry and a biscuit. In the meantime, my dear Lucien, here are cigars—contraband, of course; try them, and persuade the minister to sell us such instead of poisoning us with cabbage-leaves."

" *Peste !* I will do nothing of the kind; so long as they came from government you would find them execrable. Besides, that does not concern the home but the financial department. Address yourself to M. Humann, Section of the Indirect Contributions, Corridor A, No. 56."

" On my word! " said Albert, " you astonish me by the extent of your acquaintance. Take a cigar."

" Really, my dear viscount," replied Lucien, lighting a manilla at a rose-coloured taper that burned in a stand beautifully enamelled, " how happy you are to have nothing to do; you do not know your own good fortune! "

" And what would you do, my dear pacificator of kingdoms," replied Morcerf, with a slight degree of irony in his voice, " if you did nothing? What! private secretary to a minister, plunged at the same time into European cabals and Parisian intrigues; having kings, and better still queens to protect, parties to unite, elections to direct; achieving more from your cabinet with your pen and your telegraph than Napoleon did from his battle-fields with his sword and his victories; possessing five-and-twenty thousand livres a year, besides your place; a horse for which Château-Renaud offered you four hundred louis, and which you would not part with; a tailor who never disappoints you; having access to the Opera, the Jockey Club, and the Variétés,—in all that can you not find enough to amuse you? Well, I will amuse you."

" How? "

" By introducing to you a new acquaintance."

" A man or a woman? "

" A man."

" I know so many already."

" But you do not know this man."

" Where does he come from,—the end of the world? "

" Farther still, perhaps."

" The devil! I hope he does not bring our breakfast with him."

" Oh, no; our breakfast is cooking in the maternal kitchen. You are hungry, then? "

" Humiliating as such a confession is, I am. But I dined at M. de Villefort's, and lawyers always give you very bad dinners. You would think they felt some remorse; did you ever remark that? "

" Ah! depreciate other persons' dinners; you ministers give such splendid ones."

" Yes; but we do not invite people of fashion. If we were not forced to entertain a parcel of country boobies because they think and vote with us, we should never dream of dining at home, I assure you."

" Well, take another glass of sherry and another biscuit."

" Willingly. Your Spanish wine is excellent. You see we were quite right to pacify that country."

" Yes; but Don Carlos."

" Well, Don Carlos will drink Bordeaux; and in ten years we will marry his son to the little queen."

" You will then obtain the Golden Fleece, if you are still in the ministry."

" I think, Albert, you have adopted the system of feeding me on smoke this morning."

" Well, you must allow it is the best thing for the stomach; but I hear Beauchamp in the next room. You can dispute together, and that will pass away the time."

" About what? "

" About the papers."

" My dear friend," said Lucien, with an air of sovereign contempt, " do I ever read the papers? "

" Then you will dispute the more."

" M. Beauchamp," announced the servant.

" Enter, enter! " said Albert, rising and advancing to meet the young man. " Here is Debray, who detests you without reading you, so he says."

" He is quite right," returned Beauchamp; " for I criticise him without knowing what he does. Good-day, commander! "

" Ah! you know that already," said the private secretary, smiling and shaking hands with him.

" *Pardieu!* "

" And what do they say of it in the world? "

" In which world? we have so many worlds in the year of grace 1838."

" In the critico-political world, of which you are one of the leaders."

" They say that it is quite fair; and that you sow so much red that you must reap a little blue."

" Come, come! that is not bad! " said Lucien. " Why do you not join our party, my dear Beauchamp? With your talents you would make your fortune in three or four years."

" I only await one thing before following your advice,—that is, a minister who will hold office for six months. My dear Albert, one word; for I must get poor Lucien a respite. Do we breakfast or dine? I must go to the Chamber, for our life is not an idle one."

" We breakfast only. I await two persons; and the instant they arrive we shall sit down to table."

" And what sort of persons do you expect to breakfast? " said Beauchamp.

" A gentleman, and a diplomatist."

" Then we shall have to wait two hours for the gentleman, and three for the diplomatist. I shall come back to dessert;

keep me some strawberries, coffee, and cigars. I shall take a cutlet on my way to the Chamber."

"Do not do anything of the sort,—for were the gentleman a Montmorency, and the diplomatist a Metternich, we will breakfast at eleven; in the meantime, follow Debray's example, and take a glass of sherry and a biscuit."

"Be it so; I will stay. I must do something to distract my thoughts."

"You are like Debray; and yet it seems to me that when the minister is out of spirits, the opposition ought to be joyous."

"Ah, you do not know with what I am threatened. I shall hear this morning M. Danglars make a speech at the Chamber of Deputies; and at his wife's this evening I shall hear the tragedy of a peer of France. The devil take the constitutional government! Since we had our choice, as they say at least, how could we choose that?"

"I understand; you must lay in a stock of hilarity."

"Do not run down M. Danglars's speeches," said Debray; "he votes for you, for he belongs to the opposition."

"*Pardieu!* that is exactly the worst of all. I am waiting until you send him to speak at the Luxembourg, to laugh at my ease."

"My dear friend," said Albert to Beauchamp, "it is plain that the affairs of Spain are settled, for you are most desperately out of humour this morning. Recollect that Parisian gossip has spoken of a marriage between myself and Mademoiselle Eugénie Danglars; I cannot in conscience therefore let you run down the speeches of a man who will one day say to me, 'Monsieur the Viscount, you know I give two millions to my daughter.'"

"Ah, this marriage will never take place," said Beauchamp. "The king has made him a baron and can make him a peer, but he cannot make him a gentleman; and the Comte de Morcerf is too aristocratic to consent for the paltry sum of two millions to a *mésailliance*. The Vicomte de Morcerf can wed only a marchioness."

"Two millions! it is a nice little sum," replied Morcerf.

"It is the capital stock of a theatre on the boulevard, or a railroad from the Jardin des Plantes to La Râpée."

"Never mind what he says, Morcerf," said Debray; "do you marry her. You marry a ticket to a money-bag, it is true; well, but what does that matter? It is better to have a blazon less and a figure more on it. You have seven martlets on your arms. Give three to your wife, and you will still have four;

that is one more than M. de Guise had, who so nearly became King of France, and whose cousin was Emperor of Germany."

"On my word, I think you are right, Lucien," said Albert, absently.

"To be sure; besides, every millionaire is as noble as a bastard,—that is, he can be."

"Do not say that, Debray," returned Beauchamp, laughing, "for here comes Château-Renaud, who, to cure you of your mania for paradoxes, will pass the sword of Renaud de Montauban, his ancestor, through your body."

"He will sully it then," returned Lucien; "for I am low—very low."

"Oh, heavens!" cried Beauchamp, "the minister quotes Béranger; what shall we come to next?"

"M. de Château-Renaud! M. Maximilian Morrel!" said the servant, announcing two new guests.

"Now, then, to breakfast," said Beauchamp; "for if I remember, you told me you only expected two persons, Albert."

"Morrel!" muttered Albert,—"Morrel! who is he?" But before he had finished, M. de Château-Renaud, a handsome young man of thirty, gentleman all over,—that is, with a figure of a Guiche and the wit of a Montemart,—took Albert's hand. "My dear Albert," said he, "let me introduce to you M. Maximilian Morrel, captain of Spahis, my friend, and what is more, my preserver. And besides all that, he carries his credentials in his own person. Salute my hero, viscount." And he stepped on one side, exhibiting the large and open brow, the piercing eyes, and black mustache of the fine and noble young man whom our readers have already seen at Marseilles under circumstances sufficiently dramatic not to be forgotten. A rich uniform, half French, half Oriental, set off his broad chest, decorated with the order of the Legion of Honour, and his graceful and stalwart figure. The young officer bowed with easy and elegant politeness.

"Monsieur," said Albert, with affectionate courtesy, "M. le Comte de Château-Renaud knew how much pleasure this introduction would give me; you are his friend, be ours also."

"Well said!" interrupted Château-Renaud; "and pray that should the case require it, he may do as much for you as he did for me."

"What has he done?" asked Albert.

"Oh! nothing worth speaking of," said Morrel; "M. de Château-Renaud exaggerates."

"Not worth speaking of!" cried Château-Renaud; "life is

not worth speaking of!—that is rather too philosophical, on my word, Morrel. It is very well for you, who risk your life every day; but for me, who only did so once—"

"What is evident in all this, Baron, is that M. le Capitaine Morrel saved your life."

"Exactly so."

"On what occasion?" asked Beauchamp.

"Beauchamp, my good fellow, you know I am starving," said Debray. "Do not set him off on some long story."

"Well, I do not prevent your sitting down to table," replied Beauchamp; "Château-Renaud can tell us while we eat our breakfast."

"Gentlemen," said Morcerf, "it is only a quarter past ten, and I expect some one else."

"Ah, true! a diplomatist!" observed Debray.

"I know not whether he be or not; I only know that I gave him a mission which he terminated so entirely to my satisfaction that had I been king I should have instantly created him knight of all my orders, even had I been able to offer him the Golden Fleece and the Garter."

"Well, since we are not to sit down to table," said Debray, "take a glass of sherry, and tell us all about it."

"You all know that I had the fancy of going to Africa."

"It is a road your ancestors have traced for you," said Albert, gallantly.

"Yes, but I doubt that your object was like theirs,—to rescue the Holy Sepulchre."

"You are quite right, Beauchamp," observed the young aristocrat. "It was only to fight as an amateur. I cannot bear duelling ever since two seconds, whom I had chosen to accommodate a quarrel, forced me to break the arm of one of my best friends, one whom you all know,—poor Franz d'Epinay."

"Ah, true!" said Debray, "you did fight some time ago; about what?"

"The devil take me, if I remember!" returned Château-Renaud. "But I recollect perfectly one thing,—that being unwilling to let such talents as mine sleep, I wished to try upon the Arabs the new pistols that had been given to me. In consequence I embarked for Oran, and went from thence to Constantine, where I arrived just in time to witness the raising of the siege. I retreated with the rest. For forty-eight hours I supported the rain during the day and the cold during the night tolerably well; but the third morning my horse died of cold. Poor brute! accustomed to be covered up and to have a stove in the stable, the Arabian finds himself unable to bear ten degrees of cold in Arabia."

"That's why you want to purchase my English horse," said Debray; "you think he will support the cold better."

"You are mistaken, for I have made a vow never to return to Africa."

"You were very much frightened, then?" inquired Beauchamp.

"I confess it; and I had good reason to be so," replied Château-Renaud. "I was retreating on foot, for my horse was dead. Six Arabs came up, full gallop, to cut off my head. I shot two with my double-barrelled gun, and two more with my pistols; but I was then disarmed, and two were still left. One seized me by the hair (that is why I now wear it so short, for no one knows what may happen), the other encircled my neck with the yataghan, when this gentleman whom you see here charged them, shot the one who held me by the hair with a pistol, and cleft the skull of the other with his sabre. He had assigned himself the task of saving the life of a man that day; chance caused that man to be myself. When I am rich I will order from Klagmann or Marochetti a statue of Chance."

"Yes," said Morrel, smiling, "it was the 5th of September,— the anniversary of the day on which my father was miraculously preserved; therefore, as far as it lies in my power, I endeavour to celebrate it every year by some action."

"Heroic, is it not?" interrupted Château-Renaud. "In brief, I was the chosen one; but that is not all. After rescuing me from the sword he rescued me from the cold, not by sharing his cloak with me, like Saint Martin, but by giving it all to me; then from hunger by sharing with me—guess what?"

"A Strasbourg pie?" asked Beauchamp.

"No, his horse; of which we each of us ate a slice with a hearty appetite. It was very hard."

"The horse?" said Morcerf, laughing.

"No, the sacrifice," returned Château-Renaud; "ask Debray if he would sacrifice his English steed for a stranger?"

"Not for a stranger," said Debray; "but for a friend I might perhaps."

"I divined that you would become mine, Monsieur the Baron," replied Morrel; "besides, as I had the honour to tell you, heroism or not, sacrifice or not, that day I owed an offering to bad fortune in recompense for the favours good fortune had on other days granted to us."

"The history to which M. Morrel alludes," continued

Château-Renaud, " is an admirable one, which he will tell you some day when you are better acquainted with him; to-day let us fill our stomachs and not our memories. What time do you breakfast, Albert? "

" At half-past ten."

" Precisely? " asked Debray, taking out his watch.

" Oh! you will give me five minutes' grace," replied Morcerf, " for I also expect a preserver."

" Of whom? "

" Of myself, to be sure!" cried Morcerf; " do you think I cannot be saved as well as any one else, and that there are only Arabs who cut off heads? Our breakfast is a philanthropic one, and we shall have at table—at least, I hope so—two benefactors of humanity."

" What shall we do? " said Debray; " we have only one Monthyon prize."

" Well, it will be given to some one who has done nothing to deserve it," said Beauchamp; " that is the way the Academy usually escapes from the dilemma."

" And where does he come from? " asked Debray. " You have already answered the question once, but so vaguely that I venture to put it a second time."

" Really," said Albert, " I do not know; when I invited him three months ago, he was then at Rome, but since that time, who knows where he may have gone? "

" And you think him capable of being here punctually? " demanded Debray.

" I think him capable of everything."

" Well, with the five minutes' grace, we have only ten left."

" I will profit by them to tell you something about my guest."

" I beg pardon! " interrupted Beauchamp; " are there any materials for an article in what you are going to tell us? "

" Yes, and for a most curious one."

" Go on, then, for I see I shall not get to the Chamber this morning, and I must make up for it."

" I was at Rome during the last Carnival."

" We know that," said Beauchamp.

" Yes; but what you do not know is that I was carried off by bandits."

" There are no bandits," cried Debray.

" Yes, there are, and most hideous, or rather most admirable ones, for I found them ugly enough to frighten me."

" Come, my dear Albert," said Debray, " confess that your

cook is behindhand, that the oysters have not arrived from Ostend or Marennes, and that, like Madame de Maintenon, you are going to replace the dish by a story. Say so at once; we are sufficiently well-bred to excuse you, and to listen to your story, fabulous as it promises to be."

"And I say to you that fabulous as it may seem, I give it to you as a true one from beginning to end. The brigands had carried me off and conducted me to a most gloomy spot, called the catacombs of St. Sebastian."

"I know it," said Château-Renaud; "I narrowly escaped catching a fever there."

"And I did more than that," replied Morcerf, "for I caught one. I was informed that I was a prisoner until I paid the sum of four thousand Roman crowns,—about twenty-four thousand livres. Unfortunately, I had not above fifteen hundred. I was at the end of my journey and of my credit. I wrote to Franz—and were he here he would confirm every word—I wrote to Franz that if he did not come with the four thousand crowns before six, at ten minutes past I should have gone to join the blessed saints and glorious martyrs in whose company I had the honour of being; and Signor Luigi Vampa—that was the name of the chief of these bandits—would have scrupulously kept his word."

"But Franz came with the four thousand crowns," said Château-Renaud. "The devil! A man whose name is Franz d'Epinay or Albert de Morcerf hasn't much trouble to get four thousand crowns."

"No, he arrived accompanied simply by the guest I am going to present to you."

"Ah! this gentleman is a Hercules killing Cacus, a Perseus freeing Andromeda?"

"No, he is a man of about my own size."

"Armed to the teeth?"

"He had not even a knitting-needle."

"But he paid your ransom?"

"He said two words to the chief, and I was free."

"And they apologised to him for having carried you off?" said Beauchamp.

"Just so."

"Why, he is a second Ariosto."

"No; he is simply the Count of Monte Cristo."

"There is no Count of Monte Cristo," said Debray.

"I do not think there is," added Château-Renaud, with the air of a man who knows the whole of the European nobility perfectly. " Does any one know anything of a Count of Monte Cristo ? "

" He comes possibly from the Holy Land, and one of his ancestors possessed Calvary, as the Montemarts did the Dead Sea."

" I think I can assist your researches," said Maximilian. " Monte Cristo is a little island I have often heard spoken of by the old sailors my father employed,—a grain of sand in the centre of the Mediterranean, an atom in the infinite."

" Precisely ! " cried Albert. " Well, he of whom I speak is the lord and master of this grain of sand, of this atom; he has purchased the title of count somewhere in Tuscany."

" He is rich, then ? "

" I believe so."

" But that ought to be visible."

" That is what deceives you, Debray."

" I do not understand you."

" Have you read the *Arabian Nights ?* "

" What a question ! "

" Well, do you know if the persons you see there are rich or poor, if their grains of wheat are not rubies or diamonds? They seem like poor fishermen, and suddenly they open some mysterious cavern filled with the wealth of the Indies."

" Well ? "

" My Count of Monte Cristo is one of those fishermen. He has even a name taken from the book; he calls himself Sinbad the Sailor, and has a cave filled with gold."

" And you have seen this cavern, Morcerf? " asked Beauchamp.

" No, but Franz has; for Heaven's sake, not a word of this before him ! Franz went in with his eyes blindfolded, and was served by mutes and women to whom Cleopatra was nothing. Only he is not quite sure about the women, for they did not come in until after he had taken some hashish, so that what he took for women might have been simply a row of statues."

The two young men looked at Morcerf as if to say, " Are you mad, or are you laughing at us ? "

" And I also," said Morrel, thoughtfully, " have heard something like this from an old sailor named Penelon."

" Ah ! " cried Albert, " it is very lucky that M. Morrel comes to aid me; you are vexed, are you not, that he thus gives a clue to the labyrinth ? "

" My dear Albert," said Debray, " what you tell us is so extraordinary."

" Ah! because your ambassadors and your consuls do not tell you of them. They have no time; they must molest their countrymen who travel."

" Now you get angry, and attack our poor agents. How will you have them protect you? The Chamber cuts down their salaries every day, so that now they have scarcely any. Will you be ambassador, Albert? I will send you to Constantinople."

" No, lest on the first demonstration I make in favour of Mehemet Ali, the Sultan send me the bowstring, and make my secretaries strangle me."

" There, now!" said Debray.

" Yes, but this does not prevent the Count of Monte Cristo from existing."

" *Pardieu!* every one exists."

" Doubtless, but not in the same way; every one has not black slaves, superb galleys, arms like those at La Casauba, Arabian horses, and Greek mistresses."

" Have you seen the Greek mistress?"

" I have both seen and heard her. I saw her at the theatre, and heard her one morning when I breakfasted with the count."

" Your extraordinary man eats, then?"

" Yes; but so little, it can hardly be called eating."

" He must be a vampire."

" Laugh if you will; that was the opinion of the Comtesse G——, who, as you are aware, knew Lord Ruthven."

" Ah, capital!" said Beauchamp. " For a man not connected with newspapers, here is the pendant to the famous sea-serpent of the *Constitutionnel*."

" Wild eyes, the iris of which contracts or dilates at pleasure," said Debray; " facial angle strongly developed; magnificent forehead; livid complexion; black beard; sharp and white teeth; politeness unexceptionable."

" Just so, Lucien," returned Morcerf; " you have described him, feature for feature. Yes, keen and cutting politeness. This man has often made me shudder! and one day when we were viewing an execution I thought I should faint, more from hearing the cold and calm manner in which he spoke of every description of torture than from the sight of the executioner and the culprit."

" Did he not conduct you to the ruins of the Colosseum to suck your blood?" asked Beauchamp.

" Or, after having delivered you, did he not make you sign a flame-coloured parchment by which you yielded your soul to him, as Esau sold his birthright?"

"Rail on, rail on at your ease, gentlemen!" said Morcerf, somewhat piqued. "When I look at you Parisians, idlers on the Boulevard de Gand or the Bois de Boulogne, and think of this man, it seems to me we are not of the same race."

"I am highly flattered," returned Beauchamp.

"At the same time," added Château-Renaud, "your Count of Monte Cristo is a very fine fellow, always excepting his little arrangements with the Italian banditti."

"There are no Italian banditti!" said Debray.

"There are no vampires!" cried Beauchamp.

"There is no Count of Monte Cristo!" added Debray. "There is half-past ten striking, Albert!"

"Confess you have dreamed this, and let us sit down to breakfast," continued Beauchamp. But the sound of the clock had not died away when Germain announced, "His Excellency the Count of Monte Cristo." The involuntary start every one gave proved how much Morcerf's narrative had impressed them, and Albert himself could not prevent himself from feeling a sudden emotion. He had not heard a carriage stop in the street, or steps in the ante-chamber; the door had itself opened noiselessly. The count appeared, dressed with the greatest simplicity; but the most fastidious dandy could have found nothing to cavil at in his toilet. Every article of dress—hat, coat, gloves, and boots—was from the first makers. He seemed scarcely five-and-thirty. But what struck everybody was his extreme resemblance to the portrait Debray had drawn. The count advanced, smiling, into the centre of the room, and approached Albert, who hastened towards him, holding out his hand. "Punctuality," said Monte Cristo, "is the politeness of kings, according to one of your sovereigns, I think; but it is not that of travellers, however they may wish. But I hope you will excuse the two or three seconds I am behindhand; five hundred leagues are not to be accomplished without some trouble, and especially in France, where it seems it is forbidden to beat the postilions."

"Monsieur the Count," replied Albert, "I was announcing your visit to some of my friends, whom I had invited in consequence of the promise you did me the honour to make, and whom I now present to you. They are M. le Comte de Château-Renaud, whose nobility goes back to the twelve peers, and whose ancestors had a place at the Round Table; M. Lucien Debray, private secretary to the Ministre de l'Intérieur; M. Beauchamp, an editor of a paper, and the terror of the French government, but of whom, in spite of his celebrity, you have not heard in Italy, since his paper is prohibited there; and M. Maximilian Morrel, captain of Spahis."

At this name the count, who had hitherto saluted every one with courtesy, but at the same time with a coldness and formality quite English, made in spite of himself a step forward, and a slight tinge of red coloured his pale cheeks. " You wear the uniform of the new French conquerors, monsieur," said he; " it is a handsome uniform." No one could have said what caused the count's voice to vibrate so deeply, and what made his eye flash, which was in general so calm and so clear, when he had no motive for veiling its expression.

" You have never seen our Africans, Monsieur the Count? " said Albert.

" Never," replied the count, who was by this time perfectly master of himself again.

" Well, beneath this uniform beats one of the bravest and noblest hearts in the whole army."

" Oh, M. de Morcerf! " interrupted Morrel.

" Let me go on, captain! And we have just heard," continued Albert, " of a recent action of monsieur, and one so heroic that although I have seen him to-day for the first time, I request you to allow me to introduce him as my friend."

At these words it was still possible to remark in Monte Cristo that fixed gaze, that passing colour, and that slight trembling of the eyelid which with him betrayed emotion.

" Ah! you have a noble heart? " said the count; " so much the better."

This exclamation, which answered to the count's own thought rather than to what Albert was saying, surprised everybody, and especially Morrel, who looked at Monte Cristo with surprise. But at the same time the intonation was so soft that however strange the exclamation might seem, it was impossible to be offended at it.

" Why, then, should he doubt it? " said Beauchamp to Château-Renaud.

" In fact," replied the latter, who with his aristocratic glance and his knowledge of the world had penetrated at once all that was penetrable in Monte Cristo, " Albert has not deceived us; the count is a singular being. What say you, Morrel? "

" *Ma foi!* he has an open look about him that pleases me, in spite of the singular remark he has made about me."

" Gentlemen," said Albert, " Germain informs me that breakfast is ready. My dear count, allow me to show you the way."

They passed silently into the breakfast-room; every one took his place.

"Gentlemen," said the count, seating himself, "permit me to make a confession which must form my excuse for any unconventionalities of which I may be guilty. I am a stranger, and a stranger to such a degree that this is the first time I have ever been in Paris. The French way of living is utterly unknown to me, and up to the present time I have followed the Eastern customs, which are entirely in contrast to the Parisian. I beg you, therefore, to excuse me if you find anything in me too Turkish, too Italian, or too Arabian. Now, then, gentlemen, let us breakfast."

"With what an air he says all this!" muttered Beauchamp; "decidedly he is a great man."

"A great man in his country," added Debray.

"A great man in every country, M. Debray," said Château-Renaud.

CHAPTER XL

THE BREAKFAST

The count was, it may be remembered, a most temperate guest. Albert remarked this, expressing his fears lest at the outset the Parisian mode of life should displease the traveller in the most essential point.

"My dear count," said he, "I fear that the fare of the Rue du Helder is not so much to your taste as that of the Place d'Espagne. I ought to have consulted you on the point, and have had some dishes prepared expressly to suit your taste."

"Did you know me better," returned the count, smiling, "you would not give one thought of such a thing for a traveller like myself, who has successively lived on macaroni at Naples, polenta at Milan, olla podrida at Valencia, pilau at Constantinople, karrick in India, and swallows' nests in China. I eat everywhere, and of everything,—only I eat but little; and this day, on which you reproach me for abstinence, is my day of appetite, for I have not eaten since yesterday morning."

"What!" cried all the guests, "you have not eaten for four-and-twenty hours?"

"No," replied the count; "I was forced to go out of my road to obtain some information near Nîmes, so that I was somewhat late, and I did not choose to stop."

" And you ate in your carriage? " asked Morcerf.

" No; I slept, as I generally do when I am weary without having the courage to amuse myself, or when I am hungry without feeling inclined to eat."

" But you can sleep when you please, monsieur? " said Morrel.

" Very nearly."

" You have a receipt for that? "

" An infallible one."

" That would be invaluable to us in Africa, who have not always food to eat, and rarely anything to drink."

" Yes," said Monte Cristo; " but unfortunately my receipt, excellent for a man like myself, who leads an exceptional life, would be very dangerous applied to an army, which might not awake when it was needed."

" May we inquire what is this receipt? " asked Debray.

" Oh, yes," returned Monte Cristo; " I make no secret of it. It is a mixture of excellent opium, which I brought myself from Canton in order to have it pure, and the best hashish which grows in the East,—that is, between the Tigris and the Euphrates. These two ingredients are mixed in equal proportions and formed into pills. Ten minutes after one is taken, the effect is produced. Ask M. le Baron Franz d'Epinay; I think he tasted them one day."

" Yes," replied Morcerf, " he said something about it to me."

" But," said Beauchamp, who in his capacity of journalist was very incredulous, " you always carry this drug about you? "

" Always."

" Would it be an indiscretion to ask to see those precious pills? " continued Beauchamp, hoping to take him at a disadvantage.

" No, monsieur," returned the count; and he drew from his pocket a marvellous *bonbonnière*, formed out of a single emerald, and closed by a golden lid, which unscrewed and gave passage to a small ball of a greenish colour, and about the size of a pea. This ball had an acrid and penetrating odour. There were four or five more in the emerald, which would contain about a dozen. The *bonbonnière* passed round the table; but it was more to examine the admirable emerald than to see the pills that the guests handed it around.

" And is it your cook who prepares these pills? " asked Beauchamp.

"Oh, no, monsieur," replied Monte Cristo; "I do not thus intrust my real enjoyment to the discretion of the incapable. I am a tolerable chemist, and prepare my pills myself."

"This is a magnificent emerald, and the largest I have ever seen," said Château-Renaud, "although my mother has some remarkable family jewels."

"I had three similar ones," returned Monte Cristo. "I gave one to the Grand Seigneur, who mounted it in his sabre; another to our Holy Father the Pope, who had it set in his tiara opposite to one nearly as large, though not so fine, given by the Emperor Napoleon to his predecessor, Pius VII. I kept the third for myself, and I had it hollowed out, which reduced its value, but rendered it more commodious for the purpose I intended it for."

Every one looked at Monte Cristo with astonishment; he spoke with so much simplicity that it was evident he spoke the truth or that he was mad. However, the sight of the emerald made them naturally incline to the former belief.

"And what did these two sovereigns give you in exchange for these magnificent presents?" asked Debray.

"The Grand Seigneur, the liberty of a woman," replied the count; "the pope, the life of a man,—so that once in my life I have been as powerful as if Heaven had made me come into the world on the steps of a throne."

"And it was Peppino you saved, was it not?" cried Morcerf; "it was for him that you obtained pardon?"

"Perhaps," returned the count, smiling.

"Monsieur the Count, you have no idea what pleasure it gives me to hear you speak thus," said Morcerf. "I had announced you beforehand to my friends as an enchanter of the *Arabian Nights*, a wizard of the Middle Ages; but the Parisians are so subtle in paradoxes that they mistake for caprices of the imagination the most incontestable truths, when these truths do not form a part of their daily existence. For example, here is Debray who reads, and Beauchamp who prints every day that a member of the Jockey Club has been stopped and robbed on the Boulevard; that four persons have been assassinated in the Rue St. Denis or the Faubourg St. Germain; that ten, fifteen, or twenty thieves have been arrested in a café on the Boulevard du Temple, or in the Thermes de Julien,—and who yet contest the existence of the bandits of the Maremma, of the Campagna di Romana, or the Pontine Marshes. Tell them yourself that I was taken by bandits, and that without your generous intercession I should now have been sleeping in the catacombs of St. Sebastian, instead of receiving them in my humble abode in the Rue du Helder."

"Bah," said Monte Cristo, "you promised me never to speak of that misfortune."

"It was not I who made that promise," cried Morcerf; "it must have been some one else whom you have rescued in the same manner, and whom you have forgotten. Pray speak of it, for if you decide to relate that event you will perhaps not only repeat a few things that I already know, but will also acquaint me with much of which I am still in ignorance."

"It seems to me," returned the count, smiling, "that you played a sufficiently important part to know as well as myself what happened."

"Well, you promise me, if I tell all I know, to relate in your turn all that I do not know?"

"That is but fair," replied Monte Cristo.

"Well," said Morcerf, "for three days I believed myself the object of the attentions of a mask whom I took for a descendant of Tullia or Poppœa, while I was simply the object of the attentions of a *contadine*, and I say *contadine* to avoid saying peasant. What I know is that like a fool, a greater fool than he of whom I spoke just now, I mistook for this peasant a young bandit of fifteen or sixteen, with a beardless chin and slim waist, and who just as I was about to imprint a chaste salute on his lips placed a pistol to my head, and aided by seven or eight others, led, or rather dragged me, to the catacombs of St. Sebastian, where I found a highly educated chief of brigands perusing *Cæsar's Commentaries*, and who deigned to leave off reading to inform me that unless the next morning before six o'clock I should have contributed to his money-box four thousand piastres, at a quarter past six I should cease to exist. The letter is still to be seen, for it is in Franz d'Epinay's possession, signed by me, and with a postscript of M. Luigi Vampa. This is all I know; but I know not, Monsieur the Count, how you contrived to inspire with such respect the bandits of Rome, who respect so few. I assure you, Franz and I were lost in admiration."

"Nothing more simple," returned the count. "I had known the famous Vampa for more than ten years. When he was quite a child, and only a shepherd, I gave him, for having shown me the way to a place, some pieces of gold; he, in order to repay me, gave me a poniard, the hilt of which he had carved with his own hand, and which you may have seen in my collection of arms. In after years, whether he had forgotten this interchange of presents, which ought to have cemented our friendship, or whether he did not recollect me, he sought to take me; but on the contrary it was I who captured him and a dozen of his band. I might have handed him over to Roman justice, which is somewhat expeditious, and which would have been especially so with him; but I did nothing of the sort,—I suffered him and his band to depart."

"On the condition that they should sin no more," said Beauchamp, laughing. "I see with pleasure that they have scrupulously kept their word."

"No, monsieur," returned Monte Cristo; "upon the simple condition that they should respect myself and my friends. Perhaps what I am about to say may seem strange to you who are socialists, and vaunt humanity and your duty to your neighbour; but I never seek to protect society, which does not protect me, and which I will even say generally occupies itself about me only to injure me; and thus while I give them a low place in my esteem, and preserve a neutrality towards them, it is society and my neighbour who are indebted to me."

"Bravo!" cried Château-Renaud; "you are the first man I ever met sufficiently courageous to preach egotism pure and simple. Bravo, Monsieur the Count, bravo!"

"It is frank, at least," said Morrel. "But I am sure that Monsieur the Count does not regret having once deviated from the principles he has so boldly avowed."

"How have I deviated from those principles, monsieur?" asked Monte Cristo, who could not help looking at Morrel with so much intensity that two or three times the young man had been unable to sustain the clear and piercing eye of the count.

"Why, it seems to me," replied Morrel, "that in delivering M. de Morcerf, whom you did not know, you did good to your neighbour and to society."

"Of which he is the brightest ornament," said Beauchamp, drinking off a glass of champagne.

"Monsieur the Count," cried Morcerf, "you are at fault,— you, one of the most formidable logicians I know; and you must see it clearly proved that instead of being an egotist, you are a philanthropist. Ah! you call yourself Oriental, a Levantine, Maltese, Indian, Chinese; your family name is Monte Cristo; Sinbad the Sailor is your baptismal appellation; and yet the first day you set foot in Paris you instinctively possess the greatest virtue, or rather the chief defect of us eccentric Parisians, —that is, you assume the vices you have not, and conceal the virtues you possess."

"My dear viscount," returned Monte Cristo, "I do not see in all I have done anything that merits, either from you or these gentlemen, the pretended eulogies I have received. You are no stranger to me, for I was acquainted with you: I had given up two rooms to you; I had invited you to breakfast with me; I had lent you one of my carriages; we had witnessed the Carnival together; and we had also seen from a window of the Place del Popolo the execution that affected you so much that you nearly fainted. I will appeal to any of these gentlemen; could I leave my guest in the hands of a hideous bandit, as you term him? Besides, you know, I had the idea that you could introduce me into some of the Paris salons when I came to France. You have sometimes perhaps looked upon this resolution as a vague and fugitive project, but to-day you see it is a solid reality, to which you must submit under penalty of breaking your word."

"I will keep it," returned Morcerf; "but I fear that you will be much disappointed, accustomed as you are to picturesque events and fantastic horizons. Among us you will not meet with any of those episodes with which your adventurous existence has so familiarised you. Our Chimborazo is Montmartre; our Himalaya is Mount Valérien; our Great Desert is the Plain of Grenelle, where they are now boring an Artesian well to water the caravans. We have plenty of thieves, though not so many as reported; but these thieves stand in far more dread of a policeman than a lord. France is so prosaic, and Paris so civilised a city, that you will not find in its eighty-five departments—I say eighty-five, because I do not include Corsica— you will not find, then, in these eighty-five departments a single hill on which there is not a telegraph, or a grotto in which the commissary of police has not put up a gas-lamp. There is but one service I can render you, and for that I place myself entirely at your orders; that is, to present, or make my friends present you everywhere. Besides, you have no need of any one to introduce you,—with your name and your fortune and your talent" (Monte Cristo bowed with a somewhat ironical smile) "you can present yourself everywhere, and be well received. I can be useful in one way only; if knowledge of Parisian habits, of the means of rendering yourself comfortable, or of the bazaars, can assist, you may dispose of me to find you a suitable residence. I dare not offer to share my apartments with you as I shared yours at Rome—I, who do not profess egotism, but am yet egotistical *par excellence*,—for except myself, these rooms would not contain a shadow, unless it were the shadow of a woman."

"Ah," said the count, "that is a most conjugal reservation;

I recollect that at Rome you said something of a projected marriage. May I congratulate you?"

"The affair is still only a project."

"And he who says 'project' means certainty," said Debray.

"No," replied Morcerf, "my father is most anxious about it; and I hope ere long to introduce you, if not to my wife, at least to my intended,—Mademoiselle Eugénie Danglars."

"Eugénie Danglars!" said Monte Cristo; "tell me, is not her father M. le Baron Danglars?"

"Yes," returned Morcerf; "a baron of recent creation."

"What matter," said Monte Cristo, "if he has rendered the state services which merit this distinction?"

"Enormous services," answered Beauchamp. "Although in reality a Liberal, he negotiated a loan of six millions for Charles X. in 1829, who made him a baron and chevalier of the Legion of Honour; so that he carries the ribbon, not, as you would think, in his waistcoat-pocket, but in his button-hole."

"Ah!" interrupted Morcerf, laughing, "Beauchamp, Beauchamp, keep that for the *Charivari*, but spare my future father-in-law in my presence." Then, turning to Monte Cristo, "You just now pronounced his name as if you knew the baron?"

"I do not know him," returned Monte Cristo; "but I shall probably soon make his acquaintance, for I have a credit opened with him by the house of Richard and Blount of London, Arstein and Eskeles of Vienna, and Thomson and French at Rome."

As he pronounced the last two names the count glanced at Maximilian Morrel. If the stranger expected to produce an effect on Morrel he was not mistaken; Maximilian started as if he had received an electric shock. "Thomson and French!" said he; "do you know that house, monsieur?"

"They are my bankers in the capital of the Christian world," returned the count, quietly. "Can my influence with them be of any service to you?"

"Oh, Monsieur the Count, you could assist me perhaps in researches which have been up to the present fruitless. That house in past years did ours a great service, and has, I know not for what reason, always denied having rendered us this service."

"I shall be at your orders," said Monte Cristo, inclining himself.

"But," continued Morcerf, "*à propos* of Danglars, we have strangely wandered from the subject. We were speaking of a suitable habitation for the Count of Monte Cristo. Come, gentlemen, let us all propose some place; where shall we lodge this new guest in our great capital?"

"Faubourg St. Germain," said Château-Renaud. "The count will find there a charming hotel, with a court and garden."

"Bah! Château-Renaud," returned Debray, "you know only your dull and gloomy Faubourg St. Germain. Do not pay any attention to him, Monsieur the Count; live in the Chaussée d'Antin,—that's the real centre of Paris."

"Boulevard de l'Opéra," said Beauchamp; "on the first floor, a house with a balcony. Monsieur the Count will have his cushions of silver brought there, and as he smokes his chibouque see all Paris pass before him."

"You have no idea, then, Morrel?" asked Château-Renaud; "you do not propose anything?"

"Oh, yes," returned the young man, smiling; "on the contrary, I have one; but I expected the count would be tempted by one of the brilliant proposals made him; yet as he has not replied to any of them I will venture to offer him a suite of apartments in a charming hotel, in the Pompadour style, that my sister has inhabited for a year, in the Rue Meslay."

"You have a sister?" asked the count.

"Yes, monsieur, a most excellent sister."

"Married?"

"Nearly nine years."

"Happy?" asked the count again.

"As happy as it is permitted to a human creature to be," replied Maximilian. "She married the man she loved, who remained faithful to us in our fallen fortunes,—Emmanuel Herbaut." Monte Cristo smiled imperceptibly. "I live there during my leave of absence," continued Maximilian; "and I shall be, together with my brother-in-law Emmanuel, at the disposition of Monsieur the Count whenever he thinks fit to honour us."

"One minute!" cried Albert, without giving Monte Cristo the time to reply. "Take care; you are going to shut up a traveller,—Sinbad the Sailor, a man who comes to see Paris,—to the routine of family life. You are going to make a patriarch of him."

"Oh, no," said Morrel; "my sister is five-and-twenty, my brother-in-law is thirty. They are gay, young, and happy. Besides, Monsieur the Count will be in his own house, and only see them when he thinks fit to do so."

"Thanks, monsieur," said Monte Cristo. "I shall content myself with being presented to your sister and her husband, if you will do me the honour to introduce me; but I cannot accept the offer of any one of these gentlemen, since my habitation is already prepared."

"What!" cried Morcerf; "you are then going to a hotel; that will be very dull for you."

"Was I so badly lodged at Rome?" said Monte Cristo, smiling.

"*Parbleu!* at Rome you spent fifty thousand piastres in furnishing your apartments; but I presume that you are not disposed to spend a similar sum every day."

"It is not that which deterred me," replied Monte Cristo; "but as I determined to have a house to myself, I sent on my *valet de chambre*, and he ought by this time to have bought the house and furnished it."

"But you have, then, a *valet de chambre* who knows Paris?" said Beauchamp.

"It is the first time he has ever been in Paris. He is black, and cannot speak," returned Monte Cristo.

"It is Ali!" cried Albert, in the midst of the general surprise.

"Yes; Ali himself, my Nubian mute, whom you saw, I think, at Rome."

"Certainly," said Morcerf; "I recollect him perfectly. But how could you charge a Nubian to purchase a house, and a mute to furnish it? he will have done everything wrong, poor fellow."

"Undeceive yourself, monsieur," replied Monte Cristo; "I am quite sure that on the contrary he will have chosen everything as I wish. He knows my tastes, my caprices, my wants; he has been here a week, with the instinct of a hound, hunting by himself; he will have arranged everything to suit me. He knew I should arrive to-day at ten o'clock; since nine he awaited me at the Barrière de Fontainebleau. He gave me this paper; it contains the number of my new abode. Read it yourself," and Monte Cristo passed a paper to Albert.

"Ah, that is really original," said Beauchamp.

"And very princely," added Château-Renaud.

"What! do you not know your house?" asked Debray.

"No," said Monte Cristo; "I told you I did not wish to be behind my time; I dressed myself in the carriage, and descended at the viscount's door."

The young men looked at each other. They did not know whether it was a comedy Monte Cristo was playing, but every word he uttered had such an air of simplicity that it was impossible to suppose that what he said was false; besides, why should he tell a falsehood?

" We must content ourselves, then," said Beauchamp, " with rendering Monsieur the Count all the little services in our power. I, in my quality of journalist, open all the theatres to him."

" Thanks, monsieur," returned Monte Cristo; " my steward has orders to take a box at each theatre."

" Is your steward also a Nubian? " asked Debray.

" No, he is a countryman of yours, if a Corsican is a countryman of any one's. But you know him, M. de Morcerf."

" Is it that excellent M. Bertuccio, who understands hiring windows so well? "

" Yes; you saw him the day I had the honour of receiving you. He has been a soldier, a smuggler,—in fact, everything. I would not be quite sure that he has not been involved with the police for some trifle,—a stab with a knife, for instance."

" And you have chosen this honest citizen for your steward," said Debray. " Of how much does he rob you every year? "

" On my word," replied the count, " not more than another, I am sure. He answers my purpose, knows no impossibility, and so I keep him."

" Then," continued Château-Renaud, " since you have an establishment, a steward, and a hotel in the Champs Elysées, you want nothing more but a mistress."

Albert smiled. He thought of the fair Greek he had seen in the count's box at the Argentina and Valle theatres.

" I have something better than that," said Monte Cristo; " I have a slave. You procure your mistresses from the Opera, the Vaudeville, or the Variétés; I purchased mine at Constantinople. It cost me more, but I have nothing to fear."

" But you forget," replied Debray, laughing, " that we are Franks by name and frank by nature, as King Charles said; and that the moment she puts her foot in France your slave becomes free."

" Who will tell her? "

" The first person who sees her."

" She speaks only Romaic."

" That is another thing."

" But at least we shall see her," said Beauchamp; " or do you keep eunuchs as well as mutes? "

" Oh, no," replied Monte Cristo; " I do not carry Orientalism so far. Every one about me is free to quit me, and when he leaves me will no longer have any need of me or any one else; it is for that reason, perhaps, that they do not quit me."

They had long since passed to dessert and cigars.

"My dear Albert," said Debray, rising, "it is half-past two. Your guest is charming; but there is no company so good but that one must leave it, and sometimes for bad company. I must return to the minister's. I will tell him of the count, and we shall soon know who he is."

"Take care," returned Albert; "no one has been able to accomplish that."

"Oh, we have three millions for our police. It is true they are almost always spent beforehand; but no matter, we shall still have fifty thousand livres to spend for this purpose."

"And when you know, will you tell me?"

"I promise you. *Au revoir*, Albert. Gentlemen, good-morning."

As he left the room, Debray called out loudly, "My carriage!"

"Bravo!" said Beauchamp to Albert; "I shall not go to the Chamber, but I have something better to offer my readers than a speech of M. Danglars."

"For Heaven's sake, Beauchamp," returned Morcerf, "not a word, I beg of you; do not deprive me of the merit of introducing him and explaining him. Is he not peculiar?"

"He is more than that," replied Château-Renaud; "he is one of the most extraordinary men I ever saw in my life. Are you coming, Morrel?"

"As soon as I have given my card to Monsieur the Count, who has promised to pay us a visit at Rue Meslay, No. 14."

"Be sure I shall not fail to do so," returned the count, bowing. And Maximilian Morrel left the room with the Baron de Château-Renaud, leaving Monte Cristo alone with Morcerf.

CHAPTER XLI

THE PRESENTATION

WHEN Albert found himself alone with Monte Cristo, "Monsieur the Count," said he, "allow me to commence my cicerone-ship by showing you a specimen of a bachelor's apartments. You, who are accustomed to the palaces of Italy, can amuse yourself by calculating in how many square feet a young man who is not the worst lodged in Paris can live. As we pass from one room to another, I will open the windows to let you breathe."

Monte Cristo had already seen the breakfast-room and the salon on the ground-floor. Albert led him first to his studio, which was, as we have said, his favourite apartment. Monte Cristo was a worthy appreciator of all that Albert had collected here; old cabinets, Japan porcelain, Oriental stuffs, Venice glass, arms from all parts of the world,—everything was familiar to him, and at the first glance he recognised their date, their country, and their origin. Morcerf had expected he should be the guide; on the contrary, it was he who under the count's guidance followed a course of archæology, mineralogy, and natural history. They descended to the first floor; Albert led his guest into the salon. The salon was filled with the works of modern artists; there were landscapes by Dupré, with their long reeds and tall trees, their lowing oxen and marvellous skies; Delacroix's Arabian cavaliers, with their long white burnooses, their shining belts, their damaskeened arms, their horses, who tore each other with their teeth while their riders contended fiercely with their maces; *aquarelles* of Boulanger, representing Notre Dame de Paris with that vigour that makes the artist the rival of the poet; there were paintings by Dias, who makes his flowers more beautiful than flowers, his suns more brilliant than the sun; designs by Decamps, as vividly coloured as those of Salvator Rosa, but more poetic; pastels by Giraud and Müller, representing children like angels, and women with the features of virgins; sketches torn from the album of Dauzat's *Travels in the East*, that had been made in a few seconds on the saddle of a camel, or beneath the dome of a mosque,—in a word, all that modern art can give in exchange and as recompense for the art lost and gone with ages long since past.

Albert expected to have something new this time to show to the traveller, but to his great surprise the latter, without seeking for the signatures, many of which indeed were only initials, named instantly the author of every picture in such a manner that it was easy to see that each name was not only known to him, but that the style of each had been appreciated and studied by him. From the salon they passed into the bedchamber; it was a model of taste and simple elegance. A single portrait, signed " Léopold Robert," shone in its carved and gilded frame. This portrait attracted the Count of Monte Cristo's attention, for he made three rapid steps in the chamber, and stopped suddenly before it. It was the portrait of a young woman twenty-five or twenty-six years old, with a dark complexion, and light and lustrous eyes, veiled beneath their long lashes. She wore the picturesque costume of the Catalan fisherwomen, —a red and black bodice, and the golden pins in her hair. She was looking at the sea, and her shadow was defined on the blue ocean and sky. The light was so faint in the room that Albert did not perceive the paleness that spread itself over the count's visage, or the nervous heaving of his chest and shoulders. Silence prevailed for an instant, during which Monte Cristo gazed intently on the picture.

"You have there a most charming mistress, viscount," said the count, in a perfectly calm tone; "and this costume—a ball costume, doubtless—becomes her most admirably."

"Ah, monsieur!" returned Albert, "I would never forgive you this mistake if you had seen another picture beside this. You do not know my mother. She it is whom you see here; she had her portrait painted thus six or eight years ago. This costume is a fancy one, it appears, and the resemblance is so great that I think I still see my mother the same as she was in 1830. The countess had this portrait painted during the count's absence. She doubtless intended giving him an agreeable surprise; but strange to say, this portrait seemed to displease my father, and the value of the picture, which is, as you see, one of the best works of Léopold Robert, could not overcome his dislike to it. It is true, between ourselves, that M. de Morcerf is one of the most assiduous peers at the Luxembourg, a general renowned for theory, but a most mediocre amateur of art. It is different with my mother, who paints exceedingly well, and who, unwilling to part with so valuable a picture, gave it to me to put here, where it would be less likely to displease M. de Morcerf, whose portrait, by Gros, I will also show you. Excuse my talking of family matters; but as I shall have the honour of introducing you to the count, I tell you this to prevent your making any allusions to this picture. The picture seems to have a malign influence, for my mother rarely comes here without looking at it, and still more rarely does she look at it without weeping. This disagreement is the only one that has ever taken place between the count and countess, who are still as much united, although married more than twenty years, as on the day of their wedding."

Monte Cristo glanced rapidly at Albert as if to seek a hidden meaning in his words; but it was evident the young man uttered them in the simplicity of his heart.

"Now," said Albert, "that you have seen all my treasures, allow me to offer them to you, unworthy as they are. Consider yourself as in your own house; and to put yourself still more at your ease, pray accompany me to the apartments of M. de Morcerf, to whom I wrote from Rome an account of the services you rendered me, and to whom I announced your promised visit. And I may say that both the count and countess anxiously desire to thank you in person. You are somewhat *blasé*, I know; and family scenes have not much effect on Sinbad the Sailor, who has seen so many others. However, accept what I propose to you as an initiation into Parisian life,—a life of politeness, visiting, and introductions."

Monte Cristo bowed without making any answer; he accepted the offer without enthusiasm and without regret, as one of those conventions of society which every gentleman looks upon as a duty. Albert summoned his servant and ordered him to acquaint Monsieur and Madame de Morcerf of the arrival of the Count of Monte Cristo. Albert followed him with the count. When they arrived at the ante-chamber, above the door was visible a shield, which by its rich ornaments and its harmony with the rest of the furniture indicated the importance the owner attached to this blazon. Monte Cristo stopped and examined it attentively.

"Azure seven merlets, or, placed bender," said he. "These are doubtless your family arms? Except for the knowledge of blazons, that enables me to decipher them, I am very ignorant of heraldry,—I, a count of a fresh creation, fabricated in Tuscany by the aid of a commandery of Saint Stephen, and who would not have taken the trouble had I not been told that when you travel much it is necessary. Besides, you must have something on the panels of your carriage to escape being searched by the custom-house officers. Excuse my putting such a question to you."

"It is not indiscreet," returned Morcerf, with the simplicity of conviction. "You have guessed rightly. These are our arms,—that is, those of my father; but they are, as you see, joined to another shield, which has gules, a silver tower, which are my mother's. By her side I am Spanish; but the family of Morcerf is French, and I have heard, one of the oldest of the south of France."

"Yes," replied Monte Cristo, "these blazons prove that; almost all the armed pilgrims that went to the Holy Land took for their arms either a cross, in honour of their mission, or birds of passage, in sign of the long voyage they were about to undertake, and which they hoped to accomplish on the wings of faith. One of your ancestors had joined the Crusades; and supposing it to be only that of Saint Louis, that makes you mount to the thirteenth century, which is tolerably ancient."

"It is possible," said Morcerf; "my father has in his study a genealogical tree which will tell you all that, and on which I made commentaries that would have greatly edified Hozier and Jaucourt. At present I no longer think of it; and yet I must tell you that we are beginning to occupy ourselves greatly with these things under our popular government."

"Well, then, your government would do well to choose from the past something better than the things that I have noticed on your monuments, and which have no heraldic meaning whatever. As for you, viscount," continued Monte Cristo to Morcerf, "you are more fortunate than the government, for your arms are really beautiful, and speak to the imagination. Yes, you are at once from Provence and Spain; that explains, if the portrait you showed me be like, the dark hue I so much admired on the visage of the noble Catalane."

It would have required the penetration of Œdipus or the Sphinx to have divined the irony the count concealed beneath these words, apparently uttered with the greatest politeness. Morcerf thanked him with a smile, and pushed open the door above which were his arms, and which, as we have said, opened into the salon. In the most conspicuous part of the salon was another portrait. It was that of a man from thirty-five to thirty-eight years old, in the uniform of a general officer, wearing the double epaulette of gold and silver that indicates superior rank; the ribbon of the Legion of Honour round his neck, which showed he was a commander; and on the breast, on the right, the star of a grand officer of the order of the Saviour; and on the left that of the grand cross of Charles III., which proved that the person represented by the picture had served in the wars of Greece and Spain, or, what was just the same thing as regarded decorations, had fulfilled some diplomatic mission in the two countries.

Monte Cristo was engaged in examining this portrait with no less care than he had bestowed upon the other, when another door opened and he found himself in the presence of the Comte de Morcerf himself. He was a man of forty to forty-five years; but he seemed at least fifty, and his black mustache and eyebrows contrasted strangely with his almost white hair, which was cut short in the military fashion. He was dressed in plain clothes and wore at his button-hole the ribbons of the different orders to which he belonged. This man entered with a tolerably dignified step and with a species of haste. Monte Cristo saw him advance towards him without making a single step. It seemed as if his feet were fixed to the ground as his gaze was fixed on the Comte de Morcerf.

"Father," said the young man, " I have the honour of

presenting to you M. le Comte de Monte Cristo, the generous friend whom I had the good fortune to meet in the critical juncture of which I have told you."

"You are most welcome, monsieur," said the Comte de Morcerf, saluting Monte Cristo with a smile; "and monsieur has rendered our house, in preserving its only heir, a service which insures him our eternal gratitude."

As he said these words, the Comte de Morcerf pointed to a chair, while he seated himself in another opposite the window. Monte Cristo, while he took the seat Morcerf offered him, placed himself in such a manner as to remain concealed in the shadow of the large velvet curtains, and there he read on the careworn and livid features of the count a whole history of secret griefs written in each wrinkle planted by time.

"Madame the Countess," said Morcerf, "was at her toilet when she was informed of the visit she was about to receive. She will however be in the salon in ten minutes."

"It is a great honour for me," returned Monte Cristo, "to be thus, on the first day of my arrival in Paris, brought in contact with a man whose merit equals his reputation, and to whom fortune has for once been equitable; but has she not still on the plains of Mitidja, or in the mountains of Atlas, a marshal's staff to offer you?"

"Oh," replied Morcerf, reddening slightly, "I have left the service, monsieur. Made a peer at the Restoration, I served through the first campaign under the orders of Maréchal Bourmont. I could therefore expect a higher rank; and who knows what might have happened had the elder branch remained on the throne? But the Revolution of July was, it seems, sufficiently glorious to allow itself to be ungrateful; and it was so for all services that did not date from the imperial period. I tendered my resignation; for when you have gained your epaulettes on the battle-field, you do not know how to manœuvre on the slippery ground of the salons. I have hung up my sword and cast myself into politics. I have devoted myself to industry; I study the useful arts. During the twenty years I served, I often wished to do so, but I had not the time."

"These are the ideas that render your nation superior to any other," returned Monte Cristo. "A gentleman of high birth, possessor of an ample fortune, you have consented to gain your promotion as an obscure soldier, step by step,—this is uncommon; then become general, peer of France, commander of the Legion of Honour, you consent to begin a second apprenticeship, without any other hope or any other desire than that of one day becoming useful to your fellow-creatures,—this indeed is praiseworthy, nay, more, it is sublime."

Albert looked on and listened with astonishment; he was not used to see Monte Cristo give vent to such bursts of enthusiasm.

"Alas!" continued the stranger, doubtless to dispel the slight cloud that covered Morcerf's brow, "we do not act thus in Italy; we grow according to our race and our species, and we pursue the same lines, and often the same uselessness all our lives."

"But, monsieur," said the Comte de Morcerf, "for a man of your merit, Italy is not a country, and France opens her arms to receive you; respond to her call. France will not perhaps be ungrateful to all the world; she treats her children ill, but she always welcomes strangers."

"Ah, father!" said Albert, with a smile, "it is evident you do not know M. le Comte de Monte Cristo; he despises all honours, and contents himself with those that are written on his passport."

"That is the most just remark," replied the stranger, "I ever heard made concerning myself!"

"You have been free to choose your career," observed the Comte de Morcerf, with a sigh; "and you have chosen the path strewed with flowers."

"Precisely, monsieur," replied Monte Cristo, with one of those smiles that a painter could never represent nor a physiologist analyse.

"If I did not fear to fatigue you," said the general, evidently charmed with the count's manners, "I would have taken you to the Chamber; there is to-day a debate which would be very interesting to those who are strangers to our modern senators."

"I shall be most grateful, monsieur, if you will at some future time renew your offer; but I have been flattered with the hope of being presented to the countess, and I will therefore wait."

"Ah! here is my mother," cried the viscount.

Monte Cristo turned round hastily and saw Madame de Morcerf at the entrance of the salon, at the door opposite to that by which her husband had entered, pale and motionless; when Monte Cristo turned round, she let fall her arm, which for some unknown reason had been resting on the gilded door-post. She had been there some moments and had overheard the last words of the visitor. The latter rose and bowed to the countess, who inclined herself without speaking.

"Ah! good heavens, madame!" said the count, "are you unwell, or is it the heat of the room that affects you?"

" Are you ill, mother? " cried the viscount, springing towards Mercédès.

She thanked them both with a smile. " No," returned she; " but I feel some emotion on seeing for the first time the man without whose intervention we should have been in tears and desolation. Monsieur," continued the countess, advancing with the majesty of a queen, " I owe to you the life of my son, and for this I bless you. Now I thank you for the pleasure you give me in thus affording me the opportunity of thanking you as I have blessed you, from the bottom of my heart."

The count bowed again, but lower than before; he was even paler than Mercédès. " Madame," said he, " Monsieur the Count and yourself recompense too generously a simple action. To save a man, to spare a father's feelings or a mother's sensibility, is not to do a good action, but a simple deed of humanity."

At these words, uttered with the most exquisite sweetness and politeness, Madame de Morcerf replied, " It is very fortunate for my son, monsieur, that he found such a friend, and I thank God who has brought these things to pass." And Mercédès raised her fine eyes to heaven with so fervent an expression of gratitude that the count fancied he saw tears in them. M. de Morcerf approached her.

" Madame," said he, " I have already made my excuses to Monsieur the Count for quitting him, and I pray you renew them. The sitting commences at two; it is now three, and I am to speak."

" Go, then, and I will endeavour to make our guest forget your absence! " replied the countess, with the same tone of deep feeling. " Monsieur the Count," continued she, turning to Monte Cristo, " will you do us the honour of passing the rest of the day with us? "

" Believe me, madame, I feel most grateful for your kindness, but I came to your door this morning in my travelling-carriage. How I am established in Paris I do not yet know, and hardly know where,—a trivial matter, I admit, but causing me some inquietude."

" At least, we shall have this pleasure another time," said the countess; " you promise that? "

Monte Cristo inclined himself without answering; but the gesture might pass for assent.

" I will not detain you, monsieur," continued the countess; " I would not have our gratitude become indiscreet or importunate."

" My dear count," said Albert, " I will endeavour to return

your politeness at Rome, and place my coupé at your disposal until you have had time to provide yourself with carriages."

" A thousand thanks for your kindness, viscount," returned the Count of Monte Cristo; " but I suppose that M. Bertuccio has suitably employed the four hours and a half I have given him, and that I shall find a carriage of some sort ready at the door."

Albert was used to the count's manner of proceeding; he knew that like Nero he was in search of the impossible. Nothing, now, that the count might do could surprise him; but wishing to judge with his own eyes how far the count's orders had been executed, he accompanied him to the door of the hotel. Monte Cristo was not deceived. As soon as he appeared in the Comte de Morcerf's ante-chamber, a footman, the same who at Rome had brought the count's card to the two young men and announced his visit, sprang into the vestibule, and when he arrived at the door the illustrious traveller found his carriage awaiting him. It was a coupé of Koller's building, and with horses and harness for which Drake had, to the knowledge of all the lions of Paris, refused on the previous day eighteen thousand livres.

" Monsieur," said the count to Albert, " I do not ask you to accompany me to my house, as I can only show you a habitation fitted up in a hurry, and I have, as you know, a reputation to keep up for impromptu achievements. Give me, therefore, one more day before I invite you; I shall then be certain not to fail in my hospitality."

" If you ask me for a day, count, I know what to anticipate; it will not be a house I shall see, but a palace. You have decidedly some *génie* at your control."

" Good! spread that idea," replied Monte Cristo, putting his foot on the velvet-lined steps of his splendid carriage, " and that will be worth something to me among the ladies."

As he spoke he sprang into the vehicle, the door was closed, and he started off at a gallop, but not so rapidly but that he could notice the almost imperceptible movement which stirred the curtains of the apartment in which he had left Madame de Morcerf.

When Albert returned to his mother, he found her in the boudoir, reclining in a large velvet armchair—the whole room so obscure that only the shining spangle, fastened here and there to the drapery, and the angles of the gilded frames of the pictures, gave a kind of light to the room. Albert could not see the countenance of the countess, which was lost in a thin veil she had put on her head, and which descended around her features like a cloud of vapour; but it seemed to him as though her voice had altered. He could distinguish amid the perfumes of the roses and heliotropes in the flower-stands the sharp and fragrant odour of volatile salts, and he remarked in one of the chased cups on the mantel-piece the countess's smelling-bottle, taken from its shagreen case; and he exclaimed in a tone of uneasiness as he entered, "My dear mother, have you been unwell during my absence?"

"No, no, Albert! but you know these roses, tuberoses, and orange-flowers throw out at first, before one is used to them, such violent perfumes."

"Then, my dear mother," said Albert, putting his hand to the bell, "they must be taken into the ante-chamber. You are really unwell; just now, when you came into the room, you were very pale."

"Was I pale, Albert?"

"Yes; a paleness that suits you admirably, mother, but which did not the less alarm my father and myself!"

"Did your father speak of it?" inquired Mercédès, eagerly.

"No, madame; but do you not remember that he remarked the fact to you?"

"Yes, I do remember," replied the countess.

A servant entered, summoned by Albert's ring of the bell.

"Take these flowers into the ante-room or dressing-room," said the viscount. "They make the countess unwell."

The footman obeyed his orders. A long pause ensued, which lasted until all the flowers were removed. "What is his name of Monte Cristo?" inquired the countess, when the servant had taken away the last vase of flowers. "Is it a family name, or the name of the estate, or a simple title?"

"I believe, mother, it is merely a title. The count purchased an island in the Tuscan Archipelago, and, as he told you to-day, has founded a commandery. You know the same thing was done for Saint Stephen of Florence, Saint George Constantinian of Parma, and even for the order of Malta. Except this, he has no pretension to nobility, and calls himself a chance count, although the general opinion at Rome is that the count is a man of very high distinction."

"His manners are admirable," said the countess; "at least, as far as I could judge in the few moments he remained here."

"They are perfect, mother; so perfect that they surpass by far all I have known in the leading aristocracy of the three proudest nobilities of Europe,—the English, Spanish, and German."

The countess reflected a moment; then, after a slight hesitation, she said, " You have seen, my dear Albert,—I ask the question as a mother,—you have seen M. de Monte Cristo in his house; you are quick-sighted, have much knowledge of the world, more tact than is usual at your age,—do you think the count is really what he appears to be? "

" What does he appear to be? "

" Why, you have just said,—a man of high distinction."

" I told you, my dear mother, he was esteemed such."

" But what is your own opinion, Albert? "

" I must tell you that I have not come to any decided opinion respecting him, but I think him a Maltese."

" I do not ask you of his origin, but what he is."

" Ah! what he is; that is quite another thing. I have seen so many remarkable things in connection with him that if you would have me really say what I think, I shall reply that I really do look upon him as one of Byron's heroes, whom misery has marked with a fatal brand,—some Manfred, some Lara, some Werner, one of those relics, in short, of some ancient family, who, disinherited of their patrimony, have achieved fortune by the force of their adventurous genius, which has placed them above the laws of society."

" You say—"

" I say that Monte Cristo is an island in the midst of the Mediterranean, without inhabitants or garrison,—the resort of smugglers of all nations, and pirates of every flag. Who knows whether or not these industrious worthies do not pay to their feudal lord some dues for his protection? "

" That is possible," said the countess, reflecting.

" Never mind," continued the young man; " smuggler or not, you must agree, mother dear, as you have seen him, that the Count of Monte Cristo is a remarkable man, who will have the greatest success in the salons of Paris. Why, this very morning, at my abode, he began his entrance into society by striking every man of us with amazement, not even excepting Château-Renaud! "

" And what do you suppose is the count's age? " inquired Mercédès, evidently attaching great importance to this question.

" Thirty-five or thirty-six, mother."

" So young! it is impossible," said Mercédès, replying at the same time to what Albert said as well as to her own private reflection.

" It is the truth, however. Three or four times he has said to me, and certainly without the slightest premeditation: At such a period I was five years old, at another ten years old, at another twelve; and I, induced by curiosity which kept me alive at these details, have compared the dates, and never found him inaccurate. The age of this singular man, who is of no age, is then, I am certain, thirty-five. Besides, mother, remark how vivid his eye, how raven-black his hair; and his brow, through so pale, is free from wrinkles,—he is not only vigorous, but also young."

The countess bent her head as if beneath a heavy wave of bitter thoughts. "And has this man displayed a friendship for you, Albert?" she asked with a nervous shudder.

"I am inclined to think so."

"And—do—you—like—him?"

"Why, he pleases me in spite of Franz d'Epinay, who tries to convince me that he is a being returned from the other world."

The countess shuddered. "Albert," she said in a voice which was altered by emotion, "I have always put you on your guard against new acquaintances. Now you are a man, and are able to give me advice; yet I repeat to you, Albert, be prudent."

"Why, my dear mother, it is necessary in order to make your advice practicable that I should know beforehand what I have to distrust. The count never plays; he only drinks pure water tinged with a little sherry, and is so rich that he cannot, without intending to laugh at me, try to borrow money. What, then, have I to fear from him?"

"You are right," said the countess; "and my fears are weakness, especially when directed against a man who has saved your life. How did your father receive him, Albert? It is necessary that we should be more than complaisant to the count. M. de Morcerf is sometimes preoccupied,—his affairs make him anxious; and he might, without intending it—"

"Nothing could be in better taste than my father's demeanour, madame," said Albert; "nay, more, he seemed greatly flattered at two or three compliments which the count very skilfully and agreeably paid him with as much ease as if he had known him these thirty years. Each of these little tickling arrows must have pleased my father," added Albert, with a laugh. "And thus they parted the best possible friends; and M. de Morcerf even wished to take him to the Chamber to hear the speakers."

The countess made no reply. She fell into so deep a reverie that her eyes gradually closed. The young man, standing up before her, gazed upon her with that filial affection which is more tender and endearing with children whose mother are still young and handsome. Then, after seeing her eyes closed, and hearing her breathe gently, he believed she had dropped asleep, and left the apartment on tiptoe, closing the door after him with the utmost precaution. " This devil of a fellow ! " he muttered, shaking his head; " I said at the time he would create a sensation here, and I measure his effect by an infallible thermometer. My mother has noticed him, and he must therefore perforce be remarkable." He went down to the stables, not without some slight annoyance when he remembered that the Count of Monte Cristo had laid his hands on a " turnout " which sent his bays down to number two in the opinion of connoisseurs. " Most decidedly," said he, " men are not equal; I must beg my father to develop this subject in the Chamber of Peers."

CHAPTER XLII

MONSIEUR BERTUCCIO

DURING this time the count had arrived at his house. It had taken him six minutes to perform the distance; but these six minutes were sufficient to induce twenty young men who knew the price of the equipage they had been unable to purchase themselves, to put their horses to a gallop in order to see the rich foreigner who could afford to give ten thousand livres apiece for his horses. The house Ali had chosen, and which was to serve as a town residence to Monte Cristo, was situated on the right hand as you ascend the Champs Elysées. A thick clump of trees and shrubs rose in the centre, and masked a portion of the front; around this shrubbery two alleys, like two arms, extended right and left, and formed a carriage-drive from the iron gates to a double portico, on every step of which stood a porcelain vase filled with flowers. This house, isolated from the rest, had besides the main entrance another in the Rue Ponthieu. Even before the coachman had hailed the *concierge*, the massy gates rolled on their hinges; they had seen the count coming, and at Paris, as everywhere else, he was served with the rapidity of lightning. The coachman entered and descended the half-circle without slackening his speed, and the gates were closed ere the wheels had ceased to sound on the gravel. The carriage stopped at the left side of the portico; two men presented themselves at the carriage-window. The one was Ali, who, smiling with an expression of the most sincere joy, seemed amply repaid by a mere look from Monte Cristo; the other bowed respectfully, and offered his arm to assist the count in descending.

"Thanks, M. Bertuccio," said the count, lightly springing up the three steps of the portico; "and the notary?"

"He is in the small salon, excellency," returned Bertuccio.

"And the cards I ordered to be engraved as soon as you knew the number of the house?"

"Monsieur the Count, it is done already. I have been myself to the best engraver of the Palais-Royal, who did the plate in my presence. The first card struck off was taken, according to your orders, to M. le Baron Danglars, Rue de la Chaussée d'Antin, No. 7; the others are on the mantel-piece of your excellency's bedroom."

"Good; what o'clock is it?"

"Four o'clock."

Monte Cristo gave his hat, cane, and gloves to the same French footman who had called his carriage at the Comte de Morcerf's, and then he passed into the small salon, preceded by Bertuccio, who showed him the way.

"These are but indifferent marbles in this ante-chamber," said Monte Cristo. "I trust they all will soon be taken away."

Bertuccio bowed. As the steward had said, the notary awaited the count in the small salon. He was a simple-looking lawyer's clerk, elevated to the extraordinary dignity of a provincial scrivener.

"You are the notary empowered to sell the country-house that I wish to purchase, monsieur?" asked Monte Cristo.

"Yes, Monsieur the Count," returned the notary.

"Is the deed of sale ready?"

"Yes, Monsieur the Count."

"Have you brought it?"

"Here it is."

"Very well; and where is this house that I purchase?" asked the count, carelessly, addressing himself half to Bertuccio, half to the notary. The steward made a gesture that signified "I do not know." The notary looked at the count with astonishment. "What!" said he, "does not Monsieur the Count know where the house he purchases is situated?"

"No," returned the count.

"Monsieur the Count does not know it?"

"How should I know it? I have arrived from Cadiz this morning. I have never before been in Paris; and it is the first time I have ever even set my foot in France!"

"Ah! that is different; the house you purchase is situated "
Auteuil." At these words Bertuccio turned pale.

"And where is Auteuil?" asked the count.

"Two steps from here, monsieur," replied the notary; "a little beyond Passy,—a charming situation, in the heart of the Bois de Boulogne."

"So near as that?" said the count; "but that is not in the country. What made you choose a house at the gates of Paris, M. Bertuccio?"

"I!" cried the steward, with a strange expression. "Monsieur the Count did not charge me to purchase this house. If Monsieur the Count will recollect—if he will think—"

"Ah, true," observed Monte Cristo; "I recollect now. I read the advertisement in one of the papers, and was tempted by the false title, 'a country-house.'"

"It is not yet too late," cried Bertuccio, eagerly; "and if your excellency will intrust me with the commission, I will find you a better at Enghien, at Fontenay aux Roses, or at Bellevue."

"Oh, no," returned Monte Cristo, negligently; "since I have this, I will keep it."

"And you are quite right," said the notary, who feared to lose his fee. "It is a charming place,—running water, fine trees, a comfortable habitation, although abandoned for a long time, without reckoning the furniture, which, although old, is yet valuable now that old things are so much sought after. I suppose Monsieur the Count has the tastes of the day?"

"To be sure," returned Monte Cristo; "it is very convenient, then?"

"It is more,—it is magnificent."

"*Peste!* let us not lose such an opportunity," returned Monte Cristo. "The deed, if you please, Monsieur the Notary." And he signed it rapidly, after having first run his eye over that part of the deed in which were specified the situation of the house and the name of the proprietors. "Bertuccio," said he, "give fifty-five thousand livres to monsieur." The steward left the room with a faltering step, and returned with a bundle of banknotes, which the notary counted like a man who never gives a receipt for money until after legal examination.

"And now," demanded the count, "are all the forms complied with?"

"All, Monsieur the Count."

"Have you the keys?"

"They are in the hands of the *concierge*, who takes care of the house; but here is the order which I have written him to install Monsieur the Count in his new possession."

"Very well;" and Monte Cristo made a sign with his hand

to the notary, which said, " I have no further need of you; you may go."

" But," observed the honest notary, " you are mistaken, I think, Monsieur the Count; it is only fifty thousand livres, everything included."

" And your fee? "

" Is included in this sum."

" But have you not come from Auteuil here? "

" Yes, certainly."

" Well, then, it is but fair that you should be paid for your loss of time and trouble," said the count; and he made a gesture of polite dismissal. The notary left the room backwards, and bowing down to the ground; it was the first time he had ever met such a client.

" See this gentleman out," said the count to Bertuccio. And the steward followed the notary out of the room.

Scarcely was the count alone, when he drew from his pocket a book closed with a lock, and opened it with a key which he wore round his neck, and which never left him. After having sought for a few minutes, he stopped at a leaf which contained a few notes and compared them with the deed of sale which lay on the table, and reviving his recollections, " ' Auteuil, Rue de la Fontaine, No. 28.' It is indeed the same," said he; " and now, am I to rely upon an avowal extorted by religious or by physical terror? However, in an hour I shall know all. Bertuccio! " cried he, striking a light hammer with a pliant handle on a small gong. " Bertuccio! " The steward appeared at the door. " M. Bertuccio," said the count, " did you not once tell me that you had travelled in France? "

" In some parts of France,—yes, excellency."

" You know the environs of Paris, then? "

" No, excellency, no," returned the steward, with a sort of nervous trembling which Monte Cristo, a connoisseur in all emotions, rightly attributed to great disquietude.

" It is unfortunate," returned he, " that you have never visited the environs, for I wish to see my new property this evening; and in going with me you might have given me some useful information."

" To Auteuil! " cried Bertuccio, whose copper complexion became livid,—" I go to Auteuil? "

" Well, what is there surprising in that? When I live at Auteuil you must come there, as you belong to my service."

Bertuccio hung down his head before the imperious look of his master and remained motionless, without making any answer.

" Why, what has happened to you? Are you going to make me ring a second time for the carriage? " asked Monte Cristo, in the same tone that Louis XIV. pronounced the famous, " I have been almost obliged to wait."

Bertuccio made but one bound to the ante-chamber and cried in a hoarse voice, " His excellency's horses! "

Monte Cristo wrote two or three notes; and as he sealed the last the steward appeared. " Your excellency's carriage is at the door," said he.

" Well, take your hat and gloves," returned Monte Cristo.

" Am I to accompany you, Monsieur the Count? " cried Bertuccio

Certainly, you must give your orders, for I intend residing at the house."

It was unexampled for a servant of the count's to dare to dispute an order of his; so the steward, without saying a word, followed his master, who got into the carriage and signed him to follow, which he did, seating himself respectfully on the front seat.

CHAPTER XLIII

THE HOUSE AT AUTEUIL

MONTE CRISTO had remarked that as they descended the stair-case Bertuccio signed himself in the Corsican manner,—that is, had formed the sign of the cross in the air with his thumb,—and as he seated himself in the carriage, muttered a short prayer. Any one but a curious man would have had pity on seeing the steward's extraordinary repugnance for the count's projected drive beyond the walls; but it seemed the count was too curious to excuse Bertuccio this little journey. In twenty minutes they were at Auteuil; the steward's emotion had continued to increase as they entered the village. Bertuccio, crouched in a corner of the carriage, began to examine with a feverish anxiety every house they passed.

" Tell them to stop at Rue de la Fontaine, No. 28," said the count, fixing his eyes on the steward, to whom he gave this order.

Bertuccio's forehead was covered with perspiration; but he obeyed, and leaning out of the window he cried to the coachman, " Rue de la Fontaine, No. 28."

No. 28 was situated at the extremity of the village; during the drive night had set in, or rather a black cloud charged with

lectricity gave to that early darkness the appearance and
olemnity of a dramatic episode. The carriage stopped; the
ootman sprang off the box, and opened the door.

"Well," said the count, "you do not get out, M. Bertuccio,—
ou are going to stay in the carriage, then? What are you
hinking of this evening?"

Bertuccio sprang out and offered his shoulder to the count,
rho this time leaned upon it as he descended the three steps of
he carriage.

"Knock," said the count, "and announce me."

Bertuccio knocked; the door opened, and the *concierge*
ppeared. "What is it?" asked he.

"It is your new master, my good fellow," said the footman;
nd he held out to the *concierge* the notary's order.

"The house is sold, then?" demanded the *concierge;* "and
his gentleman is coming to live here?"

"Yes, my friend," returned the count; "and I will endeavour
o give you no cause to regret your old master."

"Oh, monsieur," said the *concierge,* "I shall not have much
ause to regret him, for he came here but seldom. It is five
ears since he was here last; and he did well to sell the house,
or it did not bring him in anything at all."

"What was the name of your old master?" said Monte Cristo.

"M. le Marquis de Saint-Méran. Ah, I am sure he has not
old the house for what he gave for it."

"The Marquis de Saint-Méran!" returned the count. "The
ame is not unknown to me; the Marquis de Saint-Méran!"
nd he appeared to meditate.

"An old gentleman," continued the *concierge,* "a stanch
ollower of the Bourbons; he had an only daughter, who married
I. de Villefort, who had been the *procureur du roi* at Nîmes,
nd afterwards at Versailles."

Monte Cristo glanced at Bertuccio, who became whiter than
he wall against which he leaned to prevent himself from falling.
"And is not this daughter dead?" demanded Monte Cristo;
I fancy I have heard so."

"Yes, monsieur, twenty-one years ago; and since then we
ave not seen the poor marquis three times."

"Thanks, thanks," said Monte Cristo, judging from the
eward's utter prostration that he could not stretch the cord
urther without danger of breaking it. "Give me a light."

"Shall I accompany you, monsieur?"

"No, it is unnecessary; Bertuccio will light me." And
Ionte Cristo accompanied these words by the gift of two pieces

of gold, which produced a torrent of thanks and blessings from
the *concierge*.

" Ah, monsieur," said he, after having vainly searched on the
mantel-piece and the shelves, " I have no candles."

" Take one of the carriage-lamps, Bertuccio," said the count,
" and show me the apartments."

The steward obeyed in silence; but it was easy to see from
the manner in which the hand that held the light trembled, how
much it cost him to obey. They went over a tolerably large
ground-floor, a first floor consisting of a salon, a bathroom, and
two bedrooms; by one of these bedrooms they arrived at a
winding staircase that opened on to the garden.

" Ah! here is a private staircase," said the count; " that is
convenient. Light me, M. Bertuccio, and go first; we will see
where it leads to."

" Monsieur," replied Bertuccio, " it leads to the garden."

" And, pray, how do you know that?"

" It ought to do so, at least."

" Well, let us be sure of that."

Bertuccio sighed, and went on first; the stairs led, in fact, to
the garden. At the outer door the steward paused. " Go on,
M. Bertuccio," said the count. But he to whom he spoke was
stupefied, bewildered, stunned; his haggard eyes glanced round
as if in search of the traces of some terrible event, and with his
clinched hands he seemed striving to shut out some horrible
recollections.

" Well!" insisted the count.

" No, no," cried Bertuccio, setting down the lantern at the
angle of the interior wall. " No, monsieur, it is impossible;
can go no farther."

" What does this mean?" demanded the irresistible voice of
Monte Cristo.

" Why, you must see, Monsieur the Count," cried the steward,
" that this is not natural,—that having a house to purchase,
you purchase it exactly at Auteuil; and that, purchasing it at
Auteuil, this house should be No. 28, Rue de la Fontaine. Oh!
why did I not tell you all? I am sure you would not have
forced me to come. I hoped your house would have been some
other one than this; as if there was not another house at Auteuil
than that of the assassination!"

" Ah, ah!" cried Monte Cristo, stopping suddenly, " what
words did you utter? Devil of a man, Corsican that you are
—always mysteries or superstitions. Come, take the lantern,
and let us visit the garden; you are not afraid with me, I hope?"

Bertuccio raised the lantern and obeyed. The door, as it opened, disclosed a gloomy sky, in which the moon strove vainly to struggle through a sea of clouds that covered her with their sombre wave, that she illumined for an instant, and was then lost in the darkness. The steward wished to turn to the left.

"No, no, monsieur," said Monte Cristo; "what is the use of following the alleys? Here is a beautiful lawn; let us go on straight forwards."

Bertuccio wiped the perspiration from his brow, but obeyed; however, he continued to take the left hand. Monte Cristo, on the contrary, took the right hand; arrived near a clump of trees, he stopped. The steward could not restrain himself. "Move, monsieur,—move away, I entreat you; you are exactly on the spot!"

"What spot?"

"Where he fell."

"My dear M. Bertuccio," said Monte Cristo, laughing, "recover yourself; we are no longer at Sartène or at Corté. This is not a *maquis* but an English garden,—badly kept, I own, but you must not calumniate it for that."

"Monsieur, I implore you, do not stay there!"

"I think you are going mad, Bertuccio," said the count, coldly. "If that is the case, I warn you I shall have you put in a lunatic asylum."

"Alas, excellency," returned Bertuccio, joining his hands, and shaking his head in a manner that would have excited the count's laughter, had not thoughts of a superior interest occupied him and rendered him attentive to the least revelation of this timorous conscience,—"alas, excellency, the evil has arrived!"

"M. Bertuccio," said the count, "I am very glad to tell you that while you gesticulate you wring your hands and roll your eyes like a man possessed by a devil that will not leave him; and I have always remarked that the devil most obstinate to be expelled is a secret. I knew you were a Corsican; I knew you were gloomy, and always brooding over some old history of the vendetta; and I overlooked that in Italy, because in Italy those things are thought nothing of. But in France assassination is generally held to be in very bad taste; there are gendarmes who occupy themselves with such affairs, judges who condemn, and scaffolds which avenge."

Bertuccio clasped his hands, and as in all these evolutions he did not let fall the lantern, the light showed his pale and altered countenance. Monte Cristo examined him with the same expression with which at Rome he had viewed the execution o Andrea, and then, in a tone that made a shudder pass throug the veins of the poor steward, "The Abbé Busoni, then, tol me an untruth," said he, "when after his journey in France, i 1829, he sent you to me with a letter of recommendation, i which he enumerated all your valuable qualities. Well, I sha write to the abbé; I shall render him responsible for his *pro tégé's* misconduct, and I shall soon know all about this assass nation. Only I warn you that when I reside in a country, conform to all its code, and I have no wish to embroil myse with French justice for your sake."

"Oh, do not do that, excellency; I have always served yo faithfully," cried Bertuccio, in despair. "I have always bee an honest man, and as far as lay in my power I have don good."

"I do not deny it," returned the count; "but why are yo thus agitated? It is a bad sign; a quiet conscience does no occasion such paleness in the cheeks and such fever in th hands—"

"But, Monsieur the Count," replied Bertuccio, hesitatingly "did not M. l'Abbé Busoni, who heard my confession in th prison at Nîmes, tell you I had a heavy reproach to mak against myself."

"Yes; but as he said you would make an excellent stewar I concluded you had stolen,—that was all."

"Oh, Monsieur the Count!" returned Bertuccio, contempt ously.

"Or, as you are a Corsican, that you had been unable to resi the desire of making a *peau*, as you call it."

"Yes, my good master," cried Bertuccio, casting himself the count's feet; "it was simply a vengeance, nothing else."

"I understand that; but I do not understand what it is th galvanises you in this manner."

"But, monsieur, it is very natural," returned Bertucci "since it was in this house that my vengeance was accom plished."

"What! my house?"

"Oh, Monsieur the Count, it was not yours then."

"Whose, then? M. le Marquis de Saint-Méran, I think th *concierge* said. What had you to revenge on the Marquis Saint-Méran?"

"Oh, it was not on him, monsieur, it was on another."

"This is strange," returned Monte Cristo, seeming to yie to his reflections,—"that you should find yourself without an

1814 he married. When the emperor returned from the island of Elba, my brother instantly joined the army, was slightly wounded at Waterloo, and retired with the army behind the Loire."

"But that is the history of the Hundred Days, M. Bertuccio," said the count; "unless I am mistaken, it has been already written."

"Excuse me, excellency, but these details are necessary, and you promised to be patient."

"Go on; I will keep my word."

"One day we received a letter. I should tell you that we lived in the little village of Rogliano, at the extremity of Cape Corse. This letter was from my brother. He told us that the army was disbanded, and that he should return by Châteauroux, Clermont-Ferrand, Le Puy, and Nîmes; and if I had any money, he prayed me to leave it for him at Nîmes, with an innkeeper with whom I had dealings."

"In the smuggling line?" said Monte Cristo.

"Eh, Monsieur the Count? Every one must live."

"Certainly; continue."

"I loved my brother tenderly, as I told your excellency, and I resolved not to send the money, but to take it to him myself. I possessed a thousand livres. I left five hundred with Assunta, my sister-in-law, and with the other five hundred I set off for Nîmes. It was easy to do so; and as I had my boat and a lading to take in at sea, everything favoured my project. But after we had taken in our cargo, the wind became contrary, so that we were four or five days without being able to enter the Rhone. At last, however, we succeeded, and worked up to Arles; I left the boat between Bellegarde and Beaucaire, and took the road to Nîmes."

"We are getting to the story now?"

"Yes, your excellency; excuse me, but, as you will see, I only tell you what is absolutely necessary. Just at this time the famous massacres of the south of France took place. Two or three brigands, called Trestaillon, Truphemy, and Graffan, publicly assassinated everybody whom they suspected of Bonapartism. You have doubtless heard of these massacres, Monsieur the Count?"

"Vaguely; I was far from France at that period. Go on."

"As I entered Nîmes, I literally waded in blood; at every step I encountered dead bodies, and bands of the murderers, who killed, plundered, and burned. At the sight of this slaughter and devastation I became terrified,—not for myself (for I, a simple Corsican fisherman, had nothing to fear; on the contrary, that time was most favourable for us smugglers); but for my brother, a soldier of the empire, returning from the army of the Loire, with his uniform and his epaulettes, there was everything to apprehend. I hastened to the innkeeper. My presages had been but too true; my brother had arrived the previous evening at Nîmes, and at the very door of the house where he was about to demand hospitality, he had been assassinated. I did all in my power to discover the murderers, but no one durst tell me their names, so much were they dreaded. I then thought of that French justice of which I had heard so much, and which feared nothing; and I went to the *procureur du roi*."

"And this *procureur du roi* was named Villefort?" asked Monte Cristo, carelessly.

"Yes, your excellency; he came from Marseilles, where he had been deputy *procureur*. His zeal had procured him advancement, and he was said to be one of the first who had informed the government of the departure from the island of Elba."

"Then," said Monte Cristo, "you went to him?"

"'Monsieur,' I said, 'my brother was assassinated yesterday in the streets of Nîmes, I know not by whom, but it is your duty to find out. You are the head of justice here; and it is for justice to avenge those she has been unable to protect.' 'Who was your brother?' asked he. 'A lieutenant in the Corsican battalion.' 'A soldier of the usurper, then?' 'A soldier of the French army.' 'Well,' replied he, 'he has smitten with the sword, and has perished by the sword.' 'You are mistaken, monsieur,' I replied; 'he has perished by the poniard.' 'What do you want me to do?' asked the magistrate. 'I have already told you,—avenge him.' 'On whom?' 'On his murderers.' 'How should I know who they are?' 'Order them to be sought for.' 'Why? your brother has been involved in a quarrel, and killed in a duel. All these old soldiers commit excesses, which were tolerated in the time of the emperor, but which are not suffered now; for our people of the south do not like either soldiers or disorder.'

"'Monsieur,' I replied, 'it is not for myself that I entreat your interference,—I should grieve for him or avenge him; but my poor brother had a wife, and were anything to happen to me, the poor creature would perish from want,—for my brother's pay alone kept her. Pray try and obtain a small government pension for her.' 'Every revolution has its catastrophes,' returned M. de Villefort; 'your brother has been the victim of this. It is a misfortune, and government owes nothing to his family. If we are to judge by all the acts of vengeance that the followers of the usurper exercised on the partisans of the king, when in their turn they were in power, your brother would be to-day in all probability condemned to death. What has happened is quite natural, and is only the law of reprisals.' 'What!' cried I, 'do you, a magistrate, speak thus to me?' 'All these Corsicans are mad, on my honour,' replied M. de Villefort; 'they fancy that their countryman is still emperor. You have mistaken the time; you should have told me this two months ago,—it is too late now. Depart instantly, or I will compel you to do so.' I looked at him an instant to see if there was anything to be gained by renewed entreaties; but this man was of stone. I approached him and said in a low voice, 'Well, since you know the Corsicans so well, you know that they always keep their word. You think that it was a good deed to kill my brother, who was a Bonapartist, because you are a Royalist! Well, I, who am a Bonapartist also, declare one thing to you, which is that I will kill you! From this moment I declare the vendetta against you; so protect yourself as well as you can, for the next time we meet your last hour will have come!' And before he had recovered from his surprise, I opened the door and escaped."

"Ah, ah!" said Monte Cristo, "with your innocent appearance you do those things, M. Bertuccio, and to a *procureur du roi!* And did he know what was meant by this terrible word 'vendetta'?"

"He knew so well that from that moment he never went out unattended, but shut himself up in his house, and caused me to be searched for everywhere. Fortunately, I was so well concealed that he could not find me. Then he became alarmed, and dared not reside any longer at Nîmes; so he solicited a change of residence, and as he was in reality very influential, he was nominated to Versailles. But, as you know, a Corsican who has sworn to avenge himself cares not for distance; so his carriage, fast as it went, was never above half a day's journey before me, who followed him on foot. The most important thing was not to kill him only—for I had an opportunity of doing so a hundred times—but to kill him without being discovered; at least, without being arrested. I no longer belonged to myself, for I had my sister-in-law to protect and provide for. During three months I watched M. de Villefort; for three months he took not a step out of doors without my following him. At length I discovered that he went mysteriously to

Auteuil. I followed him thither, and I saw him enter the house where we now are; only, instead of entering by the great door that looks into the street, he came on horseback or in his carriage, left carriage or horse at the little inn, and entered by the gate you see there!"

Monte Cristo made a sign with his head that he could discern amid the darkness the door to which Bertuccio alluded.

"As I had nothing more to do at Versailles, I went to Auteuil and gained all the information I could. If I wished to surprise him, it was evident that this was the place in which to lie in wait for him. The house belonged, as the *concierge* informed your excellency, to M. de Saint-Méran, Villefort's father-in-law. M. de Saint-Méran lived at Marseilles, so that this country-house was useless to him; and it was reported to be let to a young widow, known only by the name of 'the Baroness.'

"One evening, as I was looking over the wall, I saw a young and handsome woman who was walking alone in that garden, which was not overlooked by any windows; and I guessed that she was awaiting M. de Villefort. When she was sufficiently near to distinguish her features, I saw that she was from eighteen to nineteen years of age, tall and very fair. As she had a loose muslin dress on, and as nothing concealed her figure, I saw that she would ere long become a mother. A few moments after, the little door was opened, and a man entered; the young woman hastened to meet him. They threw themselves into each other's arms, embraced tenderly, and returned together to the house. This man was M. de Villefort; my opinion was that when he should go away, especially if he went in the night, he would have to traverse the whole of the garden alone."

"And," asked the count, "did you ever know the name of this woman?"

"No, excellency," returned Bertuccio; "you will see that I had no time to learn it."

"Go on."

"That evening," continued Bertuccio, "I could have killed the *procureur du roi;* but I was not sufficiently master of the localities. I was afraid that I might not kill him instantly, and that should his cries give the alarm, I could not escape. I deferred the undertaking until his next visit; and in order that nothing should escape me I took a chamber looking into the street, along which ran the wall of the garden. Three days after, about seven o'clock in the evening, I saw a servant on horseback leave the house at full gallop and take the road that led to Sèvres. I conjectured he was going to Versailles, and I was not deceived. Three hours after, the man returned covered with dust; his errand was performed. Ten minutes later another man, on foot, muffled in a mantle, opened the little door of the garden, which he closed after him. I descended rapidly; although I had not seen Villefort's face, I recognised him by the beating of my heart. I crossed the street and stopped at a post placed at the angle of the wall, by the aid of which I had once before looked into the garden. This time I did not content myself with looking, but I took my knife out of my pocket, assured myself that the point was sharp, and sprang over the wall. My first care was to run to the door; he had left the key in it, taking the simple precaution of turning it twice in the lock. Nothing, then, prevented my escape by this door. I examined the localities. The garden formed a long square; a terrace of smooth turf extended in the middle, and at the corners were tufts of trees with thick and massive foliage that mingled with the shrubs and flowers. In order to go from the door to the house, or from the house to the door, M. de Villefort was compelled to pass by one of these clumps.

" It was the end of September; the wind blew violently. The faint gleams of the pale moon, hidden at every instant by the masses of dark clouds that were sweeping across the sky, whitened the gravel walks that led to the house, but were unable to pierce the obscurity of the thick shrubberies, in which a man could conceal himself without any fear of discovery. I hid myself in the one nearest to the path Villefort must take, and scarcely was I there when amid the gusts of wind I fancied I heard groans; but you know, or rather you do not know, Monsieur the Count, that he who is about to commit an assassination fancies he hears low cries in the air. Two hours passed thus, during which I imagined I heard these moans repeated. Midnight struck. As the last stroke died away, I saw a faint light shine through the windows of the private staircase by which we have just descended. The door opened, and the man in the mantle reappeared. The terrible moment had come! but I had so long been prepared for it that my heart did not fail in the least. I drew my knife from my pocket again, opened it, and prepared myself to strike. The man in the mantle advanced towards me, but as he drew near I saw that he had a weapon in his hand. I was afraid, not of a struggle, but of a failure. When he was only a few paces from me I saw that what I had taken for a weapon was only a spade. I was still unable to divine for what reason M. de Villefort had this spade in his hands, when he stopped close to the clump, glanced round, and began to dig a hole in the earth. I then perceived that he hid something beneath his mantle, which he laid on the grass in order to dig more freely. Then, I confess, curiosity became mixed with my hatred; I wished to see what Villefort was going to do there, and I remained motionless, holding my breath. Then an idea crossed my mind, which was confirmed when I saw the *procureur du roi* draw from under his mantle a box two feet long and six or eight inches deep. I let him place the box in the hole he had made; then, while he stamped with his feet to remove all traces of his occupation, I rushed on him and plunged my knife into his breast, exclaiming: 'I am Giovanni Bertuccio; thy death for my brother's; thy treasure for his widow! Thou seest that my vengeance is more complete than I had hoped!' I know not if he heard these words; I think he did not, for he fell without a cry. I felt his blood gush over my face; but I was intoxicated, I was delirious, and the blood refreshed instead of burning me. In a second I had disinterred the box; then, that it might not be known that I had done so, I filled up the hole, threw the spade over the wall, and rushed through the door, which I double-locked, carrying off the key."

"Ah!" said Monte Cristo, "it seems to me this was a little assassination combined with robbery."

"No, your excellency," returned Bertuccio; "it was a vendetta followed by a restitution."

"And was the sum a large one?"

"It was not money."

"Ah! I recollect," replied the count; "did you not say something of an infant?"

"Yes, excellency; I hastened to the river, sat down on the bank, and with my knife forced open the lock of the box. In a fine linen cloth was wrapped a new-born child. Its purple visage and its violet-coloured hands showed that it had perished from suffocation; but as it was not yet cold I hesitated to throw it into the water that ran at my feet. In fact, after a moment I fancied I felt a slight pulsation of its heart; and as I had been assistant at the hospital at Bastia, I did what a doctor would have done,—I inflated its lungs by blowing air into them. And at the expiration of a quarter of an hour I saw it breathe, and heard a feeble cry; in my turn, I uttered a cry, but a cry of joy. 'God has not cursed me, then,' I cried, 'since he permits me to save the life of a human creature in exchange for the life I have taken away.'"

" And what did you do with the child? " asked Monte Cristo. " It was an embarrassing load for a man seeking to escape."

" I had not for a moment the idea of keeping it; but I knew that at Paris there was a hospital where they receive these poor creatures. As I passed the barrier I declared I had found this child on the road, and I inquired where the hospital was. The box confirmed my statement; the linen proved it belonged to wealthy parents; the blood with which I was covered might have proceeded from the child as well as from any one else. No objection was raised, but they pointed out to me the hospital, which was situated at the upper end of the Rue d'Enfer; and after having taken the precaution of cutting the linen in two pieces, so that one of the two letters which marked it was wrapped round the child, while the other remained in my possession, I rang the bell and fled with all speed. A fortnight after I was at Rogliano, and I said to Assunta, ' Console thyself, sister; Israel is dead, but he is avenged.' She asked what I meant, and when I had recounted all to her, ' Giovanni,' said she, ' you should have brought this child with you. We would have replaced the parents it has lost, have called it Benedetto; and then in consequence of this good action, God would have blessed us.' In reply I gave her the half of the linen I had kept, in order to reclaim him if we should become more prosperous."

" What letters were marked on the linen? " said Monte Cristo.

" An H and an N, surmounted by a baron's torse."

" By heaven, M. Bertuccio, you make use of heraldic terms! Where did you study heraldry? "

" In your service, excellency, where one learns everything."

" Go on; I am curious to know two things."

" What are they, monseigneur? "

" What became of this little boy? for I think you told me it was a boy, M. Bertuccio."

" No, excellency, I do not recollect telling you that."

" I thought you did; I was mistaken."

" No, you were not, for it was in fact a little boy. But your excellency wished to know two things; what was the second? "

" The second was the crime of which you were accused when you asked for a confessor, and the Abbé Busoni came to visit you at your request in the prison at Nîmes."

" The story will be very long, excellency."

" What matter? You know I take but little sleep; and I do not suppose you are very much inclined for it either."

Bertuccio bowed and resumed his story. " Partly to drown the recollections of the past that haunted me, partly to supply the want of the poor widow, I eagerly returned to my trade of smuggler, which had become more easy by reason of that relaxation of the laws which always follows a revolution. The coasts of the South especially were poorly guarded, in consequence of the disturbances that were perpetually breaking out in Avignon, Nîmes, or Uzés. We profited by the kind of respite government gave us to establish connections along the seaboard. Since my brother's assassination in the streets of Nîmes, I had never entered the town; the result was that the innkeeper with whom we were connected, seeing we would no longer come to him, was forced to come to us, and had established a branch to his inn on the road from Bellegarde to Beaucaire, at the sign of the Pont du Gard. We had thus, in the direction of Aigues-Mortes, Martiques, and at Bouc, a dozen places where we left our goods, and where, in case of necessity, we concealed ourselves from the gendarmes and custom-house officers. Smuggling is a profitable trade when a certain degree of vigour and intelligence is employed; as for myself, brought up in the mountains, I had a double motive for fearing the gendarmes and custom-house officers,—as my appearance before the judges would cause an inquiry, and an inquiry always looks back into the past. And in my past life they might find something far more grave than the selling of smuggled cigars or barrels of brandy, without a permit. So preferring death to capture, I accomplished the most astonishing deeds, which more than once showed me that the too great care we take of our bodies is almost the only obstacle to the success of those projects which require a rapid decision and vigorous and determined execution. In fact, when you have once devoted your life, you are no longer the equal of other men, or rather, other men are no longer your equals; and whosoever has taken this resolution feels at once that his strength is ten times as great, and that his horizon is enlarged."

" Philosophy, M. Bertuccio!" interrupted the count; " you have done a little of everything in your life."

" Oh, your pardon, excellency."

" No, no; but philosophy at half-past ten at night is somewhat late. Yet I have no other observation to make, except that what you say is correct, which is more than can be said for all philosophy."

" My journeys became more and more extensive and more productive. Assunta took care of all, and our little fortune increased. One day when I was setting off on an expedition, ' Go,' said she; ' at your return I will give you a surprise.' I questioned her, but in vain; she would tell me nothing, and I departed. Our expedition lasted nearly six weeks. We had been to Lucca to take in oil, to Leghorn for English cottons; and we landed our cargo without opposition, took our profits, and returned home full of joy. When I entered the house the first thing I beheld in the centre of Assunta's chamber was a cradle that might be called sumptuous compared with the rest of the furniture, and in it a baby of seven or eight months old. I uttered a cry of joy; the only moments of sadness I had known since the assassination of the *procureur du roi* were caused by the recollection that I had abandoned this child. For the assassination itself I had never felt any remorse. Poor Assunta had divined all. She had profited by my absence, and furnished with the half of the linen, and having written down the day and hour at which I had deposited the child at the hospital, had set off for Paris and had reclaimed it. No objection was raised, and the infant was given up to her. Ah, I confess, Monsieur the Count, when I saw this poor creature sleeping peacefully in its cradle, I felt my eyes filled with tears. 'Ah, Assunta,' cried I, 'you are an excellent woman, and Heaven will bless you.'"

"This," said Monte Cristo, "is less correct than your philosophy; it is true that this is only faith."

"Alas! your excellency is right," replied Bertuccio, "and God made this infant the instrument of our punishment. Never did a perverse nature declare itself more prematurely; and yet it was not owing to any fault in his bringing up. He was a most lovely child, with large blue eyes of that deep colour that harmonises so well with the general fairness of the complexion; only his hair, which was too light, gave his face a singular expression, which redoubled the vivacity of his look and the malice of his smile. Unfortunately, there is a proverb that says that 'red is either altogether good or altogether bad.' The proverb was but too correct as regarded Benedetto; and even in his infancy he manifested the worst disposition. It is true that the indulgence of his mother encouraged him. This child, for whom my poor sister would go to the town five or six leagues off to purchase the earliest fruits and the most tempting sweetmeats, preferred to the oranges of Palma or the preserves of Genoa the chestnuts stolen from a neighbour's orchard or the dried apples in his loft, although he could eat as well of the nuts and apples that grew in my garden. One day when Benedetto was about five or six, our neighbour Wasilio, who, according to the custom of the country, never locked up his purse or his valuables,—for, as your excellency knows, there are no thieves in Corsica,—complained that he had lost a louis out of his purse; we thought he must have made a mistake in counting his money, but he persisted in the accuracy of his statement. That day Benedetto, who had left the house in the morning, to our great anxiety, did not return until late in the evening, when we saw him approach dragging a monkey after him, which he said he had found chained to the foot of a tree. For more than a month the mischievous child, who knew not what to wish for, had taken it into his head to have a monkey. A boatman who had passed by Rogliano, and who had several of these animals, whose tricks had greatly diverted him, had doubtless suggested this idea to him. 'Monkeys are not found in our woods chained to trees,' said I; 'confess how you obtained this animal.' Benedetto adhered to his falsehood, and accompanied it with details that did more honour to his imagination than to his veracity. I became angry; he began to laugh. I threatened to strike him, and he made two steps backwards. 'You cannot beat me,' said he; 'you have no right, for you are not my father.'

"We never knew who had revealed this fatal secret, which we had so carefully concealed from him; however, it was this answer, in which the child's whole character revealed itself, that almost terrified me, and my arm fell without touching him. The boy triumphed; and this victory rendered him so audacious that all the money of Assunta, whose affection for him seemed to increase as he became more unworthy of it, was spent in caprices she knew not how to contend against, and follies she had not the courage to prevent. When I was at Rogliano everything went on properly; but no sooner was my back turned than Benedetto became master, and everything went wrong. When he was only eleven he chose his companions from among the young men of eighteen or twenty, the worst characters in Bastia, or indeed in Corsica; and they had already for some pieces of mischief been several times threatened with a prosecution. I became alarmed, as any prosecution might be attended with serious consequences. I was compelled at this period to leave Corsica on an important expedition; I reflected for a long time, and with the hope of averting some impending misfortune I resolved that Benedetto should accompany me. I hoped that the active and laborious life of a smuggler, with the severe discipline on board, would have a salutary effect on his character, well-nigh, if not quite corrupted. I spoke to Benedetto alone and proposed to him to accompany me, endeavouring to tempt him by all the promises most likely to dazzle the imagination of a child of twelve years old. He heard me patiently, and when I had finished, burst out laughing.

"' Are you mad, uncle?' (He called me by this name when he was in a good humour.) 'Do you think I am going to change the life I lead for your mode of existence,—my agreeable indolence for the hard and precarious toil you impose on yourself? exposed to the bitter frost at night and the scorching heat by day, compelled to conceal yourself, and when you are perceived, to receive a volley of balls,—and all to earn a paltry sum? Why, I have as much money as I want; Mother Assunta always furnishes me when I ask for it! You see that I should be a fool to accept your offer.' I was stupefied by such audacity and such reasoning. Benedetto rejoined his associates; and I saw him from a distance point me out to them as a fool."

"Sweet child!" murmured Monte Cristo.

"Oh! had he been my own son," replied Bertuccio, "or even my nephew, I would have brought him back to the right road, for the knowledge that you are doing your duty gives you strength; but the idea that I was striking a child whose father had killed made it impossible for me to punish him. I gave my sister, who constantly defended the unfortunate boy, good advice; and as she confessed that she had several times missed money to a considerable amount, I showed her a safe place in which to conceal our little treasure for the future. My mind was already made up: Benedetto could read, write, and cipher perfectly,—for when the fit seized him, he learned more in a day than others in a week; my intention was to enter him as clerk in some ship, and without letting him know anything of my plan, to convey him some morning on board. After I should have done that, and recommended him to the captain, his future would depend upon himself. I set off for France, after having fixed upon the plan. All our cargo was to be landed in the Gulf of Lyons; and these operations were becoming more and more difficult, for we were in 1829. Tranquillity was completely re-established, and the vigilance of the custom-house officers was redoubled; and their strictness was increased at this time in consequence of the fair of Beaucaire, which had just opened.

"Our expedition was successfully started. We anchored our vessel, which had a double hold in which our goods were concealed, amid a number of other vessels that bordered the banks of the Rhone from Beaucaire to Arles. On our arrival there we began to discharge our cargo in the night, and to convey it into the town by the help of the innkeepers with whom we were connected.

Whether success rendered us imprudent, or whether we were betrayed, I know not; but one evening, about five o'clock, our little cabin-boy hastened, breathless, to inform us that he had seen a detachment of custom-house officers advancing in our direction. It was not their vicinity that alarmed us,—for detachments were constantly patrolling along the banks of the Rhone—but the care, according to the boy's account, which they took to avoid being seen. In an instant we were on the alert; but it was too late. Our vessel was surrounded, and among the custom-house officers I observed several gendarmes, and as terrified at the sight of their uniforms as I was brave at the sight of any other, I sprang into the hold, opened a port, and dropped into the river, dived, and only rose at intervals to breathe, until I reached a cutting that led from the Rhone to the canal that runs from Beaucaire to Aigues-Mortes. I was now safe, for I could swim along the cutting without being seen, and I reached the canal in safety; I had designedly taken this direction. I have already told your excellency of an innkeeper of Nîmes who had set up a little inn on the road from Bellegarde to Beaucaire."

" Yes," said Monte Cristo, " I perfectly recollect him; I think he was your associate."

" Precisely," answered Bertuccio; " but he had, seven or eight years before this period, sold his establishment to a tailor at Marseilles, who, having almost ruined himself in his old trade, wished to make his fortune in another. Of course we made the same arrangements with the new landlord that we had with the old; and it was of this man that I intended to ask shelter."

" What was his name? " then inquired the count, who seemed to become somewhat interested in Bertuccio's story.

" Gaspard Caderousse; he had married a woman from the village of Carconte, and whom we did not know by any other name than that of her village. She was suffering from the marsh-fever, and seemed dying by inches. As for her husband, he was a strapping fellow, forty or forty-five years old, who had more than once in time of danger given ample proof of his presence of mind and courage."

" And you say," interrupted Monte Cristo, " that this took place towards the year—"

" 1829, Monsieur the Count."

" In what month? "

" June."

" The beginning or the end? "

" The evening of the 3rd."

" Ah," said Monte Cristo, "the evening of the 3rd of June, 1829. Go on."

" It was from Caderousse that I intended demanding shelter; and as we never entered by the door that opened on to the road, I resolved not to break through the rule, and climbing over the garden hedge, I crept among the olive and wild fig trees. And fearing that Caderousse might have some one there, I entered a kind of shed in which I had often passed the night, and which was separated from the inn only by a partition in which holes had been made in order to enable us to watch an opportunity of announcing our presence. My intention was, if Caderousse was alone, to acquaint him with my arrival, finish the meal the custom-house officers had interrupted, and profit by the threatened storm to return to the Rhone and ascertain the state of our vessel and its crew. I stepped into the shed; and it was fortunate I did so, for at that moment Caderousse entered with a stranger.

" I waited patiently, not to overhear what they said, but because I could do nothing else; besides, the same thing had occurred often before. The man who was with Caderousse was evidently a stranger to the south of France; he was one of those merchants who come to sell jewellery at the fair of Beaucaire, and who during the month the fair lasts, when there is so great an influx of merchants and customers from all parts of Europe, often have dealings to the amount of one hundred thousand to one hundred and fifty thousand livres. Caderousse entered hastily. Then, seeing that the room was, as usual, empty and only guarded by the dog, he called to his wife. ' Holloa, Carconte!' said he, ' the worthy priest has not deceived us; the diamond is real.' An exclamation of joy was heard; and the staircase creaked beneath a feeble step. ' What do you say?' asked his wife, pale as death. ' I say that the diamond is real, and that this gentleman, one of the first jewellers of Paris, will give us fifty thousand livres for it. Only, in order to satisfy himself that it really belongs to us, he wishes you to relate to him, as I have done already, the miraculous manner in which the diamond came into our possession. In the meantime, please to sit down, monsieur, and I will bring you some refreshment.'

" The jeweller examined attentively the interior of the inn and observed the visible poverty of the persons who were about to sell him a diamond that seemed to have come from the casket of a prince. ' Relate your story, madame,' said he, wishing no doubt to profit by the absence of the husband, so that the latter could not influence the wife's story, and to see if the two recitals tallied. 'Oh!' returned she, 'it was a gift of Heaven, which we were far from expecting! My husband was a great friend, in 1814 or 1815, of a sailor named Edmond Dantès. This poor fellow, whom Caderousse had forgotten, had not forgotten him; and at his death he bequeathed this diamond to him.' 'But how did he obtain it?' asked the jeweller; 'had he it before he was imprisoned?' 'No, monsieur; but it appears that in prison he made the acquaintance of a rich Englishman. And as in prison he fell sick, and Dantès took the same care of him as if he had been his brother, the Englishman, when he was set free, gave this stone to Dantès, who, less fortunate, died, and in his turn left it us, and charged the excellent abbé who was here this morning to deliver it.' 'The same story!' muttered the jeweller; 'and improbable as it seems at first, the history may be true. There's only the price we are not agreed about.' 'How not agreed about?' said Caderousse. 'I thought we agreed for the price I asked.' 'That is,' replied the jeweller, 'I offered forty thousand livres.' 'Forty thousand!' cried La Carconte; 'we will not part with it for that sum. The abbé told us it was worth fifty thousand without the setting.' 'What was the abbé's name?' asked the indefatigable questioner. 'The Abbé Busoni,' said La Carconte. 'He was a foreigner?' 'An Italian, from the neighbourhood of Mantua, I believe.' 'Let me see this diamond again,' replied the jeweller; 'the first time you are often mistaken as to the value of a stone.' Caderousse took from his pocket a small case of black shagreen, opened, and gave it to the jeweller. At the sight of the diamond, which was as large as a hazel-nut, La Carconte's eyes sparkled with cupidity."

"And what did you think of this fine story, eavesdropper?' said Monte Cristo; "did you credit it?"

"Yes, your excellency. I did not look on Caderousse as a bad man, and I thought him incapable of committing a crime or even a theft."

"That did more honour to your heart than to your experience, M. Bertuccio. Had you known this Edmond Dantès, of whom they spoke?"

"No, your excellency, I had never heard of him before, and never but once afterwards; and that was from the Abbé Busoni himself, when I saw him in the prison at Nîmes."

"Go on."

"The jeweller took the ring; and drawing from his pocket a pair of steel pliers and a small set of copper scales, taking the stone out of its setting, he weighed it carefully. 'I will give you forty-five thousand,' said he, ' but not a halfpenny more; besides, as that is the exact value of the stone, I brought just that sum with me.' ' Oh, that's no matter,' replied Caderousse, ' I will go back with you to fetch the other five thousand livres.' ' No,' returned the jeweller giving back the diamond and the ring to Caderousse,—' no, it is worth no more; and I am sorry I offered so much, for the stone has a flaw in it, which I had not seen. However, I will not go from my word, and I will give forty-five thousand.' ' At least, replace the diamond in the ring,' said La Carconte, sharply. ' Ah, true,' replied the jeweller, and he reset the stone. ' No matter,' observed Caderousse, replacing the box in his pocket, ' some one else will purchase it.' ' Yes,' continued the jeweller; ' but some one else will not be so easy as I am, or content himself with the same story. It is not natural that a man like you should possess such a diamond. He will inform against you. You will have to find the Abbé Busoni; and abbés who give diamonds worth two thousand louis are rare. Justice would seize it, and put you in prison; if at the end of three or four months you are set at liberty, the ring will be lost, or a false stone, worth three livres, will be given you, instead of a diamond worth fifty thousand livres, perhaps fifty-five thousand, but which you must allow one runs considerable risk in purchasing.' Caderousse and his wife looked eagerly at each other. ' No,' said Caderousse, ' we are not rich enough to lose five thousand livres.' ' As you please, my dear sir,' said the jeweller; ' I had, however, as you see, brought you the money in bright coin.' And he drew from his pocket a handful of gold, which he made to sparkle in the dazzled eyes of the innkeeper, and in the other hand he held a packet of bank-notes.

" There was visibly a severe struggle in the mind of Caderousse; it was evident that the small shagreen case, which he turned and re-turned in his hand, did not seem to him commensurate in value with the enormous sum which fascinated his gaze. He turned towards his wife. ' What do you think of this? ' he asked in a low voice. ' Let him have it; let him have it! ' she said. ' If he returns to Beaucaire without the diamond, he will inform against us; and as he says, who knows if we shall ever again see the Abbé Busoni? ' ' Well, then, so I will! ' said Caderousse; ' so you may have the diamond for forty-five thousand livres. But my wife wants a gold chain, and I want a pair of silver buckles.' The jeweller drew from his pocket a long flat box, which contained several samples of the articles demanded. ' Here,' he said, ' I am very plain in my dealings; take your choice.' The woman selected a gold chain worth about five louis, and the husband a pair of buckles worth perhaps fifteen livres. 'I hope you will not complain now?' said the jeweller. 'The abbé told me it was worth fifty thousand livres,' muttered Caderousse. 'Come, come; give it to me! What a strange fellow you are!' said the jeweller, taking the diamond from his hand. 'I give you forty-five thousand livres,—that is, two thousand five hundred livres of income,—a fortune such as I wish I had myself; and you are not satisfied!' 'And the forty-five thousand livres,' inquired Caderousse, in a hoarse voice, 'where are they? Come, let us see them!' 'Here they are,' replied the jeweller; and he counted out upon the table fifteen thousand livres in gold, and thirty thousand livres in bank-notes. 'Wait while I light the lamp,' said La Carconte; 'it is growing dark, and there may be some mistake.'

"In fact the night had come on during this conversation, and with the night the storm which had been threatening for the last half-hour. The thunder was heard growling in the distance; but neither the jeweller, nor Caderousse, nor La Carconte seemed to heed it, possessed as they were with the demon of gain. I myself felt a strange kind of fascination at the sight of all this gold and all these bank-notes; it seemed to me that I was in a dream, and as it always happens in a dream, I felt myself riveted to the spot. Caderousse counted and again counted the gold and the notes; then handed them to his wife, who counted and counted them again in her turn. During this time, the jeweller made the diamond play and sparkle beneath the ray of the lamp; and the gem threw out flashes of light which made him unmindful of those which—precursors of the storm—began to play in at the windows. 'Well,' inquired the jeweller, 'is the cash all right?' 'Yes,' said Caderousse. 'Give me the pocket-book, La Carconte, and find a bag somewhere.'

"La Carconte went to a cupboard, and returned with an old leathern pocket-book from which she took some greasy letters and put in their place the bank-notes, and a bag in which were at the moment two or three crowns of six livres each, and which in all probability formed the entire fortune of the miserable couple. 'There,' said Caderousse; 'and now, although you have wronged us of perhaps ten thousand livres, will you have your supper with us? I invite you with good-will.' 'Thank you,' replied the jeweller; 'it must be getting late, and I must return to Beaucaire. My wife will be getting uneasy.' H drew out his watch, and exclaimed, '*Morbleu!* nearly nine o'clock! Why, I shall not get back to Beaucaire before midnight! Good-night, my dears. If the Abbé Busoni should by any accident return, think of me.' 'In another week you will have left Beaucaire,' remarked Caderousse, 'for the fair finishes in a few days.' 'True; but that is no consequence. Write to me at Paris, to M. Joannes, in the Palais-Royal, Stone Gallery, No. 45; I will make the journey on purpose to see him.'

"At this moment there was a tremendous clap of thunder accompanied by a flash of lightning so vivid that it quite eclipsed the light of the lamp. 'Oh, dear!' exclaimed Caderousse. 'You cannot think of going out in such weather as this.' 'Oh, I am not afraid of thunder!' said the jeweller. 'And then there are robbers,' said La Carconte; 'the road is never very safe during fair time.' 'Oh, as to the robbers,' said Joannes, 'here is something for them;' and he drew from his pocket a pair of small pistols, loaded to the muzzle. 'Here,' said he, 'are dogs who bark and bite at the same time; they are for the first two who shall have a longing for your diamond, Father Caderousse.'

"Caderousse and his wife again interchanged a meaning look. It seemed as though they were both inspired at the same time with some horrible thought. 'Well, then, a good journey to you!' said Caderousse. 'Thank you,' replied the jeweller. He then took his cane, which he had placed against an old cupboard, and went out. At the moment when he opened the door, such a gust of wind came in that the lamp was nearly extinguished. 'Oh!' said he, 'this is very nice weather; and two leagues to go in such a storm!' 'Remain,' said Caderousse; 'you can sleep here.' 'Yes; do stay,' added La Carconte, in a tremulous voice; 'we will take every care of you.' 'No; I must sleep at Beaucaire. So once more, good-night!' Caderousse followed him slowly to the threshold. 'I can neither see heaven nor earth!' said the jeweller, who was outside the door. 'Do I turn to the right or to the left hand?' 'To the right,' said Caderousse. 'You cannot go wrong; the road is bordered by trees on both sides.' 'Good; all right!' said a voice almost lost in the distance. 'Close the door,' said La Carconte; 'I do not like open doors when it thunders.' 'Particularly when there is money in the house, eh?' answered Caderousse, double-locking the door.

"He came into the room, went to the cupboard, took out the bag and pocket-book, and both began for the third time to count their gold and bank-notes. I never saw such an expression of cupidity as the flickering lamp revealed in the two countenances. The woman especially was hideous; the feverish tremulousness she usually had was redoubled; her countenance had become livid, and her eyes resembled burning coals. 'Why,' she inquired in a hoarse voice, 'did you invite him to sleep here to-night?' 'Why?' said Caderousse, with a shudder; 'why, that he might not have the trouble of returning to Beaucaire.' 'Ah!' responded the woman, with an expression impossible to render; 'I thought it was for something else.' 'Woman, woman, why do you have such ideas?' cried Caderousse; 'or if you have them, why don't you keep them to yourself?' 'Well,' said La Carconte, after a moment's pause, 'you are not a man!' 'What do you mean?' added Caderousse. 'If you had been a man, you would not have let him go from here.' 'Woman!' 'Or else he should not have reached Beaucaire.' 'Woman!' 'The road takes a turn,—he is obliged to follow it,—while alongside of the canal there is a shorter road.' 'Woman! you offend the good God! There! listen!' And at this moment there was heard a tremendous peal of thunder, while the livid lightning illumined the room; and the thunder, then rolling away to a distance, seemed to leave reluctantly the cursed abode. 'Jesus!' said Caderousse, crossing himself.

"At the same moment and in the midst of the silence so full of terror which usually follows claps of thunder, they heard a knocking at the door. Caderousse and his wife started and looked aghast at each other. 'Who's there?' cried Caderousse, rising and drawing up in a heap the gold and notes scattered over the table, and which he covered with his two hands. 'It is I!' shouted a voice. 'And who are you?' 'Eh, *pardieu!* Joannes the jeweller.' 'Well, and you said I offended the good God!' said Carconte, with a horrid smile, 'why, it is the good God who sends him back again.' Caderousse fell back, pale and breathless, in his chair. La Carconte on the contrary rose, and going with a firm step towards the door, opened it, saying as she did so, 'Come in, dear M. Joannes.' 'Upon my word!' said the jeweller, drenched with rain, 'it seems as if I was not to return to Beaucaire to-night. The shortest follies are best, my dear Caderousse. You offered me hospitality, and I accept it, and have returned to sleep beneath your friendly roof.' Caderousse stammered out some words while he wiped away the damp that started to his brow. La Carconte double-locked the door behind the jeweller.

CHAPTER XLV

THE RAIN OF BLOOD

" As the jeweller returned to the apartment, he cast around him a scrutinising glance; but there was nothing to excite suspicion, if it did not exist, or to confirm it, if already awakened. Caderousse's hands still grasped his gold and bank-notes; and La Carconte smiled upon her guest as pleasantly as she could. ' Heyday!' said the jeweller, ' you seem to have had some fears respecting the amount of your receipts, since you go over them again after my departure.' ' No, no,' answered Caderousse; ' but the circumstances by which we have become possessed of this wealth are so unexpected as to make us scarcely credit our good fortune, and it is only by placing the actual proof of our riches before our eyes that we can persuade ourselves the whole affair is not a dream.' The jeweller smiled. ' Have you any other guests in your house?' inquired he. ' No,' replied Caderousse, ' we do not lodge travellers; we are so near the town that nobody would think of stopping here.' ' Then I am afraid I shall very much inconvenience you!' ' Oh, dear me, no! indeed, my dear monsieur, you will not,' said La Carconte; ' not at all, I assure you.' ' But where will you manage to stow me?' ' In the chamber overhead.' ' But is not that your chamber?' ' Never mind that! we have a second bed in the room adjoining this.' Caderousse stared at his wife with much astonishment.

" The jeweller, meanwhile, was humming a song as he stood warming his back by the fire which La Carconte had lighted in the fireplace to dry the wet garments of her guest. She also spread a napkin at the end of the table and placed on it the slender remains of their dinner, to which she added three or four fresh eggs. Caderousse had once more parted with his treasures; the bank-notes were replaced in the pocket-book, the gold put back into the bag, and the whole carefully locked in the strong-box. He then began pacing the room with a pensive and gloomy air, glancing from time to time at the jeweller, who stood steaming before the fire, and as soon as he got dry on one side, turning the other.

" ' There,' said La Carconte, as she placed a bottle of wine on the table, ' supper is ready whenever you are inclined to partake of it.' ' But you are going to sit down with me, are you not?' asked Joannes. 'I shall not take any supper to-night,' said Caderousse. 'We dined very late,' hastily interposed La Carconte. 'Then it seems I am to eat alone?' remarked the jeweller. 'Oh, we shall have the pleasure of waiting upon you,' answered La Carconte, with an eager attention she was not accustomed to manifest even to guests who paid for what they took.

"From one minute to another Caderousse darted on his wife keen, searching glances, but rapid as the lightning-flash. The storm still continued. 'There! there,' said La Carconte; 'do you hear that? Upon my word, you did well to return.' 'Nevertheless,' replied the jeweller, 'if by the time I have finished my supper the tempest has at all abated, I shall make another attempt to complete my journey.' 'Oh,' said Caderousse, shaking his head, 'there is not the slightest chance of its abating; it is the *mistral*, and that will be sure to last till to-morrow morning.' He then sighed heavily. 'Well!' said the jeweller, as he placed himself at table, 'all I can say is, so much the worse for those who are abroad.' 'Ah!' chimed in La Carconte, 'they will have a wretched night of it.'

"The jeweller began to eat his supper, and La Carconte continued to pay him the little attentions of a careful hostess. Ordinarily so whimsical and cross-grained, she had become a model of painstaking politeness. Had the jeweller been previously acquainted with her, a change so marked certainly would have surprised him, and would not have failed to excite in him some suspicion. Caderousse, meanwhile, continued to pace the room and seemed unwilling to look at his guest; but as soon as the stranger had completed his repast, he went to the door and opened it. 'The storm seems over,' said he. But as if to contradict his statement, at that instant a violent clap of thunder seemed to shake the house to its very foundation, while a sudden gust of wind, mingled with rain, extinguished the lamp he held in his hand. Caderousse shut the door and returned to his guest, while La Carconte lighted a candle by the smouldering ashes that glimmered on the hearth. 'You must be tired,' said she to the jeweller; 'I have spread a pair of white sheets on your bed. Go up to your room, and may you sleep well!'

"Joannes waited a moment to assure himself that the storm was not abating; and when he saw that the thunder and the rain were increasing, he bade his hosts good-night and ascended the staircase. He passed over my head, and I heard every step creak as he went up. La Carconte followed him with eager eyes, while Caderousse on the contrary did not even look in that direction.

"All these details, which since that time have been gathered up in my mind, made but little impression on me when they were taking place before my eyes; in fact, all that had happened (with the exception of the story of the diamond, which certainly did wear an air of improbability) appeared quite natural; but worn out as I was with fatigue, and fully purposing to proceed onwards as soon as the tempest abated, I determined to take advantage of the comparative silence and tranquillity that prevailed to obtain the refreshment of a few hours' sleep. Overhead I could accurately distinguish every movement of the jeweller, who, after making the best arrangements in his power for passing a comfortable night, threw himself on his bed, and I could hear it creak and groan beneath his weight. Insensibly my eyelids grew heavy; deep sleep stole over me; and having no suspicion of anything wrong, I sought not to shake it off. For the last time I looked in upon the room where Caderousse and his wife were sitting; the former was seated upon one of those low wooden stools which in country places are frequently used instead of chairs. His back being turned towards me, I could not see the expression of his countenance; neither should I have been able to do so had he been placed differently, as his head was buried between his two hands. La Carconte continued to gaze on him for some time in contemptuous silence; then shrugging up her shoulders, she took her seat immediately opposite to him. At this moment the expiring embers threw up a fresh flame from the kindling of a piece of wood that lay near; and a bright gleam was thrown on the scene and the actors in it. La Carconte still kept her eyes fixed on her husband; but as he made no sign of changing his position, she extended her hard bony hand and touched him on the forehead.

"Caderousse shuddered. The woman's lips seemed to move as though she were talking; but either because she spoke in an undertone, or because my senses were dulled by sleep, I did not catch a word she uttered. I could no longer even see except through a mist and with that uncertainty in which perceptions are blended with dreams. Finally my eyes closed, and I lost consciousness. How long I had been in this unconscious state I know not, when I was suddenly aroused by the report of a pistol followed by a fearful cry. Unsteady footsteps sounded on the floor of the chamber, and the next instant a dull, heavy weight seemed to fall powerless on the staircase. I had not yet fully recovered my recollection when again I heard groans mingled with half-stifled cries, as if from persons engaged in a deadly struggle. A last cry, more prolonged than the others, which gradually was subdued to groans, effectually aroused me from my drowsy lethargy. Hastily raising myself on one arm, I looked around, but all was dark; and it seemed to me as if the rain must have penetrated through the flooring of the room above, for some kind of moisture appeared to fall, drop by drop, upon my forehead, and when I passed my hand across my brow, I felt it wet and clammy.

" To the fearful noises that had awakened me had succeeded the most profound silence,—unbroken, save by the footsteps of a man walking about over my head. The staircase creaked under his step. The man descended to the lower room, approached the fireplace, and lighted a candle. It was Caderousse, his face pale and his shirt red with blood. Having obtained the light, he hurried upstairs again, and once more I heard his rapid and uneasy step in the chamber above. Ere long he came below holding in his hand the small shagreen case, which he opened, to assure himself it contained the diamond, and seemed to hesitate as to which pocket he should put it in; then, as if dissatisfied with the security of either pocket, he deposited it in his red handkerchief, which he carefully rolled round his head. After this he took from his cupboard the bank-notes and gold he had put there, thrust the one into the pocket of his trousers, and the other into that of his waistcoat, hastily tied up a small bundle of linen, and rushing towards the door, disappeared in the darkness of the night.

" Then all became clear and manifest to me; and I reproached myself with what had happened as though I myself had done the guilty deed. I fancied that I still heard faint moans; and imagining that the unfortunate jeweller might not be quite dead, I determined to go to his relief by way of atoning in some slight degree, not for the crime I had committed, but for that which I had not endeavoured to prevent. For this purpose I applied all the strength I possessed to force an entrance from the cramped spot in which I lay to the adjoining room; the badly arranged planks which alone divided me from it yielded to my efforts, and I found myself in the house. Hastily snatching up the lighted candle, I hurried to the staircase; towards the middle of it I stumbled over a human body lying quite across the stairs. It was the body of La Carconte! The pistol I had heard had doubtless been discharged at the unfortunate woman, whose throat it had frightfully lacerated, leaving a gaping wound from which, as well as the mouth, the blood was welling in sanguinary streams. Finding the miserable creature past all human aid, I strode past her and ascended to the sleeping-chamber, which presented an appearance of the wildest disorder. The furniture had been knocked over in the deadly struggle that had taken place there; and the sheets, to which the unfortunate jeweller had doubtless clung, were dragged across the room. The murdered man lay on the floor, his head leaning against the wall, weltering in a gory stream, poured forth from three large wounds in his breast; in a fourth wound was a large kitchen-knife of which the handle only was visible.

"I stumbled over the second pistol, which had not been discharged,—the powder probably being damp. I approached the jeweller, who was not quite dead; and at the sound of my footsteps, causing as they did the creaking of the floor, he opened his eyes, fixed them on me for a moment, moved his lips as though trying to speak, and expired. This appalling sight almost bereft me of my senses; and finding that I could no longer be of service to any one in the house, my only desire was to get away. I rushed to the staircase, clasping my burning temples with both hands, and uttering cries of horror. Upon reaching the room below, I found five or six custom-house officers and two or three gendarmes,—an armed troop. They immediately seized me, and I did not even attempt any resistance; I was no longer master of my senses. I tried to speak, but could utter only inarticulate cries. I saw some of the party pointing at me, and lowered my eyes to look at myself; I was covered with blood. That warm rain that I had perceived falling on me through the staircase was the blood of La Carconte. I pointed with my finger to the place where I had been concealed. 'What does he mean?' asked a gendarme. One of the revenue officers went to the place I had indicated. 'He means,' replied the man, upon his return, 'that he effected his entrance by means of this hole,' showing the place where I had broken my way through the planks into the house.

"Then I understood that they took me for an assassin. I recovered my voice and my strength. I tore myself from the two men who held me, and cried out, 'It is not I! it is not I!' A couple of gendarmes held the muzzles of their carbines against my breast; 'Stir but a step,' said they, 'and you are a dead man!' 'Why should you threaten me with death,' cried I, 'when I have already declared my innocence?' 'You will tell your little story to the judges at Nîmes. Meanwhile, come along with us; and the best advice we can give you is to do so unresistingly.' Resistance was far from my thoughts. I was utterly overpowered by surprise and terror; and without a word I suffered myself to be handcuffed and tied to a horse's tail, in which disgraceful plight I arrived at Nîmes.

"It seems I had been tracked by a *douanier*, who had lost sight of me near the inn; feeling assured that I intended to pass the night there, he had returned to summon his comrades, who arrived just in time to hear the report of the pistol, and to take me in the midst of such proofs of my guilt that I at once understood the difficulty I should have in proving my innocence. One only chance was left me, that of beseeching the magistrate before whom I was taken to cause every inquiry to be made for a certain Abbé Busoni, who had stopped at the inn of the Pont du Gard on the morning previous to the murder. If, indeed, Caderousse had invented the story relative to the diamond, and there existed no such person as the Abbé Busoni, then, indeed, I was lost past redemption unless Caderousse should be taken and should make a confession.

"Two months passed away in which—I ought to say in praise of my judge—search was everywhere made for the person I had desired to see. I had already lost all hope. Caderousse had not been taken. My trial was to come on at the approaching sessions; when, on the 8th of September,— that is to say, precisely three months and five days after the event,—the Abbé Busoni, whom I no longer hoped to see, presented himself at the prison, saying that he understood one of the prisoners wished to speak to him. He had learned of the affair at Marseilles, he said, and had hastened to comply with my desire. You may easily imagine with what eagerness I welcomed him; I related to him the whole of what I had seen and heard. I felt some degree of nervousness as I entered upon the history of the diamond; but to my inexpressible astonishment, he confirmed it in every particular, and to my equal surprise, he seemed to place entire belief in all I stated. And then it was that, won by his mild charity, perceiving him acquainted with all the habits and customs of my own country, and considering also that pardon for the only crime of which I was really guilty might come with a double power from lips so benevolent and kind, I besought him to receive my confession, under the seal of which I recounted the affair of Auteuil in all its details. That which I had done by the impulse of my best feelings produced the same effect as though it had been the result of calculation. My voluntary confession of the assassination at Auteuil proved to him that I had not committed that of which I stood accused. When he quitted me, he bade me be of good courage, and rely upon his doing all in his power to convince my judges of my innocence.

"I had speedy proofs that the excellent abbé was engaged in my behalf, for the rigours of my imprisonment were gradually alleviated, and I was told that my trial was to be postponed to the assizes following those now being held. In the interim it pleased Providence to cause the apprehension of Caderousse, who was discovered in some distant country and brought back to France, where he made a full confession, attributing to his wife the conception and instigation of the deed. He was sentenced to the galleys for life; and I was immediately set at liberty."

"And then it was, I presume," said Monte Cristo, "that you came to me as the bearer of a letter from the Abbé Busoni?"

"It was, your excellency; the benevolent abbé took an evident interest in all that concerned me. 'Your mode of life as a smuggler,' said he to me one day, 'will be the ruin of you if you persist in it; let me advise you when you get out of prison to choose something more safe as well as respectable.' 'But how,' inquired I, 'am I to maintain myself and my poor sister?' 'A person, whose confessor I am,' replied he, 'and who entertains a high regard for me, applied to me a short time since to procure him a confidential servant. Would you like such a post? If so, I will give you a letter of introduction to the friend I allude to.' 'Oh, *mon père*,' I cried, 'what goodness!' 'But you must swear to me that I shall never have occasion to regret my recommendation.' I extended my hand to take the oath. 'It is needless,' he said; 'I know and I like the Corsicans,—that is my reliance.' Here, take this,' continued he, after rapidly writing the few lines I brought to your excellency, and upon receipt of which you deigned to receive me into your service; and now I ask with confidence whether your excellency has ever had cause to complain of me?"

"On the contrary, Bertuccio, I have ever found you faithful, honest, and deserving. One fault I find with you, and that is your not having placed sufficient confidence in me."

"Indeed, your excellency, I know not what you mean!"

"Simply this; how comes it, that having both a sister and an adopted son, you have never spoken to me of either?"

"Alas! I have still to recount the most distressing period of my life. Anxious as you may suppose I was to behold and comfort my dear sister, I lost no time in hastening to Corsica; but when I arrived at Rogliano I found the house in mourning; there had been a scene so horrible that the neighbours remember and speak of it to this day. Acting by my advice, my poor sister had refused to comply with the unreasonable demands of Benedetto, who was continually tormenting her for money as long as he believed there was a sou left in her possession. One morning when he had demanded money, threatening her with the severest consequences if she did not supply him with what he desired, he disappeared throughout the whole of the day, leaving the kind-hearted Assunta, who loved him as if he were her own child, to weep over his conduct and bewail his absence. Evening came; and still, with all the patient solicitude of a mother, she watched for his return.

" As the eleventh hour struck, he returned with two of his ordinary companions. As poor Assunta rose to clasp her truant in her arms, she was seized upon by three ruffians, and one of them—I shudder with the fear that it may have been that infernal child—cried out, ' Let us put her to the torture; she will then tell us where the money is.'

" It unfortunately happened that our neighbour, Wasilio, was at Bastia, leaving no person in his house but his wife; no one else could hear or see anything that took place within our dwelling. Two of the brutal companions of Benedetto held poor Assunta, who, unable to conceive that any harm was intended to her, smiled upon those who were soon to become her executioners. The third ruffian proceeded to barricade the doors and windows; then returning to his infamous accomplices, the three united in stifling the cries uttered by the poor victim at the sight of these alarming preparations. This effected, they put the brazier to Assunta's feet, expecting thus to compel her to declare where our little treasure was concealed. In the struggles made by my poor sister her clothes caught fire, and they were compelled to let go their hold in order to preserve themselves. Covered with flames, Assunta rushed wildly to the door; but it was fastened. She flew to the windows; but they were barricaded. Then her neighbour heard frightful cries, —Assunta calling for help. Then her voice was stifled; her cries subsided to moans; and on the following morning, when after a night of anguish and terror Wasilio's wife could muster up courage to venture abroad, she caused the door of our dwelling to be opened by the public authorities, and Assunta, although dreadfully burned, was found still breathing. Every drawer and closet in the house had been forced open, and everything worth carrying off stolen from them. Benedetto never again appeared at Rogliano, neither have I since that day either seen or heard anything concerning him.

" It was subsequently to these dreadful events that I waited on your excellency, to whom it would have been folly to have mentioned Benedetto, since all trace of him seemed entirely lost; or of my sister, since she was dead."

" And what have you thought of that event? " inquired Monte Cristo.

" That it was a punishment for the crime I had committed," answered Bertuccio. " Oh, those Villeforts are an accursed race! "

" I believe it," murmured the count, in a melancholy tone.

" And now," resumed Bertuccio, " your excellency may perhaps be able to comprehend that this place, which I revisit for the first time, this garden, where I have killed a man, might well excite in me those disagreeable emotions of which you desired to know the cause. For, in short, I am not sure but that before me, there at my feet, lies M. de Villefort in the grave which he had dug for his child."

" Everything, in fact, is possible," said Monte Cristo, rising from the bench on which he had been sitting; " even," he added in a low tone, " that the *procureur du roi* is not dead. The Abbé Busoni did right to send you to me; and you have also done well in relating to me your history, as it will prevent my forming any erroneous opinions concerning you in future. As for that Benedetto, who so grossly belied his name, have you never made any effort to trace out whither he has gone or what has become of him? "

" Never! If I had known where he was, instead of going to him I should have fled as from a monster. I have never heard his name mentioned by any person; I hope he is dead."

" Do not hope it, Bertuccio," said the count. " The wicked do not die so, for God seems to keep them in his care, that he may use them as instruments of his vengeance."

" So be it," said Bertuccio. " I ask only that I may never see him again. And now, Monsieur the Count," added the steward, bending humbly forward, " you know all; you are my judge on earth as the Almighty is in Heaven. Have you no words of consolation for me? "

" My good friend, I can say to you what the Abbé Busoni would say to you. Villefort, the man you killed, merited the punishment he received at your hands as a just reward for the wrongs he had done you, and it may be, for other crimes likewise. Benedetto, if still living, will become the instrument of some divine retribution, and then will be punished in his turn. As far as you yourself are concerned, I see but one point in which you are really guilty. Ask yourself wherefore, after rescuing the infant from its living grave, you did not restore it to its mother. There was the crime, Bertuccio."

"True, monsieur; there, as you say, I acted wickedly, for as to that I was a coward. My first duty, as soon as I had succeeded in recalling the babe to life, was to restore it to its mother; but in order to do so I must have made close and careful inquiry, which would in all probability have led to my own apprehension. And I clung to life, partly on my sister's account, and partly from that feeling of pride inborn in our hearts, which makes us wish to come off untouched and victorious in the execution of our vengeance. Perhaps, too, the natural and instinctive love of life made me wish to avoid endangering my own. Oh! I am not brave like my poor brother."

Bertuccio hid his face in his hands as he uttered these words, while Monte Cristo fixed on him a long and indescribable gaze. After a brief silence, rendered still more solemn by the time and place, the count said in a tone of melancholy wholly unlike his usual manner, " In order to end properly this conversation, which will be our last about these adventures, I will repeat to you some words I have heard from the lips of the Abbé Busoni himself; ' For all ills there are two remedies,—time and silence.' Now, M. Bertuccio, leave me to walk alone for a few moments in this garden. That which awakens painful emotion in you, an actor in that terrible scene, gives me a sensation almost pleasant and increases the value of this estate. The trees, you see, M. Bertuccio, are pleasant only as they make a shade; and the shade itself is pleasant only as it is filled with reveries and visions. Here I have bought a garden, thinking to buy a simple enclosure shut in by walls; but suddenly that enclosure becomes a garden full of ghosts, which were not mentioned in the contract. Now I like ghosts; I have never heard it said that so much harm had been done by the dead during six thousand years as is wrought by the living in one single day. Retire within, Bertuccio, and sleep in peace. Should your confessor be less indulgent to you in your dying moments than you found the Abbé Busoni, send for me if I am still on earth, and I will find words to soothe your soul as it makes ready to start on that rough voyage to what is called Eternity."

Bertuccio bowed respectfully and turned away, sighing heavily. When he had quite disappeared, Monte Cristo arose; and taking three or four steps onwards, he murmured, " Here, beneath this plane-tree, is where the infant's grave was dug. There is the little door opening into the garden. At this corner

is the private staircase communicating with the sleeping-apart-
ment. There will be no necessity for me to make a note of these
particulars, for there before my eyes, beneath my feet, all around
me, I have the plan sketched with all the living reality of truth."

After making the tour of the garden a second time, the count
regained the house and re-entered his carriage; while Bertuccio,
who perceived the thoughtful expression of his master's features,
took his seat beside the driver without uttering a word. The
carriage proceeded rapidly towards Paris.

That same evening, upon reaching his abode in the Champs
Elysées, the Count of Monte Cristo went over the whole building
with the air of one long acquainted with each nook or corner.
Nor, although preceding the party, did he once mistake one
door for another, or commit any error in choosing the proper
corridor or staircase to conduct him to a place or suite of rooms
he desired to visit. Ali accompanied him on this nocturnal
inspection. Having given various orders to Bertuccio relative
to the improvements and alterations he desired to make in the
house, the count, drawing out his watch, said to the attentive
Nubian, "It is half-past eleven o'clock; Haydée will soon
arrive. Have the French attendants been notified?"

Ali extended his hands towards the apartments destined for
the fair Greek, which were so isolated that when the door was
concealed behind tapestry one might go all over the house
without suspecting that in that locality were a salon and two
chambers, occupied. Ali, having pointed to the apartments,
counted three on the fingers of his left hand, and then, placing
it beneath his head, shut his eyes and feigned to sleep.

"I understand," said Monte Cristo, well acquainted with Ali's
pantomime; "you mean to tell me that three female attendants
are waiting in the sleeping-chamber."

"Yes," said Ali, by repeatedly nodding his head.

"Madame will be fatigued this evening," continued Monte
Cristo, "and will no doubt wish to retire to rest immediately
upon her arrival. Desire the French attendants not to weary
her with questions, but merely to pay their respectful duty and
retire. You will also see that the Greek servants hold no communication with those of this country."

Ali bowed. Just at that moment voices were heard hailing
the *concierge*. The gate opened; a carriage rolled down the
avenue, and stopped at the flight of steps leading to the house.
The count descended, and presented himself at the already
opened carriage-door. He offered his hand to a young woman
completely enveloped in a mantle of green and gold. She raised

the hand extended towards her to her lips, and kissed it with a mixture of love and respect. A few words passed between them in that sonorous language in which Homer makes his gods converse. The woman spoke with an expression of deep tenderness, while the count replied with an air of gentle gravity. Preceded by Ali, who carried in his hand a candle of rose-coloured wax, the woman, who was no other than the lovely Greek who had been Monte Cristo's companion in Italy, was conducted to her apartments, while the count retired to the pavilion reserved for himself. In another hour every light in the house was extinguished, and it might have been thought that all its inmates slept.

CHAPTER XLVI

UNLIMITED CREDIT

ABOUT two o'clock on the following day a *calèche*, drawn by a pair of magnificent English horses, stopped at the door of Monte Cristo, and a man dressed in a blue coat with buttons of the same colour, a white waistcoat over which was displayed a massive gold chain, and brown trousers, with hair so black and descending so low over his eyebrows as to leave it doubtful whether it were not artificial, so little did its jetty glossiness assimilate with the deep wrinkles stamped on his features,—a man, in a word, who, although evidently more than fifty years of age, desired to be taken for not more than forty, bent forward from the carriage-door, on the panels of which were emblazoned the armorial bearings of a baron, and directed his groom to inquire at the porter's lodge whether the Count of Monte Cristo resided there, and if he were within. While waiting, the occupant of the carriage surveyed the house, the garden so far as he could distinguish it, and the livery of the servants who passed to and fro, with an attention so close as to be somewhat impertinent. The glance of this individual was keen, but evincing rather cunning than intelligence; his lips were straight, and so thin that as they closed they were compressed within the mouth, —in short, the size and prominence of his cheek-bones,—a never-failing proof of craftiness,—the flatness of his forehead, and the enlargement of the back of his skull, which extended far beyond his large and vulgarly-shaped ears, combined to give, in the eyes of a physiognomist, a character almost repulsive to the face of that man, so highly respected by the people for his magnificent horses, the enormous diamond he wore on his shirt-front, and the red ribbon extended from one button-hole to the other of his coat.

The groom, in obedience to his orders, tapped at the window of the porter's lodge, saying, " Does not the Count of Monte Cristo live here? "

" His excellency does reside here," replied the *concierge* ; " but—" added he, glancing an inquiring look at Ali. Ali returned a sign in the negative.

" But what? " asked the groom.

" His excellency does not receive visitors to-day."

" Then take my master's card,—M. le Baron Danglars! Be sure to give the card to the count, and say that in going to the Chamber my master came out of his way to have the honour of calling upon him."

" I do not speak to his excellency," replied the *concierge* ; " the *valet de chambre* will carry your message."

The groom returned to the carriage. " Well? " asked Danglars. The man, somewhat crestfallen by the rebuke he had received, detailed to his master all that had passed between himself and the *concierge*.

" Oh! " said the baron, " this gentlemen is a prince, then, who must be called excellency, and must not be approached but by his valet. However, it does not signify; he has a letter of credit on me, so I must see him when he requires his money."

Then, throwing himself back in his carriage, Danglars called out to his coachman, in a voice that might be heard across the road, " To the Chamber of Deputies! "

Through the blinds of his pavilion, Monte Cristo, warned in time, had seen the baron, and had studied him, by the aid of an excellent lorgnette, with no less scrutiny than M. Danglars himself had given to his examination of the house, the garden, and the liveries. " That fellow has a decidedly bad counten-ance," said the count, in a tone of disgust, as he shut up his glass into its ivory case. " How comes it that all do not retreat in aversion at sight of that flat, receding, serpent-like forehead, round, vulture-shaped head, and sharp-hooked nose, like the beak of a buzzard? Ali! " cried he, striking at the same time on the brazen gong. Ali appeared. " Summon Bertuccio! " said the count.

Almost immediately Bertuccio entered the apartment. " Did your excellency desire to see me? " inquired he.

" I did," replied the count. " You no doubt observed the horses standing a few minutes since at the door? "

"Certainly, your excellency; I noticed them for their remarkable beauty."

"Then how comes it," said Monte Cristo, with a frown, "that when I desired you to purchase for me the finest pair of horses to be found in Paris, there are in Paris two other horses as handsome as mine, and those horses are not in my stables?"

At the look of displeasure and the count's angry tones, Ali turned pale and held down his head. "It is not your fault, my good Ali," said the count, in the Arabic language, and in a tone of such gentleness as none would have given him credit for being capable of feeling,—"it is not your fault. You do not profess to understand the choice of English horses."

The countenance of Ali recovered its serenity.

"Permit me to assure your excellency," said Bertuccio, "that the horses you speak of were not to be sold when I purchased yours."

Monte Cristo shrugged his shoulders. "It seems, Monsieur the Intendant," said he, "that you have yet to learn that all things are to be sold to such as care to pay the price."

"Monsieur the Count is not, perhaps, aware that M. Danglars gave sixteen thousand livres for his horses?"

"Very well! then offer him thirty-two thousand; a banker never loses an opportunity of doubling his capital."

"Is your excellency really in earnest?" inquired the steward.

Monte Cristo looked at his steward as if astonished at the question. "I have to pay a visit this evening," replied he. "I desire that these horses, with completely new harness, may be at the door with my carriage."

Bertuccio bowed, and was about to withdraw; but when he reached the door, he paused and said, "At what o'clock does your excellency intend to make that visit?"

"At five o'clock," replied the count.

"I beg your excellency's pardon," interposed the steward, in a deprecating manner, "for venturing to observe that it is already two o'clock."

"I know it," was Monte Cristo's only reply. Then turning towards Ali, he said, "Let all the horses in my stables be led before the windows of madame, that she may select those she prefers for her carriage. Request her also to oblige me by saying whether it is her pleasure to dine with me; if so, let dinner be served in her apartments. Now leave me, and desire my *valet de chambre* to come hither."

Scarcely had Ali disappeared when the valet entered the chamber.

"M. Baptistin," said the count, "you have been in my service one year, the time I generally give myself to judge of the merits or demerits of those about me. You suit me very well." Baptistin bowed low. "It only remains for me to know whether I also suit you?"

"Oh, Monsieur the Count!" exclaimed Baptistin, eagerly.

"Listen, if you please, till I have finished speaking," replied Monte Cristo. "You receive fifteen hundred livres per annum for your services here,—more than many a brave subaltern, who continually risks his life for his country, obtains. You have food such as many clerks and place-men who work ten times harder than you do would wish to have. Though yourself a servant, you have other servants who take care of your linen and your clothes. Besides your fifteen hundred livres of wages, you steal from me annually, upon the purchases you make for my toilet, fifteen hundred livres besides."

"Oh, your excellency!"

"I am not complaining, M. Baptistin; it is reasonable. Nevertheless, I desire that to be stopped. You could find nowhere else a situation such as your good fortune has given you. I do not ill-use my people; I never swear; I do not put myself in a rage; I always pardon mistakes,—never negligence or forgetfulness. My orders are generally short, but clear and precise; I prefer to repeat them twice, or even three times, rather than have them imperfectly comprehended. I am rich enough to find out all that I want to know, and I give you notice, I am very curious. If, then, I learn that you have spoken of me kindly or unkindly, commented on my actions, or watched my conduct, you will leave me at that moment. I never warn my servants more than once. You are warned; go." Baptistin bowed and was proceeding towards the door. "I forgot to mention to you," said the count, "that I lay yearly aside a certain sum for each servant in my establishment; those whom I am compelled to dismiss lose, of course, this money, while their portion goes to the fund accumulating for those domestics who remain with me, and among whom it will be divided at my death. You have been in my service a year; your fortune has been begun. Continue it."

This address, delivered in the presence of Ali, who stood wholly unmoved, produced an effect on M. Baptistin only to be conceived by those who have studied the character and disposition of French domestics. "I assure your excellency," said he, "at least it shall be my study to merit your approbation in all things; and I will take M. Ali as my model."

"Pray do no such thing," replied the count, in the most frigid tone; "Ali has many faults mixed with most excellent qualities. Do not, then, take example from him, for Ali is an exception. He receives no wages; he is not a servant,—he is my slave, my dog. If he should fail in his duty I should not dismiss him, I should kill him."

Baptistin opened his eyes.

"Do you doubt it?" said Monte Cristo. He then repeated to Ali in the Arabic language what he had just been saying to Baptistin in French. The Nubian smiled assentingly to his master's words, then kneeling on one knee, respectfully kissed the hand of the count. This corroboration of the lesson he had just received put the finishing stroke to the stupefaction of M. Baptistin. The count then motioned to the *valet de chambre* to retire, and to Ali to follow him into his study, where they conversed a long time. At five o'clock the count struck thrice upon his gong. When Ali was wanted, one stroke was given; two summoned Baptistin, and three Bertuccio. The steward entered. "My horses!" said Monte Cristo.

"They are harnessed to the carriage, your excellency Does Monsieur the Count wish me to accompany him?"

"No, only the coachman, Ali, and Baptistin."

The count descended to the door of his mansion, and beheld his carriage drawn by the very pair of horses he had so much admired in the morning attached to the carriage of Danglars. As he passed them he said, "They are extremely handsome certainly, and you have done well to purchase them, although you were somewhat late."

"Indeed, your excellency, I had much difficulty in obtaining them, and they have cost a large sum of money."

"Does the sum you gave for them make the animals less beautiful?" inquired the count, shrugging his shoulders.

"Nay, if your excellency is satisfied, all is as I could wish it. Whither does Monsieur the Count desire to be driven?"

"To the residence of M. le Baron Danglars, Rue de la Chaussée d'Antin."

This conversation had passed as they stood upon the terrace, from which a flight of stone steps led to the carriage-drive. As Bertuccio was moving away, the count called him back. "I have another commission for you, M. Bertuccio," said he. "I am desirous of having an estate by the seaside in Normandy,—for instance, between Havre and Boulogne. You see I give you a wide range. It will be absolutely necessary that the place you may select have a small harbour, creek, or bay, into which my *corvette* can enter and remain at anchor. She draws only fifteen feet of water. She must be kept in constant readiness to sail immediately at whatever hour of day or night I give the signal. Make the requisite inquiries for a place of this description; and when you have met with an eligible spot, visit it, and if it possess the advantages desired, purchase it at once in your own name. The *corvette* must now, I think, be on her way to Fécamp, is she not?"

"Certainly, your excellency; I saw her put to sea the same evening we quitted Marseilles."

"And the yacht?"

"Was ordered to remain at Martigues."

"'Tis well! I wish you to write from time to time to the captains in charge of the two vessels so as to keep them on the alert."

"And the steamboat? Has your excellency any orders to give respecting her?"

"She is at Châlons, is she not?"

"Yes."

"The same orders as for the two sailing-vessels."

"I understand."

"When you have purchased the estate I desire, I mean to establish relays at intervals of ten leagues on the road to the north and on the road to the south."

"Your excellency may fully depend upon me."

The count gave an approving smile, descended the terrace steps, and sprang into his carriage, which, drawn by the beautiful animals so expensively purchased, was whirled along with incredible swiftness, and stopped only before the hotel of the banker. Danglars was engaged at that moment, presiding over a railroad committee. But the meeting was nearly concluded when the name of his visitor was announced. As the count's title sounded on his ear, he rose, and addressing his colleagues, many of whom were members of one Chamber or the other, he said, "Gentlemen, I must beg you to excuse my quitting you thus; but, if you will imagine it, the house of Thomson and French, at Rome, have sent to me a certain Count of Monte Cristo, and have opened for him with me an unlimited credit. It is the drollest thing I have ever met with in the course of my extensive foreign transactions; and you may readily suppose, it has roused my curiosity. I took the trouble this morning to call on the pretended count. If he were a true count he wouldn't be so rich. Monsieur was not to be seen! How does that strike you? Isn't that the style of royalty, or of a pretty woman giving herself out as Maître Monte Cristo? As for the rest, the house, situated in the Champs Elysées, and which, I am informed, belongs to him, appeared to me quite respectable. But an unlimited credit," continued Danglars, with his villanous smile, " makes the banker with whom it is opened very exacting. I hasten, then, to see our man. I think it is a hoax. But they don't know down there with whom they have to deal. He laughs best who laughs last."

Having delivered himself of this pompous address, uttered with a degree of energy that left him almost out of breath, the baron left his guests and withdrew to a salon finished in white and gold, which was much admired in the Chaussée d'Antin. He had ordered the visitor to be ushered into that room, expecting him to be overwhelmed by its dazzling splendour. He found the count standing before some copies of Albano and Fattore that had been passed off on the banker as originals, and which, though but copies, were entirely out of harmony with the gaudy gilding that covered the ceiling. The count turned as he heard the entrance of Danglars into the room. With a slight inclination of the head, Danglars signed to the count to be seated in an armchair covered with white satin embroidered with gold. The count obeyed.

" I have the honour, I presume, of addressing M. de Monte Cristo."

The count bowed. " And I am speaking to Baron Danglars, Chevalier of the Legion of Honour, and Member of the Chamber of Deputies,"—repeating all the titles he had found on the baron's card.

Danglars felt all the irony contained in the address of his visitor. For a minute or two he compressed his lips as though seeking to conquer his rage ere he trusted himself to speak. Then, turning to his visitor, he said, " You will, I trust, excuse my not having called you by your title when I first addressed you, but you are aware we are living under a popular form of government, and that I am myself a representative of the liberties of the people."

" So much so," replied Monte Cristo, " that while preserving the habit of styling yourself baron, you have deemed it advisable to lay aside that of calling others by their titles."

" Upon my word," said Danglars, with affected carelessness, " I attach no sort of value to such empty distinctions; but the fact is, I was made baron, and also Chevalier of the Legion of Honour, in consequence of some services I had rendered government, but—"

" You have relinquished your titles after the example set you by MM. de Montmorency and Lafayette? Well, you cannot possibly choose more noble models for your conduct."

" Why," replied Danglars, embarrassed, " I do not mean to say I have altogether laid aside my titles; with the servants, for instance,—there I think it right to preserve my rank with all its outward forms."

" Yes, to your servants you are ' Monseigneur;' to journalists you are ' Monsieur;' and to your constituents ' citizen.' These are distinctions very proper under a constitutional government. I understand perfectly."

Danglars bit his lips; he saw that he was no match for Monte Cristo in an argument of this sort, and he hastened to turn to subjects more familiar to him.

" Monsieur the Count," said he, bowing, " I have received a letter of advice from Thomson and French, of Rome."

" I am glad to hear it, Monsieur the Baron,—for I must claim the privilege of addressing you as your servants do; it is a bad habit, acquired in countries where barons still are found, simply because they are no longer created. But as regards the letter of advice, I am charmed to find that it has reached you; it relieves me of the necessity of introducing myself, which is always embarrassing. You have, then, you say, received a letter of advice?"

" Yes," said Danglars; " but I confess that I do not quite understand it."

" Indeed?"

" And for that reason I did myself the honour of calling upon you, in order to beg you would explain some part of it to me."

" Do it now, monsieur; I am here, and am prepared to understand you."

" Why," said Danglars, " in the letter—I believe I have it about me "—here he felt in his breast-pocket—" yes, here it is! Well, this letter gives M. le Comte de Monte Cristo unlimited credit on our house."

" And what is there that requires explaining in that simple fact, may I ask, Monsieur the Baron?"

" Nothing, monsieur, but the word ' unlimited.' "

" Well, isn't that a French word? You know they are Anglo-Germans who wrote the letter."

" Oh, as for the composition of the letter there is nothing to say; but as regards reliability it is somewhat different."

" Is it possible," asked the count, assuming an air and tone of the utmost simplicity,—" is it possible that Thomson and

French are not looked upon as safe and solvent bankers? The devil! that is annoying, for I have considerable property in their hands."

"Thomson and French are bankers of the highest repute," replied Danglars, with an almost mocking smile; "and it was not of their solvency or capability I spoke; but of the word 'unlimited,' which in financial affairs is so vague—"

"That it is unlimited, do you mean?" cried Monte Cristo.

"Precisely what I was about to say," said Danglars. "Now, what is vague is doubtful; and says the wise man, "where there is doubt there is danger!'"

"Meaning to say," rejoined Monte Cristo, "that though Thomson and French may be inclined to commit acts of folly, M. le Baron Danglars is not disposed to follow their example."

"How so, Monsieur the Count?"

"Simply thus: the banking-house of Thomson and Co. sets no bounds to its engagements, while that of M. Danglars has its limits; truly, he is as wise as the sage he just now quoted."

"Monsieur!" replied the banker, drawing himself up with a haughty air, "the amount of my capital or the extent and solvency of my engagements has never yet been questioned."

"It seems, then, reserved for me," said Monte Cristo, coldly, "to be the first to do so."

"By what right?"

"By right of the explanations you have demanded, which appear to betray hesitation."

Danglars bit his lips. It was the second time he had been defeated by this man, and this time on his own ground. His mocking politeness was an affectation, and touched upon the border which is so near to impertinence. Monte Cristo, on the other hand, smiled with the best grace in the world, and exhibited, when he wished, a certain appearance of simplicity, which gave him many advantages.

"Well, monsieur," resumed Danglars, after a brief silence, "I will endeavour to make myself understood by requesting you to inform me for what sum you propose to draw upon me?"

"Why, truly," replied Monte Cristo, determined not to lose an inch of the ground he had gained, "my reason for desiring an 'unlimited' credit was precisely because I did not know what amount of money I might wish to have."

The banker now thought the time had arrived for him to take the upper hand. Flinging himself back in his armchair, he said with an arrogant and purse-proud air, "Let me beg of you not to hesitate in naming your wishes. You will then be convinced

so from the attention you appeared to be bestowing on mine when I entered the room. If you will permit me, I shall be happy to show you my picture gallery, composed entirely of works by the ancient masters,—warranted as such. I cannot endure the modern school of painting."

" You are quite right in objecting to them, for they have generally one great fault,—that they have not yet had time to become old."

" Or will you allow me to show you several fine statues by Thorwaldsen, Bartoloni, and Canova,—all foreign artists? As you may perceive, I think but very indifferently of our French sculptors."

" You have a right to be unjust to them, Monsieur,—they are your countrymen."

" But all that may be postponed until we shall be better acquainted. For the present, I will confine myself, if agreeable to you, to introducing you to Madame la Baronne Danglars. Excuse my impatience, Monsieur the Count; but a person of your wealth and influence cannot receive too much attention."

Monte Cristo bowed in sign that he accepted the proffered honour, and the financier immediately rang a small bell, which was answered by a servant in a showy livery.

" Is Madame the Baroness at home? " inquired Danglars.

" Yes, Monsieur the Baron," answered the man.

" And alone? "

" No, Monsieur the Baron, Madame has visitors."

" Have you any objection to meet any persons who may be with madame, or do you desire to preserve a strict incognito? "

" No, indeed," replied Monte Cristo, with a smile; " I do not arrogate to myself the right of so doing."

" And who is with madame,—M. Debray? " inquired Danglars, with an air of good-nature that made Monte Cristo smile, acquainted as he was with the secrets of the banker's domestic life.

" Yes, Monsieur the Baron," replied the servant, " M. Debray is with madame."

Danglars nodded his head, then turning to Monte Cristo, said, " M. Lucien Debray is an old friend of ours, and private secretary to the Minister of the Interior. As for my wife, I must tell you she lowered herself by marrying me, for she belongs to one of the most ancient families in France. Her maiden name was De Sevières, and her first husband was M. le Colonel Marquis de Nargonne."

"I have not the honour of knowing Madame Danglars; but I have already met M. Lucien Debray."

"Ah, indeed!" said Danglars; "and where was that?"

"At the house of M. de Morcerf."

"Oh! you are acquainted with the young viscount, are you?"

"We were together a good deal during the Carnival at Rome."

"True, true!" cried Danglars. "Let me see; have I not heard talk of some strange adventure with bandits or thieves hid in ruins, and of his having had a miraculous escape? I forget how; but I know he used to amuse my wife and daughter by telling them about it after his return from Italy."

"Madame the Baroness is waiting to receive you, gentlemen," said the servant, who had gone to inquire the pleasure of his mistress. "With your permission," said Danglars, bowing, "I will precede you, to show you the way."

"By all means," replied Monte Cristo; "I follow you."

CHAPTER XLVII

THE DAPPLED GREYS

THE baron, followed by the count, traversed a long suite of apartments, in which the prevailing characteristics were heavy magnificence and the gaudiness of ostentatious wealth, until he reached the boudoir of Madame Danglars,—a small octagonal-shaped room, hung with pink satin covered with white Indian muslin. The chairs were of ancient workmanship and materials; over the doors were painted sketches of shepherds and shepherdesses, after the style and manner of Boucher, and at each side pretty medallions in crayons, harmonising well with the appointments of this charming apartment,—the only one in the vast hotel in which any distinctive taste prevailed. In fact, it had been entirely overlooked in the plan arranged and followed out by M. Danglars and his architect, one of the most celebrated men of the day. The ornamental part of the finishing of Madame Danglars's boudoir had been left entirely to herself and Lucien Debray. M. Danglars, however, while possessing a great admiration for the antique as it was understood during the time of the Directory, entertained the most sovereign contempt for the simple elegance of his wife's favourite sitting-room, where, by the way, he was never permitted to intrude, unless indeed he excused his own appearance by ushering in some more agreeable visitor than himself. It was not therefore in reality Danglars who presented the visitor; on the contrary it was he who was presented. And his reception was cordial or frigid, in proportion as the individual who accompanied him chanced to please or displease the baroness.

As Danglars now entered, he found Madame the Baroness (who, although past the first bloom of youth, was still strikingly handsome) seated at the piano,—a most elaborate piece of cabinet and inlaid work,—while Lucien Debray, standing before a small work-table, was turning over the pages of an album. Lucien had found time, preparatory to the count's arrival, to relate many particulars respecting him to Madame Danglars. It will be remembered that Monte Cristo had made a lively impression on the minds of all the party assembled at the breakfast given by Albert de Morcerf. That impression had not yet been effaced from Debray's mind, unsusceptible though he was; and the information which he had given the baroness about the count was modified by it. The curiosity of Madame Danglars, excited by the details formerly given by Morcerf, and by the new incidents related by Lucien, had therefore risen to a great height. That arrangement of piano and album was only one of those social deceptions by which the most serious precautions are concealed. A most gracious welcome and unusual smile were bestowed on M. Danglars; the count, in return for his gentlemanly bow, received a formal though graceful courtesy, while Lucien exchanged with the count a sort of distant recognition, and with Danglars a free and easy nod.

"Baroness," said Danglars, "give me leave to present to you the Count of Monte Cristo, who has been most warmly recommended to me by my correspondents at Rome. I need but mention one fact to make all the ladies in Paris court his notice, —he comes to Paris with the intention of remaining a year and spending six millions in that time! It sounds very much like an announcement of balls, fêtes, dinners, and picnic-parties, in all of which I trust Monsieur the Count will remember us, as he may depend upon it we shall remember him in all the entertainments we may give, be they great or small."

Spite of the gross flattery and coarseness of this address, Madame Danglars could not forbear gazing with considerable interest on a man capable of expending six millions in twelve months, and who had selected Paris for the scene of his princely extravagance. "And when did you arrive here?" inquired she.

"Yesterday morning, madame."

"Coming, as usual, I presume, from the extreme end of the globe? Pardon me; at least, such I have heard is your custom."

"Nay, madame! this time I have come only from Cadiz."

"You have selected a most unfavourable moment for your first visit to our city. Paris is a horrible place in summer! Balls, parties, and fêtes are over; the Italian opera is in London; the French opera everywhere except in Paris. As for the Théâtre Français, you know, of course, that it is nowhere. The only amusements left us are the indifferent races held in the Champ de Mars and Satory. Do you propose entering any horses at either of these races, Monsieur the Count?"

"I, madame, propose to do whatever people do in Paris, if I have the good fortune to find some one who will inform me as to French customs."

"Are you fond of horses, Monsieur the Count?"

"I have spent a portion of my life in the East, madame, and you are doubtless aware that the inhabitants of those climes value only two things,—the excellence of their horses and the beauty of their women."

"Ah, Monsieur the Count," said the baroness, "it would have been somewhat more gallant to have placed the women first."

"You see, madame, how rightly I spoke when I said I required a preceptor to guide me into French customs."

At this instant the favourite attendant of Madame Danglars entered the boudoir; approaching her mistress, she spoke some words in an undertone. Madame Danglars turned very pale, then exclaimed, "I cannot believe it; the thing is impossible."

"I assure you, madame," replied the woman, "it is even as I have said."

Turning impatiently towards her husband, Madame Danglars demanded, "Is this true?"

"Is what true, madame?" inquired Danglars, visibly agitated.

"What my maid tells me."

"But what does she tell you?"

"That when my coachman was about to prepare my carriage he discovered that the horses had been removed from the stables without his knowledge. I desire to know what is the meaning of this?"

"Be kind enough, madame, to listen to me."

"Oh! I will listen to you, monsieur, for I am curious to know what you are about to tell me. These two gentlemen shall decide between us; but first I will state the case to them. Gentlemen," continued the baroness, "among the ten horses in the stables of M. le Baron Danglars are two that belong exclusively to me,—a pair of the handsomest and most spirited creatures to be found in Paris. But to you, at least, M. Debray, I need not give a further description, because to you my beautiful pair of dappled greys were well known. Well! just when I have promised Madame de Villefort the loan of my carriage to drive to-morrow to the Bois de Boulogne, behold, the two horses have disappeared. No doubt M. Danglars has sacrificed them to the selfish consideration of gaining some thousands of paltry livres. Oh, what a villainous crowd these speculators are!"

"Madame," replied Danglars, "the horses were not sufficiently quiet for you; they were scarcely four years old, and they made me extremely uneasy on your account."

"Nonsense!" retorted the baroness; "you are well aware that I have had in my service for the past month the best coachman in Paris,—unless you have sold him with the horses?"

"My dear, I promise you another pair like them,—handsomer, if possible,—but more quiet and steady."

The baroness shrugged her shoulders with an air of ineffable contempt, while her husband, affecting not to observe it, turned towards Monte Cristo and said, "Upon my word, Monsieur the Count, I am quite sorry I was not sooner aware of your establishing yourself in Paris."

"And wherefore?" asked the count.

"Because I should have liked to make you the offer of these horses. I have almost given them away as it is; but, as I said, I was anxious to get rid of them. They were fit only for a young man."

"Monsieur," said the count, "I thank you; but this morning I purchased a very excellent pair of carriage-horses, sufficiently good, and not too dear. There they are. Come, M. Debray, you are a connoisseur, I believe, let me have your opinion upon them."

As Debray walked towards the window Danglars approached his wife. "I could not tell you before others," said he, in a low tone, "the reason of my parting with the horses; but an enormous price was offered me this morning for them. Some madman or fool, bent upon ruining himself as fast as he can, actually sent his steward to me to purchase them at any cost; and the fact is, I have gained sixteen thousand livres by the sale of them. Come, don't look so angry, and you shall have four thousand livres of the money to do what you like with, and Eugénie shall have two thousand." Madame Danglars surveyed her husband with a look of withering contempt.

"What do I see?" suddenly exclaimed Debray.

"Where?" asked the baroness.

"I cannot be mistaken; there are your horses! The very animals we were speaking of, harnessed to the count's carriage!"

"My dappled greys?" cried the baroness, springing to the window. "'Tis indeed they!" said she. Danglars was stupefied.

"Is it possible?" cried Monte Cristo, with well-feigned astonishment.

Madame Danglars whispered a few words in the ear of Debray, who approached Monte Cristo, saying, "The baroness wishes to know what you paid her husband for the horses."

"I scarcely know," replied the count; "it was a little surprise prepared for me by my steward. They cost, I think, about thirty thousand livres."

Debray conveyed the count's reply to the baroness. Danglars looked so crestfallen and discomfited that Monte Cristo assumed a pitying air towards him. "See," said he, "how very ungrateful women are! Your kind attention in providing for the safety of the baroness by disposing of the horses does not seem to have made the least impression on her. But so it is; a woman will often from mere wilfulness prefer that which is dangerous to that which is safe. Therefore in my opinion, my dear baron, the best and easiest way is to leave them to their fancies, and allow them to act as they please; and then if any mischief follows, why, at least, they have no one to blame but themselves."

Danglars made no reply; he was occupied in anticipations of the coming scene between himself and the baroness, whose threatening looks and frowning brow, like that of Olympic Jove, predicted a storm. Debray, who perceived the gathering clouds and felt no desire to witness the explosion of Madame Danglars's rage, suddenly recollected an appointment which compelled him to take his leave; while Monte Cristo, unwilling by prolonging his stay to destroy the advantages he hoped to obtain, made a farewell bow and departed, leaving Danglars to endure the angry reproaches of his wife.

"Excellent!" murmured Monte Cristo to himself, as he retraced the way to his carriage. "All has gone according to my wishes. The domestic peace of this family is henceforth in my hands. Now, then, to play another master-stroke, by which I shall gain the heart of both husband and wife,—delightful! Still," added he, "amid all this, I have not yet been presented to Mademoiselle Eugénie Danglars, whose acquaintance I should have been glad to make. But never mind," pursued he, with his peculiar smile; " that will come later. I am on the spot and have plenty of time before me."

With that reflection the count entered his carriage and returned home. Two hours afterwards Madame Danglars received a charming letter from the count, in which he entreated her to receive back her favourite dappled greys, protesting that he could not endure the idea of making his *début* in the Parisian world by disappointing a lovely woman. The horses were sent back, wearing the same harness they had worn in the morning; but in the centre of each of the rosettes worn on the heads of the animals a diamond had been placed by order of the count.

To Danglars Monte Cristo also wrote, requesting him to excuse the whimsical gift of a capricious millionaire, and to beg of Madame the Baroness to pardon the Eastern fashion adopted in the return of the horses.

During the evening, Monte Cristo quitted Paris for Auteuil, accompanied by Ali. The following day, about three o'clock, a single blow struck on the gong summoned Ali to the presence of the count.

" Ali," observed his master, as the Nubian entered the chamber, " you have frequently told me how skilful you are in throwing the lasso."

Ali drew himself up proudly, and returned a sign in the affirmative.

" Very well. With your lasso you could stop an ox? "

Ali repeated his affirmative gesture.

" Or a tiger? "

Ali bowed his head in token of assent.

" A lion? "

Ali made the movement of one throwing a lasso, and then imitated the sound of strangling.

" I understand," said Monte Cristo; " you wish to tell me you have hunted the lion? "

Ali smiled with a triumphant air.

" But do you believe you could arrest the progress of two horses running away? "

The Nubian smiled.

" It is well," said Monte Cristo. " Ere long a carriage will dash past here, drawn by the pair of dappled grey horses you saw me with yesterday; now, at the risk of your own life you must manage to stop those horses before my door."

Ali descended to the street, and marked a straight line on the pavement immediately at the entrance of the house; then he returned and showed the line to the count, who was watching him. The count patted him gently on the back, his usual mode of praising Ali, who, pleased and gratified with the commission assigned him, walked calmly towards a projecting stone forming the angle of the street and house, and seating himself thereon began to smoke his chibouque, while Monte Cristo re-entered his dwelling without further concern. But as five o'clock approached and the carriage was momentarily expected by the count, the indication of more than common impatience and uneasiness might be observed in his manner. He stationed himself in a room commanding a view of the street, pacing the chamber with restless steps, stopping from time to time to listen for the sound of approaching wheels, then to cast an anxious glance on Ali; but the regularity with which the Nubian puffed forth the smoke of his chibouque proved that he at least was wholly absorbed in the enjoyment of his favourite occupation. Suddenly a distant sound of rapidly advancing wheels was heard, and almost immediately a carriage appeared, drawn by a pair of wild, ungovernable horses, who rushed forward as though urged by the devil himself, while the terrified coachman strove in vain to restrain their furious speed.

In the vehicle was a young woman and a child of about seven or eight years of age. Terror seemed to have deprived them even of the power to utter a cry, and they were clasped in each other's arms, as though determined not to be parted by death itself. The carriage creaked and rattled as it flew over the rough stones; and had it encountered the slightest impediment to its progress, it must inevitably have upset. The carriage kept the middle of the street, and cries of terror were uttered by those who saw it coming.

Then Ali, laying down his chibouque, drew the lasso from his pocket, threw it so skilfully as to catch the forelegs of the near horse in its triple fold, suffered himself to be dragged on for a few steps, by which time the tightening of the well-cast lasso had so completely hampered the furious animal as to bring it to the ground; the horse fell on the pole and broke it, and prevented the other animal from pursuing his headlong way. Gladly availing himself of this opportunity, the coachman leaped from his box; but Ali had promptly seized the nostrils of the second horse, and held them in his iron grasp, till the maddened beast, snorting with pain, sank beside his companion. All this was achieved in much less time than is occupied in the recital. The brief space had, however, been sufficient for a man, followed by a number of servants, to rush from the house before which the accident had occurred. As the coachman opened the door of the carriage, this man assisted to alight from it a lady who was convulsively grasping the cushions with one hand, while with the other she pressed to her bosom her young companion, who had lost all consciousness of what was passing. Monte Cristo carried them both to the salon, and deposited them on a sofa. "Compose yourself, madame," said he; "all danger is over."

The woman looked up at these words, and with a glance far more expressive than any entreaties could have been, pointed to her child, who still continued insensible.

"I understand the nature of your alarm, madame," said the count, carefully examining the child; "but I assure you there is not the slightest occasion for uneasiness. Your little charge has not received the least injury; his insensibility is merely the effect of terror, and will soon cease."

"Are you quite sure you do not say so to tranquillise my fears? See how pale he is! My child! my Edouard! speak to your mother! Ah, monsieur, send for a doctor! My fortune to him who restores to me my son!"

Monte Cristo signed to the distracted mother to lay aside her apprehensions; then opening a casket that stood near, he drew forth a phial composed of Bohemian glass, containing a liquid of the colour of blood, of which he let fall a single drop on the child's lips. Scarcely had it reached them ere the boy, though still pale as marble, opened his eyes, and eagerly gazed round him. At this sight, the delight of the mother was almost a delirium. "Where am I?" she exclaimed; "and to whom am I indebted for so happy a termination to my late dreadful alarm?"

"Madame," answered the count, "you are under the roof of one who esteems himself most fortunate in having been able to save you from a continuance of your sufferings."

"My wretched curiosity has brought all this about," pursued the lady. "All Paris rang with the praises of Madame Danglars's beautiful horses, and I had the folly to wish to try them."

"Is it possible," exclaimed the count, with well-feigned astonishment, "that these horses belong to Madame the Baroness?"

"Yes, monsieur; do you know her?"

"Madame Danglars? I have that honour; and my happiness at your escape from the danger that threatened you is redoubled by the consciousness that I have been the unwilling and unintentional cause of all the peril you have incurred. I yesterday purchased these horses of the baron; but as the baroness evidently regretted parting with them, I ventured to send them back to her, with a request that she would gratify me by accepting them from my hands."

"Why, then you are the Count of Monte Cristo of whom Hermine has talked to me so much!"

"Yes, madame," replied the count.

"And I am Madame Héloïse de Villefort." The count bowed with the air of a person who hears a name for the first time. "How grateful will M. de Villefort be for all your goodness; how thankfully will he acknowledge that to you alone it is owing that his wife and child exist! Most certainly, but for the prompt assistance of your intrepid servant this dear child and myself must both have perished."

"Indeed, I still shudder at your peril."

"Oh, I hope you will allow me properly to recompense that man's devoted courage."

"I beseech you, madame," replied Monte Cristo, "not to spoil Ali, either by too great praise or rewards. I cannot allow him to acquire the habit of expecting to be recompensed for every trifling service he may render. Ali is my slave, and in saving your life he was but discharging his duty to me."

"But he risked his life!" said Madame de Villefort, on whom the count's authoritative manner made a deep impression.

"His life, madame, belongs not to him; it is mine, in return for my having myself saved him from death." Madame de Villefort was silent; perhaps she was absorbed in the contemplation of the singular individual who from the first had made so powerful an impression on her. During that interval of silence Monte Cristo scrutinised the features and appearance of the boy she kept folded in her arms, lavishing on him the most tender endearments. The child was small for his age, and unnaturally pale. A mass of straight black hair, defying all attempts to train or curl it, fell over his projecting forehead, and hung down to his shoulders, giving increased vivacity to eyes full of sly malice and juvenile wickedness. His mouth was large, and the lips, which had not yet regained their colour, were particularly thin; in fact, the deep and crafty look, forming the principal character of the child's face, belonged rather to a boy of twelve or fourteen years of age than to one so young. His first movement was to free himself by a violent push from the encircling arms of his mother, and to rush forward to the casket from which the count had taken the phial of elixir; then, without asking permission of any one, he proceeded in all the wilfulness of a spoiled child unaccustomed to restrain either whims or caprices to pull the corks out of the bottles.

"Touch nothing, my little friend," cried the count, eagerly; "some of those liquids are dangerous not only to taste, but even to smell."

Madame de Villefort became very pale, and seizing her son's arm, drew him towards her; but once satisfied of his safety, she also cast a brief but expressive glance on the casket, which was not lost upon the count. At this moment Ali entered. At sight of him Madame de Villefort uttered an expression of pleasure, and holding the child still closer towards her, she said, "Edouard, do you see that good man? He has shown very great courage and resolution, for he exposed his own life to stop the horses that were running away with us, and would certainly have dashed the carriage to pieces. Thank him, then, my child,—for had he not come to our aid, neither you nor I would be alive at this moment."

The child stuck out his lips and turned away his head in a disdainful and contemptuous manner, saying, "He's too ugly!"

The count witnessed all this with internal satisfaction, and a smile stole over his features as he thought that such a child bade fair to realise one part of his hopes; while Madame de Villefort reprimanded her son with a moderation which certainly would not have satisfied Jean Jacques Rousseau had the little Edouard been called Emile.

"This lady," said the count, speaking to Ali in the Arabic language, "is desirous that her son should thank you for saving both their lives; but the boy refuses, saying you are too ugly!"

Ali turned his intelligent countenance towards the boy, on whom he gazed without any apparent emotion; but the spasmodic working of the nostrils showed to the practised eye of Monte Cristo how deeply the Arab was wounded by the unfeeling remark.

"Will you permit me to inquire," said Madame de Villefort, as she rose to take her leave, "whether you usually reside here?"

"No, madame," replied Monte Cristo; "it is a small place I have purchased quite lately. My place of abode is No. 30 Avenues des Champs Elysées; but I see that you have quite recovered from your fright, and you are no doubt desirous of returning home. Anticipating your wishes, I have desired the same horses you came with to be put to one of my carriages, and Ali — he whom you think so ugly"—continued he, addressing the boy with a smiling air, "will have the honour of driving you home, while your coachman remains here to attend to the necessary repairs of your *calèche*. As soon as that important business is concluded, I will have a couple of my own horses harnessed to convey it direct to Madame Danglars."

" But I dare not return with those dreadful horses," said Madame de Villefort.

" You will see," replied Monte Cristo, " that in the hands of Ali they will be gentle and docile as lambs."

Ali had indeed given proof of this,—for approaching the animals, who had been raised to their feet with considerable difficulty, with a sponge soaked in aromatic vinegar he rubbed their foreheads and nostrils, covered with sweat and foam; and almost immediately they began to breathe noisily, and a shudder, lasting several seconds, passed over their bodies. Then, undisturbed by the noisy crowd collected round the broken carriage, Ali quietly harnessed the pacified animals to the count's chariot, took the reins in his hands, and mounted the box; when lo! to the utter astonishment of those who had witnessed the ungovernable spirit and maddened velocity of the same horses, he was actually compelled to apply his whip in no very gentle manner ere he could induce them to start. And even then all that could be obtained from the celebrated dappled greys, now changed into a couple of dull, sluggish, stupid brutes, was a slow, pottering pace, kept up with so much difficulty that Madame de Villefort was more than two hours returning to her residence in the Faubourg St. Honoré. As soon as she arrived and had satisfied the first emotions of the family, she wrote the following letter to Madame Danglars:—

DEAR HERMINE,—I have just had a wonderful escape from the most imminent danger; and I owe my safety to the very Count of Monte Cristo we were talking about yesterday, but whom I little expected to see to-day. I remember how unmercifully I laughed at what I considered your eulogistic and exaggerated praises of him; but I have now ample cause to admit that your enthusiastic description of this wonderful man fell far short of his merits. But I must endeavour to render the account of my adventures somewhat more intelligible. You must know, then, my dear friend, that when I had proceeded with your horses as far as Ranelagh, they darted forward like mad things and galloped away at so fearful a rate that there seemed no other prospect for myself and my poor Edouard but that of being dashed to pieces against the first object that impeded their progress, when a strange-looking man,—an Arab or a Nubian, at least a black of some nation or other,—at a signal from the count, whose domestic he is, suddenly seized and stopped the infuriated animals, even at the risk of being trampled to death himself; and certainly he had a most wonderful escape. The count then hastened to us and carried us into his house, where by some skilful application he speedily recalled my poor Edouard (who was quite insensible from terror) to life. When we were sufficiently recovered he sent us home in his own carriage. Yours will be returned to you to-morrow. I am afraid you will not be able to use your horses for some days; they seem thoroughly stupefied, as if sulky and vexed at having allowed this black servant to conquer them. The count, however, has commissioned me to assure you that two or three days' rest, with plenty of barley for their sole food during that time, will bring them back to a condition as flourishing—that is to say, as frightful—as they were in yesterday. Adieu! I cannot return you many thanks for the drive to-day; but after all, I ought not to blame you for the misconduct of your horses, more especially as it procured me the pleasure of an introduction to the Count of Monte Cristo; and certainly that illustrious individual, apart from the millions at his disposal, seemed to me a problem so curious and so interesting that I intend to study it at all hazards,—even at the hazard, if necessary, of another ride behind your horses. Edouard has supported the accident with admirable courage. He did not utter a single cry, but fell lifeless into my arms; nor did a tear fall from his eyes after it was over. You will still say that I am blinded by maternal affection; but there is a soul of iron in that poor little body so frail and delicate. Valentine sends many affectionate remembrances to your dear Eugénie, and with best love to her and yourself, I remain, Ever yours truly,—HÉLOÏSE DE VILLEFORT.

P.S.—Do contrive some way for my meeting the Count of Monte Cristo at your house. I must see him again. I have just made M. de Villefort promise to call on him, and expect that he will return the call.

Nothing was talked of throughout the evening but the adventure at Auteuil. Albert related it to his mother; Château-Renaud recounted it at the Jockey Club; and Debray detailed it at length in the salons of the minister; even Beauchamp accorded twenty lines in his journal to the relation of the count's courage and gallantry, which exhibited him as a hero before the eyes of all the fair members of the aristocracy of France. Many persons left their names at the hotel of Madame de Villefort with the design of renewing their visit at the right moment to hear from her lips all the circumstances of this romantic adventure. As Héloïse had predicted, M. de Villefort put on a black suit and a pair of white gloves, and ordered the servants attending the carriage to be dressed in their full livery, and forthwith drove to the hotel of the count, situated, as the reader is already informed, in the Avenue des Champs Elysées.

CHAPTER XLVIII

IDEOLOGY

If the Count of Monte Cristo had lived for a very long time in Parisian society, he would have fully appreciated the significance of the step which M. de Villefort had taken. Standing well at court, whether the king regnant was of the elder or younger branch, whether the government was Doctrinaire, Liberal, or Conservative; esteemed clever by all, just as we generally esteem those clever who have never experienced a political check; hated by many, but warmly protected by others, without being really liked by anybody,—M. de Villefort held a high position in the magistracy, and maintained his eminence like a Harlay or a Molé. His drawing-room, regenerated by a young wife, and a daughter by his first marriage scarcely eighteen, was still one of those well-regulated Paris salons where the worship of traditional customs and the observance of rigid etiquette were carefully maintained. A freezing politeness; a strict fidelity to government principles; a profound contempt for theories and theorists; a deep-seated hatred of ideality,—these were the elements of private and public life displayed by M. de Villefort.

M. de Villefort was not only a magistrate, he was almost a diplomatist. His relations with the ancient court, of which he always spoke with dignity and respect, made him respected by the new one; and he knew so many things that not only was he always carefully considered, but sometimes consulted. Perhaps this would not have been so had it been possible to get rid of M. Villefort; but like the feudal barons who rebelled against their sovereign, he dwelt in an impregnable fortress. This fortress was his post as *procureur du roi*, all the advantages of which he worked out marvellously, and which he would not have resigned but to be made deputy, and thus to substitute opposition for neutrality. Ordinarily, M. de Villefort made and returned very few visits. His wife visited for him; and this was the received thing in the world, where they assigned to the heavy and multifarious occupations of the magistrate what was really only a calculation of pride, the essence of aristocracy, —in fact, the application of the axiom, " Pretend to think well of yourself and the world will think well of you," an axiom a hundred times more useful in our society than that of the Greeks, " Know thyself,"—a knowledge for which we have substituted the less difficult and more advantageous science of knowing others.

For his friends M. de Villefort was a powerful protector; for his enemies he was a silent but bitter enemy; for those who were neither the one nor the other he was a statue of the law made man. With a haughty air, immovable countenance, look steady and impenetrable, or else insultingly piercing and inquiring,—such was the man for whom four revolutions, skilfully piled one on the other, had first constructed and afterwards cemented the pedestal on which his fortune was erected. M. de Villefort had the reputation of being the least curious and the least wearisome man in France. He gave a ball every year, at which he appeared for a quarter of an hour only,—that is to say, five-and-forty minutes less than the king is visible at his balls. He was never seen at the theatres, at concerts, or in any place of public resort. Occasionally, but seldom, he played at whist; and then care was taken to select partners worthy of him, —some ambassador, archbishop, prince, president, or some dowager duchess. Such was the man whose carriage had just now stopped before the Count of Monte Cristo's door. The *valet de chambre* announced M. de Villefort at the moment when the count, leaning over a large table, was tracing on a map the route from St. Petersburg to China.

The *procureur du roi* entered with the same grave and measured step with which he would have entered a court of justice. He was the same man, or rather the completion of the same man, whom we have heretofore seen as deputy *procureur* at Marseilles. Nature, following up her principles, had changed nothing for him in the course she had marked out for him. From slender he had become meagre; from pale, yellow; his deep-set eyes were now hollow; and his gold spectacles, as they shielded his eyes, seemed to make a portion of his face. All his costume was black, with the exception of his white cravat; and this funereal appearance was varied only by the slight line of red ribbon which passed almost imperceptibly through his button-hole, and which appeared like a streak of blood traced with a pencil. Although master of himself, Monte Cristo scrutinised with irrepressible curiosity the magistrate, whose salute he returned, and who distrustful by habit and especially incredulous as to social marvels, was much more disposed to see in the noble stranger, as Monte Cristo was already called, a *chevalier d'industrie* who had come to try new ground, or some malefactor who had broken his prescribed limits, than a prince of the Holy See, or a sultan of the *Arabian Nights*.

"Monsieur," said Villefort, in the tone assumed by magistrates in their oratorical periods, and of which they cannot or will not divest themselves in society,—"Monsieur, the signal service which you yesterday rendered to my wife and son has made it my duty to offer you my thanks. Allow me, therefore, to discharge this duty and to express to you all my gratitude." And as he said this, the severe eye of the magistrate had lost nothing of its habitual arrogance. These words he articulated in the voice of a *procureur-général*, with the rigid inflexibility of neck and shoulders which caused his flatterers to say that he was a living statue of the law.

"Monsieur," replied the count, with icy coldness, "I am very happy to have been the means of preserving a son to his mother,—for they say that the sentiment of maternity is the most holy of all; and the good fortune which occurred to me, monsieur, might have enabled you to dispense with a duty which in its discharge confers an undoubtedly great honour,—for I am aware that M. de Villefort is not lavish of the favour he bestows on me, but which, however estimable, is unequal to the satisfaction which I internally experience."

Villefort, astonished at this reply which he by no means expected, started like a soldier who feels a blow upon the armour he wears; and a curl of his disdainful lip indicated that from that moment he noted in the tablets of his brain that the Count of Monte Cristo was by no means a civil gentleman. He glanced around for something on which to resume the fallen conversation, which in falling seemed to have broken in pieces. He saw the map which Monte Cristo had been examining when he entered, and said, "You seem geographically engaged, monsieur. It is a rich study, especially for you, who, as I learn, have seen as many lands as are delineated on this map."

"Yes, monsieur," replied the count; "I have sought to make on the human race, taken as a mass, what you practise every day on individuals,—a physiological study. I have believed it was much easier to descend from the whole to a part than to ascend from a part to the whole. It is an algebraic axiom which directs us to proceed from the known to the unknown, and not from the unknown to the known; but sit down, monsieur, I beg of you."

Monte Cristo pointed to a chair, which the *procureur du roi* was obliged to take the trouble to move forward himself while the count merely fell back into his own, on which he had been kneeling when M. de Villefort entered. Thus the count was half-way turned towards his visitor, having his back towards the window, his elbow resting on the geographical chart which afforded the conversation for the moment,—a conversation which assumed, as had those with Danglars and Morcerf, a turn adapted to the persons if not to the situation.

"Ah, you philosophise," replied Villefort, after a moment's silence, during which, like a wrestler who encounters a powerful opponent, he took breath; "well, monsieur, really, if like you I had nothing else to do, I should seek a more amusing occupation."

"Why, in truth, monsieur," was Monte Cristo's reply, "man is but an ugly caterpillar for him who studies him through a solar microscope; but you said, I think, that I had nothing else to do. Now, really, let me ask, monsieur, have you? Do you believe you have anything to do; or to speak in plain terms, do you think that what you do deserves being called anything?"

Villefort's astonishment redoubled at this second thrust so forcibly made by his strange adversary. It was a long time since the magistrate had heard a paradox so strong, or rather to say the truth more exactly, it was the first time he had ever heard of it. The *procureur du roi* exerted himself to reply. "Monsieur," he responded, "you are a stranger, and I believe you say yourself that a portion of your life has been spent in Oriental countries; so that you are not aware how human justice, so expeditious in barbarous countries, takes with us a prudent and well-studied course."

"Oh, yes,—yes, I am, monsieur; it is the *pede claudo* of the ancients. I know all that, for it is with the justice of all countries especially that I have occupied myself. It is the criminal procedure of all nations that I have compared with natural justice; and I must say, monsieur, that it is the law of primitive nations, —that is, the law of retaliation,—that I have most frequently found to be according to the law of God."

"If this law were adopted, sir," said the *procureur du roi*, "it would greatly simplify our legal codes; and in that case the magistrates would not, as you have just observed, have much to do."

"It may perhaps come to this in time," observed Monte Cristo. "You know that human inventions march from the complex to the simple; and simplicity is always perfection."

"In the meanwhile," continued the magistrate, "our codes are in full force, with all their contradictory enactments derived from Gallic customs, Roman laws, and Frank usages,—the knowledge of all which, you will agree, is not to be acquired without lengthened labour; and it requires a tedious study to acquire this knowledge, and when it is acquired, a strong power of brain is necessary in order to retain it."

" I agree with you entirely, monsieur; but all that even you know with respect to the French code, I know, not only in reference to that code, but as regards the codes of all nations. The English, Turkish, Japanese, Hindu laws are as familiar to me as the French laws; and thus I was right when I said to you that relatively—you know that everything is relative, monsieur—that relatively to what I have done, you have very little to do; but that relatively to all I have learned, you have yet a great deal to learn."

" But with what motive have you learned all this? " inquired Villefort, astonished.

Monte Cristo smiled. " Really, sir," he observed, " I see that in spite of the reputation which you have acquired as a superior man, you contemplate everything in the material and vulgar view of society, beginning with man and ending with man,—that is to say, in the most restricted, most narrow view which it is possible for human understanding to embrace."

" Pray, monsieur, explain yourself," said Villefort, more and more astonished; " I really do—not—understand you—perfectly."

" I say, monsieur, that with the eyes fixed on the social organisation of nations, you see only the springs of the machine, and lose sight of the sublime Artisan who makes them act; I say that you do not recognise before you and around you any but those place-men whose brevets have been signed by the minister or the king; and that the men whom God has put above those titulars, ministers, and kings, by giving them a mission to follow out, instead of a post to fill,—I say that they escape your narrow view. It is thus that human weakness fails, from its debilitated and imperfect organs. Tobias took the angel who restored him to sight for an ordinary young man; the nations took Attila, who was doomed to destroy them, for a conqueror similar to other conquerors; and it was necessary for both to reveal their missions, that they might be known and acknowledged. One was compelled to say, ' I am the angel of the Lord;' and the other, ' I am the hammer of God,' in order that the divine essence in both might be revealed."

" Then," said Villefort, more and more amazed, and really supposing he was speaking to a mystic or a madman, " you consider yourself as one of those extraordinary beings whom you have mentioned? "

" And why not? " said Monte Cristo, coldly.

" Your pardon, monsieur," replied Villefort, quite astounded;
" but you will excuse me if when I presented myself to you, I
was unaware that I should meet with a person whose knowledge and understanding so far surpass the usual knowledge
and understanding of men. It is not usual with us, corrupted
wretches of civilisation, to find gentlemen like yourself, posses-
sors, as you are, of immense fortune,—at least, so it is said; and
I beg you to observe that I do not inquire, I merely repeat,—it
is not usual, I say, for such privileged and wealthy beings
to waste their time in social speculations or in philosophical
reveries, fitted at best to console those whom fate has deprived
of the good things of this world."

" Really, monsieur," retorted the count, " have you attained
the eminent situation in which you are, without having admitted, or even without having met with exceptional beings;
and do you never use your eyes, which must have acquired so
much skill and certainty, to divine at a glance the kind of man
who has come before you? Should not a magistrate be not
merely the best administrator of the law, not merely the most
crafty expounder of the chicanery of his profession, but a steel
probe to search hearts, a touchstone to try the gold which in
each soul is mingled with more or less of alloy? "

" Monsieur," said Villefort, " upon my word, you overcome
me. I never heard a person speak as you do."

" Because you remain eternally encircled in a round of
general conditions, and have never dared to raise your wing
into those upper spheres which God has peopled with invisible
or exceptional beings."

" And you allow then, monsieur, that those spheres exist,
and that these exceptional and invisible beings mingle with us? "

" Why should they not? Can you see the air you breathe,
and without which you could not for a moment exist? "

" Then we do not see those beings to whom you allude? "

" Yes, we do; you see them whenever God pleases to allow
them to assume a material form. You touch them, come in
contact with them, speak to them, and they reply to you."

" Ah! " said Villefort, smiling, " I confess I should like to be
warned when one of these beings is in contact with me."

" You have been served as you desire, monsieur, for you have
been warned just now, and I now again warn you."

" Then you yourself are one of these marked beings? "

" Yes, monsieur; and I believe that until now no man has
found himself in a position similar to mine. The dominions of
kings are limited either by mountains or rivers, or a change of

manners, or an alteration of language. My kingdom is bounded only by the world,—for I am neither an Italian nor a Frenchman nor a Hindu nor an American nor a Spaniard; I am a cosmopolite. No country can say it saw my birth; God alone knows what country will see me die. I adopt all customs, speak all languages. You believe me to be a Frenchman, for I speak French with the same facility and purity as yourself. Well, Ali, my Nubian, believes me to be an Arab; Bertuccio, my steward, takes me for a Roman; Haydée, my slave, thinks me a Greek. You may therefore comprehend that being of no country, asking no protection from any government, acknowledging no man as my brother, not one of the scruples that arrest the powerful, or the obstacles which paralyse the weak, paralyses or arrests me. I have only two adversaries,—I will not say two conquerors, for with perseverance I subdue even them,—they are time and space. There is a third, and the most terrible,— that is, my condition as a mortal being. This alone can stop me in my onward career, and before I have attained the goal at which I aim; all the rest I have taken into account. What men call the chances of fate,—namely, ruin, change, circumstances,—I have anticipated them all; and if any of these should overtake me, yet they will not overwhelm me. Unless I die, I shall always be what I am; and therefore it is that I utter the things you have never heard, even from the mouths of kings,—for kings have need of you, and other persons fear you. For who is there who does not say to himself in a society as incongruously organised as ours, ' Perhaps some day I shall have to do with the *procureur du roi ?* '"

"But must you not say that, monsieur?—for the moment you become an inhabitant of France, you are naturally subjected to the French law."

"I know it, monsieur," replied Monte Cristo; "but when I visit a country, I begin to study, by all the means which are available, the men from whom I may have anything to hope or to fear, until I know them as well, perhaps better, than they know themselves. It follows from this that the *procureur du roi*, be he who he may, with whom I should have to deal would assuredly be more embarrassed than I should."

"That is to say," replied Villefort, with hesitation, "that human nature being weak, every man according to your creed has committed—faults."

"Faults or crimes," responded Monte Cristo, with a negligent air.

"And that you alone among men, whom you do not recognise

as your brothers,—for you have said so," observed Villefort, in a tone that faltered somewhat,—" you alone are perfect."

" No, not perfect," was the count's reply; " impenetrable, that's all. But let us leave off this strain, sir, if the tone of it is displeasing to you; I am no more disturbed by your justice than you are by my second-sight."

" No, no, by no means," said Villefort, who was afraid of seeming to abandon his ground. " No; by your brilliant and almost sublime conversation you have elevated me above the ordinary level. We no longer talk; we discourse. But you know how the theologians in their collegiate chairs, and philosophers in their controversies, occasionally say cruel truths. Let us suppose for the moment that we are discussing social theology and theological philosophy; I will say to you, rude as it may seem, ' My brother, you sacrifice greatly to pride; you may be above others, but above you there is God.'"

" Above us all, monsieur," was Monte Cristo's response, in a tone and with an emphasis so deep that Villefort involuntarily shuddered. " I have my pride for men,—serpents always ready to erect themselves against every one who may pass without crushing them. But I lay aside that pride before God, who has taken me from nothing to make me what I am."

" Then, Monsieur the Count, I admire you," said Villefort, who for the first time in this strange conversation applied that aristocratic formula to the unknown personage, whom, until now, he had only called *monsieur.* " Yes; and I say to you, if you are really strong, really superior, really holy,—or impenetrable, which you were right in saying amounts to the same thing,—be arrogant, monsieur, that is the characteristic of predominance. But you have unquestionably some ambition."

" I have had one, monsieur."

" And what was it? "

" I too, as happens to every man once in his life, have been taken by Satan upon the highest mountain in the earth; and when there he showed me all the kingdoms of the earth, and as he said before, so said he to me, ' Child of earth, what wouldst thou have to make thee adore me? ' I reflected long, for a gnawing ambition had long preyed upon me, and then I replied, ' Listen: I have always heard of Providence, and yet I have never seen him, nor anything that resembles him, or which can make me believe that he exists. I wish to be Providence myself, for I feel that the most beautiful, noblest, most sublime thing in the world, is to recompense and punish.' Satan bowed his head and groaned. ' You mistake,' he said; ' Providence does exist, only you have never seen him, because the child of God is as invisible as the parent. You have seen nothing that resembles him, because he works by secret springs, and moves by hidden ways. All I can do for you is to make you one of the agents of that Providence.' The bargain was concluded. I may have lost my soul; but what matters it?" added Monte Cristo. "If the thing were to do again, I would again do it."

Villefort looked at Monte Cristo with extreme amazement. "Monsieur the Count," he inquired, "have you any relatives?"

"No, sir, I am alone in the world."

"So much the worse."

"Why?" asked Monte Cristo.

"Because then you might witness a spectacle calculated to break down your pride. You say you fear nothing but death?"

"I did not say that I feared it; I only said that that alone could check me."

"And old age?"

"My end will be achieved before I grow old."

"And madness?"

"I have been nearly mad; and you know the axiom, *non bis in idem*. It is an axiom of criminal law, and consequently you understand its full application."

"Monsieur," continued Villefort, "there is something to fear besides death, old age, and madness. For instance, there is apoplexy,—that lightning-stroke which strikes but does not destroy you, and yet after which all is ended. You are still yourself as now, and yet you are yourself no longer; you who like Ariel touch on the angelic, are but an inert mass, which like Caliban touches on the brutal; and this is called in human tongues, as I tell you, neither more nor less than apoplexy. Come, if so you will, Monsieur the Count, and continue this conversation at my house, any day you may be willing to see an adversary capable of understanding and anxious to refute you, and I will show you my father, M. Noirtier de Villefort, one of the most fiery Jacobins of the French Revolution,—that is to say, a man of the most remarkable audacity, seconded by a most vigorous temperament; a man who perhaps has not, like yourself, seen all the kingdoms of the earth, but who has helped to overturn one of the most powerful; a man who, like you, believed himself one of the envoys, not of God, but of the Supreme Being,—not of Providence, but of fate. Well, monsieur, the rupture of a blood-vessel in the lobe of the brain has destroyed all this,—not in a day, not in an hour, but in a second. M. Noirtier, who on the previous night was the old Jacobin, the old senator, the old Carbonaro, laughing at the guillotine, laughing at the cannon, laughing at the dagger; M. Noirtier, playing with revolutions; M. Noirtier, for whom France was a vast chess-board from which pawns, rooks, knights, and queens were to disappear, so that the king was checkmated,—M. Noirtier, so redoubtable, was the next morning *poor M. Noirtier,* the helpless old man, at the tender mercies of the weakest creature in the household, that is, his grandchild, Valentine; a dumb and frozen carcass in fact, who only lives without suffering, that time may be given to his frame to decompose without his consciousness of its decay."

"Alas, sir!" said Monte Cristo, "this spectacle is neither strange to my eyes nor my thought. I am something of a physician, and have, like my fellows, sought more than once for the soul in living and in dead matter; yet like Providence it has remained invisible to my eyes, although present to my heart. A hundred writers since Socrates, Seneca, Saint Augustine, and Gall have made in verse and prose the comparison you have made; and yet I can well understand that a father's sufferings may effect great changes in the mind of a son. I will call on you, sir, since you bid me contemplate, for the advantage of my pride, this terrible spectacle, which must spread so much sorrow throughout your house."

"It would have done so unquestionably, had not God given me so large a compensation. In presence of the old man who is dragging his way to the tomb, are two children just entering into life,—Valentine, the daughter by my first wife, Mademoiselle Renée de Saint-Méran, and Edouard, the boy whose life you have this day saved."

"And what is your deduction from this compensation, monsieur?" inquired Monte Cristo.

"My deduction is," replied Villefort, "that my father, led away by his passions, has committed some fault unknown to human justice, but marked by the justice of God; and that God, wishing to punish but one person, has visited this justice on him alone."

Monte Cristo, with a smile on his lips, had yet a groan at his heart, which would have made Villefort fly had he but heard it.

"Adieu, monsieur," said the magistrate, who had risen from his seat; "I leave you, bearing a remembrance of you.—a remembrance of esteem, which I hope will not be disagreeable to you when you know me better; for I am not a man to bore my friends, as you will learn. Besides, you have made an eternal friend of Madame de Villefort."

The count bowed and contented himself with seeing Villefort to the door of his cabinet, the *procureur* being escorted to his carriage by two footmen, who on a signal from their master followed him with every mark of attention. When he had gone, Monte Cristo drew a hard breath from his oppressed bosom, and said, " Enough of this poison; let me now seek the antidote." Then sounding his bell, he said to Ali, who entered, " I am going to madame's apartments; have the carriage ready at one o'clock."

CHAPTER XLIX

HAYDÉE

THE reader will remember who were the new—or rather, old—acquaintances of the Count of Monte Cristo who lived in the Rue Meslay; they were Maximilian, Julie, and Emmanuel. The anticipation of that pleasant visit which he was about to make, of those few happy moments he was to enjoy, of that ray of Paradise gleaming across the hell to which he had voluntarily committed himself, had, from the moment in which he had lost sight of Villefort, illumined the face of the count with a most charming expression of happiness; and Ali, who had responded quickly to the call of the bell, seeing that face so beaming with a joy so rare, withdrew on tiptoe and holding his breath, as if he feared to frightened away the pleasing thoughts which seemed to him to hover around his master.

It was the hour of noon, and Monte Cristo had set apart one hour to be passed with Haydée. It seemed as if happiness could not gain a sudden admission to that soul which had been so long oppressed; that it needed to prepare itself for gentle emotions, as other souls need to be prepared for violent emotions. The young Greek, as we have already stated, occupied apartments wholly unconnected with those of the count. The rooms had been fitted up in strict accordance with the Eastern style, —that is to say, the floors were covered with the richest carpets Turkey could produce, and the walls hung with brocaded silk of the most magnificent designs and texture; while around each chamber luxurious divans were placed, with piles of soft and yielding cushions that could be arranged at the pleasure of those who used them. Haydée had four women in her service,—three French and one Greek. The three French women remained constantly in a small waiting-room, ready to obey the first sound of a small golden bell, or to receive the orders of the Romaic slave, who knew sufficient French to transmit her mistress's orders to the three other waiting-women, who had received instructions from Monte Cristo to treat Haydée with all the respect and deference they would pay to a queen.

The young girl was in the inner room of her apartments,—a sort of boudoir, circular, lighted only from above, through panes of rose-coloured glass. She was reclining upon cushions covered with blue satin spotted with silver; her head, supported by one of her exquisitely moulded arms, rested on the divan immediately behind her, while the other was employed in adjusting to her lips the coral tube of a rich nargile, through whose flexible pipe the vapour ascended fully impregnated with the rich odours of the most delicious flowers. Her attitude, though quite natural for an Oriental, would have evinced perhaps, in the case of a French woman, a slight affectation of coquetry. Her dress, which was that of the women of Epirus, consisted of a pair of white satin trousers, embroidered with pink roses,— exposing to view two small feet, which might have been taken for Parian marble but for their playing with two little sandals turned up at the point, and adorned with gold and pearls; a blue and white striped vest, with large open sleeves, trimmed with silver loops and buttons of pearls; and a species of bodice, which, of a heart-shaped pattern in front, exhibited the whole of the ivory throat and upper part of the bosom, and was fastened below by three diamond buttons. The junction of the bodice and trousers was entirely concealed by one of those many-coloured scarfs, whose brilliant hues and rich silken fringe have rendered then so precious in the eyes of Parisian belles. A small cap of gold, embroidered with pearls, was placed on one side of her head; while on the other a natural rose, of purple colour, mingled with the luxuriant masses of her hair, which was so black that it appeared to be blue. The beauty of the countenance was peculiarly and purely Grecian; there were the large dark melting eyes, straight nose, the coral lips, and pearly teeth, that belonged to her race and country. And to complete the whole, Haydée was in the very springtide and fulness of youthful charms; she was nineteen or twenty years old.

Monte Cristo summoned the Greek attendant, and bade her inquire whether it would be agreeable to her mistress to receive his visit. Haydée's only reply was to direct her servant by a sign to withdraw the tapestried curtain that hung before the door of her boudoir; the framework of the opening thus made served as a sort of border to the graceful tableau presented by the reclining young girl. As Monte Cristo approached, she leaned upon the elbow of the arm that held the nargile, and extending to him her other hand, said with a smile of captivating sweetness, in the sonorous language spoken by the women of Athens and Sparta, " Why demand permission ere you enter? Are you no longer my master, or have I ceased to be your slave? "

Monte Cristo returned her smile. " Haydée," said he, " you know—"

" Why do you address me so coldly? " asked the fair Greek. " Have I by any means displeased you? If so, punish me as you will; but do not speak to me so formally! "

" Haydée," replied the count, " you know that we are now in France, and that you are consequently free! "

" Free! " repeated the young girl; " free to do what? "

" Free to leave me."

" Leave you! and why should I leave you? "

" That is not for me to say; but we are now about to mix in society,—to see the world."

" I have no wish to see any one."

" Nay, but hear me, Haydée. You cannot remain in seclusion in the midst of this gay capital; and should you see one whom you could prefer, think not I would be so selfish or unjust as to—"

" I have never seen men handsomer than you; and I have loved only you and my father."

" My poor child! " replied Monte Cristo, " that is merely because you have hardly spoken to any one but your father and myself."

" Well! what occasion is there for me to speak to any one else? My father called me *his joy;* you style me *your love;* and both of you call me *your child!* "

" Do you remember your father, Haydée? "

The young Greek smiled. " He is here, and here," said she, touching her eyes and her heart.

" And where am I then? " inquired Monte Cristo, laughingly.

" You? " cried she, " you are everywhere! "

Monte Cristo took the delicate hand of the young girl in his, and was about to raise it to his lips, when the simple child of nature hastily withdrew it, and presented her fair cheek instead. " You now understand, Haydée," said the count, " that from this moment you are absolutely free; that you are mistress; that you are queen. You are at liberty to lay aside or continue the costume of your country, as it may suit your inclination; you will remain here when you wish, and you will go abroad when you wish. There will always be a carriage awaiting your orders; and Ali and Myrto will accompany you whithersoever you desire to go. There is but one favour I would entreat of you."

" Oh, speak ! "

" Preserve most carefully the secret of your birth. Make no allusion to the past; nor upon any occasion be induced to pronounce the name of your illustrious father nor that of your poor mother ! "

" I have already told you, my lord, that I will see no one."

" It is possible, Haydée, that so perfect a seclusion, though conformable with the habits and customs of the East, may not be practicable in Paris. Endeavour, then, to accustom yourself to our manner of living in these northern climes, as you did to those of Rome, Florence, Milan, and Madrid; it may be useful to you one of these days, whether you remain here or return to the East."

The young girl raised her tearful eyes towards Monte Cristo, as she said with touching earnestness, " Whether *we* return to the East, you mean, do you not, my lord? "

" My child," returned Monte Cristo, " you know well that if we part, it will be by no wish of mine. The tree does not leave the flower; the flower leaves the tree."

" My lord," replied Haydée, " I will never leave you, for I am sure that I could not live without you."

" Poor child ! In ten years I shall be old; and you will still be young."

" My father had numbered sixty years, and the snows of age were on his head, but I admired and loved him far better than all the gay, handsome youths I saw about his court."

" Then tell me, Haydée, do you believe you shall be able to accustom yourself to our present mode of life? "

" Shall I see you? "

" Every day."

" Well, then ! what are you asking me, my lord? "

" I fear that you may feel lonely."

" No, my lord, for in the morning I shall expect your coming, and in the evening shall remember that you have been with me; and besides, when alone I have grand remembrances,— I see again immense plains and far horizons with Pindus and Olympus in the distance; and then I have in my heart three sentiments which leave no room for *ennui*,—they are sorrow, love, and gratitude."

" You are a worthy daughter of Epirus, Haydée, and your charming and poetical ideas prove well your descent from that race of goddesses who claim your country as their birthplace; depend on my care to see that your youth is not blighted, or suffered to pass away in ungenial solitude, for if you love me as a father, I too love you as my child."

"Let not my lord be deceived; the love I bear you resembles in no degree my feelings towards my father. I survived *his* death; but were any evil to befall you, the moment in which I learned the fatal tidings would be the last of my life."

The count, with a look of indescribable tenderness, extended his hand to the animated speaker, who carried it reverentially and affectionately to her lips. Monte Cristo, thus soothed and calmed into a befitting state of mind to pay his visit to the Morrels, departed, murmuring as he went these lines of Pindar, "Youth is a flower of which love is the fruit; happy is he who, after having watched its silent growth, is permitted to call it his own." The carriage was ready according to orders; and stepping lightly into it, the count drove off at his usual rapid pace.

CHAPTER L

THE MORREL FAMILY

IN a very few minutes the count reached No. 7 in the Rue Meslay. The house was of white stone, and in a small court before it were two small beds full of beautiful flowers. In the *concierge* that opened the gate the count recognised Coclès; but as he had but one eye, and that eye had considerably weakened in the course of nine years, Coclès did not recognise the count. The carriages that drove up to the door were compelled to turn to avoid a fountain that played in a basin of rockwork, in which sported a large number of gold and silver fishes,—an ornament that had excited the jealousy of the whole quarter, and had gained for the house the appellation of *le Petit Versailles*. The house, raised above the kitchens and cellars, had besides the ground-floor two stories and attics. The whole of the property, consisting of an immense workshop, two pavilions at the bottom of the garden, and the garden itself, had been purchased by Emmanuel, who had seen at a glance that he could make a profitable speculation of it. He had reserved the house and half the garden, and building a wall between the garden and the workshops, had let them with the pavilions at the bottom of the garden; so that for a trifling sum he was as well lodged, and as completely shut out from observation as the most exacting proprietor of a hotel in the Faubourg St. Germain. The dining-room was of oak; the salon, of mahogany and blue velvet; the bedroom, of citron wood and green damask. There was a study for Emmanuel, who never studied, and a music-room for Julie, who never played. The whole of the second story was set apart for Maximilian; it was precisely the same as his sister's apartments, except that the dining-room was changed into a billiard-room, where he received his friends. He was superintending the grooming of his horse, and smoking his cigar at the entrance of the garden, when the count's carriage stopped at the door.

Coclès opened the gate, and Baptistin, springing from the box, inquired whether Monsieur and Madame Herbaut and M. Maximilian Morrel would see M. le Comte de Monte Cristo.

"M. le Comte de Monte Cristo?" cried Morrel, throwing away his cigar and hastening to the carriage; "I should think we would see him! Ah! a thousand thanks, Monsieur the Count, for not having forgotten your promise." And the young officer shook the count's hand so warmly that the latter could not be mistaken as to the sincerity of his expressions; he saw that he had been expected with impatience, and was received with pleasure.

"Come, come!" said Maximilian; "I will serve as your guide,—such a man as you are ought not to be introduced by a servant. My sister is in the garden plucking the dead roses; my brother is reading his two papers, *La Presse* and *Les Débats*, within five steps of her; for wherever you see Madame Herbaut you have only to look within a circle of four yards and you will find M. Emmanuel, and 'reciprocally,' as they say at the Ecole Polytechnique." At the sound of their steps a young woman of from twenty to twenty-five years, dressed in a silk *robe de chambre*, and busily engaged in plucking the dead leaves off the splendid rose-tree, raised her head. This woman was Julie, who had become, as the clerk of the house of Thomson and French had predicted, Madame Emmanuel Herbaut. She uttered a cry of surprise at the sight of a stranger; and Maximilian began to laugh. "Don't disturb yourself, Julie," said he. "Monsieur the Count has only been two or three days in Paris; but he already knows what a woman of fashion of the Marais is, and if he does not you will show him."

"Ah, monsieur!" returned Julie, "it is treason in my brother to bring you thus; but he never has any regard for his poor sister. Penelon! Penelon!"

An old man, who was digging busily at one of the beds of

roses, stuck his spade in the earth and approached, cap in hand, and striving to conceal a quid of tobacco he had just thrust into his cheek. A few locks of grey mingled with his hair, which was still thick and matted, while his bronzed features and determined glance announced the old sailor who had braved the heat of the equator and the storms of the tropics. "I think you hailed me, Mademoiselle Julie?" said he. Penelon had still preserved the habit of calling his master's daughter "Mademoiselle Julie," and had never been able to change the name to Madame Herbaut.

"Penelon," replied Julie, "go and inform M. Emmanuel of this gentleman's visit, while Maximilian conducts him to the salon." Then, turning to Monte Cristo, "I hope you will permit me to leave you for a few minutes," continued she, and without awaiting any reply disappeared behind a clump of trees, and entered the house by a lateral alley.

"I am sorry to see," observed Monte Cristo to Morrel, "that I cause no small disturbance in your house."

"Look there," said Maximilian, laughing; "there is her husband changing his jacket for a coat. I assure you that you are well known in the Rue Meslay."

"Your family appears to me a very happy one!" said the count, as if speaking to himself.

"Oh, yes, I assure you, Monsieur the Count, they want nothing that can render them happy. They are young and cheerful; they are tenderly attached to each other; and with twenty-five thousand livres a year they fancy themselves as rich as the Rothschilds."

"Five and twenty thousand livres is not a large sum, however," replied Monte Cristo, with a tone so sweet and gentle that it went to Maximilian's heart like the voice of a father; "but they will not be content with that. Your brother-in-law is a barrister; a doctor?"

"He was a merchant, Monsieur the Count, and had succeeded to the business of my poor father. M. Morrel, at his death, left five hundred thousand livres, which were divided between my sister and myself, for we were his only children. Her husband, who when he married her had no other patrimony than his noble probity, his first-rate ability, and his spotless reputation, wished to possess as much as his wife. He laboured and toiled until he had amassed two hundred and fifty thousand livres; six years sufficed to achieve this object. Oh, I assure you, Monsieur the Count, it was a touching spectacle to see these young creatures, destined by their talents for higher stations, toiling together, and unwilling to change any of the customs of their paternal house, taking six years to accomplish that which innovators would have effected in two or three. Marseilles still resounds with their well-earned praises. At last, one day Emmanuel came to his wife, who had just finished making up the accounts. 'Julie,' said he to her, 'Coclès has just given me the last *rouleau* of a hundred livres; that completes the two hundred and fifty thousand livres we had fixed as the limits of our gains. Can you content yourself with the small fortune which we shall possess for the future? Listen to me. Our house transacts business to the amount of a million a year, from which we derive an income of forty thousand livres. We can dispose of the business, if we please, in an hour, for I have received a letter from M. Delaunay, in which he offers to purchase the good-will of the house, to unite it with his own, for three hundred thousand livres. Advise me what I had better do.' 'Emmanuel,' returned my sister, 'the house of Morrel can only be carried on by a Morrel. Is it not worth three hundred thousand livres to save our father's name from the chances of evil fortune and failure?' 'I thought so,' replied Emmanuel; 'but I wished to have your advice.' 'This is my counsel: Our accounts are made up and our bills paid; all we have to do is to stop the issue of any more, and close our office.' This was done instantly. It was three o'clock; at a quarter past a merchant presented himself to insure two ships. There was a clear profit of fifteen thousand livres. 'Monsieur,' said Emmanuel, 'have the goodness to address yourself to M. Delauney. We have quitted business.' 'How long ago?' inquired the astonished merchant. 'A quarter of an hour,' was the reply. And this is the reason, monsieur," continued Maximilian, " that my sister and brother-in-law have only twenty-five thousand livres a year."

Maximilian had scarcely finished his story, during which the count's heart had seemed ready to burst, when Emmanuel entered, having meanwhile put on a hat and coat. He saluted the count with the air of a man who is aware of the rank of his guest, then after having led Monte Cristo round the little garden, he returned to the house. A large vase of Japan porcelain, filled with flowers that impregnated the air with their perfume, stood in the salon. Julie, suitably dressed, and with her hair coquettishly arranged (she had accomplished this feat in less than ten minutes), received the count on his entrance. The songs of the birds were heard in an aviary hard by,—the branches of false ebony trees and rose acacias forming the border of the blue velvet curtains. Everything in this charming retreat, from the warble of the birds to the smile of the mistress, breathed tranquillity and repose. The count had felt from the moment he entered the house the influence of this happiness, and he remained silent and pensive, forgetting that he was expected to recommence the conversation which had ceased after the first salutations had been exchanged. He perceived the pause, and by a violent effort tearing himself from his reverie, "Madame," said he at length, "I pray you to excuse my emotion, which must astonish you who are accustomed to the happiness I meet here; but satisfaction upon a human countenance is so new a sight to me, that I could never be weary of looking at yourself and your husband."

"We are indeed very happy, monsieur," replied Julie; "but we have also known unhappiness, and few have ever undergone more bitter sufferings than ourselves."

The count's features now displayed an expression of curiosity.

"Oh, all this is a family history, as Château-Renaud told you the other day," observed Maximilian. "This humble picture would have but little interest for you, accustomed as you are to behold the pleasures and the misfortunes of the wealthy and illustrious; but such as we are we have experienced bitter sorrows."

"And God has poured balm into your wounds, as he does for all those who are in affliction?" said Monte Cristo, inquiringly.

"Yes, Monsieur the Count," returned Julie, "we may indeed say he has, for he has done for us what he does for only his elect,—he sent us one of his angels."

The count's cheeks became scarlet, and he coughed so as to have an excuse for putting his handkerchief to his mouth.

"Those born to wealth and who have the means of gratifying every wish," said Emmanuel, "know not what is the real happiness of life; just as those who have been tossed on the stormy waters of the ocean on a few frail planks can alone estimate the value of a clear and serene sky."

Monte Cristo rose, and without making any answer,—for the tremulousness of his voice would have betrayed his emotion,— walked up and down the room with a slow step.

"Our magnificence makes you smile, Monsieur the Count," said Maximilian, who had followed him with his eyes.

"No, no," returned Monte Cristo, very pale, and pressing one hand on his heart to still its throbbings, while with the other he pointed to a crystal cover, beneath which a silken purse lay on a black velvet cushion. "I was wondering what could be the use of this purse which appears to contain a paper at one end, and at the other a large diamond."

"Monsieur the Count," replied Maximilian, with an air of gravity, "those are our most precious family treasures."

"The stone seems very brilliant," answered the count.

"Oh, my brother does not allude to its value, although it has been estimated at one hundred thousand livres; he means that the articles contained in this purse are memorials of the angel of whom I spoke just now."

"This I do not comprehend; and yet I may not ask for an explanation, madame," replied Monte Cristo, bowing. "Pardon me, I had no intention of committing an indiscretion."

"Indiscretion! Oh, you make us happy by giving us an occasion of expatiating on this subject. Did we intend to conceal the noble action this purse commemorates, we should not expose it thus. Oh! would we could relate it everywhere and to every one! so that the emotion of our unknown benefactor might reveal his presence."

"Ah, really!" said Monte Cristo, in a half-stifled voice.

"Monsieur," returned Maximilian, raising the glass cover and respectfully kissing the silken purse, "this has touched the hand of a man who saved my father from suicide, us from ruin, and our name from shame and disgrace, — a man by whose matchless benevolence we, poor children doomed to want and wretchedness, can at present hear every one envying our happy lot. This letter" (as he spoke, Maximilian drew a letter from the purse and gave it to the count)—"this letter was written by him the day that my father had taken a desperate resolution, and this diamond was given by the generous unknown to my sister as her dowry." Monte Cristo opened the letter and read it with an indescribable feeling of delight. It was the letter written (as our readers know) to Julie, and signed "Sinbad the Sailor."

"Unknown, you say; is the man who rendered you this service unknown to you?"

"Yes; we have never had the happiness of pressing his hand," continued Maximilian. "We have supplicated Heaven in vain to grant us this favour, but all the affair has had a mysterious direction which we cannot comprehend; all has been guided by a hand invisible but powerful as that of an enchanter."

"Oh!" cried Julie, "I have not lost all hope of some day kissing that hand as I now kiss the purse which he has touched. Four years ago Penelon was at Trieste,—Penelon, Monsieur the Count, is the old sailor whom you saw in the garden, and who from quartermaster has become gardener,—Penelon, when he was at Trieste, saw on the quay an Englishman who was on the point of embarking on board a yacht; and he recognised him as the person who called on my father on the 5th of June, 1829, and who wrote me this letter on the 5th of September. He felt convinced of his identity, but he did not venture to address him."

"An Englishman!" said Monte Cristo, who grew uneasy at the attention with which Julie looked at him. "An Englishman, you say?"

"Yes," replied Maximilian, "an Englishman, who represented himself as the confidential clerk of the house of Thomson and French, at Rome. It was this that made me start when you said the other day, at M. de Morcerf's, that Messrs. Thomson and French were your bankers. That happened, as I told you, in 1829. For God's sake, tell me, did you know this Englishman?"

"But you tell me, also, that the house of Thomson and French have constantly denied having rendered you this service?"

"Yes."

"Then is it not probable that this Englishman may be some one who, grateful for a kindness your father had shown him, and which he himself had forgotten, has taken this method of requiting the obligation?"

"Everything is possible on such an occasion, even a miracle."

"What was his name?" asked Monte Cristo.

"He gave no other name," answered Julie, looking earnestly at the count, "than that at the end of his letter,—'Sinbad the Sailor.'"

"Which is evidently not his real name, but a fictitious one."

Then noticing that Julie was struck with the sound of his voice, "Tell me," continued he, "was he not about my height, perhaps a little taller and slenderer, with his neck confined in a high cravat,—closely buttoned and laced, and always carrying a pencil in his hand?"

"Oh, do you then know him?" cried Julie, whose eyes sparkled with joy.

"No," returned Monte Cristo, "I only guessed. I knew a Lord Wilmore, who was constantly doing acts of generosity."

"Without revealing himself?"

"He was an eccentric being, and did not believe in the existence of gratitude."

"Oh, Heaven!" exclaimed Julie, clasping her hands. "In what did he believe, then?"

"He did not believe in it at the period when I knew him," said Monte Cristo, touched to the heart by the accents of Julie's voice; "but perhaps since then he has had proofs that gratitude does exist."

"And do you know this gentleman, monsieur?" inquired Emmanuel.

"Oh, if you do know him," cried Julie, "can you tell us where he is,—where we can find him? Maximilian, Emmanuel! if we do but discover him, he must believe in the gratitude of the heart!"

Monte Cristo felt tears start into his eyes, and he again walked hastily up and down the room.

"In the name of Heaven!" said Maximilian, "if you know anything of him, tell us what it is."

"Alas!" cried Monte Cristo, striving to repress his emotion. "If Lord Wilmore was your unknown benefactor, I fear you will never again see him. I parted from him two years ago at Palermo, and he was then on the point of setting out for the most remote regions; so that I fear he will never return."

"Oh, monsieur, this is cruel of you," said Julie, much affected; and tears came into her eyes.

"Madame," replied Monte Cristo, gravely, and gazing earnestly on the two liquid pearls that trickled down Julie's cheeks, "had Lord Wilmore seen what I now see, he would become attached to life, for the tears you shed would reconcile him to mankind;" and he held out his hand to Julie, who gave him hers, carried away by the look and accent of the count.

"But this Lord Wilmore," said she, clinging to the last hope, "had a country, a family, relatives,—in short, he was known to some one? Could we not, then—"

"Oh, make no inquiries, madame," said the count; "do not build chimerical hopes on that word of mine. No; Lord Wilmore is probably not the man whom you seek. He was my friend; he had no secrets from me, and he would have confided this also to me."

"And he told you nothing?"

"Nothing."

"Never a word which might lead you to suppose—"

"Never."

"And yet you instantly named him."

"Ah, in such a case one supposes—"

"Sister, sister," said Maximilian, coming to the count's aid,

" Monsieur is quite right. Recollect what our excellent father so often told us: ' It was no Englishman that thus saved us.' "

Monte Cristo started. " What did your father tell you, M. Morrel? " said he, eagerly.

" My father thought that this action had been miraculously performed; he believed that a benefactor had arisen from the grave to save us. Oh, it was a touching superstition, monsieur; and although I did not myself believe it, I would not for the world have destroyed my father's faith in it. How often did he muse over it and pronounce the name of a dear friend,— a friend lost to him for ever! and on his death-bed, when the near approach of eternity seemed to have illumined his mind with supernatural light, this thought, which had until then been but a doubt, became a conviction, and his last words were, ' Maximilian, it was Edmond Dantès!' "

At these words the count's paleness, which had for some time been increasing, became alarming. He could not speak; he looked at his watch like a man who has forgotten the time, said a few hurried words to Madame Herbaut, and pressing the hands of Emmanuel and Maximilian, " Madame," said he, " I trust you will allow me to visit you from time to time; I value your friendship and feel grateful to you for your welcome, for this is the first time for many years that I have thus yielded to my feelings; " and he hastily quitted the room.

" This Count of Monte Cristo is a singular man," said Emmanuel.

" Yes," answered Maximilian, " but I feel sure he has an excellent heart, and that he likes us."

" His voice went to my heart," observed Julie; " and two or three times I fancied I had heard it before."

CHAPTER LI

PYRAMUS AND THISBE

NEAR the middle of the Faubourg St. Honoré, and at the back of one of the most distinguished-looking mansions in this rich neighbourhood, where the various hotels vie with each other for elegance of design and magnificence of construction, extended a large garden, whose widely-spreading chestnut-trees raised their heads above the walls, high and solid as those of a rampart, scattering each spring a shower of delicate pink and white blossoms into the large stone vases placed at equal distances upon the two square pilasters supporting an iron gate of the time of Louis XIV. This noble entrance, however, notwithstanding its striking appearance and the graceful effect of the geraniums planted in the two vases, as they waved their variegated leaves in the wind, and charmed the eye with their scarlet bloom, had fallen into utter disuse from the period when the proprietors of the hotel (and many years had elapsed since then) had confined themselves to the possession of the hotel, with its thickly-planted courtyard opening into the Faubourg St. Honoré, and the garden shut in by this gate, which formerly communicated with a fine kitchen-garden of about an acre in extent. But the demon of speculation having drawn a line,—that is to say, a street,—at the extremity of this garden, and the street having received a name even before it was completed, it occurred to the owner to sell the garden for a building site on the street, and make connection with that grand artery of Paris called the Faubourg St. Honoré.

In matters of speculation, however, man proposes, and money disposes. The newly named street was never finished; and the purchaser of the kitchen-garden, having made complete payment, was unable to find any one willing to take his bargain off his hands without a considerable loss. Believing, however, that at some future day he should obtain a sum for it that would repay him not only for his past outlay, but also the interest upon the capital locked up in his new acquisition, he contented himself with letting the ground temporarily to some market-gardeners, at a yearly rent of five hundred livres. Thus, then, as already stated, the iron gate leading into the kitchen-garden had been closed up and left to the rust, which bade fair to destroy its hinges ere long, while to prevent the ignoble glances of the diggers and delvers of the ground from presuming to sully the aristocratic enclosure belonging to the hotel, the gate in question had been boarded up to a height of six feet. True, the planks are not so closely adjusted but that stolen views may be obtained between their interstices; but that house is rigidly proper, and has no fear of indiscreet curiosity.

In that garden, where the most choice and delicate of fruits and vegetables once reared their heads, a scanty crop of lucerne alone bears evidence of cultivation. A small, low door opening on the projected street gives entrance to the enclosed space, which has finally been abandoned on account of its sterility, and which for a week past instead of yielding one half of one per cent. on its cost, as it had previously, yields nothing at all. Towards the hotel the chestnut-trees we have before mentioned rise high above the wall, without in any way affecting the growth of other luxuriant shrubs and flowers that eagerly press forward to fill up the vacant spaces, as though asserting their right to enjoy the boon of light and air also. At one corner, where the foliage is so thick as almost to shut out the daylight, a large stone bench and sundry rustic seats indicate that this sheltered spot is either a place of assemblage or a favourite retreat of some inhabitant of the hotel, which is faintly discernible through the dense mass of verdure that partially conceals it, though situated but a hundred paces off. In short, the choice of this mysterious retreat is abundantly justified by the absence of all glare; the cool, refreshing shade; the screen it affords from the scorching rays of the sun, that find no entrance there even during the burning days of hottest summer; the warbling of birds; and the seclusion from both the noise of the street and the bustle of the hotel.

On the evening of one of the warmest days spring had yet bestowed on the inhabitants of Paris, might be seen, negligently thrown upon the stone bench, a book, a parasol, and a work-basket from which hung a partly embroidered cambric hand-kerchief; while at a little distance from these articles was a young woman, standing close to the iron gate, endeavouring to discern something on the other side through the openings in the planks, while the earnestness of her attitude and the fixed gaze with which she seemed to seek the object of her wishes, proved how much her feelings were interested in the matter. At that instant, the little side door leading from the enclosure to the street was noiselessly opened; and a tall powerful young man, dressed in a common grey blouse and velvet cap, but whose carefully arranged hair, beard, and mustaches, all of the richest and glossiest black, but ill accorded with his plebeian attire, after casting a rapid glance around him, in order to assure him-self that he was unobserved, entered, and carefully closing and securing it after him, proceeded with a hurried step towards the iron gate.

On seeing him present whom she had been expecting to see, though probably not in such a costume, the young girl started in terror, and was about to make a hasty retreat. But the young man with the eye of love had already seen through the openings in the gate the movement of the white robe, and observed the fluttering of the blue sash fastened around the slender waist of his fair neighbour. He sprang to the wall, and applying his mouth to an opening, exclaimed, " Fear nothing, Valentine; it is I! "

The young girl drew near. " Oh, monsieur," she said, " why have you come to-day so late? It is almost the dinner-hour, and I have been compelled to exercise my utmost skill to get rid of the incessant watchfulness of my stepmother, as well as the espionage of my maid, who no doubt is employed to report all I do and say. Nor has it cost me a little trouble to free myself from the troublesome society of my brother, under pretence of coming hither to work undisturbed at my embroidery, which I fear will not soon be finished. So excuse yourself as well as you can for having made me wait; and after that tell me why I see you in so singular a dress, which almost prevented my recognising you."

" Dear Valentine," said the young man, " you are so far beyond my love that I dare not speak of it to you; and yet every time I see you I want to tell you that I adore you, so that the echo of my own words is sweet in my heart when I am no longer with you. Now I thank you for your reproaches; they are altogether charming, for they show me, I don't dare to say that you awaited me, but that you thought of me. You wish to know the cause of my delay and the reason of my disguise; I will explain, and I hope that you will pardon. I have chosen a trade."

" A trade! Oh, Maximilian, how can you jest at a time when we have such deep cause for uneasiness? "

" Heaven keep me from jesting with that which is far dearer to me than life itself! But listen to me, Valentine, and I will tell you all about it. Tired out with ranging fields and scaling walls, and seriously alarmed at the idea suggested by yourself, that if I should be caught hovering about here your father would very likely have me sent to prison as a thief,—which would taint the honour of the entire French army,—and dreading no less the surprise that might be occasioned by the sight of a captain of Spahis hovering eternally about this spot where there is neither a citadel to besiege nor a stockade to defend,—I have become a gardener, and have adopted the costume of my calling."

" What nonsense you talk, Maximilian! "

" On the contrary, it is, I believe, the wisest action of my life, for it affords us every security."

" I beseech of you, Maximilian, to tell me what you mean."

" Simply, that having ascertained that the piece of ground on which I stand was to let, I made application for it, was readily accepted by the proprietor, and am now master of this fine crop of lucerne! Think of that, Valentine! There is nothing now to prevent my building myself a little hut on my plantation, and residing not twenty yards from you. Imagine my happiness! I can scarcely contain myself. Do you understand, Valentine, that such things can be paid for? Impossible, is it not? Well, all that happiness, all that comfort, all that joy, for which I would have given ten years of my life, cost me—guess how much? —five hundred livres per year, payable quarterly! Henceforth we have nothing to fear. I am on my own ground, and have an undoubted right to place a ladder against the wall, and to look over when I please; and I may tell you that I love you, without fear of being taken off by the police,—unless, indeed, it offends your pride to listen to professions of love from the lips of a poor working-man, clad in a blouse and cap."

A faint cry of mingled pleasure and surprise escaped from the lips of Valentine, who almost instantly said in a saddened tone, as though some envious cloud darkened the joy which illumined her heart, " Alas, no, Maximilian! this must not be, for many reasons! We should presume too much on our own strength, and like others perhaps be led astray by our blind confidence in each other's prudence."

" How can you for an instant entertain so unworthy a thought, dear Valentine? Have I not, from the first blessed hour of our acquaintance, schooled all my words and actions to your sentiments and ideas? And you have, I am sure, the fullest confidence in my honour. When you spoke to me of your experiencing a vague and indefinite sense of coming danger, I placed myself devotedly at your service, asking no other reward than the pleasure of being useful to you; and have I ever since by word or look given you cause of regret for having selected me from among those who would willingly have sacrificed their lives for you? You told me, my dear Valentine, that you were engaged to M. d'Epinay; and that your father was resolved upon completing the match; and that from his will there was no appeal, as M. de Villefort was never known to change a determination once formed. Well, I kept myself in the background, awaiting, not by my own resolution nor yours, but the ordering of Providence. And meanwhile you love me; you have had pity on me and avowed it. I thank you for that sweet word; I ask only that you will repeat it from time to time,— it will enable me to forget everything else."

" Ah, Maximilian, that is the very thing that makes you so bold, and which renders me at once so happy and unhappy that I frequently ask myself which is to be preferred,—the unhappiness occasioned by the harshness of my stepmother, and her blind preference for her own child, or the happiness full of danger which I enjoy in seeing you."

"Danger!" cried Maximilian; "can you use a word so hard and so unjust? Is it possible to find a more submissive slave than myself? You have permitted me to converse with you from time to time, Valentine, but forbidden my ever following you in your walks or elsewhere; I have obeyed. And since I found means to enter this enclosure, to talk with you through this door, to be close to you without seeing you, have I ever sought to touch even the hem of your rob through these openings? Have I ever attempted to throw down this wall,—an obstacle so trivial to my youth and my strength? I have never complained of your reserve, never expressed a desire. I have held to my promise like a knight of the olden time. Come, admit so much at least, that I may not think you unjust."

"It is true," said Valentine, passing through a small opening in the planks the end of one of her delicate fingers, to which Maximilian pressed his lips,—"it is true. You are an honourable friend; but still you acted from motives of self-interest, my dear Maximilian, for you well knew that from the moment in which you had manifested an opposite spirit all would have been ended between us. You promised to bestow on me the friendly affection of a brother,—on me, who have no friend but yourself upon earth, who am neglected and forgotten by my father, harassed and persecuted by my stepmother, and left to the sole companionship of a paralysed and speechless old man, whose withered hand can no longer press mine, whose eye alone converses with me, and whose heart doubtless retains for me some lingering warmth. Oh, how bitter a fate is mine, to serve either as a victim or an enemy to all who are stronger than myself, while my only friend and supporter is but a living corpse! Indeed, Maximilian, I am very miserable, and you are right to love me for my sake and not your own."

"Valentine," replied the young man, deeply affected, "I will not say you are all I love in the world, for I dearly prize my sister and brother-in-law; but my affection for them is calm and tranquil, in no manner resembling that I feel for you. At the mere thought of you my heart beats more quickly, my blood flows with increased rapidity through my veins, and my breast heaves with tumultuous emotions; but I solemnly promise you to restrain all this ardour, this fervour and intensity of feeling, until you yourself shall require me to render them available in serving or assisting you. M. Franz is not expected to return home for a year to come, I am told; in that time many favourable and unforeseen chances may befriend us. Let us, then, hope for the best,—hope is so sweet a comforter. Meanwhile, Valentine, while reproaching me with selfishness, think a little of what you have been to me,—the beautiful and cold statue of a modest Venus. In return for that devotion, that obedience, that restraint, what have you promised me,—you? Nothing. What have you granted me? Very little. You tell me of M. Franz d'Epinay, your betrothed lover; and you shrink from the idea of being his wife. Tell me, Valentine, is there nothing else in your heart? What! I pledge my life to you, I give you my soul, I devote to you even the lightest pulsation of my heart. And when I am thus wholly yours; when I say to myself that I shall die if I lose you,—you, you do not shudder with fright at the bare thought of belonging to another! Oh, Valentine, Valentine! if I were in your place, if I knew myself loved as you are sure that I love you, a hundred times at least should I have passed my hand between these iron bars, and said to poor Maximilian, ' Yours, yours only, Maximilian, in this world and the next!' "

Valentine made no reply; but her lover could plainly hear her sobs and tears. A rapid change took place in the young man's feelings. " Oh, Valentine, Valentine! " he exclaimed, " forget my words if there is anything in them to give you pain."

" No," she said, " you are right; but do you not see that I am a poor creature, at home abandoned almost as a stranger, —for my father is almost a stranger to me,—whose will, since I was ten years old, has been broken day by day, hour by hour, minute by minute, by the iron will of those by whom I am oppressed? No one knows what I suffer, and I have not spoken of it except to you. Outwardly, and in the eyes of the world, all goes well with me,—every one is kind to me; but in fact every one is my enemy. The general remark is, ' Oh, it cannot be expected that one of so stern a character as M. de Villefort could lavish the tenderness some fathers do on their daughters, but she has had the happiness to find a second mother in Madame de Villefort.' The world, however, is mistaken; my father abandons me from utter indifference, while my stepmother detests me with a hatred the more terrible as it is veiled beneath a continual smile."

" Hate you! you, Valentine! " exclaimed the young man; " how is it possible for any one to do that? "

" Alas! " said Valentine, " I am obliged to own that my stepmother's aversion to me arises from a very natural source,—her overweening love for her own child, my brother Edouard."

" How is that ? "

" How is it ? It seems strange to me to speak of money matters in a conversation with you; but, my friend, I think her hatred towards me springs from that source. She has no fortune; while I am already rich, as heiress to my mother, and my possessions will be doubled by the wealth of Monsieur and Madame de Saint-Méran, which will some day fall to me. Well, I think that she is envious. Oh, my God! if I could only give to her the half of that fortune and find myself in the home of M. de Villefort as a daughter in the house of her father, I would certainly do it without hesitation ! "

" Poor Valentine ! "

" I seem to myself as though living a life of bondage, yet at the same time am so conscious of weakness that I fear to break the restraint in which I am held, lest I fall utterly powerless and helpless. Then, too, my father is not a person whose orders may be infringed with impunity. He is powerful against me; he would be powerful against you, even against the king,— protected as he is by an irreproachable past and by a position almost impregnable. Oh, Maximilian! I assure you if I do not struggle, it is because you also, as well as I, would be overwhelmed in that struggle."

" But why, Valentine, do you despair, and regard the future with dread ? "

" Ah, my friend! because I judge it from the past."

" Still, consider that although I may not be, strictly speaking, what is termed an illustrious match for you, I am for many reasons not altogether so much beneath your alliance. The days when such distinctions were so nicely weighed and considered no longer exist in France; and the first families of the monarchy have intermarried with those of the empire. The aristocracy of the lance has allied itself with the nobility of the cannon. Well, I belong to the latter class; I have a promising future in the army; I possess a fortune limited but independent; and my father's memory is revered in our country as that of a most honourable merchant. I say our country, Valentine, because you were born not far from Marseilles."

" Name not Marseilles, I beseech you, Maximilian; that one word brings back my mother to my recollections,—my angel mother, who died too soon for myself and for all who knew her, but who, after watching over her child during a brief period in this world, now, I hope at least, contemplates her with pitying tenderness from those realms of bliss to which her pure spirit has flown. Ah, were she still living, we need fear nothing, Maximilian, for I would confide our love to her, and she would aid and protect us."

"I fear, Valentine," replied the lover, "that were she living I should never have had the happiness of knowing you. You would then have been too happy; and Valentine happy would have regarded me disdainfully from the height of her grandeur."

"It is you who are unkind,—ay, and unjust, too, now, Maximilian," cried Valentine; "but there is one thing I wish to know."

"And what is that," inquired the young man, perceiving that Valentine hesitated and seemed at a loss how to proceed.

"Tell me, Maximilian, whether in former days, at Marseilles, there ever existed any misunderstanding between your father and mine?"

"Not that I am aware of," replied the young man; "unless, indeed, some ill-feeling might have arisen from their being of opposite parties,—your father being, as you know, a zealous partisan of the Bourbons, while mine was wholly devoted to the emperor. There could not have been any other difference between them. But why that question, Valentine?"

"I will tell you," replied the young girl, "for it is but right that you should know all. Then I must begin by referring to the day when your being made an officer of the Legion of Honour was publicly announced in the papers. We were all sitting in the apartment of my grandfather, M. Noirtier. M. Danglars was there also; you recollect M. Danglars, do you not, Maximilian?—the banker, whose horses ran away with my stepmother and little brother, and very nearly killed them. While the rest of the company were discussing the approaching marriage of Mademoiselle Danglars, I was occupied in reading the paper aloud to my grandfather; but when I came to the paragraph concerning you, although I had done nothing else but read it over to myself all the morning (you know you had told me all about it the previous evening), I felt so happy, and yet so nervous, at the idea of pronouncing your beloved name aloud and before so many people, that I really think I should have passed it over but for the fear that my so doing might create suspicions as to the cause of my silence. So I summoned up all my courage, and read it as firmly and steadily as I could."

"Dear Valentine!"

"Well, as soon as my father caught the sound of your name he turned round quite hastily. I was so certain—you see how foolish I am—that every one had been struck by your name as by a thunderbolt that I thought I saw my father give a start, and even M. Danglars, too,—though that of course was an illusion.

"'Morrel! Morrel!' cried my father, 'stop a bit;'" then, knitting his brows into a deep frown, he added, 'Can that be one of the Morrels of Marseilles,—those furious Bonapartists who gave us so much trouble in 1815?'

"'I fancy,' replied M. Danglars, 'that the individual alluded to in the journal mademoiselle is reading is the son of that former ship-owner.'"

"Indeed!" answered Maximilian; "and what said your father then, Valentine?"

"Oh, such a dreadful thing I dare not repeat it."

"Tell it, nevertheless," said the young man, smiling.

"'Ah,' continued my father, still frowning, 'their idolised emperor treated these madmen as they deserved; he called them "food for cannon," which was precisely all they were good for. And I am delighted to see that the present government is vigorously applying this salutary principle. Though it should keep Algiers only for that purpose, I would congratulate the government, even though that policy be costly.'"

"The sentiments expressed were somewhat unfeeling," said Maximilian; "but do not blush, dear friend, at that speech of M. de Villefort, for I can assure you that my father was not behind yours in the heat of his political expressions. 'Why,' said he, 'does not the emperor, who does so many fine things, form a regiment of judges and lawyers and send them always to the front of battle?' You see, Valentine, that for mildness of thought and picturesqueness of expression there is not much choice between the two parties. But what said M. Danglars to this burst of party spirit on the part of the *procureur du roi*?"

"Oh, he laughed, and in that sinister way peculiar to him and which to me seems ferocious; and a moment later they got up and went out. Then for the first time I observed the agitation of my grandfather; and I must tell you, Maximilian, that I am the only person capable of discerning emotion in that poor paralytic. I suspected that the conversation that had been carried on in his presence (for no one pays attention to him, poor man) had made a strong impression on his mind,—for naturally enough it must have pained him to hear the emperor he so devotedly loved and served spoken of in that depreciating manner."

"The name of M. Noirtier," said Maximilian, "is one of the celebrated names of the empire. He was a statesman of high standing; and I know not whether you are aware, Valentine, that he took a leading part in every Bonapartist conspiracy set on foot during the restoration of the Bourbons."

"Oh, I have often heard whispers of things that seem to me most strange,—the father a Bonapartist, the son a Royalist; what can have been the reason of so singular a difference in parties and politics? But to resume my story: I turned towards my grandfather, as though to question him as to the cause of his emotion; he looked expressively at the newspaper I had been reading. 'What is the matter, dear grandfather?' said I. 'Are you pleased?' He gave me a sign in the affirmative. 'With what my father said just now?' He returned a sign in the negative. 'Perhaps you liked what M. Danglars remarked?' Another sign in the negative. 'Oh, then, you were glad to hear that M. Morrel' (I dared not say Maximilian) 'has been made an officer of the Legion of Honour?' He signified assent. Only think of the poor old man's being pleased that you, a stranger to him, had been made an officer of the Legion of Honour! Perhaps, though, it was foolishness on his part, for he is falling, they say, into a second childhood! but I love him better for that sign of assent."

"How singular," murmured Maximilian, "that your father should apparently hate the very mention of my name, while your grandfather, on the contrary— Strange things are these partisan loves and hatreds!"

"Hush!" cried Valentine, suddenly, "conceal yourself! Go, go! Some one comes!"

Maximilian leaped at one bound into his crop of lucerne, which he commenced pulling up in the most pitiless manner, under the pretext of being occupied in weeding it.

"Mademoiselle! mademoiselle!" exclaimed a voice from behind the trees. "Madame is searching for you everywhere; there are visitors in the drawing-room."

"Visitors!" inquired Valentine, much agitated, "who are they?"

"A great lord, a prince, as they tell me,—M. le Comte de Monte Cristo."

"I will come directly," said Valentine, aloud.

The name caused an electric shock to the individual on the other side of the iron gate, on whose ear the "I will come!" of Valentine sounded the parting knell of all their interviews.

"Now, then," said Maximilian, leaning thoughtfully on his spade, "how does it happen that the Count of Monte Cristo is acquainted with M. de Villefort?"

CHAPTER LII

TOXICOLOGY

IT was really the Count of Monte Cristo who had just arrived at Madame de Villefort's for the purpose of returning the visit of the *procureur du roi;* and at this name, as may be easily imagined, the whole house was in confusion. Madame de Ville-fort, who was alone in her drawing-room when the count was announced, desired that her son might be brought thither instantly to renew his thanks to the count; and Edouard, who had heard this great personage spoken of unceasingly the last two days made all possible haste to come to him,—not in obedience to his mother, nor from any feeling of gratitude to the count, but from sheer curiosity, and that he might make some remark by help of which he might find an opportunity for saying one of those small pertnesses which made his mother say, " Oh, that sad child! but pray excuse him, he is really *so* clever."

After the first customary civilities, the count inquired after M. de Villefort.

" My husband dines with the chancellor," replied the young wife. " He has just gone; and I am sure he will much regret having lost the pleasure of seeing you."

Two visitors who were there when the count arrived, having gazed at him with all their eyes, retired after that reasonable delay required both by politeness and curiosity.

" Ah! what is your sister Valentine doing? " inquired Madame de Villefort of Edouard; " tell some one to bid her come here, that I may have the honour of presenting her to the count."

" You have a daughter, then, madame? " inquired the count; " very young, I presume? "

" The daughter of M. de Villefort," replied the young wife, " by his first marriage,—a fine well-grown girl."

" But melancholy," interrupted Master Edouard, snatching the feathers out of the tail of a splendid paroquet that was screaming on its gilded perch, in order to make a plume for his hat. Madame de Villefort merely cried, " Silence, Edouard! " She then added, " This young madcap is, however, very nearly right, and merely re-echoes what he has heard me say with pain a hundred times; for Mademoiselle de Villefort is, in spite of all we can do to rouse her, of a melancholy disposition and taciturn habit which frequently injure the effect of her beauty. But she does not come, Edouard; go and ascertain the reason."

" Because they are looking for her where she is not to be found."

" And where are they looking for her? "

" With Grandpapa Noirtier."

" And do you think she is not there? "

" No, no, no, no, no, she is not there! " replied Edouard, singing his words.

" And where is she, then? If you know, why don't you tell? "

" She is under the great chestnut-tree," replied the spoiled child, as he gave, in spite of his mother's cries, live flies to the parrot, who appeared to relish that sort of game. Madame de Villefort stretched out her hand to ring, intending to direct her waiting-maid to the spot where she would find Valentine, when the young lady herself entered the room. She appeared much dejected; and any person who considered her attentively might have observed the traces of tears in her eyes.

Valentine, whom we have in the rapid march of our narrative presented to our readers without formally introducing her, was a tall and graceful girl of nineteen years of age, with bright chestnut hair, deep blue eyes, and that languishing air so full of distinction which characterised her mother. Her white and slender fingers, her pearly neck, her cheeks tinted with varying hues, gave her at the first view the aspect of one of those lovely Englishwomen who have been so poetically compared in their manner to a swan admiring itself. She entered the room, and seeing near her stepmother the stranger of whom she had already heard so much, saluted him without any girlish awkwardness, or even lowering her eyes, and with a grace that redoubled the count's attention. He rose to return the salutation.

" Mademoiselle de Villefort, my stepdaughter," said Madame de Villefort to Monte Cristo, leaning back on her sofa and motioning towards Valentine with her hand.

" And M. le Comte de Monte Cristo, King of China, Emperor of Cochin-China," said the young imp, looking slyly towards his sister.

Madame de Villefort at this really did turn pale, and was very nearly angry with this household plague who answered to the name of Edouard; but the count on the contrary smiled, and appeared to look at the boy complacently, which caused the maternal heart to bound again with joy and enthusiasm.

" But, madame," replied the count, continuing the conversation, and looking by turns at Madame de Villefort and Valentine, " have I not already had the honour of meeting you and mademoiselle? The idea occurred to me a moment since, and as mademoiselle entered the sight of her was an additional ray of light thrown on a confused remembrance; excuse me the word."

"I do not think it likely, monsieur; Mademoiselle de Villefort is not very fond of society, and we very seldom go out," said the young wife.

"Then it was not in society that I met with mademoiselle and yourself, madame, and this charming little fellow. Besides, the Parisian world is entirely unknown to me, for, as I believe I told you, I have been in Paris but very few days. No; but perhaps you will permit me to call to mind—stay!" The count placed his hand on his brow as if to collect his thoughts. "No—it was somewhere—away from here—it was—I do not know—but it appears that this recollection is connected with a lovely sky, and some religious fête. Mademoiselle was holding flowers in her hand; the child was chasing a beautiful peacock in a garden; and you, madame, were under the trellis of some arbour. Pray come to my aid, madame; do not these circumstances bring to your mind some reminiscences?"

"No, indeed," replied Madame de Villefort; "and yet it appears to me, monsieur, that if I had met you anywhere the recollection of you must have been imprinted on my memory."

"Perhaps Monsieur the Count saw us in Italy," said Valentine, timidly.

"Yes, in Italy,—it was in Italy most probably," replied Monte Cristo; "you have travelled then in Italy, mademoiselle?"

"Yes; madame and I were there two years ago. The doctors were afraid for my lungs, and prescribed the air of Naples. We went by Bologna, Perusa, and Rome."

"Ah, yes; true, mademoiselle," exclaimed Monte Cristo, as if this simple indication was sufficient to determine his recollection. "It was at Perusa on the day of the Fête-Dieu, in the garden of the Hôtel des Postes, that chance brought us together, —you, Madame de Villefort, your son, mademoiselle, and myself; I now remember having had the honour of meeting you."

"I perfectly well remember Perusa, monsieur, and the Hôtel des Postes and the fête to which you allude," said Madame de Villefort; "but in vain do I tax my memory, of whose treachery I am ashamed, for I really do not recall to mind that I ever had the pleasure of seeing you before."

"It is strange; but neither do I recollect meeting with you," observed Valentine, raising her beautiful eyes to the count.

"But I remember it," said Edouard.

"I will assist your memory, madame," continued the count, "The day had been burning hot; you were waiting for horses.

which were delayed in consequence of the festival. Mademoiselle was walking in the shade of the garden, and your son disappeared in pursuit of the bird."

"And I caught it, mamma, don't you remember?" said Edouard, "and I pulled three feathers from its tail."

"You, madame, remained under the arbour formed by the vine; do you not remember that while you were seated on a stone bench, and while, as I told you, Mademoiselle de Villefort and your young son were absent, you conversed for a considerable time with somebody?"

"Yes,—in truth, yes," answered the young wife, turning very red, "I do remember conversing with a man wrapped in a long woollen mantle; he was a medical man, I think."

"Precisely so, madame; that man was myself. For a fortnight I had been at that hotel, during which period I had cured my *valet de chambre* of a fever and my landlord of the jaundice; so that I had really acquired a reputation as a skilful physician. We talked a long time, madame, of different subjects,—of Perugino, of Raphael, of manners, costumes, of the famous *aqua-tofana*, of which they had told you, I think you said, that certain persons in Perusa had preserved the secret."

"Yes, true," replied Madame de Villefort, hastily, and with a degree of uneasiness; "I remember now."

"I do not recollect now all the various subjects of which we discoursed, madame," continued the count, with perfect calmness; "but I remember distinctly that falling into the error which others had entertained respecting me, you consulted me as to the health of Mademoiselle de Villefort."

"Yes, really, monsieur; you were in fact a medical man," said Madame de Villefort, "since you had cured the sick."

"Molière or Beaumarchais would reply to you, madame, that it was precisely because I was not that I had cured my patients; for myself, I am content to say to you that I have studied chemistry and the natural sciences somewhat deeply, but still only as an amateur, you understand."

At this moment the clock struck six. "It is six o'clock," said Madame de Villefort, evidently agitated. "Valentine, will you not go and see if your grandpapa will have his dinner?"

Valentine rose, and saluting the count, left the room without replying a single word.

"Oh, madame!" said the count when Valentine had left the room, "was it on my account that you sent Mademoiselle de Villefort away?"

"By no means," replied the young woman, quickly; "but

this is the hour when we give to M. Noirtier the sad repast which supports his melancholy existence. You are aware, monsieur, of the deplorable condition of my husband's father?"

" Yes, madame, M. de Villefort spoke of it to me,—a paralysis, I think."

" Alas, yes! there is an entire want of movement in the frame of the poor old man; the mind alone is still active in this human machine, and that is faint and flickering like the light of a lamp about to expire. But excuse me, sir, for talking of our domestic misfortunes; I interrupted you at the moment when you were telling me that you were a skilful chemist."

" No, madame, I did not say so much as that," replied the count, with a smile; " quite the contrary. I have studied chemistry because having determined to live in Eastern climates, I have been desirous of following the example of King Mithridates."

" *Mithridates, rex Ponticus*," said the young scamp, as he cut some beautiful portraits out of a splendid album, " the individual who breakfasted every morning with a cup of poison *à la crême*."

" Edouard, you naughty boy!" exclaimed Madame de Villefort, snatching the mutilated book from the urchin's grasp; " you are unendurable; you disturb the conversation. Leave us, and join your sister Valentine in Grandpapa Nortier's room."

" The album," said Edouard.

" What do you mean? the album!"

" I want the album."

" Why have you cut out the pictures?"

" Oh, it amuses me."

" Go; go directly."

" I won't go unless you give me the album," said the boy, seating himself doggedly in an armchair, according to his habit of never giving way.

" Take it, then, and disturb us no longer," said Madame de Villefort, giving the album to Edouard, who then went towards the door, led by his mother.

The count followed her with his eyes. " Let us see if she shuts the door after him," he muttered.

Madame de Villefort closed the door carefully after the child, the count appearing not to notice her; then casting a scrutinising glance around the chamber, the young wife returned to her chair, in which she seated herself.

" Allow me to observe, madame," said the count, with that

kind tone he could assume so well, " you are really very severe with that charming child."

" Oh, sometimes severity is quite necessary," replied Madame de Villefort, with a true maternal emphasis.

" It was his Cornelius Nepos that Master Edouard was repeating when he referred to King Mithridates," continued the count; " and you interrupted him in a quotation which proves that his tutor has by no means neglected him, for your son is really advanced for his years."

" The fact is, Monsieur the Count," answered the mother, agreeably flattered, " he has great aptitude, and learns all that is set before him. He has but one fault,—he is somewhat wilful; but referring to what he said, do you believe that Mithridates used these precautions, and that these precautions were efficacious? "

" I think so, madame, because I—I who now address you— have made use of them that I might not be poisoned at Naples, at Palermo, and at Smyrna; that is to say, on three several occasions when but for these precautions I must have lost my life."

" And your precautions were successful? "

"Completely so."

" Yes, I remember now your mentioning to me at Perusa something of this sort."

" Indeed! did I? " said the count, with an air of surprise remarkably well counterfeited; " I really did not remember it."

" I inquired of you if poisons acted equally and with the same effect on men of the North as on men of the South; and you answered me that the cold and sluggish habits of the North did not present the same susceptibility to poison as the rich and energetic temperaments of the natives of the South."

" And that is the case," observed Monte Cristo. " I have seen Russians devour without being visibly inconvenienced vegetable substances which would infallibly have killed a Neapolitan or an Arab."

" And you really believe the result would be still more sure with us than in the East, and that in the midst of our fogs and rains a man would habituate himself more easily than in a warm latitude to this progressive absorption of poison."

" Certainly; it being at the same time understood that one is protected only against that poison to which he has accustomed himself."

" Yes, I understand that; and how would you habituate yourself, for instance, or rather how did you habituate yourself? "

"Oh, very easily. Suppose you knew beforehand the poison that would be made use of against you; suppose the poison was, for instance, brucine—"

"Brucine is extracted from the *Brucæa ferruginea*, is it not?" inquired Madame de Villefort.

"Precisely, madame," replied Monte Cristo; "but I perceive I have not much to teach you. Allow me to compliment you on your knowledge; such learning is very rare among ladies."

"Oh, I am aware of that," said Madame de Villefort; "but I have a passion for the occult sciences, which speak to the imagination like poetry, and are reducible to figures like an algebraic equation. But go on, I pray you; what you say interests me extremely."

"Well," replied Monte Cristo, "suppose, then, that this poison was brucine, and you were to take a milligramme the first day, two milligrammes the second day, and so on. Well, at the end of ten days you would take a centigramme; at the end of twenty days, adding another milligramme, you would take three centigrammes,—that is to say, a dose which you would support without inconvenience, but which would be very dangerous for any other person who had not taken the same precautions. Well, then, at the end of a month, when drinking water from the same *carafe*, you would kill the person who at the same time as yourself had drank this water, without your perceiving, otherwise than from slight inconvenience, that there was any poisonous substance mingled with this water."

"Do you know any other counter-poisons?"

"I do not."

"I have often read, and read again, the history of Mithridates," said Madame de Villefort, in a tone of reflection, "and have always considered it as a fable."

"No, madame, contrary to most history, it is a truth; but what you tell me, madame, what you inquire of me, is not the result of a chance question,—for two years since you asked me the same questions, and said too that for a very long time this history of Mithridates occupied your mind."

"True, monsieur. The two favourite studies of my youth were botany and mineralogy; and subsequently, when I learned that the use of simples frequently explained the whole history of a people, and the entire life of individuals in the East, as flowers illustrate all their thoughts of love, I have regretted I was not a man, that I might have been a Flamel, a Fontana, or a Cabanis."

"And the more, madame," said Monte Cristo, "as the Orientals do not confine themselves, as did Mithridates, to make a cuirass of his poisons, but they also make them a dagger. Science becomes in their hands, not only a defensive weapon, but still more frequently an offensive one. The one serves against all their physical sufferings; the other against all their enemies. With opium, with belladonna, with brucæa, snakewood, the cherry-laurel, they put to sleep all those who would keep them awake. There is not one of those women,—Egyptian, Turk, or Greek,—whom here you call 'good women,' who do not know how, by means of chemistry, to stupefy a doctor, and in psychology to amaze a confessor."

"Really!" said Madame de Villefort, whose eyes sparkled with strange fire at this conversation.

"Eh, indeed! Yes, madame," continued Monte Cristo, "the secret dramas of the East begin and end thus, from the plant which can create love to the plant that can cause death; from the draught which opens heaven before your eyes to that which plunges a man in hell! There are as many shades of every kind as there are caprices and peculiarities in human, physical, and moral nature; and I will say further, the art of these chemists knows how to accommodate the remedy and the ill to its yearnings of love or its desires for vengeance."

"But, monsieur," remarked the lady, "those Oriental societies, in the midst of which you have passed a portion of your existence, are as visionary as the tales that come from their strange land. A man can easily be put out of the way there, then; it is indeed the Bagdad and Bassora of M. Galland. The sultans and viziers, who rule over those societies, and who constitute what in France we call the government, are in fact Haroun-al-Raschids and Giaffars, who not only pardon a poisoner, but even make him a prime minister if his crime has been an ingenious one, and who under such circumstances have the whole story written in letters of gold, to divert their hours of idleness and *ennui*."

"By no means, madame; the fanciful exists no longer in the East. There are there now, disguised under other names, and concealed under other costumes, agents of police, magistrates, attorney-generals, and bailiffs. They hang, behead, and impale their criminals in the most agreeable manner possible; but some of these, like clever rogues, have contrived to escape human justice and succeed in their fraudulent enterprises by cunning stratagems. Among us a simpleton possessed by the demon of hate or cupidity, who had an enemy to destroy, or some near relative to dispose of, goes straight to the grocer's or druggist's, gives a false name, which leads more easily to his detection than his real one, and purchases under a pretext that the rats prevent him from sleeping five or six grams of arsenic; if he is really a cunning fellow, he goes to five or six different druggists or grocers, and thereby becomes only five or six times more easily traced. Then, when he has acquired his specific, he administers duly to his enemy or near kinsman a dose of arsenic which would make a mammoth or mastodon burst, and which without rhyme or reason makes his victim utter groans which alarm the entire neighbourhood. Then arrive a crowd of policemen and constables. They fetch a doctor, who opens the dead body, and collects from the entrails and stomach a quantity of arsenic in a spoon. Next day a hundred newspapers relate the fact, with the names of the victim and the murderer. The same evening the grocer or grocers, druggist or druggists, come and say, ' It was I who sold the arsenic to the gentleman accused;' and rather than not recognise the guilty purchaser, they will recognise twenty. Then the foolish criminal is taken, imprisoned, interrogated, confronted, confounded, condemned, and cut off by hemp or steel; or if she be a woman of any consideration, they lock her up for life. This is the way in which you Northerners understand chemistry, madame. Desrues was, however, I must confess, more skilful."

"What would you have, monsieur?" said the lady, laughing; "we do what we can. All the world has not the secret of the Medicis or the Borgias."

"Now," replied the count, shrugging his shoulders, "shall I tell you the cause of all these stupidities? It is because at your theatres, by what at least I could judge by reading the pieces they play, they see persons swallow the contents of a phial, or suck the button of a ring, and fall dead instantly. Five minutes afterwards the curtain falls; and the spectators depart. They are ignorant of what comes afterwards. They see neither the commissary of police with his badge of office, nor the corporal with his four men; and that persuades many weak minds to believe that things happen in that way. But go a little way from France; go either to Aleppo or Cairo, or only to Naples or Rome, and you will see people passing by you in the streets,—people erect, smiling, and fresh-coloured, of whom Asmodeus, if he were near you, would say, ' That man was poisoned three weeks ago; he will be a dead man in a month.' "

"Then," remarked Madame de Villefort, "they have again

discovered the secret of the famous *aqua-tofana* which they told me at Perusa had been lost."

" Eh, indeed, does mankind ever lose anything? The arts are removed, and make a tour of the world. Things change their names, and the vulgar do not follow them,—that is all; but there is always the same result. Poison acts particularly on one organ or the other,—one on the stomach, another on the brain, another on the intestines. Well, the poison brings on a cough, the cough an inflammation of the lungs, or some other complaint catalogued in the book of science, which however by no means precludes it from being decidedly mortal; and if it were not, it would be sure to become so, thanks to the remedies applied by foolish doctors, who are generally bad chemists, which will act in favour of or against the malady, as you please. And then there is a human being killed according to all the rules of art and skill, in regard to whom justice makes no inquiries, as was said by a terrible chemist of my acquaintance, the worthy Abbé Adelmonte de Taormine, in Sicily, who has studied these national phenomena very profoundly."

" It is frightful, but deeply interesting," said the young woman, motionless with attention. " I thought, I must confess, that these tales were inventions of the Middle Ages."

" Yes, no doubt, but improved upon in our own age. What is the use of time, encouragements, medals, crosses, and Monthyon prizes, if they do not lead society towards perfection? Yet man will never be perfect until he learns to create and destroy, like God; he does know how to destroy, and that is halfway on the road."

" So," added Madame de Villefort, constantly returning to her object, " the poisons of the Borgias, the Medicis, the Renés, the Ruggieris, and later probably that of Baron de Trenck, whose story has been so misused by modern drama and romance—"

" Were objects of art, madame, and nothing more," replied the count. " Do you suppose that the real *savant* addresses himself stupidly to the mere individual? By no means. Science loves eccentricities, leaps, and bounds, trials of strength, fancies, if I may be allowed so to term them. Thus, for instance, the excellent Abbé Adelmonte, of whom I spoke to you just now, made on this subject some marvellous experiments."

" Really l "

" Yes; I will mention one to you. He had a remarkably fine garden, full of vegetables, flowers, and fruit. From among these vegetables he selected the most simple,—a cabbage, for instance. For three days he watered this cabbage with a distillation of arsenic; on the third, the cabbage began to droop and turn yellow. At that moment he cut it. In the eyes of everybody it seemed fit for table, and preserved its wholesome appearance. In the knowledge of the Abbé Adelmonte alone it was poisoned. He then took the cabbage to the room where he had rabbits,—for the Abbé Adelmonte had a collection of rabbits, cats, and guinea-pigs as fine as his collection of vegetables, flowers, and fruit. Well, the Abbé Adelmonte took a rabbit, and made it eat a leaf of the cabbage. The rabbit died. What magistrate would find, or even venture to insinuate anything against this? What *procureur du roi* has ever ventured to draw up an accusation against M. Magendie or M. Flourens, in consequence of the rabbits, cats, and guinea-pigs they have killed? Not one. So, then, the rabbit dies, and justice takes no notice. This rabbit dead, the Abbé Adelmonte has its entrails taken out by his cook and thrown on the dung-hill; on this dunghill is a hen, who pecking these intestines is in her turn taken ill, and dies next day. At the moment when she is struggling in the convulsions of death a vulture is flying by (there are a good many vultures in Adelmonte's country); this bird darts on the dead bird and carries it away to a rock, where it dines off its prey. Three days afterwards this poor vulture, who has been very much indisposed since that dinner, feels very giddy suddenly while flying aloft in the clouds, and falls heavily into a fish-pond. The pike, eels, and carp eat greedily always, as everybody knows; they feast on the vulture. Well, suppose the next day one of these eels, or pike, or carp is served at your table, poisoned as they are in the fourth degree. Well, then, your guest will be poisoned in the fifth degree, and will die at the end of eight or ten days of pains in the intestines, sickness, or abscess of the pylorus. The doctors open the body and say, ' The subject has died of a tumour on the liver, or of typhoid fever ! ' "

" But," remarked Madame de Villefort, " all these circumstances which you link thus one to another may be broken by the least accident; the vulture may not pass in season, or may fall a hundred yards from the fish-pond."

" Ah, just there is the province of art. To be a great chemist in the East we must direct chance; and this is to be achieved."

Madame de Villefort was deep in thought, yet listened attentively. " But," she exclaimed suddenly, " arsenic is indelible, indestructible; in what way soever it is absorbed, it will be found again in the body of the creature from the moment when it has been taken in sufficient quantity to cause death."

"Precisely so," cried Monte Cristo,—"precisely so; and this is what I said to my worthy Adelmonte. He reflected, smiled, and replied to me by a Sicilian proverb, which I believe is also a French proverb, ' My son, the world was not made in a day, but in seven. Return on Sunday.' On the Sunday following I did return to him. Instead of having watered his cabbage with arsenic, he had watered it this time with a solution of salts, having their basis in strychnine, *strychnos colubrina*, as the learned term it. Now, the cabbage had not the slightest appearance of disease in the world, and the rabbit had not the smallest distrust; yet five minutes afterwards the rabbit was dead. The fowl pecked at the rabbit, and the next day was dead. We were the vultures, so we opened the fowl, and this time all particular symptoms had disappeared; there were only general symptoms. There was no peculiar indication in any organ,—an excitement of the nervous system only; a case of cerebral congestion. The fowl had not been poisoned; she had died of apoplexy. Apoplexy is a rare disease among fowls, I believe, but very common among men."

Madame de Villefort appeared more and more reflective. "It is very fortunate," she observed, " that such substances could only be prepared by chemists, for otherwise, indeed, one half the world would poison the other half."

"By chemists and persons who have a taste for chemistry," said Monte Cristo, carelessly.

"And then," said Madame de Villefort, endeavouring by a struggle, and with effort, to get away from her thoughts, "however skilfully it is prepared, crime is always crime; and if it avoid human scrutiny, it does not escape the eye of God. The Orientals are stronger than we are in cases of conscience, and have prudently abolished hell,—that is the difference."

"Really, madame, this is a scruple which naturally must occur to a pure mind like yours, but which would easily yield before sound reasoning. The bad side of human thought will always be defined by the paradox of Jean Jacques Rousseau, you know, —' the mandarin who is killed at five thousand leagues' distance by raising the tip of the finger.' Man's whole life passes in doing these things, and his intellect is exhausted by reflecting on them. You will find very few persons who will go and brutally thrust a knife in the heart of a fellow-creature, or will administer to him, in order to remove him from the surface of the globe, that quantity of arsenic of which we just now talked. Such a thing is really out of rule,—eccentric or stupid. To attain such a point the blood must be warmed to thirty-six degrees, the pulse be at least at ninety, and the feelings excited beyond the ordinary limit. But if, passing, as we do in philology, from the word itself to its softened synonyme, you make an elimination; if instead of committing an ignoble assassination, you merely and simply remove from your path him who is in your way, and that without shock or violence, without the display of those sufferings which becoming a punishment make a martyr of the victim, and of him who inflicts them a butcher in every sense of the word; if there be no blood, no groans, no convulsions, nor, above all, that horrible and compromising instantaneousness of the deed, —then one escapes the clutch of the human law, which says to you, ' Do not disturb society I ' This is the mode in which they manage these things and succeed in Eastern climes, where there are grave and phlegmatic persons who care very little for the matter of time in conjunctures of importance."

" Yet conscience remains I " remarked Madame de Villefort, in an agitated voice, and with a stifled sigh.

" Yes," answered Monte Cristo, " happily, yes, conscience does remain; and if it did not, how wretched we should be I After every action requiring exertion it is conscience that saves us, for it supplies us with a thousand good excuses, of which we alone are judges; and these reasons, how excellent soever in producing sleep, would avail perhaps but little to save our lives before a tribunal. Thus Richard III., for instance, was marvellously served by his conscience after the putting away of the two children of Edward IV.; in fact, he could say, ' These two children of a cruel and persecuting king, who have inherited the vices of their father, which I alone could perceive in their juvenile propensities,—these two children are impediments in my way of promoting the happiness of the English people, to whom they would undoubtedly have done harm.' Thus was Lady Macbeth served by her conscience, when she sought to give her son, and not her husband, whatever Shakespeare may say, a throne. Ah, maternal love is a great virtue, a powerful motive,—so powerful that it excuses a multitude of things; so that after the death of Duncan, Lady Macbeth would have been very miserable without her conscience."

Madame de Villefort listened with avidity to these appalling maxims and horrible paradoxes, delivered by the count with that ironical simplicity which was peculiar to him. After a moment's silence she said, " Do you know, Monsieur the Count, that you are a very terrible reasoner, and that you look at the world through a somewhat distempered medium? Is it, then, because you have studied humanity through alembics and crucibles? For you are right, you are a great chemist; and the elixir you administered to my son, which recalled him to life almost instantaneously—"

"Oh, do not place any reliance on that, madame. *One* drop of that elixir sufficed to recall life to a dying child, but three drops would have impelled the blood into his lungs in such a way as to have produced most violent palpitations; six would have suspended his respiration and caused syncope more serious than that in which he was; ten would have destroyed him. You know, madame, how suddenly I snatched him from those phials which he so imprudently touched."

"Is it, then, so terrible a poison?"

"Oh, no! In the first place, let us agree that the word 'poison' does not exist; because in medicine use is made of the most violent poisons, which become, according as they are made use of, salutary remedies."

"What, then, is it?"

"A skilful preparation by my friend, the worthy Abbé Adelmonte, who taught me the use of it."

"Oh," observed Madame de Villefort, "it must be an admirable anti-spasmodic."

"Perfect, madame, as you have seen," replied the count; "and I frequently make use of it,—with all possible prudence, though, be it observed," he added, smiling.

"Most assuredly," responded Madame de Villefort, in the same tone. "As for me, so nervous, and so subject to fainting-fits, I should require a Dr. Adelmonte to invent for me some means of breathing freely, and tranquillising my mind, in the fear I have of dying some fine day of suffocation. In the meanwhile, as the thing is difficult to find in France, and your abbé is not probably disposed to make a journey to Paris on my account, I must continue to use the anti-spasmodics of M. Planché; and mint and Hoffmann's drops are among my favourite remedies. Here are some lozenges which are made expressly for me; they are compounded doubly strong."

Monte Cristo opened the tortoise-shell box, which the young woman presented to him, and imbibed the odour of the lozenges with the air of an amateur who thoroughly appreciated their composition. "They are indeed exquisite," he said; "but as they are necessarily submitted to the process of deglutition,—a function which it is frequently impossible for a fainting person to accomplish,—I prefer my own specific."

"Undoubtedly; and so should I prefer it, after the effects

I have seen produced. But of course it is a secret; and I am not so indiscreet as to ask it of you."

"But I," said Monte Cristo, rising as he spoke,—"I am gallant enough to offer it you."

"Oh, monsieur!"

"Only remember one thing: a small dose is a remedy; a large one is poison. One drop will restore life, as you have witnessed; five or six will inevitably kill, and in a way the more terrible, inasmuch as poured into a glass of wine, it would not in the slightest degree affect its flavour. But I say no more, madame; it is really as if I were advising you."

The clock struck half-past six, and a lady was announced, —a friend of Madame de Villefort, who came to dine with her.

"If I had the honour of seeing you for the third or fourth time, Monsieur the Count, instead of for only the second," said Madame de Villefort; "if I had the honour of being your friend, instead of having only the happiness of lying under an obligation to you,—I should insist on detaining you to dinner, and not allow myself to be daunted by a first refusal."

"A thousand thanks, madame," replied Monte Cristo, "but I have an engagement which I cannot break: I have promised to escort to the Académie a Greek princess of my acquaintance who has never seen your grand opera, and who relies on me to conduct her thither."

"Adieu, then, sir, and do not forget my recipe."

"Ah, in truth, madame, to do that I must forget the hour's conversation I have had with you, which is indeed impossible."

Monte Cristo bowed and left the house. Madame de Villefort remained immersed in thought. "He is a very strange man," she said, "and in my opinion is himself the Adelmonte he talks about."

As to Monte Cristo, the result had surpassed his utmost expectations. "Good!" said he, as he went away; "this is a fruitful soil, and I feel certain that the seed sown will not be cast on barren ground." Next morning, faithful to his promise, he sent the desired prescription.

CHAPTER LIII

" ROBERT LE DIABLE "

THE pretext of an opera engagement was the more plausible since there chanced to be on that very night a more than ordinary attraction at the Académie Royale. Levasseur, who had been suffering under severe illness, made his reappearance in the character of Bertram; and as usual, the announcement of the most admired production of the favourite composer of the day had attracted an audience consisting of the very *élite* of Parisian fashion. Morcerf, like most other young men of rank and fortune, had his orchestral stall, with the certainty of always finding a seat in at least a dozen of the principal boxes occupied by persons of his acquaintance; he had, moreover, his right of entry into the box of the " lions." Château-Renaud rented a stall near his own, while Beauchamp, in his editorial capacity, had unlimited range all over the theatre. It happened that on that particular night the minister's box was placed at the disposal of Lucien Debray, who offered it to the Comte de Morcerf, who, upon Mercédès's refusal of it, sent it to Danglars, with an intimation that he should probably do himself the honour of joining the baroness and her daughter during the evening, in the event of their accepting the box in question. The ladies received the offer with too much pleasure to dream of a refusal. To no one else is a free opera-box so acceptable as to a millionaire.

Danglars had however declared that his political principles and his position as a member of the opposition would not permit him to use the minister's box; the baroness had therefore despatched a note to Lucien Debray, bidding him call for them, since she could not go to the opera with Eugénie alone. And in fact, if the two women had gone thither without an escort the world would have put a bad construction on it; but should Mademoiselle Danglars go to the opera with her mother and her mother's lover, the world would have no fault to find. We must take the world as we find it.

The curtain rose as usual to an almost empty house, it being one of the absurdities of Parisian fashion never to appear at the opera until after the performance has begun, so that the first act is generally played without the slightest attention being paid to it, that part of the audience already assembled being occupied in observing the new arrivals; while the noise of opening and shutting doors, with the mingled buzz of many conversations, makes it impossible to hear anything else.

" See," said Albert, as the door of a box on the first circle opened, " there is the Comtesse G——."

" And who may she be, pray ? " inquired Château-Renaud.

" Oh, baron! an unpardonable question! You ask who is the Comtesse G—— ? "

" Ah, to be sure! " replied Château-Renaud; " I remember now,—your lovely Venetian, is it not ? "

" Herself."

At this moment the countess perceived Albert and returned his salutation with a smile.

" You are acquainted with her, it seems ? " said Château-Renaud.

" Yes. Franz presented me to her at Rome," replied Albert.

" Well, then, will you do for me in Paris what he did for you in Rome ? "

" With much pleasure."

" Silence! " exclaimed the audience.

This manifestation on the part of the spectators of their wish to be allowed to enjoy the rich music then issuing from the stage and orchestra, produced no effect on the two young men, who continued talking as though they had not even heard it.

" The countess was present at the races in the Champ de Mars," said Château-Renaud.

" To-day ? "

" Yes."

" Bless me! I quite forgot the races. Did you bet ? "

" Oh, a trifle,—fifty louis."

" And who was the winner ? "

" Nautilus. I betted on him."

" But there were three races, were there not ? "

" Yes; there was the prize given by the Jockey Club,—a gold cup, you know; and a very singular circumstance occurred in that race."

" What was it ? "

" Silence! " again vociferated the music-loving part of the audience.

" Why, that it was gained by a horse and rider utterly unknown on the course."

" Is it possible ? "

" True as day. Nobody had observed a horse entered by the name of Vampa, or a jockey styled Job, when a splendid roan and a jockey about as big as your fist presented themselves at the starting-post. They were obliged to stuff at least twenty pounds' weight of shot in the small rider's pockets to make him heavy enough; but with all that he outstripped Ariel and Barbare, against whom he ran, by at least three whole lengths."

" And was it not found out at last to whom the horse and jockey belonged? "

" No."

" You say that the horse was entered under the name of—"

" ' Vampa.' "

" Then," answered Albert, " I am better informed than you are; I know who is the owner of that horse! "

" Silence there! " came from the audience. And this time the tone and manner in which the command was given betokened such growing hostility that the two young men perceived for the first time that the mandate was addressed to them. Turning round, they searched the crowd for some one person who would take upon himself the responsibility of what they deemed an impertinence; but as no one responded to the challenge, the friends turned again towards the stage. At this moment the door of the minister's box opened, and Madame Danglars, her daughter, and Lucien Debray, took their places.

" Ha, ha! " said Château-Renaud, " here come some friends of yours, viscount! What are you looking at there? Don't you see they are trying to catch your eye? " Albert turned round just in time to receive a gracious wave of the fan from Madame the Baroness; as for Mademoiselle Eugénie, she scarcely vouchsafed to waste the glances of her large black eyes even upon the business of the stage.

" I tell you what, my dear fellow," said Château-Renaud, " I cannot imagine what objection you can possibly have to Mademoiselle Danglars—that is, setting aside her want of ancestry and somewhat inferior rank, which, by the way, I don't think you care very much about. She seems to me a very fine-looking girl."

" Handsome, certainly," replied Albert, " but not to my taste, which, I confess, inclines to a softer, gentler, and more feminine style than hers."

" Bless my heart! " exclaimed Château-Renaud, who, as a man thirty years old, assumed a paternal air towards Morcerf, " you young people are never satisfied. Why, what would you have more? Your parents have chosen you a bride who might serve as the living model of the ' Hunting Diana,' and yet you are not content."

" No, for that very resemblance affrights me. I should have

liked something more in the manner of the Venus of Milo or Capua; but this chase-loving Diana continually surrounded by her nymphs gives me a sort of alarm, lest she should some day entail on me the fate of Actæon."

And indeed it required but one glance at Mademoiselle Danglars to discover the significance of Morcerf's remark. She was handsome, but, as Albert had said, with a beauty somewhat too pronounced. Her hair was raven black, but amid its natural waves might be discerned a certain resistance to the hand that sought to control it; her eyes, of the same colour as her hair, were richly fringed and surmounted by well-arched brows, whose great defect, however, consisted in an almost habitual frown, while her whole physiognomy wore an expression of firmness and decision little in accordance with the gentler attributes of her sex; her nose was precisely what a sculptor would have given to a chiselled Juno; her mouth, which might have been found fault with as too large, displayed teeth of pearly whiteness, rendered still more conspicuous by the over-redness of her lips, beside which her naturally pale complexion seemed even more colourless. But that which completed the almost masculine look Morcerf found so little to his taste was a dark mole of much larger dimensions than these freaks of nature generally are, placed just at the corner of her mouth; and the effect tended to increase the expression of unbending resolution and self-dependence that formed the characteristics of her countenance. The rest of Mademoiselle Eugénie's person was in perfect keeping with the head just described; she indeed reminded you of the " Hunting Diana," as Château-Renaud observed, but with something still more resolute and masculine in her beauty. As regarded her attainments, the only fault to be found with them was the same that a fastidious connoisseur might have found with her beauty,—that they were such as belonged to the other sex. She spoke two or three languages, was a good artist, wrote poetry, and composed music. To the latter art she professed to be entirely devoted, studying it with one of her school-friends, who, without fortune, had every disposition to become—as she was assured she might—an excellent singer. A celebrated composer was said to take an almost paternal interest in this young woman last mentioned, whom he stimulated to work diligently in the hope that she might find a fortune in her voice. The possibility that Mademoiselle Louise d'Armilly might sometime go upon the stage prevented Mademoiselle Danglars from appearing with her in public, although still receiving her at home. But though Louise had not in the house of the banker the independent position of a friend, her position was superior to that of the ordinary governess.

The curtain fell almost immediately after the entrance of Madame Danglars into her box; the band quitted the orchestra for the accustomed interval allowed between the acts; and the audience were left at liberty to promenade the salon or lobbies, or to pay and receive visits in their respective boxes. Morcerf and Château-Renaud were among the first to avail themselves of this opportunity. For an instant the idea struck Madame Danglars that this eagerness on the part of the young viscount arose from his impatience to join her party; and she whispered to her daughter that Albert was hurrying to pay his respects to them. The latter, however, shook her head, smiling. At the same moment, as if to show that her incredulity was well founded, Morcerf was seen in a box in the first circle; it was the box of Comtesse G——.

"Ah! you have arrived, monsieur," cried the countess, extending her hand to him with all the warmth and cordiality of an old acquaintance; "it was really very good of you to recognise me so quickly, and still more so to bestow your first visit on me."

"Be assured," replied Albert, "that if I had been aware of your arrival in Paris, and had known your address, I should have paid my respects to you long ere this. Allow me to introduce my friend, Baron de Château-Renaud, one of the few gentlemen now to be found in France. I have just learned from him that you were at the races in the Champ de Mars yesterday."

Château-Renaud bowed to the countess.

"Ah! you were at the races, monsieur?" inquired the countess, eagerly.

"I was, madame."

"Well, then," pursued Madame G——, with considerable animation, "you can probably tell me to whom belonged the winner of the Jockey-Club stakes?"

"I am sorry to say I cannot," replied the baron; "I was just asking the same question of Albert."

"Are you very anxious to know, Madame the Countess?" asked Albert.

"To know what?"

"The owner of the winning horse?"

"Exceedingly; only imagine—but do you know, Monsieur the Viscount, who he is?"

"Madame, you were about to relate some story. You said 'only imagine.'"

" Well, then, listen! You must know I felt so interested for the splendid roan horse, with his elegant little rider so tastefully dressed in a pink satin jacket and cap, that I could not help praying for their success with as much earnestness as though the half of my fortune were at stake; and when I saw them outstrip all the others and come to the winning-post in such gallant style, I actually clapped my hands with joy. Imagine my surprise, when upon returning home I met on the staircase the jockey in the pink jacket! I concluded that by some singular chance the owner of the winning horse must live in the same hotel as myself; but, lo! as I entered my salon I beheld the gold cup awarded as a prize to the unknown horse and rider. Inside the cup was a small piece of paper, on which were written these words, ' From Lord Ruthven to Comtesse G——.' "

" Precisely; I am sure of it," said Morcerf.

" Sure of what? "

" That the owner of the horse was Lord Ruthven himself."

" What Lord Ruthven do you mean? "

" Why, our Lord Ruthven,—the Vampire of the Theatre Argentina! "

" Truly? " exclaimed the countess; " is he here, then? "

" To be sure; why not? "

" And you visit him?—meet him at your own house and elsewhere? "

" I assure you that he is my most intimate friend, and M. de Château-Renaud has also the honour of his acquaintance."

" But what makes you think it is he who took the prize? "

" Was not the winning horse entered by the name of ' Vampa '? "

" What of that? "

" Why, do you not recollect the name of the celebrated bandit by whom I was made prisoner? "

" Ah! that is true."

" And from whose hands the count extricated me in so wonderful a manner? "

" To be sure."

" His name was Vampa. You see, then, that it is he."

" But what could have been his motive for sending the cup to me? "

" In the first place, because I had spoken much of you to him, as you may believe; and in the second, because he delighted to see a countrywoman, and to see her take so lively an interest in his success."

" I hope you never repeated to him all the foolish remarks we used to make about him? "

" I should not like to affirm upon oath that I have not. Besides, his presenting you the cup under the name of Lord Ruthven proves his knowledge of the comparison instituted between himself and that individual."

" Oh, but that is dreadful! Why, the man must mortally hate me."

" His action is hardly that of an enemy."

" No; certainly not."

" Well, then——"

" And so he is in Paris? "

" He is."

" And what effect does he produce? "

" Why," said Albert, " he was talked of for a week. Then the coronation of the Queen of England took place, and the theft of Mademoiselle Mars's diamonds; and two such interesting events turned public attention into other channels."

" My dear fellow," said Château-Renaud, " it is clear that the count is your friend, and you speak of him accordingly. Do not believe what Albert is telling you, Madame the Countess; so far from the sensation excited in the Parisian circles by the appearance of the Count of Monte Cristo having abated, I take upon myself to declare that it is as strong as ever. His first astounding act upon coming among us was to present a pair of horses, worth thirty thousand livres, to Madame Danglars; his second, the almost miraculous preservation of Madame de Villefort's life; now it seems that he has carried off the prize awarded by the Jockey Club! I therefore maintain, in spite of whatever Morcerf may advance, not only that the count is the object of universal interest at this present moment, but that he will be still more so a month hence if he continues to display those eccentricities which seem to be his ordinary characteristics."

" Perhaps you are right," said Morcerf; " meanwhile, who has taken the Russian ambassador's box? "

" Which box do you mean? " asked the countess.

" The one between the pillars on the first tier; it seems to have been entirely made over."

" So it does," said Château-Renaud. " Was any one there during the first act? "

" Where? "

" In that box."

" No," replied the countess; " it was certainly empty during the first act." Then, returning to the subject of their previous conversation, she said, " And so you really believe it was your Count of Monte Cristo who gained the prize ? "

" I am sure of it."

" And who afterwards sent the golden cup to me ? "

" Undoubtedly."

" But I do not know him," said the countess; " I have a strong inclination to return it."

" Do no such thing, I beg of you; he would only send you a second goblet, formed of a magnificent sapphire, or hollowed out of a gigantic ruby. It is his manner of acting, and you must take him as you find him."

At this moment the bell rang to announce the drawing up of the curtain for the second act. Albert rose to return to his place.

" Shall I see you again ? " asked the countess.

" If you will permit me to make a second visit in the next pause in the opera, I will do myself the honour of coming to inquire whether there is anything in which I can be useful to you in Paris ? "

" Pray take notice," said the countess, " that my present residence is 22 Rue de Rivoli, and that I am at home to my friends every Saturday evening. So now, you gentlemen cannot plead ignorance."

The young men bowed, and quitted the box. Upon reaching their stalls they found the whole of the audience in the *parterre* standing up and directing their gaze towards the box formerly possessed by the ambassador of Russia. A man of from thirty-five to forty years of age, dressed in deep black, had just entered, accompanied by a woman dressed after the Eastern style; the woman was young and surpassingly beautiful, while the rich magnificence of her attire drew all eyes upon her.

" By heavens ! " said Albert, " it is Monte Cristo himself, with his Greek ! "

The strangers were indeed no other than the count and Haydée. The sensation excited by the beauty and dazzling appearance of the latter soon communicated itself to every part of the theatre; the ladies leaned forward from the boxes to see the glitter of that cascade of diamonds. During the second act there was the continual buzzing sound which in a crowded assembly marks the occurrence of some striking event. No one thought of calling for silence. That woman, so young, so beautiful, so dazzling, was the most interesting spectacle that was presented. Upon this occasion an unmistakable sign from Madame Danglars intimated her desire to see Albert in her box as soon as the curtain should fall on the second act; and neither the politeness nor good taste of Morcerf would permit his neglecting an invitation so unequivocally given. At the close of the act he therefore proceeded to the baroness's box. Having bowed to the two ladies, he extended his hand to Debray. By the baroness he was most graciously welcomed, while Eugénie received him with her accustomed coldness.

"My dear fellow!" said Debray, "you have come in the very nick of time to help a fellow-creature regularly beaten and at a standstill. There is madame overwhelming me with questions respecting the count; she insists upon it that I can tell her his birth, education, and parentage, where he came from, and whither he is going. Being no Cagliostro, by way of getting out of the scrape, I said ' Ask Morcerf; he has the whole history of Monte Cristo at his fingers' ends;' whereupon the baroness made you a sign to come hither."

"Is it not almost incredible," said Madame Danglars, "that a person having at least half a million of secret-service money at his command, should possess so little information?"

"Let me assure you, madame," said Lucien, "that had I really the sum you mention at my disposal, I would employ it more profitably than in troubling myself to obtain particulars respecting the Count of Monte Cristo, whose only merit in my eyes consists in his being twice as rich as a nabob. However, I have turned the business over to Morcerf, so pray settle it with him,—it does not concern me any longer."

"I am very sure no nabob would have sent me a pair of horses worth thirty thousand livres, wearing on their heads four diamonds valued at five thousand livres each."

"He seems to have a mania for diamonds," said Morcerf, smiling; "and I verily believe that like Potemkin he keeps his pockets filled to strew them along the road as little Thumb did his flint-stones."

"Perhaps he has discovered some mine," said Madame Danglars. "I suppose you know he has an order for unlimited credit on the baron's banking establishment?"

"I was not aware of it," replied Albert, "but I can readily believe it."

"And he has stated to M. Danglars his intention of staying only a year in Paris, during which time he proposes to spend six millions. He must be the Shah of Persia, travelling *incognito*."

"Have you remarked the extreme beauty of that young woman by whom he is accompanied, M. Lucien?" inquired Eugénie.

"I really never met with a woman so ready to do justice to the charms of another as yourself." Lucien raised his lorgnette to his eye. "Charming!" said he.

"Who is this young person, M. de Morcerf?" inquired Eugénie; "does anybody know?"

"Mademoiselle," said Albert, replying to this direct appeal, "I know a little on that subject, as well as on most points relative to the singular person of whom we are now conversing. That young woman is a Greek."

"So I should presume by her dress; if therefore you know no more than that one self-evident fact, all the spectators in the theatre are as well-informed as yourself."

"I am extremely sorry you find me so ignorant a *cicerone*," replied Morcerf; "but I am obliged to confess that I have nothing further to communicate,—yes, I do know one thing more, namely, that she is a musician, for one day when I chanced to be breakfasting with the count I heard the sounds of a *guzla*,—sounds which certainly could have been made only by her."

"Then your count entertains visitors, does he?" asked Madame Danglars.

"Indeed he does, and in a most noble manner, I can assure you."

"I must try and persuade M. Danglars to invite him to a ball or dinner, or something of the sort, that he may be compelled to ask us in return."

"What!" said Debray, laughing; "do you really mean you would go to his house?"

"Why not? My husband could accompany me."

"But do you know this mysterious count is a bachelor?"

"You have ample proof to the contrary, if you look opposite," said the baroness, as she laughingly pointed to the beautiful Greek.

"No, no!" exclaimed Debray; "that female is not his wife. He told us himself she was his slave. Do you not recollect, Morcerf, his telling us so at your breakfast?"

"Well, then," said the baroness, "if slave she be, she has all the air and manner of a princess."

"Of the *Arabian Nights?*"

"If you like; but tell me, my dear Lucien, what is it that constitutes a princess? Diamonds, and she is covered with them."

"To me she seems overloaded," observed Eugénie. "She

would look far better if she wore fewer; and we should then be able to see her finely-formed throat and wrists."

" See how the artist peeps out! " exclaimed Madame Danglars; "my poor Eugénie, you must conceal your passion for the fine arts."

" I admire all that is beautiful in art or nature," returned the young lady.

" What do you think of the count, then? " inquired Debray; " he is not much amiss according to my ideas of good looks."

" The count? " repeated Eugénie, as though it had not occurred to her to observe him sooner,—" the count? oh, he is so dreadfully pale! "

" I quite agree with you," said Morcerf; " and in that very paleness lies the secret we want to find out. The Comtesse G—— insists upon it he is a vampire."

" Then the Comtesse G—— has returned to Paris, has she? " inquired the baroness.

" There she is, mamma," said Eugénie; " almost opposite to us, with that profusion of beautiful light hair."

" Yes, yes, there she is! " cried Madame Danglars; " shall I tell you what you ought to do, Morcerf? "

" Command me, madame; I am all attention."

" Well, then, you should go and bring your Count of Monte Cristo to us."

" What for? " asked Eugénie.

" What for? Why, to converse with him, of course; if you have no curiosity to hear whether he expresses himself like other people, I can assure you I have. Have you really no desire to see him? "

" None whatever," replied Eugénie.

" Strange girl! " murmured the baroness.

" He will very probably come of his own accord," said Morcerf. " There! do you see, madame, he recognises you and bows."

The baroness returned the salute in the most smiling and graceful manner.

" Well," said Morcerf, " I sacrifice myself. Adieu; I will go and see if there is any chance of speaking to him."

" Go straight to his box; that will be the simplest plan."

" But I have never been presented."

" Presented to whom? "

" To the beautiful Greek."

" You say she is only a slave? "

" While you assert that she is a princess. No, no, I cannot

venture to enter his box; but I hope that when he sees me leave you, he will come out of his box."

"It is possible; go."

Morcerf bowed and went out. Just as he was passing the count's box, the door opened, and Monte Cristo came forth. After giving some directions to Ali, who stood in the lobby, the count observed Albert, and taking his arm walked onwards with him. Carefully closing the box-door, Ali placed himself before it, while a crowd of wondering spectators assembled round the Nubian.

"Upon my word," said Monte Cristo, "Paris is a strange city, and the Parisians a very singular people. One might suppose he was the only Nubian they had ever beheld. See them crowd around poor Ali, who doesn't know what it means. I assure you that a Frenchman might show himself in public, either in Tunis, Constantinople, Bagdad, or Cairo, without drawing a circle of gazers around him."

"That shows that the people of the East have too much good sense to waste their time and attention on objects undeserving of either. However, as far as Ali is concerned, I can assure you that the interest he excites arises from the fact that he belongs to you, who are at this moment the most celebrated person in Paris."

"Really? and what has procured me so flattering a distinction?"

"What? Why, yourself, to be sure! You give away horses worth a thousand louis; you save the lives of ladies of high rank and beauty; you send to the race-course, under the name of Major Brack, horses of pure blood and jockeys not larger than marmots; then, when you have carried off the golden trophy of victory, instead of setting any value on it, you give it to the first handsome woman you think of!"

"And who has filled your head with all this nonsense?"

"Why, in the first place, I heard it from Madame Danglars, who, by the bye, is dying to see you in her box, or to have you seen there by others; secondly, I learned it from Beauchamp's journal; and thirdly, from my own imagination. Why, if you sought concealment, did you call your horse Vampa?"

"That was an oversight, certainly," replied the count; "but tell me, does the Comte de Morcerf never visit the opera? I have been looking for him, but without success."

"He will be here to-night."

"In what part of the house?"

"In the baroness's box, I believe."

" That charming young woman with her is her daughter? "

" Yes."

" Indeed! then I congratulate you."

Morcerf smiled. " We will discuss that subject at some future time," said he. " But what think you of the music? "

" What music? "

" That which you have just heard."

" Oh, it is admirable, as the production of a human composer, sung by a party of bipeds without feathers, as Diogenes styled mankind."

" Why, my dear count, it would seem that you can hear at pleasure the seven choirs of paradise."

" You are partly right; when I wish to listen to sounds so exquisitely attuned to melody as mortal ear never yet listened to, I go to sleep."

" Very well; you are wonderfully well situated for that. Sleep, my dear count, sleep; the opera was invented for no other end."

" No; in fact your orchestra is too noisy. To sleep after the manner I have mentioned, calm and silence are necessary; a certain preparation must also be called in aid."

" Ah! the famous hashish? "

" Precisely. Viscount, when you want to hear music come and take supper with me."

" I have already enjoyed that treat when breakfasting with you," said Morcerf.

" Do you mean at Rome? "

" I do."

" Ah, then, I suppose you heard Haydée's *guzla;* the poor exile frequently beguiles a weary hour in playing over the airs of her native land."

Morcerf did not pursue the subject, and Monte Cristo himself fell into a silent reverie. The bell rang at this moment for the rising of the curtain.

" You will excuse my leaving you," said the count, turning in the direction of his box.

" What! Are you going? "

" Pray say everything that is kind to Comtesse G—— on the part of the vampire."

" And what message shall I convey to the baroness? "

" That, with her permission, I propose doing myself the honour of paying my respects in the course of the evening."

The third act had now commenced; and during its progress the Comte de Morcerf, according to promise, made his appearance in the box of Madame Danglars. The Comte de Morcerf was not one of those persons whose aspect would create interest or curiosity in a place of public amusement; his presence therefore was wholly unnoticed save by the occupants of the box in which he had just seated himself. The quick eye of Monte Cristo, however, marked his coming; and a slight smile passed over his lips. Haydée was entirely absorbed in the business of the stage; like all unsophisticated natures, she delighted in whatever addressed itself to the eye or ear.

The third act passed off as usual. Mademoiselles Noblet, Julie, and Leroux, executed the customary pirouettes; Robert duly challenged the Prince of Grenada; and the royal parent of the Princess Isabella, taking his daughter by the hand, swept round the stage with majestic strides, the better to display the rich folds of his velvet robe and mantle. After which the curtain again fell, and the spectators poured forth from the theatre into the lobbies and salon.

The count left his box and proceeded at once to that of Madame Danglars, who could scarcely restrain a cry of mingled pleasure and surprise. " Welcome, Monsieur the Count! " exclaimed she, as he entered. " I have been most anxious to see you, that I might repeat verbally those thanks writing can so ill express."

" Surely so trifling a circumstance cannot deserve a place in your remembrance. Believe me, madame, I had entirely forgotten it."

" But it is not so easy to forget, Monsieur the Count, that the next day you saved the life of my dear friend, Madame de Villefort, which was put in peril by those very horses."

" This time, at least, I cannot accept your flattering acknowledgments. Ali, my Nubian slave, had the good fortune to render to Madame de Villefort that eminent service."

" Was it Ali," asked the Comte de Morcerf, " who rescued my son from the hands of bandits? "

" No, Monsieur the Count," replied Monte Cristo, pressing with friendly warmth the hand held out to him by the general; " in this instance I may fairly and freely accept your thanks. But you have already tendered them, I have already received them; and in fact I am embarrassed by your continued gratitude. Do me the honour, Madame the Baroness, to present me to mademoiselle your daughter."

" Oh, you are no stranger,—at least not by name," replied Madame Danglars; " and the last two or three days we have talked of nothing else but yourself. Eugénie," continued the baroness, turning towards her daughter, "M. le Comte de Monte Cristo."

The count bowed, while Mademoiselle Danglars returned a slight inclination of the head. "You have a charming young person with you to-night, Monsieur the Count," said Eugénie. "Is she your daughter?"

"No, indeed," said Monte Cristo, astonished at the coolness and freedom of the question. "She is an unfortunate Greek, of whom I am the guardian."

"And what is her name?"

"Haydée," replied Monte Cristo.

"A Greek?" murmured Comte de Morcerf.

"Yes, indeed, count," said Madame Danglars; "and tell me, did you ever see at the court of Ali Tebelin, whom you so gloriously served, a more admirable costume than we have there before our eyes?"

"Did I hear rightly, Monsieur the Count," said Monte Cristo, "that you served at Janina?"

"I was inspector-general of the pacha's troops," replied Morcerf; "and I seek not to conceal that I owe my fortune, such as it is, to the liberality of the illustrious Albanian chief."

"But look! pray look!" exclaimed Madame Danglars.

"Where?" stammered Morcerf.

"There, there!" said Monte Cristo, as, folding his arms around the count, he leaned with him over the front of the box, just as Haydée, whose eyes were occupied in examining the theatre in search of the count, perceived his pale features close to the countenance of Morcerf, whom he was holding in his arms. This sight produced on the astonished girl an effect similar to that of the fabulous head of Medusa. She bent forwards as though to assure herself of the reality of what she beheld, then uttering a faint cry, threw herself back in her seat. The sound that burst from the agitated Greek quickly reached the ear of the watchful Ali, who instantly opened the box-door to ascertain the cause.

"Bless me!" exclaimed Eugénie, "what has happened to your ward, Monsieur the Count? She seems taken suddenly ill!"

"Very probably!" answered the count. "But do not be alarmed on her account! Haydée's nervous system is delicately organised, and she is peculiarly susceptible to the odours even of flowers; there are some which cause her to faint if brought into her presence. However," continued Monte Cristo, drawing a small phial from his pocket, "I have an infallible remedy for such attacks." So saying, he bowed to the baroness and her daughter, exchanged a parting shake of the hand with Debray and the count, and quitted the box. Upon his return to Haydée, he found her extremely pale and much agitated. As soon as she saw him she seized his hand. Monte Cristo noticed that the hands of the young girl were moist and cold.

" With whom was my lord conversing a few minutes since? " asked she, in a trembling voice.

" With the Comte de Morcerf," answered Monte Cristo. " He tells me he served your illustrious father, and that he owes his fortune to him."

" Ah, the scoundrel! " exclaimed Haydée; " it is he who sold my father to the Turks, and the fortune he boasts of was the price of his treachery! Did you not know that, my dear lord? "

" Something of this I heard in Epirus," said Monte Cristo; " but the particulars are still unknown to me. You shall relate them to me, my child. They are no doubt both curious and interesting."

" Yes, yes! but let us go hence, I beseech you! I feel as though it would kill me to remain longer near that dreadful man." So saying, Haydée arose, and wrapping herself in her burnoose of white cashmere embroidered with pearls and coral, she hastily quitted the box at the moment when the curtain was rising upon the fourth act.

" Do you observe? " said the Comtesse G—— to Albert, who had returned to her side; " that man does nothing like other people. He listens most devoutly to the third act of ' Robert le Diable,' and leaves when the fourth begins."

EVERYMAN'S LIBRARY

By ERNEST RHYS

VICTOR HUGO said a Library was 'an act of faith,' and another writer spoke of one so beautiful, so perfect, so harmonious in all its parts, that he who made it was smitten with a passion. In that faith Everyman's Library was planned out originally on a large scale; and the idea was to make it conform as far as possible to a perfect scheme. However, perfection is a thing to be aimed at and not to be achieved in this difficult world; and since the first volumes appeared there have been many interruptions, chief among them Wars, during which even the City of Books feels the great commotion. But the series always gets back into its old stride.

One of the practical expedients in the original plan was to divide the volumes into separate sections, as Biography, Fiction, History, Belles-lettres, Poetry, Philosophy, Romance, and so forth; with a shelf for Young People. The largest slice of the huge provision of nearly a thousand volumes is, as a matter of course, given to the tyrranous demands of fiction. But in carrying out the scheme, publishers and editors contrived to keep in mind that books, like men and women, have their elective affinities. The present volume, for instance, will be found to have its companion books, both in the same class and not less significantly in other sections. With that idea too, novels like Walter Scott's *Ivanhoe* and *Fortunes of Nigel*, Lytton's *Harold*, and Dickens's *Tale of Two Cities*, have been used as pioneers of history and treated in some sort as holiday history books.

As for history, Everyman's Library has been eclectic enough to choose its historians from every school in turn, including Gibbon, Grote, Finlay, Macaulay, Motley, and Prescott, while among earlier books may be found the Venerable Bede and the Anglo-Saxon Chronicle. On the classic shelf too, there is a Livy in an admirable translation by Canon Roberts, and Caesar, Tacitus, Thucydides, and Herodotus are not forgotten.

The poets next, and we may turn to the finest critic of Victorian times, Matthew Arnold, as their showman, and find in his essay on Maurice de Guerin a clue to the 'magical power of poetry.'

Hazlitt's *Table Talk* may help again to show the relationship of author to author, which is another form of the Friendship of Books. His incomparable essay, 'On Going a Journey,' makes a capital prelude to Coleridge's *Biographia Literaria*; and so throughout the long labyrinth of the Library shelves you can follow the magic clue in prose or verse that leads to the hidden treasury. In that way Everyman becomes his own critic and Doctor of Letters.

> To him all books which lay
> Their sure foundation in the heart of man . . .
> From Homer the great Thunderer, to the voice
> That roars along the bed of Jewish song . . .
> Shall speak as Powers for ever to be hallowed!

If found please return
to

Margaret Beresford
Manor Farm
Chilmark
Salisbury
Wiltshire

OR.

Margaret Beresford
Aldelmstead West
Sherborne
Dorset.